M000073634

SAILING OFF
OFF

THE
EDGE
OF

THE
WORLD

SAILING

OFF

THE
EDGE
OF

THE

WORLD

ALSO FROM MIND HARVEST PRESS

Feint
By
Michael G. Sullivan

Dream Work
By
R. Bentz Kirby

King's Highway
Fellow Traveler
Let the Glory Pass Away
The Year They Canceled Christmas
Dogs of Parsons Hollow
Dixiana
Down in Dixiana
Dixiana Darling
Reconstruction of the Fables
By
James D. McCallister

A Novel By
Michael G.
Sullivan

Mind Harvest
Press

ISBN 978-1-946052-45-2

Editing and interior design by James D. McCallister

Cover Design by Marc Cardwell (www.marccardwell.com)

FOREWORD

A little more than seven years ago, at a now-defunct, beloved pizza joint near the shop my wife and I own, I met the late Michael G. Sullivan through a mutual set of friends. And while I would one day become Michael's editor and publisher, this was our only actual conversation together; it lasted about five minutes.

Introduced as both entrepreneur and author, I found myself in the company of a writer looking for advice on how to break through both in terms of process and publication, which I had achieved. It had only taken me fourteen years, I told him, but with award-winning short stories, two novels in print and a raft of magazine articles, newspaper columns and other types of writing under my belt, all things were possible. I had done well, especially for someone who didn't truly return to his childhood craft at which I had received recognition and encouragement, until the age of thirty-five.

I never shy away from helping out others on the authorial path. When all your dreams have come true, what is left but to give back to a world which has so blessed you? That's why I always try to help the Michael Sullivans of the world realize their own dreams.

As an aspiring author as well as an attorney, my new

friend listened with glistening eyes, focused on my brief discourse as though scrutinizing an opposing litigator in the courtroom. I offered my pep talk not only on what it takes to get through composing and editing a novel manuscript, but getting it published.

None of this is easy, I said. "You have to learn to love misery," I may have added, "when it comes to paying your dues."

By this caveat I meant the course of receiving rejection slips, working with editors who may or may not think your work brilliant, and all the other psychologically trying obstacles writers must pass in order to receive their due. When we say 'process,' we are talking about much more than facing the blank page. As bad as that aspect of creativity can be, the real-world aspects of seeing books come into print are in their own way even more layered and complex, though often this complexity does not 'pay for itself;' it is merely an expression of the modern and typically destructive penchant for the acquisitions of imaginary fiat currency over what makes good art, a seemingly endless struggle which almost always results in diminishment of artistic vision.

My only recollection of Michael's response to my advice was a circumspect and polite gratitude. But I know why he didn't have much to say—his mind had already begun racing ahead to when he could return to the work. Perhaps he knew time truly was short. The event which took his life, an accident, would occur not long after.

However much time one may have left, the aspiring writer must cultivate what the Persian poet Rumi called 'the duck of urgency' to pursue such lofty, complicated and lengthy artistic goals as writing a meaningful book. I'm thankful I got through my course of art, my crucible of creativity, to a point wherein such a voice is quelled. It was the only way for me to get where I needed to be—don't give up, don't stop, time is short, the journey of a thousand miles begins with a single step, and about a hundred other motivational koans the duck quacked in my ear until I got through the next draft of my novels *Dixiana* or *Fellow Traveler*.

Michael Sullivan, on the other hand, did not make it to see his books in print. But he got them written, thank goodness. Obviously so, as you now hold one of them in your hands. And the 'process' for me in editing and publishing his work was like being touched from the great beyond by an angel proud and happy for my attention and efforts.

Seriously: bringing both *Feint* and now *Sailing Off the Edge of the World* into print has turned into one of the finest deeds I have ever accomplished with my authorial and editorial skills. The spiritual boon has been incalculable.

How do I know this, one may ask? Because Michael knows this; he looks down on all this and laughs with pleasure and delight. As he informs me from his place in the eternal hall of heroes:

Not even death could keep me from becoming the writer of my dreams. Thank you.

The best part? I have heard Michael saying these words in tones angelic, a sort of high speech to which perhaps only artists are privy. And my only response to him is this: thank you, sir, for giving me this sacred opportunity to serve. And may you all know how good a feeling this is, in your own way, one day soon.

—*James D. McCallister*
October, 2021

To my son

A just man is a man just in the right place doing his best and giving full equivalent of what he receives.

— PLATO

1

Only those who have no imagination appear as they seem, as they are inside; the rest of us, if we have any skill at all, present ourselves to the world as our own best invention.

Example—I've been editing my autobiography for years, leaving out the bad parts while giving myself star billing in events I'd often only witnessed, sucking the marrow from the meat of other people's triumphs or tragedies for my own ends. I fancied myself the author of my own existence, of reality itself. It's like how people say that some of us create our own luck.

So far, no one's caught me at my little game. But, deep down, I know it will take more than skill or manufactured luck to keep up the charade. Time is short for me to accomplish what I must here in Washington, before someone in a position to do something about me finds out they've let a dead-eyed shark into their swimming pool. Hell, for all I know, it may already be too late.

⚓

IN LESS FANCIFUL TERMS I MERELY POLISHED UP MY PAST, elevating a third-tier law school experience in Maryland to one of those lesser-known, yet still well regarded, schools on the west coast. If pressed, my subterfuge came complete with a forged transcript and other documents to support the story. On the whole I thought it less likely I'd bump into a fellow alum here in Washington if I chose a school three thousand miles away, but let's face it, the world is getting smaller every day. I can be pretty naive at times, I guess, for a reality creator such as myself.

Again: it has worked well so far, this authorship of a life. So far, I've found success at selling this version of myself in Washington on K Street; whichever version I happened to be, whichever self I needed to become as circumstances warranted, that is who appears before you. But when this method finally stops working, as my gut tells me it will, well... I guess I'll be the first person to find out the bad news.

BUT LOOK AT HOW SERIOUS I TAKE MY SUBTERFUGE: I EVEN changed my own name. Well, not changed; altered is perhaps more accurate. I dropped my surname and added an S to my middle—Paul Johns. Somehow this sounded more like the real me than my given name, which had come from a father I'd been meaning to forget, as he had forgotten me, for as long as I could remember.

I've always surprised at how easily I get away with such deceptions, which I display like shiny objects. People are understandably reluctant to press about one's past. It seems rude, somehow. It's like the news anchors on TV—they can sell any story, make any set of alleged facts sound true. That's show biz.

And, if you think newsreaders are good at fudging the truth, consider the litigator in the courtroom. As a lawyer, at the necessity of cultivating such an ability goes without saying. A zealous defense, let's say, calls for serious salesmanship. You've all watched courtroom dramas. The real version is much more dry and boring, but it's still mostly performance art. Ask any lawyer. They'll tell you, unless, of course, you're one of the profane who isn't in the club; if you're one of the regular folks whose ignorance of how the privileged world of power truly works predicates the successful functioning of such a world, allowing those with all the toys to hold onto them.

Participating in such a scheme doesn't make me proud, no, far from it. My biggest problem is figuring out how I get myself some of those toys, which are still out of reach for a young associate such as myself. I would worry about how to keep all the spoils I sought later. Let's not get ahead of ourselves, here.

STILL, WITH ALL THAT BRIGHT, GLIMMERING FALSEHOOD PILED in my corner, I hadn't made much progress at Cantor and Miller. Despite his advocacy in getting me the position, working with Ben Schiller in criminal law had gotten me nowhere fast. Yes; I'm impatient. I will admit that seeing all the wealth around me in D. C. has done a number on my head.

But in the space of a brief phone call, I suddenly didn't need to worry about Ben anymore, nor his advocacy and the security it provided at work, and maybe not even work at all. Luck, from wherever its source, can be a fickle lady indeed:

Ben's wife Pamela, whom I knew well enough to have been in bed with her on a number of occasions, was the first to call with the news. She said my advocate at Cantor & Miller had suffered a heart attack at dinner the previous evening.

"Early this morning Ben died... in the hospital," she added, sounding numb. "It was too late."

I found it difficult to tell over the phone whether she had been numbed by the suddenness, or simply felt relieved at the brief drama of his life's end. Given our situation—the affair we'd been having—a little of both were possible.

"Do you want me to come over there?"

"God, no," she said, aghast, and hung up.

Right—Ben and I weren't that close. My presence would have seemed odd. Or, perhaps merely as a bringer of guilt.

Either way I got it, taking no offense. Had she made love with her husband one more time before he died? I'm not a monster. I can imagine how rotten a feeling it must be for someone now with neither a spouse nor a sympathetic lover.

The worst part of it all? For me? Ben had brought me into the firm. Worse yet, my hiring had been over the objection of at least one of the other junior partners, or so I'd heard. Now that Ben was dead, I would be let go. And soon, too.

Either way, I would also have to stop seeing Pamela. It was one thing to dabble in a rather lazy affair with another man's wife, but it would be another entirely to frolic with his widow. Besides, I genuinely liked Ben, and had enjoyed our time working together. I would have to find another job soon, so there would be little time to console her.

⚓

THE PHONE RANG AGAIN. PAMELA.

"I'm sorry for hanging up. What you suggested seemed —awful."

Understood. "You're in shock. We both are."

"Yes—I can't believe this. I can't believe any of it. I'm dreaming. Am I dreaming?"

I didn't know, but my own dream would end the second I got to the office. And that's the whole of what was really on my mind.

On the surface, it also felt hypocritical to start talking about how much we would both miss Ben, so we moved on to more practical matters.

"Can you look into Ben's life insurance today?"

I said I would, and asked if she had immediate concerns about her finances.

After a hearty laugh she said, "Other than the two mortgages and empty savings account? Not at all."

That sounded like Ben, who liked spending big and living large.

A surge of panic—I hoped she wasn't about to ask to borrow money. As a junior associate I didn't have any to give, but it would be awkward all the same to tell her I couldn't help.

No question about it: I would have to break this off sooner rather than later. It was a matter of timing, really. I'd wait until a few days after the funeral; that seemed a decent enough interval. From her tone, I already suspected she would be more than amenable to my motion before the relationship court. There had been little love between us, only raw animal passion. And if I've learned anything from relationships, sex alone offers an inadequate hook on which to hang a pair of hats.

I HAD BEEN AT MY DESK ONLY TWENTY MINUTES WHEN MR. Cantor's assistant rang to say he wanted me in his office immediately. It certainly hadn't taken them long to decide to fire me. Sometimes I get tired of being right all the time.

Mr. Cantor, one of the two founding partners at Cantor and Miller, did seem to like me, however, and so maybe I had him in my corner. And while I saw him enough at work and had been to his town house for the obligatory New Year's Eve party, we didn't really know each other. But in any case, around the office it was Miller, known as The Guillotine, who performed any bloodletting. I was surprised and curious, then, that it was Mr. Cantor who had called to give me the boot.

The door to his office was open. I went in and stood waiting for him to notice me.

He seemed surprised by my appearance in his doorway. As though he had to search for my name: "Yes—Paul?"

I hoped he couldn't see my jangled nerves. I had risked everything to get this job, and now here it was slipping away already. "You asked for me, Mr. Cantor."

His eyes held a curious sheen. "A moment to finish this, please."

With that he went back to reading his messages, a small snowdrift on his desk which had accumulated during his recent vacation. He had a deep tan, the kind you only get from days at the shore. His voice had a Virginia softness about it that invited one to listen close and with care. It was the voice of a man who expected to be heard the first time. He exuded dignity, money, power. Everything I wanted.

While my boss made me wait like a servant, I surveyed the photos on the wall behind his desk, which included a black and white photograph of a navy destroyer. Ben had told me how proud Mr. Cantor was of having been a naval officer. I would remember to speak with admiration of our men in uniform and the armed services they provide. Cantor's appearance even suggested a military bearing. He kept his hair cut in a near-flattop, was in trim shape, rose each day at 5am, he said, as he had done as a young enlisted man. "Discipline makes the difference," he had been heard to repeat like a meditation mantra.

On the wall across from me hung documents of more recent times, a collage of signed photographs of Mr. Cantor with various congressmen and senators, a personal history of power-playing going back twenty-plus years. But no matter where my vision fell, I did not find a photo of Elizabeth Cantor, his wife.

After several minutes of watching him grunt and scrutinize his messages, I cleared my throat to remind my employer I was still there. We both knew what this was about, so I saw little reason to drag it out. Put the blindfold on; let me have a last cigarette, ready, aim… fired.

Mr. Cantor screwed the cap onto his pen and laid it down with great care, like a jeweler putting a fine ring back into its case. He performed even the most ordinary tasks with great deliberation, indeed, a discipline and economy of movement I studied with great interest.

His mouth, dry, crackled as he at last spoke. "I'm sorry to have to tell you this news." He paused to take a sip of water from a tumbler at his elbow. "But, our friend and colleague Ben Schiller, well—he passed away this morning."

It wouldn't do to say his widow had already telephoned from the hospital, so I feigned surprise. As I sunk down onto the sofa I asked about the details with what I hoped sounded like the right note of shock tinged with sadness.

"Heart attack." Mr. Cantor, appropriately rueful, leaned back and lit a cigarette, even though smoking had long been disallowed in the building. "But hearing of such an outcome only makes me want another one of these. Do you smoke?"

"On occasion."

"You should quit altogether, then," as rich menthol smoke

plumed from his nostrils and he put away the pack, "if you aren't hooked."

"I'm stunned to hear about Mr. Schiller." And I was sorry, even though I was more concerned about where I would find another job than the death of my friend Ben. He'd been a heart attack waiting to happen. But Ben was the past, and I now needed a new advocate at the firm. Who better than a full partner? "What do you need me to handle?"

Mr. Cantor smiled. "I like a man who doesn't dwell on sentiment, not when there is business waiting to be conducted. I'd say Jenkins needs your attention first."

"I'll let the court know that we'll need to reschedule the trial," an embezzlement case.

I considered asking about Mrs. Schiller, but doing so could invite trouble—rumors of the affair may have reached Mr. Cantor. A law firm is in many ways like a small town, where gossip spreads like a bad cold in a classroom of children.

"You worked with Ben doing criminal defense for almost a year now, isn't it?"

I noticed Mr. Cantor used the past tense. How quickly Ben had slipped into history, and I guessed I was about to follow right after him. This was bad—the mourning period for Ben, all of five minutes, seemed officially over. He'd never been a particularly big earner at the firm, so I supposed public expressions of grief would be kept to a minimum. "Yes, it will be a year in April."

Mr. Cantor tamped out his cigarette and waved a hand to clear away the smoke. "A whole year," he said, without irony. "How about that."

Here it comes, I thought. I could feel sweat gathering on my upper lip, but I didn't dare wipe it away.

"With Ben gone—well. There really isn't a position here for you doing criminal work, Paul."

I could almost hear the firing squad loading their rifles. "I hadn't considered that," I said, lying. "I guess I'm still overwhelmed by his passing."

"A tragedy—we'll all miss Ben. Certainly."

"No one more than me."

"And of course the firm must carry on best it can." Mr. Cantor smiled without reassurance, and I smiled back because that's what men do in these situations. It lets the other fellow know you aren't going all warm and gooey over a trivial event in the grand scheme like the death of a colleague. Like the old joke says, even five hundred dead lawyers at the bottom of the ocean would make but an excellent start.

AT LAST ERIC CANTOR GOT DOWN TO BUSINESS:

"I'm sure you know TateAir is our biggest client and, as luck would have it—" He paused to again drink water, three big swallows. "I think you, among all of us here at the firm, may be in a unique position to do our client a good turn."

The firing squad seemed to stand down. Could I take off my blindfold now? "I'm afraid I don't understand."

Cantor seemed amused. "Sure you do."

Confusion and relief swirled in my head like bats in an attic. I let myself relax for the first time and ease back into the red leather couch facing his desk. I could see almost all the way to Georgetown through the large window behind my boss. The nation's capitol lay all around us. We were at the center of the world, or at least everyone in DC acted that way.

"As you've no doubt heard, my friend Jack Tate, at seventy-three, has had an epiphany of some sort. The result is a wish to sell his airline; the wisdom of doing so is not for us to say. What you may not have heard is that we've found a buyer."

The deal would be sweet for the firm. Rumors had swirled about who would benefit most. I told him I had not heard of a buyer, probably the first true thing I'd said. What would a stakeholder ask?

"Is it the buyer we want?"

He chuckled and said, yes, he thought so. "But, here's the rub: like a cross-country pilot, we've run into a bit of a head-wind. And it's at the FAA."

My anxiety began to return. Perhaps I had taken my blind-fold off too soon. I knew now where this was leading, but I feigned ignorance. "What can we do about that?"

Mr. Cantor eyed his half-cigarette in the cut glass ashtray, licked his lips, thought better of lighting another. "Now, as we do compile dossiers on our young lawyers—their hobbies, the clubs they belong to, things like that—I happen to know you have a connection at the agency."

"I can't help feeling a little odd at being surveilled."

"As though background checks aren't a part of everyone's life now. It's good business. We never know when an outside interest of one of the associates might enhance our value to a client."

I already knew where this was going, but still played dumb. "And in my case—?"

Mr. Cantor, with a quizzical frown, leaned across his desk. "Is your sister not married to an FAA functionary named Arthur Peck? I believe that she is," answering his own question. "Yes, I do believe she is."

Arthur was a mid-level bureaucrat at the FAA. One didn't have to be Sherlock Holmes to see where this was going. The firm's private investigators had done their job and turned up a shiny penny. The thought of it all chilled me to the bone— what about the rest of my history? I had never mentioned Arthur to Ben, not that I recalled. They just knew, Mr. Cantor and Ben. Maybe they went over my dossier together. The more I thought about it, of course they did.

The thought then crossed my mind that Ben might also have known about the affair. Well, if he did, he never let on. It started about five minutes after I showed up, so I felt like only a player in an ongoing drama. His demeanor had been uniformly warm up until our last lunch.

Maybe he didn't give a damn what she did. They'd been married for over twenty years, and you wonder in some marriages if those things don't matter so much, not after all that time.

Further, he had a history of heart problems; she said it had been years since they'd slept together. But of course she would say that. Such a rationalization, true or not, assuaged the guilt Pamela had at times displayed.

I felt guilty as hell, too. Sure. Ben, a friend. How could I not? I owed him my whole career. And yet…

There was another possibility, though. Maybe Cantor had known about Arthur all the time, and that's why he let Ben hire me. Perhaps there had been no need for me to tell all those lies about where I had gone to law school and done my clerkship.

Or maybe it was my willingness to lie which had convinced them I was their man. Someone who would lie on his resume wouldn't think twice about compromising his brother-in-law.

I was starting to wonder who had fooled whom.

Mr. Cantor seemed a little disappointed he had to lay all this out to me in such minute detail. "Good connections, Paul, are quite valuable in this town. Like strands of gold."

"I'm aware of this."

"Of course you are." He smiled. "It's not like a mission in the jungle. All we'd like you to do is wrangle information out of Mr. Peck regarding the holdup of the TateAir merger. Simple as that."

My brother-in-law would take some handling, at least with the lip service he paid to his 'duty' as a public servant, one rather proud of his position. I would have to tread carefully. "Arthur's scrupulous about conflicts of interest."

"As we knew about your relationship to him, this is another fact of which we're aware."

Clarity descended like an angel—Cantor and Miller needed a double-agent who could manipulate an underpaid bureaucrat into granting their petition. Having already demonstrated my willingness to do pretty much whatever it took to get this job, I wondered:

Maybe they're on to me. Have been the whole time.

Herein lay a bit of trouble with little fabrications such as the ones I've engineered about myself. One is never quite sure who knows which truth.

Mr. Cantor, with a wave of his hand, hoped to make any objections disappear as he had done with the smoke from his cigarette. "Now, I can see your inner sense of conflict. But, we don't peddle influence here."

"So what is it you want me to do?"

"We require our client's point of view put before the people who need to hear it—the right people. Certainly, Mr. Peck wouldn't object to such a fair-minded, by-the-book proposal?"

"No, I don't think he could justify doing so."

Cantor's veil of conviviality cooled into the stony gray face of a statue. "Well, he has found enough reasons for doing so thus far. And we've got to do, you and I, is chip away at this pernicious resistance—it simply won't do."

I mulled the situation: The second I bring up the merger, Arthur will object. He's married now, though. And my sister, well, she wants a house in a place like Potomac, they could never afford. Not on his bureaucrat's salary.

⚓

I TOLD CANTOR I FELT QUITE CERTAIN ARTHUR WOULD BE something of a problem, but he was also a person who sometimes expressed feelings that the world hadn't quite appreciated him fully. It's the disappointments we suffer in life, even the imagined ones, that make us vulnerable.

"Now that's a piece of information we didn't have." His grin split his face like a triumphant rising sun. "An important one."

Our tone became officious. "I can't guarantee any miracles—"

"—no—"

"—but I'll certainly speak to him about it."

"Just make sure he knows why we believe this merger is good not only for the airline industry, but for the public. And the country."

Mr. Cantor came around from behind his desk and joined me on the couch. "You'll be working with Enid Pearl over in M&A. She's handling the tax side of things, but I think she could use a little help from someone like you—a person who knows how things operate in the real world."

A coldness settled in my gut. His eyes bore into mine. "Do I, though?"

He laughed, though I meant nothing humorous. "I'm sure you're thinking how boring corporate law will be compared with criminal defense work, but you're mistaken. Criminal law is mere sociology, but corporate law is where all the real lawyers play chess." He stared out at Georgetown as he spoke. He seemed carried away by this snippet of obscure wisdom, his voice taking on a more sententious air, a lecturer. "You see, civil cases are won by the lawyers capable of finding the game-changers, the sneaky little obscure connections among players in cases no one else has even begun to consider."

And now my role became clear. I needn't worry about my lack of experience in mergers and acquisitions. I was a linchpin, one I now hoped would remain as 'important' as he had suggested.

"Ever do any sailing, Paul?" Mr. Cantor glanced at the picture of his sailboat sitting on his desk where other men had pictures of their family. "Nothing like it."

I felt ashamed I had never been sailing, and until today, had never even known anyone who owned a sailboat. If I admitted to this it seemed my whole life with its endless worries about money, its bad haircuts and cheap shoes, would be laid across Mr. Cantor's desk, ready for an autopsy. I thought about lying, but it would be too easy for him to trip me up with some damn nautical term or other. Was starboard right or left? What was a square hitch?

There was nothing for it but to confess. I felt my face go red. "No, I haven't."

"No matter. We'll soon make a sailor out of you."

He said this as if he meant it, and I believed him. Once I brought home this airline merger, I could already see myself on sunny weekends sailing the Chesapeake Bay with Mr. Cantor.

"Did you get in any time on the water while on vacation?"

"Almost every day. Mrs. Cantor, she hates the ocean... which, of course, makes sailing the perfect hobby for me."

We both laughed like two men who understood the limits of our relations with women.

"Sometimes we have folks from the office—young people like yourself—come down to the bay house for a weekend. You should now be among them."

"I'd like that very much."

"Perhaps I could take you, your sister and her husband to dinner one evening. How do you feel about La Ferme?"

I'd heard of that restaurant, as well known for being expensive as it was for its food, a display of wealth important to the DC players who patronized it and the other elite eateries in town, of which there were ample. "I'm sure they'd like that very much."

"I'll have Manon make reservations for us." Mr. Cantor got up and looked at his calendar. "Let's say Thursday, at eight sharp, if she can get us in then."

I thought how pleased Arthur and Brenda would be to have dinner at La Ferme, but it occurred to me that perhaps it wouldn't be such a good idea after all. What made me valuable to Mr. Cantor was my connection to Arthur—if the two of them met, wouldn't I become the suddenly dispensable middleman? And, there was no reason yet to tell Arthur how important his help was to the firm. No sense in giving him a swelled head.

No—I'd make up some excuse to put off the dinner. I'd have to be careful not to let Arthur know how much I needed him. Our relationship up to now had been cordial and cool. I couldn't come on too strong.

"You can bring someone if you like."

"Thank you. I will."

For a brief moment I considered asking Patty Swain, a clerk in the prosecutor's office. We had often flirted with each other when I was over there. But, she wouldn't fit in at La

Ferme. And besides, I had to think of some plausible reason why Arthur couldn't go to dinner.

"We'll make the reservations for six, then." Mr. Cantor made a note on his calendar with his fountain pen. There was no computer on his desk. Those were gadgets for law clerks and secretaries, not senior partners.

He blotted the ink with a piece of paper. "I'd like you to introduce yourself to Ms. Pearl tomorrow. She'll tell you what needs doing on a more prosaic level."

"I've already met Ms. Pearl." I had seen her in the elevator a number of times, but we had never spoken.

"Very attractive, don't you think? And bright too," he added quickly to chase away any whiff of sexism. "You'll learn a great deal from her."

"I'm sure I will."

"And, Paul, I'd prefer that you keep this business about your brother-in-law just between us for now."

"I understand."

"I know you do." He sat down again to go back to his messages. "Talk to Manon about arranging an office for you near Enid's."

Well—all that turned out a long way from being fired. But Cantor still left me feeling on the spot; as if he had the goods on me. All accomplished liars have irritable and active imaginations, with mine being no different. I closed the door behind me, the sweat on my upper lip almost, *almost* dry.

⛵

THE BRUNETTE WOMAN AT THE RECEPTION DESK GLANCED UP briefly at me before going back to her crossword puzzle. Meanwhile, I couldn't take my eyes off her.

Manon was the receptionist for the senior partners and

corporate lawyers. Those of us on the twelfth floor rarely caught a glimpse of her. Quite elegant and beautiful, Manon; some hinted that she might be sleeping with Mr. Cantor. If true, he certainly had exquisite taste.

After thirty seconds of watching her struggle with the puzzle, I leaned across her desk and said, "'Centaur'."

"Excuse me?"

I pointed to the newspaper. "That's the answer to five across."

She seemed more annoyed than pleased. "You sound so sure."

"Maybe I'm a genius."

"If that were the case you'd be a partner, not an associate."

I laughed. She had me dead to rights. "I did that puzzle this morning. That's the only reason I know."

She seemed to accept my explanation and smiled. I could sometimes resist showing off in front of a woman, but never one as attractive as Manon.

"I'm transferring from the criminal defense section downstairs. Mr. Cantor says you can find me an office."

She folded her paper neatly in half and laid it to one side. "I didn't hear anything about that from Eric."

I was surprised to hear her refer to Mr. Cantor as Eric. Perhaps she was sleeping with him after all, or perhaps exercising the prerogatives of an attractive woman in a powerful position.

I stole a glance at her legs. "He said I should see you about it."

Noticing my downward gaze she asked, icy, "Seen enough?"

Like all men, I persuaded myself she appreciated the attention. "For now."

A standoff. Then the ice broke, and she gave me a sly

smile. "There's a corner office available, but it's supposed to be for partners only." She tapped a brightly polished red nail against a floor plan that showed a smallish office marked *available*.

I noticed she hadn't said I couldn't have the office, only that I *shouldn't* have it. Certainly there was an invitation to mischief in there somewhere. "So I'll be a naughty boy in there, then."

She lifted an eyebrow. "I'll make the arrangements."

I tried to sound as if I were joking so I could retreat if she was offended by my offer: "What if I were to make amends for all this bother with a decent lunch at, say, Chez Brown?"

She seemed to think it over. "Make it dinner, and we'll talk."

We were walking on the same tightrope now, each watching the other for a misstep which could bring this playful business to an abrupt end. We shook hands. I held hers for a moment, long enough to feel the steady and insistent pulse in her wrist. "We have a deal."

She withdrew her hand and tugged at her skirt to signal that I was to behave myself.

The telephone rang and she picked it up after letting it ring a bit. "Cantor and Miller... oh, yes. Thank you, Senator. Mr. Cantor is heartbroken over the news about Mr. Schiller. Yes, yes. I will certainly extend your condolences..."

I knew it was reckless of me to flirt with Manon, but the fact that she might be having an affair with Mr. Cantor only made her even more appealing. It was precisely her unavailability I found irresistible. Of course, that's what had first drawn me to Pamela Schiller—the sinful, electric, afternoon pleasures which only a hungrily unfaithful wife can bring.

without looking up from a legal pad covered in notes. That was one of the techniques people in the firm used to show you how unimportant you were. I had been through this so often I had learned to stare dreamily off into space until my tormentor got bored and finally said something of importance. It rarely took longer than a minute or two of noncommittal grunts and uh-huhs on my part to bring these little discourses to an end.

Her vibe throughout remained icy. *This is going splendidly*, I thought.

Her blond hairdo, cut brutally short in one of those severe styles which leave little room for traditional femininity, nonetheless complimented her hard, oval face, one which had likely been cute as a button before law school and the legal trade had hammered the innocent out of her. Her black-rimmed glasses reinforced that impression.

Against my will I had to agree with Cantor; she was still attractive. I could imagine channeling some of her energy into a different direction. And with the Pamela situation irrevocably changed—I saw our relationship only in terms of a secretive affair, and without that context it held no interest or excitement—perhaps Enid would be the next pearl on my string of conquests.

Why I got off so much on having other men's wives and girlfriends is probably grist for some psychoanalyst's mill. I don't spend much time on such navel-gazing matters. No time—I am in the water with sharks, like those sailors from the USS Indianapolis. I'm only trying to stay alive, not explore my neuroses. I just *am*. That is my secret.

TIME FOR BUSINESS.

"As you know, Mr. Cantor has asked me to partner with you," a careful choice of words, "on bringing home the TateAir merger."

She folded her hands in front of her. Sighed. "That's the rumor."

"I'd call it 'news.'" I smiled, winked. "I believe you're handling the tax side of things."

Now she placed her hands palms-down on the desk to either side of her legal pad. "First of all, Paul, you're working for me. I'm lead counsel on the merger," she added, in case I didn't understand the chain of command. "And that means I'm responsible for all aspects of its success, taxation-related or otherwise."

"How about failure?" I couldn't resist a little display of insubordination. "Will you also be taking that responsibility?"

One eyebrow shot up, but this was the only sign she gave that my dart had struck home. "The merger is going—fine, so far." She began jotting down some notes to signal she had more important things to do than to waste her time talking to me. "But if Mr. Cantor says we need you, then I guess we do."

"Mr. Cantor is under the impression you're having some difficulties getting the FAA to sign off." I rolled that little grenade across the floor to see how she would react to it.

"It's nothing unusual for the FAA to scrutinize a transaction of this magnitude with great care. But, I'm mystified that he thinks someone with a background in criminal defense will be of much help with this."

"It's possible, Enid, I have talents of which you're unaware."

Unimpressed, she put her notes away and gave me a hard glare. "I didn't ask to have you assigned to me, but since you're here and I can't do anything about it, I'd like you to prepare a memorandum on some loans made by the Tate

Family Trust to the Barbara Tate Trust. I think they total around two million dollars, were made over the past three years."

"What's the issue?"

"Mr. Tate would like to write them off as bad debt, and I've assured him he could. Put a memo together confirming my opinion, and then we'll see how much of a 'partnership' this relationship is." Without waiting for any more witty responses she stood to indicate our little chat had ended. "My assistant will give you the files."

I scribbled some notes in my pocket notebook. "I think I've got it."

"You do know enough about tax law to recognize the elements of a gift, I assume?" Her tone left no doubt that she felt I was out of my league in tax matters.

"Actually, I do." Of course in reality I had no idea what constituted a gift under the law in the District, but I didn't think it would be tough to find out. I've faked my way through some unbelievably complex legal situations simply by cramming like a hungover final-exam college student right before meetings, often in which people's lives and freedom were on the line. "I think you'll be surprised by all I can do."

"Let's hope so."

"No need for hope. That's a guarantee."

"In any case, I'm having breakfast with the Tate's at the Mayflower Hotel Thursday morning, so I'll need your memo on my desk by tomorrow afternoon."

"Consider it done."

I went to offer my hand, but Enid had already all-but pushed me out the door. She closed it with enough force to punctuate her dislike of even being in the same room with me. The sound echoed in the quiet M&A hallway.

Now, this was going to be a challenge on multiple fronts.

But the risk-reward I had run on this deal in my head gave me the tingles. So much money on the table. How would I snag some for myself?

I SPENT THE REST OF THE DAY LOOKING AT THE TWO FILES I HAD been given. After a little research and a phone call to an old pal who indeed knew about such tax situations, it didn't take long to realize Ms. Pearl's advice to the Tates may have been mistaken. I admit taking a secret pleasure in this conclusion, and looked forward to presenting her with this error the next day.

However, I needed to be sure of myself before I challenged her. She was, after all, the firm's senior tax attorney. And it seemed odd that something so obvious to me, indeed far from an expert in tax environments, had flown right by her.

I brought the files home with me so I could work on them, but not until after I took Bismarck for a run and got my thoughts together.

The light of the setting sun outside lay golden across the neighborhood. As I got into the park, the smell of the city fell away. With both of us in top shape, we followed the trail along Rock Creek Park for a mile and a half before turning around. Glorious, the light and the cool air on my face. Once the endorphins kicked in, I forgot everything but the blood pumping in my healthy veins. When I run, it feels like freedom. Maybe sailing with Mr. Cantor one day would offer similar pleasures.

WHEN WE RETURNED TO MY BLOCK, BOTH THE DOG'S TONGUE and mine were both hanging out with fatigue—the best kind.

I felt strong and centered, albeit pensive. Much had happened in only a short time, and the reality started to sink in. The last thing I tend to do is let reality get too tight a grip on my plans and schemes, however, so I dismissed it as brusquely as Enid had dismissed me.

As the dog and I came strolling in cool-down mode around the corner, I was surprised, or maybe not, to see Pamela Schiller sitting on the doorstep. We had not spoken since the late-night call. She had been busy with all the details and duties of tending to a sudden death—arrangements, phone calls, insurance and bureaucracy, family. It goes without saying that a secret lover, at least in such times, represents anything but 'family.'

We embraced in silence, awkward rather than tender; it didn't help my being damp with perspiration. I invited her inside. Bismarck licked her hand and followed her down the steps. He had seen her a few times over the past few months, during our stolen hours here or in a hotel room.

As there was only one chair, Pamela sat on my bed. She had been horrified the first time we had had a tryst here. Had no idea I lived such an 'ascetic' life, as she put it.

"I'm sorry to drop by like this, but I needed to talk."

"I'm glad you came." I wasn't.

"This is a mess."

"What—us?"

"All of it."

I shook my head. "Not to the rest of the world. Not the 'us' part." I needed to probe, to make sure our affair had remained discrete. "Right?"

"Inner turmoil is closer to it."

I gave her the most sincere smile I could. "I'm so sorry about Ben."

Her face took on a brittle cast, stony and stolid, as though if I touched her she would crumble into dust. "Thank you."

While Ben was alive it was difficult for her to get away, so there had never been unannounced visits. We planned each meeting with great care so she would not be seen coming here. That caution had added to the allure of it all. But this visit held no thrill. It had only a formal air, a necessarily funereal one rather than erotic and dangerous.

I wondered if I should go sit next to her on the bed. As is so often the case with men and women, I had no idea what she expected of me—more sex? A new life partner? Surely neither.

Pamela began to cry. "I didn't want to come. Everything is so up in the air."

I went to comfort her, but she waved me away. I stood at a respectable distance. "I'm sure things aren't really as bleak as they look right now."

"Are you serious? Ben was my whole world. We were nothing in comparison." In a flash she realized how this sounded. She again broke down, trashing another in a series of tissues. "Not that it might have seemed that way to you."

I told her I understood, more than she knew.

How ill equipped we are to say anything genuine, anything worthwhile, in these moments. I could only think of other clichés exposing how shallow our relationship really was. Other than sex, we didn't have much in common. And the sex, good as it was, wasn't enough to weather this storm.

She dried her eyes. "I usually don't cry. Not ever. Now I can't seem to stop…"

"It's a different look for you, that's for sure."

And now, a chuckle. Sad, but a laugh nonetheless. "Yes. I can only imagine how alluring."

She put her handkerchief back into her purse and I was relieved. I hoped it meant an end to her tears. "Ben and I had a good marriage. We had a lot of fun at first. Maybe everybody does...?"

"I wouldn't know."

She gazed over into the tiny kitchen, the only other room in the apartment. "He was always good with the children, too."

I thought for a moment she had forgotten to whom she was speaking. "Recalling happier times is healthy."

Or, not. She seemed crushed by the weight of past good times. "We went to Nova Scotia for our honeymoon. It was late September, and already so cold. When we opened the door of our cabin, we saw snow, an early snowfall. It was so beautiful, so strange—when we left home, from Maryland at the time, it had still felt like summer. The change in weather underscored the transition we had made. And I'd never been so happy in my life." She hung her head. "I wish it had been me who died."

"Well, I certainly enjoyed working with Ben," I said, pulling back from the emotional edge, and to let her know I too found him human and vital and a friend. "And I imagine a handsome young Benjamin seemed quite the catch."

It wasn't necessary; she was lost in memories probably only half true. After all, memories are a kind of painting we make of our past, leaving things off the canvas we no longer want while adding details we'd like to see instead.

"Mother liked him right away. I was dating another boy when we met, one I'd known since high school. At first I wasn't attracted to Ben, but my mother said give him a chance. I did, and found she was right. He was a good husband and a good father," she repeated with emphasis.

Pamela looked over at me as though she had remembered someone else was in the room. "But we had lost something."

"That happens with couples."

"So it seems."

I assumed she offered all this to explain our affair, assuage the guilt she obviously felt. I wondered if I had been the only one, not that it mattered. I hadn't asked, but couldn't help being curious. "Everyone at the firm liked him. His reputation was stellar." I babbled, now, trying not to get in the way of her reveries.

"Ben thought you a clever lawyer. And, he liked you personally. We both did." She scratched Bismarck behind the ears. He leaned all his weight against her legs.

I had to ask. "Did he tell Cantor about my brother-in-law?"

"Yes, when the merger began to stall. But, he said Eric already knew about your connection at the FAA." Left unanswered was the question of how Ben had learned about my brother-in-law in the first place.

I had to put her on the stand. "Did Ben ever say anything about the FAA before the firm hired me?"

Lost in a fresh reverie, she gave a small shrug. "I have no idea." Pamela stood and straightened her skirt. She leaned forward and kissed me on the cheek. "I've got to go. Thank you for listening to me."

"Probably best to end things, now. It's not like we were having a love affair."

"Do you really want to know what Ben liked about you, why he hired you?"

I said I'd be interested.

"That you're a heartless bastard."

However true, it still stung. "Pamela, I'm a lawyer. That's like the pot calling the—the kettle—"

"Oh, I found it attractive at first. I think Ben did, too. To us it looked like strength. But, now?"

I followed her outside without speaking, nor did she finish articulating her moment of truth. What was there to say? I let my hand touch her back for a brief second as Pamela got in and shut the door of her Mercedes. Without looking back, she drove away up Wisconsin Avenue.

I watched her taillights and wondered if she knew the car was leased to the firm, and that the lease terminated upon the death of the partner. I hoped Mr. Cantor would break the news to her gently.

3

Early on Wednesday I rose with the sun, got in an enjoyable walk with the dog. After a quick shower and a generic-brand toaster pastry I hustled over to the office and began studying the Pearl Memorandum, as I thought of my assignment. It sounded like one of those spy novels that were once all the rage, back when people still read books.

As I began to research and write, however, I found myself with more questions than answers. I ended up spending most of the morning on the telephone trying to piece together the complex history of the Tate loans. By noon I knew enough to draft my memo, although after reading it over, I doubted what I had produced would satisfy Enid Pearl. I sent over my assessment, which was that we could have a slight problem with a few intra-family loans, and waited.

⚓

I HAD ONLY GOTTEN HALFWAY THROUGH MY CATALOGUE OF USED sailboats when my telephone rang. Ms. Pearl wanted to see me at once. The word her assistant used? "Immediately."

I struggled not to laugh as I made my way to her office, feeling like a naughty schoolboy about to face the principal. Ms. Pearl's assistant couldn't suppress a rather alarmed look at my grin as she motioned me into the inner office.

I knocked on the door even though it was open. I could see my memorandum lying on her desk. It was covered in notes written in red ink, the favorite color of angry people everywhere.

Enid, on the telephone, gestured with her free hand to the leather chair in front of her desk. I sat holding my research to my chest to shield me from the blows I knew were about to come.

Enid hung up and replaced her earring. She had an odd smile. "Quite a memo."

"You seem to have some notes for me."

She tried to appear upbeat, even chipper, but I could see beneath the practiced smile that she fumed. "I look the liberty of making comments where I thought you were off the mark."

Thinking she meant for me to examine her copious notes, I reached for the memo. "Well, let's see where I went wrong."

She put her hand over the documents to stop me. "No one can blame you for making a mistake. You're new to transactional law."

True enough. And yet: "There was no mistake."

Her already fake smile faltered. She waited.

"Based on my research, it appears Barbara Tate made one interest payment on the loans and no payment on principal." I tapped the pile of paper on her desk. Ms. Pearl might know a great deal about taxes, but I knew about evidence. "The transfers were gifts meant to appear as loans to avoid the gift tax."

"I don't think you understood your assignment."

I asked how.

"You were to confirm my opinion that the transfers were indeed loans." The cheery voice was gone now, replaced by words squeezed through clenched teeth. "That was your purpose here."

Ms. Pearl was calling the loans *transfers*. At least I understood her thinking. I kept my hand on the research I had brought with me. Like a detective's ankle gun, it was there if I needed it.

"I appreciate your disappointment, but the law is quite clear. The normal presumption of a loan is reversed in those cases where the transfers are made between related parties."

"Mr. Johns, you'll either agree to rework this memo or be fired. I'll call Cantor right now." She reached for the telephone, but not with much enthusiasm. "Those are your choices. Don't you understand you could put the merger in jeopardy?"

Now I wondered if Mr. Cantor had informed her the real purpose of my being here was to get my brother-in-law to move the Tate FAA application along. I guessed not, or we wouldn't be having this conversation. In any event, Mr. Cantor wasn't about to fire me. Not until I delivered Arthur, anyway.

"Before you do that, I should point out that the promissory notes totaled nine million, the 'transfers' made over a period of eleven years," I said. "With interest and penalties, the total tax liability is more like fifteen million banana skins," trying to lighten the mood, "which is starting to sound like real money."

Enid withdrew her hand from the phone. "You yourself said there were promissory notes for each loan. That doesn't sound like a gift."

"A gift someone's attempting to disguise as a loan, maybe." I examined my copies of the paperwork. "See here—five of them don't even meet the formal requirements in the District for a promissory note."

"That's your first mistake—they were probably executed in Virginia." Ms. Pearl leaned back in her chair, pleased with how easy it had been to trip me up.

This was starting to be fun. All I had to do now was keep laying my cards on the table, one at a time. Like in a game of poker, one of us was bluffing. Which one would soon be clear. "Yes. But, these documents don't meet the requirements there, either."

She froze in mid-recline. Folded her hands in her lap. "And yet I've already told Jack Tate we thought he could take the bad debt deduction on these."

"Who is 'we'?" I shrugged. "I'd never have let him think that."

Ms. Pearl eyed her copy of my memo with the busy red scrawls over it. "Be that as it may: redo your memo. Work all night, if necessary." She tapped her finger on the desk to emphasize her point. "But for God's sake, make it conform to the man's expectations."

"Doing so won't change anything about the law. I do have an idea, though."

"This should be interesting."

I ignored her sarcasm. "We'll have the Tates agree that five of the promissory notes are probably unenforceable, and so of diminished value and concern. The remaining four notes total three and a half million dollars. Ms. Tate's home in the District is worth almost that."

"What are you getting at?"

"Simple. I suggest she deed it over to the Tate Family Trust and we call the debt settled. Mr. Tate could then write off the uncollected balance, although I would strongly recommend against that. That might encourage the IRS to look more deeply into all this. That's the sword dangling over our heads."

Enid Pearl's crystal blue eyes widened with alarm. "How do you know what her house is worth?"

"I checked the tax assessor's rolls."

"I think Barbara Tate might find that a bit invasive, don't you?"

"And I think her father would prefer to avoid paying fifteen million in taxes... don't you?"

"I don't doubt it for a moment."

Checkmate.

Ms. Pearl slid my memo off to one side. No longer playing the bully, a hint of self-pity now crept in her voice. "Well, there's nothing to do but tell them I was mistaken."

"But we also have a solution to the problem."

"Mr. Tate already thinks I can't get this damn merger through as it is."

For only a moment, a brief one, I wished for her sake she had been right about the promissory notes. I could feel her anxiety from across the table. "One question's been troubling me since I first looked at this file."

"Do tell," she said, weary.

"Who is it we really represent, here?"

Ms. Pearl canted her head to one side, made no effort to hide her annoyance. "You mean 'whom' do we represent. And in this case, it's the Tates, of course."

"Both of them?"

The impatient, imperious Ms. Pearl returned in full bloom. "The firm has represented them both for almost twenty years."

"We can't represent them both in this case. The Tate Family Trust is the creditor. The Barbara Tate Trust is the debtor. Even the client can't waive that conflict." It was obvious this had never occurred to Ms. Pearl. Or to anyone else at the firm, so eager were they to please their most important clients.

"I don't want to have to tell one of them at breakfast tomorrow that they have to hire another firm." Her eyes bulged with a fear she couldn't hide, even from a new subordinate. "Mr. Cantor will have my head."

"You don't have to tell him."

"Go on."

"Your advice will make it clear who your client is. I think our solution is a good one. It will certainly convince the IRS that a good faith effort was made to collect on these loans. That'll at least sidestep the gift tax issue."

Enid seemed to brighten up when I used the word *loans*. "You've been very thorough in investigating this."

"I'm a criminal defense lawyer—remember? In my work, people's lives are often at stake."

We both smiled, she rather wanly, me in full triumph.

"Yes, I think Seth said something about that."

I could only imagine what Seth, a man I didn't even know, had said about me. I felt a wave of paranoia and self consciousness as I stood to collect my papers. "Well, it's time for the old steam whistle, and I've got to go home and let out my dog. The last time I was late, he chewed the handle of my tennis racket clean through."

"Do you play?"

"I haven't in years, but I was on the team in college." Another of my little fibs. My mother did make me take lessons in high school, but that had been the extent of the tennis. We were both sure I would meet rich girls on the courts, but all the young women I encountered were as poor as I was—they were there for the same reason.

"I'll mention it to Seth. He's always looking for someone to play with."

"Sure. Sounds great." In truth I didn't care to meet Seth, nor play tennis with him. In fact, I wished a Seth wasn't even in Enid's picture. Her eyes were beautiful, never more than when fierce with indignation. I could imagine all sorts of post-merger meetings with her, none of which would have anything to do with the law we practiced by day. "A good challenge is always welcome."

THE NEXT MORNING I AWOKE WITH A ROCK IN MY STOMACH. It only got worse as I rode in a cab to the Mayflower Hotel to meet the Tates; the President's motorcade held up the side-street traffic for several moments.

When at last I came hurrying into the dining room, Ms. Pearl and our clients, the Tates, were already seated. When she saw me appear over Jack Tate's right shoulder, her eyes widened in surprise. I was the last person she expected to see.

My greeting: "Enid, I wanted to give you these." I handed her copies of the nine promissory notes. Nodding to the Tates, I continued, "And I wanted to apologize for my mistake in thinking they could be deducted as bad debt."

Enid got my meaning. "Anyone can make a mistake. I believe you know the Tates already—?" She introduced me.

Barbara Tate held a spoon poised over her cup as she spoke. "I don't think we've met, Mr. Johns. But you seem to know a great deal about me."

"It's all about doing my job."

Mr. Tate, smiling, extended his hand. "Sit down and join us, son." He snapped his fingers and a server appeared. "We have an additional guest. Tea or coffee, young man?"

"Thank you. I'd love a cup of Earl Grey."

The waiter decamped to procure my tea. "Now, my baby girl Babs here isn't very fond of you, Mr. Johns." Jack Tate laughed at his daughter's petulance. Mr. Tate watched closely to see how I reacted. "She thinks you're being too picky about these *loans*, as we've always referred to them."

"I was asked to perform due diligence."

Jack Tate's eyes twinkled in a face ruddy and wrinkled, as though he'd spent more of his life outdoors than inside an office building. He seemed impish, as though enjoying his daughter's discomfort in some perverse parental way. His manner was more working class than refined. His suit didn't appear tailored; he had not had a manicure like Mr. Cantor back at the office. "Be that as it may, Ms. Pearl says you believe Babs must give up her house because of those damn promissory notes. Now you can't expect her to think very highly of you when you go around saying things like that, can you?"

"The significance of me being 'picky' is about fifteen million dollars in gift tax and penalties." I kept my eyes on Mr. Tate. "But let's not shoot the messenger."

"There was no gift, Mr. Johns, and the promissory notes prove that." Babs put down her spoon. "I don't see how being a criminal defense lawyer qualifies you to render an opinion on transactions that took place before you were even out of law school. I think you may be a little out of your depth in this business."

"Don't be a snob. Mr. Johns is here to help us through this." Mr. Tate, brusque, signaled the waiter for another round cup of coffee and for my tea.

"Actually, Ms. Tate, if you'll let me take you through the law on this, I think—"

"It's Ms. Wolcott, if you please." Babs smiled around the table as if to say, if I couldn't get her name straight, how could I possibly know anything about the legal situation?

"I'm sorry, *Ms. Wolcott*, but I understood that in your most recent divorce you asked the court to restore your maiden name, and," I checked my pocket notebook like a detective investigating a crime, "the motion was granted on November 10th of last year."

A silence settled around the table. It lasted through the server's visit, a dapper young man whose silent and meticulous bearing suited the high-dollar nature of the dining room.

After the server left, Mr. Tate chuckled. "Paul's got you there, Babs." He put three lumps of sugar into his coffee and stirred it with his spoon. He had the serenity of a man without a care in the world. "Someone's certainly done his homework."

"Actually, my background as a criminal defense lawyer makes me ideal for this issue." I squeezed lemon into my tea, stirred, sipped. "The defective promissory notes coupled with no payments made by you, and no effort made by your father to collect on the debt, is the sort of thing I saw in garden variety fraud cases all the time."

I hoped I hadn't gone too far. Enid, who had been sitting in stony silence, looked further shocked by the nasty turn this breakfast had taken. My using the word 'fraud' had brought everyone up short… except for Jack Tate.

Babs spoke first. "Are you suggesting my father and I committed fraud?"

"Not at all. I'm saying that's how the Internal Revenue Service will view these transactions." The tea felt good on my tight throat. When I gamble I go big, and my nerves felt stretched thin.

"I thought the statute of limitations stopped them from going back into your returns after three years." Babs seemed to have lost her appetite for grapefruit and for insulting me. Someone had been coaching her on the finer points of tax law. That someone wasn't a good coach, though. I hoped it wasn't Enid Pearl.

"Generally that's true, but in this case they'll allege civil fraud, which will allow them to go back to the first loan. They'll argue they couldn't discover the true nature of these transactions precisely because of the fraudulent returns you filed, and I suspect a judge will agree with them."

"The right judge will," Tate said. "Or rather, the wrong one."

"Yes," I agreed, nodding, trying to make sure the father saw I was still their legal counsel and could be trusted, at least to a certain extent. "The wrong judge."

"Well, I've heard enough," Mr. Tate said.

Enid, meanwhile, had turned the color of the fine-dining white tablecloth. "Jack, please let me apologize. I had no idea this issue would be so—so—"

"Apologize? Ms. Pearl, I think we should do just as your Paul Johns here says. Once the whining is done, Babs will sign her house over to the trust, and that will be that." Mr. Tate tossed his napkin into his plate and called for the check, signaling that the meeting was at an end.

"Actually, there is something else," I said. "Because her house now belongs to the trust, we'll have to show that Ms. Tate pays a reasonable monthly rent."

Babs boiled over. *"I'll be damned if I'll pay rent to live in my own house."*

Her father spoke softly, gently. "You must, dear, or the rental value of the property will constitute an additional gift to reinforce the case against us. Right, Mr. Johns?"

My earlier anxiety now vanished. Ms. Tate, or Babs, or whatever the hell her name was, could rage all she liked. But in the end, they would do as I had suggested. The merger was too important. Tate was already rich, but the deal would make him—and his female heir, if she had any sense—much more wealthy. "That's correct, sir."

"At least I can write off part of the debt she didn't pay." Mr.

Tate seemed pleased to have salvaged this mess. He showed us how a skilled businessman, the kind who goes the distance, feints and swerves away from an approaching disaster. But, most of all? How he keeps his cool throughout. *Fifteen million? Big deal. It'll all work out.* And so on.

"I'd recommend against doing so."

"Why?"

"The trust holds a great deal of TateAir common stock. Claiming such a deduction can only invite scrutiny from the IRS."

Tate grunted and nodded. "What else?"

"If they want to go after the gift tax they think you owe, they may very well put a lien on the shares owned by the trust. That could create problems for the merger Ms. Pearl is putting together." Putting all the pieces of this puzzle together, as well as maintaining an affect of confidence, had worn me out, I suddenly realized.

"You've really thought this through, Mr. Johns. Color me impressed." Mr. Tate and I shook hands again. "I'd like you to come by the office one day next week."

"I'll see what Ms. Pearl has scheduled for me," I said in genuine deference, or at least the appearance of it. I had already committed a breach of etiquette as it was—a junior associate showing up to meet with a client without the approval of a supervising partner had been my first gamble of the day.

"Just tell us when you'd like him to come by." Ms. Pearl offered Mr. Tate her hand. She seemed relived that all of this was winding up in a way that left her blameless.

Barbara Tate came around the table. "I'm sorry if I was rude. This whole business has had me on edge." We shook hands. "Perhaps you and Ms. Pearl would like to come by for a drink some time?"

"I'd like that." I let go of her soft, well-tended hand and nodded to Enid, who seemed to like the idea as well. "Let's get it scheduled."

ENID AND I CHOSE TO WALK BACK TO THE OFFICE TOGETHER, AT first in silence.

"It's obvious Tate is one of those successful men who'd never feel comfortable taking advice from a woman," Enid finally said at a crosswalk.

"It's unfair. But, he'll change with the times, or else become irrelevant." I needed to forge a bond with her. "You didn't get where you are by accident."

And yet, Tate's attitude seemed to have eroded my boss's self confidence. Far from being resentful, she seemed genuine in her happiness to have me deal with him. "That was good lawyering in there. I appreciate you for taking the blame for my mistake."

I gave an offhand shrug. "We're a team at Cantor and Miller."

"Well—the gesture meant a great deal to me."

Back at the office I found myself unable to sit still. After flipping through the sailboat catalog twice, I left for an early lunch. I wondered how I could turn TateAir into my own personal windfall. After his reception of me this morning, forging a relationship with Mr. Tate seemed possible. That much I knew.

When I returned from a lunch in which I'd walked more than eaten, I found a surprise on my desk: a green vase with a single long stemmed yellow rose. An unsigned card read only, *Thank you.*

I remembered in the Paris photograph how Enid had been

holding the same rose. I smiled at the thought of her knowing I would make the connection. Trusting that someone is as smart as you is like finding the thread of an invisible web between yourself and that person. I wondered what other threads I might find between us.

Knowing I don't cook, my sister Brenda often invited me over for dinner, typically on Thursdays. No subterfuge needed; no surprise visit from me to put my brother-in-law on the defensive. A normal family dinner. I maintained the strategic high ground—for now.

I wanted to bring up the question of why the TateAir merger had stalled in Arthur's department, but I had to do it in such a way it didn't appear as if I were trying to use my connection, tenuous as that was, to manipulate him. I brought along an especially expensive cheesecake, Arthur's favorite dessert. Simple, perhaps, but possibly effective.

⛵

WHEN BRENDA MET ME AT THE DOOR SHE LOOKED AS IF SHE might have been crying. She hugged me as usual and took the cheesecake, so I didn't think any more of it. Marriage gave everyone reasons to weep.

Arthur sat in the living room watching television, a political roundtable on PBS. He had been married to my sister for three years now, but every week when I came by their place he behaved in a manner so formal it was as though we were meeting for the first time. This evening was no different. At my appearance he switched off the television, stood, brushed lint from his slacks, came over with hands clasped and stood stiff as we shook hands and exchanged greetings like unfamiliar colleagues, not family.

I found my brother-in-law an odd duck; I always had. I often wondered why Brenda had married him. After I graduated from law school, Bismarck and I had lived in their back bedroom for a few months, but the experience—I rarely saw Arthur—gave me little insight into their marriage. His manner was as distant and formal with Brenda as everyone else. I couldn't imagine what living with such a cold fish must be like.

None of it mattered—Arthur's facilitation of the TateAir approval, and what a favorable outcome would mean to me, loomed paramount in my mind over our tenuous personal connection.

Once we sat down to eat Brenda, a traditionalist from childhood, said a blessing. Arthur wasn't a Catholic, so he unrolled his napkin into his lap as we bowed our heads. By the time I opened my eyes, he was already buttering a roll.

"Saw in the paper that your boss died," he said, dry as a desert wind.

I made the sign of the cross before answering. "It was a surprise to everyone. He was only forty-eight."

Arthur, never one to mince words, grunted and went *tsk-tsk*. "He looked older. All that extra weight, perhaps?"

Brenda offered me the platter of roasted chicken. It had a delicious scent, rosemary, sage, like Thanksgiving. "How's his poor wife holding up?"

"Poor indeed. I think he left her with very little money."

"That's not good. But, I meant emotionally."

"At the funeral she seemed to be bearing up pretty well." True enough.

Brenda eyed me across the table. She had seen me with Pamela once or twice, but I didn't believe she suspected about the affair. Her sense of marital propriety was positively Victorian. To her it would be inconceivable for a married woman to behave in such a manner, as well the brother, a good boy, who had just prayed alongside her.

"It must be difficult to lose your husband after you've been together for so long."

I took some broccoli from the serving dish and squeezed a lemon slice over the florets. "The conventional wisdom is that the last day of a marriage is often happier than the first."

Unamused: "How would you know—you got divorced after six months."

Arthur laughed, a true chortle. I admitted she had a point. He laughed again.

"We mustn't laugh about someone else's misfortune, dear." Ever my defender, Brenda chided her husband for his tastelessness. "I just meant he doesn't know what a lasting marriage requires. That's all."

"Ann wanted to have children." For Brenda, marriages had to have substantial reasons for ending, not stupid, selfish ones like bad sex, or too much drinking, or plain old boredom. To a devout Catholic, marital dissatisfactions such as these did not enter into the calculation. What was wedded remained wedded, lest drawing the ire of a vengeful Old Testament deity. "But I didn't. Simple as that."

"I hear she's married to a doctor now." Arthur was enjoying himself, no doubt about that. This was as close as he came to having a sense of humor. Cruel things amused him. "Brenda sees her at the hospital sometimes."

"I was going to tell you about that." My sister's face flushed as if caught in a lie. "She got married last month to one of our staff surgeons."

"Does she seem happy?"

Brenda shrugged. "Very much so."

"Did she ask about me?"

"Yes. I told her you were with Cantor and Miller now. That you're working on really big cases. She said to say hello."

"How lovely."

While I felt a failure at marriage, I can't say that I missed Ann Greene the Weeping Machine—she'd cry when I worked too many hours, when we didn't have sex for a few weeks, when I wanted sex too often, when my sister called too late at night, when someone I represented got off, when someone I represented went to jail for life, whenever the wind blew. Ann, a sweet soul too burdened for this world, represented the great flood in my life. The marriage lasted for six months, until all the tears finally washed me away.

I felt a pang like regret, a foreign sensation I quickly dismissed. "I'm happy for her—truly. Please tell her that. I was a terrible husband. She deserves better."

Smug, my sister's husband poured more wine into his glass and passed the bottle to her, who waved him off. "Ann probably got a clue about that while you still lived together."

I needed Arthur too much. I had to let his insults slide. "I suppose neither of us knew why we got married. We were certainly proof that opposites attract. At least for a little while, anyway."

Brenda had heard enough. "Well, I've got to be at work at midnight, so I'm off to have a nap. I expect you boys will clean up when you're done…?"

Arthur and I rose and sat down again. I slid my empty glass towards the center of the table. He filled it halfway and handed it back.

"I wish she didn't have to work nights."

"I think that comes with being a nurse."

"A noble vocation. To be sure."

"Does she really need to work?"

"It's that she wants to. We're doing all right." Arthur gave a little frown. "Now that Ben Schiller's gone—rest his soul—I'm surprised they're keeping you on. You were his protégé, weren't you?"

"Something like that."

"I recall you said the other partners didn't seem enthusiastic about your joining the firm."

"Apparently the only partner who counts is quite enthusiastic about my staying on."

"Oh—you must mean Cantor."

Arthur had a curious way of making you feel as if you ought to be ashamed of yourself, but without knowing why. A stab of anxiety—he could be way ahead of me. "That's right."

"Perhaps he's found a new reason to retain you?"

Arthur, as a man attracted to government service, wasn't that bright. A given. But, what if he were harboring an inner Blue Tick hound who catch the scent of danger coming his way while still a mile off. It was possible he had fooled me into believing him more naive than in reality.

"They liked the way I handled a recent gift tax case for one of our biggest clients."

"How fortunate for you." Arthur snickered as though he didn't believe a word I'd said. He took a bite of the dessert, swooned. "Wait until they discover your taste in cheesecake."

"I hoped you'd enjoy it."

He took another bite. A crumb of crust clung to his lower lip. Arthur brushed it away with a crooked finger. "You're no longer doing criminal defense work at the firm?"

"Like you said. With Ben gone, there wasn't as much room for me there." I hoped that would end our little game of Twenty Questions. "But again, Mr. Cantor and I, we talked, and—"

"—and let me surmise that you're now working on the TateAir Merger. In some fashion."

Damn. He's way ahead of me. "They shuffled me over to the mergers and acquisitions section for now."

"Ever since the TateAir file landed on my desk, I've been wondering when they'd get around to putting you on it." Arthur cut himself another slice of cheesecake, a sliver, just one more taste. "And here you are."

"Thought it was just a good guess."

He ignored me. "Now, of course I haven't said anything to Brenda."

"Not sure I understand." How quickly Arthur had turned the tables. No need for me to be coy any longer, but I still couldn't bring myself to come out and say what was on my mind. "Not quite up to speed on TateAir yet."

His gray eyes, sad and hooded, nonetheless pierced right through me. "Let's stop pretending we don't know why you're here. Shall we?"

There it was. "All right. Cards on the table."

He waited.

"It'd certainly be helpful if you could take a fresh look at what's holding up the merger—what's *really* holding it up, if we're being honest."

He shrugged as if to say *no big secret*. "I can tell you what's behind the delay: my boss doesn't like the fact that one of the investors served in the Iranian Parliament. From time to time, this individual has been highly critical of the current administration. And so on."

I should have known the real problems weren't about gifts or loans or taxes. "That's definitely a complication above my pay grade."

"The problem is fairly straightforward—if the merger were to go through, the administration worries our former

Persian parliamentarian, a representative of a government foresworn to destroy the West and its allies, would have control over a substantial amount of the aircraft leasing business on the east coast. And that's not sitting well with certain highly-placed actors at the State Department."

"I've only just joined the team, so I haven't looked into the investor dossiers." I hoped that plea of ignorance would give me time to look into all this—the issues suddenly seemed much bigger than the two of us at the dinner table. "But this sounds serious."

"Then I suggest you make time for study. Forget the money involved, the Tate family, your firm's bottom line—this merger could present a back-door national security risk."

Arthur poured more wine, but I decided to become careful about my drinking, leaving it untouched. I thought Arthur might be testing me, since he knew the booze had been a bit of a problem. I never thought of myself as an alcoholic, but they say once in the throes of it, one rarely recognizes the situation the way others do.

"I'll take a deep dive into all this first thing tomorrow." I wanted Arthur to know how seriously I took his advice. "I need to know what I'm walking into."

He clucked in assent. "What you must remember in deals like this is that you lawyers are the keys for your clients, but we regulatory people are the locks you boys have to open. Your clients pay you a great deal of money to get the locks open, and the lock gets—well, the lock has to be satisfied with a measly GS-12 salary." Arthur beamed a Cheshire Cat grin. "Hear how unfair that sounds?"

"I do." Hearing him spell out the situation made it seem like possible misdirection. I had to be careful. "Understood."

"Here's the way I see it." Arthur leaned forward and lowered his voice. "I think tomorrow you go and tell Mr.

Cantor how we've spoken, that it looks promising; and, furthermore, how you think you deserve a rather substantial bonus once the FAA approves the merger."

I expressed shock. "Well, now. How much did you have in mind?"

"I'm not so sure I would assign an actual dollar amount. At this point."

"Arthur, I'm only a junior associate. I don't tell senior partners anything, especially not that I expect a freaking bonus." Now I wanted a drink of that wine and took it, draining my glass. "He'll fire me on the spot."

"Nonsense. What do you suppose this deal is worth to your firm?"

I told Arthur I guessed maybe three, four million a month in billing. "The entire M and A floor is working on it."

"Hourly fees are peanuts on a deal like this. No, there's a success fee out there somewhere, and that's the real money. Not for you of course. Nor for me. For the partners."

I had no idea about this fabled fantasy money Arthur was talking about, but he seemed certain. I thought how different this conversation had been from the one I had rehearsed in my mind on the drive over here. "That's within the realm of possibility."

"And that, my friend, is the understatement of the evening. Paul, I want you to trust me on this. I suspect Cantor will find you a canny, perhaps even wise junior associate."

He rose and began clearing the table. I helped carry the plates into the kitchen of their fairly modest home in Silver Spring, where I put them into the sink. I opened the dishwasher to begin loading, but he shooed me away and said he would finish up.

"So—is it about national security, or money?"

"Let me worry about the State Department. As for you,

play out that scene with Mr. Cantor first thing tomorrow. He'll understand about the bonus." Arthur led me to the front door and held out his hand, which I took with reluctance. "You won't be fired—I promise."

SLEEP ELUDED ME ALL NIGHT.

One thing was certain; Arthur was not the innocent I had thought—in fact, he seemed the opposite, as though playing both sides against the middle, with a hell of a personal payout waiting for him on the other end. I wondered if he had done this sort of dance before, but then I remembered the modesty of their lifestyle. Thought about my sister pulling the grave-yard shift at the hospital.

No, this was Arthur's shot at a payday. And he knew it. He had been lying in wait for me like a deer hunter hidden by foliage.

The mere thought of bring up a bonus with Mr. Cantor made me queasy. I was the one being squeezed now, by Arthur on the one hand and Mr. Cantor on the other. I was certain my boss would fire me and, maybe even get Arthur fired, too.

God, when this all blows up in our faces, what will Brenda think?

I tried to come up with any other way of proceeding, but Mr. Cantor not only needed my in-law to push the merger along, Arthur wanted the 'bonus,' meanwhile I wanted to keep my job. I had no idea how to frame the conversation—I didn't know if I should say I wanted the bonus, or that *Arthur* wanted it.

When I finally got up, groggy and nervous, I asked

Bismarck what he thought I should do. He answered by bringing me his leash; I envied the simple life of a dog.

⛵

A FEW MINUTES AFTER TEN, MR. CANTOR'S ASSISTANT CALLED to say he wanted to see me in his office. No need to make an appointment.

At my appearance this time, Cantor stood and wordlessly pointed to the couch. He asked Manon, who had given me a sly, sexy smile as she escorted me to the office, to close the door behind her.

"How's the wind blowing?"

"Sir?"

He looked disappointed. "How did your dinner go?"

I brought a pad and pencil with me even though I guessed he wouldn't want any notes taken at this meeting. My voice trembled. "With Arthur Peck?"

"No. The Easter Bunny." Mr. Cantor leaned back and folded his arms, waiting.

"He said he'd look into the issues surrounding the merger." I had no idea what else I should say. "He said he was—amenable to the process."

Mr. Cantor smiled. After a brief internal negotiation, he reached behind him for a cigarette. He now carried a hint of urgency in his voice. "What will it take?"

I could barely speak. "He—Arthur, that is—feels that to bring this home, I should receive a—some kind of an —incentive."

"A substantial bonus of some sort?" He smiled. "Before or after the merger goes through?"

"Sooner rather than later, I guess."

"My suspicion of our Mr. Peck being a free-market capitalist have proven correct." He lit his cigarette and blew thoughtful smoke high into the air above him. He scoffed at the simplicity of it all: "Fish in a barrel."

"He suggested the bonus be paid when the FAA approves the merger. Not when it's finalized."

"Did he say how substantial this bonus of yours should be?"

"He didn't express a specific expectation." I could barely believe I was talking like this to Mr. Cantor in his own office.

"Does he take the metro into work in the morning?"

"Yes."

"From a split level in—where does he live?"

I nodded. "Silver Spring."

Cantor laughed, low and knowing. His eyes twinkled. "Why don't you telephone our Mr. Peck. Let him know I agree with him; but that 'your' bonus will be paid when, not if, the FAA approves the merger." My boss took out his pen and scribbled a note. "And not a moment sooner."

Bad idea. Contemporaneous notes are usually admissible into evidence, I thought. "I'll call him right away."

"By the way—is there still a need for me to arrange dinner with your dear brother-in-law? Since we're moving right along?"

"Arthur said they can't make it. He and my sister are riding over to Chevy Chase to see his parents."

"Don't be too clever now, Paul."

I started to say *how do you mean*, but figured that would only seem like cleverness. We both understood that a go-between has to protect his sources. "No, of course not, Mr. Cantor."

"In any case, 'clever' did not get me here behind this desk with my name on the building. Something did, but it certainly wasn't subterfuge. Understood?"

I did, sort of, or at least told him so. Cantor dismissed me with a brusque, "Keep me posted, son."

I TELEPHONED ARTHUR ON HIS PERSONAL LINE TO REPORT about my conversation with Cantor. I tried not to sound astonished. "He thought my bonus was a splendid idea."

Arthur replied, "I told you so," and instructed me that once I received it, I was to sign the bonus over to my sister. I was to use her maiden name, and tell her it was a belated wedding gift. That was to make it more difficult to trace the money back to him if anything went wrong.

I said, "You bet. Soon as it's possible. Which depends now on you."

Moving right along. But inside, I felt used and ineffective. I wasn't running the show at all—Arthur was the one who had thought of everything. And that meant I needed more information about what sort of DC viper's nest I had stumbled into, before the venom made its way to my heart.

W hen the cooler air of September began to push out the tropical August that drapes itself over Washington each summer, Mr. Cantor at last invited me to sail the Chesapeake Bay with him in his forty-two foot Valiant sailboat. He needed at least one person to crew for him, especially on gusty days, but his affection for sailing in rough weather had scared off most of the other young lawyers in the firm.

Once on the water I found him a skillful, if somewhat reckless, sailor, but also a good teacher. After two more sailing afternoons with him in which we discussed the movement of the merger, it wasn't long before I knew the boat top-down from the main sail; I stood on deck watching the wind as closely as he did.

Cantor seemed a different person onboard his boat, less guarded. He still found time to talk about work, of course, especially the TateAir business. In his opinion Arthur was dragging his heels so he could ask for more money, but he was wrong about that. Arthur Peck was a man of his word, but he was also a cautious bureaucrat.

"Speed kills," Arthur said whenever I'd ask him to push our petition along, and he was right. "But we're making progress." Sure—toward a fat payout for the bureaucrat I once thought held integrity. Everyone would do well to remember whose presence in the equation was making this deal possible. That's all I knew.

"You take the helm. Steer for that point of land to the northeast." Cantor slid out from behind the wheel, sat basking in the sun on the port side of the cockpit. "That'll keep the wind on our beam."

I tried to mimic the easy way he steered the boat, but found I was headed directly into the wind. As if to call attention to my ineptitude the sails flapped their noisy disapproval, but Cantor only continued smoking his cigarette, here without shame or inner conflict as in the office, while he gazed out at the choppy surface of the bay. I was quite sure Eric heard the sails, but he always gave me a chance to correct a mistake before he again became my sailing mentor.

Grunting with the effort, I managed to get the boat turned east; the sails swelled with contented majesty and the power of the wind. The bow rose up as our speed increased. I could feel the hull of the Sundance pushing against the sea, with its ungodly, unimaginable wellspring of force and pressure behind it.

Often when we sailed together, my 'big boss' and I would go long stretches without speaking. Cantor had mentioned on our first afternoon out here about sailing with his father; I guessed in these long moments of silence he may have been awash in memories of such sailing trips, in a wooden boat he said had 'rotted into nothingness,' a phrase of such specificity I suspected he always used it when telling the story, after his father suddenly passed away.

I found it hard to imagine Eric as a boy. To me he was one

of those people who sprang to life as he was now; urbane, charming, intelligent and remote.

"I heard a nasty rumor." Mr. Cantor spoke without turning away from the water and I pondered he may be thinking out loud. "There's another investor sniffing around TateAir."

I nearly gasped. "Since when?"

"A few days ago."

"But why wouldn't Enid tell me?"

"Because I asked that she not."

I tried to feel the current through the rudder as I turned the boat five more degrees to the east to bring her up into the wind. "She did as you wished. I haven't heard a whisper."

Cantor, grim, reported that "a friend, highly placed in New York," told him a particular hedge fund believes TateAir may be undervalued. "This is a curveball."

I didn't want to appear naïve, but I honestly didn't understand his point. "But, the deal is already in place. The company's already been sold, essentially. It's merely a regulatory issue." I felt idiotic bringing up the sole reason for our relationship. "As you know."

"Understood; but our process is taking too long. Once a deal loses momentum, the vultures start circling." He took off his sunglasses, made sure I could see the steely glint in his eyes. "You've got to find out why, despite our considerable efforts and pledges, your brother-in-law seems loathe to move it along."

That seemed to be as much as he was willing to say in response to my jejune responses. There had been an offer and it had been accepted, but no money had changed hands yet— how could it, with Arthur holding things up? We were in that dangerous time just before consummation, when people often question their judgement, actions, true wants and needs. The tension at the firm on the M&A floor ran as strong as the current against the hull. I had had no idea why. Now I did.

⛵

As we came about to return home, I now spoke to Cantor's back—he had retaken the wheel. "I'm doing what I can, but Arthur is cautious to a fault."

"As established."

"A petition that jumps out of order is always suspect."

"Are those your words? Or his?"

"His," I said, stopping myself from adding *of course, you dolt*. What the hell did I know about airline regulatory hoodoo over at the FAA? Such experience had not played into my selection for this role, only proximity through marriage.

"I'm wondering where this hedge fund is getting its information." The wind quickly carried away the blue smoke as Mr. Cantor exhaled, but his words made their way to my ears. "That's our problem."

Rumors of a traitor unnerved even the faithful, and I felt myself a suspect. I groped in my shirt pocket for my own cigarettes, but had left them on the navigation table back at the dock. Yeah—I had started smoking again, one night at dinner when we'd both had a bit too much to drink, which for me means a second glass of anything. Now I'm back to a pack a day. Once the merger goes through I'll quit again, and this time for good. This time I had taken up smoking Gaulois, the expensive French cigarettes Mr. Cantor preferred. I could barely afford the habit. Mr. Tate and my boss weren't the only players eager for the deal to succeed.

"Won't such attention result in a better price for TateAir, and more billable work for us—right?"

He could barely disguise his anger at my inability to see

what was so obvious to everyone else. "What it means is there may very well be a hostile takeover. And, if it succeeds, we almost certainly won't be representing TateAir any longer."

Even I could do the math on that. Losing our biggest client could be calamitous for the firm.

"Why would anyone give the hedge fund inside information?" As soon as the words were out of my mouth I knew the answer: for money, of course. Duh. "Well. No need to answer that."

Cantor stubbed out his cigarette and flicked it into the water instead of the old coffee can we typically used for our butts. "Think of the fat finder's fee dangled before anyone who could deliver this deal. That's how these funds operate."

As I watched his cigarette drift away in our wake, I imagined the trillions of them which must clog every waterway in the world. "It isn't anyone at the firm—right?"

He barked a sharp, rueful laugh. "Don't be so sure of that."

Now, *I* knew I couldn't be trusted. All I could wonder at the moment, however, was how much he also felt that way.

Cantor saw my stricken expression. "No, Paul. I don't mean you."

"Then who?"

"Someone who also has access to all the TateAir's financial reports."

The gravity of it struck me: "Such a level of knowledge suggests one of the partners."

Facial muscles contorted beneath skin turned ruddy by weekends on the water. "Rather than an associate like yourself?"

"I don't know who else it would leave, besides Enid."

"A sound theory, then. Unfortunately."

A stony look passed between us. I got a cold knot in my stomach. "Sir, I promise I've kept our confidences."

He put his gaze back on the horizon and requested a minor course correction, which I implemented. Our speed increased. Cantor understood the vagaries of the wind on the Chesapeake Bay as well as he knew the law. Perhaps better.

We spent a time sailing in silence, letting the possibilities settle in both our minds. I suspected it wasn't my acumen he found reassuring, rather my lowly status at the firm which convinced him I could be trustworthy. What did I know about TateAir, enough that a hedge fund would pay me? Not enough. Not yet.

⛵

IN THE COURSE OF TAKING DEPOSITIONS I HAD LEARNED THAT people reveal themselves in their most off-hand comments. These revelations were like mental fingerprints, the ones they hadn't bothered to wipe clean. I would listen to Cantor from here on out with even sharper ears than I had before. Much more could be at stake here for me than I may have realized. Much more. As I held our course to keep the wind aft of the beam, I tried to push thoughts of a miracle finder's fee under my legal Christmas tree as far from my mind as possible, which wasn't far at all.

"I'd like you to talk to your Mr. Peck again. See if he can speed things along," Cantor finally said as we tacked west and began our approach to the marina. "And it goes without saying I prefer that you not discuss this hedge fund business to anyone at the firm."

"Not even Ms. Pearl?"

"No. You and I will sort it out on our own."

There it was—I had been his invited to join him in a secret society.

Eric Cantor looked across the cockpit and smiled. It was a

practiced smirk which managed to nonetheless charm peti-tioners and partners alike, almost against their will. I had seen him deploy this smile in a variety of situations, and he nearly always got his way.

And, wasn't he getting his way with me now? Wasn't I turning Arthur into our man over at the FAA? And wasn't I only too willing to keep this hedge fund business quiet?

"I'll call Arthur from the house as soon as we get back."

He nodded. "I feel an urgency now, son, that was not there when we began. Is it clear what I mean by 'urgency'?"

"Clear as the spray from our keel."

Paternal, he patted me on the shoulder, took a deep breath of warm ocean air, and steered us back home.

I tried to relax and enjoy the rest of the journey across the bay, but couldn't shake feeling annoyed and anxious. I thought the real message today, whether he meant it or not, may have been *every man for himself.*

Indeed, there's only so much room in a lifeboat when the ship starts sinking, and once the merger was complete—after which he'd need neither Arthur nor me anymore—Mr. Cantor would see me booted out of the firm in a flash. With millions on the line, who knew what extralegal means a man like Cantor might employ.

No. I was kidding myself. I wasn't really in his secret club. Once done with me, he'd dump a low-level associate like me quicker than a New York minute. Not after I had been given this apparent level of inclusion in nefarious deeds like bribing public officials. I would have to think of some way to blunt the axe waiting to lop off my head as soon as the merger succeeded.

I held an advantage: Cantor wouldn't believe me capable of dimensional thinking like him. I knew it the second he praised me for my 'partner' level conceptual acumen, a back-handed compliment coming from a master of the universe like him.

We approached the dock, smooth as silk. "Forget calling Peck. I'd rather you speak with him in person."

"I'll pay him a visit first thing Monday morning."

Telephone calls leave records, records that would be like footprints leading to the firm. I was starting to think like a criminal, and I felt like one, too—but what was the heist we were pulling, exactly?

"No, not at his office. Why don't you take him to Chez Brown for lunch instead."

I thought about Arthur's love of good wine. "He'd enjoy that."

"Accounting will have a credit card ready for you in the morning. You're going to have expenses."

"That fast?"

He shrugged. There came the charismatic smirk. "I had already approved it."

Junior associates didn't have firm credit cards—well, it's always nice to be needed. "I'll make the reservation."

"Ask for Carlos. If you tell him this is my lunch, he'll find a table."

So this is what it's like to be a K Street lawyer. It felt exactly as I had imagined it would. I enjoyed the sense of being above the day-to-day chores that hobble most people; those things were being covered for me now. I became keen on never losing such privilege. "I'll get Arthur moving."

"You're wondering why I haven't said anything to Jack Tate about this hedge fund business. Of course, if it were a bona fide offer, I'd be bound to tell him about it, but this is merely a rumor. Hell, it's not even that. It's what we used to call in the navy 'scuttlebutt.'" Mr. Cantor laughed a conspiratorial laugh. "Remember—hearsay is never admissible."

"Actually, it is often admissible… if you find the right exception," I reminded him. I wondered how many years it had been since he had been inside a courtroom. Like a prize-fighter, you lose your edge pretty quickly once you stop climbing into the ring.

"Of course it is, but not in this case." He laughed again and it seemed disloyal of me not to join in, so I did. I wondered which of us was the more duplicitous.

I still didn't understand why we couldn't tell Jack Tate about the possibility of another buyer for the company. Wasn't it up to him to decide if the offer was worth pursuing or not? There was something about this merger that I didn't see, like that part of an iceberg that sits below the surface of the water. Of course, that's the part that sinks you.

⛵

He gave me the wheel back for me to steer the boat into the marina. Cantor sat watching as I approached the shallow cut which was the only way into the harbor. The tide was lower than I would have liked, so I pushed the throttle forward and we caught for a moment on the soft mud. I gave her more throttle and we lurched free.

Mr. Cantor still said nothing. I was ready to hand the wheel over to him, but he didn't move and I wasn't going to ask him to relieve me. There was a three-knot current coming out of the harbor so I had to keep the throttle open as we approached the slip. I could see I was going too fast, so I used reverse to bring the bow around and the front bumper just nudged the pier.

As Mr. Cantor tied off the bowlines, he nodded his silent approval of my handling of the boat. We made a good crew.

Would it extend to a long-term professional relationship? Time would tell.

⛵

As we turned down the gravel driveway that led to the white clapboard bay house, I saw Manon's black Toyota sedan parked under an oak tree. Mr. Cantor had suggested I bring Manon along on one of these sailing afternoons. If Mrs. Cantor got the impression that Manon was my girlfriend, he said, it wouldn't be a bad thing.

"My wife," he further explained, "is suspicious of men who remain single after a certain age."

I saw no reason why I shouldn't do as he asked; I had grown rather fond of Mrs. Cantor. I suppose I was deceiving her somewhat about Manon being my significant other, but that was different from outright lying.

Manon was almost the exact opposite of Mrs. Cantor: attractive, fit, well-tended in her own regard, but also coldly patrician and remote, when she wished. Manon offered the promise of rebellious sex, and sex is the wild card in even the most carefully planned life. You can never tell exactly when it will turn up or what damage it will do. Manon was that frivolous, powerful element which could undermine all the years of careful planning, of building a career, of raising children, of business dinners and good credit ratings; the essentials couples believe hold them together. A sexpot like her had men thinking about throwing all that away, and women thinking how fragile their relationships with men really were. She was the answer to the question wives asked when husbands chucked it all and disappeared.

I had determined a measure of suspicion in Mrs. Cantor's eyes at the sight of my sexy 'girlfriend.' Perhaps even jealousy, but that was only my ego talking. Nevertheless, her cool demeanor had melted a few times when we had been alone; little pats on the forearm, compliments, and so on. Maybe she understood that I was a mere beard in this situation, which would take more dignity for her to endure than I could imagine. You never knew what was really going on inside people. I was living proof of that.

As part of the subterfuge at the Cantor's bay house Manon and I pretended to be an old-fashioned couple, one which didn't believe in premarital sex, and so we requested separate rooms. As we were both Catholics, Mrs. Cantor seemed to find that plausible—or at least she pretended she did.

As I considered the possibilities, and tried to imagine the delicate negotiations which must accompany long-term marriages between powerful couples, maybe it was enough for her that Cantor had gone to the trouble of disguising his relationship with Manon. Perhaps it was that simple courtesy of using me as a prop which had convinced his wife he still respected their marriage, enough for her to turn a blind eye to a the presence of another woman beautiful enough to have caused tremors in even the most secure of relationships. I had no clue about how such a marriage worked, or perhaps any marriage at all—mine, ephemeral as it was, almost didn't count as actual experience.

⛵

ON SUNDAY MORNING AS THE FOUR OF US HAD BREAKFAST together, I told Mrs. Cantor we had to get back early for Sunday Mass, and went upstairs to pack.

When I came back downstairs, my boss's wife presented us with chicken salad leftovers from last night's dinner. "Put it in a cooler. It's the mayonnaise you have to worry about. It goes bad so quickly."

Manon promised not to let it stay in the car too long. "It was delicious."

"Yes," Mrs. Cantor said, staring at my alleged girlfriend. "It would be a tragedy to let it spoil."

I don't know why, but I always felt overwhelmed with sadness when driving away from that house. Being there was a kind of dream for me, one I didn't want to wake up from—I had to have the life Cantor had.

⛵

ON THE WAY TO MY APARTMENT MANON ASKED IF WE COULD stop by her place to pick up some things she wanted to take to the cleaners. When we got to her condo I carried her suitcases upstairs. Three was the minimum number she needed even for a weekend trip.

She went into her bedroom and yelled that I could help myself to some wine. It was a bit early for that, but I thought: why not; I didn't have anything to do for the rest of the day.

I opened a bottle of Chateau Neuf De Pape sitting on the counter. I guessed it was a gift from Mr. Cantor, as Manon certainly couldn't afford such a vintage. As I poured myself a glass, I remembered I had left the chicken salad in the car. Just then Manon called out that she would like a glass of wine, too.

"Would you mind bringing it in here to me?"

When I did I discovered her lying in bed, one bare leg sticking out, a lazy arm behind her head.

I hesitated in the doorway. It was early for sex as well, I thought. But once I brought the glass over to her bedside table, and saw the pools of her blue eyes looking up at me, her dark hair spilling across the pale pink of her pillowcase, I stopped thinking.

LATER, WHILE MANON WAS IN THE SHOWER, I NOTICED A handwritten note on her dresser. I recognized the off-white linen bond and indigo blue ink—Eric Cantor's personal stationery.

It was the usual nonsense such men write to their illicit paramours: *Soon I'll be free, and we can live our lives together, I miss you when we're apart,* and so on and on for two florid pages. These operatic emotional bits were followed by rather overheated memories of their sex life, which on the whole sounded far less interesting than what I had just experienced.

I blew out my lips. Manon and I were both using the poor man, but he didn't have the sense to realize it. Eric Cantor suddenly seemed master not of the world, but of nothing.

The thought of him as such a dupe felt disappointing, really. I had never imagined Mr. Cantor could be so much like other men, so easily misled by his own baser impulses. And for heaven's sake, he should have known better than to put something like this testimony in writing—who knew what could come from such a document in the wrong hands? As I heard Manon turn off the water in the bathroom, I quickly folded the letter and slipped it into my jacket pocket.

6

A bout the time I arrived at the restaurant, the morning rain stopped. In front stood Arthur already waiting, the curved wooden handle of his oversized black umbrella hanging from one insouciant wrist. His look of anticipation was like that of a man awaiting a much-needed cargo ship which now approached the dock.

"Right on time," he said with an odd air, as though my punctuality could be an indicator of suspicious motivations.

"But a go-getter like you believes in being early," I said, gesturing to him.

He took my hand in his customary too-firm, almost painful grasp. He laughed. "I guess this isn't only about lunch."

"A not-unreasonable supposition."

"Why don't we get our table first?"

Agreeing we should refrain from discussing the merger petition out the sidewalk in front of God and everyone, a line which made him guffaw as though I were a standup comic, I led the way inside the plush interior of the restaurant.

Carlos, who greeted me not only with elegant enthusiasm but by name, made a further fanfare of showing us to our table. As we sat down I saw Arthur's little smile disappear; impressed at my station in a restaurant of such renown, his antennae seemed to wiggle.

I ordered two martinis. Arthur protested about a high-octane cocktail at such a tender hour, but I told him they were the best in town and insisted he try a sip or two.

"On Mondays they feature fresh crab legs." I couldn't stop myself from playing the Man About Town. "Highest recommendation."

The drinks arrived. Wincing, Arthur made a polite sip at his martini like a bird drinking from a shallow puddle.

Conspiratorial, at last he couldn't help himself: "Just how often do you come here?"

"Oh—you don't want to see my expense account. It's criminal." As a server snapped open my napkin and placed it into my lap, Carlos presented a menu.

I didn't bother to open it. "The trout is stunning." I didn't much care for fish, but that's what Mr. Cantor always ordered. Nonchalant, I shrugged as though I ate a thirty-dollar plate of seafood for lunch five times a week. "I guess that's what I'll try today, Carlos."

His voice held a breathy, dignified approval: "*Oh*—excellent choice, Mr. Pauls. Wine?"

"Just the martinis."

"Very good."

Dazzled, Arthur placed his order like a child at an ice cream shop.

Once the crusty bread and dipping oils came out, he took a more generous sip of his drink and smiled. "Things are starting to move."

A cold bolt of adrenaline hit my gut. I held my gaze on a delicious set of nylon legs across the way for more than one reason. "Is that right?" As though I had already closed two mega-mergers that morning. "Anything I need to know?"

"I've sent a request for further documentation to your Ms. Pearl. Nothing too extensive, you understand."

"Meaning—?"

"Enough to show our due diligence. Just enough."

Time to get serious. "Too much at stake here to be coy."

He groaned as though weary. "Well. There is one major problem. Unfortunately."

Endive salads arrived; we both declined a re-fill on the cocktails. Instead of asking him to go on, I continued to play it cool and took a bite. "Whoa—this sesame dressing is sublime."

He tried a mouthful of greens and agreed. "It's dazzling," and seemed to mean it. Arthur enjoyed his gustatory pleasures. "Savory-sweet."

"So—what are we facing?"

"Well, my boss," a senior FAA official and more recent political appointee than a lifetime bureaucrat like Arthur, "said she might want a study done on the impact the merger would have on air fares."

I suffered a stab of adrenaline. We both knew that if the FAA called for a study of any kind, the merger would collapse. "That could take months."

"Eighteen months, to be exact." He went back to his salad. "And then there's the review process."

Now I knew what Mr. Cantor meant when he said how, if these things lose momentum, the vultures start to appear.

But I couldn't be entirely sure if Arthur's boss had truly mentioned doing a study, or my shrewd brother-in-law had made it up to convince me we were getting good value for our 'bonus' money. An entire industry based in this town operated worldwide selling protection from imaginary threats, after all.

"Well, we certainly want to avoid a study." I tried to sound unconcerned, but my mouth was so dry I could barely speak. I asked him how we could quell this desire on the part of his boss.

"I'm doing what I can to dampen her enthusiasm. But, if she calls for one, she'll farm it out to a consulting firm—"

"—one which'll then hire her for high six-figures once she leaves the administration?"

"That's the way it goes in this town." Smarmy: "But I shouldn't need to tell you that."

I smiled in cynical agreement. "No."

I could see that in his mind demanding a bonus from us was merely skipping the middle step his boss was taking; how you steered consulting business to a firm, later joined that firm after you leave the government. It was the revolving door that swept dollars into any bureaucrat's pockets willing to play ball. In a perverse way, though, Arthur was more honest than most of them. At least he wasn't hiding his greed behind some ethical fig leaf.

Settling into the groove of white-tablecloth dining for lunch instead of the cafeteria, he lifted a finger to signal Carlos that we were ready for our entrées.

I tried to play it cool. "Say—I wonder if your boss would be satisfied if you were to present her with an analysis of the impact of past mergers on fare prices?" I thought this might appeal to Arthur for two reasons; first, it would speed up the approval process and secondly, he could claim he had done the analysis, meanwhile getting a gold star for having shown initiative.

Arthur's enthusiasm was obvious. "Gosh, Paul, I think that just might work."

"Just the barebones statistics, that kind of thing. Would it move the needle?"

He shrugged. "We can always hope."

I mentioned a professor over at GW who could whip up a report in a few days. I added a nod to integrity so Arthur wouldn't feel compelled to make a speech about how this all had to be in the public's best interest. "You'd write it up in your own way, of course."

"I think his help would really move it along."

Arthur finished his drink. Now I nodded to Carlos for another round. This time when the martinis arrived, I heard no protest from Arthur.

"To the success of the merger." We toasted the TateAir deal. "Mr. Cantor appreciates everything you've done for us."

"Those statistics could give your bosses a lot of cover, if there's any flack on the Hill."

"I'll get on it this afternoon."

"Look at the time. I'm supposed to be back for a conference call at two." Arthur made as if to reach for his wallet to pay for lunch. It was one of the rituals that had to be observed if we were to go on pretending I hadn't bought him completely.

"Nonsense. Put it away."

I signed the bill, left the serving team a generous tip and walked Arthur, who face shone with the flush of two drinks, outside to put him into a cab.

On my way back to the office, I stopped off at a shop on Pennsylvania Avenue and bought myself two new ties. One had orange and black strips that one could almost mistake for a Princeton tie, if one didn't look too closely. Now all I had to do was get the professor at GW—or any professor—to produce the necessary paperwork.

I FOUND MS. PEARL IN THE CONFERENCE ROOM.

"Seth would like to see you."

"Seems unusual."

"He is a partner, after all."

"If only a junior one."

"He needs your help, Paul."

"But the merger—"

"I'm not asking." *Just do it*, her stern face said.

I didn't have any fear of Enid but thought I'd put on a show of obeisance, if only to keep the peace. I had much more important matters on my mind, but I hustled on over to Seth Meyrinck's office anyway.

WITH BARELY A WORD OF CORDIALITY, AT MY ARRIVAL SETH announced: "I need you to file a notice of appearance in this case."

"Why me?"

"Because Enid thinks highly of you."

I asked how complicated the case.

"Not much to it, really." He rested his hand on a stack of file folders. "It's some Pro Bono thing I was appointed to."

He gave me the lowdown: A woman of means in Anacostia, it seemed, purchased an enormous truckload of furniture while later failing to make payments upon it. Way beneath my current radar, but what could I do?

"Here's her contract, along with the complaint Sherwood Furniture filed against her. I've already filed an answer admitting she didn't pay, so all you have to do is show up for the hearing on their motion for summary judgment. Get her to agree to some schedule of reduced payments and they'll enter into a consent decree. That's all that ever happens in these cases."

Seth still hadn't asked me to sit down. "But Mr. Cantor said he wants me to focus on the TateAir business until the merger is approved. I think I should clear this with him first—don't you?"

"No. I'm a partner." Seth pushed the case file across his desk. "Now file the notice of representation today. Leave a copy of it on my desk."

I reached for the file. "Is that all, sir?"

"No—as a matter of fact, it isn't." Seth tented manicured fingers in front of lips gone fleshy with privilege and power, a body pear-shaped despite his tennis prowess. "I voted against bringing you into this firm. I still think it was a mistake."

My self-esteem threatened to plummet. "I appreciate such refreshing candor out of a fellow attorney."

He ignored my sarcasm. "And, for as long as you're here, you'll do what the partners—any partner—assigns you. Is that clear?"

"As the morning sky."

With that, I left. I wondered what Enid could see in someone so crassly manipulative and hateful.

On the way back up to my office I considered going over Seth Meyrinck's head to Cantor, but that would only make things worse; it would look as if I couldn't handle myself. No, I'd have to find another way to deal with him.

BACK AT MY DESK I GOT BACK TO MY OWN BUSINESS. I telephoned my contact at George Washington University, who recommended a stats professor who'd done work for this and other firms; was amenable to such work, as well the rewards it brought.

Once I got hold of the Ph.D. in question, Allison Kohlhagen, I told her what I needed for the FAA. I asked to focus only on mergers which had resulted in reduced fares.

Allison said such specificity, as well as the tight deadline, wouldn't be cheap.

Understanding the tenets of negotiation, I played it ambiguous. "Now, our budget has limits."

"Be that as it may." She told me what it would take. I tried not to gasp at the number.

Here I needed to make a decision: act my age and rank, or pretend I held more power over the purse strings than I did.

I dove in head first: "Thanks to the onerous condition that the firm needs results by next Monday—that's a hard, drop-dead deadline—I suspect we can meet your price."

A low chuckle. "I've known Eric Cantor for years," she said, a reveal. "I assume he sent you to me?"

I hated being caught unaware like this. "Actually—no. Your reputation proceeded you without his guidance."

Another laugh, this one of *yeah-sure* disbelief. "Have it your way. Point me to the data you want stacked and sorted. I'll try to make it pretty for you."

WITH OUR AIRLINE STATISTICS BEING GROUND AND SIFTED INTO fine data, at last I began reading the novel of the season, the Sherwood Furniture file. As I mulled over this situation, I understood what had happened—Enid Pearl had conspired to move me away from the action, lest I end up seeming like the prime mover on TateAir.

God help me, I thought. *Who among us* doesn't *have everything riding on this merger?*

The facts in the case were as Seth described them. The defendant, Bethany Stark, bought furniture 'on time' from Sherwood Furniture, which had also provided the in-house financing for this, likely one of their biggest sales of the year.

For thirteen happily cash-flowing months, Stark had in fact made payments… but then stopped. Sherwood, as these things tended to go, had sued for the return of the furniture and all back payments due. In the answer he had filed, Seth admitted Mrs. Stark had bought the furniture and stopped making the agreed-upon payments. What, then, was I supposed to do with this penny-ante case?

But next I discovered that Sherwood was also suing for unpaid insurance premiums in the amount of fifty-six dollars. My intuition flared, a warm feeling in my gut.

I telephoned Mrs. Stark, who told me that Sherwood had insisted she take out insurance on the furniture, as it served as collateral for her loan. I asked who had sold her the insurance.

"The Sherwood furniture salesman. By the way…"

"Yes?"

"My brother's attorney says he thought something didn't seem right there."

"Indeed," I agreed, but would have to look into it to know for sure. Doing so was pretty standard for this type of financing. I didn't at first see how this aspect would provide me with much of a defense. Still, the warmth in the gut had never— well, rarely—steered me wrong.

Out of curiosity more than frustration, I pulled up the insurance commission website. I didn't see Sherwood listed. After checking a couple of other sources of information, I sat up straight in my chair—apparently Sherwood *was not licensed to sell insurance in the District of Columbia.*

Like a hunting dog onto a scent, I consulted Maryland and Virginia. Sherwood lacked licensing in those states as well.

Well-well.

Now I felt certain I had a reasonable defense, until I read the penalty section of the insurance statute. It provided only for the return of any premiums paid, along with modest attorney's fees. That wouldn't be much of a bargaining chip when I tried to negotiate a settlement with Sherwood.

Nevertheless, later in the afternoon I filed a motion to amend Mrs. Stark's answer to include my defense to the claim for unpaid insurance premiums. It wasn't much, but all I had. I put the case out of my mind and wondered what my stats professor looked like—her voice had been quite alluring.

TWO WEEKS LATER, I HAD NOT ONLY GOTTEN OUR SIFTED DATA from Professor Kohlhagen and forwarded the material to Arthur, but I also got notice a hearing had been scheduled on Sherwood's motion for summary judgment and mine to amend our answer. I had barely given the case another thought. After all, it was pro bono, and I was spending all my time on the TateAir merger. Billable hours are, after all, what gets associates promoted to partner.

When I arrived at the courtroom, the lawyer for Sherwood, Irving Zucker, was already seated at the Plaintiff's table, his posture stiff and still, like a meditating monk. The pile of files in front of him was at least a foot high, as though this were a capital murder case.

His firm, I had learned, specialized in collecting delinquent debts and got paid a percentage of what they collected. Given the smalls sums involved they couldn't afford to spend much time on each case. It was a mass production operation and, of course, that's precisely where they were most vulnerable. If I could make them believe I had valid defenses that required a trial I felt sure they would settle with me.

"Your motion to amend is untimely," he said.

I cut my eyes over at Sherwood's attorney. His head was barely visible over files. "We'll see about that."

"You don't do much debt collection work, do you?"

I didn't try to hide my disdain. "As a rule? Um, no."

Smug. "You'll leave today having learned something, then."

I took my seat at the defense table. "Perhaps we both will."

When I learned the judge on the case, Susanne Collinsworth, was also a woman of color, I had insisted Mrs. Stark attend the hearing. Her presence might not help, but it certainly couldn't hurt. We all know how the theatricality of the courtroom often turns on such cosmetic details.

Promptly at nine the judge, middle-aged and stooped with the weight of jurisprudence on her shoulders, and whose stern countenance filled me with dread, took the bench. It crossed my mind she might think me pandering by bringing my client to the hearing, but this, a chance I was willing to take.

"May it please the court, your honor…" Zucker introduced himself. "The court has before it our motion for summary judgment. Mrs. Stark admits the facts we allege in our complaint and therefore we are entitled to judgment."

"And yet I see the defendant has filed a motion to amend her complaint to include certain defenses related to your claim for insurance premiums due," Judge Collinsworth said. She glanced at me with eyes wise and weary like those of Yoda, as well at Mrs. Stark with what I perceived was a not-unsympathetic look. "So how, Mr. Zucker, do you claim the facts remain uncontested?"

"The defendant's motion to amend is untimely." Irv Zucker smiled a cruel grin over at me. "It was only served on us seventeen days ago."

"Counsel, it appears Mr. Zucker is correct," the judge said with a grave air. She shook her head. "The Plaintiff, alas, has not enjoyed the requisite thirty days to respond to your motion to amend. Now, I presume you have a credible reason I should not deny your motion as untimely?"

Her rhetoric gave me hope. "Your honor is correct. The plaintiff did not get thirty days in which to reply to my motion."

Sudden, I rose from my seat and gestured, expansive, as though persuading a jury of a murderer's obvious innocence. "However, if it may please the court, let me point out that the purpose of the thirty-day rule is to give the opposing party sufficient time to develop a proper response. Now, in my motion to amend, I allege Sherwood sold collateral insurance to Mrs. Stark. Sherwood, as well, has alleged as much in its own complaint. We allege Mrs. Stark stopped making premium payments. Sherwood has alleged the same in its complaint."

"The more specific point, please, counselor," the judge said. "I've reviewed the case."

I resisted the urge to give her a wink. "The only thing we allege that is not in Sherwood's complaint is this: *the company is not properly licensed to sell insurance.* For my motion to be untimely, Sherwood would have to testify to this court that they were *unaware of the fact* that they never obtained the proper license to sell insurance in the District of Columbia. As well in Maryland and Virginia," I added, cheerful, before sitting down with a shrug. "All this seemed to us here on the defense like something of an oversight."

The judge's incredulous tone left Mr. Zucker on the hot seat. "Mr. Zucker—? Does Sherwood contend it has been unaware of the requirement that a company like this must pass through the proper regulatory procedures, like obtaining a license to sell insurance to its customers?"

"Your honor," Zucker said with a stammer, "this apparent

oversight by Sherwood is one I am just now learning about, as well one that will be corrected today. I assure you."

Irving Zucker was not out of the game just yet. "But, your Honor, Mr. Johns has only recently filed an appearance in this case. Prior to that Mrs. Stark was represented by Seth Meyrinck, a partner in Cantor and Miller. Mr. Meyrinck and I reached a settlement in this matter, a settlement which is binding on the defendant. Perhaps Mr. Johns is unaware of that agreement."

"I'm very much aware of that agreement, your honor. It is not binding because it was procured by fraud. Mr. Meyrinck, like Mr. Zucker, was quite unaware of this now admitted licensing error."

The judge arched an eyebrow. "Does the left hand at Cantor and Miller not know what the right is doing? I'd be surprised."

I cleared my throat, generated a tone of mild outrage. "Your Honor, Sherwood held itself out as an insurance agent, which they have just admitted before the court that they were not. A predicate for the settlement was that Sherwood was duly licensed to sell Mrs. Stark insurance. Since that is not the case, there can be no settlement."

It only took her about five seconds to respond. "The court agrees with Mr. Johns. If there was a settlement, it was procured by fraud and is a nullity." She studied several papers in front of her. "Thank you for those assurances about your intention to obtain a license, Mr. Zucker, but for now I am granting the defendant's motion to amend, as I find it contains nothing which should surprise Sherwood Furniture. Your answer is due fourteen days from today."

Zucker had turned pink as a rose. "Your Honor—!"

"Further, I am denying the motion for summary judgment, as clearly the facts of this case are contested, and so the matter is not one which can be dealt with by summary judgment. Do you have anything further, Mr. Johns?"

I did not.

"Mr. Zucker, is there anything *you* wish to add?"

"Not at this time, your Honor."

"Then court is adjourned." The judge rose. We all leapt to our feet.

As soon as she was gone, I turned to Mr. Zucker. "By the way, Irv, I'll include some interrogatories with my amended complaint. I believe they'll serve nicely as the basis for a class action suit against Sherwood furniture, on behalf of all customers to which you sold insurance over the last three years."

Zucker busied himself collecting his files. "She'll never certify a class in this case."

"I believe you were equally pessimistic about my Motion to Amend."

"Even if she does, the damages are peanuts."

"Not when you multiply them by four thousand, seven hundred and twenty-three."

"What's that number supposed to mean?"

"It's the number of liens Sherwood filed on furniture it had sold to people like Mrs. Stark. The average cost of insurance over the financing period was just under four hundred dollars. The statute provides for treble damages plus attorney's fees."

"You've been a busy boy, Mr. Johns." Zucker's words were meant as an insult, but with a touch of grudging admiration, too. "Good luck with all that."

"You mentioned a settlement to the judge. I'd like to propose one to you now."

Now his flushed cheeks turned pale. "But, I'd to have to call Sherwood first."

"I thought you might. You could offer them this: if Mrs. Stark chooses to file a complaint with the insurance commission, which is an option on the table, it's likely Sherwood will *never* get its license. That's the true value of the settlement."

The short version of what happened next: By eleven o'clock I concluded an agreement with Irving Zucker and headed back to the office, triumphant.

⚓

AT THE OFFICE I HAD BARELY TAKEN OFF MY OVERCOAT WHEN Seth Meyrinck, sweating and blustery, announced himself from the doorway.

I greeted him as I took special care in folding my camel hair polo coat so the creases would fall right. I didn't want it to wrinkle. I had quite a few more payments to make on it.

"Well?"

"You've obviously heard something already."

"I'd say so—Irv Zucker is filing a grievance against me."

"Because—?"

"Because you didn't honor the settlement he and I had made."

I sat down at my desk. I heard a toilet flush in the senior partners' bathroom. "Irv Zucker is in no position to file a complaint against you. Or anyone."

"Who told you to file a Motion to Amend, anyway?"

"No one."

"I told you to run everything by me before you filed it."

"Actually, you said provide a copy of my Notice of Representation." I began looking at messages that had been left on my desk while I was at court. "Which I did."

Seth loomed over me. I could smell his expensive cologne. Specks of spittle had gathered at the corners of his mouth. "Enid warned me you were an arrogant little bastard."

"I'd call it confidence." I shrugged. "I did my homework. Like a good lawyer should."

Seth, beet-red, seemed out of breath. "You won't talk your way out of this, slick."

"No?"

"No. I'll see you fired. Your brown-nosing on that sailboat with Cantor won't help you this time."

Seth Meyrinck was kidding himself. He didn't have enough pull to get me fired, nor could he know how intimate I'd become with Cantor. His threats held all the weight of gossamer. The real reason for all this outrage, I suspected, was my increasingly cordial relationship with Ms. Pearl, and all the after-hours fun it portended. Or so I had been imagining, at least when Manon wasn't sprawled naked across my bed with Bismarck licking her bare toes.

I set aside my messages and gave him my full attention. "The court characterized Sherwood's conduct as fraud. I've already ordered a transcript of the hearing, so there won't be any grievance filed against you."

"You didn't hear the call from Zucker."

"And you weren't in the courtroom today. He's letting off some steam. I'm guessing after such an embarrassing and costly hearing that Sherwood fired him."

"This is a highly regarded law firm, Johns. This scheming, bullying style of yours just doesn't fit here. That may have been fine when you were a criminal defense lawyer, but in corporate we don't act that way."

I wanted to tease more anger out of him. "I'm afraid I don't have the first clue what you're going on about."

"I mean, throwing your weight around on the TateAir business because Mr. Cantor thinks you're some hot shot criminal litigator, and now turning a stupid pro bono case into a class action. Hell, now Enid's afraid to do anything without asking you first. You're a damn *associate*, for Christ's sake."

So I was right about his jealousy over Enid. "I assure you I understand that Ms. Pearl is lead counsel."

"Stop calling her Ms. Pearl, for God's sake. You spend more time with her than I do." Seth's rage was starting to sound a bit like despair. I despised him for showing such glaring weakness. I felt surprised he had made it in life as far as he had. He needed to read more Sun Tzu.

I thought I'd bring the subject back round to where it had started in the first place. "Mr. Zucker got caught with his trousers down around his ankles this morning in front of that judge. He won't file a grievance against you for the same reason you won't get me fired."

"For someone who lied about where he went to law school, I detect unearned arrogance." Seth waited with unconcealed delight to see how I received the news. "Oh, that's right—I checked out your past."

I had to admit he had caught me off guard, but a real liar is never without an explanation for anything.

And yet, I couldn't bring myself to tell him some lame story that might explain my enhanced resume, since by now no one but this jerk gave the slightest damn about where I went to law school. No, I thought I'd let him make a fool of himself by outing me to Mr. Cantor. "Actually, you should consider yourself lucky I spotted Sherwood's licensing problem. Had you settled without raising that defense, it would've been malpractice on your part."

He mouthed an epithet under his breath. His face turned red.

As for me, calm and collected, I leaned back in my chair. "I saved a firm of this stature from embarrassment—and that's a fact. Not spin, my friend."

Bitter, he deflated like a limp party balloon left behind hours after the last guest has gone home. "A lucky guess on your part."

"Hardly. That's what litigation is—you look into every corner to see what the other fellow has hidden. It's the lawyer who sniffs out the details no one else does who wins." I tried to remember where I had heard that before, but drew a blank.

"Don't lecture me."

I continued, nonchalant. "And I just happened to find Sherwood selling insurance without a license. You see, even a lawyer like me, from a third rate law school out west, can find a crumb of something valuable every now and then." I had to rub that in even though I was being as petty as him now. "Rooting around in the dirt with the rest of you East Coast elites."

Something about my tone seemed to chill him to the bone. His eyes were now calculating how much damage he may have done not only by handing me this case, but by confronting me. "Cantor already knows. Doesn't he?"

I ignored his stark, personal revelation. "You didn't have all the facts in the Sherwood case before you threw in the towel. And by the way, I don't suppose Irv Zucker told you we settled the case, did he?"

"He told me they dropped all claims against Mrs. Stark, and gave her clear title to the furniture."

"I don't mean that part."

"He said you threatened them with a class action suit, but I told him you were bluffing."

"No—I wasn't bluffing at all."

In a chastened voice, Seth asked me to explain.

"Under the order in the Stark case, Sherwood has agreed to apply for a license to sell insurance. If I bring a class action against them, they won't get that license until the case is settled… so that's what they did."

"Did what?"

"Sherwood settled my class action claim."

"But you haven't even filed it yet."

"No, but they know I'd win if I did, so we just skipped the courtroom theatrics and got right to the money."

Seth took a stagger-step forward. *"What are you talking about?"*

"They're going to pay the firm nine hundred-thousand in fees, issue a coupon to everyone who bought insurance from them over the last three years—a coupon good for six months of premium payments. Of course, to use it, one must waive any claim against Sherwood."

"That sounds good for our firm, but not quite so good for Sherwood's customers."

"Oh? Before I went into that courtroom this morning, those same customers had nothing. Those coupons are found money to them."

Seth seemed determined to find fault with my triumph. "The court will never approve it."

"I think they will. You see, we're donating three hundred-thousand of that fee to the bar indigent defense fund. Now, what judge wouldn't like that? Not to mention that it's tax deductible."

"I assume you got Cantor's approval on all this?"

"He contributed the idea of the donation to the bar. Said it would keep the court from getting indigestion over the size of our fee."

Seth grappled with the math on it all, and I don't mean the money.

At last he held out his hand, which trembled. He could use one of those martinis like I shared with Arthur. "I'm sorry I went off like that. I'll be glad when this damn TateAir deal is over, and Enid is more like her old self. Surely you understand."

I shook his hand. And why not? His veiled confession about 'Ms. Pearl' made me realize how interested in her I had now become. "Bygones it is, then."

7

Upstairs in the guest room the Cantors now reserved almost exclusively for me, I looked out of the window to admire the view of the bay. Instead, my gaze was drawn to a vehicle pulling down the drive: Enid Pearl, along with my nemesis Seth Meyrinck in the passenger seat. I hadn't seen him since our little meeting earlier in the week, but I was sure it had been him avoiding me.

As she got out of the car, Enid noticed me standing at the window. I quickly stepped behind the curtain, which, of course, only made me look even more foolish. I stood still for a moment hoping that might make me invisible.

She turned as I heard Elizabeth Cantor greeting them below and announcing that, yes, I had come down for the weekend, too. I hoped she wouldn't mention anything about my having brought Manon along, a fact which would soon become evident.

The juggling of romantic interests—before dropping one girlfriend, picking up another, all while trying to keep them up all spinning in the air—had taken on an all-too familiar feeling. I always seem to be trying to corral the women in my life, even ones like Enid with whom I wasn't yet sleeping. With certain women, I had found the possibilities for such outcome often hiding behind more demure or reluctant appearances. You had to tease it out of them, sometimes, those suppressed carnal graces.

DOWNSTAIRS I FOUND THE THREE OF THEM ALREADY IN THE kitchen. I feigned surprise. "Who called this meeting?"

"Paul, how lovely." Enid held out her hand. We both wore our at-work faces because the other two were watching, Mrs. Cantor as much as Seth, although for different reasons. "I didn't realize you'd be here."

I dropped her hand. "And I didn't know you were coming, either."

"We just decided on the spur of the moment to drive down."

I chanced a glance at her companion—a little frown had appeared between Seth's bushy eyebrows. "Paul."

"Seth."

I opened a familiar cupboard to take down a glass—this should show Enid and Seth how frequent a guest I had become at Mr. Cantor's bay house. "Would anyone like a drink of water? Or, something stronger?"

"Water for me, at this hour, anyway." Mrs. Cantor took the glass I offered and filled it from the tap. "I adore your new sweater. I don't think I've seen that one before. Doesn't he look stylish, Enid?"

I flushed at the mention of my sweater because I had only put it on when I saw Enid arriving. The cashmere garment had me cost me more than I usually spent on groceries for the month.

"Indeed he does." Enid smiled at Mrs. Cantor.

I suddenly felt like a boy in his Sunday school suit being inspected by doting aunts. "Enough fawning, ladies. If you please."

But the more I observed her, Enid's discomfort at finding me here now seemed obvious. I wondered if I had done something to offend her. Maybe Seth's low opinion of me was starting to rub off and temper her obvious attraction. Of course, by now he would have told her about the embellishment of my background.

"Are you going sailing with us this afternoon? The wind's blowing around twelve knots." Even as I spoke I realized how absurd I must sound with my nautical jargon, but I couldn't stop myself from showing off in front of Enid. I was glad Mr. Cantor wasn't there to see me making such a spectacle of myself. I couldn't have been more ridiculous if I had burst into a sailor's jig right there in the kitchen.

I thought I saw Mrs. Cantor smile in my direction, a tolerant expression I had seen before when I had tripped over my tongue. She was fond of me precisely because I was rough around the edges, unlike the other lawyers at the firm. I think that and my utter inability to disguise my ambition amused her.

"Seth doesn't much care for sailing." Enid squeezed Seth's arm to show me on whose team she played. "But I might come along."

"Actually, sailing doesn't care for me. I can get seasick just looking at a painting of the ocean." Seth laughed at himself and I joined in, even though I would have given anything to see him doubled over the handrail in ten-foot seas. "Elizabeth, why don't you and I go to the farmer's market and get something for dinner while they're off sailing?"

"I'd like that. There's still some late-season corn. And let's get some blue crabs, too." Mrs. Cantor smiled at Seth. "I'm with you. If I never set foot on that boat again, it will be fine with me."

As the two of them laughed, I imagined an afternoon with Enid. I wished it would be the two of us on the boat, alone. Maybe Mr. Cantor would fall overboard, for some reason.

MANON CAME INTO THE KITCHEN WEARING A SHORT RED SKIRT, a white silk blouse, and her typical affect of raw feminine power. With the mane of thick black hair pulled away from her face, her hoop earrings glistened whenever she moved her head. Even without makeup she was startlingly beautiful.

"Why, Manon, how nice to see you here, too." Enid, tentative, extended her hand as the word 'too' hung in the air. "Don't you look wonderful."

Enid's discomfort was now so complete I suspected even she knew of Manon's relationship with Mr. Cantor. I wondered which she would find more despicable—my pretense as Manon's weekend date, or the truth of my having slept with her. Perhaps both were equally reprehensible in her mind. I hoped before the weekend was over I would get a chance to explain things.

Demure. "Well—I came down last night with Paul."

"How nice the two of you could get away." Enid turned back to me. "The weather is supposed to be perfect."

"Could I get a coffee?" Manon sat down at the kitchen table. I stood behind her without pulling out her chair. She reached up and took my hand. "Would you pour me a cup, dear?"

I recoiled when Manon touched me; I hoped no one noticed. She had never done anything like that before. Playing it up for... whom? Enid? Mrs. Cantor, I suppose.

I brought her coffee and sat down. She stirred three spoonfuls of sugar into her cup and sipped.

"How was the trip down?" Small talk with Enid would have to do. I had truly begun to want her, and the thought of her and a weak yes-man like Seth together made me quiver with disgust. Enid was too good for this chump.

"You know how it is on weekends across the bridge—bumper to bumper." She went to look for something in her purse and ended our conversation.

"Seth, would you mind taking our bags upstairs?" She looked at Mrs. Cantor. "Are we staying in the room at the head of the stairs?"

"Actually, Paul stays in there when he's down." Mrs. Cantor smiled at me as if I were her son home from college. "He's got his things spread everywhere. Armenta doesn't even want to go in to clean his room after these sailing weekends." Mrs. Cantor chortled and patted me on the shoulder to show everyone she forgave my shortcomings. "I thought you and Seth would be comfortable out in the guesthouse."

"That will be fine." Enid's pronunciation of 'fine' made it obvious she didn't like being relegated to the guesthouse, and especially not to make way for some parvenu junior associate like me. She was probably imaging Manon and me in that bed upstairs, doing whatever it is that junior associates and receptionists do. I could feel her resentment across the room. But I found myself enjoying the moment. The remote Ms. Pearl didn't seem quite so remote just now.

I walked around the table to Manon. "Would you like more coffee, dear?" As I bent forward I caught the scent of her perfume. Chloe. It seemed exactly right for her.

At first Manon seemed a bit startled by my surprising show of affection, but she quickly got into character. Her hair brushed against the side of my face and she squeezed her eyes with faux affection. "Yes, please."

"Eric's already onboard the boat, so anyone going sailing better get moving." Mrs. Cantor began to collect the cups on the table. I helped her put them and the other dishes in the sink for her housekeeper to clean.

"When the wind is like this," I said, "he'll want to shove off soon."

"And he'll need his first mate at his side," again patting me maternally. Whatever Mrs. Cantor thought of the Manon subterfuge, and in truth I couldn't imagine putting up with having the girlfriend hanging around, she did seem to like me.

As Seth hustled their bags down to the guesthouse, Enid lingered in the kitchen. "Well, if we're going sailing, I better change. Are you going as well, Manon?"

"I wouldn't miss it. Eric's a master sailor."

Receptionists don't use their boss' first name; not, that is, unless they're sleeping with them. Perhaps Manon had simply grown tired of playing the Lady in Waiting to the official Mrs. Cantor, but in any case, no formal reactions came from the wife of the man sleeping with his assistant.

Mrs. Cantor, finished with the kitchen, embraced Enid. "I'm so glad you and Seth could come down." That seemed the signal that it was time to go, and we all left the kitchen.

I had never admired Mrs. Cantor more. I realized people don't have their dignity stripped from them; they must consent to give it away themselves, and she wasn't about to do that. Instead of being humiliated by what Manon had said, Elizabeth's grace under duress had only made me feel ashamed for my own part in this shabby business.

But there was no backing out now, and besides, even Mrs. Cantor had made her deal with the devil—just as Manon and I had. I was quite sure my faux girlfriend wasn't the first set of long legs at the office to catch Mr. Cantor's eye. But like many women, still Mrs. Cantor soldiered on in her marriage. I hadn't been married long enough to even have any affairs, much less understand how one put up with knowing one's life partner is out screwing around. Reasons, I supposed, but hers remained obscure.

⛵

MANON, ENID AND I STROLLED DOWN THE CANTORS' expansive lawn to the dock where the Sundance was moored. We had each brought an extra pair of shoes, as Mr. Cantor didn't allow anyone in street shoes near his pristine deck. Like all good sailors, he kept his boat in perfect trim. Why wouldn't he? If you could afford it, you better be able to keep it looking shiny and new.

Once TateAir went through, what would Eric buy for himself next?

What would I, for that matter?

With the tide in, it posed no difficulty for the girls to climb aboard. I had learned to clamber over the rail no matter the tide, as Mr. Cantor did, with a gracefulness to his pear-shaped body not seen at the office.

I caught Enid admiring my physicality. She had it bad as I did. All in good time.

It felt wonderful to be back on board the boat again. For a moment, I almost resented having the women onboard. When it was only the two of us Mr. Cantor sailed hard, the sharp bow spray misting us as we'd laugh like mad, our voices lost in the wind and the waves pounding against the boat.

Twice, in fact, he had turned the Sundance over on its side, and both times the ten tons of lead in the keel had righted her once the wind spilled out of the sails. Terrified the first time, I felt sure we would both drown. Mr. Cantor, however, didn't seem to notice how afraid I was. He simply ordered me to make sure my safety harness was tethered.

The second time it happened, I felt the excitement of being close to real trouble—the tipping point before you fall into the abyss—but it was a crisis one felt confident could be survived; that my luck would hold. We both enjoyed the adrenaline rush of sailing almost off the edge. It's what we had in common. But it wouldn't be like that today. Not with the ladies beside us.

⛵

As soon as we were out in the bay, Mr. Cantor had me raise the main sail. Just as I began to pull on the halyard he turned the boat sharply away from the wind, and I nearly lost my balance on the wet deck. I grabbed at anything to keep from going overboard. The girls in the cockpit had a good laugh.

Once I steadied myself, I saw that Eric laughed, too. As I knew, he had done it on purpose to show off for Manon and Enid. As with the exuberance and risk-taking when we were alone, where women were concerned, an overgrown adolescent such as Eric Cantor would no doubt need to show off for them.

The thought crossed my mind that he suspected me of poaching Manon. Perhaps a little sailing humiliation was meant to put me in my place. Maybe Manon had told him everything in order to make him jealous—who knew? You could never be sure about these things, even if you asked outright. Sex is the careless bullet that always seems to ricochet around the room. The last time Manon and I had made love, it occurred that I may have learned nothing from prior mistakes.

I finished raising the sail and made my way back to the cockpit. Blood trickled down where I'd barked my shin.

"Oh—you've cut your leg." Enid ripped off her scarf and pressed it against my shin. "Does it hurt?"

That my M&A colleague seemed to care about my slight wound was more unsettling than Mr. Cantor's little trick.

Gentle, I pushed her hand away. "It's nothing. But now I'm afraid we've ruined this lovely scarf."

"Never mind about that." She called over to Eric: "Where do you keep your medical kit?" Her tone held a certain determination.

"It's down below, in the head. And hurry up—this jackass is bleeding all over my cockpit."

Mr. Cantor laughed and I did too, the way we did when it was only the two of us sailing and one of us got hurt. A sailboat is a marvelous place for injuries—the salt spray in the air promotes fast healing. But now my leg began to throb in earnest, and any amusement dried up. His tomfoolery had gotten someone injured: me.

Enid reappeared with the first-aid kit. "The cut's deep. He might need stitches."

"It's all fun and games," I said, looking at my boss, "until someone gets hurt."

That seemed to land. Eric blinked twice, his smile faltering. "Well, Nurse Nightingale is certainly making a fuss over nothing."

I thought I saw Manon stifle a laugh. I knew how closely she would be watching the two men today. Always one to put things in their proper prospective, she held up one corner of the scarf. "You're right about one thing. This is ruined."

While Enid cleaned and dressed my cut with not one but two large bandages, Manon and Mr. Cantor watched in amused silence.

We sailed on for a few hours more, but a pall seemed to settle, and if any of us were really enjoying ourselves, it wasn't outwardly apparent.

At last, on the way back to the marina, Manon remembered she was supposed to be my girlfriend.

"How's your cut?" She lay long, manicured fingers upon my forearm. "Does it hurt?"

Enid watched from across the deck. I winked at her. "The medical officer on duty squared me away."

Meanwhile, Mr. Cantor watched from the cockpit. Steering, he had his back to us, yet I could see how he had stiffened at my proximity to Manon. If only he knew the whole truth.

AFTER A QUIET DINNER OF SURF AND TURF SERVED WITH TWO elegant wines, one white and one red, I announced that my leg was bothering me and asked to be excused like the teenaged son of well-to-do parents.

From my room at the head of the stairs I could hear the clatter of dessert plates, the muted chatter from the dining room. Carefully, I cracked open the window and lit a cigarette, the smoke from which I inhaled with a greedy and furtive urgency. Mrs. Cantor didn't allow smoking in the house. I was a scofflaw.

A creak came from the door hinges; light, sudden, spilled into the room. Thinking it Mrs. Cantor, I pitched the butt out the window and started fanning with furious abandon.

As I turned to apologize I saw not Mrs. Cantor, but Enid.

"That's a filthy habit." She stood outlined in the pale light from the hallway. "I came up to see about that leg."

"It's fine... thanks to you." I closed the window, swept a dusting of ash from the sill. I couldn't help smiling at that blatant untruth. "And, I'm planning to quit these coffin-nails soon enough. Honest."

"Of course. That's what they all say."

Enid shut the door behind her. It took a moment for my eyes to adjust to the almost total darkness.

She came over to me. Her tone turned serious again, like a doctor inquiring after an especially exasperating patient. "Really, now—how's the leg?"

"A bit sore, but other than that I'm good to go." I did a little soft-shoe routine to demonstrate my fitness for duty. "See?"

"That was a stupid stunt Eric pulled today."

"You saw he did that on purpose?"

She nodded.

"He was only showing off."

"For whom?"

"For you… and Manon."

Honesty descended like a fine mist. Enid sat on the bed. "You know something? I think Elizabeth almost believes Manon is your girlfriend."

"I would hope so."

"That's a pretty lousy stunt, too… don't you think?"

"You mean *you* don't think she's my girlfriend?" I tried to sound hurt that Enid couldn't imagine Manon falling for me.

"Paul? You're terribly charming, but I happen to know a junior associate like you doesn't have enough money for a girl like her."

"No?"

"No. Whatever that little gold-digger is, she's not your 'girlfriend'. Not in the way people usually mean the term."

Enid crossed her legs. I could almost forget Seth was downstairs. I wondered if she knew how much I wanted her.

"You're quite the scold today."

"I know you admire Eric, but that doesn't mean you have to act as his beard. Don't you find it a bit undignified?"

I gasped. "Just lay it right out there."

If she sensed my affection for her, she certainly hid it well. She seemed oblivious to what seemed to me an obvious vibe, one palpable here in the darkness. "Please. You're a damn smart lawyer and he knows that. He was tremendously impressed by what you did with the Sherwood case."

"I can't say the same for your fiancé." I couldn't bring myself to mention his name.

"Seth was hugely embarrassed you turned his pro bono case into a nice fee for the firm."

"How smart a lawyer do you think I am?"

"Smart enough." She smoothed a crease in her skirt. "It also doesn't help that he thinks I have a crush on you."

I could make out her oval face in the moonlight, her full lips, lovely green eyes. Maybe it was that half darkness that allowed to us speak our minds. "Do you?"

Enid stood to go. "I've been unhappy before, Paul. I don't need any more of that."

I thought of the fellow who had taken her picture in Paris and wondered if it was he who had schooled her in unhappiness. I knew I was edging out onto thin ice, but I couldn't seem to stop myself. "And Seth will make you happy?"

"He won't make me unhappy."

"That's not quite the same thing, is it?"

"It's more than a man like you could do for me."

"You haven't even given me a chance."

"And I won't anytime soon, either."

We had become two lawyers pleading our personal injury case, and like all defendants who represent themselves, we had fools for clients. "Well, we can't always control who we're attracted to, now, can we?"

"No—but we can control how we respond to it."

At the door she paused in the sudden, harsh light spilling from the hallway. She glanced around, lowered her voice. "Here's what I know about this current situation: Manon is the first girlfriend Eric has ever brought into this house."

"Meaning what?"

"He wants to get caught."

I asked her for additional clarity on this knowledge.

"Isn't it obvious? He's trying to force Elizabeth to ask him for a divorce, because he's too much of a coward himself to ask."

"A divorce would cost him millions." I offered this wisdom as proof certain that Enid must be mistaken. Any exploration of my relationship with her would have to wait until another day. My masquerade as Manon's boyfriend, I now fully understood, had seen to that.

"Elizabeth has her own money."

"Spoken like a lawyer."

"It's a verifiable fact." She told me Elizabeth's maiden name, an East Coast family going back to the country's founding. "With or without Eric Cantor, she has a substantial family trust."

"Is it enough?"

"Enough to keep her in wine and tummy-tucks? Especially as the owner of, say, this bay house? Yes."

I intended to say more when Enid, abrupt, hurried back downstairs.

I stood at the open door—I could hear Mr. Cantor joking about 'the patient upstairs,' and then he and Seth laughed.

I turned out the light but couldn't sleep, so I got up to sneak one last cigarette. While at the window I saw Enid strolling back to the guesthouse with Seth. They stopped on the gravel pathway and kissed.

Somehow I had never imagined them as lovers. What in hell did I think they were? I guess I had always managed to drive around that particular pothole. At least, until now.

I shut the window and pulled down the shade. I was always on the lookout for emotional disasters, and if I saw even the slightest sign of a storm approaching, I'd sound the alarm to abandon ship. In how many different ways was a coward, I wondered in a moment of clarity? I shook off the doubt.

⛵

I AWOKE TO THE PLUMP THWACKING OF BALLS STRIKING THE high-tension strings of tennis rackets. Even without looking, I could tell from the measured rhythm of the play they were both good. The set went on—either they really were well-matched, or one of them was sandbagging.

When I raised the shade I saw Seth and Elizabeth Cantor, both of them wearing tennis whites, on the red clay court near my side of the house. I cracked the window and lit my first cigarette of the day. I watched their competition through a veil of smoke which threatened to give away my position.

They played a rather conventional game; moving their opponent to the far side of the court before hitting the ball deep into the opposite corner. I had played in high school. I enjoyed the game for what it showed you about people. It wasn't that hard to beat even far better players, not if you watched in the early sets for their weaknesses. Move close-in on people with a stronger serve; use long rallies to frustrate big hitters. Not much more to it than that. The thing was to turn their strengths into weaknesses.

Sailing, now, here was a real sport—you competed against nature itself, not another spindly, weak human being like you. We are too fragile to be too threatening, whether on a tennis court, or a court of law. Our egos tell us otherwise, but next to the waves of the ocean, the wind, the clouds and the sky, we are nothing.

Like all talented jocks, I observed Seth play like a bully, with aggression. He drilled the ball at her and hollered *HUH* as though he were John McEnroe. Seth had one of those booming serves that kicked up when it struck the court.

Mrs. Cantor had moved back to deal with the force of his serves, but doing so left her out of position for his return.

I opened the window a bit more. A telltale plume of blue smoke spiraled above my head like a ghost as I called down, "Who's winning?"

"Put that cigarette out, you bad boy, and come down here to take my place."

"Before breakfast?"

Mrs. Cantor draped a white towel around her neck and sat down to catch her breath. "Yes—I need to get inside to make it for everyone."

"I'll be right down."

I enjoyed the times we had played. I liked the graceful way she hit the ball, and the knowing way she'd say, "You let me win." She played a country club style game, one where you weren't supposed to care much about winning. It was about the doing, a kind of Zen enterprise with which to while away a privileged hour or two, if the sun weren't too terribly dire that day.

I groped around for my racket under a pile of clothes lying in the corner of my room. Then, I slipped on a pair of faded blue shorts and my favorite T-shirt with the Ducati logo on it. Seth was the last person with whom I wished to interact, but I headed downstairs anyway.

OUTSIDE I FOUND SETH, WITH A SMUG GRIN, STRETCHING AND flexing as though he were in the finals at Wimbledon.

As Elizabeth left the court, she tossed a fresh ball my way. "He beat me in straight sets. See what you can do with him."

I wouldn't be satisfied unless I could give Seth what-for here on this court as well as in that furniture case. What did I have to my advantage?

I noted the sun cresting the tree line. Ah—that would put it in Seth's eyes, give him difficulty when he served with that high toss of his. Another five minutes and he'd be half-blind. Perfect.

"Mind if we hit a few first?"

"Sure." Seth twirled his racket, one with the oversized head; the kind pros favored, though his dumpy physique belied such status. "But as you saw, I'm warmed up already."

I hit a low forehand shot to his backhand. To prove his earlier point, he returned my soft-serve with serious power. But given the way he stepped into the ball, I expected that; I met it on the rise and pounded it to his backhand.

This time he made the return, but with a bit less zest and spin. He hadn't anticipated I would jump on his shot.

"I'm ready." I'd already learned what I needed to about his game, didn't want him to see any more of mine before we started keeping score. Besides, I was already out of breath. Elizabeth had begun to walk back to the house, but stopped after she saw our first few strokes and sat down again.

I called to her, *"What about breakfast?"*

"Just get on with this little contest."

Seth laughed. "Yes. Let's."

"You serve." I hit three balls over to my opponent. He had been playing for the better part of an hour, but his hair was still perfectly in place. It reminded me I had forgotten to comb my shaggy, corkscrewed bed-hair.

He tossed the ball high into the air and arched his back like a catapult ready to fling the ball, but instead he let it drop to the court. As he tried again I immediately moved towards the service line and hit a low cross-court return. Seth was so surprised to see me standing in the middle of the court that he hit his shot wide.

"Love-fifteen." Mrs. Cantor seemed to be enjoying herself.

"You son of a bitch."

"What?" Innocent, bouncing from foot to foot.

"Now the damn sun is in my eyes."

"Do you forfeit?"

Seth cursed and served again. This time he struck the ball clean and hard. It was all I could do to return it with a junk shot that made it over the net, just-this-much, before falling unmolested onto the court and rolling across toward him.

Seth looked at the ball, then at me, with something between surprise and disgust. I thought I heard Elizabeth laugh. "That's love-thirty."

By now frustration, along with the sun, worked equally to interfere with Seth's game; I broke his serve without too much difficulty. Now I was getting my second wind. I had never had a particularly strong serve, but I could place it pretty much where I wanted. This often put me in position to hit a winning return.

To this end, I nailed my first serve deep into Seth's backhand so I could slide to my right and hold a nice angle for his return. I watched the ball leave his racket and continued with it all the way into my own. I didn't have to lift my head up to know my return was a winner. When I did look, Seth made a swing at the ball but smacked his racket against the ground; on my next serve I put enough English on it so that the ball spun wide when Seth moved to force it toward my backhand.

"Gracious, boys. Gold medals for all." Elizabeth walked off towards the house. "Nobody get hurt, now."

"We won't be very long, not the way I'm playing today," Seth called after her, the implication being that his A-game was primed to return.

To this end I let him win a few games, to let him think he had me. Then I took two straight sets, pounding them back and running the older Seth Meyrinck, also thirty pounds too heavy, from one side to the other. I always did fight above my own weight.

When the game was over I walked to the net to shake his hand, but he busied himself putting his racket into its carrier. "Good match," he muttered without making eye contact.

On the walk back to the house I started coughing from all the exercise and remembered I had promised Enid I would quit smoking. Well, neither of us took that seriously I'm sure. But suddenly I saw her point—I had little knife-points sticking into both lungs. It would pass.

As the smell of frying bacon filled my being with hunger, I discovered Seth would not join us for breakfast. Enid made excuses, said he was packing. I tried not to talk about beating him, but Elizabeth kept asking about the game. With Mr. Cantor working on the boat and Manon still in bed, it was only the three of us in the kitchen.

I thought of what Enid had said last night about how another game, the pretense over Manon, degraded Elizabeth. Her continuing her duties with grace and good cheer made her seem strong to me, not a victim. Weren't we all doing what we had to not only to survive, but prosper? And then, you had the fraternal aspects of such transactions. You couldn't explain that part to women, not if one spent all day on it, nor if you filed a brief the length and weight of the phone book.

Enid served a poached egg from the warming dish. "You

must play well, because Seth was the captain of his team at Dartmouth."

"Actually, he's a better player than I am."

"Please, no false modesty. It doesn't become you."

"No, I mean it. He is a better player. I noted a few weak spots in his game, and played to those. Simple as that."

"Like you noticed that business about Sherwood and the insurance regulations?"

"That was just good lawyering. Like any competent litigator would have discovered."

Elizabeth stared at me from across the table. She smiled. "I understand more and more why Eric thinks so much of you. Peas in a pod."

Meanwhile, I tingled yet again at having Enid to myself without Seth around. I couldn't stop wondering what she would be like in bed. I was starting to feel like a dam in danger of breaking over this lustful obsession with my immediate supervisor. As though the situation weren't already complicated enough...

As I was packing, Elizabeth appeared in my room. She sat down on the antique chest by the window.

"It reeks of cigarettes in here. I wish you wouldn't smoke in the house."

I froze in the motion of tossing a T-shirt into my overnight bag. "I'm sorry."

Something in her glistening, sad-smiling eyes said, *please don't speak*.

I stuffed my last wrinkled shirt into my bag. She again stood, this time to hug me.

"What is this?"

"I've never been good at games, Paul. But you seem to enjoy them so very much."

"Again—I got lucky with Seth."

"I'm not talking about this morning's tennis match."

She seemed to be giving me another quiet opportunity to come clean, perhaps. A guilty conscience can stoke all manner of paranoia. I liked Elizabeth—I wanted to tell her the truth, but how could I?

She asked, "Have you ever noticed how 'lucky' very determined, smart and resourceful people also seem ?"

"Are you suggesting I somehow manufacture my own luck?"

She laughed without answering.

"Here, I packed lunch for you and Manon." She handed me a bag with two wax paper-wrapped sandwiches alongside two deli-sized dill pickle slices. "I see why you like her. She's quite lovely."

I took the lunch bag from her. I felt as if she was still waiting for me to tell her the truth about Manon. Here I was lying to her about the same woman about which her husband had been lying for over two years.

And yet, was I being untruthful? I was simply pretending for Elizabeth that Manon was my girlfriend—call it a lie of omission. That was enough of a rationalization to get me out of the room with this woman deceived yet dignified, an unnerving dignity which made me question my own. "Yes, she's quite a lady, that Manon."

"In every way, I suspect."

My cheeks flushed. "Yes. Quite so."

"Well—good. That's wonderful for everyone."

Elizabeth knew my weaknesses as well anyone, but I suppose that wasn't difficult for her, since she felt me so much like her husband. I had no clue now what she thought of me, but I supposed one day, one way or another, I'd find out.

In any case, later that night in bed with Manon I would need to do my best to ignore the stickier aspects of our tangled web of relationships. In fact, after we were finished, I suggested she go back home to her own place.

"Sure," she said with a shrug. "See you tomorrow."

God forbid I actually fall in love with a woman like this— Manon was far too much like me, the more I thought about it.

M y reputation at the firm now preceded me.
Early Monday morning at my desk I had just
finished chewing up my first antacid tablet when Derrick
Bishoff, a fellow junior associate, knocked and sauntered
through the door.

"Interested in arguing a motion in District Court for me?"

"What is it?"

"Personal injury case."

"Why me?"

He grinned. "I like your style, dude. What can I say?"

I had never argued a personal injury case before, but my
success with the Sherwood motion made me feel confident I
could handle it. With the hearing set for Tuesday at nine I'd
need the case files right away, which he happened to have
under his arm.

"I thought you might like a chance to go up against a really
good lawyer—Marcia Herring," a well-known litigator.

I whistled. "Herring? More like a mako shark."

"That's her rep, sure. But after the schooling you gave that
schmuck Zucker on the furniture case? I doubt little Marcia
scares you."

"Irv did walk out of court that day with his pants down."

"Legendary, my man. Marcia won't know what hit her."

My antennae wriggled at a hint of sarcasm in Derrick's
tone. I knew he and Seth Meyrinck were friends, so caution

seemed wise—they could be looking for any chance to humiliate me in front of Mr. Cantor.

With all that in mind I should have said no, but you know me—if ambition always walks ahead of us, there you will find me hurrying after it, eager for the chance to again prove myself in court.

"I'll look it over."

"I'll need a firm answer by lunch-thirty at the latest."

After Derrick left, I mulled and meditated on this latest wrinkle. No gain without risk. A win against Marcia would seal the deal on my rep, here at the firm and elsewhere. I had to go for it.

I CHECKED THE COURT ROSTER TO SEE WHO'D BE HEARING motions this week. I groaned—I'd face not only a mako shark but the Honorable Lucious Symmons, a toad-like judge with a gravel-thick growl, an impatient demeanor, notorious for being rude and demonstrative to handsome young lawyers like me.

Nothing to be done about my handsome face and confident bearing, so I looked into all personal injury cases the judge had decided in the last five years, to get a feel for facts and rhetoric he might find persuasive.

Doing so wasn't encouraging; the judge's judicial philosophy, if he had one, seemed to be that the district court judge represented a sort of feudal lord who could do as he pleased, precedent be damned.

I did notice, however, that female attorneys—like Ms. Herring, my opposing counsel in this case—fared well in front of the learned judge. This news raised a red storm flag up a pole buffeted by strengthening winds of judicial conflict.

Symmons also seemed to find ways to mention his status as an alumnus of Princeton at almost every opportunity. I decided I would wear a dark blue suit with a starched white shirt and that faux Princeton tie I'd purchased for just such an occasion. As far as he knew, I would be an Ivy League man from the knot in my Paul Stuart tie to the soles of my Allen Edmond shoes. I had paid enough for the costume. Time to use it.

After a quick stroll into Enid's office to ask if I could have the day to prepare for this sudden hearing she agreed, albeit with reluctance. She considered litigation a waste of time, thought litigators were rather lazy prima donnas and show-offs. I felt certain she found my zeal to take on this case puzzling.

When I mentioned Derrick Bishoff's name as the source of this request, Enid suffered a flash of brief, unhidden surprise, but said nothing. That confirmed my suspicion Seth had put his buddy up to this, to give me an impossible case so I could be humbled in court by Ms. Herring. But, I liked taking on a case no one expected me to win. In the courtroom, with its theatrics and magic, making the impossible seem possible was a good litigator's stock in trade.

⛵

I SPENT THE DAY STUDYING THE FILINGS IN THE CASE. BY EIGHT o'clock in the evening, I understood the issues and our position on each of them. Our client, a company which ran a chain of motels throughout the country, had reduced security services. As a result, crime around its properties had risen sharply. During discovery it had come out that it had done so in order to cut costs. The plaintiff, an attractive eighteen-year old girl, had been raped and shot at one of the now less-than-secure motels. Our defense, however, was that the company could not be held liable for the unpredictable acts of third-party criminals. Foreseeability is the key to imposing liability on anyone.

I thought our defense was well supported by the case law. I had even suggested to Derrick we move to have the case dismissed under Rule 56. At first he resisted the idea, because he felt it would make settlement more difficult if we lost. I finally convinced him that, even if we lost, the motion would strengthen our appeal. The facts were against us, so we would almost surely lose at trial... but the law, however, was on our side, which meant we'd win on appeal.

I had shrugged, nonchalant. "It's all a question of who'll blink first, really."

"Seth wasn't kidding about you." Derrick shook his head. "But Marcia Herring doesn't have a blinking-bone in that body of hers."

I believed him. I'd seen Ms. Herring on television a number of times. While short, she presented more than a match for the indifferent corporations which injured and ignored her clients. Her bright red lipstick highlighted the perpetually angry expression on her face. I'd seen lawyers like her before; they were camera-hog actors only one step above ambulance chasers, really, rarely bothering to understand the law governing their case.

Before leaving the office I had the IT people put together a compilation of Ms. Herring's trials which had been televised. Since I couldn't sleep I stayed up all night watching her intimidate judges, badger witnesses, and cow opposing counsel, all while charming jurors into delivering verdicts that landed her in the win column. Now I knew what to expect.

ONCE THE LIGHT BEGAN TO APPEAR OUTSIDE MY BEDROOM window, I gave up on sleep. After a brief dog-walk I showered, put on my Princeton outfit and tried to pull myself together with a mug of coffee the size of a movie theater soft drink.

As I perfected the knot, I admired my appearance. By now I had at least one tie from every Ivy League school. One of the surprising things I'd learned is how few asked if you had actually ever attended these schools. I suppose it would be too embarrassing for everyone if you were found out.

It's the way it was explained to me by the guy who gave me the idea, a boozy old litigator at some bar at lunch one day. I had seen him changing his tie from a Columbia to a Cornell, both top five schools, and asked what was up. "An old trick," he said, downing a martini like I'd served Arthur at lunch and chewing up three mints before hustling out of the bar. "It's all a game… it's all bullshit," the seasoned attorney had said with a wink. I often wondered if he had been real. Some kind of law-angel imparting wisdom and vanishing in a puff of fairy dust.

Back down to earth, I shined my new Allen Edmonds and looked over the entire package in the mirror. Nervous but excited, I had begun to perspire already, but I was good to go. Soon as I refilled my giant coffee followed by two doses of antacid, I would eat opposing counsel alive.

WHEN I CHARGED INTO COURTROOM 4C WITH MY HEAD HELD high, however, only the bailiff had arrived to witness my grand entrance. Before going back to reading the day's sports stats, the gray-haired court officer, likely inches from retirement, lowered his newspaper long enough to decide I posed no threat. To him, I looked like a kid. Probably someone's law clerk.

Well—isn't he in for a surprise.

Now seated at the defense table, I snapped open my brief-case with what I hoped sounded like sufficient authority. If the bailiff decoded my message, he didn't show it. I poured water into the paper cups one always found in court and took a long drink. Sighed. Waited.

Would the judge and Ms. Herring be able to tell, simply by looking at me, that I'd never argued a personal injury case? I decided I would be polite but reserved, as any Princeton man should be. Now that I had my script—any script—I began to feel better.

As I re-read the brief we had filed in support of our motion, I noticed none of the cases citations were from the District of Columbia, which in itself wasn't unusual. Still, I would have preferred a few local cases which supported our position.

I didn't have long to ponder, because once the doors opened behind me there stood Ms. Herring, wearing a power dress shimmering redder than her glossy lipstick. Two more women, law clerks, followed her into the courtroom like vassals trailing behind a potentate. Both clerks wore bow ties and dark slacks. They sported identical Dutch Boy haircuts. Their near-genderless twinned appearance made them look like members of the Heaven's Gate cult.

I stood and went to the plaintiff's table to introduce myself. Ms. Herring glanced first at me, then at my outstretched hand, before turning away without speaking. Her law clerks snickered.

"Nice to meet you as well."

She replied without making eye contact, "I don't like to make small talk before litigation. If you please."

"As you wish."

As I eased back down into my chair I noticed the bailiff had lowered his newspaper to give Marcia a smug smile. She greeted him by his first name; he asked if there was anything she needed. She asked if his son was still playing basketball at Vanderbilt. Meanwhile, I had drunk so much water I needed the bathroom, but afraid the judge would take the bench while I was away, I chose to suffer.

"*All rise.*"

The bailiff had a surprisingly forceful voice for such an old man. When he spoke, we all leapt to our feet as Judge Symmons appeared from a door at the rear of the courtroom. He glanced around with dark eyes suggesting a sour mood.

When he spied Ms. Herring, however, a faint smile forced back a frown which seemed etched into the deep folds around the corners of his mouth. His pale skin looked like nothing so much as melting wax.

The moment he caught sight of me, that smile disappeared. For an instant he looked like a man who had tasted sand in his oyster, found a hair in his iced tea. If he admired my Princeton tie, he didn't let on.

"*Be seated,*" the bailiff boomed out with operatic solemnity. If I hadn't been so nervous, I would have laughed.

Marcia stood and began addressing the court. "Good morning, your honor. First, let me apologize that the court is having its time wasted today. Judge Symmons, you see before you a copy of the defendant's Rule 56 motion to dismiss, which I will show is based not only on a misunderstanding of the law, and an egregious misstatement of the facts at hand in this case."

Before I knew it I was on my feet. "Objection, your honor." When I looked at Ms. Herring she seemed astonished I would show such temerity in interrupting her. Trust me, she was no more astonished than me at my behavior. I had made my first motion, but had no idea what I would say next.

But, I was in the flow. I turned off my thinking brain to act in the moment, fully present. "As Ms. Herring correctly noted, the court has before it the defendant's motion to dismiss. And while I'm grateful to Ms. Herring for offering to introduce that motion to the court, we prefer to argue our own motion before having it mischaracterized in such a reductive and shallow manner."

Judge Symmons, pale, seemed barely able to catch his breath after the long climb up the three steps to his chair. Between gasps, a voice breathy and weak came to the court: "I don't think an experienced trial lawyer like Ms. Herring needs instruction from you, Mr. Johns." Bushy eyebrows rose above the Judge's thick glasses. "Any more impertinence here this morning and I'll deny your motion without a hearing."

"I stand corrected, your honor." I sat down and tried to understand what the hell was going on. But a Princeton man must never appear flustered, so I arranged a confident smile on my face; I tried to look as though the judge had paid me the greatest of compliments instead of dressing me down.

The Judge's good humor seemed to return the moment he spoke to my opposing counsel. "You may proceed, Ms. Herring."

"Thank you, your honor. As I was saying, the defendant, a conglomerate which owns six-hundred eighty motels in the United States, and over two hundred in Canada, asserts in its motion it cannot be held liable for the acts of third parties. This is simply a misstatement of the law."

I jumped to my feet again. "Your honor, I must again

object. Counsel is attempting to argue the defendant's motion. I must insist that she confine herself to arguing the plaintiff's case."

This time I remained standing. I watched as the judge shifted his weight from one side of his chair to the other as if he were trying to gain momentum before dressing me down. No wonder they called him the Walrus.

"Young man, this is the second time I've had to caution you about interrupting counsel. There will not be a third time." The judge eyed the bailiff with an ominous glare. "Do you understand me?"

In response, the bailiff rested his hand on his holster.

I continued on as if I hadn't noticed the dark clouds rolling my way. "Your honor, you have before you my client's motion. Only I am authorized to present their views to this court. As the court has pointed out, Ms. Herring is an experienced trial lawyer and knows that as well as I do."

The Walrus swiveled in his chair, leaned back and looked to the ceiling for wisdom. At first I thought he might have fallen asleep, but soon he began to mumble through teeth clenched and yellow. "Since you're so eager to speak, Mr. Johns, perhaps you should hurry up and enlighten the court on why I should dismiss this young victim's complain against your corporate client."

Having the judge refer to the plaintiff as "this young victim" was not a good sign. "Your honor, the facts remain uncontested. No one denies, for example, that Ms. Johnson went to the motel on New York Avenue to spend the day with her boyfriend."

The judge was aghast. "What does the fact she was about to see her boyfriend have to do with this case?" He blustered like Wilford Brimley going for an acting nomination. "*Son, are you trying to impugn this girl's character?*"

Who would have thought the old Walrus so gallant a protector of young women? "Absolutely not, your honor. I mention this detail because the boyfriend, as we'll soon see, represents a crucial witness in this case."

All five-foot-one of Ms. Herring seemed to appear beside me like a ghost. Her objection, all but shouted in my ear, only caused the smallest of flinches, the slightest dimming of the fire in my eyes.

"Mr. Sands—I mean, Mr. Johns," an error which threw Symmons off his bluster a bit, "just told this court the facts are, they're uncontested, so—how can—no, I'm sorry." He made a show of shuffling papers, found his focus. "This boyfriend in question cannot possibly be an important fact witness. It is Ms. Johnson who was raped and shot. Her prior sexual conduct will have no part in this case."

"But, Judge Symmons, if it pleases the—"

"Mr. Sands, I caution you to tread carefully. This court will not allow this hearing to be turned into a campaign to smear a young girl's reputation."

Of course, all this theater was classic Marcia Herring, this feint, this ploy. In only five minutes of court time she had managed to make me look as dastardly as the rapist's accomplice. I needed to pull myself together.

"May I proceed, your honor?"

"Involving prior sexual conduct?"

I held out my hands. "Of course not."

Marcia snorted with mirth, meanwhile the Walrus threw a dismissive gesture in my general direction, a wriggling cluster of fat sausage fingers. "Go on, then."

"Your honor, perhaps it might be more direct for me to merely point out to the court that there is no prior case in the District of Columbia where a landlord was held liable for the criminal acts of a third party. In fact, in a case exactly on point, Roosevelt versus Spring Oaks Condominiums, the Virginia Court of Appeals held in this way: since it is entirely unforeseeable where a criminal may strike, it would be simply unconscionable to impose liability for such unfortunate, albeit *entirely unforeseeable*, acts of malice which occupy our days litigating the rule of law."

A wall of silence from the bench.

"Now, while my client regrets the injuries sustained by Ms. Johnson, precedent calls for one ruling and one ruling only, that this court may not impose liability on a landlord for the criminal actions of a third party not under the defendant's control."

I surprised myself at how persuasive it sounded. I nodded to Ms. Herring, who pouted, and sat down.

"Mr. Johns, you're quite right about one thing; there is no case exactly on point in the District. However, you fail to mention that the Virginia case on which the motion relies is thirty-eight years old. Since that time, why, a veritable host of cases have expanded landlord liability, for everything from faulty steps to crimes committed by the landlord's employees."

Now Marcia and the Walrus colluded on a pair of smirks. I wondered where they would go for lunch later.

I pressed ahead. "Ms. Herring is simply reinforcing our position, your honor. First, she concedes there's no case on point to support her position and then she cites the phantom of expanding landlord liability, but the cases she cites, they all have *just one thing* that this case does not."

Here I paused to watch the two of them as they waited for my punch line. "That's right. In every case cited by Ms. Herring, the plaintiff was injured by a person or property *under the control of the landlord*. Now, no one contends the defendant had any control over the career criminal who raped and shot Ms. Johnson. In his statement to the police, the assailant *admitted* he was simply walking by the motel when he observed Ms. Johnson exit her car and walk towards her room. The exact quote from his statement," I produced from a document on the table, "reads that he'd never even seen the motel before, had no familiarity with the property. 'I just pulled over there at random'—these are his exact words. No connection whatsoever with the motel, thereby no connection to our client." I thought that might be enough for the Walrus to chew on for a while.

A little wind had gone out of the judge's billowing black sails. His honor seemed almost pleading now with Marcia to say something, anything, to give him an opening to rule against me. "Don't you have anything to add, Ms. Herring?"

With her usual energy and aplomb, opposing counsel leapt to her high heels. "It's no wonder that Mr. Sands—I mean, Mr. Johns—characterizes landlord liability as a phantom because his client, the gravely misnamed Rest Easy Motel chain, also thinks they hold no duty or obligation, obviously, to the people who pay to stay there."

This opening line by Ms. Herring seemed to delight the Walrus who barely suppressed a laugh. "Go on."

"Mr. Johns makes much of the fact that no case in the District explicitly holds a landlord liable for the acts of a criminal on the landlord's property, and that is true. However, in a recent Maryland Court of Appeals case, the court held that while there was no specific statute holding landlord's liable for criminal acts on their property, to do so would be consistent with the evolving law of landlord liability. It should be noted that prior to that decision, the District and Maryland had nearly identical case law on this issue. As such, we ask today that this court recognize a singular fact: to hold the Rest Easy motel chain liable for those crimes that happened on their property requires no new law, but is instead entirely consistent with *the spirit of common law* as it has evolved and been interpreted by this court now for decades."

Absolutely beaming now, the Walrus rotated his mass so he could get a better look at me, to see if I was aware of the mortal blow my case had been dealt. "That sounds awfully persuasive to the court. Have you anything to add, Mr. Sands?" Unlike the judge's earlier invitation to Ms. Herring, he seemed almost daring me to open my mouth.

But my fear was long gone, and with it perhaps also any good sense I might have had left:

"Thank you, your honor. But my name is Johns, not Sands." I again rose to my feet. This might be my last chance. "Ms. Herring, it seems, hopes to ride the horse of eloquence over the obstacle of foreseeability; I can see that she has had good training in matters of rhetoric, as have I in my education," fingering the striped Princeton tie. "However, much as we all regret the injuries suffered by Ms. Johnson, the law stands as an absolute bar to any recovery from this defendant. We would point out to the court that in her suit Ms. Johnson did not sue her assailant, the man who actually raped and shot her. Instead, she elected to sue my client, whose only fault apparently lies in having deep pockets available for picking by a claim best described as frivolous. While Ms. Herring would confer legislative authority on the proceedings today and allow us in our hubris to enact new law, we, on the other hand, are confident this court will reject her attempt to lure it into trespassing on legislative prerogatives."

I stopped here because I thought I saw a look of concern cross the brow of the judge. Could it be that he actually understood what I was saying?

Ms. Herring rose without waiting for an invitation from the court. "We are delighted that Mr. Johns has reminded the court that the touchstone of liability in the District, as elsewhere, is foreseeability. Now," she turned to receive a sheaf of pages from one of the clerks with which she gestured noisy for the remainder of her remarks, "appended to plaintiff's Reply Brief is a copy of select pages from the deposition of the manager of the Rest Easy Motel at the time of the assault. We direct the court's attention to pages twenty-six through thirty, lines four-zero-seven through five-zero-two."

Here Ms. Herring paused so the judge and I could refer to our copies of the deposition, which we both rattled in finding the passage. I dreaded reading it again. Now had an inkling of where Ms. Herring was headed.

"There you'll see that Mr. Hayden, the manager, testified that in order to cut costs, the motel fired its lone security guard. He goes on to say corporate headquarters turned down his request to build a fence across the back of the property and perhaps, most tellingly, the motel had an occupancy rate at the time of one hundred and seven percent." Marcia glared before continuing so I could not possibly miss the scorn she felt for my client and, perhaps, for me as well. "The court may rightly wonder, just as I did, how a motel could have an occupancy rate exceeding one hundred percent, since in grade school we all learned one hundred percent is the whole of anything. But it seems the laws of arithmetic don't apply to the Rest Easy Motel, your honor."

The Walrus leaned forward so far with anticipation he nearly fell out of his chair. "Go on, go on, Ms. Herring."

"You see, if rooms are rented more than once a day, you can actually have an occupancy rate that exceeds one hundred per cent." Ms. Herring paused again to let the utter horror of this new disclosure sink in. "You see, your honor, prostitutes frequently rent rooms by the hour at the Rest Easy Motel. I will hand up to the court the police incident reports for prostitution at that address."

The Walrus fell back into his chair, pressed down by this shocking revelation. My opponent stared at me to see if I felt any shame at representing such a disgusting client.

Of course I didn't.

Here's the real-world situation: Ms. Herring is a worker in the victim's industry, and me? A part of the corporate defense world. Despite her ostensible coming sainthood as a victim's advocate I found her moral posturing ridiculous, but I did admire her ingenuity in dredging up those police incident reports. I made a mental note to remember that trick. She had certainly caught me off guard with it. I was beginning to understand now how she had won so many trials, why she was so feared.

His honor, on the other hand, seemed dumbstruck that a practice so vile as prostitution was underway not more than three miles from his courtroom. "This court does not share your belief, Mr. Johns, that it is without authority to address the gross negligence of your client, negligence that may very well have ruined the plaintiff's life." The judge seemed to have recovered his simmering dislike of the Rest Easy Motels and me. "As such, I am ready to rule on your motion."

I thought I heard the sound of a cash register ringing at the plaintiff's table, but I wasn't entirely out of bullets just yet. "Before the court rules, your honor, I would remind the court that the Rest Easy Motel also asserts that Ms. Herring, in her zeal to cast the widest possible net over the defendant, has sued the wrong party."

Now it was my turn to look at Ms. Herring and see how she liked seeing her case slip away. She didn't seem as concerned as I thought she should be by now, which worried me. "You see, your honor, each Easy Rest motel is independently owned and operated by the local franchisee. The business license of each motel is held in the name of that franchisee." Now I had them. Or, I didn't, but this was my last, best shot. "Therefore, liability, if there is any, *must be confined to the specific motel where Ms. Johnson was injured*. Not the corporation."

The old Walrus furrowed his brow in an unconvincing imitation of deep thought, but he needn't have bothered because the ever-energetic Ms. Herring sprang into rebuttal as if she had been waiting all morning for this moment.

"You honor, Mr. Johns tells us, apparently with a straight face, that these motels are independently owned and operated. Independent or not, these businesses are nonetheless under the total control, dominion and license of the corporate headquarters of Rest Easy Motels located in Dallas, Texas. Furthermore, the court will see in the motel manager's deposition that occupancy rates were reported to corporate headquarters daily, so they knew of the problem with prostitutes using the motel. Next, the decision to fire the security guard and not build a fence around the property was made in Dallas, Texas. Finally, room rates are set by corporate, advertising campaigns, logos and interior decor is as well. In other words, the franchisee simply collects money for the franchisor."

Those two law clerks with her had certainly done their homework. I was running out of straw-man arguments, and the judge was running out of patience.

I repeated myself: "In a recent ruling, the Ninth Circuit Court of Appeals held that, absent a specific statute, a court may not impose liability on a landlord for the criminal acts of a third party." I wanted to remind his honor of the gravity of the mistake he was about to make. "It's plain as day."

For a moment I thought Judge Symmons was having a heart attack; his face grew red, his eyes bulged out of their sockets and he could barely breathe. I wondered why the bailiff didn't rush to help him. "Mr. Johns, where is the Ninth Circuit located?"

"That court sits in California, your honor." I had no idea where this was going, but it didn't seem very encouraging. The bailiff smiled at Ms. Herring and folded his arms over his chest as if he were settling in for some real entertainment.

"And where is my court located?"

"In the District of Columbia, your honor."

The Walrus nodded to Ms. Herring to assure her he would make short work of me and the prostitute-infested motels I represented. "And what circuit is my court in?"

"The Fourth, your honor."

"Well, perhaps you could climb down off your California surfboard long enough to tell me what the Fourth Circuit holds on this issue, and not try to hide behind the ruling of some court out on the West Coast." I had no idea if he expected me to say something or just stand there and take it. "You've got your law right, but your geography is all mixed up."

That was too much for the bailiff and Ms. Herring—they both let out audible guffaws. The Walrus shot them a stern but understanding glance, and they grew quiet.

I certainly knew how to handle a bully like Symmons. I would simply maintain my composure and let the judge make a spectacle of himself. "Your honor, we are surprised to learn that this court feels rulings by the Ninth Circuit have no precedential value whatsoever."

The judge, smelling an appeal headed his way, decided to clean up the record of this hearing. "I did not say Ninth Circuit rulings have no precedential value. I simply said we look first to the Fourth Circuit."

I enjoyed watching the old blowhard squirm. The bailiff and Ms. Herring weren't laughing now.

I brought my own smile back and beamed it around the courtroom like a lighthouse beacon piercing the darkness of the Chesapeake Bay. "I don't disagree, your Honor, but as Ms. Herring was gracious enough to concede, the Fourth Circuit has not ruled on this issue... so we are compelled to look elsewhere."

I began to relax but too soon, as it turned out. Once again, Ms. Herring was more than up to the task:

"Like his geography, Mr. Johns's knowledge of procedure seems rather limited. You see, we are here on Diversity Jurisdiction grounds only, removed from state court by Mr. Johns's client because they reside in a state different from the plaintiff. They hoped that bit of forum shopping would help them escape the reach of state law. However, the plaintiff has brought state law claims and as Mr. Sands said—I mean, Mr. Johns—foreseeability is the touchstone of liability in state law cases, and this does not change merely because we find ourselves today in federal court."

The Walrus had heard enough. "The court is ready to rule. Defendant's motion for Summary Judgment is hereby denied. Will counsel for the Plaintiff please prepare an order for the court?"

"Of course, your honor." Ms. Herring shut her briefcase with a startlingly loud and triumphal snap. The Judge raised himself from his chair.

"All rise." The bailiff eyed me to see if I had any more disrespectful tricks up my sleeve.

"Mr. Johns, perhaps we can have a word before you leave?" Ms. Herring was suddenly all smiles.

"I can't imagine there's anything more to say." I didn't want to look like a sore loser, but that's exactly how I felt.

"I thought you might want to tell your client that we're happy to settle."

"What's the price of this happiness?"

"I'd say three million sounds about right." Ms. Herring sent her law clerks away so we could talk *mano-a-mano*. "I'm sure after what happened here today you can't possibly want to try this case."

Now we were playing poker, and she held all the cards. This would require some creative bluffing on my part. "I won't recommend a settlement of that size. Sorry."

"Oh, really. What figure *would* you recommend?"

The fact that she was fishing for a number told me they would take a good deal less, but it would need to be an amount easily divided by three since her fee was one third of the settlement. Now, I had no authority from my client to offer anything, and I was sure Derrick Bishoff would kill me when he learned what I had done, but I felt I should seize the moment to settle this case. "Let's see. I'm sensing something more like six hundred thousand."

Ms. Herring's smile disappeared. "I hardly think so."

I stood to go, shoving paper into my briefcase. "I'm sorry you found our offer unacceptable. I feel the court made significant errors today, and we intend to challenge them. I'm sure you're aware that Judge Symmons is not the most revered jurist in this district, but he is the most reversed—in the last three of them, the court of appeals noted his apparent lack of impartiality when dealing with corporate defendants in tort cases such as yours."

Marcia couldn't hide the concern in her eyes. "Go on."

I adjusted my cuffs, straighten the tie. "Marcia, we both know the girl's injuries have nothing to do with it, because they're not compensable under the law."

"That girl's life was ruined by your client, and all because they wanted to save a few bucks on minimum-wage security guards."

"I don't want to appear unfeeling, but that argument is wasted on me. You'd best save it for a jury of your client's peers."

"What are you, some kind of moral midget?"

I ignored her ableist shaming of those afflicted by dwarfism. "Ms. Herring, you did not sue the rapist; you sued my wealthy corporate client. So any discussion of morality would be better left to someone other than two trial lawyers."

"Rest Easy certainly has the right kind of lawyer."

Marcia meant it as an insult, but I considered it a compliment. "I appreciate your candor."

Then she blurted: "How about a million?"

I began to glow inside—I had manufactured some more of that mysteriously willful luck of mine. "Nine hundred-thousand. That's as firm an offer as I'm authorized to make."

She nodded. "All right."

So that was the price of morality. Her fee would be three hundred thousand dollars—not bad for a morning's work.

"Good game," I said as though we were Little Leaguers after a close match under the lights at the neighborhood playground. We shook hands.

"You son of a bitch," Marcia said under her breath, holding my hand a beat too long, enough for me to notice the hot blood beating beneath her skin. "We'll meet again someday."

"I look forward to it. Maybe a drink instead of in the courtroom?"

"Don't flatter yourself."

ON THE CAB RIDE BACK TO THE OFFICE, THE THOUGHT SETTLED that I would be fired. By the time I arrived, all the coffee and excitement of the morning had me vibrating like a high-tension line.

I ran into Manon who presented me with a bundle of mail, brushing my hand with her fingertips as she did so. "How'd it go, handsome?"

During our walk-and-talk down the hallway I pretended to go through the mail, but I was too distracted to recognize a single address. "Not too good. Not at all."

"Everybody knows about the hearing already."

"Oh—they do, do they?"

"I'm sorry. Marcia Herring's a tough one for anybody to go against."

I told her I knew it going in; I left out the part about my own hubris playing a role in the downfall. "I learned a lot today. But, it didn't help to have Judge Symmons all but sitting on her lap like a puppy."

"Don't let it get you down. Derrick asked you to argue that motion because he knew it was a loser."

"You haven't heard the whole story, yet. It's not as dire as the ruling suggests."

"Did you settle the case?"

I told her I had.

"Derrick and Seth will both have a fit."

"That's what I'm counting on."

Manon smiled and briefly grasped my hand, a quick and furtive gesture. Thoughts of matters other than the hearing, like the soft skin covering Manon's beautiful body, flooded into my head. "That's my go-getter."

"Why don't you come over for dinner tonight?"

"I'd like that very much."

"I'll fry you a steak. You'll need the protein for later…"

Manon was fun. When you were with her, you felt as if

you were the only man in her life… even though you knew it wasn't true. But maybe it should be.

As I passed Seth Meyrinck's office I recognized Derrick Bishoff's voice; I thought I heard my name mentioned.

I stopped to hear the two of them discussing what had happened in court this morning. Derrick would repeat something Ms. Herring or the Walrus had said, and the two of them would laugh like mad. I assumed the bailiff was their informant but, of course, he knew nothing of the settlement I had negotiated with Ms. Herring.

I listened for another moment before knocking. When Seth saw me, he blanched.

Ever the charmer, however, he quickly regained his composure. "Paul—get in here, buddy." Seth smiled and offered a chair. "Say, how'd that hearing go this morning?"

A smirk crept across Derrick's face like a lengthening afternoon shadow. "Yeah, what happened?"

"Actually, quite well." I picked up one of the tennis magazines Seth always had lying around and flipped to a story about funding for elementary school tennis programs. I waved the article at them as though it were an important brief. "This is fascinating stuff. I've got a nephew who loves watching Wimbledon. I wonder if six is too early to get them started training?"

Derrick said with a snide air, "Speaking of courts, I heard Judge Symmons really laid into you." He tried to sound sympathetic. "The old grizzly bear can be—well, a real bear. To a young lawyer. Like you."

"And Marcia Herring's no picnic either," Seth chimed in with a snicker.

"All that matters is our client is pleased."

Seth's smirk vanished. "How could our client be pleased?"

"Who doesn't love saving money?"

Derrick looked concerned, his earlier good humor evaporating at the mention of our client. "What the hell are you talking about?"

"I telephoned Rest Easy General Counsel in Dallas to tell him our motion had been denied."

"Wait—no one told you to do that." Derrick's face flushed with a mixture of anger and anxiety.

"No one told me not to." I dropped the tennis magazine. No need now for any props or diversions. Seth had retreated behind his desk.

Derrick shook his finger in my face. "Johns, only lead counsel have contact with the client. You know that."

"Yes; but I thought I should take responsibility for losing the hearing. After all, you trusted me to argue a motion that I'm sure you would have won." I hoped that bit of sarcasm wasn't too subtle for a bonehead like Derrick Bishoff. "I took the heat for you."

"I could have you fired for this." We both knew by now Derrick's bluff held little weight, which made this bit of theater all the more laughable. It was the third time I'd been threatened with being fired, and despite my earlier anxiety I didn't take the thought as seriously anymore. Not from a junior partner like Derrick, anyway.

"Well, are you going to tell us what Dallas had to say?"

And now time for the coup de grace. "Sure. General Counsel told me they had set aside five million in reserves to settle the case, so when I told him I had settled it for nine hundred-thousand… they were delighted."

Derrick looked at me gape-mouthed, as though I had slapped him openhanded. I suddenly saw him for what he was

—with his ill-fitting suit and scuffed shoes, he slumped in the corner like an experienced loser.

Seth seethed, his words a harsh whisper: "You had no authority to settle anything. They may have taught you to make a move like that wherever the hell you went to law school, but here, we don't operate that way."

"I suppose it's worth noting that Dallas is calling Mr. Cantor this afternoon to tell him they want me that from now on, I'm to handle *all* their litigation." I paused at the door, trying not to sound too smug. "But I'll suggest to him instead that he tell them how much you both disapprove of the settlement."

Neither of my colleagues seemed in a mood to laugh now.

"Now hold on a minute," Derrick said. "I shouldn't have said all that, but you had no right to settle that damn case."

"Listen, pal, I was trying to get our wheels out of the ditch," I said. "Or to use another metaphor, trying to turn chicken shit into chicken salad."

Derrick looked to his friend for help, but Seth had moved on; now he busied himself testing the tension of the gut on what appeared to be a new racket. He shrugged. "You really could have created liability for the firm, if it hadn't gone down like it did."

"I know what you mean. But it didn't happen, thank the good lord above."

I hoped to sound contrite, but hit such a false note that both of them looked insulted. I tried again. This time I was right on key. "I'll certainly keep that in mind in the future. You both can depend on me."

But as I walked away, I realized I hadn't improved the delivery, only dialed up the sarcasm. They deserved it, but I tried not to entertain the thought of them somehow pulling retribution on me.

One thing could kill my deal with Mr. Cantor, that much I knew: him finding out about his junior associate bedding down with the girlfriend. Manon and I would need to be extremely careful, now. I almost regretted inviting her over tonight. Almost.

On Friday afternoon, my phone rang—Arthur Peck had finally telephoned to let me know the FAA had approved the merger. But before I could say anything, he asked straight-out when he could expect to receive his considerable recompense.

Caught off-guard, I mumbled I'd have to discuss it with Mr. Cantor.

"You putting me off, Paul?"

"Nothing of the sort."

A threat: "It's not too late to monkey-wrench this situation from my end, you know."

In the hopes he'd get the hint, I pledged to see him soon 'off-campus' to discuss further and hung up.

After all my months of late nights at the office, other sharks were circling for their dinner. My part would almost certainly be effusive praise for my work on the merger, followed by a slender severance package. And in case I made a fuss over the unfairness of my being let go, an oblique, or not-so oblique, reference to the lies of my past would give them cover. It was time to find a lifejacket for the storm sure to come.

⚓

AFTER I FRESHENED UP IN THE RESTROOM, I STROLLED TALL, straight and self-assured into Mr. Cantor's office. As usual, he blathered on the telephone in his low-pitched, warm voice. When he noticed me standing in the doorway, he winked with good cheer and motioned me toward the couch.

We had been waiting for this day for quite some time. Months had passed since I first sat on this couch. Only now, my perception was different: the large corner office with its window looking over the city, the leather couch, the antique desk, the oil paintings and photos hung where you couldn't miss them... I now saw them all as nothing but props in the ongoing K Street Lawyer theatrical production.

The other difference? I had delivered TateAir. But now I knew too much to keep around. Surely that would be my fate.

Or... could there be another, gorgeous, long-legged reason he'd be getting rid of me?

"Brad, my brightest young associate has arrived, so let's finish this conversation at the club tomorrow, where I can peer into those demonic eyes of yours in person." Mr. Cantor howled at his colleague's response, hung up and turned to me still amused.

He noticed my pensive countenance. "Why so glum? I hope nothing's wrong with our project, not this close. I hoped to be enjoying a victory lap of a different sort out on the links tomorrow." Cantor's favorite charity golf tournament happened the next day. I was to be his caddy.

"Actually, Arthur called just now, and the news couldn't be better. The FAA will announce the merger approval, well, as soon as the markets close, which is in..." I checked my watch. "About seven minutes. So—we did it, sir."

I watched and waited in silence for his response, but Cantor's expression didn't flicker, except that the smile had cooled, and his eyes, they had gone fully dead and cold like an experienced hunter who'd dropped his game without breaking a sweat. The man had waited almost a year for this, a huge payday for all involved, and here he sat immobile, as though made of granite; as if I had told him news as ordinary as the expectation of sunrise in the morning.

At last he spoke: "Well done."

I let out my breath. "Yes. Thank you, sir."

Mr. Cantor swiveled his chair around and looked out the window. "Here's the truth, son. Forget your connection to our favorite brother-in-law—I don't know anyone in the firm who could have done this better than you. Not even half as well. True story."

Not typically a man to give out praise, my boss, so I thought this must be his way of expressing his excitement over the deal being at last done. I thanked him again, waited for the chance to discuss Arthur's fee.

"Now that our private backslapping's over, let's commemorate this little victory, shall we?"

Without waiting for me to answer, Cantor picked up his telephone and ordered Manon to assemble all of the firm's lawyers in the main conference room at six sharp, with light hors-d'oeuvres and champagne for everyone. I heard Manon answer, "Sir-yes-sir," in her mock military manner.

Hearing her voice filled me with dread. I wondered how much he suspected. As Manon held no true feelings for the man, I considered our indiscretion stacked on top of his own as a minor trespass. In a way it was a compliment to him, if you thought about it—I agreed in his taste in women. I had demonstrated so with a vigorous enthusiasm on quite a few occasions, in fact.

I was embarrassed to even bring up the subject of the bribe because of how obvious it made Arthur's unseemly impatience. Then it occurred to me that Mr. Cantor might suspect I had inflated the bonus so I could skim off a slice for myself. Then again, he might think I was a fool for not taking a bit of the bonus for myself. More than once, after all, he had said you can never completely trust a completely honest man.

Cantor, as if reading my mind: "Want to wager our Mr. Peck probably has his abacus out right now?"

"Arthur happened to mention 'my' bonus."

We both laughed at my brother-in-law's eagerness, as much for its lack of style as its blatant and unseemly corruption. "I'll have accounting cut you a check tomorrow morning. Bring this boat into port, Paul." With a curt nod from my boss, I was now free to go.

Clean and neat. If there was ever any trouble over this, all anyone would find is evidence my firm paid me a bonus I had used to bribe a government official. Mr. Cantor's fingerprints wouldn't show up anywhere. He'd feign as much surprise as anyone that his brightest young associate could have been capable of such behavior. I'd be expected to fall on my sword alone.

"My tee-time is at eight sharp," Cantor called after me. "Let's not be late." I stopped myself from barking *sir-yes-sir*.

As I passed through the reception area, I told Manon anyone looking could find me outside enjoying a smoke. Her little shrug seemed to say, *Who would come looking for you now that TateAir is squared away?*

I walked the three blocks to Farragut Square. How many bag lunches had I eaten in this park, winter and summer? A sense of staleness came over me, of routine.

My cell phone rang, startling me out of a reverie.

I answered and found myself surprised to discover Mr. Tate himself on the line. I had no idea he had my number.

With a furtive quality to his voice, he asked if I was free to talk. I said I was. "I'm standing in the park."

Mr. Tate sounded distant and odd for a man about to sell his shares in the company for nearly a billion dollars. "How about that news today, eh?"

"The firm is having a party to celebrate."

"Eric invited me."

"I'd hope so."

He laughed. "I'm paying for the champagne, so I might as well drink some. Yes?"

I didn't really know what I was supposed to say, or not say, to the firm's biggest client. "I'm sure you're delighted, sir. Enjoy the moment."

"Yes," but again, the odd tone. "Paul, when I see you later, I'd like to pretend we didn't talk today. As far as what's on my mind, let's have you come by my office early next week —Monday."

I agreed that I would. "I'll see you at the party."

Mr. Tate hung up without answering. My skin began to crawl with uncertainty. Whatever was at stake for this man seemed about more than the considerable amount of money about to come his way.

Skittish, I had begun walking back to the office when I remembered I still hadn't smoked a cigarette. No time for that now, as I was almost back to 1825 K Street. Perhaps the nicotine would have only made me more nervous, not less.

As the afternoon wore on, I received well-wishers in my office and could hear noise from the conference room as the caterers arrived and set up. Before long, lawyers, paralegals and clerks alike had begun lining up for champagne.

I thought about remaining in my office—hiding, let's call it —but Manon spotted me lurking in the doorway and waved me over.

I made my way through the bustling, cheerful crowd to her. She had already changed into a black cocktail dress. I supposed she kept a few of those at the office, because a girl like Manon never knew when a party was going to break out.

"Where's your drink?" She raised an eyebrow and held out her glass. "Want a sip of mine?"

"I don't think Mr. Cantor would like that." I looked around for Enid Pearl, who'd been noticeably absent today.

Meanwhile, Manon had gotten rather good at reading my mind. "Your girlfriend isn't here yet."

"I thought you were my girlfriend."

We both laughed at the absurdity.

"You could do worse."

"I have."

A server passed by. I snatched a glass of champagne from his tray. Standing closer to Manon than was wise, I couldn't help a glance down her plunging neckline. "You look wonderful, as always."

"Settle down. You've seen those before." She stepped closer to me. "Want to see them again tonight after this is over?"

"I'm quite sure Mr. Cantor will be taking you home, or somewhere, later tonight." I took a sip and smiled, but I felt nothing inside. Our relationship was what it was. What I liked most about Manon, I suspect, was her willingness to see things as they really were.

"Wait—are you *jealous*?" She laughed again and finished her drink. A waiter keeping an eye on us presented another.

"What would you say if I were?'

"I'd say that would ruin everything for both of us." She gave my free hand a hasty, furtive squeeze. "I like you best among all the boys I know. Can't you tell?"

"What if I said I was falling in love with you?" I was only half-joking.

"You're too insecure to possess a woman like me." Now her assessment of reality had turned blunt and perceptive. "Now someone like Ms. Pearl, she'd be good for you... but she's too prissy."

I asked her to explain the context here of 'prissy.'

"For a boy who likes to play like you do? Definitely too prissy."

I couldn't help but smile at this nod to our uncomplicated, adventurous sex life. Manon, a carnal sorceress of some skill, seemed to beam me with a bolt of warmth that flooded into my lower body. I grunted and shifted in the Italian leather shoes I'd bought to supplement my little courtroom costumes, like the Princeton get-up which had gotten me nowhere with Judge Symmons. The shoes looked fabulous, but were rubbing blisters on my little toes. I suddenly understood why women complained about the high heels. Style over comfort sometimes felt like a poor trade-off.

⛵

ALL THE WARMTH IN MY GUT DISSIPATED AS I SPOTTED MS. Pearl and Seth coming into the conference room. He held his hand on the small of her back, was guiding her through the crowd.

I thought the gesture unseemly; whatever happened outside of the office, here they were colleagues. She should have batted his chubby paw away from her body the way he smacked his fuzzy yellow-green tennis balls across the net.

As they drew near, Enid held out her hand. "Congratulations, Paul."

The noise and hubbub from a crowd growing tipsy had become so loud I leaned forward so she could hear me. "For what?"

She stayed close so we could talk. "Getting that FAA business done."

"We had a bit of luck on that."

"You and your illustrious 'luck'."

I chuckled, but her eyes held something more like irritation. For all her knowledge and success in M&A, here I had come along and just 'made it all happen' by dint of a family relationship. For some, learning the hard lesson that the only way to win is through cheating takes time to settle in the gut. Enid, for her part, looked as though she'd swallowed a rock.

"I'm no different than you in the equation," I said. "I'm an employee of the firm. And on this case, I was asked to carry water. What would you have done?"

"Nice work. Once again." Seth crushed my hand in a powerful grip, a lion's paw. I could feel the calluses on his palm. Holds his tennis racket too tight, I thought. Hard to put topspin on the ball that way.

"That's very generous of you."

"Like you said, we're part of an equation here. And at the end of the day, it has to add up."

He gave my hand an unpleasant extra squeeze before he let it go. I wondered again what Enid saw in him.

I glanced back for Manon, but she had slipped away. I had scared her off with that love talk. Maybe I wasn't as adept at manipulating reality as Seth and Enid seemed to think. Once again alone, I wandered over to refill my glass, which I downed and refilled yet again. *Hey—it's a party, right?*

⛵

Mr. Cantor came into the room. At his appearance, sudden, silence slowly took hold; heads and bodies turned.

He had changed his suit from earlier. He also looked like he might have gone to the spa for a haircut, facial, and manicure. He glowed like a pink baby who had just been scrubbed in a hot bath.

Once the big boss got the attention of the room, he held out his hands and began:

"I just want to say a few words, and then you can all go back to your champagne. As you have doubtless heard by now, the FAA today approved the TateAir merger. Needless to say, this has been a long and difficult process, more so than we anticipated… but you all contributed to its successful conclusion." Mr. Cantor raised his glass and we all toasted ourselves. "And so I salute you."

A small cheer arose from the lawyers of Cantor and Miller.

"Now, having spread the love wide, let's get more specific." He searched the crowd until finding me. "I'd be remiss if I didn't single out one of our junior associates, Paul Johns, for special mention tonight. Besides his exemplary efforts on several other important cases, his tireless work with the FAA was instrumental in getting this project approved for our client. Now, we may begin calling Paul one of our most *accomplished* junior associates."

"Go get 'em, buddy," Seth called out. "Tremendous job." At his behest came another small wave of applause. I felt my face flushing red and raised my glass in thanks.

Here Mr. Cantor looked around for our client, but he had yet to arrive. "And I'm sure Jack Tate would join me in saying you did a brilliant job on this." Mr. Cantor raised his glass again and we all joined him in another toast. "Now, let's all keep up the good work until the last signature, the last document is filed, and the final checks are cut."

That prompted a hearty cheer. Nothing like a little grease for the wheels to bring out the more heroic aspects of the bossman's benevolence.

Enid had returned to my side. "Eric is so impressed with you."

"So much he's even letting me caddy for him tomorrow at the golf tournament."

"You can't be that naive. He isn't trying to demean you."

"Do tell."

"He's asked you to do that so you can meet important people."

"I wish it were that simple."

She held my arm with her free hand as though she wanted to shake some sense into me. "Is it true that you have a chip on both shoulders?"

She waited to see what I thought of that. I had nothing to say.

"You can relax. The people here admire what you've accomplished. You're on your way—somewhere."

Of course she had no idea I was nothing but a glorified bagman for the firm about to pay Arthur his bribe. On my way, all right. To be Eric Cantor's fall guy, should the need arise.

I suddenly felt the urge to flip the script on this conversation. I knew this wasn't the moment for me to make this move, but there would never be a good time. And besides, I liked daring her to step off the plank with me. "Does 'somewhere' include you?"

"You have the most irritating mix of arrogance and insecurity." She stared me full in the face. "Like almost no one I've ever known."

"But that doesn't answer my question."

She smiled and held up her empty glass. I saw the guard in her eyes drop; my intuition had been correct. "Good things to those who wait."

"Let me get you another drink."

"Thank you," she said.

And just like that, a relationship with Enid seemed possible. Now I did feel like being congratulated.

I GRABBED HOLD OF A SERVER BEARING A TRAY FULL OF champagne flutes and took two, but when I returned to where we had been standing, Enid, fresh drink in hand, appeared locked in conversation with one of our fellow M&A drones. She glanced my way, shrugged her shoulders. I smiled to let her know I understood and went off to find something to eat.

Starving, I loaded cocktail shrimp onto my plate. Even before I heard the voice, I felt someone behind me.

"I see you're helping yourself." Mr. Tate had arrived.

I presented him with my plate. "Try some. You paid for them."

"I don't care for shellfish. I'll have a glass of bubbly, though. Pretty damn good champagne."

Already a bit drunk, I could but agree. I'm sure he could smell the baby-vomit reek of the champagne on my breath from several feet away.

After taking a sip: "You've got to give it to that Eric."

"How so?"

"His taste in the finer things, like this champagne." Seeing

Manon across the room, he nudged me in the ribs and added, "In everything. Isn't that right, Mr. Johns?"

I ignored the reference to Manon. "He's one hell of a good lawyer. I've learned much from him."

"Not too much, I hope."

"How much knowledge is too much?"

"Oh, my boy—may you never find out the answer." Mr. Tate drained his glass. His words held no hint of cocktail party banter. "Let's go find our Mr. Cantor, our mastermind, and get a real drink into our successful stomachs."

I followed Mr. Tate through the crowd until we came upon my boss, basking in a semicircle of subordinates blowing smoke.

"Eric," Mr. Tate said, "tell me you've got something stronger than this French fizzy water, fine as it may be."

Mr. Cantor cupped his ear and leaned toward us. "Excuse me?"

"I said, let's go to your office where we can talk." Mr. Tate spoke loud enough so the petitioners near us heard him. They all dispersed like smoke in a stiff breeze. Everyone here knew their place. Everyone but me. The hubbub of the party faded behind us as Mr. Cantor led our group of co-conspirators down the hall.

WHEN WE ARRIVED AT MANON'S DESK OUTSIDE HIS DOOR, however, Mr. Cantor hesitated. "I think I'd better speak to Jack alone."

"Of course."

"No, Eric. I want him in on this."

The two powerful men suffered a brief a standoff, two

bosses each used to getting his way. I yielded by acting as though it were no big deal either way.

Cantor shrugged. "At your discretion, Jack."

Jack Tate's response held an air of grim portent. His words filled me with dread: "It had better all be at my discretion."

Inside the office, I could feel tension between them. "Perhaps Mr. Cantor is right, and I should leave."

"Nonsense, Paul. Find yourself a seat." Mr. Tate waved me over, patted the couch next to him. To Cantor he said, "Now. Any brandy here on K Street worth drinking?"

With a smug half-smile, Mr. Cantor produced a bottle of Remy Martin XO from the cabinet behind him. He poured three generous measures into crystal tumblers which felt as though they each weighed a pound. "You should know the answer to that. You of all people."

Mr. Tate chortled, but without mirth. "How much would you say we've 'contributed' to this firm in the last eighteen months?"

Mr. Cantor's flinty eyes flitted toward mine for the answer. I cleared my throat, felt above my station talking such numbers with two of the richest men I knew. "We're just shy of twenty-five million in billings, I believe."

Tate whistled. "We're close to talking about real money here, aren't we?" He raised his glass to Mr. Cantor. "But a damn fine drink indeed. That much is certain."

"We earned those billings. Rather successful work, I might add."

"Successful for whom, Eric?"

"Well, now. You'll have to be a little less coy if you want an actual answer to such a question." I admired the way Mr. Cantor appeared unconcerned about Jack Tate and whatever it was he wanted to say. He took out a cigarette and tapped it against his desktop. "Is our success not mutual?"

"I know it's been successful for you, but how about for me?"

"Does success in your world not resemble seven-hundred and fifty million dollars? What more could you want? Besides, you've already signed the contract." With that simple move Mr. Cantor tried to make Jack Tate appear greedy, but no one in the room considered that a vice. "The time for such philosophical rumination may be upon us, but doing so changes nothing about our current reality."

"What if the news today isn't the FAA approval?"

A chill descended in the room. Mr. Cantor set down his cognac with a hard *clunk*. "Enough games."

"All right. Long story short, I've got another buyer, one who thinks the company's undervalued by at least seventy million. Maybe more." Mr. Tate sat back and finished his drink. "I'd be a fool to leave that kind of money on the table. Why, we're inching ever closer to a billion, aren't we?"

"We not only had an independent valuation done, but you signed the contract after the board approved it. Westbrooke," the buyer, "will sue you, as will your own board."

"They can try."

My boss's face had turned the color of a brick, like the one I now felt down in my gut. "When I put together those investors, Jack, you were only too happy to sell to them." Mr. Cantor looked at his watch, a trick I'd seen him use many times to rush a conversation he didn't want to continue. "I'm happy to pour you another splash of this cognac, but, well, you can't back out now on the deal. It would be—suicide."

"Here's what's odd. Their offer you negotiated came in right at the minimum we said we'd accept. And I'm in this business to earn a dollar and a cent, as we used to say in the old neighborhood. Not settle for minimums."

Mr. Cantor seemed to have a counter for every punch Jack

threw at him. "I found that investment group, they made you an offer and you accepted it. No one forced your hand."

"That's right. Relying on your firm's advice, I took the offer because you assured me it was a fair price for the company. Which I now know is total crap, Eric."

Despite Jack Tate's growing anger and Mr. Cantor's own red face, my boss kept his tone unchanged. The stakes might as well have been a weak golf score. "Jack, Jack, Jack—if you had second thoughts about selling the company, you should have come to me sooner. This is just a damn shame."

"I don't have second thoughts about selling—I'm having second thoughts about the price the buyer's offering." Mr. Tate got up and poured himself another drink. Mr. Cantor had barely touched his. I nursed mine along because the tension in the air, along with all the champagne, made me want to puke.

Mr. Cantor, a former litigator, undermined each of Mr. Tate's objections. "You could have found another buyer."

"There *were* no other offers... according to Cantor and Miller."

"That's precisely my point. That you have one now is immaterial to the process already in motion. I'm sorry." Mr. Cantor eased back in his chair, a signal that this unpleasantness was at an end. He shot the cuffs of his white shirt, checked a pair of diamond cufflinks, glanced at his Rolex. "Now, if you don't mind, I promised Elizabeth I'd be home by nine."

"I'm sure she won't mind if you're a few minutes late. Not with a deal of this size on the line."

Meanwhile, I squirmed on the couch, breathing their smoke and wanting one of my own. *Mr. Cantor may have met his match in Jack Tate. I could be here all night...*

Mr. Cantor became expansive and collegial, always his last

card. If things weren't going well, he would simply over-whelm his opponent with the illusion of agreement. "Leaving all that money on the table is awful, but once the sale goes through you'll have still have more than you can ever spend." This was classic Cantor, swing the narrative around until catching a breeze, one born of a shared past, blowing off the beam; smooth sailing lay just ahead. He outlined any number of ways the firm could continue to help, as well. "'Not bad for a poor kid from Baltimore'—isn't that what you always say about yourself?"

"Baltimore was another lifetime ago, Eric. You and Eliza-beth were living off Massachusetts Avenue—"

"—when you and Tricia were still so young you had to live with her parents."

I hadn't realized how far they went back. I felt more like an interloper than ever.

The men shared a silent moment of nostalgia. The mention of his wife, long dead as I had learned, seemed to have drained the anger out of Jack Tate. "Money certainly won't bring her back."

In the awkward silence he finished his drink, held out his glass for another. Cantor refreshed mine as well.

"No. More money isn't going to make us any happier now, Jack. And neither will this expensive liquor."

"You're right." His body heavy with age, weight and alco-hol, Mr. Tate lifted himself off the couch with some difficulty. He had begun to slur his words. "But I still wish this thing had turned out differently."

"It turned out pretty well." Mr. Cantor stood and held his old friend by the elbow, caught my eye and gave a furtive wink. "I think you'll wake up tomorrow and feel the same. Don't you, Paul?"

"No question, sir. I know I will."

A brief negotiation ensued over getting Mr. Tate home. It seemed he had driven himself over in his six-figure Bently.

"That won't do at all, my old friend. Paul?"

"I'll find a sober law clerk to drive him home."

"Good man."

I squeezed past Mr. Tate, who patted me on the shoulder. When I looked back, I saw the two of them embracing, followed by a handshake in which their fingers seemed to creep into each other's cuffs.

I wondered what I had just been through—an elaborate ritual between rich men, a theatrical play for someone not in the club? Tossing around seventy million here, a billion there? I had no idea. But I did feel fairly full of myself, sitting between those powerful players. I simply didn't know yet if I was truly in their club, or still a mere errand boy.

I found a law clerk, Andrew or Anton, something with an A, still at work on the twelfth floor. I instructed the harried young man to meet me in the parking garage.

"But I've got to finish editing these briefs."

"I don't care if it's your grandmother's funeral. Downstairs," I ordered.

Once Jack Tate and I were in the lobby, I had security bring the car around. As I held open the passenger door he shook my hand and said in a confidential tone, "Much more to discuss, my boy. I'll be in touch."

As the valet handed me the keys I slipped him a substantial tip, the way Jack Tate would have. I helped the airline mogul into the back seat and gave the address to his house to the law clerk, who glowered with ill-will—he likely felt the same way about this chore as I did about being asked to caddy.

I watched with interest as the dark blue Bently disappeared down Connecticut Avenue. What would all my service on this deal truly mean for me? I couldn't shake the feeling I wasn't yet home free.

⛵

By the time I got back to the party, the only revelers still drinking were the single lawyers, along with a few married ones who wished they weren't.

I spotted Enid standing with a group of women who worked with her in the tax section. As I made my way towards her, Seth sidled up to report under his breath that Manon had departed with Mr. Cantor.

I feigned surprise at their lack of discretion, but as I pushed past him, I felt a hand on my shoulder.

"No time for old tennis partners?" Seth, a glass of champagne in each hand, swayed on his feet. I had never seen him this drunk.

"I was going to see a friend…?"

"It wouldn't be that friend with the ample assets over there, would it?" Seth raised one of his glasses in the direction of Enid.

I tried not to sound annoyed, but I had no time to waste on more games. Not tonight. "Settle down. I think you've had too much."

"Don't be coy, Johns." Seth drained a glass and reached to put it on the conference room table but instead dropped it on the carpet, which he didn't seem to notice. "It looks as though our junior associate has made something of himself after all."

I glanced past him to see if Enid was still there. "Sorry if I've offended you by being successful at my work."

Enid caught my eye and winked. That absurd little gesture made my head swim more than all the alcohol. I became determined to wriggle free of Seth.

"You know what I've observed about you?" Seth's voice had grown loud, and the people around us were starting to take notice. "The stupid thing about you, Paul Johns," my name like an epithet, "is that *you* think you're *better* than everyone else. Well, you ain't, pal. And I'm gonna prove it to everyone."

With that Seth lurched away and began addressing the room, flinging his arms in a wide circle. "And you know why that's funny?" He waited for someone to answer, but we were all too embarrassed for him. "It's because you're some little nobody from nowhere, who's managed to fool a lot of really smart people…" The room had fallen silent. "You're nothing but an actor."

"So I guess all this success makes me a pretty good one, huh? Is there an Academy Award in my future?"

"See? This is what I'm talking about."

I shrugged at a few folks, mimed a gesture—the raising of the wrist. Seth, who glimpsed my pantomime, laughed so hard he began to cough. Several people tried to quiet him, but he was having none of it.

"I don't know how you did it, buddy, but you fooled everybody."

I put a hand on Seth's elbow to steady him a bit, but he pulled away from me with such force that he knocked a tray of drinks out of a waiter's hand. Mortified by what he had done, Seth stumbled out of the room, with Enid scurrying close behind.

With Seth safely gone, I turned to the now quiet group of people behind me. I smiled to let them know I could be a good sport about these things. After all, he was drunk, and who hasn't made an ass out of himself when he's had too much? "He's mad over that furniture store business. That's all."

I could see by their faces that they, too, had been

wondering from where I had come to rise to such a position, but unlike Seth, they had been too timid or polite to say it.

Derek Bishoff, a glad-hander of the first order, said, "Seth's the one who stepped in it on Sherwood Furniture. Don't pay any attention to him."

"Done."

I looked around for a waiter but they were all huddled against the far wall, as if they had been blown there by the force of Seth's outburst. I raised my empty glass to signal I'd like another. The bravest of the servers ventured over to fill it.

"To TateAir," someone called out in triumph.

I looked around to see who had said that. It was Enid, who had returned without Seth.

Everyone responded to her toast by raising their glasses. "*To TateAir.*"

The Seth business appeared to be forgotten, at least for now.

How adroitly Ms. Pearl had come to my rescue. I nodded to let her know I appreciated what she had done. I guessed we were even, now, for my taking the blame for her mistake on the Tate Family loans.

A FEW MINUTES LATER, SHE CAME OVER TO SAY GOODNIGHT. Enid had already put on her coat, so I knew I'd have little time.

"Seth made a fool of himself tonight. I'm sorry."

"He only said what everyone's been thinking."

"You're wrong about that. He's just envious because you're a better lawyer than he'll ever be."

"I doubt he believes that."

"You've worked very hard, and it's paid off."

"At times work seems all I do."

"Seth says that about me, too."

"Where is he?"

"I put him in a cab to go home. Which is where I should go."

"I'm sorry you have to leave."

"So am I." She turned up the collar of her coat, took off her glasses and put them in her purse. Until that moment I hadn't realized how blue her eyes were.

She held out her hand and told me goodnight. I continued holding it long enough for her to tilt her head to one side, as though to ask what on earth I thought I was doing.

"Why don't we go over to the bar at the Mayflower, have a nightcap?"

Enid's little frown seemed to say no, but then: "I'd enjoy that."

I followed her out of the room and into the elevator. Even though we were the only passengers, after the door closed we remained standing close to each other, as close as we'd ever been. Neither of us moved until the door opened at the lobby.

Out on the sidewalk, the November wind felt sharp against my face. I began shivering like mad, but wasn't about to lose the lovely momentum because of the weather.

"Don't you want to go back for your overcoat?"

"Despite being a lawyer, I'm warm-blooded."

She barked a cynical laugh.

We set off to walk the four blocks to the hotel, which we did without speaking, only an occasional glance, our elbows bumping, and once when I touched her on the arm to stop her from crossing against a light. I longed for more contact, as much as possible.

WHEN WE ARRIVED AT THE HOTEL BAR I HELD THE DOOR FOR her, followed her inside with my hand on the small of her back. She didn't stiffen when she felt my hand. In fact, she seemed almost to sink back against my touch.

The heat inside the lobby felt wonderful. Feeling began to return to my fingers, which I rubbed together.

She took my hands in hers. "See—they're freezing. I knew we should have gotten your coat."

For the second time this evening I felt myself overwhelmed by her presence, her smell, those eyes. One thing the cold had done was sober me up. "I'm fine. Let's get that drink."

In the bar we squeezed ourselves through a crowd to order a brandy for myself and for her a Black Russian, which I had once heard Seth mention was her favorite cocktail. When our drinks arrived, I steered her towards a booth just vacated by a party.

As we waited for the busboy to finish removing the glasses she said, "Some of that business with Seth, well, it's my fault."

I sipped my brandy and smiled as it chased the cold out of my hands and feet. "He had too much too fast. That's all."

"He thinks you're responsible for the problems we're having."

"Problems? At work?"

"No—at home."

I didn't feel like pretending. "I guessed as much."

She reached across the table and touched my hand. "Do you remember the last time we were here?" She meant the morning with Jack Tate and his daughter. "When you took the blame for my mistake?"

I tried to sound modest. "That's what a good law clerk does."

"Seth said then you were a show-off." Enid laughed. "He was already jealous of you."

"Jealous?"

"Of you having such nerve." Her tone turned more demure. "And he seemed to know before I did that—I harbored feelings for you."

My hand found hers. She squeezed back. "I'm flattered."

Enid recovered her hand and looked at her watch. "But it's one o'clock already, and you have to caddy for Eric in only a few hours. I'm sorry I kept you out so late." She made to leave, standing to put on her coat. "I'll see you at work."

I stood as well, but it was to lean in and kiss her, a smooth motion which occurred without thinking; it just happened. As did the rest of the night together in a room upstairs which cost me more than I could afford, at least until I got my bonus, or whatever was left after Arthur took his cut. None of that remained on my mind, however, not once the card-key slipped into the lock, and the door to Enid Pearl at last opened.

AS INSTRUCTED, THE FRONT DESK TELEPHONE CALL JARRED ME awake at a brutal six o'clock. I lifted Enid's arm, rolled over to answer it. After I hung up, she was still asleep, a light snore.

We hadn't been to sleep all that long. While much more reserved in bed than Manon, it hadn't taken long for us to get into a particularly satisfying groove. The naughtiness of our indiscretion seemed to fuel her passion.

I went into the bathroom for a cigarette to clear out the residue of too much brown liquor from my hungover throat. With the first taste of smoke my gorge rose, but I didn't vomit. Nevertheless, Mr. Cantor would have to find another caddy today.

I thought I would ask Enid if she wanted to go to the zoo

after breakfast, or anything else fun she'd enjoy. I wondered if I was making too much of last night. There was still the matter of her fiancé, not to mention the fact that I was sleeping with Manon, but none of that seemed important.

"You better get a move on if you're going to caddy for Eric." Enid yawned and brushed her hair away from her face. "Yuck—you've been smoking. I can smell it."

"My electric razor caught on fire." I laughed, and she did as well. "What would you like for breakfast?"

"Eggs and hash brown potatoes and toast." She sat up in bed. "And I want tea with cream and honey."

"You're hungry." I ran my hand over my chin. "I better shave for real if we're going downstairs to eat."

"Let's eat in the room. I'm not ready to see other people just yet." She pulled the blankets up to her chin. "I want us to be alone for a little longer."

As I reached for the telephone to call room service I noticed our clothes on the floor beside the bed. "I think I'll tidy up a bit before the waiter arrives."

"I'm surprised you're still here."

"What do you mean?"

"Tell me you didn't wake up and think about leaving."

"Oddly enough, I didn't. But that was only because you had me in a headlock for most of the night."

"I wanted to make sure you didn't go anywhere."

She got out of bed, a lovely sight, and went into the bathroom. As I rang room service, I heard the shower running.

As with many of my expenses, I charged everything on the firm credit card. No one would be going over expense accounts too carefully. Not now.

When Enid opened the door steam rolled into the room and she called out, "Seth, will you get my purse for me?"

I handed the purse to her through the partially opened door. "Don't you mean 'Paul'?"

"Yes—I'm so sorry. Let me make it up to you…"

Once she pulled me inside the steam to join her, I also decided I wasn't quite ready to leave this hotel room.

10

My boss, whose forgiveness over the caddying no-show came immediately: "I made other arrangements because I knew you'd be hungover as a sailor, son," he said with a fatherly chuckle. We discussed the Tate situation, our private meeting in his office. I told him about Jack wanting me to come and meet with him at his office.

None of that bothered him; in fact, he felt it a good opportunity for information gathering.

He did make an important suggestion regarding my meeting with Jack Tate: that I take the Cantor family Jaguar, which had been washed and detailed only yesterday. It wouldn't do, he said, for me to pull up to the TateAir building in my nine year-old Fiat, what with rust showing through its chipped paint.

"You are my emissary, Paul. You must fly the colors, so to speak."

"Understood, sir." Better than he knew.

Before I pulled out of the garage, I luxuriated in the fine leather and workmanship of the automobile. I would have my own one day soon. And a sailboat, too.

Being meticulous, I checked the glove box for the registration and insurance documents. In doing so I was surprised to see the car belonged to Elizabeth Cantor. Maybe she did have all the money, as Enid had suggested.

On the drive over I considered why Mr. Tate might want to see me. I'd met with him before, but never alone. The merger was ready to close, I'd done my part with the FAA, and I could think of no reason for it. That is, not unless a further problem were about to appear. Despite the contentious meeting in the office, Mr. Cantor seemed unconcerned.

I hoped no one had noticed that I had put my night with Enid at the Mayflower Hotel on the TateAir account. I'd heard that, rich as Eric Cantor was, he fired people for cheating on their expense accounts. Well, I *was* with Ms. Pearl and she *was* lead counsel on the merger, so it could be reasonably expensed. I mean it wasn't as though I'd taken Manon to the hotel for a tumble. Now those tracks I would have had the sense to cover myself.

Furthermore, I doubted I'd be taking Enid there again, or anywhere. After we left the Mayflower that morning, it felt clear to me that she saw me as a one-time thrill ride; that we were to go back to business as usual. Why I thought she might offer more, I had no idea.

I PARKED THE JAGUAR IN FRONT OF THE BUILDING AND HANDED the keys to the attendant at the reception desk. When I told her my name, she said Mr. Tate, who was expecting me, could be found in the tenth floor conference room.

"Right on time," he said tapping a basic Timex on his wrist, not a bejeweled ornament like most of the rich men I knew. "Let's chat in here, shall we?"

I followed him into the main conference room and took off my overcoat. Before I could settle into my seat, an assistant appeared and asked Mr. Tate if there were anyone else she should call into the meeting.

"No. And if we're disturbed, that person will be fired."

She looked as surprised by his tone as I did. She stammered yes-sir and made a hasty retreat.

This could be bad. I knew he was frustrated with the firm because of the size of our bills, as well that business of the millions he 'lost' by not taking the other offer. But, that little scene had held a strange quality, more like theater than anything real. As for the billings, alas, he would also have to take that up with Mr. Cantor.

"Coffee? Or, is it tea with you?"

I declined a beverage. I ran through everything I thought he might want to address with me, but I couldn't come up with anything concrete. I opened my briefcase and took out a legal pad.

"You can put that away. And you'll understand why in a minute."

Now more confused than ever, I did as he asked. "Do you mind if I smoke?"

"Your know the city's banned all indoor smoking. I own the damn building, and even I can't smoke in it."

We both laughed and I put my cigarettes to one side. "How can I help you, sir?"

"I've got a very peculiar little problem, and I think you're just the man to solve it."

"Listen, sir. I apologize for the delay in getting FAA approval. We were doing our best."

"I've got the bills to prove it. And last month, you put in more hours than anyone."

"I'm the logistics man on this job. That's why I put in so many hours each month."

"I didn't ask you over here to talk about your firm's bills."

"I'm relieved to hear that." I took out a cigarette and rolled it between my fingers, hoping to absorb nicotine by osmosis. Mr. Tate could be brusque, but he and I had always gotten along. You never had to guess what he was thinking. He was the exact opposite of Mr. Cantor. "I can't help with that, anyway."

"Ever hear of The Dorfmann Fund?"

I went through my mental Rolodex, but came up empty. "I don't think so."

"Not surprising. They're a little-known group of investors in California, pension money, mostly. They're the competing buyer for TateAir. And, as you already know, they're willing to pay more than the group Eric brought in."

"I'm sure your shareholders are delighted."

"Seventy-million times more delighted, in fact. "

His angry conversation with Mr. Cantor the night of the party held actual weight. "Who wouldn't be?"

"Except for one thing."

I already knew the answer. "The contract."

"That's right."

I said he'd have to take it to Mr. Cantor. "I'm only a junior associate errand boy, Mr. Tate."

"Son," he said, shaking his head. "If I didn't think you were key to the success of this enterprise, I wouldn't have let you in on any of it." He sipped coffee from a mug with the TateAir logo. "I'm certain your little group of folks is paying my old pal Eric a hefty finder's fee for bringing the deal to them. And that's not fair to TateAir. Nor to me personally."

"Conflict of interest is a serious charge." I had to tread carefully here. It wouldn't do to side with Mr. Tate against the man I worked for, at least not yet. Virtue should struggle, at least for a bit, before being overcome by temptation. Here was my life raft floating in the rough seas between Jack Tate and Mr. Cantor. "Especially between old friends."

"It certainly is, and I don't want to get in a brawl with my own lawyer. Not in the middle of this deal." Mr. Tate drew a triangle on the polished surface of the table with his finger. "That's where you come in."

I assumed the three sides of the triangle represented Mr. Tate, Mr. Cantor and little me. My voice came out small and halfway frightened: "But sir, I don't understand."

Apparently my attempt at playing innocent had not been convincing. "I think you do. It's simple—I've got to get out of that contract so I can sell to Dorfmann." Mr. Tate wiped away the triangle with the palm of his hand. "I need the additional money the other buyer will bring me—no. I *want* it, son. I *earned* it. I'll never have another airline to sell. I know someone your age can't understand, but... this is my shot. I gotta take it," sounding like an aging boxer still dreaming of that championship belt. "I won't get another chance."

A moment had arrived—was it time to drop all pretense? My gut didn't truly know, nor did my head. "You have to know what this will do to Mr. Cantor, and the rest of the firm. What about your friendship?"

"I could ask the same of him and his behavior." His eyes went dead. "Otherwise, all I can tell you is that I play a long game, son. A damned long game."

God only knew what had gone on between them over the decades. I inwardly gasped as I grappled with the implications of moving such pieces around on a chessboard for such a long time. "And if I manage to get you out of the contract? Somehow?"

A grin split his face—he realized he had me. "Ten percent sound reasonable?"

"Ten percent...?"

Of the seventy million, I heard him say, his voice faraway as all the blood drained out of my head. "Sound fair?"

I did a quick calculation. At my present salary, such an amount represented about eighty years of income. My mouth went dry. At the thought of being handed seven million bucks all at once, as well the destruction I would have to bring on people who had put me in this position, I feeling more akin to panic than elation swept throughout my body.

ONCE I COULD BREATHE AGAIN, I TOLD HIM I FELT FLATTERED by the amount of the bribe. I wondered, though, if we could figure out a better name for the transaction. finder's fee didn't quite cover it; but, as he replied, what else could one call it?

I had to at least pretend to defend Mr. Cantor. "Our firm drafted that contract. There's no way you could break it."

"No?"

"Not unless you want the current buyers to sue the company, and you personally."

"I've thought all that through."

"You have to realize Mr. Cantor's not being so much obstinate as cautious—in your favor, sir."

Tate scoffed. "I always thought a good lawyer could find a way out of anything, if he wanted to. But our Eric doesn't seem to want that."

"Would you, if you were him?"

He ignored my appeal to his humanity. "But if you find a way to get us out of that contract, you walk away a rich, young, former associate attorney with the world as his oyster. One in no need of Eric Cantor or his firm." Mr. Tate leaned his back against the plate glass window overlooking the nation's capitol. Folded his arms. "Or his mistress, for that matter."

The panic threatened to return. Tate knew everything. "You're blackmailing me."

Now Jack Tate chortled as though I were Robin Williams doing funny voices. "Paul, do you remember the first time I met you?"

"At the Mayflower."

"And you showed up to take the heat for a mistake Enid Pearl made? I knew it couldn't have been out of chivalry. Your eyes betrayed you—I saw what was lurking there. You were a chess player, and in that moment, Enid was your queen. Right then I knew you were the person I'd go to if Eric, the dullard that he is, ever tried to double-cross me. Which is where we find ourselves now. It's tragic; but I can't let him get away with it."

"He's been an advocate of mine," I said quietly.

"Don't kid yourself. You're about as meaningful to him as a janitor." Jack Tate leaned forward. He grabbed the blue linen of my suit jacket. "You don't know what else he's already gotten away with, son."

My blood chilled. "I have no idea what to say, sir. This is all above my pay grade."

"Not for long. Say," he said, checking his watch. "It's noon. Lunchtime. Know what that means?" Mr. Tate went to mix himself a drink from the wet bar at the end of the room. "Too early for you? I bet you could use it."

He continued to read me with accuracy. "Vodka tonic?"

He opened the cabinet with its a setup of premium-label liquor. "I've got some Russian potato water that'll knock those socks off your feet."

He returned with two cocktails. My hand shook as I took mine.

"I also like what I've heard about you in the courtroom." He saluted me with his drink, a healthy three fingers of bourbon. "You're two for two in pulling fat back out of the fire."

That's who he was looking for—someone who knew his way around a courtroom? No, a lawyer willing to throw his boss under the bus for seven million dollars. Which meant he was looking for me. As Cantor and Miller had wanted someone who wouldn't mind passing along a bribe to a well-placed bureaucrat.

But: I wasn't a player scanning my eyes over the chessboard and thinking many moves ahead, with the power to actual make anything happen, not on the level these men were playing. Jack and Eric were the ones in charge of the pieces. That's all I was to these folks—a useful pawn.

"Now, Paul," he said with a smile. "Take me through the firm's response to my decision not to sell."

I pondered and sipped. "First we'll go to District Court to get an order compelling the sale—a declaratory judgment, really. The judge will examine the contract; he'll declare the buyers have a right to go forward with the purchase." I took another drink. Crystal-clear white lightning, just what I needed. "It would be nearly impossible to avoid."

"Then it looks as if you have your work cut out for you." Mr. Tate drained his glass. "Ready for another?"

I finished my drink and held the empty glass out to him. I had begun to feel better. "If the buyers do file that motion, the firm will send one of their senior litigators down to argue it, I'm sure."

"I've thought of that. I'll tell Eric I want you to argue the motion. After all, no one knows this deal better than you. And, you're on a hot streak. Mr. Hot Streak. That's you."

Mr. Tate handed me another drink, stronger than the first.

"You do have the right to select your own counsel." They

couldn't very well say 'no' to Mr. Tate. After all, he was our biggest client, as they never tired of telling me. "Still, Mr. Cantor might insist on a senior partner arguing such an important motion."

"He would if he wanted to win, but he doesn't. He wants me to lose." Mr. Tate set his glass on the polished black surface of the conference table. "Will you believe me if he agrees to let you argue our response to the seller's motion?"

The second drink made it difficult for me to think clearly. "I don't know."

"If Eric lets a junior associate argue this—even one as admittedly gifted as you, Paul—then you'll know he wants me to lose. And that's exactly why he's going to let you do it."

I had to admit Mr. Tate had a point. "It would certainly be unusual to allow a junior member of the firm to argue something like this."

"How about this: if Eric says you can argue the motion, then I have your word you'll go for the win, no matter what they tell you to do."

"You're asking me to disobey the instructions of a partner."

"I'm asking you to do what's right for your client. Isn't that what lawyers are supposed to do?"

"Of course it is." I hadn't had so much to drink that I couldn't see the storm I was sailing into now. If I didn't follow Mr. Cantor's instructions and lost, I would be fired immediately. Dead broke. Starting from scratch.

Mr. Tate held out his hand. "You know there's no reward without risk. And what a reward it will be—for both of us."

Surely Mr. Cantor wouldn't let me argue this. Jack had to be wrong. "I can't promise you anything."

"What do you have to lose? That's an Ivy League firm, Johns, and, no insult intended, but I don't think you exactly went to Harvard. You'll never make partner... and if I know that, you ought to know it."

News of my phony résumé had also reached Mr. Tate. No surprise. My options, already limited, dwindled to none.

I was still thinking it over when Mr. Tate again spoke. "Then you'll try?"

"If Mr. Cantor agrees that I argue the motion."

"He will. I've never been wrong about Eric Cantor in my life."

We shook hands. I put on my overcoat and stood up to go. I needed at least that much confirmation my boss and sailing partner was double-crossing Jack to, what? Justify my own double-crossing of Mr. Cantor?

"If I do stop the sale, how do I know you'll pay me?"

"I didn't build an entire airline by being a cheat, son. We shook hands on it, didn't we?"

"Lawyers tend to prefer signatures."

"This is a handshake deal only. You ought to know that."

I did. And that was good enough for me. It had been a long time since I'd trusted anyone, so it still left me feeling uncomfortable to put that much faith in Jack Tate, but, no turning back now. Actually, there never had been, but I was only now waking up to that fact.

BY THE TIME I GOT BACK TO THE OFFICE THE DAY WAS WINDING down. Manon had left a note, however, that I was to see Mr. Cantor the moment I returned. I laughed at the breathy urgency of her message, three underscores beneath the word *immediately*. As though he hadn't told me the same thing before I left...

I needed to collect my thoughts. I went into the bathroom

to comb my hair. As I looked at myself in the mirror, I noticed how out of shape I'd become. I had not only put on weight, but looked as if I hadn't seen the sun in a year. My runs with Bismarck, the world's loneliest dog, had become two-block strolls. Maybe when all this was over, I'd get fit, quit smoking, ease off the throttle of the liquor. I brushed my teeth so Mr. Cantor wouldn't smell the booze—as though drinking on the job had been my worst sin of the day! My head spun at the web of deceit I'd helped create.

When I got to Mr. Cantor's office, I found him flipping through a sailboat catalog. I knocked, gently.

"Paul. Come in." He held up a two-page spread for me to admire. "I've just chosen a new Valiant. A fifty-two footer. Very beamy too. The Sundance II."

"What a beauty."

"Interesting meeting with Mr. Tate this afternoon."

"Only Jack would think three-quarters of a billion was too little." He snorted and went back to his catalog. "Did you know it takes over a year to build one of these?"

"He did reiterate that he thought the company was under-valued." I sat down without waiting to be asked. I took out a cigarette and lit it. He raised his eyebrows ever so slightly as I exhaled smoke into the air—I usually waited for him to light up first. It was a look like a parent gives a child who puts elbows onto the table.

Mr. Cantor laid the catalog on his desk. "Jack will be happy with the bag of money I've found for him. I've instructed Enid to wrap up the merger ASAP."

I leaned forward and reached for the sailboat catalogue. "How much does she cost?"

"Enid Pearl?"

"No. The Sundance II."

"Oh," he said, amused. "About ten grand a foot. That's all."

Mr. Cantor retrieved his catalogue. "But you know what they say—if you have to ask, you can't afford it."

"But sir, Mr. Tate is adamant that his company is undervalued. I couldn't move him off that point."

"Paul, listen to yourself. Jack's been my client for twenty years. I remember him when he had two airplanes in a cow field where Dulles is now. He built that company into what it is, and now he's having second thoughts about selling. That's natural enough. This has nothing to do with money—it's about his manhood."

I watched to see how Mr. Cantor took this news: "Be that as it may, but he says his other buyer is serious. And he wants to sell to them."

Cantor's cheeks flushed, but he kept his voice steady. "There was no other buyer interested two years ago when I found Westbrooke. That's the important point, the only point. That, and the fact of Jack having signed a binding agreement with them, one which will be enforced."

I thought I noticed a slight change in his calm tone, a slight quaver. I wasn't sure if he was growing exasperated with Mr. Tate, or with me. "He wasn't lying at the party, sir. The buyer who contacted Mr. Tate is a California hedge fund. And like he said, they're offering seventy million over Westbrooke's offer."

"It doesn't matter who they are or what they're offering. Jack has already sold his company." There was no mistaking Mr. Cantor's tone now. He was tired of this back and forth with Jake Tate. "*It's too late.*"

It was time to retreat. I didn't know if Mr. Tate was right about Mr. Cantor having been flipped by Westbrooke or not, but something suspicious was in the air. "But he's not backing down, sir."

"Did that S-O-B tell you he thought I sold him out for

some huge finder's fee? That old bastard's as paranoid as they come."

"He didn't suggest anything like that. It's a bottom-line issue."

Mr. Cantor at last lit a cigarette and dropped his gold lighter on his desk. He blew smoke in the air and smiled that charming smile I had seen a hundred times... and indeed, it now looked like overconfidence. "Let no weaving spiders come here, Paul. Jack Tate isn't the last multimillionaire client you'll be representing here at Cantor and Miller. That's my advice to you personally. Now, tell me the truth."

Strategy time: If my lie that Mr. Tate hadn't said anything about a finder's fee were uncovered, Mr. Cantor might suspect me of lying and wonder about my loyalty. Since he already thought Jack didn't trust him there seemed no harm in telling the truth, or at least enough of the truth to reassure my boss I was still on the home team. "Yes, he did mention something about how rich your end would be. And, whether the figure had—colored your judgement, in his words. He's wringing his hands about it, in fact."

Mr. Cantor leaned back in his chair. He seemed almost relieved I had told him. "Why, it would be a conflict of interest to take an undisclosed fee of that sort."

"I said as such to him."

I didn't know who to believe, but in truth, it wasn't Eric Cantor's style to take so obvious a bribe as the one for which I now found myself angling. That was too gauche. That might be all right for Arthur Peck, but it wouldn't do for someone like him. I was convinced there was a success fee of some kind, but not the sort Mr. Tate suspected. It would be more nuanced than what I'd been offered.

Then again, maybe we were both wrong. In any case, I had to be careful in lying to someone as clever as Mr. Cantor—the

Manon Gambit, as I had come to think of our side-affair, had been good practice. Outright lies are too hard to remember; lies of omission, on the other hand, were easier to manage. Always tell the truth, sure, but nudge it along in the direction you want it to go.

"Bottom line: The company's already been sold. You got the FAA to approve the deal and that's the end of it."

"How large will the company be after the merger?"

"About three times its current size." Mr. Cantor glanced at his watch to let me know our chat was at an end. "Why do you ask?"

"Just wondering."

So that was it. After the merger Cantor and Miller would grow from eighty-seven lawyers to over two hundred. That was the success fee. The firm would get all the work from the new, much bigger company. Of course there was nothing wrong with that. At least not anything you could pin on Mr. Cantor. No, things would just shake out that way. It was simply a coincidence that Westbrooke, which also owned Piedmont Air, had bought the company for the lowest bid the TateAir board had agreed to accept. And, of course, Mr. Cantor as TateAir's long time counsel knew what that number needed to be. Knowing that number would have saved Westbrooke millions, seventy of them to be exact. It was a coincidence, that's all.

I stubbed out my cigarette in Mr. Cantor's crystal ashtray and rose to go.

"Now, Paul, don't listen to anything Jack Tate says. He's an old drunk who doesn't know when to quit. And, for god's sake, not a word of this to anyone."

Did he suspect me already? He already knew what I was capable of, so perhaps he did have doubts. "You can depend on me, Mr. Cantor."

"I know, son. And thank you for that."

When I got back to my office I found a check made out to me on my desk in the amount of two-hundred and fifty thousand dollars, my bonus money, but meant for Arthur. I slipped it into my trial practice notebook. No point in telling Arthur about it yet. Things were too unstable for that just now. All in good time. Who knew, maybe I would need the FAA approval to slow down, now. For my own sake.

11

Despite Mr. Cantor's instructions for me to keep quiet about Mr. Tate's unhappiness with the current contract, news of such magnitude spread quickly throughout the firm. I may even have been the one who mentioned it to my assistant, who was by general agreement acknowledged to be The Office Gossip.

I admit I enjoyed watching all the Chicken Littles scrambling after any tidbit of news about the merger. Now, whenever I passed one in a corridor they'd ask under their breath if I thought the deal would go through, and I would reply, "Gosh, why wouldn't it? I certainly hope so," in a loud, confident voice I hoped might be overheard by any senior partner who might have strayed from his corner office.

But as soon as I got to my desk? I'd lock the door and, like any good double agent, dive back into my research on how I could undermine the TateAir contract.

A problem—none of the cases I pursued looked promising. I read the one hundred and twenty-seven page agreement until I had memorized nearly every line. It seemed like an impregnable vault contained my seven million dollars of found money. The firm had certainly done a good job of locking Mr. Tate into the merger.

I considered telling Jack that Westbrooke had an absolute right to buy his company, but the thought of all the money coming my way simply wouldn't let me quit.

And then it occurred to me that if I used all of the tricks I had learned from Mr. Cantor, I might pull this off. Perhaps he would even recognize some of them. I couldn't help smiling at the thought of that. How better to flatter the teacher than by emulation?

I TURNED OFF MY COMPUTER AND OPENED THE DOOR TO LET some air into the shoebox I called an office. If I craned my head far enough out of the door, I could sometimes hear Seth Meyrinck's voice booming from around several corners. How many times had I watched him saunter past, looking smug? I wondered if that famous nonchalance of his would survive the scene he created at the party.

I heard him finally arrive. As I pretended to read the *Wall Street Journal*, I held it low enough so as to peer over the top to watch for him.

He slouched down the hallway, looking as though he had forgotten to shave. His brown suit and overcoat made him look like a walking paper bag—a crumpled one.

It wasn't long before before he appeared in my doorway. At the sight of his sheepish expression I tried not to be too obvious in how much I was enjoying myself. One ought to convey graciousness in times like these. Besides, now that I had gone over to the other side, it was doubly important that I keep a lid on my feelings. It wasn't difficult.

"I should apologize for that scene the other night."

I pretended I didn't understand and continued smiling. "What do you mean?"

"Come on—I drank too much and made a total ass of myself."

"Who hasn't?"

He couldn't seem to go on, the act of apologizing to someone like me being too humiliating. Seth cocked his head to one side and a pained look came over him. He couldn't believe I was going to drag this out. "But that business about a third-rate law school, and all that. Way out of line."

I hoped my delight in Seth's predicament wasn't too obvious. "I haven't given it a second thought." I wanted to add, *and since I slept with your fiancée, I'd say I more than came out ahead on the deal*, but such a childish indiscretion would be far from wise. "Forget it."

"That's good of you." Seth adjusted his tie and pulled at his cuffs, ran a hand over his unshaven chin. "No idea why I went off like that."

My jaw had begun to ache from holding the frozen smile in place. "You only said what everyone's being thinking."

"That's not true." Seth didn't bother to put much conviction into his words. He was on automatic pilot now, going through a pro forma act of contrition. Suddenly he looked exhausted, the way he did after I had beat him at tennis. Lying can be exhausting; who would know better than me?

I disliked everything about him; the way he dressed, the way he spoke, his sense of entitlement and, of course, the fact that he was sleeping with Enid. Here, a little spritz of honesty to mask the scent of all this hypocrisy: "Look, you and I don't much care for each other, and I don't see any reason why we should go on pretending we do."

"I'm sorry you feel that way. That's what I'm trying to fix, here." Seth frowned as though he had been genuinely wounded by what I'd said. I was sure he thought everyone liked him. It took all my strength not to laugh. His attempt to convey bruised innocence was so wide of the mark that at first I thought he was doing it as a joke, like the unnervingly accurate impressions he did of Mr. Cantor and Mr. Miller, but then I realized he was being serious which, of course, made it even more absurd. Apropos of nothing he continued, "Enid and I are trying to work out our problems, so I didn't want there to be any hard feelings about Friday."

"What does Enid have to do with me?"

"She thinks quite highly of you. For some reason," with a sullen smirk.

Were they really trying to work things out? When had they decided that? Hell, I'd spent the night with her only three days ago.

I looked at my watch to put an end to this conversation the way I had seen Mr. Cantor do so many times. I'd had enough of Seth for one morning. In a curious way I almost liked him better when he'd been insulting me. At least then he was believable. "I've got to get moving on this pile of Tate paper."

"We're good then?" Seth held out his hand.

I filled both hands with TateAir documents so I could escape the ritual of shaking the bastard's hand. I tried to sound equally insincere. "You bet, big guy. Bygones, and all."

His face relaxed. He seemed relieved. "Magnanimous. Enid said you'd react just like this."

I shrugged. "We've been working together for months, now. She's seen all my schtick."

"I'll bet she has."

If only you knew.

⛵

AFTER ANOTHER HOUR STOOPED OVER MY DESK, I TOOK A stroll past the reception desk, where I found Manon applying a fresh coat of fingernail polish. Whether she didn't notice me, or perhaps pretended not to, I kept going to the elevator without a word.

When I got out at the twelfth floor I saw Enid already at work in the main conference room.

"Well—hello there."

"I've been waiting for you to come in."

"I'm not late for a meeting, am I?" I had on my business-as-usual face. "I've been chained to the desk all morning."

"No, you're not late." She moved the pile of merger documents in front of her to one side. "You acted so strangely at breakfast Saturday, I didn't know what was wrong."

"That isn't so," I lied, the way you do when you want to avoid something difficult. Again it struck me how men and women inhabit different emotional planets. "Maybe I felt conflicted, somewhat."

"Paul, I was talking to my mother last night about you, and that's when I remembered I called you Seth when I asked you to get my purse."

"It could have been worse; you could have called me Seth while we were in bed." I sat down at the far end of the table.

"Please don't be like that."

"Like what?"

"Don't be coarse." She reached across the table to take my hand in hers, but I was too far away so she simply folded her hands. "I'm trying to tell you how sorry I am."

"Apparently this is the day for apologies. Seth just told me how sorry *he* was about the party."

"He is sorry. He told me so."

"How very mature of him." Just the thought being discussed like that was enough to make me detest them both. Had she told him about our spending the night together? Was that when they decided to try to work things out?

"Paul, I'm the one who feels conflicted. Don't you see?"

"What does it matter? You're engaged. I knew at the Mayflower, so no harm, no foul." I wanted to say something that I knew would hurt her, something that would leave her thinking she meant nothing to me. "You were just sowing some wild oats before getting tied down."

"Please stop being so glib. You sound stupid and childish." Now it was her who sounded angry. "I've said I'm sorry. You can accept that, or you can go on enjoying how right you were in your opinion of me."

Before I could say anything more, Enid's assistant appeared to say that Mr. Cantor needed to see me right away.

Not knowing exactly what to do regarding Enid, I mumbled something about how I had better go and see what the big boss wanted. We were both thankful for the interruption. I realized then what a stupidly complicating act it had been to seduce Enid Pearl. Bygones.

⚓

I found Mr. Cantor in his office reading a letter. When I came in he immediately handed it to me. "Read this nonsense, Paul," he said with a distressed tone.

It was a letter, CC'd to Mr. Cantor, from Jack Tate to the Westbrooke Group. It announced his intention to break the contract to sell his company. He offered no explanation for his decision, only hints that he suspected Westbrooke's offer of being somehow improper.

"I tried to warn you he was serious."

"How like Jack to blow smoke down a rat hole to see who'd run out."

I had no idea what he meant. I handed the letter back to Mr. Cantor and sat down. This meant war, and during wartime traitors ended up before a firing squad. "Looks like he's moving ahead against all advice."

"Jack's crazier than we thought."

"I don't know what to say." I certainly was being truthful about that. That Jack would declare war so openly had caught me completely off guard. "What's the response from Westbrooke?"

"I've been on the phone all morning with the lawyers. They've given us until the end of the week to withdraw the letter, after which the deal will proceed."

"Have you spoken with Mr. Tate?"

"Jack isn't taking my calls."

I asked what we should do from here.

"I'm sending you back over there right now to tell that old lying sack of…" Mr. Cantor thought better of what he was going to say. "Remind Jack again he has no grounds to void the sale. We drafted that contract. His board approved it. The FAA even approved it, thanks to you."

"I can't imagine he'll see me if he won't speak to you, Mr. Cantor." Did Eric suspect something? Why on earth did he think Jack would speak to me again? Mr. Cantor was enough of a schemer himself to know another one by sight.

"He seems to have taken a liking to you." Mr. Cantor picked up the letter and read it again. "I want you to make him understand that if he tries to block this sale, they'll sue him personally."

"I'll certainly try." I looked at the picture of the destroyer Mr. Cantor had served on in the navy and thought of the first time I had been in this office. How in awe of him I was then. And here I was betraying him. How do these things go so wrong? Seven million reasons later, maybe I'd figure it out.

"Now, don't listen to any of Jack's nonsense about another

buyer. That's just an old man's reluctance to let go of a company he started."

"I'll do my best." If this ended badly and the court ordered the merger to go forward, I would be finished as a lawyer in this town. I'd be drawing up wills and doing uncontested divorces in Charleston, West Virginia, if not even further away from the big leagues.

"A lot of people are counting on this deal going forward." Mr. Cantor stopped speaking and seemed lost in thought. It was as if he'd forgotten I was in the room. "I've worked over three years on it, and I don't expect some greedy geriatric to torpedo it." Mr. Cantor narrowed his eyes. "My old 'friend' is getting nearly a billion dollars, Paul. He's going to risk all that for, what? Another sixty or seventy million? It's preposterous."

What was it that Mr. Cantor always said? Money is the most relative of all things. "He believes the company is seriously undervalued," I reminded him.

"He doesn't know what he's talking about. I found the Westbrooke people, and I know that price is fair."

"It does look odd that we're taking a position contrary to the wishes of our client." As I said this I edged towards the door. "That's my big stumbling block."

"Jack Tate doesn't know what the hell he wants. Here's what this is all about. Jack owns the majority of the company's voting stock. This new offer is the same as the Westbrooke offer, only they're offering more for the voting shares and less for the others."

"How can you be sure of that?" Suddenly I found myself less eager to help Mr. Tate. If it were true that Jack was trying to cheat his own shareholders, then I certainly didn't want to get caught up in any of that. It was getting harder and harder to know who to believe.

"Let's just say I know Jack Tate maybe too well, and I'll bet he's taking home a lot more money under this new offer, with the non-voting shareholders finding a lot less in their envelopes."

I tried not to imagine myself in the middle of a shareholder dispute that would drag on for years. "That certainly sounds unethical."

"It is. And if Jack has any brain cells left undamaged by alcohol, he'll withdraw this letter."

"I'd better be on my way."

"It's crucial, both to the firm and to me personally, that you change his mind."

"I understand that, sir." There was an almost erotic thrill to being the deceiver, the trusted confidante who, in reality, is a mole. How perfectly that name fit. Here I was burrowing under the foundation of Cantor and Miller while everyone was scurrying around above me. "Want me to take the Jaguar again?"

He smiled. "Certainly, my boy. Already getting used to it, eh?"

"It's a sweet ride."

"Tell you what. You get Jack Tate settled down, and I'll sign the damn title over to you. Deal?"

I gave a big, theatrical thumb's up, but on the inside I felt only anxiety as my pawn got moved from one square to another and back again. Something would soon need to break this stalemate.

THE CAR SMELT OF MANON'S PERFUME. WHEN I STARTED THE engine, I could barely hear it idling beneath the hood. The bonnet, I think they call it in England. I liked that. I closed the windows to seal out the world and enjoyed the feel of money.

Maybe I'd buy a Jaguar when this was over. I didn't want Cantor's leftovers, though god forbid Manon heard me say it like that.

No need to go directly over to TateAir; it would be better to keep Mr. Cantor waiting as long as possible for my next report. I should at least make it look as though I had spent time trying to talk Jack out of rejecting the sale.

Instead, I headed out to the beltway and got off at the Silver Spring exit. As I pulled into the driveway, I sounded the horn. Brenda came out.

"Where'd you steal that?" She cast an admiring glance at the green Jaguar.

"It's Mr. Cantor's. I told him I was thinking of getting one, and he tossed me the keys to take it out on the beltway."

"Maybe you better pay your law school loans off first."

"I'll have some money soon."

So I really had made up my mind to do what Jack Tate had asked. It had been in the back of my mind that I might not, but now I realized I was actually going through with Tate's scheme.

The thought frightened me. There were a hundred ways to fail and only one way to succeed. What do gamblers call that, long odds? But, of course, the payout is always highest at that window.

"That would be a nice change." Brenda laughed in a not unkind way as I followed her inside. "Want some coffee?"

"I've already had ten cups this morning." I held my hands out so she could see how they shook. "No, thanks."

"Good thing you're not a surgeon."

We went inside the split-level and sat down at the kitchen table. "How is that woman you're working with?"

I lit a cigarette. "Why do you ask?"

"Because you never mention her any more. You used to talk about her all the time."

I tried to sound nonchalant but, of course, there was no fooling Brenda. "You mean Enid Pearl?"

"That's her name? I never heard you call her that before." Brenda made a note on one of the bills she was getting ready to pay. "You used to always call her Ms. Pearl."

What a clever little spymaster Brenda was. "What's your point?"

"I just found it odd how you used to talk about her all the time, and then suddenly nothing." Brenda looked at me in a way I remembered from years ago when we were little children when I tried to tell her a fib, but knew it would be useless. My lying had improved considerably since then.

"We've started seeing each other." I hoped that would satisfy Brenda, at least for now. And is that what you called it, seeing each other? Seeing each other naked was more like it. "Nothing serious."

"I thought you said she was engaged."

"Yes, that's right. I did say that." I puffed furiously on my cigarette and tried to hide in a cloud of blue smoke. Why on earth did I tell her that? What's the Miranda warning? Anything you say can and will be used against you?

"That can't be very nice for her fiancé."

"You might worry more about how stressful it is for your brother." There, I had taken the moral high ground and that was no mean trick for someone fooling around with a woman who is engaged.

"Yes, I'm sure sleeping with a beautiful blonde is horrible for you." Apparently Brenda was not entirely sympathetic to my situation.

Brenda's sarcasm seemed to clear my head and I realized

this wasn't mere idle curiosity on her part. "How do you know she's blonde?"

"She came to my yoga class last week. Didn't she tell you? She's very pretty. I see why you like her."

"No, she didn't mention it." I tried not to give away how surprised I was. Brenda was in her element now. Nothing pleased her quite so much as knowing something I didn't. And why would Enid drive completely across town to go to a yoga class. And how did she know my sister would be there? Oh, yes, pillow talk. I had mentioned that Brenda took yoga classes at the Y.

"That's odd, don't you think?"

"No, actually I don't think it's odd at all." I tried to think of some way to change the subject, but before I could speak Brenda started up again.

"She's certainly got a crush on you."

"Did she say that?" It didn't sound like Enid to bare her soul to a perfect stranger, even if that stranger was my sister.

"She didn't have to. She was almost blushing when she told me you work together."

"I hope you didn't say anything bad about me?" My mind was spinning with the possibilities; Brenda with her gossip about my divorce and troubles with alcohol. I lit another cigarette.

"Of course not." Brenda smiled slyly to suggest she wasn't about to let me know all she had said to Enid. "Have you told her about Manon?"

"What's there to tell?" Oh, god, why had I told Brenda about that, too? Jesus, would I ever learn to be keep things to myself?

"She might like to know you have a girlfriend."

"Manon is not my girlfriend, and, Enid's engaged, for Christ's sake."

"Yes, and she told you that."

"You don't even know her." I stood up so Brenda would see I'd had enough of this.

"I'm not thinking of her."

"Well you're certainly not thinking of me." I put my cigarette out and jingled Mr. Cantor's car keys.

"I am thinking of you and the way you treat people who care about you." Old family wounds were always just out of sight for us, like unmarked curves on an icy mountain road. Brenda was talking about me and her now. I hadn't been the best brother.

"Thank you for your concern." I tried to sound as sarcastic as I possibly could and we both laughed. No one knew me better than Brenda, and that wasn't always a good thing.

My sister followed me outside. Before I got to the car, she took my arm and stopped me from leaving.

"You've been mooning over that girl for a year. She's very nice and I just want you to be happy."

"Are you happy?" That was my return of serve.

"Not particularly. Arthur's staying with friends for a bit."

"How long have you been separated?" I couldn't say I was surprised. I had always wondered why she married Arthur in the first place. She was pretty enough and had always had plenty of boyfriends, all of them more charming than the graceless Arthur Peck.

"Three weeks. Arthur and I are trying to sort some things out."

This seemed to be the season for sorting things out. First there was Enid and Seth, and now Brenda and Arthur. I wondered how much my brother-in-law's bribe money played into it all.

"Is that what you want?"

"I'm not exactly sure." She rubbed her eyes. "I don't know which end is up, right now."

"I know you'll get it worked out."

I wanted to get going before she burst into tears, so I started the car and began backing out into the street. I needed to make sure Brenda got the 'bonus' money now, not Arthur. She didn't make enough at her job to afford even this modest house, not in the DC suburbs. Another complication.

Brenda stood watching as I drove off. I could still see her in the rearview mirror as I turned out of the subdivision and headed for the beltway ramp, her posture one of stress and concern. At least she hadn't pestered me about the chain smoking.

It was a relief to be in the car again, but I couldn't get over Enid going to Brenda's yoga class. Why hadn't she said anything to me about meeting her? But what difference did any of that make now? It was clear that I'd be with neither Enid nor Manon, not in the long term.

I missed my exit to the TateAir offices because I was thinking of Enid and Brenda, and it was nearly lunchtime when I caught up with Jack Tate. Not that time mattered; Jack and I dwelled in a different dimension from the others now, one of secrecy, collusion and privilege.

MR. TATE, LAUGHING AT MY QUICK REAPPEARANCE, TOOK ME out to his favorite restaurant. He ordered a bottle of Malbec, a heavy Argentinian red wine which had a finish more like alcohol than fruit.

As I watched him drain his glass, I thought of what Mr. Cantor had said about his drinking. The trouble with being a quisling: the duality and deception brought any and all doubts about the people around you into high relief. Still, there was something fearless about Jack I liked. I wasn't sure who he was playing against whom, but I suspected him capable of anything.

Over giant prawns he told me he had written Westbrooke to tell them why he wouldn't go forward with the sale. He had started the company thirty years ago with ten thousand dollars, he explained, borrowed from his father-in-law. The company had struggled for years until a smart young lawyer named Eric Cantor, Tate said with a wry smile, had described the tax advantages of leasing their planes.

"You see, TateAir's success is just a creation of the tax code."

"Give yourself more credit than that."

Jack filled our glasses again. "That's the problem. Eric thinks he invented this business, and in a way I guess he did. But I didn't build this company up to give it away to the first guy willing to give Eric Cantor a finder's fee for screwing his own client."

I told Jack I didn't think Mr. Cantor would do that, but now I wasn't so sure. I'd seen him lie often enough during settlement negotiations and later, on the way back to the office, he'd laugh about how gullible the people he'd deceived. It always left me wondering if I was one of those people.

One thing I knew first hand: lying becomes a habit, something you do almost unconsciously after a while, simply because that's how you move through life.

Now, here I had Jack Tate cashing out for hundreds of millions of dollars, with Mr. Cantor receiving peanuts despite his contribution to all the success. Maybe he did feel he was owed more.

But... trying to convince Jack Tate of my boss's trustworthiness seemed counterintuitive. Why would I? The less Jack trusted Mr. Cantor, the more he would need me. That's the way these things work.

It was odd, too, that we were trying to enforce a contract our client no longer wanted. I was so busy trying to think how I might get him out of a merger he had already agreed to that I could barely listen. I don't think he appreciated how difficult doing so would be—every time I tried to tell him of my concerns, he said he knew I'd figure it out.

Then I remembered the valet at the Mayflower Hotel. Jack had given him one of those twenty-dollar tips to bring his car up first. He expected me to win because, like that valet, I was going to be paid if I did as he asked. That's why he didn't want to talk about it. As far as he was concerned, it was over. If I wanted that money, and he knew I did, I would find a way to beat Westbrooke and Mr. Cantor.

Easy to say, but knowing the law would be against us, I had a real challenge before me. I was going to have to come up with something Westbrooke would never consider, perhaps even outside the law. I didn't know what that was, and I wouldn't have long to find it, either. If Jack didn't withdraw his letter, Westbrooke was sure to sue to compel the sale. But watching him finish his second self-satisfied glass of wine made me feel quite sure he wasn't about to withdraw anything.

As our entrees arrived, we talked about what Mr. Tate would do after he sold the company. He spoke of founding a new company—something to do with finance, naturally—but I wasn't listening. I had other things on my mind.

On the drive back to the office I rehearsed what I would say to Mr. Cantor. He would want to know every word Jack Tate had said. Of course, that was out of the question, so I would have to come up with some believable dialogue: I begged Jack to listen to reason, and he just as vigorously refused to change his mind.

I had to leave Mr. Cantor with *some* hope that Jack might change his mind between now and Friday, however. That would delay the filing of the suit to compel the sale, mainly to give me more time to reason, or maybe intuit, a way of coming out on top of this rich man's increasingly complicated quagmire.

12

Back at the office I found Mr. Cantor in a meeting with Westbrooke's lead counsel, Mark Dresser.

Manon, who broke the news, did so sounding rather alarmed. "Eric said to send you in immediately," she said with a strained whisper. "His eyes had that hard look."

"What's the tone?"

"Can't you tell already?" She pointed at the boss's door. Inside, the sound of upraised voices. "Get in there."

I gulped, knocked, and entered.

Mr. Cantor, looking strained, introduced me to Mr. Dresser, but when I reached over to shake his hand, he ignored the gesture with a hard glare.

"For the love of God, Eric, you let subordinates just come traipsing in whenever they feel like it?"

Cantor shook his head. "Now, Mark, Mr. Johns is our point man with Jack Tate. Let's all sit down and have a chat."

Dresser remained unimpressed. A heavyset man in his mid-fifties, he had a stout, powerful body inside a suit with the drape and cut of a tailored affair which easily cost ten times my own Brooks Brothers ensemble. His fingers, short and stubby, constantly jabbed in the air as he spoke. His thick forehead jutted out over his eyes. A beast, albeit an articulate one, they had gone to Yale together, but couldn't have been more different: where Mr. Cantor deployed a kind of lethal charisma, Mr. Dresser seethed with barely-coiled rage.

"Your client withdraws that letter by Friday, or we're going after him personally, and his board, too." Sweat rolled down his forehead. I worried he might be feeling unwell, on the verge of a stroke. "You tell that to Jack Tate," like a schoolyard invitation to a fight at recess. "Or else."

"Marc, settle down. Paul's just come back from meeting with Jack." Cantor gave me a warm smile. "Tell us how it went... this time."

"But, Mr. Cantor, I can't."

A wall of silence from them both. Dresser had finally settled into a stone-faced countenance. At last Cantor said, "Go on."

"My conversation with Mr. Tate, it's, well—it's privileged." I didn't relish instructing a senior partner on the rules of privilege, but Mr. Cantor certainly knew better than to ask me to repeat a conversation with our client in front of opposing counsel.

"That's ordinarily true, yes yes, but in this case, we're waiving the privilege rule." Mr. Cantor seemed impatient with my invocation of the rule, but repeating my conversation with Mr. Tate in front of Marc Dresser was not only unethical, it could hurt our case. Now I began to understand Jack wasn't being paranoid when he suspected Mr. Cantor of betraying him. "Please tell Marc what he said."

There seemed no harm in repeating those parts of the conversation I wanted Marc Dresser to hear, especially since I wasn't about to tell the truth. "He said he'll think about it—"

"*He'll think about it?*" Marc Dresser looked as though he could kill me. "What in the actual hell?"

"—but he continues to insist the current offer is far too low and thus unacceptable, the contract be damned."

I had barely finished before Mr. Dresser pushed all of his girth out of his chair. He pointed a fat, accusing finger in my general direction. "He's already accepted the goddamn offer, young man. Did you not remind him that it's a little late to negotiate for more money?"

"Marc, no need to be insulting. I have confidence Paul knows what he's doing."

Cantor's soothing voice seemed to calm our fellow attorney, at least for the moment. "All right. Go on."

"Mr. Tate alleges now that the Westbrooke people used inside information in making their bid." I said this knowing it would cause Mr. Dresser to start shouting again. I wanted to take his measure, as I had watched Seth hit a few tennis balls before owning him on the court that morning. "In fact, he claims he's certain of it. That he has some sort of evidence."

Dresser didn't disappoint. Spittle flew from his mouth as he spoke and his lips curled away from his teeth. "Son, you better know what you're talking about, or I'll sue your ass for defamation."

"I think you mean you'll sue Mr. Tate, don't you?"

"No, I mean you, you wise little bastard." To Mr. Cantor he said, "What sort of brain-dead law clerks do you having working here?"

Cantor had had enough. "Paul is an associate, but he's even more than that—we sail together. I insist that you show him respect."

I sat down on the leather couch and took out a cigarette. "Do you smoke, Mr. Dresser?"

The question caught him completely off guard. "Excuse me?"

"I asked if you'd like one." I offered him one of my Gauloises.

He stared at the cigarette as though I'd offered him a writhing, poisonous snake. "When I'm done with you and Jack Tate, that smoke will be coming out of your ass."

Sweat had coursed down Mr. Dresser's thick neck to stain his blue shirt collar. Meanwhile, Mr. Cantor had gone oddly quiet. If they didn't sue by Friday, I could be certain they were trying to find out what I knew. And why Mr. Cantor was being so uncharacteristically silent? I might just have stumbled onto a thread I could keep pulling until something unraveled.

But no judge would stop a merger simply because a junior associate suspected Westbrooke had insider help in putting together their lowball bid. No, I'd have to find another angle, a feint which would leave the court with no choice but to halt the sale. I had no idea what yet, but guessed I had at least bought myself a few days' time.

I blew smoke towards Mr. Dresser. "Here's my view: I suggest that before you threaten Mr. Tate, you review Westbrooke's bid to see if it was based on this alleged inside information." I knew I couldn't prove Westbrooke had used insider information in formulating their bid, but nothing would frighten them more than thinking I could. "You have to admit it was quite a coincidence that the bid came in exactly at the low end of what the board would accept."

"TateAir is a publicly traded company, so if the bid process were somehow tainted, the SEC would certainly investigate," as Dresser called my bluff. "Have you filed a complaint with the SEC?"

I smiled and shrugged. "I thought it best to give us a chance to do an internal investigation first, but if you wish, I can do so tomorrow."

Mr. Dresser looked confused, like a man dealing with someone who doesn't understand English. "I don't think that's necessary. Those damn things can go on for years."

I sank back into the depths of Mr. Cantor's red leather couch. My little ploy had paid off, at least for now. It certainly was starting to look as if Mr. Tate hadn't imagined this conspiracy. What's that saying? That a paranoid is merely someone who's gotten wind of what's really going on?

Like the sun coming out from behind a storm cloud, Mr. Dresser smiled. His tone turned conciliatory. "Listen, John…"

"It's Paul."

"Of course—Paul." Mr. Dresser sat down. The couch creaked under him. "Now, it's clear you've done a damn fine job of representing TateAir, but Jack, god love him, he's hurting his own shareholders, which means he's hurting himself. Am I right, Eric?"

Mr. Cantor now looked gray and ill-at-ease, as though he wanted to be anywhere else. He held out his hands and nodded as if to say, *yes yes.*

"There you have it." Mr. Dresser slapped me playfully on the knee. "Eric tells me Jack listens to you, so why don't you just tell him he's got to close or risk this blowing up into consequences he won't enjoy."

"I already know his answer. He'd like to hear from you first about the results of your internal inquiry."

Mr. Dresser's smile faded as quickly as it had appeared. "That could take awhile. Westbrooke wants to close now."

I had to be careful not to overplay my hand. "Why don't we agree that two weeks from today we'll deliver a letter to Jack—I mean, Mr. Tate—stating the findings of the inquiry."

Mr. Dresser thought over my offer. I could see he was beginning to sense there was a trap here. He was no fool, but for the time being I had blunted his anger. "And if I don't find anything, will Tate withdraw his letter?"

Now I was on the spot. How quickly Marc had turned the tables on me. If I said yes, I bound Mr. Tate to my decision. If I said no, Marc would see that I was stalling. I had to choose.

I extended my hand to show enthusiasm for our new agreement. "Of course I'll do my best to persuade him."

"What's really at the heart of all this, Paul?"

"It's as Mr. Cantor suspected—he's an old man making a last attempt at gaining more financial leverage, however shortsighted."

Marc took my hand in his and squeezed it hard. "That's more like it. You've yourself got a deal."

I could barely move my fingers. The son of a bitch had nearly broken my hand. "I'll leave you gents with it, then."

"Yes—go home, get some rest. We've got a lot to do tomorrow." Suddenly Mr. Cantor seemed like himself again. "Perhaps we'll celebrate by getting in some sailing this weekend. Enid's coming down."

I tried to sound only mildly interested; sailing, staying here in DC, Enid, no Enid, I was golden either way. I hoped it came off as confidence. "I thought Mr. Meyrinck didn't care for sailing."

"She's coming alone."

"Really, now."

"Do try to get down. Let's say Friday for dinner."

Charming as ever, Mr. Cantor walked me out to the hallway. All the insinuation of insider information being traded seemed behind us now, like a passing squall that leaves your sailboat once again back in the bright sun. To the accomplished men of Yale in the office just now, I was only a parrot mouthing Jack Tate's crazy ideas no one took seriously. Not from a junior associate like me, one who wasn't even Ivy League.

BUT WHEN WE GOT TO THE ELEVATOR, MR. CANTOR TOOK ME aside. I felt blindsided by what came next:

"So listen, Paul—this morning Pamela Schiller stopped by my office."

I hadn't called Pam in ages. But to my credit, nor had she reached out. I guessed the thought of her having spent the last months of Ben's life bedding down with me on any number of occasions had left her with guilt. "How is she?"

"Upset about the financial mess Ben left her with—no money, two mortgages. That sort of conundrum."

I nodded with sympathy, but I couldn't let on I knew much about Pamela's finances. "Tough position."

"Anyway, she's still got it in her head that Ben's life insurance should go to her." Mr. Cantor looked at me, almost as if waiting for some explanation. "I explained to her that we carry 'key man' insurance on all partners, but, that's to protect the firm, not the family. And that I was sorry."

Knowing Pamela as I did, I couldn't imagine any explanation would satisfy her, especially not since I had told her about the million-dollar policy the firm held on her husband. I held out my hands in sympathetic helplessness. "Cantor and Miller remains the beneficiary. I would've thought she knew."

"Well, she's started making unpleasant accusations about how we got FAA approval of the TateAir merger."

"In what sense?"

"She knows your brother-in-law works there."

A bit of an oh-hell moment rolled through my gut. "I may have mentioned Arthur to Ben."

"You were close."

"That's right. It would have been casual."

"Of course. But, actually… she says you told her."

"I had dinner with them at their home often. She must have overheard." Knowing Mr. Cantor was watching my every word, looking for any inconsistency which would expose me as a liar, I said this as casually as I could. But, now I had to assume he knew I'd been sleeping with her. A chilling thought: I wondered what else he knew.

"So what shall we do about this?"

"The million dollar policy is real money to her, but in context, the TateAir deal is worth many times that." I wanted to sound like a cold-hearted realist doing the calculus of risk and reward without regard to who gets hurt. Mr. Cantor always responded to that jeweler's eye view of the world. He would think I was trying to steer money to Pamela if I made her case too forcefully so I had to appear to be an honest broker. "But as you once told me, money is relative. No matter how much."

Mr. Cantor, always one for getting straight to the point. *"Are you suggesting we give her the million dollars?"*

I shrugged. "We don't want the FAA approval challenged. Do we?"

"I thought you might say that." He looked at me as though he were trying to figure out whose side I was on. Perhaps I had overplayed my part and he had seen through my little performance. He was no fool.

At last he said, "Well, too bad. We've already spent the money."

I knew some of it had been used to pay me my bonus, so I had to tread lightly here. "Perhaps we could use the firm's line of credit." I offered this more as a question than a suggestion. There were rumors that the firm's finances were strained.

"You might as well hear it now—I've taken an option on a building on Pennsylvania Avenue, and, for the moment anyway, the deal has exhausted our credit."

I asked if the lease here had come up.

"No, but I want out of it. If we're going to grow, we'll need more space."

This was the first I'd heard of his plans to break our lease, one I knew to be held by Mrs. Cantor. And for all my finagling and chess moves, I still held affection for Pam. "I still think we should settle with Mrs. Schiller."

"Out of respect to Ben?"

"Call it what you will. How long was he here? Twenty-five years?"

Cantor nodded. "We'll offer her two hundred-fifty. It would be the decent thing to do."

I pushed the button on the elevator. "The decent thing. Yes."

"And, I'd like you to make the offer to her."

"Certainly."

I thought about tipping off Pamela that she should hold out for more money, but it was so unlike Mr. Cantor to reveal his settlement strategy I thought he might be laying a trap. Much as I wanted to help Pamela, she would have to fend for herself. I had bigger fish to fry. "I'll call her tonight."

"Oh, and Paul: be very careful of Mark Dresser. He's a top notch litigator."

"I thought it went well in there." A lie.

"I've know Mark for thirty years. He doesn't like being fooled with."

"And I don't care for being insulted."

"That's just his way. But, Paul—be careful with him. And with Jack Tate."

I STOPPED IN A RESTAURANT NEAR THE OFFICE TO HAVE A DRINK. I fought my way up to the bar and ordered a scotch on the rocks. Finding a quiet nook amidst the happy hour bustle of suits with ties yanked and voices bellowing, I wanted to mull over what had happened, and why Mr. Cantor had seemed so quiet.

But the minute my drink arrived, I found myself thinking of Enid. Why was she going to the Cantor's bay house alone? Maybe it had something to do with last Friday's tryst at the Mayflower. Then I remembered she wasn't wearing her engagement ring when I saw her this morning.

My god, you don't break off your engagement just because you fell into bed with someone at work—do you?

I had finished my first round and was about to order another when I spied two familiar faces—Mr. Cantor and Mark Dresser being seated in a booth near the bar.

They hadn't seen me over in the shadows. What an opportunity!

I slipped into the crowd, mingled my way through until I could lean against a wall near enough to their table to eavesdrop. And while I couldn't hear them well, every now and again my name floated above the din of happy hour bar chatter. From the tone, it didn't sound as if either of them was all that fond of me.

Mr. Cantor wasn't kidding—I needed to be careful as a monk crossing an icy stream.

Well—at least I knew now not to trust my boss any farther than I could throw that Jaguar of his. If I was to survive, I would need to reset the chessboard on these powerful players. But, how...?

13

For the first time in my life, I stopped worrying about money. Thanks to an expense account I had begun to abuse, money was there whenever I needed it. I started taking a cab to the office.

Everything this week had gone on the firm card; bar tabs, car fare, my dry cleaning—everything. I signed my credit card bills with a slashing, uncaring signature. If Manon wanted to spend the night at an expensive hotel, that is where we went. We ordered a huge meal from room service but left it untouched, because being around all this unbridled luxury made us think more of vigorous sex than food. We did it all again the next night.

As for my worries about running up the tab, with so much money at stake neither Eric Cantor nor Jack Tate were about to quibble over pennies. Had basically told me as much.

So, I spent. What would you have done? Wait—don't answer that.

During the day, Enid and I lunched at the best restaurants. Ours, I soon discovered, was an unspoken agreement; we wouldn't mention the night we spent together, but would remain friends and colleagues. I don't know how such agreements occur among clandestine lovers, but they do.

After lunch, we were back to work as usual. Only the occasional glint in her eye told me she remembered how good it had been. Whereas Manon in bed behaved like a starving tiger, Enid had been more of a purring house cat, all warmth and affection, a gradual eruption of passion. I yearned for more, but made no moves. I had much more lucrative issues on the table than pursuing a certain-to-fail office romance.

Around that office, with the deadline approaching for Jack to withdraw his opposition to the merger, the whole firm found itself in the grip of a kind of controlled hysteria, the sort which infects passengers on a slowly sinking ship. All the senior folks understood if the merger didn't go through, the firm stood to default on the proposed new building lease, while also having no recourse as to renewing the old one—a Big Pharma group with hundreds of well-paid lobbyists had already signed their own letter of intent to move into our current building the second we vacated. In that instance, Eric and the other partners would be forced to downsize. The tension from the bosses seeped into the lower levels of paralegals, clerks and assistants.

The mood was dour enough, in fact, that some of the junior partners were already sending out feelers for other jobs. Of course, this was all done on the Q.T. No one wanted to be seen as the first one climbing into the lifeboats.

By Friday I had begun a kind of sequestration in my tiny office in my attempt to find cases which would help my situation, but the law was unusually clear on one point: a contract means what it says. I would soon need to generate that luck of mine, the type I seemed able to call on whenever the stakes got high... and none might ever be higher for me than Tate-Air. Eric and Jack weren't the only players with everything on the line. I had an entire lifetime ahead. I didn't even have it yet, but occasionally I'd think about the grand life I intended for myself. Seven million might only represent the start of what I'd need.

⛵

AT NOON MR. CANTOR POKED HIS HEAD INTO MY OFFICE TO remind me we were leaving in an hour for the bay. "I could use a wingman on the drive, if you don't mind."

"Sounds great."

I wanted to come up with an excuse to get out of the weekend this time, but everything I thought to say seemed obvious. I would go and act as though nothing was wrong. I was so worried about finding some way to stop the merger I couldn't think about anything else, and I needed desperately to work on Saturday. Well, nothing I could do about it now.

Not to mention Enid's presence. Who knew what that portended, though again, I tried to put our complicated relationship out of my mind.

Furthermore, I was sure Mark Dresser would have his team working all weekend. He didn't seem like someone who would spend his time on a hobby so frivolous as sailing, not with millions on the line. The thought crossed my mind Mr. Cantor invited me out to the bay house to make sure I would't be ready for Westbrooke's motion.

Just before one o'clock I ate a protein bar—a far cry from the sensational lunches of earlier in the week—and changed out of my suit to meet Mr. Cantor in the parking garage.

Downstairs he seemed unusually relaxed, clapping me on the shoulder and seeming fatherly and proud, somehow. I doubted it had to do with me—perhaps it was the alcohol I caught on his breath, or maybe he was merely confident I couldn't possibly defeat Marc Dresser.

As soon as we left town he put down the top, even though

214 | MICHAEL G SULLIVAN

it was rather chilly. I tried to light a cigarette, but only succeeded in getting ash in my eye. Mr. Cantor laughed and expertly lit his own with one hand, passed it on to me for me to catch a mercy light.

We didn't talk much. At that speed, the wind was deafening. I often wondered why Mr. Cantor never got a ticket. Luck, I guessed. He certainly had plenty of that.

Not to mention the boozing: After we got out of the DC traffic he produced a flask and took himself a good nip. He offered it to me the way folks do, but I said no. If he kept on, someone would need to drive us the rest of the way.

THANKS TO TRAFFIC GETTING THROUGH ANNAPOLIS AND ACROSS the bridge, not to mention with the flask long empty, we arrived at his bay house in one piece just as the sun was disappearing behind the tallest trees.

Before getting out Mr. Cantor chewed up a couple of breath mints. He was more cautious of his wife than being pulled by a state trooper. Everyone has their own method of risk calculation, I supposed.

Mrs. Cantor, with reserved body language and a muted demeanor, came out to greet us in the driveway. She hugged us both and led us into the kitchen. The hug she had shared with her husband had been as dry and brief as the one she'd given me.

"I've made tea." She presented a china teapot service on the table. "Aren't you boys frozen after driving with the top down?"

"Not at all," her husband said, a volume to his voice born of alcohol. "We're grown men. We can take a little nip in the air."

As she poured tea into my cup she said, "Dear, have you boys been drinking?"

Mr. Cantor looked across the table at me and laughed. "Had a Friday martini at lunch. I tried to get Paul to join me, but all he does these days is work."

"There's a lot that needs doing." I took a sip of my tea. I could taste the orange blossom honey. Mrs. Cantor knew from our Sunday brunches it was my favorite. "I really shouldn't even be here now."

"Nonsense. The TateAir merger will close next week." As Mrs. Cantor began to pour his tea, Mr. Cantor put his arm around her waist. "Let's go out to dinner tonight. What do you say?"

Mrs. Cantor stepped gracefully out of Mr. Cantor's embrace. "I think not. And besides, Enid will be here soon."

Mr. Cantor didn't touch his tea. "Can't she go with us?"

"I think she wants to talk."

"I hope not to me." Mr. Cantor winked at me in that conspiratorial way men use when trying to escape from a commitment to a woman. "Or about work, for that matter."

"I'm sure not to you, Eric."

I hoped Mrs. Cantor didn't know Enid and I had slept together, but if she didn't already, I was certain she would soon. What would Elizabeth think of me then? I've spent half my life regretting things I did, and the other half wondering why I did them. "Wait—is anything wrong?"

"If you must know, Paul, she and Seth are having a spot of —trouble."

The way Elizabeth looked at me said it all. Enid had already told her about our night together. "I'm sorry to hear that. I thought they were solid."

Elizabeth hadn't taken her eyes off me since the discussion turned to Enid's problems. Of course Mrs. Cantor, herself a victim of spousal infidelity, would see me as the villain in this little domestic drama. "It's all rather sudden. Only since last week."

Oh, boy. I could feel a new level of trouble brewing. I knew I shouldn't have slept with Enid. She wasn't a girl who could enjoy sex for the fun. No, she was going to make herself and me miserable over this, I was sure of that. Once I noticed she had stopped wearing her engagement ring, I should have realized. Jesus, why not take an ad out in the *Post* announcing we had slept together.

"Wait—what? I thought she and Seth were doing fine." Mr. Cantor, who had not touched his tea, took out a bottle of bourbon from a cupboard. Elizabeth looked on with deep disapproval. "I think I'd better have a bracer to deal with the extreme shock," sounding more mirthful than upset.

"You only say that because you don't pay attention to these things." Despite her sour face, Elizabeth produced a cut crystal glass for her husband. He proceeded to pour a generous serving of bourbon. He smiled and handed his wife the bottle for her to put away, even though he sat closer to the cabinet. As he killed the first finger and a half, she got up, dutiful, and put the liquor away. Jack Tate had nothing on his old friend Eric. Not today, anyway.

He took another good sip. "Seems like I'd have heard something about a breakup, the way everyone gossips back on K Street."

Mrs. Cantor's disapproval had turned to acceptance. "Well, I told you I didn't think Seth was right for her. He's too predictable. She needs someone more..." And here she found my eyes again. "Well. Perhaps I don't know her well enough to guess what she needs in a man."

Mr. Cantor laughed. "How about Paul here? He's about as unpredictable as they come."

It wasn't entirely clear if he was only referring to my relationships with women. My traitor's antenna was working overtime. Was he on to me? An uneasy conscience can make you betray yourself.

Elizabeth slid a plate of pralines across to me. "I can't speak for Paul. All I know is that Enid is too spirited for someone like Seth."

"You make her sound like a horse that needs to be broken."

"For heaven's sake, Eric. That might be the way you view women, but it certainly isn't mine."

Mr. Cantor laughed and I joined in, even though I didn't feel much like it. "Now, Elizabeth, please don't turn their problems into some feminist rallying cry against all men."

"Not all men. Only philanderers, liars, and the like."

She could have been referring to either of us, or both.

Suddenly I wished I hadn't let Mr. Cantor talk me into coming down to the bay. I had visited so often, from time to time the two of them forgot I was in the room and would air a bit of dirty laundry in front of me. In a way I suppose I should have been flattered, but I had enough drama of my own without sharing theirs, too.

"I think we're going to have good sailing tomorrow. I'd like to run up to Saint Michaels. What do you say, Paul?"

"I'd be up for that."

"It'll be a good workout for us."

Actually, I was a bit concerned because the water was always so rough getting out to Saint Michaels, but I was relieved that Mr. Cantor had managed to change the subject in such an adroit fashion. No way he knew about me and Manon, and I prayed he couldn't possibly suspect how I was trying to sabotage the merger.

"There it is, then. We'll shove off around nine." Mr. Cantor finished his drink. His speech had begun to slur, and it wasn't even five o'clock. "The wind is supposed to be out of the west at about fifteen to twenty knots, so, it may be a bit choppy going out. But you, you're not afraid."

"No." But on the inside? The choppy bay waters near Saint Michaels would certainly make a believable location for a less-experienced seamen, and a traitor, to end up overboard in a tragic mishap. Surely I was being paranoid. "It'll be a good learning experience, I'm sure."

He looked over at his wife and went to take another drink, forgetting he had killed the brown liquor. He set the tumbler down with a loud *clunk*. "This kid's not afraid of anything. Are you, Paul?"

"I don't know about 'anything,' but I can take some chop."

"I don't doubt you can, son."

In truth I knew potential six-to-eight foot seas would have my stomach rolling more than the Sundance itself. But Mr. Cantor was a terrific sailor. All I had to do was follow his orders and we'd be fine.

Now I wondered whether I could sail the boat back by myself. If anything were to happen to him in those cold waters on the way to St. Michael's. A hungover sailor slips and falls, hitting his head and tumbling into the water before his first mate even noticed. It sounded plausible.

I needed air. "I think I'll take a walk by the shore."

"And I think I need to get some food into my husband. Join us?"

My stomach right now felt too tight to eat. "I'll grab a snack when I get back."

"That's fine, son," Mr. Cantor said. "You go and get relaxed. We have a big day ahead tomorrow."

I brought my suitcase up to the room at the head of the stairs. I opened the windows and the room filled with the smell of the sea. I sat on the bed, changing into a pair of running shoes. Whatever tomorrow would bring, the stakes now seemed about more than money. Much more.

THE SUN HAD CREPT LOW IN THE SKY AND THE TEMPERATURE began to drop even more. Before I went downstairs, I put on a jacket over my sweater and closed the windows. I forced myself not to smoke in the room, honoring Elizabeth's house rules. She'd been betrayed enough.

The Cantors weren't in the kitchen, so I went outside and followed the gravel path past the guesthouse where Enid had stayed with Seth. The tide had gone out; the sea lay calm in anticipation of tomorrow's winds.

One Saturday back in the summer Mr. Cantor and I had anchored out in the bay to spend the night onboard the Sundance. As soon as it got dark we ate, had two bottles of good red wine between us. Even though you could hear the sea banging against the hull, straining to get in, I slept well at anchor. Out on the bay, I always felt as if I was away from the problems that seemed to plague my life on shore. Mr. Cantor felt that way too. He didn't need to say it aloud. I could see it in his eyes, his body language.

As I came up over the rise full dark had fallen. I saw head-lights coming up the driveway. It had to be Enid.

My first thought was to wait here out in the field to give her time to go inside without seeing me, but I decided against it. I wanted to see her, to be alone with her, if even for a minute. I had to admit I missed her when we were apart. I had no future with Manon. But Enid...

I raised a hand as her headlights spilled across me standing in the yard. She rolled down her window. "You startled me."

"Need help with your bag?"

"Thank you. Would you mind putting it in the guesthouse?"

"Why don't you stay with us? Plenty of room."

"I don't think that would be wise—do you?"

What was the right answer to that? Did she want me to ask her to stay at the main house, or agree that she shouldn't? I had hoped we could put this business off, at least until after the hearing on the merger. Well, this was no different than anything else in my life. Events were always crashing over me like waves, and I was always scrambling to get back to dry land. "I'll put your things away over here, then."

She pulled on over into one of the parking spots near the guest house. I took out her bags and set them inside beside the bed. I knew somehow Enid was here to make our situation impossibly complicated, or at least add another layer to a colossal train wreck in the making. It didn't take a crystal ball to see that.

When I went back outside, she stood looking beautiful despite the garish yellow from the porch light. I wanted her again. I couldn't help myself.

"You sure you don't want to stay in the big house? With me?"

Enid slapped my face, hard, and went striding off without a word. Well—that answered that.

IN THE MAIN HOUSE I FOUND ONLY ENID AND MRS. CANTOR, sipping tea in the kitchen amidst the makings of a light meal on the table of cheeses, fruit, crackers and so on. I guessed Mr. Cantor had retreated to his study. Wise.

"What happened to your face?" Mrs. Cantor put her hand to my reddened cheek.

"I bumbled into a tree. Dark outside."

Enid stirred sugar into her tea. "You don't have to lie."

I thought I was being gallant by fibbing, but you can never tell about these things. "It doesn't hurt."

"You mean, it doesn't hurt to lie?" Enid looked at Mrs. Cantor who didn't seem at all surprised by what she was hearing. "Understood."

I sat down across from Enid and rubbed my cheek as if to reinforce my claim on her sympathy. "If you insist on being honest, it hurts like hell."

Mrs. Cantor went to the sink and began to run water over a towel. "I'll get you a cold cloth. I'll put some ice in it."

"It's really nothing." My eyes found Enid's. "You could at least say you're sorry."

"But, I'm not."

"Sometimes a man deserves a good slap in the face," Mrs. Cantor said, not without a trace of sympathy. Gentle, she placed the towel against my cheek and held it there. "You'll be fine."

I took over the towel and held it against my eye. "I suppose I should have turned the other cheek?"

"If you had, I'd have slapped that one as well."

Mrs. Cantor put her hand on Enid's shoulder. "I'm sure you don't mean that."

Her bitterness came out in a torrent. "Look at him, sitting there. He's thinking, aren't these women crazy, aren't they ganging up on poor me! But, he hasn't a clue about anything. *Sometimes I'd like to slap every man I see in the face.*"

"Well, I'm glad it's not only me who excites these warm feelings of affection." My little joke fell flat before this audience.

Enid's hand shook as she raised her cup to her lips. "The

only thing special about you is that you seem to be even more clueless than most men."

Mrs. Cantor laughed and squeezed Enid's shoulder. As usual, she was able to make everyone feel at ease again. "I must say I've wanted to slap Eric any number of times. Maybe now I will."

"Enid—I'm sorry I upset you." I hadn't the slightest idea what I was apologizing for, but it was always a handy thing to do when female trouble came calling. I prayed Enid wouldn't ask for specifics so she could prove to Mrs. Cantor how oblivious I really was. "Truly."

"And, I'm sorry I slapped you." Enid spoke so softly that at first I thought I might have imagined I heard her apologize. "Sincerely."

"Now, that's better." Mrs. Cantor went to the pantry and came back with a bottle of red wine. "I think we could all do with a drink."

Enid and I nodded in agreement. "I suppose you and Eric are going sailing tomorrow?"

By changing the subject Mrs. Cantor had announced the official end of my spate with Enid, or at least its public phase. I was quite certain there would be more to come. "Yes, we're going over to Saint Michael's."

"Be careful. The wind is always strong there this time of year." Mrs. Cantor served me a generous pour. "And the current will be running against you."

"We'll be fine."

"Eric thinks he can sail into anything."

"He certainly does." I took a sip of Chateau Neuf De Pape, Mr. Cantor's favorite. One thing you could say about my boss, he had excellent taste—in women, wine, and sailboats. "But now he has another experienced seaman at his side."

"That's why I stopped sailing with him—because I thought

he was reckless. But I suppose the danger's the same reason you enjoy it." Mrs. Cantor took a long sip of wine and turned to Enid. "Why are men like that?"

"Like what?" The minute those words were out of my mouth I knew they were an invitation for the two of them to unload all that they disliked about men in general, and me and Mr. Cantor in particular. I tried to think of something to change the subject, but before I could speak, Enid added her bit to the conversation.

"Because they're never happy with what they have, that's why." Enid's tone left no doubt that her judgment on men was final and there would be no appeal. I suddenly felt like the accused in a criminal trial where I was being tried for the sins of all men everywhere. If these two were the judges, I felt little doubt as to who would be found guilty.

"When Eric first bought the Sundance he loved that boat, but now every time he goes out, I swear he's trying to sink her." Elizabeth held her glass up to the light as though the answer to her husband's strange behavior might be found in the ruby-red wine. "Paul, do you realize you're the only person willing to sail with him anymore?"

I said that wasn't true; that I was only teacher's pet for this season. "There'll be another Paul at his side one day."

She took a sip of her wine and I could see she was thinking whatever was wrong with him was wrong with me as well. "I remember when his recklessness used to scare you."

"I've learned to trust his skills. And my own." Of course that was the wrong thing to say. It implied criticism of Elizabeth for not trusting her husband. We certainly weren't just talking about seamanship any more. "But I understand why his style of sailing might not appeal to everyone."

"Sometimes I think the two of you are simply showing off for each other. The weather tomorrow is too dangerous to sail to Saint Michaels, any fool knows that, but neither of you are willing to admit to the other that you're nervous about it." Mrs. Cantor sounded dismayed at our stupidity, yet couldn't help admiring our stubbornness. "You'd risk your lives before you'd back down."

"Men." Enid leaned forward on the kitchen table and looked straight at me. "Sometimes I suspect you fellows enjoy each other's company more than being with us."

"Women also enjoy each other's company. It's not a conspiracy." I offered this observation knowing it wouldn't be received in the manner intended.

"What does that prove?" Enid pulled back from me as if the stupidity of my answer had so repelled her she had to retreat back into her chair.

"I was only saying that everyone needs relationships like the one I have with Eric. It's called friendship."

"Do you know why men and women can never really be friends?"

During an interim of uncomfortable silence I thought of a million reasons why men and women could never be friends, but I wasn't about to offer any of those. I tried to think of a more innocuous remark to regain a lighter mood. "Because we see the world differently?"

"No." Enid seemed almost pleased that I had answered incorrectly. "I'll tell you why. It's because of sex."

I began to wonder just how much Enid herself had had to drink. Surely we weren't going to discuss sex, not in front of Elizabeth?

Apparently I had misjudged the depth of their friendship, because Enid plowed on without any hint of embarrassment. "When a man looks at a woman, any woman, he thinks about one thing—whether he can 'lay' her. Isn't that so?"

"I wouldn't say 'any' woman," I offered in correction,

feeling the need to defend all those other unjustly accused men not present.

"Don't try and turn this into a joke." Enid poured more wine into her glass. "That's only a way of trivializing what I'm saying."

"I apologize."

Enid wiped her hair away from her eyes. "Look at me and you—before we slept together we were doing fine, and now everything between us is ruined."

"I don't think everything is ruined." I offered this as cautiously as any good soldier walking across a minefield. Then I thought, my god, she's going to recite everything she imagines is ruined in front of Mrs. Cantor. Wasn't it enough that she had just blurted out we had slept together? "After all, TateAir will be fine. Don't you think?"

"Oh, all business, are we? Well, you're not the one whose whole life is in tatters."

"Now listen—we're all adults here. It was a mistake, I admit it. But, it takes two to tango. And so we should call this a draw, in my opinion."

Elizabeth chortled and killed her glass of wine. Enid put her face in her hands. "You bastard."

Before giving either one of them a chance to further roast me I pretended to have a headache from being struck, excused myself to lie down until dinner.

As I climbed the stairs to my room I could hear Mrs. Cantor and Enid talking. Enid's voice shook; she had begun crying.

I stopped at the head of the stairs to listen to what they were saying. From what little I could hear it sounded as if they were unsure who was worse, Mr. Cantor or me. Now I wondered if Elizabeth and Enid both weren't delighted at the prospect of dangerous seas for us tomorrow out on the Sundance.

⛵

UPSTAIRS, I CRACKED THE BEDROOM WINDOW SO I COULD smoke after all. I wondered if I could drop down to the ground below without breaking an ankle, disappear into the night before anyone knew I was gone. But it would be a twenty-mile hike to the closest public transportation.

Cold winter air filled the room. I sat smoking in the dark looking out over the fields to the waters of the bay now visible in the moonlight. The surface looked agitated with whitecaps; I could feel the wind picking up. Mrs. Cantor was right; it would be rough sailing to Saint Michaels tomorrow. But it was bad form for sailors to discuss the weather with anything other than a cheerful disdain. You had to learn to muzzle your fear.

I liked that about sailing. I especially enjoyed when Mr. Cantor and I left the harbor when all the other boats were clinging to the dock. I would stand in the cockpit with the wind blowing ocean spray in my face as I steered the Sundance into the bay; Mr. Cantor would let both the headsail and the main sail out and the boat would surge forward like a horse out of the starting gate. All I could hear was the wind and the waves and the lines clattering above us like monkeys in the forest canopy. With twenty knots of gusting wind, the boat would cut through the water until a wave lifted us, after which we'd heel over and surf along with water rolling over the hull into the cockpit, the wind spilling out of the sails and off we'd go again. Without speaking we seemed to egg each other on to get more out of the boat, heedless of the risks we were taking. And, of course, that is exactly what sailing should be.

My cigarette began to taste dry and sour. I stubbed it out, dressed for dinner and contemplated what sort of gut check I'd soon face, both downstairs and tomorrow on the water.

DOWNSTAIRS I FOUND EVERYONE ASSEMBLED IN THE DINING room. Enid wore a black dress I had never seen before. She looked beautiful.

I took my seat next to her without saying anything. Rather than continue our earlier conversation in front of Mr. Cantor, I felt confident propriety would prevail. Most of us were lawyers. We knew how to put on a show.

"There's my boy." Mr. Cantor, who seemed to have sobered up somewhat, offered me a carafe of red wine.

"Not too much. I want to be sharp tomorrow."

"We'll need to be."

I filled Enid's glass and then my own. She failed to thank me, or even make eye contact.

During dinner I tried to start a conversation with her, but she wasn't going to be drawn into it. Instead, I made a few mindless comments about how delicious I found the duck. Mrs. Cantor agreed, saying Armenta had prepared it, l'orange-style, to perfection.

Before I knew it, the meal was over.

Mr. Cantor looked at his watch. "I want to get another look at that weather blast from NOAA," he said, muttering about windspeed and chop. He left the dining room with a slight wobble in his step. The carafe had long been emptied, with most of it going down his own hatch. If he were anything like me, his hangover after an afternoon of liquor followed by red wine would be deadly. That I had begun to question his judgement now went without saying.

Enid, of course, decline my offer to walk her to the guest cottage. Instead I held the door for her as she stepped out into the night. I watched as her black dress disappeared into the darkness along the cinder path that led to the guesthouse. The 'wrongness' of our sordid night together had forever soured any chance with her.

⛵

WITH A STIFF, HOWLING NORTH WIND OUTSIDE MY WINDOW, sleep eluded me. Maybe I should have had more of that wine after all—I'd been drinking like a fish all week. My hands trembled, but I suspected from nerves as much as alcohol withdrawal.

When at last I checked my watch, it was only three in the morning. We wouldn't go out until nine, so unless I got to sleep I had six hours to kill. With the nerves and the acid sloshing in my stomach, I thought I'd pad quietly into the kitchen and have a glass of warm milk.

Downstairs I found a robed Elizabeth sitting at the table with a cup of tea, reading on her tablet. Rather than being startled by me, her eyes flicked up from the glowing screen and she merely smiled.

"Sorry. Didn't mean to intrude."

"You're not."

"What are you reading?'

"*Excellent Women* by Barbara Pym." Mrs. Cantor touched and swiped on the screen to show me the cover. "Heard of it?"

I shook my head. "Not much time for casual reading."

"I wouldn't expect that you had." Mrs. Cantor went to the

counter and brought another cup to the table. "Have a cup. It's chamomile. Won't keep you awake."

"Too late for that anyway."

"Nervous?"

I sat down at the small round table, but wished I had stayed in bed. It was clear she was disappointed in me for the way I had treated Enid. "Something along those lines."

The kettle must have still been hot; it whistled almost as soon as she lit the blue gas flame beneath it. My boss's wife handed me the steaming china cup along with a container of honey and a spoon, which I declined.

"By the way—you might as well plan to sleep in."

"Weather not clearing up?"

"Either way, Eric isn't going sailing."

"You sure about that?"

She stared, gauging my reaction. "He's taking me into town instead. I want new pillows for the new couch in the living room."

"Color me surprised."

"He'll be far too hungover to sail anyway. You must surely have known that already."

I felt relief. Now neither of us would end up drowning in frigid water. "And here I thought he put the Sundance above everything."

"When my husband has crossed a line, I let him know. And the decisions he's been making lately, they seem reckless."

"I'm not sure I disagree. I'm just not in the same position to tell him as you."

She smiled. "That's right. You aren't. You have to work around him—don't you?"

"Sometimes that's the only way."

While all that could have been about TateAir, in no way was Elizabeth Cantor talking about Eric's penchant for dangerous sailing. In a flash, I now knew she had seen the note he had written to Manon.

How did I know? Because after I'd taken it from Manon's dresser, I decided to leave it in her guest room on our last visit here. Planted evidence, in this case merely relocated rather than fabricated out of whole cloth, can really make a case. Actually, sometimes it's the best evidence possible. That's what my career in jurisprudence had thus far taught me, among other juicy, if troubling, tidbits about how the legal world really works.

All this was mere strategy: always divert the enemy's attention from your real attack. While I worked to undo the TateAir merger, now Mr. Cantor had his grubby hands full on the home front regarding the girlfriend situation. It wasn't checkmate, not in this complicated scenario, only a skirmish in the longer battle ahead.

But, what difference would this revelation make? I knew from Manon he had made big talk about planning to dump Elizabeth, soon as he could. All I'd done was take the liberty of speeding up the process. In life, timing is everything. Besides, Elizabeth, a woman of the means and of the world, must surely have already suspected.

But here, she seemed calm and cool, untroubled by the rough marital seas ahead. "You know Eric thinks the world of you. He wants you to believe he can do anything, I guess, so you'll be in a position of confidence about your own future. But, he's fifty-six years old, he's drinking too much, and it's time to live a little further away from the edge."

"Before he sails off it?" I pondered aloud.

"It's not only him who likes dancing along the edge of disaster," she said.

I felt a chill. We were no longer talking about sailing or Manon.

"I understand that better than most."

"If you don't, you'll soon have to learn where that line is for yourself." She poured herself more tea. "Did he tell you he's putting the boat up for sale? After the TateAir business is done, he and I are going to Europe to look for a house in Spain. I've always wanted to live there."

I thought of the sailboat catalog, the Sundance II he planned to order. "That's rather sudden, isn't it?"

"I've wanted to live in Spain for years."

"I meant on the part of your husband."

"Eric agreeing to it? Yes, that's rather sudden. You see, this house is mine, and so is our townhouse in the city."

"I had no idea."

"Didn't you know my father started Cantor and Miller? Only then it was 'The Gottfried Firm.'"

He married into it, I thought. Eric Cantor had built nothing. He was nothing better than one of those legacy frat-boy types with a fat trust fund. I suddenly felt only revulsion for him.

"I hold the lease on the firm's office space, too."

I laughed, but only to myself. She held all the purse strings. As though speaking to a judge: "No wonder he's so agreeable about your trip into town."

"As well as Spain." She shook her head. "When I married Eric, my father brought him into the firm. Now, he makes a very nice living, but he spends more than he makes. So we decided last night that's he's going to downsize a bit. He's going to start taking more time off now, too."

"Living in Europe should help with that."

Mrs. Cantor smiled. "You remind me of Eric when I first met him. He was ambitious like you. And, he thought he was smarter than everyone, *and* had a chip on both shoulders like you... In a way, Paul, you make him uneasy."

"I never get that sense."

"Oh, my, yes—it's because he remembers what he was capable of when he was your age."

"Are you saying he doesn't trust me?"

"Not exactly." But her eyes said differently. "Should he not trust you?"

"My entire career is riding on the fact of his trust. So, no."

Perhaps Jack Tate was right after all. Maybe Mr. Cantor did need money badly enough to sell out his client. If the merger fell through there would be no new sailboat, no Manon, no bigger law firm, only the comfortable misery of following his rich wife around the world.

"However he came by his position," I continued, "your husband is still a tremendous lawyer."

"That's sweet of you to say. He thinks you're quite adept, and daring, as well. But perhaps too much for your own good."

"How so?"

"He says you're addicted to risk-taking. And too ambitious."

"I don't come off that way. Do I?"

"Not too much. As he put it, you often seemed only as ambitious as, say, Lucifer."

I sat mute. Every drop of blood drained from my face.

She burst into laughter. "Oh, Paul. Drink your tea." She laughed again. "It's not as though yours is an uncommon condition in a place like DC."

Why was she telling me all this? She wanted me to know that her husband had his doubts about me, but why? Maybe because she knew it was me who had left Manon's note where it would be found.

"I hope he still has faith I can bring the TateAir deal home."

"He's knows you're careful. This business with Mark Dresser has him worried, though."

"How so?"

"Because he thinks you're obsessed with showing his old classmate that you're a better lawyer than either of them. The way you showed Seth how you could beat him, an experienced player on the court, during a casual Saturday morning match."

"You make me sound like some sort of scheming, egomaniacal monster."

"Oh, no. We're both very fond of you."

"That's a relief to hear. I feel the same."

"But there's one more thing you should know." Mrs. Cantor stood and stretched, put her teacup in the sink. "Poor Manon will have to be let go on Monday."

Now the chill returned. I had a vision—not of Mr. Cantor moving pieces on a chessboard, but his wife Elizabeth. "That will come as a shock."

"No doubt. And since it would be rather awkward for Eric to tell her," Mrs. Cantor said with a tone which had become unmistakably officious, "I feel it best if the news comes from you."

"From me?"

"Since you also enjoy such a close relationship with her."

I could have seen the train coming. She had turned over all her cards, including an ace in the hole. "It's a casual friendship. Nothing more."

"Like with Enid?"

"It's nothing like that. No."

"Then I'll let Eric know you'll take care of it?"

What could I say? Elizabeth Cantor, as I had discovered, had been my true boss all along. "Consider it done."

"Good, Paul. I can't thank you enough. And as for Enid, she'll be fine. As will Seth, once they've reconciled."

"But I thought I had ruined everything."

234 | MICHAEL G SULLIVAN

Nothing is ever that simple, that straightforward, her face seemed to say. "Go get some rest. If you can."

My cup of tea deep in the nighttime had proven more valuable than I could have guessed. After calling and arranging for a taxi to take me to the train station, an expensive ride, I'd escape before anyone else got up. I'd leave Mr. Cantor a note, apologizing and explain how I simply had to get back to work, and for him to enjoy the day. I had no idea if he knew his sailing trip had been called off, but at first light Elizabeth would let him know.

Considering the power she wielded, I was glad she seemed to like me well enough. I doubted that emotion would last, though. Not if I was successful at what I was trying to pull off.

The only question left unanswered: which of the players in this drama would find themselves among the casualties of the TateAir merger, leaving a select few sitting pretty among the winners?

If I were in the former group, the merger would go forward. Mr. Cantor would almost certainly divorce Elizabeth, Manon would become the new Mrs. Cantor, and I would be sent packing for my various levels and acts of outright duplicity. If, on the other hand, I won the day and the merger derailed, Mr. Cantor couldn't afford to leave Elizabeth.

As for me? Without a job but wealthy indeed, at least by my current standards.

Meanwhile Cantor and Miller, unfortunately, would lose its biggest client. For a time they would stagger, like a drunk wobbling along until falling down in a heap, before pulling in the shingle and scattering the lawyers to the four winds. Mr. Cantor would head off to Spain with Elizabeth, but fall asleep each night dreaming of Manon. Enid and I, then, would ride off into the sunset.

No—that part didn't seem in the realm of possibility. Nor

with Manon, but then, she was far too much like me for us to have any real relationship.

After serious consideration, I chose to ignore Mrs. Cantor's request that I fire Manon. After all, she was a partner's wife, not a partner; I took my orders from her husband. Sometimes while waiting in your sailboat for a storm to blow over, it's wise to heave to and do nothing.

Poor Elizabeth. Reading her husband's note to Manon, with its colorful descriptions of their sex life, must have been excruciating. I wished there had been some other way. In DC-speak, at the end of the day it is what it is... depending on how one defines 'is,' of course.

I fretted Cantor had seen my fingerprints on everything: Jack Tate's coolness towards the deal, the note to Manon appearing, the specter of collusion and conflict of interest popping up as a bar to the merger. Perhaps I'd been naive about my maneuvering.

WHEN I SETTLED INTO MY OFFICE ON MONDAY, I FOUND OUT Marc Dresser had served TateAir with a Motion for a Temporary Restraining Order. The filing asked the court to prevent the airline from negotiating or accepting any new offer a from a buyer other than Westbrooke, until such time the court could ascertain the status of Westbrooke's contractual rights.

This move surprised me at first, since we had four days left on our stand-still agreement. But then, such an aggressive salvo seemed in keeping with Marc's bullying style. He hoped by this bold maneuver to pressure Jack into accepting the deal.

The hearing was scheduled for Friday afternoon at three.

That meant the judge expected it to be a long one, had scheduled it as the last of the day. But a TRO hearing is limited in what the court will hear, and that was exactly the break I needed. Impetuous Marc Dresser had made his first mistake.

NATURALLY ENOUGH, ONLY MOMENTS LATER MR. CANTOR appeared in my office to ask about the motion and hearing Friday.

"Quite a bomb Marc lobbed."

"I'm not entirely surprised. Think it will work with Jack?"

My boss seemed delighted Marc had pulled this little trick. "Tough cookie, a Yale man like him. Some even call him 'ruthless'."

"Sometimes you have to be, in our world."

"Understatement."

I still had no idea how I was going to respond to the motion, so it wasn't difficult for me to convince Mr. Cantor how worried I was about it. He'd call Marc and tell him he'd hit a bullseye. "But saying I expected something like this doesn't mean I know what to do about it."

He held out his hands. "Time to think about the closing rather than all this last-minute finagling—eh?"

"I suppose so."

"Don't sound so excited."

I caught myself. "Jack's chess moves haven't sat well with me. My future here rests on this working out."

"As does that of the entire firm, my boy." Fatherly, he put his hand on my shoulder. His voice came as warm as melted butter. "Like you, I'd hoped for smooth sailing here at the end."

After Mr. Cantor left I telephoned Jack to tell him about

the hearing. He asked if I thought it would be a good idea if he was to attend, but I said no.

"What's the strategy?"

"Better to discuss in person."

"Ten-four." He hung up.

I had nothing to discuss. I had just bought time. And not much at that.

THE REST OF THE DAY WENT BY IN A BLUR OF RESEARCH: HOW best to defeat a motion for a TRO. None of the cases I pored over seemed encouraging. What I needed wasn't found in the case law I had at hand; that much became clear.

Then I remembered what Mr. Cantor had said to me the first time I had met with him in his office, about how the lawyer who sees what no one else does ending up winning. Well, I would need my X-ray glasses, because I wasn't seeing anything. Not yet.

Somewhere in those thousands of pages of merger documents had to be a morsel of information I could use to beat Marc Dresser. A much bigger job in its depth of paperwork than the pile of mere case law research before me.

Discouraged, I left the office late in the afternoon. I shuffled to Farragut Square and then onto Pennsylvania Avenue; the sharp wind took my breath away. I pulled my coat close around my neck, kept going until I found myself in front of Old Ebbitt Grill.

Even though it was still early, I went inside and ordered a bourbon to take off the chill. As soon as I had finished my first round, I waved to the bartender for another. The middle-aged man brought it to me with a spring in his step; I came there often enough for him to know I was a good tipper.

The second drink calmed me down enough so I could think more clearly about the hearing Friday. No need for me to do any more legal research. I would have to think my way out of this, plain and simple. I ordered a third cocktail, but decided as soon as it was done I'd take a cab home. Getting drunk wouldn't help matters.

The driver let me off in front of my apartment. I gave him a twenty and told him to keep the change. I'd gotten used to showing off with other people's money.

After a light meal I decided to go to bed, start fresh at first light. But try as I might, I couldn't sleep. Sometime after midnight, I dressed out in sweats, called a cab and grabbed my briefcase to go back into the office.

Against the odds it was the same driver who had picked me up earlier, a young black woman now at the end of her shift instead of the beginning.

"Wait, this feels like déjà vu."

She laughed. "You must be a doctor on call, going back into work this late."

"Nothing that exciting. Lawyer."

"Oh, you said K Street. I should've figured."

"Yeah. The neighborhood's infested with us."

⚓

BURNING THE MIDNIGHT OIL—I KNEW IT WELL. I HADN'T cheated my way through law school. I had had to work hard. Many late nights. Here was another, only with higher stakes.

Enid had done a meticulous job of researching all the Westbrooke partners. We were certain they had the financial strength to close the deal. I nevertheless pulled all her information together and compared it with their filings with the FAA in support of the merger. Then, I examined every public document containing the names of any of the partners. My eyes began to cross.

I napped on the couch in the conference room until five, when I went outside to smoke and see if the coffee shop had opened yet. Around seven I got changed into a suit and shoes I'd brought. Said, well, I just won't have shaved.

Enid popped in an hour later to say an icy good morning and ask if I needed any help. I said no. It would only make her suspicious to see I was looking into the backgrounds of the Westbrooke people.

"It's nothing from your side of things."

"Oh," she said. "Really."

"Really."

But the revelation didn't come, not until I worked all through the night on Thursday as well. When it did, I had only a few hours to get certain documents together, which I managed.

Friday morning at eight, I cabbed over to the Treasury Department clutching my research to my chest and breathless in the hope this maneuver would work. I didn't finish there until noon, which left me barely enough time to go home, shower and change. For the most important hearing of my life so far, I would definitely make time to shave.

MY HEART SANK AS I ENTERED THE COURTROOM, WHERE I discovered that Judge Harold Symmons had been assigned to hear the case. As with Marcia Herring before, the judge was also rumored to be friends with Marc Dresser. Probably another Yale man. Birds of a feather, I thought, about to peck out my eyes.

The bailiff called out, "All rise" and the Honorable Judge

himself appeared. With great difficulty he climbed the steps to his chair, hauling himself up above us; with little walrus eyes he surveyed the courtroom.

"Good afternoon, Mr. Dresser. Good to see you here again."

Then he turned towards me. He looked down at the Motion Marc had filed with the court. "You are Mr. Johns, I presume." He lowered his head so he could peer over his glasses. The judge's words fairly dripped with disapproval. "Now: you have not filed a response to Mr. Dresser's motion. Is that correct?"

"We have not, your honor." I smiled.

"After having all week to do so?"

I shrugged. "I will admit it must seem counterintuitive."

"I'll grant you that much. How on earth is the court supposed to know your position?" The judge's words toppled down from the bench like boulders from a landslide. "Don't be coy or clever, son."

As I spoke, I felt myself grow calmer. "Your honor, Mr. Dresser chose to bring this matter before the court as a motion for a temporary restraining order. Because of the short notice period for such a hearing, the rules provide no requirement for a responsive pleading."

Judge Symmons face grew red as he thought about what I had just said. To him it was tantamount to contempt of court to challenge anything the bench had to say, but he contented himself with raising a suspicious eyebrow to let me know I might have pulled a fast one on him. "I've read your motion, Mr. Dresser, and it seems persuasive to the court. As usual, you're thorough in your research; you have stated the law as I understand it to be. Let's proceed, shall we?"

Nothing like telegraphing a punch I always say. The judge

wanted to establish early on that this hearing was a mere formality—he had already made up his mind.

"May it please the court, your honor, my name is Marc Dresser. I am a partner with Swerling and Thomas, and I am here today representing the Westbrooke Group."

"The court is well acquainted with you, Mr. Dresser." The Walrus smiled with warmth.

"Good afternoon, your honor. My name is Paul Johns. I am an associate with Cantor and Miller and I am here today representing TateAir." I stood to attention and waited.

"Have you appeared before me previously, Mr. Johns?"

"I have, your honor. Mostly recently in the Rest Easy Motel case."

"You argued that Rest Easy was entitled to a default judgment in that case, I believe."

"Your honor has an impressive memory." Here it came. Apparently the old amnesiac could only remember the happy days he had spent tormenting me.

"Yes. I remember I ruled against you in that case." Judge Symmons couldn't hide the pleasure recalling this episode gave him. A slight smile animated those rubbery lips. The Walrus was hinting a similar fate awaited this case. But, now he knew I would drag his ill-considered opinion to the court of appeals again, if my hand were forced.

"Let's hear your case, Mr. Dresser."

"Your honor, attached to our motion is the one hundred and twenty-seven page contract TateAir entered into with the Westbrooke Group. The court will note that contract was executed by Jack Tate on behalf of TateAir, and by Arman Kosshoggi on behalf of the Westbrooke Group. The only condition remaining is for TateAir to execute the closing documents and for Westbrooke to transfer the agreed-upon funds."

"Who prepared the contract, Mr. Dresser?" The Old Walrus lobbed a softball to Marc so the court could nearly faint with surprise at the duplicity of TateAir.

Marc tried to sound incredulous, but it wasn't really in his emotional register. "As we make clear in our motion, your honor, Mr. Paul's firm drafted the very contract they are now attempting to disavow."

The judge's beady eyes widened with alarm at the thought of such mendacity being practiced right here in courtroom 4C. "Is this *true*, Mr. Johns?"

"Quite so, your honor." I didn't offer anything more by way of explanation. I felt certain Judge Symmons would enjoy dragging the story out of me. And besides, it might offer me a chance to slip another banana peel under the old bastard.

The judge could barely speak. His mind reeled from this perfidy that stank in the nostrils of justice. "Mr. Johns, these allegations would require me to report you to the bar for raising frivolous defenses to this motion."

"The Treasury Department doesn't find them frivolous," I deadpanned as I opened my briefcase, "as these affidavits I obtained only hours earlier now demonstrate."

"Affidavits?" Dresser leapt, best he could, to his huge feet encased in fine leather. The soles of his shoes squeaked under his weight. "Your honor, this case has nothing to do with the Treasury Department, and the court is rightfully outraged at the duplicity of counsel. This is a straightforward contract case. Westbrooke has the right to buy TateAir and is prepared to do so. Jack Tate has, without cause or justification, however, sent us a letter saying here at the last minute that he'll refuse to sell."

"Mr. Johns, I must warn you that if you attempt to introduce evidence into this hearing that the court deems irrelevant, and whose only purpose is to obfuscate the issues to delay the purchase of TateAir, I will hold you in contempt of court."

Contempt. The court was really pulling out the big guns now. I guessed it was time to lay my cards on the table, even though I would have enjoyed dragging this charade out longer.

"Your honor, I now hand the court and to opposing counsel copies of an affidavit obtained by me today, one signed by the Assistant Undersecretary of the Treasury, Ms. Roberta Tyler. Now, in this affidavit Ms. Tyler recites that after she reviewed all relevant documents in this case, she finds that the proposed merger between TateAir and Westbrooke violates the included and enumerated Treasury regulations cited therein."

I stood waiting as they scanned the document for either Marc or the Walrus to bellow with rage. I didn't have long to wait.

"Your honor," Dresser all but shrieked with indignation, "this is outrageous." He pounded his meaty fist on the table. The pencils on it danced into the air. "It's just a shabby trick perpetrated by counsel to delay the execution of the contract."

"I agree with you completely, Mr. Dresser." Nothing stimulated the Walrus like an opportunity to display righteous indignation, especially if it was in an attempt to save a case for one of his pals. "Mr. Johns, the court has warned you it will not tolerate any attempt to delay this merger that is found to be without merit."

"I'm not trying to delay it. I'm acting on behalf of our client, who has expressed reasonable concerns about the sale of his family business—his life's work."

At this, the judge's body seemed to vibrate with anger under that tent-like robe. But instead of speaking, he stared at the affidavit.

Not to be outdone, Marc Dresser, also shaking with indignation, stood once again. A bright red patch appeared on his neck and spread into his ample cheeks.

"Your honor, I ask that the court not consider this affidavit because it was not shown to us before this hearing, and because it holds no relevance to the matter before the court." Marc gripped the table in front of him with those immense hands and I felt certain he was about to rip it in half. "Lastly, in prior conversations with Mr. Cantor, I was led to believe that TateAir would withdraw its objections to the merger at this hearing. I believe Mr. Johns is not accurately representing the views of his client here today."

All that was more than enough for Judge Simmons. "I have known Eric Cantor for thirty years, and if he told you that I'm sure it's true. What do you say to respond to counsel's allegations, Mr. Johns?" The Walrus whispered something to his law clerk, who dashed out of the courtroom. Perhaps he had gone to find an axe to cut off my head. I assumed this little theatrical sidebar was solely for my benefit.

"First, your honor, opposing counsel has no standing to raise any issue with this court regarding the quality of my representation. That is a matter that rests solely with my clients. Second, I am counsel of record in this matter for our client TateAir, not Mr. Cantor, so, anything he may or may not have said to Mr. Dresser cannot be considered by this court. Lastly, since the Treasury Department asserts jurisdiction over this matter, this court is hence now precluded from exercising its typical authority over Mr. Dresser's motion."

I stood waiting for the storm that was sure to follow. No judge likes a lawyer to tell him he has no authority over a case that is before him, and no judge resented that more than the Walrus. I watched as foam collected at the edges of his mouth.

He seemed to grind my words between his teeth like so many indigestible pebbles:

"It is true that questions about counsel's representation of a client are normally reserved for resolution by the client, but in this case where there are allegations of actual fraud, I think Mr. Dresser is well within his rights to raise this very troubling issue."

Marc looked me over with a raw contempt which would have been more convincing had it not been for the fact that, like me, he was being paid to put on this show. Rented outrage is always less moving than genuine emotional pain, even when the performance is given by an actor as skilled as Marc Dresser. "Your honor, these proceedings, along with the very integrity of the court, are jeopardized by Mr. John's conduct today in this courtroom."

I'd heard enough. "Your honor, if Mr. Dresser were correct, opposing counsel would have the power to determine the suitability of my representation of my client. That would lead inevitably to lawyers, certainly not Mr. Dresser, but *some* lawyers, seemingly in the act of trying to stifle vigorous representation."

Reluctantly, the Walrus agreed I might have a point. Pained at granting me a victory, his bulk sagged back into his chair to now hear rebuttal. "Your response, Mr. Dresser?"

"Mr. Johns claims this court is without jurisdiction in this matter not because it is precluded from hearing it by virtue of preemption, but because he knows his position is without merit and therefore the court will grant our motion." Marc scribbled on his pad and waited with evident anticipation for the Walrus to pin my ears back. "Simple as that."

"The court agrees with Mr. Dresser. The fact that the Treasury Department has voiced an opinion in this matter does not preclude this court from exercising its authority, especially when, as Mr. Dresser says, your position appears to be frivolous." The judge leaned forward, back in the game now, doing all he could to salvage Marc's case. "Treasury is entitled to their opinion; I am entitled to mine."

With that bit of wisdom the judge looked down at me and smiled with contentment. At last, he had me boxed in and it was time for him to announce he would grant Marc's motion for a TRO.

My seven million dollars seemed beyond my grasp. I thought of how the lawyers at the firm would laugh behind my back, and how delighted Mr. Cantor would be to send me packing. After all, now that I had brought the Treasury Department into this, I had revealed whose side I was really on. No turning back now.

"Your honor, at this time I must direct the court's attention to the second page of the affidavit, wherein the Assistant Undersecretary declares this merger involves matters touching on our government's relationship with foreign governments, and those are exclusively the province of the executive branch. Treasury, meaning the Federal government itself, is prepared to join me in appealing any decision by this court that in any way aids the Westbrooke takeover of an American company."

The Walrus wouldn't mind ruling against me, but having Treasury join me in an appeal raised the stakes for him. Now he had to consider just how important it was to risk being embarrassed by the court of appeals yet again, this time with much higher stakes, including likely press coverage. Like all bullies, the Walrus was at heart a coward. I felt certain he was about to fold, not gracefully of course, but fold all the same.

Mr. Dresser sensed that his old pal might be getting ready to toss in the towel as well. He struggled back to his feet, waving with a frantic hand as though trying to hail a cab.

"Your honor, even if Mr. Johns is correct, the court can surely enjoin TateAir from selling to another buyer until we have a hearing on the merits of our contract claim." Desperation now crept in Marc's voice. The earlier arrogance was gone as he watched his case fall apart and the judge draw back from him. "Treasury objects to the participation of Mr. Kasshoggi because he is an Iranian national. We ask only that TateAir be prevented from selling while Westbrooke locates a partner to replace Mr. Kassogghi."

At last the Walrus had found a way to snatch my victory away. He and Marc exchanged the smiles of men who had just escaped being hanged. "That seems entirely reasonable, Mr. Dresser."

"Your honor, Mr. Dresser's suggestion would be reasonable if it were not for paragraph two-hundred-nineteen of the contract which Mr. Dresser attached to his motion. That paragraph states, and I am here quoting from memory so the court may wish to refer to the contract itself, that if any portion of this contract is found to be in violation of applicable federal or state laws or regulations, then this contract shall be declared void. As such, I have taken the liberty of preparing an order for the court's signature declaring the Westbrooke contract null and void for breach of this paragraph."

I handed a copy of the order to Marc and the original up to the court. The Walrus took it from me as if it were a soiled diaper. At least all those hours spent parsing the contract language had finally paid off.

Watching as Marc and the judge scrambled to read paragraph two hundred nineteen, I sat to enjoy seeing their heads droop once it became clear to them I had moved into checkmate. The law was the law, and we were its arbiters... were we not?

Judge Symmons raised his head. He looked like he'd been served a rotten egg for breakfast, but had no choice but to dig in. "Have you anything further to add, Mr. Dresser?"

"This is a court of equity, and Mr. Johns comes into this courtroom with unclean hands. It was his firm that negotiated the contract, it was his firm that drafted it, and it was he who got FAA approval for the merger. Now he comes here and tells this court that very contract is void for facts that were *known* to TateAir from the very beginning."

The Walrus looked surprisingly interested in these new allegations. He even took off his reading glasses so he could get a clearer look at the miscreant who was behind all this wrongdoing. I returned his accusing stare with a beatific smile. And why not? I had the two of them on the ropes, and they knew it.

"I find Mr. Dresser's assessment of the facts about you and your firm's action in this case to be not only accurate, but deeply troubling."

The judge's law clerk reappeared and whispered to the Walrus, something the judge found unpleasant because I heard him say, "Are you certain?" The clerk nodded that he was. I guessed it was about whether the judge had any grounds to find me in contempt.

Judge Symmons shooed his clerk away with a flick of his hand. "I am reluctant to sign your order, Mr. Johns, for the very reasons raised by Mr. Dresser. It is your own conduct that gives the court pause."

"Your Honor, I must point out that Mr. Kasshoggi did not reveal his role in the Iranian parliament in his FAA filings. That willful omission is, in itself, a violation of federal law. Surely this court does not want to be put in the position of aiding an agent of a foreign government sworn to the destruction of the United States and Israel. The media could easily misconstrue the purpose of such an order, as would the court of appeals."

There, all out on the table now. Even a half-blind old beast like Symmons could see where this was going if he granted Westbrooke's motion. Judges read the papers and watch cable news like most people, and as such prefer to avoid being criticized by them. I felt confident now the Walrus would find his inner cowardice sufficient cause to sign my order.

Marc Dresser was about to speak, but the judge raised his hand for silence. "After hearing arguments from both parties, the court finds the contract presented by Westbrooke to be null and void for violation of paragraph two-hundred-nineteen." The judge reached for his pen and signed my order with the briefest hint of a signature.

"But, your honor—!" My opponent looked terrified. He wasn't used to losing.

Symmons replied by raising himself up with some effort to exit to his chamber. "The law is quite clear on this. The matter is settled, for now. Court is adjourned."

I LIKE TO THINK OF MYSELF AS BEING MAGNANIMOUS, especially in difficult cases, so once the judge departed I went over to opposing counsel with my hand extended.

"Sorry, but the law is the law."

Dresser refused to shake my hand. "You have no idea what you did here today. You didn't beat me—you beat yourself. And your entire firm."

"I don't like to rub it in, but this order makes it look like the opposite has happened." Ungracious to a fault, I waved the order in his face.

"You hurt your firm with this stunt in ways you can't even

imagine, and as Eric hears what you pulled here today, you'll be fired, if not investigated." Marc slammed his briefcase shut with astonishing vigor. "I promise you that."

"And I suppose he'll be hearing it from you." The irony of this was lost on Marc.

"You bet your ass he will."

"Instead of spending your time trying to get me fired, you might suggest to Westbrooke that they make another offer to TateAir… one in which they don't use inside information to make a lowball offer."

That seemed to unnerve Marc and his whole body shuddered as he pointed a meaty finger at me. "You have no idea what you're talking about, but as I warned you earlier, now you've just bought a defamation suit for yourself and Jack Tate."

"No, I think you mean I don't have any evidence yet, and that's true enough—for now. But I do have the idea, Marc, that it'd be best for you and everyone else if I don't have to start looking a variety of effective ways of proving it."

Marc balled up his fist. I thought for a few seconds he might punch me in the face. And why not, hadn't I just stolen what he surely imagined was an easy win? Instead he stuck his finger in my chest and leaned so close to me I could feel his breath on my face. His lunch had included garlic. "I told Eric when he hired you that he was making a mistake."

I looked at my watch. It was four-fifteen. The hearing had taken only a little over an hour. That's the way things happen —you go along, every day seems the same and then, out of nowhere, it all changes.

I sent Jack Tate a text message. *We won. Westbrooke contract is void.*

It only took seconds to receive his reply. *Knew you would. Ready to sell the company. New offer came in today.*

He named a major airline. Sure enough, I checked the financial news and found it already reporting about the possible new merger. Now the deal would become the billion-dollar windfall of Jack's dreams. Good for him.

I sat in the back of the empty courtroom and thought about Jack. He really was fearless.

My telephone buzzed again. It was him. "Oh, by the way— congratulations. Check your bank account. You'll have a pending wire transfer."

I logged in to the app. The pending balance showed $7,000,423.18. The four-hundred twenty-three dollars and eighteen cents was what I had managed to save over the last two years that I had been with Cantor and Miller.

I laughed to myself. I read the court order once again and then tucked it carefully into my briefcase. It was the briefcase I had bought one day when I was out with Mr. Cantor, over a year ago. I remember being frightened and delighted at the same time by the way he spent money without any concern for how he would pay for things. How I had mistaken his recklessness for courage!

As I got up to leave, the bailiff followed me to the door.

"I see a lot of lawyers in here."

"I'm sure you do."

"Just wanted to say I never saw Judge Symmons fold as fast as that before."

"Thank you."

"You must know your stuff."

We shook hands before he closed the doors behind me. "Sometimes I get lucky. That's all."

I THOUGHT ABOUT GOING BACK TO THE OFFICE TO FACE THE music, but then again, what music?

Then I remembered how the firm had taken the option on the building on Pennsylvania Avenue. I knew if I bought the rights to the option money before word got out about the hearing, I could turn my windfall into quite a bit more.

I called the building's owners and offered them five million for the rights to the option money, if the sale fell through. They immediately agreed. After all, if Mr. Cantor went forward with the purchase, the option money would be rolled into the sale price, and I would have bought the rights to nothing. The option money only had value if Mr. Cantor didn't go forward with buying the building, and only I knew he wouldn't be able to complete the deal. Not unless Mrs. Cantor gave him the funds, and that now seemed unlikely.

All the pool balls were starting to drop now; only the magic eight remained. Either way I'd still have two million. Enough to get by, for a time.

I needed a drink, so I caught a cab to Old Ebbitt Grill. I nursed a few; now was not the time to get drunk. Around nine I looked at my watch and knew everyone would have left the office, so now it would be easier to go ahead and clean out my desk.

15

I got to the building just as the cleaning crew was finishing up in the reception area. It's always slightly unsettling in an office after everyone has gone home. It resembles nothing so much as an air-conditioned ghost town, with echoes of your own footsteps following you down each empty corridor. It was so silent even the ghost of Ben Schiller seemed to have left the building.

I was almost to my office when I noticed Mr. Cantor's light still on. I thought about turning around and going home, but he was here waiting for me. I'd ignored numerous calls and texts, but no point in putting it off any longer.

When I stepped into his office, Mr. Cantor looked up without speaking. I sat on the couch, lit an impudent cigarette and waited. But he just stared at me as if he was mulling over what was left to say.

At last: "I thought you might come back right after the hearing. I think you know we all wanted to find out what happened." Mr. Cantor's tone was quiet, almost hurt, as though he minded my bad manners almost as much as my treachery.

I fanned away the plume of blue smoke that lingered in the

air between us. The liquor had added insolence to my tone, but it was bravado I didn't really feel. "I thought Marc Dresser would fill you in. Don't conspirators usually gather after their plot fails?"

"Do you realize what you've done to me?"

"I was zealous in representing our client. Isn't that what a lawyer does?"

Sadness came over his face in a wave. For a moment I wished we could go back to the beginning and start over. I'm not a monster, after all. Perhaps if I had known my own father, I might have held more sympathy. It was what it was.

"Well, 'our' client has fired us. I assume you engineered that as well."

"I engineered nothing other than representing TateAir to the best of my abilities. Anything less would have been unacceptable."

He made a note on his ever-present legal pad. "You've destroyed this firm."

"I'm sorry."

"I assume you'll be well taken care of by Jack, though, won't you? Like I once was?"

I felt nothing. The money was the money. I just needed to get through this little scene, start thinking about my next move. I could go anywhere, even if the building option gambit failed. Two million would be sufficient. "I'm sorry to hear of further consequences. But, if Jack Tate was truly your friend, I don't see how you could have sought to undermine him as you did, sir."

Of course, it was me who'd insisted Jack notify the firm that they would no longer represent TateAir. The loss of their largest client would violate the firm's loan covenants with the bank financing the purchase of the new building, and now they would back out of their loan commitment. Eric would be forced to notify the building's owners that he was forfeiting his option money. And by Monday, my stash would become grow to twelve million.

I ached to tell Eric I had bought the right to his option money so he could see how clever I really was; how like him I'd turned out in every way. I thought he might admire what I had done. But we'd let that ride for now. No need to pile on.

I put out my cigarette in one of the glasses he used to serve drinks to clients. I had been the magician's apprentice, after all, and I knew all his tricks. He'd been able to keep us suspended in the air, levitating on invisible wires of hubris and conspiracy, but now I was the man behind the curtain pulling the strings. His act was finished, like vaudeville being ushered off into the dustbin of history by the advent of the movies.

"Johns, you've made a big mistake."

Eric hadn't called me by my last name since we had first met over a year ago. In a way, I was disappointed—we'd never go sailing again. "I don't believe that's the case, Eric. Nor will you."

My calling him by his first name for the first time made him wince. "You're a smart boy, I'll give you that. I wasn't wrong about that part. But maybe too much for your own good."

"I take that as a compliment." I looked around the room for the bottle of aged bourbon he always kept handy. "Mind if I help myself to a drink?" Without waiting for an answer, I poured myself a generous helping of bourbon. It was brown and welcoming in my glass, like molasses on a pancake. I raised my tumbler in a silent toast to myself and took a sip.

"You understand that Judge Symmons is thinking of filling

a grievance against you with bar counsel, and Marc is preparing an appeal. Don't you?"

There it was at last, the empty threat. It all seemed so beneath Eric, like the barking of a toothless dog. "And what would the basis for any of that be?"

"The mistake you made was in thinking Jack was your client. He's not. Our firm was retained by TateAir, not Jack Tate personally. While you gave him a great victory today, you did nothing for the shareholders of TateAir."

Eric sat back in his chair and gave me a moment to digest all this, but I didn't whip Marc Dresser in court only to lie down now.

"There isn't going to be any appeal, and Judge Symmons isn't going to file any grievance. You see, the merger was void the minute your friend Kassshoggi lied on his FAA disclosure."

"You found a crumb, like a lucky dog."

"But an important one. You have to admit it was damn clever getting the Treasury Department to object to the merger."

Eric couldn't help himself from doling out this bit of reluctant praise to his Frankenstein. "Yes. I have to give you that. That you found something Marc never saw coming is impressive, if it weren't so venal and destructive to us all."

It wasn't enough that I had won; I wanted Eric to admire how I had hoodwinked him. I wanted him to see how cleverly it had been planned, how exquisitely executed, but also how without malice it had all been. Couldn't he see my behavior was a tribute to him, in a way?

"And you, sir, aren't going to let Marc appeal anything, because then the court would learn it was you who conspired with Westbrooke on making the lowest possible offer the TateAir board would accept, while also fooling your 'friend' and client into believing he'd never find another buyer."

His cool began to fracture. His voice shook. *"You'll never be able to prove it."*

"I won't have to. I assume Westbrooke was going to express their gratitude to you once the merger went through by having the new, bigger airline retain you as their lead counsel. That's why you needed a new office to house all those young lawyers you were about to hire." I couldn't stop myself from laying it all out in the open for Eric to see how completely I had bested him. "A whole army of us."

Mr. Cantor's tone was the only thing that gave even a hint of how agitated he was. I was impressed by how deliberate he seemed, but I knew him well enough to know better. I had mimicked that style myself many times: so often in fact that it was becoming increasingly difficult for me to tell where I began and Eric ended. "What are you getting at, Johns?"

"I think you know the answer to that." I lit another cigarette and nearly burned myself with the gold lighter I'd bought after I left court this afternoon. I wanted a little keep-sake to remind me of the day. I tried to adjust the flame, but my hand was too unsteady. I set the lighter down on Eric's desk. "You see, it was Manon who told me everything."

That little arrow hit home. "So it *was* you who left that letter for my wife to find. You bastard."

That letter had merely been a feint to draw his attention away from my real attack. Surely he had to realize that by now? "A key piece of evidence fell into my hands. I used it. What would you have done?"

His fury boiled over. I'd never heard him raise his voice, except in triumph out on the bay. "We took you into our home. We sailed together. You had a career here—friends, a future. *We all depended on you.*"

Was it possible he didn't understand what I had done, the artistry of it? For God's sake, this wasn't some damn street mugging. Even he had to see the imagination, the creativity which had gone into what I'd done. "Maybe you shouldn't have told Manon you were going to fire me after the merger went through."

"For Christ's sake, you were sleeping with my—my—" He couldn't find a word to describe his relationship with Manon. "Don't you understand that we were in love?"

"When I planted Manon's letter at your house, when I persuaded Jack Tate that you were double-crossing him, when I brought Treasury in to oppose the merger, I felt certain I would fail because I expected you to recognize your own style. I'm disappointed you didn't realize what was happening under your own nose."

"You're exactly what Marc Dresser said you were—a conniving thief." He stopped himself from surrendering further to his anger. He had once told me all emotion is vulgar, and until now he had acted as if he really believed that.

"One who pulled the wool over your eyes, Mr. Cantor. You, and everyone."

I blew smoke into the air and smiled at Eric's simmering anger. I'm sure he was wondering who this person sitting across the room from him was. Wasn't I supposed to be groveling for my job by now, begging him not to ruin my reputation? That was twelve million dollars ago. Another dream; a separate reality.

Cantor's fury seemed to leach out of him, his body collapsing back into his chair. He had become as resigned to our contentious denouement as I was. We were two boxers exhausted from punching each other for twelve rounds.

He said this as though he knew we would both regret that news. "I'm selling the Sundance."

It was time for us to total up our damages and pay the bill. "Elizabeth told me. I say you should sail it to Spain."

"What—are you sleeping with my wife as well?" He lit a cigarette and looked out the window at the city. A heavy cloud cover reflected back the artificial orange glow of thousands of streetlights. It was almost as if he was talking to himself now. "Would it surprise me if you were? No."

"I'm not that craven."

"Could have fooled me." He managed a sad chuckle. "Believe it or not, Paul, I'll miss sailing with you."

"I will as well."

"Damn shame."

I wasn't lying; I would miss the weekends at the bay, Mrs. Cantor's kindness and their beautiful house overlooking the ocean, the soft shell crabs and fresh corn and my room that looked out over the guest cottage to the water shimmering with light, beckoning us to take to the waves in our sailboat. Then I remembered I'd left some clothes in the guest room. Perhaps now that I wasn't coming back again, Mrs. Cantor would send them to me. Or perhaps best that I leave them. I didn't play to see either of them again.

There wasn't much more to say. I killed my drink and we both stood. My former boss and mentor said, "You won't believe me, but in a way I feel sorry for you."

"We'll both be fine."

"One question, Paul. Why? For god's sake, why?"

I shrugged. "It's K Street, boss."

"So—for money."

"Like I said."

We didn't shake hands. Neither of us much cared for hypocrisy. "It's not finished," he said, but it felt more like a plea than a statement of purpose. "You'll reap the whirlwind from this perfidy, my boy."

"And when that happens, I'll just tack against the wind until I find a friendlier current."

As I walked out of his office I could feel hateful eyes staring at my back. Who could have imagined when we were out on the water together that this is the way we'd end our friendship, cluttered as had become. As sailors always say, though, the minute you come into sight of land, that's when the trouble starts.

⛵

IT WOULDN'T TAKE LONG TO CLEAN OUT MY DESK. I HADN'T stored anything too personal in its drawers.

When I got to my office, I found a note from Enid. I eased down into the chair. I opened it to see her large, perfect handwriting.

> *Dear Paul:*
>
> *I waited for you to return from court this afternoon. But when I heard what happened, I guessed you weren't going to come back anytime soon.*
>
> *I can't say if I was ever in love with you, but you did make me realize how much I have with Seth. For that, I'm grateful.*
>
> *By the way, I've given Mr. Cantor my notice. Seth and I want to start a family as soon as possible, as far away from K Street as we can get. I suggest you do the same, while you have a shred of soul left in you. But then again, it might be too late for that. I hope not.*
>
> *Enid*

I folded the blue sheet of linen stationery in half and put it back into its envelope. Rather than put it into the cardboard box along with my scant other personal items, instead I shoved it into the middle drawer to leave behind.

⛵

WHEN I GOT BACK HOME, THE APARTMENT WAS QUIET. Bismarck had been in the house so long he almost ran me over to get outside. I found a pile of dry dog turds in a corner; I left it to clean later.

After walking the dog I wrote a check to Brenda for a quarter-million dollars, made out in her maiden name, as instructed by Arthur. All debts now paid. If she needed more to start over, I now had it to give.

I was exhausted, but couldn't sleep. I switched on the television, watched a stream of late night fare in a stupor on the couch. Before finally dozing off around three, I had gone online to shop for sailboats. Maybe Eric would sell me the Sundance. He'd need money soon enough, I suspected.

⛵

RISING THE NEXT MORNING AT A PERFECTLY CIVILIZED ELEVEN, on a bright and cheerful Saturday that saw the clouds having burned off, I took my truest life companion for a much longer walk. The world had never looked so dewy and new, the light here in the city never so bright.

We stopped at a sidewalk cafe for me to sip a beer, what I explained to Bismarck that they call 'hair of the dog.' I enjoyed the bright morning sunshine. The day had started chilly, so sitting in the sun felt wonderful.

I thought about what I'd buy: a new Mercedes, perhaps a Bently like the one Jack Tate drove. A house in Mecklenburg on a big horse farm. I'd get a sweet property on the bay, too, with views like I'd enjoyed at the Cantors. Go there on weekends, invite all the friends and colleagues I'll now have as a wealthy man.

But, if the idea of spending the money inspires only a feeling of cold emptiness inside, what good is money?

I kept checking the balance.

It didn't seem real.

What money did? It certainly wasn't real anymore after you'd blown it all. At least it would take me time to squander this much.

Was that my goal in life—to acquire a pile of unreal money and spend it? If this is what dreams coming true felt like, I needed a new dream.

God help me, but I don't have one. If I ever did.

The excitement of yesterday in the courtroom had evaporated, leaving behind only a distilled sense of panic.

We left the bistro for me to buy a paper; I found a park bench in the sun. For the most part the news in the *Post* read as usual—corruption here, warfare there, murder all along the way, and no one ever truly being held to account for any of it. Having my emptiness and panic filled up by horror and cynicism courtesy the newspaper seemed a sucker bet.

Then an inside page item caught my eye: that the Rest Easy Motel chain had been sued again. The plaintiff this time, a woman from Anacostia, looked in her photograph as if she had had a recent black eye.

First thing Monday, I thought, *I'll call Rest Easy general counsel in Dallas, get my hands on the case file.* According to the article, the woman had retained my courtroom rival on the prior Easy Rest motel case, Marcia Herring. *Even if I can't get in on this somehow, maybe it will be good to see Marcia again.*

Not that trying cases mattered now. Not after TateAir.

And, why was I still thinking about Marcia, what with Manon now available? Wasn't Mr. Cantor's former mistress a part of this deal?

Yeah—I had suffered about a half-dozen messages from her, in fact, telling me how happy she was for me. How glad I had won. How much she loved me. How she couldn't wait to see me again…

Love? Before I had the money, she hadn't come close to using the word. But now that I was rich…

Let's face facts: Manon and I were both players, both liars, both out for ourselves. It would be fine, if I chose to run with her for another season or two. But I'd never be able to trust her. And when the money ran out, so would she.

But with Marcia I would be back in court, where all is theater and the law is a sideshow. Where I could work more of the rhetorical and procedural magic I had learned. To be honest, the thrill of being on the edge of defeat before the scales of justice has been the only time in my life I've felt truly alive—well, there, and a few times sailing with Mr. Cantor out on the bay.

But as I said, the courtroom was theatre, as had been my entire relationship with everyone in my life for that last few years—Ben, Pam, Eric, Elizabeth, Enid, and Manon; as well all my opposing counsel, my alleged friends at the firm.

What about reality?

I toyed with the idea of going in a new direction: performing a more true version of myself for everyone to see. Whichever 'self' that really is.

I tucked Marcia under my arm—I mean, the newspaper—and went back home to start packing up the apartment. I didn't know where we were moving, but I felt it wise to get out of DC, somehow. I had angered a few powerful people in all this, after all.

Bismarck looked up at me, his face and eyes eager and seemingly affectionate. I could trust my dog, maybe the only other creature in the world I could say that about. I scratched him behind his ears, checked the bank balance again, and started imagining on which performance stage this freshly undefined self of mine would next appear.

AFTERWORD

From late summer 2014, following the author's tragic motorcycle accident:

Thirty-seven days ago, right about now, Mike saddled up, headed for the grid with Dave Pisak, Dave Semian, Steve Kidd, Jim Ray, Johny Waters and Brian. It was a short lap, and just the first of a very long session. He's still in that session, and has had a pretty good week.

As his life is now measured, it's filled with concern over fluctuations in heart rate and blood pressure, maintenance of oxygen saturation levels, independent breaths a minute, ability to withstand a thirty degree angle on the tilt table, indications of sensitivity or movement in his arms, pain and the nature and location of it, restlessness, sleeplessness, and so on.

There's not much excitement in Mike's world as far as I can tell, but he manages to give those of us around him those moments, and in the process both encourage and aggravate his nurses and caregivers...sounds pretty much like Mike doesn't it?

But here's how he is 888 hours after his injury: he's on the ventilator pretty much full time, and will be for the fore-

seeable future. His heart rate and blood pressure are maintained with a small-dosage of drugs, he was not able to tolerate the tilt table for the period of time we hoped, but the pneumonia is gone, and there are no other incipient infections, the amount of fluid collecting in his lungs is greatly reduced, and the general edema is lessened. He's had a tracheal device inserted that will allow him to talk, but doesn't like it because it removes the ventilator support when he uses it. He'll get over that fear.

There is talk now of a step-down room, still in critical care, but a step toward rehab nonetheless. He's quite sick of the twenty four hour news talk shows, and is even bored with the music we play for him. The guys at the track sent over a small DVD player with some horrible B movies so we'll see what that does for him! I'm assuming what he'd really like is a walk with Mollie, and you can be sure that's at the top of her list as well.

— HOSPITAL REPORT BY STEPHEN SCHAR

And from Michael's funeral comes this eulogy:

Mike Sullivan was a man, in every sense of the word. He was many things to many people. To Natt and Rani, he was a father. To the rest of us gathered here, he was a friend, a great friend. Every time we met, he didn't just greet us; he burst into our lives, suffusing them with the magic of his energy. He filled our lives with fun. Our good times were better because of his presence, and our hard times were softened by the support you knew you could count on. Every man who knew Mike well, appreciated the authenticity of his character–this was a man unafraid of the world and what-

ever it held in store. And every woman who knew him well, understood this one truth: no harm could ever come to her as long as he was around. He was a natural protector: a Marine, a policeman, and a lawyer with a strong affinity for the poor, the marginalized and the dispossessed. When I think of those roles he played, I am reminded of the first night we met, some 33 years ago. We were watching a championship heavy-weight boxing match and began swapping stories about our days as Marines, cops and our own somewhat exaggerated martial prowess, when one of the other men present just shook his head and observed ruefully,"Ex-Marines age grace-lessly". We took it as a compliment! Little did I suspect at the time the strong friendship that would evolve over the years and survive even the inevitability of death.

Mike instinctively liked people. He had a way of breaking through the barriers that too often separate us—race, gender, ethnicity and economic station. He'd walk into a restaurant for the first time and, by the time he left, every Black waitress in the place would be laughing and waving him goodbye. People loved him. He could see the humor in every situation. We all have a thousand stories illustrative of that lightening quick wit.

I remember one time he called me to say he had some legal work to attend to on the Outer Banks, and suggested I motorcycle down there to join him for dinner. We stayed at an off-season hotel and ate in its practically empty restau-rant. We ordered steaks. I have never seen less appetizing steaks. When the waiter put Mike's in front of him and turned to walk away, Mike said, "Hey, wait a minute, where are the laces? You forgot the laces."

Self-deprecating and egalitarian, he disdained the pomposity of the proud. It evoked—not his animus—but his humor, the quality most feared by the proud and most revered by the humble.

He was also, perhaps, the least politically correct man I knew. He could not care less what others expected him to say or believe. That was just part of the ferocity of his independence. As communal and sociable as we know him to have been, he was also comfortable as a loner, an entrepreneur running his own business or law firm. He was a New Yorker who moved to Columbia, South Carolina where he knew no one, to start a solo practice with no safety net beneath him. This was not a man who shunned risk; he embraced it. It gave his life vitality. We did our first track day together up at Watkins Glen, we parachuted together, we kayaked across the Puget Sound. He was born for action. And if his lifestyle seemed to some as "graceless" for a man of his age, so be it. His body may have aged, but his spirit remained ever resolute, and up for any challenge.

There was another side to Mike, softer, but equally authentic. He was kind, and not in a showy way. He had shouldered his share of life's disappointments. He felt the hurt. He could see it in others and was quick to offer help. He earned the trust of his friends who, like I, sought and highly valued, his counsel. And there was a spiritual dimension, as well. He had a tattoo on his shoulder–not USMC, not a woman's name or a drawing of some sort, but a concept– "Kannegara no Michi"–Japanese for "a soul in search of God". And the inscription was in calligraphy. This was not a tattoo for others to see and appreciate. It was there simply as a reminder of our greatest challenge and destiny. His search would be unique because he always he sought the untrod path.

Mike spurned the ostentation of wealth and its possessions. Give him a motorcycle and a roof over his head and he was happy. That's all he needed. His "wealth" was the knowledge that he was in possession of himself. The pleasure he sought was not of the fleeting and perishable kind, but a more robust and virile type that derived from self-discipline and virtue. Cicero tells us that the word "virtue" comes from "vir" or man, and denotes manliness in action. That is how Mike lived and that is how he died. In his last three months as a quadriplegic, never did I hear him complain, never any self-pity.

He told me long ago that when he returned from Vietnam, he was billeted in a transit area in California, a decompression base, I gather. As a sergeant, he was assigned command of a platoon of 40-50 returning Marines. A more senior Sergeant told him to have his unit fall out in formation at 0600 the next morning. Mike informed him that some of those men had lost legs and others were pretty banged up. The sergeant replied, "When they get back out in the civilian world, others can treat them like victims or handicapped, but as long as they are in the Marine Corps, they will be treated as Marines and they will act like Marines." Mike got it, and he remembered it these past few months. It was all about nobility of character and toughness. He could endure the fear and the suffering involved because, through years of practice, he had steeled himself to defy the misfortunes to which human lives are subject.

From the moment of his accident, his survival was a long shot. But, as Seneca tells us, "The brave and wise man should not beat a hasty retreat from life; he should make a becoming exit". Death overcomes the coward as well as the brave, but it hounds the coward and merely liberates the brave. Mike neither feared death nor did he readily surrender to it. But when the time came, he was ready to die, with the strength born of a life of valor.

In closing, I would note that it is fitting that we lay him to rest on this, the 239th birthday of the Marine Corps. This Marine is not lost to us but merely posted ahead of us. We should not let the enjoyment of our friendship pass away with him. We should endeavor rather to rejoice because we possessed his friendship, than to lament because we have lost it.

The years ahead will roll on ineluctably, like the winter waves that wash away the footprints from the sands of summer. But the years will not wash away our memory of his friendship. He faced life with intelligence and honesty; with an open mind and an open heart. By his friendship, he shored up our self-respect. He saw the good in us before we even knew it was there. If this man cherished our friendship, then we could know that hidden deep inside us there must be the moral strength that engaged his respect. And so, in the years ahead, we carry forth the memory of that friendship and we honor it by doing our best to meet the standards he set for himself: to speak honestly, to act nobly and to love grandly.

— EULOGY BY PETER CONNELL

B orn on Staten Island in 1945 but much later settling in Columbia, South Carolina, Michael George Sullivan served as a United States Marine Corps rifle platoon sergeant deployed during the Vietnam conflict, as a Vermont State Trooper, and later, an attorney specializing in commercial litigation.

Along the way he wrote or co-wrote a number of publications for the South Carolina Bar Association. An avid motorcyclist, he would further refine his authorial skills by publishing a regular column in *Motorcycle Consumer News Magazine*, reporting from racing schools in Atlanta, Virginia and Las Vegas.

After his retirement in 2012 he also produced an all-but edited novel manuscript entitled *Feint*, posthumously published in 2020 from Mind Harvest Press. Another completed manuscript discovered among his papers, *Sailing Off the Edge of the World*, is now in the reader's hands. Who knows what else Michael may have left for us? Stay tuned.

Thank you,

Michael

DON'T KILL THE MESSENGER

"Someone's coming," Candace reported, excitement threading through her voice. "But I can't see them, yet."

Roda followed them toward the door and Wang sniffed the air. "Do you smell something?"

Rieka nodded. "They're gassing the room." Knowing the effort would be all but futile, she willed Roda to hurry out the door. Seconds later, it closed behind them.

"They're here!" Candace gasped.

Rieka looked down the corridor to see a squad of six Ophs running around the corner, their weapons drawn. Pinned in the short hallway, she stepped forward beside Wang.

"Shoot, shoot!" Rieka ordered. She lifted her maitu and discharged it just as they received return fire.

Earth
Herald

JAN CLARK

A ROC BOOK

ROC
Published by the Penguin Group
Penguin Putnam Inc., 375 Hudson Street,
New York, New York 10014, U.S.A.
Penguin Books Ltd, 27 Wrights Lane,
London W8 5TZ, England
Penguin Books Australia Ltd, Ringwood,
Victoria, Australia
Penguin Books Canada Ltd, 10 Alcorn Avenue,
Toronto, Ontario, Canada M4V 3B2
Penguin Books (N.Z.) Ltd, 182–190 Wairau Road,
Auckland 10, New Zealand

Penguin Books Ltd, Registered Offices:
Harmondsworth, Middlesex, England

First published by Roc, an imprint of Dutton NAL,
a member of Penguin Putnam Inc.

First Printing, July, 1998
10 9 8 7 6 5 4 3 2 1

Copyright © Jan Clark, 1998
All rights reserved

Cover art by Donato

 REGISTERED TRADEMARK—MARCA REGISTRADA

Printed in the United States of America

The author would like to acknowledge the following individuals for their help in making this book possible. Your input and support are dearly appreciated.

In return, let me take this opportunity to remind us all that—*anything* is possible.

Many thanks to: Jim Allen, Bunnie Bessel, Jan Christensen, Alec Disharoon, Dr. Arthur Ehlmann of Texas Christian University, Chuck Gatlin, Laura Anne Gilman, Mr. Coke Kohli, Jonathan Shipley, and David Williams.

ONE

"I *hate* politics. Whatever made me think I wanted to do this?" Rieka Degahv muttered to herself. She rubbed the ache in her temples and frowned at the Commonwealth News Sheet she'd been studying on the screen.

The Bournese Herald had made a deal with her uncle to purchase 27 percent of all imported produce from Earth, beginning on Commonwealth date 135.00. In exchange for that business, Alexi had agreed to hire three Bournese excavation companies to do the prep work for the next subterranean Earth city, New SubNairobi.

It sounded simple enough. But Rieka knew there were subtleties in the agreement, even if she couldn't see them. And 27 percent was a huge amount. Some other planet, probably Aurie, would suffer the consequences of such a deal. And they were sure to resent it. But who would be criticized? The Bournese Herald, the Earth Herald, the commercial middlemen, or Humans in general?

"With my luck, this will turn out to be some kind of huge disaster—and *I'll* be blamed for it." She raked a hand through her dark hair and activated her datapad. "Notebook, remind me to get some numbers on the agro business between Aurie and Bourne."

She called up the next News Sheet page. Nothing of interest appeared, so she scrolled through the next few sheets.

A communiqué has just come in for you . . . from Yadra, Triscoe's mind-voice told her.

Rieka warily pulled her attention from the computer screen and tried to decipher what her husband had meant. That he hadn't used the intercom implied the news was personal.

From Alexi?

No. I'm bringing it down.

That isn't necessary, just transfer it to—. She felt it when he stopped listening, as if a barrier had been erected. "Men," she grumbled. "It doesn't even matter what species."

Rieka tapped the proper keys to save her place, then left the desk to walk the confines of their quarters. They'd been living on the *Providence* since she'd given up her command of the *Prodigy*. The arrangement had worked out, so far, since she'd needed a way to get from planet to planet, and Triscoe's current tour would not be over for several months. But after her inauguration as Earth Herald, all that would change.

Only a few more days, she told herself. It had become her mantra.

Waiting, her least favorite pastime, served to fuel her irritation at Triscoe's strange behavior. Since he'd refused to discuss who'd sent the message, her mind worked at the small mystery. Having come from Yadra gave the impression it had been sent by someone from the Fleet. Admiral Nason was her first choice, since she hadn't yet signed her acquittal papers. But there were others who might be inclined to send a communiqué.

The only other thing Rieka could deduce from their short conversation was that they'd come close enough to the Centauri world, Indra, to drop out of their quantum-slide and power down to quarter light speed. Another ten hours or so and they'd be visiting Triscoe's parents at their home near Bedron. The next morning she and Triscoe had an appointment at Sati Labs. And then she'd be interviewing Jeniper Tarrik, the last on her list of potential Earth adjutants.

The door slid open behind her and Captain Triscoe Marteen stepped inside the room, wearing a tentative smile. His light hair matched his pale skin, in direct contrast to the deep blue-and-rust tunic of his Fleet uniform.

"Let's have it," she said, holding her hand out for the message.

He gave her a steely look, and replied, "In a minute."

"This is beginning to sound very bad, Triscoe," Rieka

warned. She tilted her head up to maintain eye contact as she stepped closer. "Is it from Nason?"

"No. It's private."

"Private?" she repeated. "My cousin, Edell?"

Triscoe shook his head. "Your mother."

Dumbstruck, she stared at him before finding her tongue. "What?"

"It's from your mother." Cautiously, Triscoe dug into his trouser pocket and pulled out a small blue disk. He held it up for her to take. "After what happened at Paden's funeral, I didn't think you should see this alone."

Rieka's heart hammered in her chest as she recalled her mother's threat to prevent her from becoming Earth Herald.

"Look, Yadra's fifteen light-years from here, Triscoe," she began, hoping her bravado would hold. "I'll admit Candace has some pretty lengthy tentacles, but we've discussed this before. Her threats are just that. She can't do a thing now. The election's over."

"Then let's have her prove that to us, together." He flashed her a carefree smile, both dimples appearing on his cheeks.

Rieka appreciated and ignored the tactic. Mentally connected by their marriage bond, she could tell his grin was completely cosmetic. She studied the proffered disk for a moment, then snatched it from his fingers. "Fine." Two strides put her back at the computer console, and she slid the disk into the proper slot. Triscoe pulled up a second chair as the small screen activated. She eased into the desk chair and glanced at him once. Grim, she thought. Now he looks ready to kill. She could only hope her expression wasn't a twin to her husband's.

"Hello, Rieka," her mother began. Rieka immediately recognized the stern expression and frosty tone. Seated behind her immense white desk, Candace meant business. That she'd chosen her home office to produce this message provided several other subtle hints as to its content. The custom desk and furnishings, as well as her expensive suit and coiffure spoke of money. A lot of money. The recording had been made in private—so Rieka figured her mother wanted no one else to know about it for as long as possible.

"This message is for you alone," Candace said, confirming her only daughter's assumption. "The communiqué is encoded with some sort of scrambling program—so my engineers have informed me—and can only be played once. So you had better listen well."

Rieka rolled her eyes. Scrambled communications were the norm, but single-play recordings were illegal. "She's such a bitch."

Triscoe nodded but didn't comment. He kept his eyes on the small screen as if memorizing every image that flashed by.

"I have told you how I feel about what you did to Paden," Candace went on, her voice bitter. "Your brother's death will be on your hands for all eternity, and I can only hope the guilt you feel will cause you to suffer as he did—for the rest of your life."

Rieka sighed. "The woman needs medical help," she muttered.

"But I do not intend to dwell on the fact you have committed fratricide. Perhaps justice will be served, and the court will one day see to it you pay for your crime. I am sending this message to you for one purpose—to stop you from committing a second crime, more heinous than the first. A crime against Humanity itself."

"What is she up to?" Triscoe wondered aloud when Candace paused for effect.

Rieka sat straighter. "I'm sure we'll find out."

"I warned you not to attempt to become Earth Herald, and you ignored me. Rieka, Rieka, do you not see the pattern? Your father, the consummate Human sympathizer, left me—and died in that 'esteemed office' because you encouraged him in his dream to make the Earth viable again. It cannot happen. Do you understand? It mustn't be allowed."

"No, I don't understand," Rieka told the recording.

"You may think I have turned my back on your little crusade, but I know you well enough to realize you want the same thing your father did—all Humans living on Earth. You are wrong. That is the worst possible thing for the Commonwealth. You may have been elected, but you will fail as badly as your father, Rieka. The Earth cannot support civilization. Period. I want you to consider abdication."

"Can you believe this?" Rieka wondered aloud.

"She apparently does."

"You do not have to believe me," Candace went on as if she'd heard the comment. Her blue eyes suddenly turned steely. "I have many expert opinions to back me up—and they have not come cheaply. Roughly ten and a half billion Humans exist in the Commonwealth, the bulk of them here on Yadra. Less than two million currently reside on the Earth—all working feverishly to complete the subterranean cities begun by your father over twenty years ago. You expect ten billion people who have lived their entire lives on worlds such as Yadra, Aurie, and Indra—to return to Earth just because their ancestors once lived there? Thank heavens they will not, but if they did, can you imagine the social upset? The economic turmoil? An exodus to Earth will cause more damage to the Commonwealth than rescuing the four billion refugees did two hundred years ago.

"Think realistically, Rieka. Your charming ideal of our species returning to its homeworld won't work. It can't work. And I will do everything in my power to stop you—should you try to go forward with that plan."

"She's out of her mind," Rieka grumbled. "She can't possibly think I'd—"

"I will grant you the planet that spawned our species has been rejuvenated. I have reports here," Candace offered, gesturing toward a console on the desk, "that tell me the oceans are healthy again. The land arable. The air sweet and clean. That is wonderful news. A tremendous accomplishment. But you mustn't take it too far.

"Consider this, daughter—the Earth is new again. Fresh. Vital. Why not make every effort to keep it that way? Encourage only limited repopulation—with essential self-supporting industries on-site. But the bulk of the Earth should remain the paradise it has become. Turn it into a resort world—if you insist the rest of the Commonwealth should be inspired to visit there on a regular basis. Rethink the marketing and turn the Blue Planet Future into a performance advertisement for vacationing on Earth—not for going there to live.

"Rieka, my people have done all the research and compiled the data. If you would discard your pride and study my documentation, you would see where you are about to go terribly wrong. What you want for Humanity cannot be allowed to happen. It will not only bring ruin, again, to our species, it will serve to upset the very foundation of the Commonwealth's economic structure."

Candace stopped and took a breath before lifting her chin and staring directly into the video pickup. "You may have saved the Commonwealth from a Procyon invasion six months ago, but I can assure you they'll only stay away for as long as we continue to appear strong. Your concept as a Reaffirmed Earth will bring the Procyons back faster than any quantum-slide. Think about that, daughter."

The screen went blank.

Rieka let out a long sigh. "That was quite a tirade."

"She certainly likes to cover herself," Triscoe commented. "By sending you a self-destructing threat, you have no grounds for retaliation."

"But it wasn't really a threat," Rieka said, turning to face him. "She never actually said she'd do anything."

He frowned. "But she implied something. Just like she implied she'd make you pay for Paden's death."

"And that's starting to make sense now, too," Rieka said. "If he hadn't been killed, I would never have considered running for Herald. And as obnoxious as he was, Paden would have been elected over either Edell or Peter. I'm sure of it. Mother's clout, if not her money, would have bought him the position. Add to that the fact she had him completely under her control; he would have been the Earth Herald in name only. His death effectively stole that power from her. It's why she blames me."

"And in light of that, I don't understand why she's opted to ask for your cooperation. You'd think she'd be looking for a way to control you just as effectively as she did Paden."

"You're right." Rieka nodded. "I'd have to guess Candace hasn't found that angle, yet. But she's right about one thing. If Earth repopulates, the Commonwealth's economy is going to react. The agro business will experience a big shift. That's already starting to happen," she added, thinking of the News Sheet. "Other industries will probably follow. I just can't see how that would hurt the general economy."

Triscoe leaned back in his chair and crossed his arms over his broad chest. "Apparently, your mother can."

"So why should she be right?" Rieka argued. "For the last two centuries Humans have been trying to recover from the Collision. We're almost there now, and because she's comfortably rich on Yadra, she doesn't want that to happen for fear it'll upset her power base." She banged her fist on the desktop. "Well too bad, Candace. You're not getting your way this time."

"She may not get her way," Triscoe echoed ominously, "but I can guarantee she'll do whatever she thinks is necessary not to let you get your way, either."

At that, Rieka smiled slowly. "She's certainly welcome to try."

Triscoe Marteen felt that same sentiment aimed at him two days later. She was stubborn, his Human wife, and quite often that particular characteristic could be endearing. But she'd been saving the "baby" issue for their arrival at Indra, announcing it to his parents almost as soon as they'd arrived.

Now, as he sat watching his bridge crew begin the mid-tour inspection, Triscoe wondered how he could possibly convince Rieka to give up on the idea of motherhood. Twanabok, the *Providence*'s medical superintendent, had told him Indran-Human hybrids were impossible, but he knew Rieka would never accept defeat.

The console at his elbow beeped softly, bringing him back to the present. Aarkmin, his executive officer, turned toward him from the navigation console. "Your appointment, Captain?"

"Yes." Frowning slightly, Triscoe pushed himself out of his chair. "You have the bridge, Commander. Page me for any reason."

Her shadowy smile did not escape his notice. Aarkmin had retrieved him from other unpleasant meetings with a simple and not necessarily urgent page. "Of course, sir," she said. He wondered if she thought rescuing him from Rieka was funny.

Not bothering to acknowledge her awareness of his apprehension, Triscoe strode from the bridge. A few moments later, the InterMAT deposited him in the Indran city of Korval. A short walk from the station put him in front of the planet's foremost genetic-research facility, Sati Labs.

The beveled-glass facade sparkled in the afternoon sun, causing him to squint as he entered the foyer. A familiar dark-haired figure walked toward him, and Triscoe leaned to welcome her with a light touch on her jawline. "I didn't forget," he said softly.

"I didn't think you would," Rieka answered lightly. "I've already signed us in. It shouldn't be much longer. There's a place to sit over here."

He followed her, noticing she'd worn a skirt today as opposed to her usual jumpsuits. Rieka claimed she'd worn the Fleet uniform for so many years she'd never be comfortable in anything else. But he knew she liked variety. Most Humans did. And the skirt had a certain appeal that slacks did not.

"That color suits you," he said. She looked at him and smiled slightly but said nothing. Studying her, Triscoe noted her hair had returned to its original nut brown color, but her skin still looked paler than he remembered. Dr. Twanabok had sworn her normal pigment tones would return within a year. His ministrations had been the key in allowing her to appear Indran when Admiral Nason had ordered her to spy on the Procyons. Twanabok had also suggested removing her breasts, but Rieka had bound them instead. For that, Triscoe was grateful. The alien structures fascinated him, as did the Human concept of recreational sex.

After their marriage's shaky start, they'd grown more comfortable with each other. But now, Triscoe felt the distinct murmurings of unrest. Rieka had left the Fleet to pursue her father's wish that Earth be managed by a Herald who both loved the planet and her peoples. Now, on the brink of achieving that goal, Rieka had already grasped at another.

And this one would be far more difficult to attain.

"The doctor we'll be speaking to is Wilmstos," she told him, once they'd settled into a pair of padded lobby chairs. "He's their . . . sounding board, I suppose you'd call it. He gets to interview the potential patients, then makes recommendations to the board." Enthusiasm sparkled in her voice, and her hands gestured as she spoke.

"Rieka," he offered hesitantly, gauging his words by the anxious amber he sensed in her subconscious. "I've been talking to Vort—just hypothetically, and—"

She cut him off with an accusing look. Slowly, she asked, "About us?"

"Not exactly," he explained. "Just about . . . possibilities."

She huffed. "It's on your face, Tris," she hissed quietly, obviously not wanting to draw the receptionist's attention. "You talked to Dr. Twanabok about our personal business, didn't you?"

"I didn't," he insisted innocently, knowing she had been asking certain questions herself. "I just inquired about the possibilities of DNA recombination among any two Commonwealth species."

"And?"

"Degahv and Marteen?" an Aurian woman announced from a nearby doorway. When they both turned to her, she offered them a sunny smile while her bibbets flushed a light pink. "Dr. Wilmstos will see you now."

Almost thankful for the interruption, Triscoe stood and followed Rieka and the woman down a short corridor to Wilmstos's office. The man was shorter than expected, Triscoe realized, as they performed the formal Indran greeting of touching palms. The top of his head looked to be almost level with Rieka's. His hair had gone white, though touches of tan were still visible in the braid that fell from just behind his left ear to his shoulder. His face appeared smooth, smile genuine.

"Captain Degahv, Captain Marteen, a pleasure," Wilmstos said. "I'm Helegi Wilmstos. Please, sit down." He gestured to a small arrangement of furniture near a corner window.

"Thank you," Rieka said as she settled onto a chair. "But please, call me Mrs. Degahv, or Rieka. I've given up my Fleet commission."

"Of course. Although we will soon be calling you Herald," the doctor added with a smile.

Triscoe couldn't help but grin at the look on Rieka's face. She still found it difficult to accept even such a subtle

compliment. How would she ever manage as a public figure? At least she didn't blush readily or have to worry
about bibbets turning dark, he mused. Perhaps, it would
just be a matter of getting used to that type of attention.
For her sake, he hoped so. Rieka hated feeling self-
conscious.

A moment of silence passed. Wilmstos said, "Before we
begin, let me say one thing. Today's interview is simply the
groundwork—nothing physical will happen. No samples or
testing. You've filed your request with us, and it's my job
to make sure we get all the pertinent information before
sending your case on to the review board. It will be up to
them to decide whether or not your situation is one that
will be mutually satisfactory for Sati Labs. Are we clear
on that?"

"Yes," Rieka said, while Triscoe nodded.

"Good." Wilmstos reached for a datapad on a nearby
table and activated it. "Now, I have here you've been married for approximately eight months. You were both captains at that time—and Rieka had since left the Fleet."

"Correct," Triscoe said.

Without looking up, Wilmstos continued. "Captain Marteen is a native Centauri from the planet Indra. And Rieka
is a native Yadran of Human descent."

"I prefer to think of myself as simply Human, if you
don't mind," she told him sternly.

"But you and two prior generations were born and raised
on Yadra, is that correct?"

"Yes, that's correct," she replied, her tone flat.

He tapped something into the small machine and continued. "Do the two of you share physical intimacy?"

Triscoe tried hard not to smile at the incredulous look
that crossed Rieka's face. Before she could utter a sound,
he said, "Frequently. That has never been a problem for
us."

"Good, good," Wilmstos said, tapping more information
into his computer. "Now, you are aware of the impossibility
of any kind of natural fertilization, are you not?"

"Yes," Rieka answered, her eyes on the doctor's datapad. "That's why we're here. We both possess the ability
to reproduce. We just want to do that with each other."

"And that's the tricky thing, Rieka," Wilmstos commented as he set aside the datapad. "What we've got here is a loving, married couple. They're compatible emotionally, mentally, physically . . . and they want to produce offspring. But the undeniable fact is—even though you may look very much alike—you are not the same species. Far from it." Wilmstos gestured with his hands. "And that is a huge obstacle."

"But is it possible?" Rieka asked.

Triscoe felt his chest constrict as he waited for Doctor Wilmstos to answer.

"Of course," he told them. He reached for the datapad again, tapped a few keys, and looked up. "Actually, just about anything is *possible* in the field of biology. *Probable* is another thing altogether."

"But you've combined closely related species before," Rieka urged. "And the results—well, the published ones anyway—have been tremendously successful."

Wilmstos nodded. "True. But there have been serious failures. And the parent species have always been indigenous. We're talking about something altogether different here."

Triscoe clamped his teeth together and nodded, relieved. He refused to argue with her in front of a stranger, but if the doctor told them trying to produce a child by artificial means even at the most basic level was ludicrous, he would not give up the opportunity to agree.

Rieka glanced at him, frowned, and turned her attention back to Wilmstos. "Are you trying to tell me that since something hasn't been tried previously—you're not willing? This is supposed to be Indra's most advanced lab."

"It is," Wilmstos told her. "But our reputation comes from the fact we are very careful about what we do. We and our clients must honor both moral and legal obligations to society."

Triscoe watched as Rieka puckered her lips in a displeased frown. "I'm simply trying to find a way to have a child with my husband," she argued. "I appreciate the necessity for being careful . . . you just aren't being very helpful."

"Are you saying we should give up?" Triscoe asked.

"No, Captain Marteen, I'm not. There are certainly things that can be done to aid in your having a baby. Quite

simply the idea of trying to genetically recombine chromosomes from *alien* species is . . . not a good one. We could
clone a child—even go so far as to alter the sex—give you
a boy. But we would only be creating a genetic reproduc-
tion of you, Rieka. I cannot recommend trying to hybridize
an Indran and Human. It is far too complex. Too
dangerous."

"Why? You've just pointed out how alike we are—aren't
there enough genetic similarities?" Rieka asked sarcastically.

Wilmstos remained unruffled, and Triscoe silently applauded him. "Of course there are. I would be a fool to
deny the obvious. Every new discovery made in the last
four decades gives credence to the theory of a common
ancestor. Most of the advanced scientific minds now agree
with that scenario. But after a few billion years of evolu-
tion, even the most hardy bacteria—and that is all our supposed forebears are guessed to have left behind—are going
to be genetically incompatible."

Wilmstos leaned forward. "The three of us are sitting
here sharing this atmosphere, but your lungs are absorbing
oxygen and releasing carbon dioxide. Triscoe and I are taking in carbon dioxide and breaking it down at the cellular
level."

She sighed. "I know that. I simply thought you could
genetically engineer the desired traits. You make a decision
on what you want—and then go with that."

"An essentially accurate assumption," agreed Wilmstos.
"But every decision made must be followed through with
utmost precision."

Triscoe felt himself frowning at the complexity of their
request. If Sati Labs started working on the problem today,
it might take years before they were ready to attempt anything involving a physical subject. "You're saying this is
like designing an entirely new species."

He nodded. "Yes, Captain. But I would not recommend
it in this case. There is no guarantee that the chemistry of
the fetus would not adversely affect Rieka in some way.
Or vice versa. The risks are simply too great."

Triscoe reached for Rieka's hand as the crestfallen look
swept across her face. He sensed her disappointment and
refused to discount it in the face of his own triumph. Not

that he didn't want to be a father. He just didn't want her desire for a child to outweigh common sense.

"I'm sorry," Wilmstos offered finally. "I simply need you to understand the facts."

She stayed silent another long moment, kneading Triscoe's palm with her fingers. *What do you think?*

He's right. The risks are too great.

She sighed. "Look, Doctor, I've done an awful lot of things in my life, a great many of them risky. What's the worst that could happen?" Without waiting for an answer, she continued. "The chromosomes wouldn't combine—or if they did, the embryo would die quickly. And if you got past that, maybe it wouldn't survive being implanted—or my body chemistry. Anything. But you'll never know what can be accomplished unless you do try.

"This is the best facility Indra has to offer, but if you're unwilling to even attempt what we ask, we'll just go somewhere else. We'll keep going until we find someone who *will* try."

"I understand," Wilmstos said finally. "But you are not looking at the entire scenario. Implanting a viable embryo with incompatible chemistry could also kill you, Rieka. And if you somehow managed to bring the fetus to term, it is possible the infant would have an abnormal appearance . . . perhaps even freakish. Above everything else, I must make sure you understand that." He looked squarely at Rieka, then Triscoe.

Rieka nodded once. "It's understood."

Wilmstos tapped his datapad again and set it aside. "I think I've got all the information I require at this point. I'll take your request to our board of directors and contact you in a few days."

Triscoe nodded, and they said their good-byes. Walking back to the InterMAT station, he realized now more than ever that he could do little to dissuade her from this crusade. Rieka saw no point in avoiding something simply because it hadn't been done. His arguments for her safety would, as in the past, be conveniently ignored.

And with all the complications and stresses of being Herald added to the equation, Triscoe saw only disaster ahead. How would he ever manage to convince her that her concept of life was not necessarily the only acceptable one?

He would love a child cloned from her Human cells just as deeply as one that they might have had—had Rieka been Centauri.

This procedure could also produce an abomination instead of the cherubic baby she envisioned. And simply carrying a hybridized child might kill her, the doctor had said. She would fight him, of course, but under no circumstances would Triscoe allow Rieka to make such a sacrifice. Whether or not Sati Labs accepted their case, he needed to find a suitable argument in order to stop her.

Unfortunately, nothing came to mind.

TWO

"I'm simply saying if you *can* control something, you should make every effort to do it completely," Ker Marteen told her as he leaned back in his chair.

Rieka studied her father-in-law for a long moment, trying to judge whether or not he was serious. "Really, Ker, that is the most moronic thing you've ever said to me. We're talking about creating babies, not inanimate objects." She sighed and looked at Triscoe. He seemed relaxed in his father's presence, or at least less tense than she'd remembered from the last time they'd all met in this house. Of course they'd been newlyweds then, and Ker had been completely opposed to the idea his son had married a Human.

"It is not moronic," the older man insisted, flipping his long silver-blond braid over his shoulder. "If you'd just look at this sensibly, you'd see that."

Rieka glanced at the expensive artwork on the wall and shook her head. "I'll tell you what I see around here, Ker. You live in this private art gallery surrounding yourself with images created by mortals. Look at this place." She gestured to various pieces in the room. "It's a shrine. And a group of individuals created it. but it's not *natural*. It's affected. Created to your whims. And that's fine," she added with a shrug. "I would be pleased with the challenge of helping to design a house or a spaceship to my specifications. But I draw the line at designing a *person*."

Ker pounded a big fist on his knee. "You're not listening." He pointed a finger at her. "You made that decision when you went to Sati Labs. I'm simply saying as long as they have agreed to try to combine your DNA with

Triscoe's, you ought to find out if they can preselect some traits. Intelligence would be nice, for one. General health. Coloring. Temperament."

Rieka lifted a hand, wanting to stop him while it was still possible. "Please. Let's change the subject. The lab hasn't even agreed, yet. If they determine they can do the job, we'll take whatever we can get. I'm not going to manipulate nature any more than absolutely necessary."

"Why ever not?"

"Because it's dangerous." Rieka huffed again and looked out the window. "Triscoe and I are not about to risk any more than we have to in order to have a child. I'm determined in this, Ker." She turned and glared at him. "You aren't going to change my mind."

Ker looked at Triscoe. "You agree with her?"

"For the most part," he replied. "The thing you don't seem to want to understand, Father, is that this is our decision, not yours. Yes, I know—this would be your first grandchild. But you must allow the two of us to be parents. Rieka has made some incredibly hard decisions in the past few months. I think the least we can do is offer a little slack."

"Thank you," she said.

Ker grumbled but offered no comment.

"Well, I see we're all getting along famously, as usual," Setana quipped from the doorway. Rieka bit back a snide comment and watched as her mother-in-law offered them all a wry smile before seating herself near Ker.

Rieka sighed and gnawed at her lip. Would she ever learn self-control the way Setana had? Triscoe's mother, the Indran Herald, possessed the *quantivasta* gift—the ability to pick up on other people's thoughts and emotions. She used that gift to manage everything and everyone with gentle determination. Rieka's experience in the Fleet taught her how to issue orders. Persuasive tactics, she supposed, could be learned. She hoped.

For some reason, that thought made her think of her father. His untimely death had given her good reason to find her own subtle ways to help both the Commonwealth and Humanity.

And Stephen Degahv had also disagreed with Candace on the most basic principles. He truly believed Humanity belonged on Earth. That the people needed a common place to connect on a most basic level—not live scattered by chance rather than choice on eight of the Commonwealth's ten member worlds.

She hadn't been on Earth the day the transport ship crashed, but she'd always known the circumstances surrounding the accident were murky. Pilot error? Mechanical or electrical failure? Rieka could never be sure of that any more than she could say for certain Candace had had nothing to do with it.

And now, out of some warped sense of responsibility, she'd been elected Earth Herald, her campaign focusing on her role as Earth's champion. Her father would have loved it. While protecting the Commonwealth from the Procyons, she'd made a shocking discovery: The meteor collision that had nearly destroyed Earth had been a deliberate attack.

Humanity had been manipulated for the past two centuries, and it had to stop.

Jeniper Tarrik sat at the table in her small apartment in Bedron staring at the News Sheet on her IndraLink screen. She blinked once and realized she hadn't actually read any part of the article. Her breakfast, now a lump of soggy mush in her bowl, had lost its appeal. In a few hours, she'd have her interview with Herald-elect Degahv. Why couldn't Jonik have waited until tonight to contact her? After all, she hadn't heard from him in months. Now, on top of being nervous, she'd become preoccupied. She couldn't help wondering what trouble he'd gotten himself into, this time. And the price tag he would quote for her help.

As the third child, Jonik had grown up with many handicaps. Both Jeniper and Edrin, their older brother, had always tried to help him however they could. But sometimes Jeniper thought he'd gone beyond help. Ever the adventurer, Jonik would never conform.

In a way, though, she envied him. She'd worked as the Earth Herald's Attaché on Indra for four years. At first, the job had challenged her, but recently Jeniper found herself bored with the routine. If the new Earth Herald didn't hire her, she'd already decided to resign her post here and find something better.

Glancing at the time, Jeniper sighed into her now-inedible breakfast. "Thanks, Jonik. I get to go to the biggest interview of my life—on empty *ribah*—then meet with you. Can't imagine a better day."

Pushing away from the table, she disposed of the uneaten food and switched off the screen she hadn't even read. On the way toward the door, she checked herself in the mirror. Her hair looked fine, as did her outfit, but the dark mauve bibbets on her forehead wouldn't do.

Hoping she could grab fifteen minutes to get herself under control, Jeniper grumbled, "This can't possibly get any worse," and closed the door behind her.

"Dammit, this is impossible!" Rieka raked her fingers through her hair and heaved a tired sigh. "I've been invited to six civic dedications—all on Earth on the same day— and a state wedding between two people I've never met. There are one, two . . . five corporate meetings I've been asked to attend. I don't know what the companies expect, or even the topic of discussion. I don't negotiate contracts. At least I don't think I do." She looked at Setana for confirmation.

"Not necessarily, though I'm sure you will be asked to mediate from time to time. A Herald whose planet means to be productive knows who is doing business with whom. And Herald sanction of a business deal can be quite significant."

"Well, I'd better mark those as "should attend," she muttered.

"You also should have several appointments scheduled for protocol briefings and at least two fittings for your inaugural dress."

"Got that." She tapped another key and glanced back at her mother-in-law. Six more entries had come in during their short conversation. "I knew I'd be busy, but this is ridiculous."

Setana smiled gently. "A new Herald is bound to get a great deal of attention, Rieka," she advised. "It will all settle down in a few weeks, I'm sure. The most important thing to remember is you must never allow the public to see you distraught. A nervous Herald is an ineffectual one."

"I'll keep that in mind," Rieka said. "Actually, this isn't that much different than commanding a Fleet ship. It's just that I had over a hundred people crewing the *Venture*. More than three hundred on the *Prodigy*. Right now, it's a solo performance until I get my staff in place."

Setana smiled. "You are *pemila kaye*." She made a complex gesture with her fingers. "That's an Indran expression which seems to fit you rather well. You are trying to be ahead of where you are," she offered with a slight frown. "Is there a Human equivalent?"

She thought about that for a moment. "Putting the cart before the horse?"

Rieka watched as Setana considered the idiom. "Why yes. That is very similar. Rieka, have you ever considered how closely Human phrases are to those of the Boo? Everything is so visual. Indran and Peratan concepts are characteristically thought processes. Really, it is quite remarkable."

Rieka shrugged noncommittally. "And what does that have to do with my being . . . *pemila kaye*?"

Setana refocused on Rieka and smiled. "You already have a staff, you know. And an office on every planet."

"Well, yes, but they're Uncle Alexi's people. I didn't think it would be right to just walk in and . . ."

"I'm sure there are people at the Earth Embassy here on Indra who would be happy to assist you in any way— even though Alexi is still the legal Earth Herald."

"I suppose so. I'm interviewing Jeniper Tarrik this morning. My Herald's Adjutant is the most pressing decision to be made."

She'd already interviewed four people for the position. Unfortunately, none of them had both the self-motivation and willingness to work Rieka sought. She needed to find someone who wanted the same things for Earth she did, and soon.

"You will find someone suitable," Setana told her.

"I'm sure I will. It would be nice, though, if I could do that sooner, rather than later." Rieka hesitated a moment, then asked the questions she'd wanted to know for weeks. "Did you know I'd be elected?"

Setana looked up from her computer screen. "I wondered if you would ask." With a wistful smile, she answered, "Yes, I did. Yillon mentioned it some time ago. After you'd announced your candidacy."

"I see. And that's why you invited me here and cleared your calendar—so we'd be able to spend time together?"

"Since there is no point in trying to cover up that fact, yes. Precisely." Intelligent brown eyes studied Rieka for a long moment. "I always knew you were quite intuitive."

Rieka glanced at her mother-in-law and realized the woman expected her to explode.

"Are you angry?" Setana asked.

"A little," she answered honestly, knowing Setana's *quantivasta* gift would sense any deceit. "I realized you couldn't tell me what you knew—but it's still hard to accept. I suppose I would have gotten very *pemila kaye,* if I'd known ahead of time."

At that, Setana laughed lightly, and Rieka joined her.

"If it is any consolation, I doubt Yillon will be predicting any significant changes in your life in the near future."

"A comforting thought," Rieka jibed. She glanced out the window toward the trees in the distance and bluntly changed the subject. "You and Ker have built this sanctuary where you can come and find a little peace. I have nothing like it."

"You will someday, I'm sure."

"Is that a prediction?"

"No. Just an idea. A thought. We all need a place to retreat when things threaten to overwhelm us."

"I used to call that place home."

"And where was that?"

"My mother's estate on Yadra. It's a huge place in the hills outside of Kilpani called Olympus. I was just a child, though. I didn't know any better." The great stone edifice surrounded by outbuildings, fields, and rolling terrain skimmed across Rieka's mind. She hadn't thought of the estate in a long time. No. She had no home. Setana's gentle advice had proven far more valuable than her mother's constant criticism.

"You're thinking of Candace?"

"Are you reading my mind?"

"No." Setana smiled. "Just your face. You look as though you've swallowed something awful."

Rieka laughed.

Setana tilted her head slightly and Rieka felt her mother-in-law's scrutiny like a tangible thing. "Was she that bad?" Setana asked. "I've only met her once or twice."

"Bad doesn't begin to describe Candace Degahv," Rieka began. Her voice turned cold. "She loved Paden because he let her tell him what to do. And she resented me because my father stood up for my independence. Now that Paden's dead, she's become even more unreasonable."

"How so?"

"At the funeral she took me aside and told me she'd make me pay for Paden's death. She's convinced I killed him."

A frown crossed Setana's brow. "But he was shot by a Procyon. You tried to save him."

"I know that—and so does everyone else in the Commonwealth. But Candace will never believe such a story. She called me a murderer and promised to see justice done. The funeral was . . . quite a show."

Setana frowned thoughtfully at Rieka. "Do you have any idea what she meant?"

"No. And until recently, I've ignored her. She threatens people all the time. But she wanted Paden to be Herald. And now I am. She sent a message to me on the *Providence* threatening to stop me from trying to make Earth viable again."

"Threatening to do . . . what?"

"She didn't say." But Rieka had recognized that look in her mother's eye. She'd seen it before. At the funeral. And the day she and her father had left for Earth.

Candace meant to have her way.

THREE

As she entered the small waiting area at the Earth Embassy, Rieka decided she wasn't particularly impressed with either its cramped size or the ecru decor. And aside from the furnishings, all of Centauri design, she was alone. Irritated by that fact, she strode past the vacant receptionist's desk and opened the door.

"Oh, you can't do that," a voice scolded her from behind.

Rieka turned and looked at the speaker, previously hidden by a profusion of greenery set in an alcove. The slight Centauri man in his middle years stood holding a watering can. Rieka wondered if she'd ever figure out why Alexi hadn't hired a completely Human staff.

"And you are . . . ?" Rieka demanded.

"I'm the receptionist here. Mr. Kelind Barq." He left the can near the plants he'd been tending, walked to the inner door, and closed it securely. He then turned and stood behind his desk like a sentry.

The man's posture reminded Rieka of a Fleet security officer, and she tried hard not to smile. She covered it by clearing her throat and offering, "Good morning, Mr. Barq."

"Good morning," the man returned. "But I have no appointment scheduled for this early in the day. Whom did you wish to see?"

Rieka watched as Mr. Barq plopped onto his chair and began tapping orders to his computer. In addition to the interview with Ms. Tarrik, she'd intended to check up on Alexi's recent business dealings and see what was required of her in order to pick up the reins efficiently. Ms. Tarrik, apparently, had not informed anyone of her impending visit, which Rieka found curious.

Mr. Barq finished with his console and looked up at her expectantly. "I'd like to see Jeniper Tarrik, if I may," she said politely.

"Have you business concerning Earth?"

"I would say so."

"A residential or commercial license?"

"No."

Barq frowned. "Construction permit of some kind?"

"No."

"Scientific research?"

Rieka shook her head.

"You look familiar," Barq told her. "Have we met before?"

"I sincerely doubt that, Mr. Barq."

"Well, I feel I should know you." Barq frowned and studied his computer screen. "I have an opening for tomorrow morning at eleven hundred hours."

"I don't want an appointment. And I know I'm a bit early. But I just need to see Jeniper Tarrik." Rieka clenched her jaw to keep from smiling. Their droll conversation was a lot like getting past Admiral Nason's secretary. A lot of double-talk and little progress. "I should be on the schedule," she repeated. "I'm sure Ms. Tarrik confirmed the appointment."

"Ms. Tarrik is the Planetary Attaché," Barq countered, shaking his head. "She's quite busy. One can't simply walk in and expect—"

The door behind him opened abruptly and a statuesque Aurian woman appeared. Jeniper Tarrik resembled her holofile exactly. She wore her hair pinned up off her neck in a trio of neat coils. Her pale blue eyes were both sharp and guileless, and, despite the row of bibbets adorning her hairline, the sprinkle of freckles across her fine-boned cheeks gave her a Human look. She glanced at Rieka then did a double take. "Captain Degahv?"

"Just Rieka—for now," she replied, offering her hand and catching a better glimpse of the woman's forehead, or what she could see of it beneath the carefully coifed red hair. The Aurie's hivelike bibbets had flushed from pink to rose but the welts had stayed relatively flat, indicating her emotional state had gone from nominal to somewhat stimulated.

"Jeniper Tarrik, Centauri's Attaché to Earth Herald Alexi Degahv." Jeniper shook hands firmly, and Rieka extended hers again, to Barq. The Centauri man had gasped but regained his composure quickly enough to accept and return the greeting.

"I am so sorry, Herald," Barq mumbled. "Please accept my apologies. I should have recognized you. I knew you looked familiar."

"Think nothing of it Mr. Barq," Rieka told him, slightly self-conscious of that title, since it wasn't yet completely hers. "I dressed this way on purpose." Not wanting to be recognized on the street, she'd made a special point of looking as ordinary as possible today. She'd worn an old jumpsuit, no jewelry, and didn't even carry her datapad.

Mr. Barq nodded hesitantly. "Please call me Barq. Everyone else does."

"It's a pleasure, Barq."

Alexi's attaché pulled herself straighter. "Please don't let us be disturbed, Barq. I imagine our guest will need my full attention while she's here."

"Of course, Ms. Tarrik."

With that, Jeniper gestured Rieka through the door. "Let me show you around, Rieka."

"First door here, conference room. Next on the left is my office. Next to that is the media room. Across here, the kitchen. Can I get you anything?" When Rieka shook her head no, Jeniper turned to the next doorway. "Here is where the rest of the staff works. Yime is on Perata at present. Mr. Giff is attending a corporate meeting between Fielmar Services and JoirWen Incorporated this morning. And Yoe is in the data center, on the fourth floor. That is where the rest of the secretarial staff works. A complement of seven there, total."

"So, with seven there plus two out of the office and one on Perata—and you and Mr. Barq, Alexi has a staff of twelve, here. Is that enough?"

"I believe so," Jeniper said. "Of course one of the junior staff is always stationed at the small office on Perata. They rotate that position on a monthly basis."

"Whatever works, I suppose."

"And the end office will be yours. It's got a wonderful view of Bedron."

Jeniper threw open the door, and they entered. The office had all the personality of a dormitory. Dark blue floor, pale blue walls, large desk with an equally large chair. Near the window, which did boast an impressive view of University Park and the city beyond, sat the usual grouping of chairs and low tables for informal conversation.

"Ugh," Rieka groaned. They would have to redecorate completely in order to achieve the comfortable, open feeling she wanted to create. Visitors here should feel as if they were on Earth, not Indra. "It's almost as bad as out front. Who decorated this place?"

"I have no idea, ma'am," the Aurian answered dryly. "It was this way when I came."

"It was a rhetorical question, Jeniper," Rieka murmured, still taking in the view. "I suppose Alexi doesn't spend much time on Indra."

"Only a few weeks out of the year."

Rieka turned. "And that must be because the office here manages quite well without him."

Jeniper looked away, and her bibbets colored slightly. "I wouldn't begin to guess the Herald's reasons for doing what he does, Cap—Rieka," she answered diplomatically.

Rieka nodded, pleased the woman had neither denied herself the compliment nor augmented it. Still, she hadn't forgotten that odd scene in the reception area. "And now that we're alone, would you mind explaining why your interview for the position of my adjutant is a secret?"

She watched Jeniper clench her fingers, then nod. "Of course. The answer is quite simple, really. The application is my business, not theirs. If I'm hired, I'll appoint one of the junior staff to take my place and leave it to him or her to fill the empty spot. If I'm not hired, routine here will go on as usual." She shrugged slightly. "Routine is important, Rieka. I do everything I can to maintain it."

Rieka found herself admiring the woman's honesty. "Mmm. Have you ever been to Earth, Jeniper?" She gestured to the chairs, and they sat.

"No, I've never been to Earth. Travel there is restricted until the Reaffirmation."

"I know that—but you're the Herald's attaché. I would

have thought Alexi might have sent you there for some reason." Jeniper shook her head. "We'll have to rectify that oversight. Can't have people working for me—and the Earth—who haven't even been there, can I?"

"I suppose not," Jeniper said. Her watery blue eyes sparkled in a way that reminded Rieka of her Aurian friend, Robert DeVark.

"How old are you?"

"Twenty-nine, ma'am."

"And why do you want to leave Indra? A bit bored here?"

"Excuse me?"

Rieka shrugged. "I was just thinking you're awfully young, and despite the importance of this embassy and your dedication to routine—you're probably not very challenged."

At that, Jeniper smiled slightly. "I don't mind routine. But I will admit looking forward to the Earth's Reaffirmation into the Commonwealth. I've been considering hiring more staff to compensate for the additional activity."

"Sounds like a good idea."

"I take it you've gone over my application."

"Yes." In fact, she'd gone over it several times. Scrutinized it. Jeniper Tarrik was qualified, dedicated, and willing to work for Earth. Rieka just needed to get over the idea of having a non-Human as her adjutant.

"And?"

"And I'd like to get to know you a bit before I decide," she admitted, intrigued that the interview had somehow pivoted. She hadn't expected to answer questions, just ask them. "I'd prefer to hire someone with a personality compatible to my own. One I can trust to make decisions in my absence."

"Very reasonable." Jeniper rose and went toward the Herald's huge desk console. "If you want to explore that aspect, then perhaps we should try working together. I could acquaint you with our data-processing system."

Rieka pushed herself up from the cushions and went to sit in Alexi's large chair. Jeniper Tarrik had to be the most intriguing person she'd met in some time. "Great. Then how about giving me a quick tutorial on this console. For the moment, I'd like to know exactly who works for me and what my uncle has been doing for Humans who live on Indra and Perata."

Five hours later, the intercom beeped. Barq's face appeared on the small screen. "You have an incoming call, Herald. Captain Triscoe Marteen from the *Providence*."

Rieka didn't bother to correct Barq. She would have to get used to it eventually. She glanced at Jeniper, then rolled her head to loosen the cramped muscles in her neck. "Put him through, Barq."

Triscoe's amused expression told her Barq had probably questioned his request to speak to her. "So what's with the formal call, Tris?" she asked. "I would have bet money you'd simply get my attention . . . the Indran way." He hadn't even nudged a sense of nearness into her thoughts.

"None of that for the new Earth Herald," he replied seriously, though Rieka could tell he was biting his tongue.

"Right," she told him, her voice oozing with sarcasm. "What do you want, then? Did I forget an appointment or something?"

"No, love. I just wondered if you'd forgotten to eat. I have. And since my inspection is now complete, I thought I'd invite you to lunch."

"Well isn't that sweet?" Rieka looked at Jeniper with a wry grin. The Aurian woman seemed uncomfortable at being privy to the personal byplay. Her bibbets flushed slightly even as Rieka watched. An idea clicked in her mind, and she asked, "On the *Providence*?"

"I suppose that could be arranged," Triscoe replied. *What's going on?*

There is someone I want you to meet. "Great, I'll be bringing a guest with me, if you don't mind."

Even on the small screen, she could see his eyes glimmer with curiosity. "Of course not. I'll meet you at InterMAT Station Four in—fifteen minutes?"

"We'll be there. Earth Embassy out." She flipped the toggle to "off" and turned to Jeniper. "What do you say we shut this down for a while and take a break. Ever been aboard a Fleet ship?"

When Jeniper didn't answer right away, Rieka wondered if she'd made other plans for lunch. Then her expression brightened. Apparently whatever Jeniper had expected to do had been overridden by an invitation to lunch with a Herald-to-be and a ship's captain. Rieka saw only the barest hint of rose in the spots on her forehead and commended her for being able to adapt quickly.

"Actually, I traveled quite a bit before I took this position."

Rieka shook her head. "Commercial passengers don't see half the interesting stuff. I think our relationship is about to become mutually educational."

It took a few minutes to shut down the terminal and put away the hard copies of the files Rieka had requested. Then they told Barq they'd be on the *Providence* until further notice and headed for the Embassy's InterMAT station.

Triscoe met them as soon as they stepped from the chamber. "Permission to come aboard, Captain?" Rieka asked.

"Granted."

She accepted the traditional Indran greeting of husband to wife, allowing his thumb to caress her lower jaw before turning her attention to her companion. "Jeniper, I'd like you to meet the *Providence*'s captain, Triscoe Marteen. Tris, this is Jeniper Tarrik. Confusing as it may seem, Humanity's Centauri Attaché is an Aurian."

"A pleasure, Captain," Jeniper said, smiling. She offered her palms in the Indran greeting.

"The pleasure is mine," he replied, touching his palms to hers. "Tarrik. The name is familiar." He gestured them to accompany him into the hallway. "Does your family do business with the Fleet?"

Jeniper nodded. "My brother Edrin owns a hydroponics company based on Aurie."

Rieka watched while he nodded thoughtfully. "Yes. I thought I recognized the name. And you resemble him, do you not? Though his hair is darker as I recall."

"It is."

Rieka remained quiet through lunch, watching both Triscoe and Jeniper. The woman had an easy rapport with just about everyone, Rieka observed. She was intelligent, inquisitive, adaptable, and highly motivated. She had all the qualities of the adjutant Rieka needed, save one: she wasn't Human.

While Rieka wrestled with that, Triscoe regaled Jeniper with the story of how Rieka and the Boos had saved the

Prodigy during the Procyon War. When they'd finished
eating, he offered to take them on a short tour.

"That would be wonderful," Rieka said. "Jeniper was
telling me earlier that she's traveled a great deal but never
really seen how a Fleet ship functions. Engineering would
be the perfect place to start."

"I have wondered, of course," Jeniper began.

"Then we'll endeavor to answer all your questions,"
Triscoe told her. "This way." They walked down the main
corridor to the nearest Chute and were deposited on quadrant B, deck two before Jeniper finished asking if they ever
had trouble with the gravity pod.

Rieka smiled wryly. The Pod, located a kilometer below
the vessel's main curved hull and manned only by Boos,
produced the gravitational field that allowed both the passengers and crew to move about normally. "Problems occur
now and then," she said. "But Memta is one of the best
engineering supers in the Fleet."

"The best," Triscoe corrected.

They followed him through the huge doors and entered
an immense room that spanned all three floors of the um-
brella-shaped vessel. The room brought back fond memories of her own engineering suites on the *Venture* and
Prodigy. Men and women from five races worked together
here on the main engineering deck. Far below in the gravity
pod, only the Boo could withstand the immense stresses
they generated with their almost magical equipment.

Rieka noted Jeniper's slight reaction as a huge Boo shuffled up to Triscoe and began to speak. "Captain has a
problem?"

"Negative. Roddik. We slide to Varannah," Triscoe told
him. "I have visitors who wish to see the curve of the dawn.
Is Memta close?"

"In the Pod. I'll super here until his return."

Lieutenant Roddik, an immense blue creature with multi-
faceted eyes and a translator box sutured to his chest,
turned toward Rieka. "Captain Herald Degahv," he gurgled, "your visage is weightless."

She offered him a grateful smile. "I am honored you
recall my visage, Roddik," she said. "And I am glad to see
you aboard."

"Always shall I work under Memta," Roddik replied. He

took a brief pull from his atmosphere compensator, and
added, "His command is the square of the nth. All
equality."

The odor of chlorine swept over her, but Rieka had
trained herself to ignore it long ago. "That is good. I would
introduce you to my friend, Jeniper Tarrik."

Rieka watched as Jeniper stood her ground while Roddik
sidled closer. He was nearly half again her height and probably outweighed her ten times over. "Honored am I Jeniper
Tarrik," he said, wiggling the fleshly folds over his gleaming
black eyes. He double-blinked and added, "The *Providence*
slides to Varannah on the dew, does it not?"

"Well, yes, I suppose it does," Jeniper replied. "Where
exactly is Varannah, Lieutenant?"

"It is the place on the horizon which touches our *ckla*.
Here we find symmetry."

"So it's really more like a feeling than an actual place."

"Yes."

"Well then, I suppose you are right."

The odor of chlorine grew heavy. While Rieka watched
Jeniper wipe her eyes, Triscoe silently asked, *What's going
on?* She knew his curiosity had been piqued even before
lunch.

Have Roddik show her around, and I'll tell you, Rieka
offered, tempting him with a quizzical grin.

A brief request from his captain was all it took to send
Lieutenant Roddik shuffling off with Jeniper. She threw
them one questioning look over her shoulder before frowning up at the Boo, probably trying to fathom what he'd
said.

"What is going on?" Triscoe repeated aloud.

"As if you couldn't guess. She's my adjutant."

Triscoe looked down at her skeptically. "You didn't introduce her that way."

"Well, that's because I haven't exactly hired her, yet."

"Rieka!" he chided.

"What?" She looked at him innocently. "She knows what
I'm doing—that this is part of her interview. I wanted to
see how she dealt with an unpredictable situation. Roddik
is about as unpredictable as they come—though Memta
would have been more intimidating."

Triscoe turned, effectively blocking her view of the suite.

"I cannot believe this behavior is coming from you. Do you realize you are manipulating this woman? You, of all people." He put his hands on his hips. "A Human who swore never to be caught acting like any of those—"

Rieka poked him in the chest. "Don't you start with me, Centauri. And I'm testing, *not* manipulating. And Jeniper knows it."

She watched as a dimple puckered in his cheek. "You are quite beautiful when you're defensive, my wife," he said softly. "Your face gets pink and your eyes start to— no, now that is definitely not a defensive move." He smiled. "I am teasing, Rieka," he added, catching her raised fist in his hand.

Triscoe kneaded her fingers gently. She knew he still didn't understand the appropriate times for things, but he was working on it. "I knew that," she lied, pulling her fist from his hand. "And Jeniper will be a wonderful adjutant. Alexi's kept her holed up as his attaché here for four years. She's ready for a challenge."

"Then why are you waiting to tell her she's got the job? She meets all your criteria. I imagine you'll know soon enough if you've made the wrong choice."

Rieka glanced up into his face and decided not to comment on that. She'd simply have to have faith in her own judgment. She sighed and made an exasperated face, then waved her hand as if to dismiss him. "Go play captain and annoy someone else, Triscoe. Jeniper and I have work to do." She turned on her heel and went to collect her soon-to-be adjutant.

"I'm such a *bimoosh*," Jeniper muttered to herself as she studied one of Olm's early watercolors. After leaving the Herald's office, both stunned and thrilled by Mrs. Degahv's decision, she'd hurried to the museum, afraid she'd missed Jonik. Her baby brother was nowhere to be seen. Thinking of little else beyond the enormity of her new position, and the fact she'd been hired almost on the spot, Jeniper examined the painting a few minutes longer, then moved on to a wall wearing an abstract oil. If Jonik's reason for wanting to see her had anything to do with money, he'd arrive soon.

She stood there, feeling a sudden connection with the

wide, abstract bands of color, and tried to concentrate on
what she'd need to do before she left Indra.

"Took you long enough to get here," a familiar voice
said.

Jeniper turned and looked into her younger sibling's face,
wondering how long he'd been studying her while she'd
thought she'd been waiting for him. His appearance had
changed enough for Jeniper to feel a jolt of maternal anxiety. He now wore his dark hair long and over his bibbets,
effectively covering all but those near his eyes. Stubble covered his jaw line. He seemed thinner than the last time
she'd seen him, and there were worry lines around his
mouth. And his clothes, though clean, looked old and
threadbare.

"I had business to attend to, Jonik," she explained with
an air of superiority. "I have a good job. And responsibilities. I realize you aren't familiar with those sorts of things,
but—"

"I didn't come here to be insulted," he grumbled, setting
himself down on a bench in front of an immense Pollock.
"Now this one I can relate to. One great big mess." He
leaned back to get a better view. "That's me."

Jeniper glanced up at the paint-splattered canvas, then
folded her skirt under her as she sat next to him. "What
sort of trouble are you in now?"

"Who says I'm in trouble?"

"I hear from Mam and Pae once a week, Jonik. And
Edrin sends a message every now and then. I hear about
what you've been doing."

Jonik shrugged and said nothing.

"You haven't asked me for money in nearly a year. I
suppose I'm due." Jeniper sighed. "How much do you need
this time?" she asked resignedly.

"Just a loan, Jen," he said.

"And like all the other loans—I'll never see a credit of
it again. How much?"

"Fifty-eight thousand."

Jeniper felt her jaw drop, and she snapped it closed.
"You are out of your mind, Jonik. What have you done?"
she whispered in disbelief. His silent reply irked her further. "I don't have that kind of money, and if I did—I
certainly wouldn't throw it away on you. Go ask Edrin. He

can put it in his books as a bad investment." She pushed herself up from the bench and headed for the museum entrance.

Jonik caught up to her on the street. "You don't understand, Sis," he told her. "This isn't just money I owe someone. It's more. She means business. If I don't pay up in less than a week's time, she'll . . . do something." His eyes grew wide and he pressed his lips together, a nervous habit he'd developed as a child.

"Grow up, Jonik."

"I'm serious."

Jeniper huffed and kept on walking. Jonik had tried this approach too many times. She no longer had a soft spot for his problems. He was a grown man now, able to look after himself. "I'm sorry you've made some bad decisions," she began. "But they've been your decisions to make. The entire family has gone out of its way to help you. This is too much." She shook her head at his incredulous expression. "Don't try to hold me accountable. I've got enough responsibilties to worry about for myself." Wasn't he tired of hearing this speech by now?

"But Jen, you don't understand," he babbled, dogging her as she crossed to the next block. "I can't go to Edrin. He's got worse problems than I do. And besides, he just gave me ten thousand six months ago."

She stopped and looked into Jonik's worried face. "Worse problems? What are you talking about?"

He jammed his hands in his pockets and wouldn't look at her. The stance reminded her of a little boy, though Jonik had just turned twenty-six. "Uh, nothing," he muttered. "Edrin expressly told me not to concern you about it. Just a temporary thing."

Jeniper could tell he was lying and wanted to shake him, but not here on a public street. Instead, she balled her fists, and, through a stiffened jaw, said, "Jonik, go to the police and tell them this woman has threatened you." He rolled his eyes. "Then go to Mam and Pae and tell them you're in trouble, again." He shook his head.

Jeniper almost caved in to his forlorn look. She was about to offer him what credit she could when she remembered Barq's advice. Living alone on Indra, Jeniper had welcomed the older man's friendship and counsel and

thought of him as a mentor of sorts. Barq had told her
Jonik would never learn to depend on himself unless he
was forced to face the consequences of his decisions alone.

Strengthening her own resolve, Jeniper set her jaw.
"Leave me alone, Jonik. I am *not* going to help you." At
that, he looked her directly in the eye. She lifted her chin
and added, "I don't know you anymore. You *aren't* my
brother." Maybe the threat of being disowned, even by her,
would wake him up.

It didn't. He shrugged. "You may get your wish," he said
cryptically. "But let me tell you something, Jen. This . . .
person craves satisfaction. Even if she finds me and . . .
does something . . . she'll still want her money. She knows
everything about me. About my family."

Jeniper felt her bibbets darken. He'd gone too far, now.
"You're not going to intimidate me. I'm through listening
to you whine. Do you understand that, Jonik?"

"I understand. Perfectly. You've sold out Aurie to work
with Humans in some *vikkat* job for an equally self-cen-
tered Herald. You only care about yourself."

Stunned by his outburst, Jeniper said nothing. She stood
on the sidewalk and watched him disappear into the crowd
of moving bodies. She had her own problems to think
about, she told herself. She had a new job and a new boss,
and she had to be ready to leave for Earth by tomorrow
afternoon. She should be concentrating on that.

But all she could think about was the color of Jonik's
one visible bibbet when he'd said the mysterious person
would "do something." He'd managed to school his expression enough to seem simply serious about the threat. But
he'd never been able to control his bibbets. When they
were kids, she could read him like a book. And just now
he'd gone maroon. He'd tried to hide it with his hair
brushed forward, but a breeze had come up, and she'd
caught a glimpse of one near the corner of his eye.

Maroon.

FOUR

Rieka massaged the banded muscles in her neck and wondered if she'd ever get rid of her headache. She thought she'd understood the eco-political system that drove the Commonwealth, but the documents in Alexi's files made her want to quit before she started.

"Okay," she said to herself, glad that Jeniper had run off on an errand. "In addition to their own planetary set-ups, each member world elects five senators, three judiciary ministers, and one Herald to coordinate Commonwealth interests." She sketched out a crude diagram with a stylus and sheet of paper, starting with three circles at the top of the page.

"Then, there's the Fleet." Rieka drew a line from each circle to a box below them marked "Fleet." "And the races on the member worlds." She wrote out the names of the eight sentient species and the member worlds they claimed as home. For the two planets that had been terraformed and had no indigenous species, Yadra and Medoura, she drew a line to the primary inhabitants there: Indrans, Aurians, and Humans.

Rieka gazed at her crude diagram. "So, the Senate writes the legislation, and the Judiciary enforces it—as long as it doesn't countermand local practices. The Heralds work as an intermediary between the citizens and the government. And all anyone really cares about is the amount of profit they can earn."

She sighed. It had seemed a lot simpler when she'd learned it in school.

A tone sounded from her console. "A message has just come in for you, Herald," Barq told her.

Glancing toward the screen, Rieka studied Barq's Centauri face, his eyes expressing a curious uncertainty. Curious herself, Rieka pushed aside her frustration with the mechanisms that ran the Commonwealth. "For me? Not for my uncle?"

"Yes," Barq replied. "It has your name on it, Herald."

"Thank you, Barq," Rieka said. She tapped the appropriate keys on the desk console to play the message. The Earth Herald's logo appeared, and she wondered for a moment if Barq had been mistaken. But then Alexi's round face sprang from the graphics and she knew she should have expected him to send a message.

"Rieka," he began, his welcoming smile somehow managing to look sincere despite showing all his teeth, "I hope you are well and beginning to find your way through the myriad of new responsibilities being Earth Herald–elect has brought. I am sure Setana has offered her assistance— which is why I did not ask you to come to Yadra before now."

She watched Alexi nod, a habit he'd developed that somehow managed to coerce people to agree with him, and Rieka found herself fascinated by the cloud of white hair on his head and how it contrasted with his steely beard and dark skin.

"So get to the point, Uncle," she muttered to herself, waiting for the message to continue.

"But circumstances here have changed, and I need you to come to Yadra right away," he went on, as if knowing she'd asked the question. "There is a matter of some urgency I must speak to you about, in person. If you have not already selected your staff, I suggest you do so before you leave—and use the time spent in transit to work out the details of how you wish to handle your office. In any event, I need you to come to Yadra as soon as possible."

"You're not going to tell me what it's about, are you, you old hustler?" she grumbled. She could simply fast-forward to the information she wanted, but Rieka dutifully let the message play, noting the day and time he wanted to see her.

"I am sure you wish to know the reason our meeting must occur as soon as possible," Alexi went on. His pudgy cheeks rounded even more when he smiled again. "I must brief you on several agreements I have pending with certain businesses and planets. There will not be ample time for this prior to your inauguration, since I am not scheduled to arrive until the day before the ceremony. I am sure you understand the necessity of coming to Yadra, first. Please notify me as soon as your ship makes orbit. I look forward to seeing you soon, Rieka."

She watched while his image was replaced by the Earth Herald's logo. A moment later the screen went dark, and Rieka sighed. Had she really thought she could tolerate all the folderol that went along with the job?

Before she had a chance to consider the question, the console beeped, and she touched the intercom button. "Yes, Barq?"

"Incoming call from Captain Marteen," Barq replied.

"Thank you." She touched the button again and frowned at the anxious look on his face. "What's wrong, Tris? Barq didn't interrogate you again, did he? I thought I'd already made it clear to him before we left for lunch."

"It wasn't Barq," he said, schooling his features to disguise whatever had been bothering him. "It's nothing. Nothing at all to worry about, love. I have good news, in fact."

He'd said the words, but his tone reminded Rieka of a time months ago when Admiral Nason had sent her on a covert mission Triscoe had opposed. "It doesn't sound very good so far," she commented.

He mustered a sickly smile. "Dr. Wilmstos from Sati Labs spoke to me a moment ago."

She sat straighter. "What did he say?"

"The board reluctantly gave the go-ahead to the experimental combination of Centauri and Human genotypes."

Rieka exhaled a breath she didn't realized she'd held. "So soon? I thought they'd take several days to decide."

"Apparently not," he said tersely.

"And that's a bad thing?" When Triscoe looked away from the camera, she felt her heart begin to thump in her chest. The fact that he hadn't communicated this mentally told her he knew something and wanted to keep it to himself. A dozen ideas coursed through her mind while she watched him hesitate, none of them what she wanted to hear.

"Before you say anything," she began, lifting a hand to

indicate he shouldn't interrupt, "I want to know why you're so upset."

"I'm not upset."

She sighed. "Triscoe, do you take me for an idiot? We wouldn't be talking like this if you weren't upset." She leaned an elbow on the desk and perched her chin on her hand. "Tell me everything."

He took a deep breath and looked into the video pickup. "They have also accepted your request—to follow through the complete process and attempt to hybridize a child."

Rieka didn't need to be in mental contact to see that something was definitely bothering him. She decided she could probably get him to tell her if she could keep him talking long enough. "You just said that. Or am I not following the conversation?"

"I said they'd decided to do the experimental lab work—and attempt the pregnancy."

She'd watched carefully as he'd explained himself. He'd actually grimaced when he'd said the word "pregnancy." "You don't want me to get pregnant, do you?" she asked softly, feeling the hairs rise on her forearms.

He sighed. "I would love for you to be pregnant, Rieka. Just . . . not this way. Not with your life at risk, and the child's. It seems so—"

"—engineered?" she finished.

He shook his head. "Futile."

She said nothing for a long moment. "I think we need to talk about this. But we'll need to do it in person. This sounds like a subject for Yillon's little white room."

"It does," he agreed, his sober tone almost frightening. "Perhaps we can sit with the *wruath* instead."

Rieka recalled the shimmery scarf he'd wrapped around her shoulders when they'd said their marriage vows aboard the *Providence*. It symbolically compelled them to be truthful with one another. "Perhaps," she agreed. "But it had better be soon. I just got a message from Alexi. He needs to have a meeting with me on Yadra in three days."

"I'm scheduled to depart for Tau Ceti tomorrow," he offered. "The *Providence* would be honored to transport you."

"Have you got room for my Planetary Adjutant?" she asked with a grin.

"And the Indran Herald."

"Sounds like a crowded ship."

"More so than you think. I've got two crews of steve-dores loading the cargo holds as we speak. We'll be 87 percent capacity by zero-eight-hundred tomorrow."

Rieka nodded. That kind of activity was nothing new. "Are we supposed to go to the lab before they close today?"

"That would seem best, since it is unclear as to when either of us will be back." He paused briefly. "Unless you'd rather wait for a while."

Rieka sat straighter in the chair. "No. Not at all. Nothing like the present, we Humans say. I'll just wrap up what I'm doing here and tell Jeniper we're going to Yadra instead of Earth. Then I'll get myself over to Sati Labs before seventeen-hundred."

"Good," he said softly. "I will see you later, then. Mar-teen out."

The screen went blank, and Rieka heaved a concerned sigh. Triscoe was always overprotective when it came to her safety, she told herself. Still, she had to admit this situation was different. No enemies. No weapons to discharge. She faced technological risks, chemical imbalances, untried techniques. But everything would turn out fine. Triscoe would forget all about his uncertainty when he held their baby in his arms. Of course he would, because this was a risk she had to take.

The Earth Herald needed an heir. That was all that mattered.

Rieka didn't know what to expect when she got to Sati Labs, but Wilmstos greeted her at the door and ushered her in with enthusiasm. He led her to a room that looked remarkably like the surgery suite on a Fleet ship.

"Doctor Saleem?" he asked, looking around the room.

An Indran female stepped out of a peripheral office. "Yes?" When she noticed them, she came forward, smil-ing. "Hello."

Rieka returned the smile. "Good afternoon, Dr. Saleem. I'm Rieka Degahv." She extended a hand, and the doctor gripped it without hesitation. "I can't tell you how much I appreciate your taking this case."

Nodding, Wilmstos interjected, "Dr. Saleem will supervise your procedure and prepare your sample. Captain Marteen is having his sample taken in the suite across the hall."

Rieka looked at him. "I didn't know he was here," she said, irritated he'd avoided her again.

"Arrived shortly before you did," Wilmstos told her. He nodded at the doctor. "I'll leave you to it, then."

With Wilmstos gone, Saleem grabbed up a datapad and gestured toward a bodypad. "If you would position yourself on the table, Mrs. Degahv, we can get started."

Rieka nodded amicably and complied, lying face up. "Don't I need to disrobe?" she asked, watching Saleem roll a large piece of equipment toward her.

"Not necessary for this," the doctor said. "The extraction needle is quite thin and the sterilization field is not encumbered by fabric."

"Great." Rieka watched her pivot the device and lower a section of it over her abdomen.

"Don't move, please," Saleem said. "You may breathe, but your legs and hips need to remain immobile."

"Okay." The lowered section clamped itself to the table, and Rieka didn't see how she could move even if she wanted to. Saleem checked the clamps, then moved around the unit to the control panel. She tapped her fingertips on its surface and explained what she was doing.

"I'm now using the sonic device to load in the exact location of your right ovary. Sterile field established. Extractor needle ready to deploy. Deploying needle. You may feel a slight—"

"—poke. Yes, I did," Rieka said tightly, trying not to complain.

Saleem ignored her. "Needle on target. Cell extraction under way."

"How much material are you taking?"

"The unit will secure one hundred viable eggs from each of your ovaries," Saleem replied.

"That sounds like a lot."

"Not really. The experiments planned for your case have a high failure projection rate simply because they have not been done before. Actually, it is arguable that two hundred cells are not enough."

"I suppose that sounds reasonable." A moment later the doctor announced the procedure had been completed, then repositioned it and extracted cells from Rieka's other ovary.

"You may feel a slight soreness for a few hours," Saleem told her as Rieka sat up.

She nodded. "When will you know anything?"

The doctor shook her head. "Unknown. Days. Possibly months. As I said, we're dealing with new territory here, Mrs. Degahv."

"I understand." She said good-bye and left the surgical suite. Down the hall, she saw Triscoe talking to Wilmstos.

"Everything went well?" Wilmstos asked as she approached them.

Rieka smiled. "I think so."

"As I was telling Captain Marteen, we'll get started first thing in the morning. I'll send reports to you every week. Hopefully, something will happen sooner rather than later."

"Hopefully," she agreed. "Thank you again, for everything."

As they left the lab, Rieka couldn't help feeling elated. Glancing up at Triscoe's serious expression, she knew in her heart he wouldn't regret what they'd done this afternoon once he held their baby.

Three days later, Rieka notified Alexi's office the *Providence* had achieved orbit. She turned to say something to Jeniper when the console on Triscoe's desk beeped with an incoming call.

"That was fast." She quirked an eyebrow while Jeniper grinned, and tapped the respond button. "Degahv."

The second eyebrow joined the first and she sat straighter. "Admiral Nason, this is a surprise."

The admiral's bibbets, clearly visible on his receding hairline, deepened from pink to rose. He smiled genuinely before speaking. "I hope I haven't interrupted anything important, Rieka," he said with a small nod. "I need to meet with you as soon as possible."

Rieka felt a wave of uneasiness pass through her at his tone. But she grinned at him, and crooned, "And it's so nice to see you, too, Admiral. You're looking well."

Nason's response was predictable. His bibbets flushed

slightly, and he looked suitably humbled. "I beg your pardon. Welcome to Yadra. I hope your trip was uneventful."

"Remarkably so," she confessed, since she hadn't had a chance to deal with Triscoe's fear for her safety.

"And congratulations."

"Thank you. I was a little worried there, for a while. But then I suppose all elected officials must endure elections." She paused, and when he didn't immediately jump in, offered, "Now that we've gotten through the social niceties, what can I do for you?"

"You learned that from Setana, no doubt."

"What?"

"Circumventing the problem at hand with social niceties, as she calls them."

Rieka watched as the admiral leaned back in his chair and crossed his arms over his chest. His smile seemed more relaxed now, and she noted that the beard he'd begun to grow when she'd seen him last had filled in. The red hair on his chin was infused with as much white as that of his head, giving him a peachy glow. "Yes, actually I did. I've noticed every Herald has a certain way of approaching a pending problem. The goatee becomes you, by the way," she told him.

"Thank you."

"And the problem is?" she prompted.

"Something I'd rather discuss in person."

She studied him for another moment before nodding and consulting her datapad. "I have a tight schedule, Admiral. I'm afraid I've only got from now until eleven-hundred open." She glanced at Jeniper, who nodded and mouthed the words: only one hour.

"That will do. I'll notify my secretary to send you in as soon as you arrive. Fleet Headquarters out."

The screen went blank, and Rieka let her jaw drop slightly in indignation. She huffed and glanced up at Jeniper. "What are you grinning about?"

"He's still giving you orders—and yet allows you to banter with him like an equal. I find that very entertaining."

"I'm sure you would—since the two of us do exactly the same thing." She pushed herself out of the chair. "I suppose I'd better change into something befitting my station if I'm to visit Fleet Headquarters. What do you think of that navy blue outfit with a white blouse?"

"That should be fine." Jeniper followed her into the sleeping room Rieka shared with Triscoe.

Rieka retrieved the outfit from the closet. "How much more work are we going to need to do on that speech?"

"It looks fairly smooth," Jeniper replied. "A bit more polishing should do it."

Rieka grunted her agreement and began to change. "And what about our schedule once we get to Earth?"

"Nothing is doubling up so badly that I won't be able to manage it. But I'm going to need at least two assistants to handle the itinerary. And we're going to have to hire local people right away to supervise the details for the social events. Entertainment. Tours. Catering. Lodging." Jeniper paused and her tone became more serious. "Oh, and remember to ask your uncle if his legal staff plans to switch over to you or stay with him once you're inaugurated. And his PR staff, too, if you think of it."

"Two of a hundred or so questions on my list," she quipped. "I doubt we'll get to them all today."

"Do try to remember the important things, at least," Jeniper countered. "That outfit does look very nice on you. The admiral will be impressed."

Rieka glanced at herself in the mirror and nodded with approval. The white collar curved upward around her neck much like her old uniform, but beyond that, there was no comparison. The silky, deep blue overvest and pants clung to her in all the right places and followed her every move. "The admiral," she murmured, though silently agreeing with Jeniper, "is rarely impressed by anything, even heroics."

Admiral Nason rose and came around his desk to greet her as she entered his sanctum. "Rieka, you're looking well. I am glad you could come on such short notice."

She grinned and shook the hand he offered, noting his silent appraisal. "It's a pleasure to see you again, Admiral. I think. You're looking fit."

He nodded and gestured for her to sit in the chair opposite his desk. He ambled back to his own seat and said, "Complete recovery. Both lungs are functioning at 96 per-

cent—or so the doctors tell me. Of course I wouldn't be
here at all if Captain Finot hadn't intervened."

Rieka's smile faded. "A noble sacrifice," she murmured.
"We all miss him."

Nason's expression remained somber for a moment. "Indeed. But I believe he knew what he was doing. The risk
he took in putting himself in the line of fire."

She cleared her throat. "Yes. Well . . . am I correct in
assuming I'm here to sign my acquittance request?"

His pale blue eyes met hers, and she noted the stern set
of his bearded jaw. "I'm afraid the admiralty was unable
to grant you all the items you asked for."

Rieka accepted that with a slight nod. "How many were
left out?" she asked, silently wondering if they'd altered
her retirement or severance pay, or both, and by how much.

"Only one item, actually," Nason answered. "I have the
hard copy here—for you to look over and sign—if you
don't wish to appeal their decision."

Rieka frowned at him and pulled herself straighter in the
chair. "Which particular point are we talking about?"

"Discharge."

"What?" she huffed, grabbing the proffered document.
"They're going to make me stay in the Fleet for another
year—until my contract expires? That's ludicrous. How can
I possibly command a ship and act as Earth Herald at the
same time? I thought we worked this out months ago."

"It's not exactly as complicated as I may have implied,"
he said softly, obviously trying to soothe the blow. "Look
on page six."

Rieka read through the paragraph that had been marked
in the margin. "It's just Article Nine that they want
changed?"

"Yes."

She glanced at Nason and noted his bibbets were uncharacteristically dark. He was worried that she'd make a stink
about this, but it really didn't matter all that much.

"I think you're worrying over a stonefoot," she said,
using an Aurian phrase that meant the problem did not
really exist. "The circumstances listed here in which I could
be recalled to duty are simply not going to happen."

Nason had the decency to look relieved, but still held

himself with an aura of caution. "I'm glad you see it that way."

"Invasion," she read. "Medical Emergency. Epidemic. Insurrection. Mutiny. These things are hardly on the horizon for the Fleet, Admiral."

He nodded. "I thought so, too, but I've given up trying to predict the future," he told her sagely. "At any rate, I'm sure you understand the value of your command experience."

"Mmm." Rieka flipped through the pages, glancing at all the other articles in the acquittal contract. "It looks like everything else is in order. If you'll hand me a stylus, I'll be glad to sign this and be done with it."

"You're sure?"

"I'm sure. Is there something else I need to know?" she asked jauntily.

Nason placed his stylus on her side of the desk in such a way to make her hesitate to pick it up. "Perhaps."

She sighed and braced herself. "Then let's have it."

Nason leaned back in his chair again, and looked at her with a curious expression. "I am not sure, exactly, if anything is happening. But I have a sense of uneasiness."

"How so?" For Nason to make this statement, something had to be up.

He shrugged. "Nothing in particular. Huge shipments have been made recently. Mostly to and from Aurie. In some instances, valuable items have been lost. Oph stocks have been rising and falling hundreds of points in a very short time." Rieka nodded; she'd seen the stock reports, too. "Something seems to be shifting in the business world. The analysts all have ideas—but who can say what is really going on? My understanding is the business community is concerned about Earth's Reaffirmation—and how the Commonwealth economy will react. Still, I can't see that as the entire reason for this odd behavior."

Rieka took a moment to gather her thoughts before she spoke. "You know my opinion of the negative attitude the Commonwealth has toward Humans." She raised a hand to stop him from interjecting before she finished the thought. "And I'll admit there's a lot of speculation going on—about how the Reaffirmation will unbalance things," she said. "Even my mother has given me the end-of-the-world scenario. But let me assure you it is not my intent to disturb the economic status quo. I think everyone is blowing this out of proportion." She paused, and added, "I did everything in my power to keep this civilization out of Procyon hands. Why would I ever jeopardize it in any way?"

She felt a welcome wave of relief when Nason smiled and pushed the stylus closer to her side of the desk. "I'm glad to hear you say it, Herald. And I trust you to do what you say."

"Thank you, Admiral." She picked up the writing instrument and leafed to the contract's last page, then signed her name with her characteristic scrawl and handed the paper back. "I see you even managed to come up with a new rank—in the event of my return to the fold."

He tucked the contract into a drawer, and she watched in amazement as he actually grinned. "That was my recommendation," he admitted.

She grinned back at him and silently hoped no one in the Fleet would ever refer to her as Captain Herald Degahv.

She left the Fleet building a few moments later and stepped to the curb to hail a taxi. Momentarily blinded in the bright sunshine, Rieka squinted and caught herself as she collided with someone standing near a car. "Excuse me," she said.

"No problem," the man replied. Then, in the space of what seemed like a heartbeat, he opened the door and shoved her into the passenger compartment.

"What the hell?" She immediately turned and pressed at the door release, but nothing happened.

Out of the sun, she could see that the vehicle's interior was plush and the divider between the passenger compartment and the driver deeply tinted. She banged on it as a man, presumably the one who'd shoved her, took his place at the control.

"What is going on here?" she demanded.

By the time Rieka realized he couldn't hear her no matter how loud she yelled, the vehicle had left the curb. She searched frantically for an intercom switch and found one among several buttons under a uniquely disguised panel.

In as pleasant a voice as she could muster, she asked,

"Where are you taking me?" They glided silently past several Fleet office buildings before he answered.

"I've been asked not to say, madam."

"Stop this car immediately and let me out."

"This is not possible."

Rieka huffed. "You'd better do as I ask if you care about your standard of living for the next thirty years."

"I'm simply doing my job, madam," the chauffeur replied. "I was told, quite specifically, to fetch the Earth Herald."

FIVE

Rieka gave up banging on the window and watched as the scenery whizzed by. They'd left Rhonique some minutes ago. Once out of city traffic, the driver pushed their speed to the maximum, 150 kph.

Despite having been kidnapped, Rieka didn't feel threatened. Quite the opposite, in fact. Her curiosity was piqued. Knowing she could mentally contact Triscoe for help if she needed it, Rieka dismissed the abduction and concentrated on who the driver's boss might be. She couldn't decide whether it had been the cavalier way the man had spoken, or the interior elegance of the car, but somehow this "kidnapping" had the feeling of a command performance.

She knew for certain when they passed Kilpani township. It went by quickly, the few buildings little more than a multicolored blur. Then the road sign told her everything she needed to know. Olympic Drive was the next exit.

The driver turned off the main highway, and, a few minutes later, she could make out the tile roof over the tree line. Situated on a modest hill, her mother's manor house, Olympus, loomed like a reclining god. She watched, transfixed, as the edifice appeared for a brief moment only to be hidden again by the trees. She remembered the pony she'd had, and the huge closet, where she had often hidden to get away from the yelling. The clash of voices echoed across her mind, her father and mother in lengthy, bitter arguments over every detail of their lives.

A strange pain pulled her from her reverie. Looking down, Rieka realized her hands had balled into fists, the knuckles white. "You have no power over me now, Can-

dace," she whispered, consciously relaxing her fingers.
"You can't hurt me anymore."

They approached the hill quickly, and her captor did not
deign to slow down until he pressed the control for the
gates to open.

He continued to reduce their speed until they came to a
stop before the three-story monument to Candace Degahv's
business acumen. The driver opened her door, and she
stepped out, glancing daggers at him before stepping between two of the four massive columns guarding the front
entryway.

Rieka paused at the door, a grotesquely ornate thing
made of wood, twisted metal, and beveled glass. Deciding
she must be expected, she turned the knob and opened it.
Stepping into the entry, Rieka was overcome by the fact
that nothing, as far as she could see, had changed. The
fragrance of fresh-cut flowers on the foyer table brought
back even more childhood memories. Even a few pleasant ones.

"Hello," she called. "Mr. Dokins? Kenna? Mother?"

"Well, Miss Rieka, they said to expect you this afternoon, but I didn't believe it until this moment."

Rieka spun and looked at her mother's housekeeper,
Kenna. The woman looked the same as she had nearly two
decades ago. Her once blond hair now looked tinged with
gray, but her dark eyes still spoke of an inner calm, and
her smile still lit her entire face.

"Kenna." Rieka stepped forward and embraced the
woman she'd known as a child. "You look wonderful. I
would have recognized you anywhere."

Kenna's hug was fierce. "I'm so glad to see you," she
said, stepping back to hold Rieka's hands. "And look at
you. All grown-up. We followed the news last year, we did.
The battle and all, and you're being a hero. And I voted
for you last month, you know. You're so much like your
father, Miss Rieka. I just know you'll be a great Herald."

"Thank you, Kenna." Letting go Kenna's hands, Rieka
blinked back unexpected tears and turned to glance into
the huge front room. "I see you never convinced Mother
to change the flooring in there."

"Marble," the housekeeper grumbled. "Most idiotic
flooring to choose for such a room. So cold. So hard. I

daresay it's gotten a few nicks since you left. But she won't cover it, and she won't replace it."

"Probably only because my father suggested both those options."

Kenna nodded. "Probably. But I'm keeping you, prattling on so. Mrs. D. said you were to come to the office as soon as you arrived."

Rieka nodded. She stepped toward the lift and pressed her palm against the panel to call the car. "It was nice to see you again."

"The same here, Miss Rieka. Now don't let her bully you."

"I wouldn't think of it." She smiled to herself as the lift ascended. How long had it been since she'd answered to "Miss Rieka"?

The office door was closed. Not bothering to knock, she barged through.

Candace looked up from some papers on her desk.

Rieka noticed the ominous glare and ignored it, knowing Candace thrived on intimidation. She'd been a kid when she last lived here and had long outgrown empty threats. "Don't ever do that again, Mother," she warned. "Abduction is a felony."

"And you expect me to believe the new Earth Herald would actually grant me an audience through a mere request?" Candace shot back.

Rieka leaned over the desk slightly, enjoying the fact her mother had to look up to her, for once. "I promise you— do it again, and I'll file charges. You'll be running your precious empire from a prison cell."

Candace had enough sense to blanch at the threat. She took a deep breath, then indicated a cushioned chair near her desk. "Sit down, Rieka. Please."

Sure she'd made her point, Rieka pulled up the chair and sat. "I received your charming message almost a week ago. Has something changed since then?"

"Actually, no." Candace sat back in her chair and crossed her manicured fingers in her lap. "I had expected a response from you and did not receive one. So I thought it necessary to speak to you while you were here."

Rieka didn't bother to mention her presence on Yadra was not public knowledge. She'd long ago realized Candace had "retainers" in well-placed positions in both the Fleet and the Commonwealth's legislature.

"I don't respond to threats," Rieka answered with a shrug. "Just a little habit I picked up."

Candace frowned slightly before she schooled her face to the appearance of calm. "I have no idea what you're talking about. I didn't threaten you."

Rieka nodded. "Right. Not in so many words. But that big, 'Do what I say, or else,' was pretty obvious, Mother." Candace's face hardened into an expressionless mask and Rieka sighed. "You seem to think I'm planning to ship every last Human back to Earth. Tomorrow. I don't know where you got that insane idea—that is *not* on my agenda."

"But there are already a dozen underground cities on Earth ready for occupation," her mother countered. "You have prepared accommodations for almost ten million people. And more cities are under construction—or on the drawing board."

"So? Ten million people on a planet is nothing. Even ten million in a *city* is not that unusual."

"But by encouraging Humans to move to Earth, you're going to deplete the workforce on every other Commonwealth holding. And what do you intend to do with your ten million residents?"

"I don't intend to do anything with them." Rieka leaned forward and put her elbows on the edge of her mother's pristine white desk. Carefully, as though she were speaking to a child, she said, "A list of jobs has been compiled—everything from farming to engineering to bankers and teachers and plumbers. People will find out about these jobs and apply for them. If they get the job, they'll come to Earth to live and be a part of the community. What's so hard to follow?"

Candace sighed. "You're oversimplifying, trying to make me look like some kind of naysayer. I'm telling you to look at the numbers, the statistics, the projections."

"I understand that you're worried your little kingdom here might loose its firm foundation. But you're welcome to invest in the Earth, Mother. If the bottom line is so damned important to you, why can't you see this as a re-markable ground-floor opportunity? Projections tell me we're going to pay off our Commonwealth debt in only twenty-five years. Thirty-eight percent of that will be from the agro businesses. It's amazing."

"And it's going to ruin the economy of ten other worlds in the process."

"Oh, don't be ridiculous."

"You are the one who is being ridiculous."

Rieka leaned back and massaged her forehead with her fingertips. "Obviously we're not communicating. This endeavor will not happen overnight." She dropped her hand and stared purposefully into her mother's dark eyes. "It will take years. I agree if I were to suddenly InterMAT a million people off every planet it would cause problems. But we aren't talking mass exodus, here. We're talking about emigration. That takes time. And I promise you, it isn't going to be racially exclusive, either. Every race that can stand the atmosphere will find themselves welcome on Earth."

They glared at each other for a long moment. When Candace did not reply, Rieka considered an idea she hadn't thought much about, before. For a split second it seemed ludicrous, then she realized the argument might have some merit. "Or is this discussion about something else, entirely?" she asked, curiosity tinging her voice.

"I don't know what you mean."

"I think you do, Mother." Rieka sat straighter. "I think you've had a hidden agenda all along and the noise you've been making is simply to keep me from seeing the obvious."

"There is no other agenda," Candace replied innocently. "My concern is for the financial security of not only my business interests, but that of the entire Commonwealth. What you don't seem to comprehend—"

"—is the race issue," Rieka finished. "I hadn't thought of it before, but I can see where it might leave you and your business associates . . . a little nervous."

Candace furrowed her brow ever so slightly. "What do you mean?"

"Oh, it can't be that hard to follow, Mother, especially since you've already thought it through." Rieka took a breath and put her theory to words. "Triscoe once told me the other races in the Commonwealth were frightened of Humans because of our spirit. Our tenacity. Our ability to rise to a challenge. When free from the limitations we've endured for two centuries, Humans will exercise that incredible drive to succeed, to discover things, to become more than what we were. And that will only happen once we live on our own planet again. We'll be walking with the Earth under our feet. We won't be the orphaned aliens anymore. We will be *home*."

"But Rieka—"

She raised a hand. "And we will thrive without that burden of prejudice. And when a Human thrives, he or she is unstoppable. Yillon predicted it—of me. He knew I could save the Commonwealth from the Procyons. And I did, much to everyone's surprise. A mere Human. Can you imagine millions of us out there—doing our best?"

For a moment, Candace looked stricken. Then, she seemed to pull herself back together, and said, "What you are not considering—"

Rieka laughed then, cutting off her mother's sentence. "Gods! You have imagined it. And that scares the hell out of you, doesn't it?"

"You just don't seem to realize the damage this can do," Candace finally blurted. "Humans, when we lived on Earth before the Collision, were horrible creatures. Why do you think we weren't contacted? Why did it take a devastating meteor strike before the Centauris insisted on providing aid?"

Candace pushed herself out of the chair and paced behind the desk. "Because Human weren't fit to be Commonwealth citizens. We were barbaric. We fought petty wars over religion and land. We abused every sense of ethics. Young people purposely poisoned their bodies while the adults did everything they could to poison the world. Pollution was incredible. The air, land, and water were unfit."

Candace stopped for a breath, and Rieka saw the intensity of her conviction. Without the thumb of alien ethics to hold them in their place, Candace believed Humans would rise up and destroy the Commonwealth as they had almost done to the Earth.

"You're right, Mother. One hundred percent. I admit it: the textbooks tell us Humanity was an abomination. But even then, it was worth saving. And we have changed in the last two centuries. Out mind-set is completely different.

Mine is the third generation to have been born in the Commonwealth—right next to Centauris and Auries and Ophs and . . . whoever. Our consciousness has been raised by simply existing in an interplanetary community. You actually shock me with your shortsightedness."

Candace waved a hand dismissing that thought. "You are so incredibly naive."

"I don't think so." Rieka walked around to her mother's side of the desk and perched on the corner. "I fought in the Procyon War, Mother. I had the opportunity to kill. And I killed from a distance because it was them or me. And during that war I also had the option to murder. But I didn't. Believe me, I had both motivation and opportunity. And even in hand-to-hand combat, I did not kill Commander K'resh-va. I left his fate in the hands of our judicial system."

Her mother's face went white for a moment. "You fought with that animal?"

Rieka ran her tongue along the inside of her lip, where the scar still remained. Smiling crookedly, she murmured, "I'm not sure who enjoyed it more."

"There. See. Exactly. You enjoyed it!" Candace aimed an accusatory finger. "This is precisely what I'm talking about, and you aren't listening."

Rieka stayed motionless, amazed that her mother felt so deeply about this. "Mother, he'd wanted to kill me for a long time. And when I found out he'd set me up in the first place and then kidnapped me," she paused, making sure Candace heard the comparison, "I wanted to kill him, too. More importantly though, I had the opportunity—but *didn't*." Knowing it would be detrimental to her case, she purposely kept to herself the part about Triscoe's intervention in the fracas.

"I don't believe you," Candace said softly.

Rieka shook her head. "About what?"

"About your innocence. You wanted to control K'resh-va's fate more than you wanted him dead. So he was placed under arrest. It's as simple as that." Candace shook her head. "But we shouldn't be talking about war. We live in peace, now. And peacetime struggles can be far more vigorous."

"But no less important," Rieka noted.

"Correct." Candace glared at her once, then turned and walked to a window. "And lives are always at stake."

"What is that supposed to mean?"

Her back to her daughter, Candace said, "Paden would have understood."

Rieka pulled her fingers through her hair and sighed. "Let's not go into that, again. Under your influence, Paden refused to believe me. He took matters into his own hands and put his life and that of Ker Marteen in jeopardy. If he'd trusted me, he would be alive right now—as Herald-elect."

Candace turned toward her, and they locked eyes. Rieka's gaze remained steady. "Quit trying to lay the blame on my shoulders, Mother. I wasn't the one who pulled the trigger. And I wasn't the one who brainwashed him not to trust his own sister."

Candace's eyes widened as she absorbed the innuendo. "Are you blaming me?"

"Is there anyone else in the room?" Rieka left the desk and faced her mother's angry grimace. "He thought the way you wanted him to think, Mother. You taught him that his father had made a mockery of being Herald and his sister would never be anything more than a public servant. You told him he would be Earth Herald after Alexi. And he believed you. You held him in your grasp like a puppeteer does a marionette. And because you couldn't influence Dad or me, you hated us."

"Don't presume to speak for me, Rieka," Candace warned. A flush of pink spread over her cheekbones and chin.

Rieka could see her mother had been pushed far enough. She doubted anyone had been as candid with her since her last argument with Stephen. But if she did nothing else, Rieka meant to show her mother that the new Earth Herald was a considerable force.

"I don't need to. You've said and done enough on your own."

"Say what you mean."

"You need help, Mother. For all your wealth and power, as a Human you don't amount to much. You poisoned your son's mind. You disowned your daughter. And I'm beginning to believe you actually had a part in creating the accident that killed Dad."

Candace gasped, but Rieka went on as if her mouth had control of her mind instead of the other way around. "Now I have the power. And after your little stunt today, you can make sure the Earth Herald's security will increase tenfold. I'll not have you threatening me. Is that clear?"

"You don't actually believe—?"

"It doesn't matter what I believe. What *you* believe matters. And the *truth* matters. The minute I have any extra time, I'm going to investigate Stephen's shuttle accident. Thoroughly."

Rieka stormed from the room and headed for the lift, Candace behind her.

"You'll never prove anything with an investigation, Rieka," Candace shouted, her voice echoing through the entryway. "You're a fool if you try to go up against me. You'll never prove anything. And if you try—I'll see to it that you'll never succeed. At anything!"

The lift door opened, but Rieka turned at her mother's last comment. Did she know about Sati Labs? "I told you I don't like being threatened, Mother," Rieka told her calmly. "But since you've screamed it across the house, and I'm sure every servant has heard you, I'll tell you this." She aimed a finger at her mother's angry face. "If anything at all happens to me, the first person the authorities are going to investigate is *you.*"

Rieka took a deep breath and let her tone take on a lighter lilt. "Good-bye, Candace. Unless you want some bad press, the car had better be waiting for me by the time I get to the front door."

"I simply can't understand why she's so obstinate, Robet," Triscoe said as they ambled down a corridor in the Fleet Administration Building. He considered it a fortunate coincidence their schedules had brought them to Yadra today. Robet DeVark had a unique way of looking at things, especially when it came to Rieka.

"Rieka's always had a mind of her own," the Aurian captain offered sagely. "She managed fairly well when she was in the Fleet because she respects authority. But now . . ." He shrugged lightly. "Now she's got the clout."

Triscoe shook his head helplessly. They both returned a lieutenant's salute as they left the building, then went into the plaza between the Fleet's two huge office buildings. There were low walls around the plantings and statues, offering places to sit, but he didn't want to discuss his personal business in public.

He slowed his pace and glanced at his red-haired Aurian friend. Robet wasn't one to offer the practical answer to any problem, though he usually did bring a hidden side to light. "Rieka hasn't changed since the election, Robet. That will be obvious to you once you see her. But she simply won't back down on this business about having a child."

"It might be better if you understood why she feels so strongly," Robet offered. He gestured to a path through a small park.

Triscoe turned with him down the shaded lane and shoved his hands into his trouser pockets. "I understand why she feels the way she does," he said finally, "though I'm not sure she's completely conscious of the motive, herself. The problem is—the Earth Herald has been a position held by her family for two centuries. She means to have an heir."

Robet shrugged. "I'm certain there are other Degahvas in the Commonwealth. She doesn't have to produce another one to keep it in the family."

"Of course. But a child raised to think a certain way about Earth would make a far better Herald than one who might be indifferent."

"That's . . . probably true," Robet conceded. "I can't understand why you're not fighting her on this, Tris. You've already given that lab your tissue samples."

"I suppose I could have been conveniently too busy to do that," he admitted. "But it would only prolong the inevitable—and Rieka would have been furious."

They approached a bench that faced a small glade. Robet sat and Triscoe joined him, wondering whose side the Aurian was on. Then he realized Robet couldn't choose sides. He had a longtime friendship with both of them.

"It really isn't that I'm so adamant about the pregnancy—I just don't want her risking her life over something so—unnecessary. And the child might suffer terribly, too."

Robet nodded. "I can't disagree with you, Tris. If there were some way gestation could take place outside her body, you wouldn't have a problem, I suppose."

"That would solve the physical risk for her," Triscoe conceded, "but not the emotional one." He leaned forward and propped his elbows on his knees. "She's picturing a perfect infant with her hair and my eyes. But in truth, they still don't know what kind of . . . thing, would come from our combined cells."

"What are you saying?"

"Robet, our species have been living side by side for nearly two hundred standard years. We've become accustomed to the physical differences between us. But we evolved on different worlds. To attempt to ignore that is simply foolhardy." Triscoe stared at the ground between his feet and watched a bug crawl up a blade of grass, silently cursing himself for being the biggest fool of all. How could he have let so much time pass without explaining to Rieka their mental link's one negative aspect?

"You mean you think the doctors wouldn't let you know if something went wrong?" Robet asked softly. "Or can you trust them that much?"

Triscoe sighed. "I trust them to do their jobs. They are the best in the Commonwealth. And we're paying them an exorbitant amount to do this research. But the thing that has begun to really worry me is—will they even know if something is wrong? In attempting to combine two alien races, they'll be creating something totally new." He raked his fingers through his hair and looked into Robet's pale blue eyes. "I don't know what to think, or feel. But I know this is wrong, Robet. Beyond my fear for Rieka's safety, I know she's wrong."

Robet stayed quiet for a long moment. His bibbets remained a steady rosy pink. "And you haven't discussed this with her?"

"I've tried. She doesn't think I'm being reasonable. She knows I'm worried for her safety and dismisses it as anxiety."

"Can't she tell, though—in your mind? That this whole thing really disturbs you?"

"Through the Singlemind? No. I don't want to worry her with this. Until now, I've been counting on Sati Labs to fail. That would be the simplest thing, wouldn't it?"

"I suppose so," Robet agreed. "But it's also conceivable that Rieka's a lot stronger than you know. Gods, Tris, remember what she went through with her arrest and the Procyons? And I might remind you she didn't have a particularly pleasant childhood either. It's entirely possible you're jumping to some wrong conclusions, yourself. You two need to talk."

Triscoe didn't think so. "My mother has advised me to wait, so I haven't made myself available for such a conversation. Rieka will simply rant that I'm being unreasonably overprotective. She'll refuse to listen, I'll become frustrated—and that won't get us any closer to solving the problem."

"You've worked this all out ahead of time, haven't you?" Robet asked, then chuckled to himself.

"How can you possibly find anything funny about this?"

"It's just," Robet began with a smile still in his voice, "ridiculous. You both know each other so well, you think you can predict what will happen. But dammit, Triscoe, if Rieka is anything at all—she's completely *un*predictable."

Triscoe thought about that for a moment before he answered. "You may be right. But you haven't talked to her since Dr. Wilmstos interviewed us. It's become . . . a given. She expects to have a baby. A perfect, healthy hybridized child."

Robet shrugged. "I guess she's confident she can overcome any obstacle—even those beyond her control."

"I don't think I will ever understand how Humans believe they can change the immutable."

Robet laughed and slapped Triscoe on the shoulder. "Sorry, friend. But I'll have to disagree with you on that one. It isn't Humans that think they can change everything, it's *women*."

SIX

Unlike the greeting she'd gotten on Indra, Alexi's receptionist on Yadra welcomed Rieka as soon as she came through the door. She was ushered immediately into a private waiting area complete with comfortable furniture and a refreshment buffet. While she helped herself to some fruit juice, the woman told Rieka that Herald Degahv would be with her shortly.

"A ruse," she murmured after the door closed. She'd been among the elite long enough to realize waiting was merely a psychological tool, appointment or no.

From what she'd seen of the outer office, Alexi ran this embassy with a bigger budget than he did on Indra. Budgeting, she thought, another thing on my list.

She opened her datapad and tapped some notes from her meeting with Nason. He'd told her once the board of admirals had signed the contract he would forward a copy to her, or else bring it himself when he attended the Reaffirmation ceremony on Earth. She added in the terms of reinstatement so she wouldn't forget to tell Jeniper or Triscoe about them. It would be a good conversation starter, anyway, she mused. She and Triscoe had had too few of them, recently.

The door opened, and Alexi bustled in with outstretched arms and a smile that bordered on sinister. "Rieka! Oh, my little Rieka. Just look at you." He beamed when she stepped forward and into his padded embrace.

Rieka endured a squeeze, a back rub, and finally several pats before he released her. "How are you? You look great," she told him.

He rocked his head from side to side. "I am fine now.

Last year was bad, you know. With the liver problem and such. And it is good that I'm retiring—and leaving the family business to you. The doctors claim that the stress of the office has not done me any good."

"I wish you wouldn't call it that."

"What?"

"The family business."

He raised his eyebrows and chuckled. "And what else is it? Earth's Herald has been a Degahv since the Collision. It was written into our constitutional agreement that only a Degahv represent the Earth to the Commonwealth—unless and until another agreement is reached. I see no reason to change what has stood for two hundred years."

She gave in to his argument and raised both hands to signal surrender. "And please accept my apology for being late. I had a—an experience—with Candace."

Alexi sobered. "Oh. I see," he murmured, his bushy brows furling over his eyes. "Nothing too horrible, I hope?"

"I'll handle her, Alexi. Now, what is so important that it can't wait for a few weeks?"

"Come. Bring your drink." He turned so quickly Rieka thought he'd lost his balance. But he hurried out the door without so much as a glance over his shoulder. She followed him into his richly paneled office. He gestured for her to sit on the sofa, then lowered himself into a cushioned armchair and heaved a sigh.

"I must lose some weight, the doctors tell me," he explained, breathing more heavily than she thought healthy. She couldn't tell if he really felt ill or was simply acting. While he'd always been rotund, Rieka decided that he did look heavier than the last time she'd seen him, only a few months ago. There was a ruddy flush to his skin, making his black eyes sparkle and his hair look even whiter than it was.

"I hope you intend to do what they say," she warned him. "There aren't many of us left, and I'd just as soon you stick around with the living as long as possible."

"Fond of your father's brother, are you?" he asked with a laugh. "I haven't seen you come visiting much in the last few years."

"We've gone over this before, Alexi. The Fleet doesn't

give captains a great deal of time off. And your schedule
has been as busy as mine. I didn't even get to see you at
the *Prodigy*'s dedication."

"I hadn't meant to be tardy," he apologized. "But it was
a fortunate happenstance, yes? Joel Ciccone's housing contract with Aurie was under dispute. I missed the attack
and arrived on the *Varannah* shortly before the Fleet left
for Medoura."

"And I suppose I'm lucky you did," she said candidly.
"I can't imagine how Triscoe must have felt with both parents on the Little One during the skirmish. If you'd been
there, too, I never would have been able to concentrate."

"How flattering." An aide knocked on the door and entered discreetly, bringing a tray of crackers and cheeses.
"Thank you, Deborah," he told her. She nodded and left.

Rieka quirked a brow at the healthy selection. Alexi had
always preferred to serve high-calorie treats to his guests
as an excuse to eat them, himself. "Now that we've caught
up on the recent past, would you mind getting to the point?
You told me you'd be available for at least three months
after the inauguration—as my advisor, I believe you put it."

Alexi drew his bushy brows together and pursed his lips
but didn't say anything. Rieka decided that wasn't a good
sign. "You're not. Well that's great, Alexi. Tell me, did you
decide this—before or after you gave me your assurances?"

He put up his hands defensively. "The circumstances now
are regretfully different than when I promised to help you
ease into the job. Immediately following my next trip to
Earth, I am going to Perata. The doctors there are quite
the experts. They've said if I don't deal with my liver problem as soon as possible—I won't have any problems at all."

It took a second for Rieka to realize he was making light
of an apparently serious illness. Her heart skipped a beat.
"It's that serious?"

"I am afraid so."

Rieka sighed and dipped her head. Her uncle had always
been there, distant perhaps, but ever-present. The thought
of his mortality hit her like a maitu stun. She rubbed her
right temple for a moment before raking her hand through
her hair. "When did you plan on telling me?"

"I . . . just did."

He looked at ease with the problem and the decisions

he'd made, so Rieka went along with him. Her father's death had been sudden, unexpected. Alexi's apparently would be slow. She wasn't sure she preferred one way over the other. In any case, she would make a point of visiting Perata as often as possible.

Looking him in the eye, Rieka said, "I want you to promise me you'll keep me up-to-date on your . . . condition."

Serious for once, he answered, "Of course."

She nodded. "Then let's get started on this tutorial. It looks like I'm going to need it." She reached for her data-pad, and turned it on.

When he smiled at her, his entire face lit up, and the rest of his body relaxed as if he'd been waiting for her to reject his offer or argue his decision. "Good. Good." He leaned forward and picked up a small chunk of cheese. "Food for thought, eh?"

"Yeah." Having missed lunch, she reached for a cracker and devoured it.

"First," he began, gesturing emphatically with his hands, "the position itself. As you know, by definition, the Earth Herald is Earth's diplomatic ambassador to the Commonwealth. Since Peter and the time of the Collision, however, none of us has actually done that—simply because Earth has had no population to speak of. So, it has been subdivided, if you will, into representing the Earth—and representing Humanity on all the other words. A difficult task.

"But we have managed fairly well," he added.

She nodded, hoping he'd get to the point. "As Herald, you are empowered by the people to act in their best interest with regard to the Commonwealth. You have no power between individual—that is to say—personal contractual agreements and the like. Such conflicts are for the courts to decide. But if there is a difficulty in conceiving an agreement or living up to one involving a government body, your involvement is mandatory if requested by either side.

"The Heralds meet annually, of course, to decide on a budget and equally mundane things. And perhaps to negotiate certain problems on a less formal level.

"But basically you are an ambassador. Humanity's foremost public-relations tool. Your position gives you great flexibility, for you can choose to mediate a dispute yourself, or go to the Judiciary—and they are compelled by the

Commonwealth Constitution to address any issue brought
forward by a Herald. But generally you will be participating
in goodwill activities. You will attend functions. Be a public
figure. A model Human. This is the best thing you can do
for Earth. Keep it in a positive light with everything running smoothly. Or the appearance of running smoothly.
Does this sound remotely familiar?"

She finished another cracker and swallowed. "Of course.
I lived with my dad for years. And recently with Herald
Marteen. But you said so yourself—Earth's situation is
unique. I may have to push the rules from time to time.
Be outspoken."

"One of your many talents," he said trepidatiously.

Rieka chuckled. "Now, something a little more pressing
is the budget. This year it was six million credits. Since we
pay a flat rate for travel and embassy real estate, I don't see
how I can possibly spend that much. Salaries and business
expenditures, as far as I can tell, come to a little over
four million."

"Yes, but you are forgetting the incredible amount of
entertaining you will do. Lunches, dinners, parties. My dear
niece, it all adds up."

She cleared her throat, and told him, "I intend to
work, too."

"Of course you do. And you will. But politics is not
physical labor. It is a business of strategy, strength of character, and patience." He smiled knowingly. "You will develop patience soon enough, I'm sure."

"Very funny. I suppose that's why everything takes so
long to get approved, or budgeted, or completed."

He frowned. "You must understand that we are required
to look at any decision from all angles. From every point
of view. If information is lacking, we must have studies
done and wait for the data to come in. This does take time,
yes. But it is necessary. We need to make the best decision
possible, especially if the Council of Ten is convened. As
a body, the Planetary Heralds are equal in power to the
Senate and Judiciary. We have even overturned their decisions on occasion. You must learn to work with them—to
your advantage."

"Are you discouraging me on purpose?" she inquired
with a sideways grin.

"You will be a wonderful Herald," he came back, his eyes wide. "I don't doubt that for a moment."

"Because I'm the antithesis of what you just described? Demanding. Straightforward. Impatient."

"No. Because you remind me of your father." He paused, then beamed at her. "He was a great Herald, Rieka. And you are very much like him."

Several things came to mind, but all she said was, "I hope so."

He leaned toward her and rested his forearms on his knees. "Now, I must tell you about the meetings I've been having with RadiMo."

She set up a new file on her datapad, typed in the Bournese Herald's name, and looked at him. "I hope you don't mind if I take notes on this, too."

"Not at all. The Bournese are interested in mining certain ores and gemstones. There are several spots on Earth they are interested in. RadiMo has been gathering information for three Bourne companies: Kimcon, BeliCo, and MiliCorp. They all intend to bid for the contract. You should plan to speak on Bourne's behalf to the Senate in the event we require legislation on the matter. It is in Earth's best interest to encourage trade with all Commonwealth planets."

Rieka shrugged. "Doesn't that go without saying? This doesn't sound terribly complicated, Alexi. I should be able to handle a mineral-rights contract."

"Good. Now, as a gesture of good faith, RadiMo is also lending his services to us. In addition to gathering information for his own planet, he has been overseeing the plans for three more subterranean cities."

"And they are?"

"New SubMoscow, SubBeijing, and SubBrasilia."

"Got them," she said, tapping at the datapad.

"You should assist RadiMo in whatever way you can, Rieka," he told her. The tone of his voice urged her to comply. "He represents the first of the member worlds not only to take an interest in capitalizing on Earth's many resources—but to offer his help as we try to repopulate."

"I hear you, Alexi," Rieka said. "And I know negotiation with the Bournese is very difficult. Almost as bad as trying to talk to a Boo. I respect what you've done so far, and I'll do my best to see that RadiMo is happy. I'll even ask Setana if she can give me any tips."

"Good. Good," he said, beaming. "She has a wealth of information in that regard. It was she, in fact, who told me of the Bourne's interest in rubies. That conversation sparked this entire relationship."

Rieka shut down her datapad and smiled at her uncle. "I'm sure she was happy to help. Is there anything else?"

"Yes. Do not trust RadiMo completely."

Rieka looked into Alexi's face. He was serious. "Say that again."

Alexi gestured vaguely with a hand. "The Bournese are very . . . literal. And also secretive. Perhaps it comes from living underground, I don't know." He shrugged. "Anyway, they have a certain talent when speaking the standard language through their translator computers that—for want of a better term—lies through omission."

"So you have to pay attention to what they don't say in addition to what they do?"

"Precisely."

Rieka returned her attention to the datapad. "Thanks, Alexi. This is exactly the type of information I need. Now, not to change the subject, but I will," she began, reactivating her datapad. "I've got a few questions. The first one is about that other deal with the Bournese—involving produce."

They went on for nearly an hour more, Rieka asking her questions and Alexi answering them. Finally, seeing he'd begun to tire, she nodded. "I think that's it, for now."

"I wish I could do more," Alexi told her, a sad note in his voice. He sat straighter and studied her. "You have selected your adjutant?"

Rieka nodded. "Her name is Jeniper Tarrik. I believe you know her."

"The Aurian who runs the office on Indra?"

She smiled. "She ran the office. We promoted her replacement just before we left."

"Are you sure you want a non-Human?"

"Yes," Rieka told him irritably. "I've met a lot of people in the last six months. She's the best person for the job— which means she actually *listens* to what I say. And unless she gives me cause to fire her, she's my adjutant—as of next week."

Alexi nodded. "That's fine, I'm sure. She never had any problems handling Indra."

Rieka winked. "Don't worry. I'm a decent judge of character. And Setana likes her, too."

"I'm sure she'll be fine," he repeated, then glanced at the wall behind her and made a strange face. "I hadn't meant to keep you so long. I will see you before you leave for Earth, yes? For dinner tonight. At my residence. And bring Triscoe and Jeniper."

"Another party for your expense account?"

Alexi laughed, a full rolling chuckle. "Perhaps."

Triscoe sat at his desk in his quarters, reading through Aarkmin's daily report without much real interest. Robet's words kept coming back to him, and he couldn't help but wonder at his friend's newfound wisdom. Robet DeVark's reputation for seeing little beyond the obvious was slowly being replaced with a mature, objective outlook. Perhaps his mother was correct when she predicted Robet would be settling down soon.

But Triscoe knew explaining the real reason for his concern would not be easy. Rieka's reaction to the one last aspect of the Singlemind he hadn't yet explained would be explosive. Not wanting to upset or distract her during the election process, he'd let the days slip by. Now he realized he might never find a proper time.

Unable to concentrate on the report, Triscoe shut down the computer just as Rieka came through the door. Immediately, he noticed her gray eyes had turned to steel. She nodded at him, her jaw set. "We have to talk."

He rose and cautiously moved toward her. A brief touch with her mind gave him a sense of anger and frustration. "All right," he said softly, gesturing toward a chair. When she sat, he gently asked, "Did you see Nason this morning?"

"Yes."

"And he gave you the acquittal papers?"

"I signed an edited version." She gestured vaguely with her hands. "No problem. I'll get a hard copy once the board of admirals okays it."

Her terse response gave him a distinctly uneasy feeling. "And you had an appointment with Alexi," he coaxed, hoping to discover the force behind her reined ire.

"Yes."

"How did that go?"

"Fine. He's seriously ill. We talked. I took notes." She tossed her datapad onto the table beside her.

He wanted to question her about that revelation, but sensed her uncle wasn't the problem. "And after that?" he coaxed.

"After that, I came back to the *Providence*. It's what happened after Nason and before Alexi that was, shall we say, disquieting."

"Rieka," he began, waiting until she looked at him to finish his question, "what happened before you met with Alexi?"

She sighed. "It isn't like it sounds—but . . . I was kidnapped."

Before he could respond to that outrageous statement, she raised a hand, her expression hard. He hadn't seen such determination since he'd stopped her from killing K'reshva.

"This time, it was relatively harmless. My mother sent her driver to 'fetch' me. But that doesn't alter the facts. I need security, Tris. I need a bodyguard."

Though he agreed with her, Triscoe knew she chafed at anyone assuming even the slightest responsibility when it came to her safety. "Are you sure that's what you want?"

"I'm sure," she replied, her voice a grating monotone. "A bodyguard is going to look conspicuous, but Candace isn't going to give up, and I don't believe she's completely rational."

Triscoe frowned. "What are you saying?" he asked softly, almost afraid of the answer.

"I'm saying this abduction was just a way to prove her point. And if I don't do what she wants—which I won't— I think she'll do something really stupid." She sighed and shook her head. "Maybe even try to have me killed."

SEVEN

Rieka knew Triscoe had been furious with her for not contacting him immediately when she'd been abducted. But two days had gone by and each silent moment now fueled her own anger. He's busied himself with ships' business day and night during their trip from Tau Ceti to Sol. He'd used every possible excuse not to be alone with her and had had almost no contact with her mind.

Which was why Rieka became curious when he entered their quarters and sat down as if to stay awhile.

She looked up from the console to acknowledge his presence, then turned some of her concentration back to the projected attendance at the Reaffirmation ceremony, pitiful though it was.

"Rieka, I need to talk to you," he began, echoing her own words from two days ago.

As she punched a key to suspend the data, a sense of apprehension tingled down her spine. "I thought you might," she said, wondering what topic had taken precedence on his agenda.

He smiled crookedly, a dimple appearing on his right cheek. "I would like you to interview several people. I'm going to hold you to your word that you will accept protection—even if I'm not the one providing it."

She shook her head, confused. "How could you have lined up job applicants in such a short time? We've been in transit for over thirty hours."

"I made inquiries before we left Yadra," he told her. Rieka thought the permanent frown he'd worn since she'd told him about the visit with her mother showed signs of cracking. "As soon as we came out of phase, I received notice that two individuals would be waiting at Earth to apply for the position of your personal bodyguard. There is another, here on the *Providence,* who wishes the job as well. A member of my crew."

She shook her head. "I can't do that. Mixing politics and Fleet personnel is strictly taboo. You know that."

"This one is willing to give up his career."

"From what rank?"

The frown became slightly more apparent. "Lieutenant."

"Who?"

"Martinez in Security."

She shook her head. "No. That's crazy." She paused a moment to think. Perhaps Martinez had a reason to want to leave the Fleet. She'd have to wait and see. "Look, the best I can do is interview them all and be fair. Let's hope your crewman isn't the most qualified."

"I am relieved to hear it—to a certain extent." She watched the frown ease slightly as he relaxed a bit against the cushions.

"I admire that kind of conviction, Tris. I just won't be party to destroying a budding career. A lieutenant, for heaven's sake." She took a breath and considered the possibility of hiring a bodyguard before she left the *Providence.* That notion felt good.

She watched Triscoe rub his hands on his thighs, a sure sign of stress. "So why are you still worried? I'll have a guard soon. Jeniper has plans to line up an entire security team once we're in Earth orbit. Everything will be fine."

"Yes. Everything will be fine."

"Except . . ." she prompted.

"Except us." His brown eyes were hard when they met hers, and Rieka realized more than just her steadfast independence bothered him.

"I told you before—I didn't feel threatened," she explained, knowing the excuse was lame. "Well, not in so many words. Being kidnapped isn't like being invited to a party. But it's happened to me before, and this time I didn't feel my life was in danger. If I had, I would have notified you right away."

Frustrated, Rieka stood and walked back to the desk. They'd gone over this before, and she still felt her judgment had been sound. Rehashing old worries did no one any good. She picked up her datapad and began to set up three files for the applicants so she could keep them straight.

"I appreciate your thoughtfulness," he said, and she sensed he wasn't being facetious. "But we have not reconciled several personal issues."

Rieka put down the datapad as he came toward her. He grabbed up her hands and held them both tightly as if fearful she would escape. "You are married to a Centauri, Rieka. A Centauri with the *quantivasta* gift. Problems cannot be ignored."

"I didn't think I was ignoring anything," she said softly, feeling an overwhelming sensation course through her at his touch. "I've set some things aside recently, so I could focus on more important . . . issues."

"I think it is more than 'things' you've set aside."

"I get it," she said, hoping her bravado held while she felt a wave of something strong and insistent work its way through her. "You mean I've ignored *you*. Well, since we left Yadra, it seems to me that *you're* the one who's been too busy to talk—or do anything else for that matter."

"I have been preoccupied with finding a way to tell you how I feel. I admit that."

She heaved a little sigh. "Okay. I take it you've come to a decision."

"Precisely. You've always been intuitive, Rieka," he murmured.

The compliment didn't boost her confidence. She felt him tug her, and she followed willingly as he moved back to the sofa.

"Sit."

She did. "I don't under—"

"Shh. Close your eyes."

It was almost a relief not to have to look at him. He'd placed her at the sofa's end, her back braced against the arm as she faced him. She felt it when he joined her, his weight shifting the cushions. He held her there, his hands gripping hers, working themselves up toward her wrists.

"Open your thoughts to me, love."

Why didn't you just say you wanted to Singlemind? she asked silently. *I would have understood.*

I don't think so. His next thoughts weren't clear enough

for her to understand in words, but he seemed both motivated and reluctant to continue.

Rieka relaxed and felt him ease into her mind. He
seemed more chaotic than she remembered. Knowing he
wouldn't believe her unless he experienced it for himself,
she purposely recalled her visit with her mother, including
how she got there.

She felt him accept it, and welcomed a small reprieve
when he finally agreed she hadn't really been in danger.
But then she felt something unexpected happen.

He receded into his mind. It left an unpleasant void between them, and she didn't know what to do.

Triscoe must have understood her confusion, because she
heard him whisper. "Come to me, Rieka."

"I don't know how."

"Let go of yourself. Fill in the empty space and come
to me."

Eyes still closed, she tried. But letting go of herself didn't
seem possible. She sensed her mind inching away and then
snapping back as if some kind of self-preservation instinct
refused to let go.

"It's not working," she whispered. "I'm trying but—"

"—don't try," he told her. "Just float. I will lead."

Floating, she guessed, would be a kind of nothingness
she could manage. Carefully, purposely, she made herself
hover not far from that instinct that kept her centered,
aware and able to withdraw into herself in a heartbeat.

"You're doing fine," he coached. "Now I'm going to
reach out to show you the path."

Not quite sure what path he meant, Rieka waited. She
felt him come back toward her, the emptiness recede, and
a kind of necessity encroach on her consciousness. She
needed to go to him. Somehow, he'd given her a compul-
sion to enter his mind. Unable to recall her motivation, she
inched forward.

"Yes. That's it."

Rieka continued, albeit slowly. Her consciousness eased
across the emptiness until it touched him. She felt the orga-
nization of his thoughts, so alien from hers. A palette of
colors and patterns and textures. The depth of his
emotions.

She felt tears sting her eyes when she touched the sensa-

tion of gold that seemed to be fused with everything around
her. Instantly, Rieka realized this was his love. It overwhelmed her, caressed her, held her in its gentle embrace.
It had no boundaries, though she could sense places where
it had been tempered with logic. She began to comprehend
the vital differences between them. Centauri love was more
complete than she'd ever imagined.

Come here, his voice silently told her mind.

She eased away from that deeply emotional part of him
and toward more rational thought, and wondered if he felt
the same things when he came to her mind. If he became
so involved with her being that he forgot how to be himself.

Where? she asked, suddenly realizing the vastness before her.

Here. A bluish area grew brighter. Feeling overwhelmed
and exhilarated, she moved toward that light.

As she reached it, Rieka felt the blue and him together,
as if she'd touched his very essence. Then, surprisingly, she
also sensed herself. Or a reflection of herself. She didn't
know which. But there seemed to be a double being within
him—as if Triscoe, by himself, was not complete.

Correct, he told her. *You are always here with me. It is
the Centauri way.*

Is this a recollection of me?

No.

Then, that means . . . what?

*Both of us exist here within me. If you die, part of me
will die, as well. It is possible I would not survive alone.*

Rieka felt her body, somewhere out there far away, shudder. During the war with the Procyons, her life had been
almost constantly in danger. Now she understood that his
fear for her safety wasn't as irrational as she'd thought. It
had to do as much with self-preservation and instinct as it
did common sense. She'd taken so many chances since
they'd exchanged their vows all those months ago. And
he'd stood by, allowing her to risk both their lives for the
greater good. How could he stand it? Why hadn't he told
her sooner?

Then another thought struck her. *But not every mate dies.
I've met widows and widowers.*

Few Centauris have the gift, he reminded her.

Rieka felt like kicking herself for not realizing that sooner. *Then why tell me now?*

She felt him hesitate as the answer came to her. He'd kept this knowledge apart from their conversation because he'd waited for her to come to the conclusion herself.

The child. Their child. Just as she held his fate in her hands, she held that child's fate, too. If something were to happen during the pregnancy, all three of them would suffer.

She absorbed the impact of that realization and felt herself recede from him. She slid through his love, again, and was surrounded with overwhelming devotion before easing back into the void. When she left him, Rieka felt her body shiver. She gasped for air, suddenly aware she'd forgotten to breathe.

"Rieka." Triscoe's hands cupped her face, and she felt his thumbs slide along her cheeks. "Rieka, don't cry. Open your eyes, love."

She blinked at him once before sliding her arms around his neck and pressing her cheek into his shoulder. She felt his arms come around her and marveled at their strength in the face of such fragility.

Promising herself to determine the necessity of everything she did from now on, Rieka allowed herself to sob quietly against him, feeling a tremor run through him almost every time she made a noise.

"I didn't do it to frighten you," he whispered finally. "I did not know any other way to make you understand."

"It isn't as thought you haven't tried," she admitted, sniffing and pulling back to look at him. His brown eyes were no different than before, but now she saw so many new things in them.

"And now I must ask you a difficult question." He paused, then asked, "Why do you wish to have a child?"

Sure she hadn't heard him correctly, Rieka made a face. "I want a family. You know that."

Triscoe nodded. "So do I. But *why* do you want one?"

She shook her head, confused. "Why does anyone?"

He offered a soft smile. "For many reason, I would guess. But you said nothing about children until after Paden died and you decided to run for Earth Herald."

She thought about that, then said, "I suppose that's an accurate observation."

"So then, why? Do you seek to replace that sense of belonging you haven't felt since your father died? Or, are you looking for an heir?"

The questions stopped her. Insulted, Rieka started to make a snide comment, then realized he was right. She turned away and tried to think.

Gently, his mind voice whispered, *I don't know, either.*

"I've been selfish, haven't I?" she asked finally, glancing up into his concerned face. "And you're right, Tris. I want an heir. And I want a child to fill an empty space." She shook her head. "But those reasons don't outweigh the risks I've been willing to take with—with our lives."

The look of relief on his face conjured feelings of both guilt and happiness. She felt a sense of pale blue serenity as he asked, "So what shall we do now?"

"Wait," she answered instantly. "It seems like the only thing we can do until a lot of questions are sorted out. I think the biggest one, for me, is understanding how my father died." His death and what caused it had been bothering her for days. Had that and Alexi's health problems brought on a sense of her own mortality? Rieka didn't know, but dwelling on it probably wouldn't help. "We should tell Wilmstos to put everything on hold until we're both emotionally ready to start a family. Maybe when your commission is over and you're not touring anymore."

She smiled faintly, and sniffed. "And we don't *have* to try to combine our genes. Ker's idea may have been a good one, after all. We could simply tell Wilmstos we want a Human child that *looks* Centauri."

Triscoe nodded and the sense of pale blue faded into a deep midnight. "I'm due back at Indra in a few days," he said. "I think it best one of us should speak to him in person."

Her smile faded. "How can you stand being married to me? It must be awful."

He shook his head. "It's wonderful." She watched him quirk his mouth. "You are the most vital, spirited, inspirational person I have ever met. You are my *wife.* In my mind that makes me the more fortunate one."

Rieka didn't realize she'd moved until she felt the warm

softness of his lips against hers. She kissed him gently at first, then as the moments passed the tenderness and respect evolved into passion.

Triscoe responded in kind. By the time she'd worked his tunic loose, she felt cool air across her shoulders and his hands on her breasts.

He was murmuring something into the skin at the base of her neck when she heard a noise in the corridor. "Tris, the door."

"Mmm. No one would enter my cabin."

"But Jeniper . . ."

He sat back. "Lock it."

Rieka got up, activated the lock, and turned back slowly, knowing his attention would be on her breasts. Indran females didn't have them, and Triscoe's fascination with them bordered on obsessive. When she returned to the sofa, both his dimples were shamelessly displayed. "What?" she asked innocently, her hands on her hips.

"I am simply enjoying the view."

Flaunting herself inches from his face, Rieka tried not to smile. "Which is precisely why you asked *me* get up to lock the door," she murmured.

He leaned forward but didn't touch her. Still, she could feel his breath on her skin when he said, "You did it, anyway."

She could only see his crown of blond hair as she looked down at him. When his lips finally made contact, Rieka gripped his shoulders. "Gods, Triscoe, you are a quick study."

I accept the compliment, he told her gallantly.

Her voice sounded raspy, even to her. "Then you should remember that after the last time, I swore I would never again make love on this sofa."

I haven't forgotten.

Taking her hand, he led her to the bedroom and set her gently on the mattress. She reached for him, but he stepped away and slowly began to remove his shoes.

Rieka groaned and stood up. He set his shoes by the bed, then turned and pushed her back on the mattress. She reached her arms around him, but he pushed her away. Taking a step back, he slowly began to undo his waistband.

"Triscoe—"

"Patience."

"You are such a tease," she complained.

His answering chuckle sent a shiver down her spine. "I learned it from you."

Jeniper rang for admittance at Captain Marteen's door and wondered what the day would be like. She and Rieka had finished the inaugural speech and were working on the Reaffirmation details, but things were not going well.

Problems seemed abundant in Damascus, and Rieka wouldn't rest until they were resolved. Two caterers had canceled. Florists had informed them the arrangements that had been ordered weeks ago were unavailable. The stadium crew had yet to complete the infield stage. Jeniper found herself nothing short of amazed. At each piece of incoming bad news, Rieka would come up with at least three alternative plans. The woman's energy in her approach to unexpected obstacles could be staggering.

Captain Marteen appeared as the door slid open. "Good morning, Jeniper," he said. "Are you ready for your first close up look at Earth? It will only be another hour or so."

"Good morning," she replied, as he stepped back and she entered. "Is it so much different than the DGI image?"

Seated on the sofa, Rieka looked up from her datapad, an intense look on her face. "Is ice different from water?"

Jeniper felt the captain's eyes on her, as if waiting for her to fall into some kind of rhetorical trap. "Yes. No. It—it depends upon how you look at it."

"Well—there you go," Rieka said.

"And here I go," the captain told them. "I'll notify you once we're nearing orbit."

Jeniper nodded and smiled at him as he left. "Your husband is . . ."

"What?"

She shrugged. "I was going to say an enigma. But then I've never known a Fleet captain personally, before. Maybe his behavior is normal, and I am simply seeing more than there is."

Jeniper thought she saw Rieka flush a bit before she answered. "You see exactly what he wants you to see. No more, no less," she replied sagely. "But basically, you're right. And I've known plenty of Fleet captains. Triscoe is . . . arcane."

Not quite sure how to respond to what she decided must be a Human term, Jeniper changed the subject. "Working on the Reaffirmation speech?"

Rieka shook her head. "I'm going over the questions to ask my potential bodyguards. Triscoe and I were just discussing whether or not to ask if they'd ever killed anyone."

Jeniper felt herself frown as she sat on one of the chairs. "Is that something you want to know? Would it make a difference?"

She knew she'd been set up when her boss grinned. "It isn't the answer that really matters, Jen," Rieka told her. "It's how the person responds to the question. If they did, are they proud of it? Or were there extenuating circumstances that warranted the act? Lots of possibilities, there—not just a yes or no."

Jeniper nodded. The thought of murder, either in self-defense or not, made her think of Jonik's predicament. Surely he was just stretching the truth in order to gain her sympathy when he'd spoken of that threat. He'd already used nearly every other ploy to persuade her to give him a loan. She'd been expecting the life-or-death gimmick for some time. Still, the thought of his bibbets when he'd walked away gave her plenty to think about.

"Are you okay?"

Jeniper gave herself a little shake as Rieka's question penetrated her reverie. "Oh, of course. I, uh . . . suppose the question is reasonable," she offered, going back to the original topic. "After all, the person is supposed to be able to defend you against any adversary."

"I thought so," Rieka agreed. "Except Triscoe wanted me to change the question to: *would* you kill someone? There's a lot more happening in the subconscious when you ask something like that."

"Perhaps you should include both questions," Jeniper suggested.

"Maybe, but the interviews have to be conducted in just under ninety minutes. Once we make orbit, neither of us is going to have a lot of time to do anything. I've got to eliminate every question I can."

Jeniper found herself making a small noise in agreement.

Once they reached a stable Earth orbit the word "busy" would be an understatement.

Rieka sat mesmerized by the blue planet on the DGI in Triscoe's quarters. She hadn't been to Earth in almost a year, and couldn't help wondering how she'd be received.

The door opened. "Permission to enter?" Jeniper asked from the corridor, though it sounded more like a statement.

Rieka shifted her attention from the three-dimensional vista. "We seem to be getting awfully formal all of a sudden," she jibed. "It isn't as if you weren't here an hour ago. Come in."

"This planet is your seat of power, Herald," Jeniper reminded her, stepping forward and following Rieka's silent gesture to sit. "You must command respect here, of all places. If you do not . . ."

"I'll be looked on as a fool," Rieka finished. Jeniper's silence made her smile. Little did her companion know she'd played the fool often enough in the past. "When you agree with me, say so, Jeniper. I've asked for your candid opinion at all times, and I expect it."

"Of course."

Rieka sighed. It would take months for this woman to feel comfortable enough to be a friend. She glanced back at the DGI. Triscoe had brought them to a high, stable orbit, and she could just make out the curve of North Africa as they approached it from the southwest.

"Do you know much Earth history?" she asked.

"What they teach in school," Jeniper replied, looking up at the planet's image.

"That's a bunch of sh—" Rieka caught herself before she embarrassed Jeniper again. "Excuse me, I'll rephrase that. The textbooks don't explain the half of it. And quite probably only a handful of people will ever know what really happened."

Jeniper leaned forward. "You're saying the Commonwealth teaches a lie?"

Rieka smiled. "Not in so many words. The lie is purely by omission. We discovered the true facts during the trouble with the Procyons six months ago. That knowledge convinced me to run for Herald."

When Jeniper said nothing, Rieka glanced at her again. The Aurian woman sat staring at the DGI with a look of wonder. "Would you like to hear the story?"

"Yes."

Relieved that it hadn't been, "Yes, ma'am," Rieka turned her attention to the screen as well. "About two hundred years ago, the Commonwealth united the civilizations on seven planets. Earth had been considered, it being so close to the Centauri system, but the people there weren't ready for nonterrestrial contact.

"Around that time, the civilization residing in the Procyon system decided they needed to move on—and the Commonwealth stood in their way. Instead of trying an overt attack, they figured their best bet would be to weaken the Commonwealth first, then pick off whatever planets they wanted. They decided to use this scenario on the only local planet with no defense."

"Earth," Jeniper supplied.

"Exactly. They found an asteroid, hollowed out one end and fit it with an ion propulsion drive. Then, they sent it on its way and sat back to watch what happened."

Jeniper turned, wide-eyed. "You mean the meteor wasn't a natural cosmic occurrence?"

"The astronomers of the time called it an anomaly," Rieka told her. "That much, at least, is in the history books. No one could explain where it came from or how it maneuvered itself to hit the Earth as it did. It was noticed months before the impact—and watched carefully. Everyone thought it would be a near miss. But just three weeks before the collision, it mysteriously changed course. Everyone figured it had been influenced by some other, equally anomalous phenomenon.

"Astronomers scrambled to figure new data trajectories. The people were warned not to panic, but nothing could be done. By that point, Humanity had banded together and started working on a plan to try to destroy it, but even if they had some way of detonating an explosion to push it off course, I'm sure the Procyons would have found a way to turn it around."

Rieka leaned forward and gestured at the DGI image. "The exact point of contact couldn't be calculated, but they worked out the correct latitude. Thirty-three degrees north.

A latitude that would affect over two-thirds of the global population.

"So the four-and-a-half-kilometer-wide rock came hurtling out of the sky at something like thirty kilometers a second. The entry angle of seventy-six degrees was way too high for anyone to hope the atmosphere might slow it down."

Rieka paused and looked at Jeniper, then stood and stepped close enough to the DGI to point to the impact site. "It hit here, about five kilometers south of an island called Cyprus in the Mediterranean Sea. The island was destroyed instantly, as were about twenty-five million people along the coast on the mainland."

"How?" Jeniper stammered. "I mean, instantly?"

"The kinetic energy was changed by the impact to heat energy. The people were incinerated, Jeniper. They estimated the temps to be upwards of a million degrees Celsius. The firestorm swept an area over seven hundred kilometers in diameter. That part of the Mediterranean coast was pretty dry. The whole thing went up in flames in a matter of minutes.

"Of course the rest of the Mediterranean suffered as well. Tsunamis—oceanic waves hundreds of meters high destroyed nearly every island and coastal town. More millions killed without a chance to save themselves."

Jeniper's bibbets got darker, but she said nothing, so Rieka went on.

"And the jolt from the impact set off hundreds of earthquakes worldwide. There's a particularly unstable area called the Pacific Rim where the continental plates move against each other. Those plates shifted. The result—more tsunamis. Underwater volcanoes erupted. No major port city made it through that time without suffering tremendous damage.

"And then there was the ash—from the fires, volcanoes, and the Collision itself. It bubbled up into the upper atmosphere and got picked up by the jet streams—prevailing movements in the air—and eventually spread out to cover the globe. Components of the ash were nitric and sulfuric acid. So when things cooled down—and they did by a good twenty degrees—the rain that fell was acidic. It wreaked havoc with pH in both fresh and salt water."

"Nothing was spared. Not plants, animals, people, water . . . even the rocks eroded under that kind of torture. In the first three months, before relief came, a billion people died. A sixth of the population. And with their deaths came disease . . ."

"I can't imagine living through anything so horrible," Jeniper whispered.

"My great-great-grandfather did. He was an astronomer—the Human who discovered the Centauri relief ship. When Delik Silva became the first Centauri to visit Earth, Peter Degahv was the man he chose to speak to. And because of his ability to stand tall in the face of adversity, old Peter took the post of Earth Herald."

"It's quite a story," Jeniper said.

Rieka smiled. "Yes, it is. And now it's come full circle. Earth has been resurrected like a phoenix from the ashes, and a Degahv is still her representative. I just hope I can manage half as well as he did."

"I am sure you'll do very well, Herald," Jeniper told her firmly. Rieka could tell she truly believed that.

Glancing back at the digital image, though, Rieka felt her jaw tense. How could one person consolidate the needs of an entire race? And then execute that agenda without disrupting the rest of the Commonwealth? "I wish I had your confidence."

"I can't understand why you don't. There are two centuries of Heralds in your family. Surely that must bring you some sense of assurance."

"But none has ever done what I have to do," Rieka said, turning away from the DGI to look directly at Jeniper. "I'll be the first Earth Herald to try to make the Commonwealth respect us for what we did. What we've done. And what we intend to do."

EIGHT

Adjutant Gundah preened the fur on her arms as she sat at the conference room table listening to the Herald's staff's weekly reports. Periodically, she glanced at the Ophs around her, but her mind calculated its own agenda. There would be many things to do before the next two weeks were out.

Cimpa, the Oph Herald, nodded at Beresh and told him to see to an agreement between the Boin clan and the Daskar. He pronounced his decisions on two short-term business deals and told his office secretary, Gabah, he wanted the arrangements for his trip to Earth on his desk by eighteen-hundred. Then he dismissed them.

Gundah pushed herself up from the table, her hollow ear jewelry clinking pleasantly, and headed toward her office. As Cimpa's adjutant, she intended to accompany him there though he had not yet included her in his party. She had always managed to profit from her position in his shadow. It would be a simple thing to do it again.

Her desk console blinked with incoming mail, so she sat and perused the files, finding a few things vaguely interesting. Once certain nothing needed her immediate attention, Gundah accessed the Commonwealth NewsNet and flipped through the various News Sheets. She took notes here and there, where business interests were concerned. TechLine stocks were unchanged. Aurie Quadrant 3 produce apparently had a good season. Three companies were reporting record profits this year.

Gundah smiled. She held a great deal of stock in two of them.

She sifted through a mass of useless information and was

about to switch off when her incoming mail icon reappeared. Curious, she opened the directory and recognized the file source as one of her people on Indra.

Her black lips pursed as her pads touched the appropriate keys. Then, as she skimmed the page, Gundah felt her ears prick up and immediately eased them back down lest someone come in the office and wonder what she was reading.

Casually, she jacked in her datapad and transferred the message onto it. Then she deleted the file from her console. She needed to read the entire missive slowly, probably several times. Then, she would decide the best action to take, although she already had the basics in mind.

An aide named Kaffah stepped into her office, the distinct odor of *ciffa* wafting in with her. "Herald wants you. Now," she said, her eyes wide.

Gundah snorted slightly and switched off her datapad. Kaffah had not yet been Advanced and knew only the academics of sex. She stood in awe of her superiors who engaged in the activity on an almost-daily basis.

"I am on my way," she told the girl, then pushed away from her desk and walked to the door. "How long to your Advancement?"

"Four more months," Kaffah said, managing to look both proud and embarrassed.

Gundah offered her a consoling growl, then said, "Always remember the males among us rut. It is a thing they do. And though it is the female's place to bear young, it is also our duty to control them in their need. Their release. You will learn how to accomplish this only with practice."

"Of course," Kaffah replied, her ears flattening to her head.

Delighted she'd completely mortified the precocious girl, Gundah strode past her and toward Cimpa's private office. Unable to bear pups of her own, she'd been servicing the Herald since she'd become his adjutant eighteen years ago.

It was a mutually beneficial practice. Long after his mate's death, Cimpa remained a remarkably functional Herald—due, Gundah thought, to her sexual services. A male in his position simply couldn't ignore his urge to rut by pounding *ciffa* every seventy-two days. And ignoring the obvious would eventually have worn on his sanity.

She opened the office door to discover an empty room. She detected the faint odor of *ciffa* and followed it to Cimpa's private bath. There, she found him leaning heavily against the sink, his eyes glazed. A huge block of *ciffa*, a refined tree sap, stood beside him, its top worn with many claw gouges. His paws were covered with the pungent white dust.

"Cimpa, *bigotch do vou kriktan*," she chided, indicating the mess with a paw. He bared his teeth at her, but she ignored that and threw the bolt on the door.

"*Vash. Vash*," he growled. "*Gundah, vash.*"

When he stood straight, she saw that his *cile* had already protruded alarmingly and the three *pictiles* were well extended, ready to engage.

"*Korik noi grunda mah*," she scolded, ambling to the half wall near the cylindrical commode and leaning on it with her arms. After taking a deep breath, she arched her back.

Cimpa leapt on her almost immediately, engaging himself and clawing at her fur. She let go the wall and grabbed at his paws. He knew better than to damage her coat. He growled, but Gundah growled louder. Now fully engaged, she felt his paws relax against hers and she released them.

"*Tondon da na*, Cimpa," she told him softly.

He growled, but this time with satisfaction. Now, as his breathing became both labored and rhythmic, she felt him stroke her back, nails held in check. She could barely feel them through her fur.

His paws made their way down her sides and reached around to knead her chest. She watched as they clenched again and tugged her wheat-colored coat. She tilted back her head and growled her displeasure. Again, he eased off.

Gundah held her position dutifully, knowing Cimpa would return to himself in a few moments. How many times had they done this, she wondered. A thousand? More? Sometimes it seemed like forever. Sometimes it felt completely new.

Another moment passed and she heard him snort, then a few seconds later she felt the *pictiles* release her as he disengaged. By the time she turned around he had restored himself completely.

He smoothed his coat and looked at her. "Again, you have my thanks, Gundah."

"I am always at your disposal. You know that," she told him. She had known his time would nearly coincide with the Earth's Reaffirmation and had wondered if he would gamble on leaving her on Oph. Obviously that was out of the question. Now, all that remained was for him to say the words.

He heaved a great sigh and flipped his left ear. "Then it is apparent that you will accompany me on my trip to Earth." He looked at her carefully, and she could almost detect a fondness for her in the way his left ear tipped forward. But perhaps it had more to do with his physical state as opposed to his emotional one.

"Of course. It is a good idea," she said. "It would be most unpleasant to have you pounding *ciffa* every hour and swollen beyond belief."

"Most unpleasant," he agreed.

"I have wondered," she began, her curiosity overcoming any hesitancy, "why do you not simply find a new mate?"

"This arrangements suits," Cimpa said, pulling himself up and expanding his chest. "A wife would wish pups. I have them. You wish only to continue as my adjutant. You perform your job to Oph—and to me, admirably. And you are sufficiently compensated."

Gundah nodded. He'd answered her question, and although the term "sufficiently" was subjective, she both understood and agreed with it. "Perhaps you would find a female who did not wish pups."

"Perhaps. But I am not looking for one." Cimpa pulled himself straighter. "I will notify you if I need you." He twitched his nose, growled softly, and left.

After making sure her coat was properly groomed, Gundah casually made her way back to her office. She reseated herself at her desk with a thoughtful sigh and reached for her datapad.

Candace's people had unearthed some news about Rieka, on Indra. Gundah hoped the report was not a repeat of anything she already knew.

It wasn't. Gundah could tell that much as soon as the name Sati Labs came up. Her breath caught when her agent reported both Rieka Degahv and Captain Marteen having visited the place twice. What were they doing there, she wondered. Sati's reputation, not to mention their fee, was beyond any other genetic-engineering lab in the Commonwealth. They were cutting edge, but staunchly ethical. Gundah couldn't imagine what Candace's daughter and her husband would be doing in such a place.

Then, a thought struck her. Outrageous as it seemed, it might be possible. They could be attempting to have a child of their combined species. Certainly Centauri and Human genomes wouldn't combine on their own. Other thoughts began to tumble in her mind.

Degahv. Sati Labs. Genetic material.

Perfect.

She touched a toggle on her console, and her secretary's voice responded almost immediately. "Zeliah, I will be accompanying Cimpa to Earth's ceremony," she began. "Inform Gabah and tell him to make the arrangements. I wish to be notified once they are finalized."

"Of course, Gundah."

"And I want you to conduct a Search. Bill it to my private expense account. Flag it urgent and express."

"Understood. Who am I searching for?"

"An Aurian. Male. Last known residence was here on Oph, but I believe he may have traveled to Indra recently."

"And the name?" Zeliah asked.

"Tarrik, I need you to find a man named Jonik Tarrik."

Having already interviewed the other two applicants, Rieka asked the third candidate the last question on her list. She and Hong Wang-Chi had been chatting in her quarters for almost thirty minutes, and the interview had gone well, she thought, until now. He looked suddenly tense and began to fidget in the chair.

"Yeah," he answered quietly. "I did kill someone once. An accident—but he's dead, anyway. And that's what counts."

She nodded her head in agreement and noted his reply on her datapad. Seeing the cautious look in his eye, Rieka said, "Well, we've gone this far, I might as well ask the circumstances."

Hong shifted in the chair. He was a big Human, close to Triscoe's height, but had to weigh half again as much.

Though he didn't look bulky, his musculature could not be ignored. The chair looked about three sizes too small.

"It was a martial-arts competition. I'd been to a lot of them, even before I started working for Norik Security. Never even hurt anybody at a competition—well, not anything more than a bruise or two. It wasn't even a top round," he explained, leaning forward and looking her in the eye. "An Aurie, his name was Freni Cabel, got assigned to me. We were at it for about twenty-five seconds—I was doing well. I threw him. That's it. I threw him. Just like I'd done a thousand times before. But for some reason he twisted in the air. I don't think I did anything to make him do that. The force of the fall, even on the mat, broke his neck. They put him on life support and started nanotherapy right away." He shrugged and said no more.

Rieka looked down at Hong's resumé. His last competition had been three years ago. "Was that at the Sepin High Trials at Pikoom?" she asked.

He nodded. "The last time I ever competed."

"But it was an accident."

Mr. Hong nodded. "Like I said though, dead is dead." After a tight sigh, he seemed to let go of the incident. The pitch of his voice rose slightly when he said, "I was on assignment on Medoura when you stopped that meteor the Procyons tried to hit us with."

Dumbfounded, Rieka nodded but made no reply. She'd seen the chaos that day on Medoura. But it would have been far worse had the Fleet not destroyed the rock she considered a twin to what had nearly annihilated the Earth two centuries ago.

"And then there's . . ." Hong began quietly, then shook his head.

"What?"

He frowned as if what he wanted to say simply wouldn't come out. "I've hurt a few people, too, Herald," he managed finally. His dark almond-shaped eyes held hers while he spoke. "I'm big for a Human. Sometimes I don't know my own strength."

"Can you explain what you mean?" she asked softly. Obviously, he felt remorse for every act that had caused someone else to suffer. Though commendable, she didn't

need a bodyguard so concerned for others that he'd put
her in danger.

"Back on Medoura. During the confusion when they
thought they'd be hit . . . the people went crazy. That's the
best way to describe it. I was on a ground-level tram in
Eskitou and the driver just—well she went crazy. She just
took off down the street with her load of passengers. There
must have been twenty of us aboard. We watched her cause
three accidents before I decided I had to do something."

He leaned toward her but looked at his hands while re-
counting the incident. Rieka sat enthralled. Neither the
Oph nor the Indran lieutenant had seemed anywhere near
as responsible.

"Her box was isolated, of course," he went on, "so I had
to break through that. I got this scar, here, from busting
through the plexi with a guy's walking stick." He showed
her the back of his left hand where a fine line ran from his
thumb to his little finger. "When I finally got the door
open—she was completely gone. I mean, she wasn't in the
real world, you know?"

Rieka nodded. "I think so."

"Medourans are sensitive people," he explained. "They
take everything personally. When I yelled at her to stop,
she accelerated. Anyway, I couldn't pull her out of her
chair—so I hit her. Hard. Knocked her out. I stopped the
tram then, and let the rest of the passengers out."

"Sounds like you saved everyone."

"Maybe, but I broke the woman's jaw. That's what the
medics told me when they finally got there."

Rieka considered that last statement and decided Mr.
Hong didn't count himself a hero as much as he did a bully.
Yet no brainless tough guy would stand watch over his
victim until paramedics arrived. She let a long moment of
silence go by before she asked, "So why have you decided
you want the position of my bodyguard?"

Hong sat up straighter and looked at her as if the answer
were obvious. "The Fleet saved us that day, Herald. All
the people on Medoura. We would have died if that meteor
had struck. And *you* were the one who figured out what
was happening."

"Who told you it was me?" Rieka asked, confused. Only

a handful of Fleet officers knew she'd been the one to deduce the Procyons' tactics.

"I know somebody who knows somebody," he replied cryptically.

"It isn't common knowledge, then?"

"No."

Relieved by that tidbit of information, she asked, "And you think you can protect me?"

He pulled himself straight, all but dwarfing the chair. "Yes, ma'am."

Realizing she'd made her decision during his story about the tram, Rieka took a moment to collect her thoughts. Hong Wang-Chi was twenty-eight years old. He'd worked for Norik Security for eight years. Before that, an excellent education on Yadra had taught him electronics, computer science, and psychology. He hadn't experienced life in the Fleet, but he did know the difference between doing something and having to do something.

"I'm used to giving orders. Do you think you can handle that?"

He offered her a cocky smile. "Not if it goes against my better judgment. If I thought you were taking too big a risk, I'd give *you* the orders."

They locked stares until Rieka laughed. "Then I suppose I should say, welcome aboard, Mr. Hong. I am using your name correctly, am I not?" she asked. "Your given name is Wang-Chi, family name Hong."

"Right."

She offered her hand, and he shook it firmly. "I'll call you Wang-Chi if you'll call me Rieka."

"Thank you, Rieka. And just Wang will do. I appreciate your confidence. And I promise I won't let you down."

Jeniper stood near the entry to the InterMAT chamber watching Captain Marteen say good-bye to his wife. She had noticed their odd behavior before, and still couldn't quite figure out what passed between the two of them. It almost seemed as though they could communicate without speaking. The Centauri *quantivasta* gift was rare, she knew. But even if Captain Marteen had it, Rieka was Human. Thought interaction didn't seem likely.

"We'll be fine in Canberra," Rieka told him. "Wang's

checked everything out with the Embassy security people and the hotel. Stop worrying."

The captain looked skeptical. Jeniper tried to hide her smile by shifting her briefcase from one hand to the other. They had a mountain of confirmations to go through for both the inauguration and Reaffirmation ceremonies. And she needed to reschedule two press conferences and organize a dinner at the Herald's hotel.

Rieka huffed and frowned at her husband. "Quit that or I'll take back what I said before about inviting your parents to stay with us before the Reaffirmation."

"I didn't *say* anything," he replied, a distinctly innocent tone in his voice. Jeniper saw a dimple appear in his left cheek. She watched Rieka's face contort into another incredulous frown.

"As if that meant something," Rieka muttered. The captain moved to stroke her chin, but his wife would have none of that. She reached to cup the back of his head and pull him down for a kiss. Self-conscious, Jeniper studied her shoes.

"See you when you get back from Mars Colony," Rieka said softly.

Jeniper could tell the captain still wasn't comfortable with leaving her, but he nodded. Wondering if she would ever find someone with whom she could be so comfortable, Jeniper scolded herself for being jealous. There was no room for that in either her job or the friendship that had taken root with her new boss.

And she needed that friendship now, she realized, in the light of Jonik's latest message. She'd received it a few hours after they'd reached Earth. Since then, thoughts of her brother were never far away. He said he'd see her soon. How could he do that? And why? What was worse, he hadn't mentioned anything about the loan he'd begged for on Indra.

Rieka turned to her, an inscrutable smile on her face. "Are we ready, then?"

"I think so," she replied.

Jeniper watched Rieka slip her datapad into a small briefcase on the console as Captain Marteen entered their destination. They stepped into the chamber. The captain looked at them both and nodded. "Two days," he said.

Jeniper smiled and meant to say good-bye, but before she could speak, she found herself looking at a wall that read: Welcome to Canberra. Knowing her new job meant a great deal of traveling, she hoped she'd get used to InterMAT transport sooner rather than later.

"Well, I expected someone would be here," Rieka murmured, openly annoyed. She heaved a disgruntled sigh and shook her head. Jeniper followed her out of the chamber and Rieka strode past the InterMAT technician and toward the outer door. It opened before she reached it.

Wang's smile apparently disarmed his boss's ire. "Transport okay?" he asked.

"A lovely way to spend nine hundred nanoseconds, Wang," she told him. "Where is everyone?"

"Downstairs. The more secure the Earth Herald's image, the better. Trust me."

"I agree," Jeniper said, smiling at him. She turned toward Rieka. "Once we're in the conference room, I'll have the Australian Administrator announce you."

Jeniper watched Rieka nod and wondered what she must be feeling. This would be her first public appearance as Herald-elect. Squeezing her briefcase a bit tighter in her hand, Jeniper followed Wang and Rieka down a short flight of stairs. She stepped around them and spoke quietly with a dark-skinned man she recognized from prior communications aboard the *Providence,* Wesley Stafford, the Australian Administrator. About a dozen journalists of nearly every race sat before them, and an untold number of holo-cameras were set up along the back wall.

After assuring Jeniper all was in order, Mr. Stafford moved to the podium and introduced Rieka, then eased aside while she came forward to greet the news people. "Good morning," she told them. "I can't tell you how glad I am to be back on Earth. Words simply aren't enough. I hope that one day soon you will all experience this feeling—of coming to a place where you are welcome simply because you are Human—and not in spite of it." She shot the journalists a wry smile. "And if you aren't Human, you're welcome anyway."

When she paused, an Aurian in the front row asked, "Were you concerned the electorate would not choose you,

Mrs. Degahv? I understand you have not completely sev-
ered your ties from the Fleet."

Rieka frowned slightly at that. "Mr.—?"

"Silkam," he supplied.

"Mr. Silkam, since I did not consult the Indran Oracle
on the matter, I was *not* sure I'd be elected," she told him,
her voice edged by a touch of humor. "And the Fleet and
I still entertain an amicable disassociation. More than that
I am not at liberty to say. But I can tell you my agenda
doesn't include commanding a starship anytime soon."

"Is it true you'll be launching a billion-credit campaign
to lure Humans back to Earth?" an Oph asked.

Jeniper smiled to herself as Rieka responded with an
openhanded gesture before speaking. They'd gone over this
type of inquiry yesterday morning. She had thought her
boss felt nervous then, but now Rieka seemed as confident
as if she'd been Herald for a decade. Jeniper could only
guess at the manner with which she'd commanded a Fleet
ship. It must have been something to see.

A few questions later, Wang nudged her, and whispered,
"We need to go."

Jeniper glanced at the wall chrono and nodded. Nearly
thirty minutes had passed. She hated taking Rieka from an
obviously positive interview, but it couldn't be helped. She
moved to stand a short distance from the podium and, before the next question could be asked, said, "Thank you
very much, ladies and gentlemen. I'm afraid that's all we
have time for today. Herald-elect Degahv has an extremely
tight schedule."

Jeniper had to gesture in order to get Rieka to leave the
podium. Stafford followed her out of the pressroom.

Wang ushered them back into the hallway and smiled
down at Jeniper. "That went well, don't you think?"

Jeniper found herself nodding, then looked at Rieka.
"You did great. The reporters all seemed pleased with
your answers."

Rieka's response was a terse laugh. "We'll see—once the
NewsNet is updated," she said. Then she looked up at
Wang. "Where to next?"

"I've arranged a tour of the city, Mrs. Degahv," Mr.
Stafford offered. "Canberra was saved from a lot of damage simply because of its position in the southern hemi-

sphere. Many of our above-ground buildings are not only maintained, but occupied as well."

Jeniper saw Rieka nod and glance at Wang. "It's all been approved," he told her. "My people will flank the touring van. I'll ride with you."

"Sounds like fun," she quipped, her tone disclaiming the words. For a moment, Jeniper wondered if she didn't want to go. Then Rieka suddenly smiled, and said, "I haven't seen Canberra in years, Mr. Stafford. And I would appreciate a tour. It's probably the most beautiful city this planet's got left."

"I'd think Sydney would like to argue with you on that, ma'am," Stafford replied. "Or possibly Winnipeg."

"I think the Herald simply means the overall effect," Jeniper supplied. "I know that from orbit the river and parks give it an esthetic appeal something like Rhonique."

"Aye, they do, Miss Tarrik," he said, smiling. "And I'm sure you'll find it that much more appealing from the ground."

Wang ushered them outside and into a waiting vehicle. Jeniper was impressed by the elevated seats and panoramic view. While the convoy assembled, she took note of the way Rieka beamed.

"Isn't it beautiful, Jen? Look at how clear the sky is. We're going to do whatever it takes to keep it that way."

"We can do with a bit of rain now and then," Stafford told her, his tone light.

"I didn't mean clouds. I meant pollution."

He smiled and glanced around. "It looks as though we're ready. Now, when we get down to the end of Brisbane and turn onto State Circle, I want you to look out to the left past Capitol Hill and see the new sculptures on the far side of the Parliament House—which is, of course, where you'll be inaugurated tomorrow."

"Herald RadiMo, this is an unexpected pleasure," Rieka said later that afternoon, bowing her head to the Bournese Herald. Wang had accompanied the Herald's *skiff* into the sitting room of her hotel suite. He stood discreetly to the side, she noticed, watching the small creature as it poked its head and shoulders from the center area of the coffin-sized floating device used for both transportation and comfort whenever the Bournese left their homeworld.

"RadiMo gives greetings to Herald-elect Degahv and wishes to inquire as to the health of Herald Degahv," the synthesized voice announced.

"The Herald Alexi is well," she replied. "And he is honored that you remember him in your greeting to his niece." This time she bowed formally, tipping her body forward from the waist. She'd dealt with few Bournese as a Fleet captain, but a short tutorial with a protocol program had hopefully honed her diplomatic skills.

"Enter my domain, Herald RadiMo," she told the small, dark being. "You are welcome and no harm will come to you."

She watched as a hole formed in the top of the *skiff*'s forward area. RadiMo's brown, fist-sized head disappeared from the center area and reappeared at the new hole, followed by narrow shoulders and forelegs. He began to tap rapidly on the miniature console before him, and the voice translated almost immediately. "You are gracious. I am comfortable."

The *skiff* edged farther into the room and settled lightly on the floor. RadiMo disappeared down the hole and emerged again a moment later from another opening.

Rieka watched while he sniffed the air. Noting the arch of what she could see of his back, she realized she'd never actually seen an entire Bourne. Computer images, yes, but never a whole living being outside a *skiff*. They were tubular, warm-blooded creatures that looked something like an otter, she decided, but with very little fur. In fact, the only hair she could see on his deep brown body was a fluff emanating from each ear and a sort of goatee below his pointy chin. RadiMo had huge eyes, dark enough brown to be considered black, but the things that most fascinated Rieka were his hands.

Bournes had eight-fingered hands, not paws. Four fingers stood out straight and two struck out the back, similar to that of birds. This opposition of digits gave them an amazing ability to grasp things. The last pair of fingers stretched over the top of the forward-facing ones. Thus, they could manipulate objects while clinging to cave walls, stalagmites, or whatever happened to offer a fingerhold. When it came to the messages emanating from their consoles, a Bourne could type faster than the machine could speak.

When the small being finished sniffing, Rieka asked, "And how are you, Herald RadiMo? How is your mate, RagiMo?"

"This creature is well," the voice replied, its sweet, child-like tone close to what Rieka figured a Bourne might actually sound like, though she'd long ago stopped trying to anthropomorphize things. "And RagiMo finds health in the birthing ring with others preparing for the event. She would ask your health."

"I am well, thank you," Rieka replied. "And I would congratulate you on your kits."

"Their arrival is not for many days, yet, though they may arrive before I return home."

Rieka nodded and sat in the chair closest to RadiMo's present position. "Alexi tells me you have been helping us plan three new cities."

"This is true."

"I understand your wish to survey the areas for the purpose of mining gemstones. It is my pleasure to assist in negotiating the contract with the Bourne."

"Rubies are cold fire."

Rieka offered a slight smile and glanced at Wang, still standing just inside the door. She had no clue what RadiMo had meant. "I'm sure. Are you interested in any others?"

"Sapphires have the warmth of water," he said.

"Yes." She waited a moment for him to speak again, then said, "You have been here on Earth many days, Radi-Mo. How much longer do you think you'll stay? When will the work be finished?"

"This is a question," the voice said. "RadiMo seeks great opportunities. Departure will wait until after the Reaffirmation."

At least another two weeks, Rieka guessed. "Earth has always been a place which offers opportunities. I hope you find what you are looking for. May I ask to have your report on the excavations of the New Subcities—Moscow, Beijing, and Brasilia?"

"You may ask."

Not sure he'd agreed with her request, but not wanting

to insult him, either, Rieka smiled softly. Offending him by pressing the point wouldn't do her any good.

She meant to ask about his plans for actually mining the gems, but RadiMo, apparently, felt the meeting had concluded. After a few parting words, he scurried back down into the *skiff*'s bowels and came up facing the door. A few adjustments of his console and he'd negotiated his way back out. Silently Rieka recalled Alexi's warning. What RadiMo had chosen *not* to say was just as important as what he had.

Wang closed the door and turned to her. "Funny little guy," he offered, "but I guess I liked him."

Rieka shook her head, laughing. "How diplomatic of you, Hong Wang-Chi," she said, trying not to sound too disapproving since her own response to RadiMo was almost identical. "I'm so glad you waited until he left to share your opinion."

NINE

Jeniper stood near the window, feeling distinctly on edge. Late this afternoon, the *Prospectus* had arrived with Herald Degahv aboard, and she had been invited to dine with Captains Marteen and DeVark, Rieka and Alexi.

But socializing with powerful people didn't bother her half as much as the latest message she'd received from Jonik. He had actually followed her to Earth. He expected her to meet him in an old mining village northeast of Canberra. Bywong, he'd called it. Before the Collision, it had been a tourists' point of interest, if one was interested in panned-out gold mines. She couldn't imagine the state it might be in after two centuries of neglect.

Questions bounced around in her mind. Why had he come? How had he paid for his ticket? What purpose did it serve to keep pestering her? She'd already told him he'd get no money.

Jeniper turned as Rieka entered the suite with her three male companions. "Jen, there you are. Why weren't you at the reception this afternoon?"

Jeniper smiled and stepped closer. "I got there a little late—another problem with the TechLine supplier at Damascus—but I did attend," she replied. "I must have spoken to half the people there. You just weren't one of them."

"I've been working you like a dog, I know," Rieka said, her expression concerned. Jeniper wondered how one worked a dog, but didn't think it prudent to ask. "But once we settle in New SubDenver, you'll be able to hire a decent staff. Then you'll only have me to deal with."

Jeniper saw a smirk appear on Rieka's face and nodded at the implication. "You're not a bad boss."

Rieka chuckled. "Compared to whom?"

She intended no response to that question, and apparently Rieka wasn't looking for one. Instead, the Human woman turned and gestured toward an Aurian in a Fleet uniform standing near Captain Marteen. A silver stripe ran down his arm, indicating the rank of captain as well. "Robet, if you're not too immersed over there, there's someone I'd like you to meet."

The man excused himself from his discussion, turned, and walked toward them. Jeniper felt a *ribah* flip deep in her chest as she looked at him. Red hair, ice-pale eyes, and the most attractive row of bibbets she'd ever seen. And apparently either he didn't care about his image, or didn't choose to flaunt it. He smiled easily at them as he approached.

Rieka extended her hand, and he took it. "Jeniper, I'd like you to meet an old friend, Captain Robet DeVark. Robet, this is my Planetary Adjutant, Jeniper Tarrik."

"A pleasure, Miss Tarrik," the captain said. He extended his right hand in the typical Earth welcome. Impressed, she took it, and he gripped her hand firmly. "A Human custom, I know," he told her. "But when on any Commonwealth planet, one should assume the local etiquette. Don't you think?"

Jeniper smiled as he let her hand go, and the warmth of his palm lingered. "I think, Captain, that your primary purpose in this particular handshake is in deference to Mrs. Degahv."

She noticed his bibbets darken to mauve and felt her own darken in turn. Rieka, apparently oblivious, laughed and clapped him on the shoulder. "I told you she was sharp, Robet."

"Sharp as a *tack,* was the term," he said, looking both entertained and embarrassed.

"Mmm," Rieka replied, quirking an eyebrow. "I suppose I might have said something like that." Jeniper watched as Rieka turned back to her. "Don't mind Robet's mouth, he often regrets what he says."

"I should think a Fleet captain would be in control at all

times," Jeniper found herself saying, glancing again at the captain's bibbets. They'd faded to pink.

"All times," he agreed, smiling. "Please call me Robet."

"Well, I'll leave you two to get better acquainted," Rieka told them. "And I expect you to discuss things other than your association with me." She looked pointedly at Robet. "Dinner should be ready in a minute. You can go in and sit down, if you like. I'll collect Triscoe and Alexi."

Though she'd originally expected to feel somewhat self-conscious at dinner, Jeniper found it the opposite. Robet DeVark regaled her with stories about Rieka and Triscoe, many of which were of great interest to Alexi as well. Her former boss looked tired, Jeniper decided, and noticed Rieka inquiring as to his comfort several times. She wondered if his health had anything to do with his retirement, but knew better than to ask such a personal question at the table.

Jonik's call still buzzing in the back of her thoughts, Jeniper reluctantly declined Robet's invitation to visit the *Prospectus* after dinner. Taking in his disappointed expression, she looked him in the eye.

"I have an appointment, Robet. But I would love to see your ship, another time."

"Sure. Can I walk you out to the taxis, then?"

"There's really no need—"

"It isn't a bother, Jeniper," he insisted. "And I thought I'd walk a bit after that meal." He tapped his stomach. "The *ribah* aren't what they used to be. My third's been giving me trouble for months. Usually a walk settles it."

She nodded and allowed him to accompany her down to ground level, and then outside. Jeniper decided she liked him rather more than she thought wise. He was charming, witty, and handsome. She particularly liked his bibbet pattern. And the way he smiled. And the way he looked at her.

When a taxi rolled up and its door slid open, Jeniper turned. "It's been very nice meeting you, Robet," she told him, noting the way his pale blue eyes swept over her face. "I hope I'll get to see you again sometime."

"The pleasure's been mine," he replied. "And you can count on it."

She smiled and stepped into the vehicle. "Bywong village, please," she told the computer. It responded with an affirmative tone when she slipped her bank card into the slot, and Jeniper breathed a small sigh of relief. Jonik hadn't said if this place could be reached by city services. She looked up and waved as the door closed and felt a jolt of delight run through her when Robet winked and waved back.

Thoughts of Captain DeVark stayed with her until she reached the dilapidated remains of Bywong. Ordering the vehicle to wait until she returned, Jeniper got out and looked around. Though lit by three tall lamps in the parking area, every structure was dark inside. All looked as if they had suffered too many years of neglect to stand even a moment more. With the car humming pleasantly behind her, Jeniper spotted a modern-looking module-type building. Glancing around once more, she headed toward it.

The door opened when she turned the handle. "Hello? Jonik?" And waiting a few seconds and receiving no reply, she stepped over the threshold and peered about in the darkness. Littered with construction materials and tools, the structure looked to be a covered work area—for whom, she had no idea. Perhaps, with the expected rush of visitors to Earth, the Australian Administrator's office had decided to renovate the village into a modern tourist attraction.

A draft came through the open door, and Jeniper shivered. Right now it held no attraction at all.

"Jonik, are you here? Answer me, you two-toned *bimoosh*."

Name calling had always unnerved him, but it did not have any effect, that night. Wondering if she had misunderstood him and had come to the wrong place, or perhaps arrived on the wrong evening, Jeniper carefully moved toward what looked like a computer workstation.

As she came around the desk, she noticed a blinking light. The station was functional. Another step and she realized the console's screen had been set to "suspend," not "off." The small oval cursor shone steadily in the lower left corner.

Not knowing what else to do, Jeniper touched a key. She sucked in a small breath when the screen sprang to life, though that was exactly what she'd expected it to do.

Jonik's face appeared, and for once, he did not even wear

his counterfeit smile. "Jeniper," he began, "I wasn't able to get here tonight. I hope you understand."

Not knowing whether or not she understood, or even wanted to, Jeniper impatiently muttered, "Get on with it."

"I need to warn you—she's coming to Earth. You're not safe, Jen. I don't think you believed me before, so please, believe me, now. She's not giving me any slack, and I'm sure she's able to make good on her threats. She's got people on her payroll everywhere. Please be very, very careful. Wherever you go—whatever you do, take a weapon with you. I'll try to find a way to meet with you as soon as I can. Until then, take care of yourself."

When the screen went blank, momentarily blinding her in the darkness, Jeniper felt all three of her *ribah* flip, one after the other. She had to force herself to let go the console and walk back to the door. Trembling with both cold and fear, Jeniper hurried back to the taxi. As the vehicle turned and headed toward Canberra, she could only hope Jonik was safe and that he'd try to contact her again.

Standing in front of Parliament House on Canberra's Capitol Hill, Rieka took a deep breath and stepped to Alexi's side. She raised her right hand and rested her left on the book he'd placed on the podium.

"I, Rieka Amelia Pirez Degahv, do solemnly swear to uphold the rights of Humans, once native citizens of Earth, a member world in the Commonwealth of Planets; to further the interests of the Human planet, Earth, and to promote peace and goodwill among all Commonwealth residents.

"As Earth Herald, I will make myself an advocate for Humanity. I promise to promote my people in every possible instance, both on and off the homeworld. And I promise to make myself as accessible as possible—so that any Commonwealth citizen, Human or not, might use my office to secure assistance, in whatever form, from the local or planetary authorities."

She lowered her right hand and looked out on the thousands that had gathered on the lawn. Her uncle slipped the huge, sealed volume from beneath her left hand and set it on a small shelf inside the podium. Then, he said, "As Earth Herald, I, Alexi Mikhail Bordeux Degahv, do hereby transfer all powers of my position to my niece, Rieka Amelia Pirez Degahv, who has sworn to uphold this office in the name of Earth and Humanity."

He then gripped her by the shoulders and kissed both her cheeks. When he hugged her, she squeezed him back and felt the crowd's approving applause roll over them.

"Congratulations," he said, offering her his hand. She shook it and turned to Triscoe who nodded. He caressed her cheek, then leaned and kissed it.

I am very proud, he told her, the thought infused faintly with a golden hue.

Alexi had turned back to the assembly and lifted the huge book sealed in cryofilm from the lectern. "As tradition dictates, I turn over the possession of this, the Commonwealth Constitution, including all amendments, to the current Earth Herald—Rieka Degahv."

Another wave of applause swelled as Rieka accepted the book, now over two centuries old. She cradled it carefully in her arms and stepped closer to the microphone.

"Fellow Humans, brothers and sisters of the Commonwealth, tradition dictates that I give a speech now, promising great challenges ahead and providing assurances of the bounty that is sure to come from our united efforts. That speech I will not give today."

A low rumbling emanated from the audience, and Rieka squeezed the book tighter. "For the last two centuries we have struggled with the greatest challenge a planet and its citizens can face. We were orphans, existing in the shadows of those on whose planet we lived. Now, we seek the rewards of a habitable homeworld where peace and prosperity are available to all. Fourteen days from today we will rededicate Earth. I urge you to join me then and celebrate all that Humanity has to offer."

She waited while the applause swelled, then faded before she continued. "This planet owes the Commonwealth a great deal. I have challenged myself to make sure that debt is repaid within my lifetime. But while we attend to our finances and the bottom line, let us not forget the reason any of us are here at all." She paused for effect and looked out on the people.

"The Human spirit, my friends, is dauntless. Since before recorded history, it has conquered disease, despair, and devastation on an order so great as to be almost incomprehensible. Let us look forward from this day to a brighter future. One where we can celebrate who we are and what we have become.

"I invite you all to visit the Site and to attend the Reaffirmation in Damascus. Until then, be well."

The crowd applauded again, and Rieka couldn't tell whether it was for the content or the short duration of her speech. She smiled and waved for several minutes. When it became almost embarrassing to accept their acclaim, she nodded and waved one last time, then turned and stepped down off the dias.

Wang was there, along with a half dozen guards. They surrounded her as she made her way inside Parliament House, followed by Triscoe. Alexi, and Jeniper. The only downside of the day, Rieka thought, was that Setana and Ker hadn't been able to be there.

"That was excellent. Excellent," Alexi told her, as they strolled to the InterMAT terminal. "The people love you, my dear."

"That remains to be seen, Uncle," she told him. "I can hardly declare success after five minutes in office." She heard a soft chuckle in her mind and glanced at Triscoe. He seemed to be trying desperately not to smile, but a dimple showed, nonetheless.

"But the people consider you a hero," Alexi insisted. "They know already you are a Degahv who will fight for them. And they respect this."

"Respect is good," she admitted, casting a glance at her now official Planetary Adjutant, who had looked grim all morning. "I suppose veneration will come in time."

Jeniper nodded. "Possibly," she agreed.

"It was a joke, Jen," Rieka told her.

"Of course."

Sensing something wasn't right, Rieka leaned toward Jeniper, and said softly, "We've got three hours before the party tonight. I'll want to talk to you before then."

"Of course," she repeated.

Tightening her grip on the book she'd inherited, Rieka sighed and entered the InterMAT chamber with Triscoe. Something had happened to Jeniper after dinner last night. She knew it as well as she knew the Earth orbited the Sun.

And just as immutably, she could tell Jeniper didn't want her to know what was wrong.

An hour later, Rieka sat at a writing table near a window in her hotel suite. Wang lounged on a nearby sofa, talking quietly to one of his men on his private comlink. The datapad she'd been using waited patiently while she looked out at Canberra, imagining how things must have been two centuries before.

The door chime sounded, bringing her back to the present.

"Come," she said, her voice drowned out by Wang's baritone as he spoke the same word. When Jeniper came in the door, Rieka added, "We've got to stop doing that, Wang." He nodded agreeably but said nothing.

To Rieka's surprise, Jeniper stayed near the entry. "Herald," Jeniper began, "I have some people with me who would like to meet you."

"Really?" Rieka couldn't imagine what Jeniper meant. "I'm sure I don't have anything scheduled before the party."

"You'll want to see them," Jeniper told her. To Wang she added, "They've already been cleared by your staff." Jeniper opened the door wider and stepped back to accommodate five young people.

"This is the Blue Planet Future's Performance Committee," Jeniper announced. "Herald Degahv, I am proud to introduce you to Dale, Samantha, Po, Maria, and Kathy."

Rieka looked into the most hopeful faces she'd ever seen. "I'm so glad you came," she said, smiling as she shook each of their hands in turn. "Come in and sit down."

Leading the way to the living area, Rieka gestured for the young people to make themselves comfortable. She offered refreshments, but they declined. Rieka pulled a chair away from the dining table and sat. "So, tell me a little about yourselves," she said.

"I'm Po," the littlest one began, his dark almond-shaped eyes barely visible below straight, black bangs. "I'm eight. My parents are electronics. They're in New SubAtlanta. Kathy wants to marry Hans."

"I do not!" an older girl snapped. "And your parents are electricians, not electronics. I'm Kathy, Herald. I'm thir-

teen, and I sing alto. My parents are wheat growers here
in Australia. And I do not want to marry Hans. I just like
him, that's all.''

Rieka nodded sagely. "I understand completely how others mistake things about us, Kathy," she said. "And I'm
glad you took the time out of your busy schedule to come
and visit me." She looked at the three other young people.
"And, Dale, isn't it?" she asked the redheaded boy. "What
do you do?"

"I'm a dancer. And I get to be assistant stage manager
sometimes."

"That sounds challenging."

"Yes, ma'am."

"And your name is Maria?" Rieka asked of the pretty,
dark-haired girl sitting next to Po.

"Yes, ma'am, Maria Fortua. I sing soprano. I'm fourteen,
and I don't have a dad anymore, but my mother works in
the Seven Seas pavilion at World Zoo. Her name is Dr.
Angela Fortua."

Rieka nodded, and softly said, "I'm sure you're very
proud of her—just as she's proud of you. I don't have a
dad either, and I know that can be tough, sometimes."
Maria studied her hands and shrugged. "What do you like
best about being in the Blue Planet Future?"

Maria thought about that for a moment, then said,
"Coming home. I don't mind performing and traveling to
the other planets. But I like Earth the best."

Grinning, Rieka said, "Me too." She turned to the last
member of the group. "And you are Samantha?"

"Yes, ma'am. Samantha Mackay. I sing soprano and
dance. I'm seventeen and my family lives just outside of
Winnipeg—so when I'm not traveling with the BPF, I live
at home."

Rieka nodded, studying the blue-eyed blond. "Jeniper
called you the Performance Committee. What is that?"

Samantha shrugged. "We get to help design the shows.
And then we critique the performances during final re-
hearsals. The show changes every six months. That's how
long any one of us can be on the committee."

"So you rotate the privilege. That sounds fair." She
looked at the youngest boy. "Po, you're the littlest. What
do you think about all this?"

"The committee is boring," he replied seriously. "Even more boring than lessons. But it makes you learn how to be fair—'cause if you're mad at someone, you have the power—and then they have the power when it's their turn. You know?"

"I think so," Rieka told him.

Jeniper stepped closer, and said, "I promised Mrs. Gambo to have you back in an hour. Sorry to cut short the visit, but we need to get moving or you'll be late."

Rieka stood as the young people rose and followed Jeniper to the door. "It was very nice to meet all of you. I'm looking forward to your performance tonight."

They followed Jeniper into the hall, then Maria stopped and turned. "Good-bye, Mrs. Degahv." It looked as though she meant to say more, but she only shrugged.

"If you want, you can write to me on the comnet," Rieka said. "Jeniper has the address."

Maria's expression brightened. "Really?"

"Knowing how she'd struggled at that age without her father, Rieka nodded. "Really."

Have I told you you look quite delectable in that dress? The words, wrapped in a warm, rosy color, came to her mind above the noise of the milling crowd.

Triscoe, standing some distance away, looked up from his conversation with Administrator Stafford. Rieka made a face at him when his eyes dropped to her low neckline, then resumed her conversation with Wint Zevak, a Vekyan hydroponics supplier. She couldn't fault him for inquiring as to Earth's possible needs, though she wished he'd be a little less dogmatic.

"Well actually, Zevak—and you probably already know this—we do a great deal of agro production on the surface," she told him, hoping she used the right words so as to avoid any misunderstanding. Some Vekyans could be painfully literal. "But there are certain products, most notably those staples in the Vekyan and Aurian diets, that can't be produced without artificial cultivation—here on Earth, that is. I can't see why we wouldn't set up a few test labs in a couple of subcities."

"This would be acceptable," Zevak said. He uncurled his

tongue and carefully speared the piece of fruit floating in his drink.

"I'll have to speak to the architects and overall designers, of course," she went on, "to make sure it's feasible to plan such a facility into the structure. And I'm afraid I just don't have time for that in my schedule for at least three weeks. But I can tell you it wouldn't hurt to invest a little thought in this. Set up a meeting with my adjutant," Rieka advised, wondering if Zevak would have better luck pinning Jeniper down. Probably not.

"Thank you for the information, Herald," Zevak told her. "I will have my designers draw up some preliminary plans." He bowed slightly, dipping his great head toward her, then stepped back and disappeared into the crowd. She noticed Alexi, seated for once, in a lively discussion with Dzan, the Boolian Herald, who stood towering over him. Wondering at that odd pair, she scanned the crowd until she spied Jeniper at the buffet table.

Irritated that Jeniper had managed to avoid her after her visit with the children, Rieka slowly made her way through the mass of bodies. When she finally got close enough, she touched the Aurian woman on the arm. "I need to speak to you."

Jeniper turned, a worried look crossing her brow before she brightened. Rieka thought her half smile looked strained, but said nothing more.

"I'm just getting a bite to eat," Jeniper told her. "Can I get you something?"

"No. Thank you. All I want is to talk to you."

"Certainly." Jeniper scooped up a half dozen *kimbie* and set them on her plate. The large Aurian sea seeds, soaked in brine until they burst, rolled about, and Rieka wondered if any would fall off the plate before they reached the table. Jeniper collected her fluted glass and turned. "Which way?"

Rieka was about to suggest they head for her table when an uproar sounded across the room. At least two voices raised above the noise from the milling crowd, which now hushed considerably.

"You didn't plan this, did you?" Rieka jibed. She signaled Jeniper to follow and looked around to find Wang and several of his people hurrying toward the disturbance.

The crowd parted before her as they stormed toward the angry voices. An Oph female and a Human man continued to argue despite the fact they were causing a scene.

"What is going on here?" she demanded as her bodyguard stepped up to her shoulder. She glanced at Wang, her look telling him she'd handle this, and hoped he had the sense to behave.

The man turned from his opponent and had the decency to look embarrassed when he recognized her. "I am Luis Mendoza, Herald," he said with a curt bow. "I beg your forgiveness for creating this disturbance."

Jeniper tried to interject something, but Rieka raised her hand, and said, "We'll see about that, Mr. Mendoza. What is the problem?"

"I am a farmer. North American continent. And this Oph is Grulah. She is from Aurie's Quadrant Two."

"A farmer as well, I suppose."

"Of course," Grulah told her. She looked down her nose at Rieka before glaring up at Wang.

Taking in the silent affront, Rieka could understand how Mendoza had gotten into an argument with this Oph. She looked back at him. "And what seems to be the problem?" she repeated.

"Grulah has challenged that her beef is of better quality than that which I, or anyone else, produces on Earth. Herald Degahv—cattle evolved on Earth! How can they not be—"

"—yes, I understand." She glanced again at Wang, who responded by rolling his eyes. Though this threat to honor could escalate, he obviously didn't think it likely. The most important thing she could do, she realized, was not offend anyone. "Perhaps we could discuss this later. My adjutant here, Miss Tarrik, can schedule an appointment."

"There is nothing to discuss, Herald Degahv," Grulah spit. "Aurie has been the premiere producer of all agricultural products for centuries. Our animals are the best to be found anywhere. To imply that beef from Earth could possibly be superior—is ludicrous."

"There, you see!" Mendoza shouted.

"Yes, I do see," Rieka told him quietly. She allowed a look of disgust to mar her expression in the hope that these two would realize they had chosen the wrong time and place for such a debate. "I see a great deal, Mr. Mendoza. And so do all my guests."

Mendoza suddenly looked contrite. "I beg your pardon, ma'am."

"You may beg my pardon—and that of everyone else here, but the problem isn't solved, is it?" She looked back at Grulah and noticed Triscoe standing not too far away. "While I applaud your loyalty to your profession, I remind you that this venue is no place for such rivalry."

"I understand," Mendoza said softly.

"Now Grulah, I'm sure you do realize the creatures to which you refer, did, as Mr. Mendoza has pointed out, evolve on Earth. I will grant that in two hundred years both Oph and Aurian animal-husbandry techniques may have improved the original stock. But that remains to be seen." She turned to Mendoza. "I suggest that you postpone this debate and let the consumer decide who has the better product."

"Of course," Mendoza echoed, his dark eyes flashing the challenge.

Grulah took a deep breath and held it for what seemed like an interminable amount of time. Finally, she exhaled, "I shall look forward to proving my point," she said. "If you will excuse me." She bowed slightly, then headed for the door. A security man followed at a discreet distance.

"My sincerest apologies, Herald," Mendoza offered, inclining his head toward her. A relieved sigh deflated him for a moment before he puffed out his chest again, this time with pride. "I too, will look forward to—seeing her proved wrong!"

Rieka studied him for a moment. "Mr. Hong's men will accompany you to the exit. Good evening, Mr. Mendoza."

"Good evening, ma'am," he said respectfully. "It was a pleasure to meet you—despite the circumstances." A huge blond woman took his arm and turned him toward the door.

"Wasn't that fun?" Triscoe asked her as he stepped closer.

"Can't remember when I had a better time," she replied dryly.

"It looks as though we're secure for now, Boss," Wang told her. She could tell when he frowned and put his finger to his ear that he was using his own security net. "Uh-huh. Okay. Thanks." Wang looked back at her. "The Blue Planet Future is ready. Could I get you to return to your table?"

Flanked by Wang, Jeniper, and Triscoe, Rieka returned to her chair. They seated themselves, and she leaned toward Jeniper. "Later, I mean it."

Triscoe nudged her as the youth band struck up their first song. *What is wrong?*

Something's going on with Jeniper. I haven't been able to talk to her.

Something bad?

I don't know.

They listened to the next song, a duet performed by Samantha and a talented young man. Rieka was glad Alexi had endorsed the group. The Blue Planet Future, made up of youth who had been born on Earth while their parents readied it for repopulation, had become ambassadors in their own right.

When the duet ended, Wang moved closer and touched her arm. "There seems to be a problem with RadiMo," he said.

"What now?" she mumbled, and excused herself from the table. Po and a group of the younger children lined themselves up and started to sing.

"What's the problem?" she asked the Centauri attendant stationed near the Bournese Herald's *skiff*.

Wang caught up with her as the man replied, "I don't know, ma'am. Herald RadiMo went down a hole, squealed terribly, and switched on his red light."

"Do you have a remote control for the *skiff*?" Wang asked. The attendant nodded. "Then let's take it out into the hall before this song is finished."

She watched him guide the floating platform out a pair of double doors, while at the same time listening to the Future's singers and a muffled but distinct Bournese wail.

Once out in the hall's quiet, Rieka leaned close to the *skiff*. "Herald RadiMo, it is Herald Degahv. Are you ill?"

She heard a series of snorts and clicks but could make nothing out. Softly Wang said, "The translator boards are all inside the unit."

Rieka nodded. "RadiMo, I do not speak Bournese. You must translate for me to understand the difficulty."

Slowly, a portal opened and he crept toward her. She backed away from the hole and stood at a discreet distance. "The noise," the synthetic voice finally said.

"Is it quiet enough here, or would you rather depart?"

"Departure is preferred."

Rieka nodded and offered him a soft smile. "Your comfort and happiness are my concern. Do not trouble yourself to stay."

His fingers moved quickly over the board. "RadiMo thanks Herald Degahv for her graciousness."

"Anytime. I hope you enjoyed the party before the music started."

"It proved . . . interesting. Good evening." He slunk back down the hole, and the attendant accompanied the *skiff* down the hall.

Rieka heaved a sigh and looked up at Wang. "Aliens." She chuckled, shaking her head. "I'll never figure them out."

TEN

Triscoe watched Rieka walk across the suite's bedroom, marveling at how a mere garment could capture his attention. "Where did you get that dress?"

"You're awfully interested in my wardrobe, recently," she commented. Then, after glancing his way, answered, "Rhonique. There's a little shop not far from the Fleet Administration Building. On Senate Boulevard."

"Perhaps you should open an account there," he told her. There must have been something in his voice that caused her to chuckle. "What?"

"Triscoe, dear heart, I love you, but I don't ever think you're going to understand the Human concept of romance."

Indignant, he stood straighter. "And what gives you that idea?"

"Obviously, this dress—or rather *me* in it, is something you find attractive."

"Almost to the point of distraction, if you must know." He watched her breasts push against the fabric when she heaved a sigh and wondered whether or not she'd worn anything under the shimmery, deep blue material.

"It's the neckline," she told him. "Anyway, the point is—if you find me sexy in this thing," she lifted the skirt a bit and let it fall, "and want to open an account at the store where I bought it—that's fine."

He frowned. Rieka had completely lost him, again. "Didn't I just say that?"

"No. You said *I* should open an account there."

Confused, he sat and nudged off his shoes. "Why . . . shouldn't you?"

"Because *you* should."

Triscoe dropped his chin into his hand to think. Finally, he gave up. Again. "I fail to understand why I would wish to open an account in a women's dress shop. I have no intention of wearing a dress—or is that *your* idea of romance?" he finished warily, hoping humor might actually enable them to communicate.

He watched her fidget and make a strange, disgruntled noise. "No. Don't be ridiculous."

Triscoe felt as if he were in his first conversation with a Boo. Nothing followed or made any sense at all. "I think *you're* being ridiculous. How would I know what style to choose? What size?"

"You like this one, don't you?"

"Unquestionably, but I don't see why you would want more of the same." He found himself shaking his head, again.

Rieka sat down across from him and leaned forward, her elbows on her knees. Her eyes twinkled, silently challenging him to grasp an obviously Human concept. "You pick out presents for me—to please you. I'll buy things for you that please me. Get it?"

He took a moment to think it through. "This sounds like a paradox. I should buy things for me to give to you. And this is romantic?"

"No. Yes." She made a face. "Well, not the way you put it."

He liked her confused scowl. At least it made him feel as if they'd found an equal, if not precarious, footing. "Perhaps," he suggested, "we should just both go around without any clothes and the problem will be solved."

"Very funny."

He sighed. "Really, I am not that dense. I believe I understand the concept, now, although I am skeptical."

"I'll take what I can get."

Triscoe was smiling softly at her, his eyes consuming everything about her from the jeweled comb in her hair to her satin slippers, when his TC clicked. He switched it on. "Marteen."

"Saw you leave the party a little early," Robet's voice reverberated in his head. "Wanted to say good-bye before I left for Dani."

"That was thoughtful, Robet." He watched Rieka put her hand to her mouth.

"Tell him I'm sorry I didn't get to say good-bye," she whispered.

"Rieka says good-bye, Robet. And she'll try to find a way to spend some time with you when you return for the Reaffirmation."

"Ugh! I can't," she huffed. "My schedule is—" He waved at her to be quiet.

"Tell her I understand."

"He understands, love."

Rieka rolled her eyes and went to the bar for a beverage.

"Anyway," Robet's voice continued, "I missed Jeniper, too. I really like her, Tris. She's a fascinating woman."

"Yes, I suppose she is," he agreed uneasily.

"I know you're leaving tonight, too, but I thought you might pass on a message. I had intended to speak to her before I left."

"And what's the message?"

"See you in two weeks."

"That's it?"

"Yes. I didn't want to seem to pushy. I don't think she'd appreciate that."

"That's rather thoughtful of you," Triscoe told him dryly. "I'll ask Rieka to give her the message. Anything else?"

"No. I suppose I'll see you in two weeks, too."

"Undoubtedly. Marteen, out."

Robet switched off his end of the communication, and Triscoe leaned back into the sofa's cushions. "Robet asks you to tell Jeniper he'll see her in two weeks—and he's sorry for not telling her good-bye."

"I'll be happy to. I think it's very sweet," Rieka said.

"You know I don't approve of your pairing them up."

"Yes." Her gray-blue eyes flashed at him, and she lifted her chin. "I could tell you weren't overjoyed when I sat them together at dinner last night, but for heaven's sake, Triscoe, it's been months. Robet's a big boy. He's bounced back from that . . . that leap of stupidity. Jeniper is a nice, safe girl. And she's Aurian. They'll get along just fine, given a chance."

"A chance is all he needs. You know his reputation."

"Stop. That isn't nice. Robet is capable of a meaningful relationship. He's friends with us, after all."

Triscoe closed his eyes and rolled his head on his shoulders to ease the tightness in his neck. "I don't feel particularly 'nice' at the moment," he told her. "You've berated me over this 'romance' concept—again. I can't seem to fathom why I should buy clothes for you to wear—or vice versa. You've gone against my better judgment in pairing Robet and Jeniper. And now, I have to leave you when I would much rather—"

He heard her soft footfall and drew a deep breath when she put her finger on his lips. She then traded her lips for her finger and slid into his lap. "Me too," she said finally, her voice uncharacteristically deep. "Let's make a truce for now," she told him, nibbling her way along his chin toward his ear. "When you leave, we still may not agree, but at least we'll both be . . . satisfied."

Triscoe slipped his fingers beneath the skirt's long slit. "Deal."

Rieka tried to shove her way around Wang as he blocked the cockpit door. "I said let me pass, Wang-Chi."

"And I said you are not going to pilot this craft."

She huffed and put her hands on her hips. "I've already cleared it with the pilot. And you've had your people go over the ship. We're all going to be as safe as if we were home in bed. Now, *let me pass.*"

"You said you'd take orders from me," he persisted.

"You're forgetting about the part where my life might be in danger. It isn't, here. For heaven's sake, we're only taking this tiny shuttle on a puddle jump." Rieka waved a hand in his face to help make her point.

"You are not cleared to pilot this ship, Herald."

Rieka set her jaw. "Actually, I am. I have a current Commonwealth pilot's license for everything from a shuttle like this—to the *Prodigy*. And for your information, Mr. Hong Wang-Chi," she added, using his complete name the way a parent would to an obnoxious child, "in addition to being Earth Herald and your boss, I am *still* a Fleet captain."

Knowing it would take him a second to digest that interesting tidbit, Rieka rushed past him. Lieutenant Verde looked over her shoulder and saluted.

"Welcome aboard the *Kimbell,* Herald," she said. "She's small, but she's a good little ship."

"Why thank you, Lieutenant," Rieka said, throwing a glance at Wang as she returned the salute and assumed the captain's chair. Verde had already moved to the copilot's seat. "I haven't flown one of these in a couple of years. Please don't allow my position in the Fleet or the Council of Ten to intimidate you. If I forget to do something—I expect you to tell me."

Verde looked skeptical. "I doubt that, ma'am. You've been piloting ships for years."

Rieka's laugh sounded more like a sigh. "I'll take that as a compliment."

Wang hovered in the cockpit door and Verde glanced at him. "Is there something I can do for you, sir?" she asked.

"No," he grumbled, glaring at Rieka.

"Really, Wang," she offered, doing the preflight check, "you're safe with me. I promise I won't crash the *Kimbell.*"

"You'd better not. Half your staff is along. And we've got another four passengers, too."

Rieka happily tapped the console and studied the systems reports. She hadn't realized how much she missed spaceflight, and no amount of Wang's grumbling would dent her enjoyment of it. "Which reminds me," she told him over her shoulder, "send Jeniper up here as soon as we level off in the exosphere." She glanced at Verde. "About ten minutes from now."

Rieka watched Wang's reluctant return to the cabin, then waited, her fingers poised over the controls, until Verde announced, "We're cleared." A moment later the *Kimbell* shot down the short runway and angled up through the clouds.

When they hit the first elevation mark, twenty kilometers, Verde said, "You're doing great, Captain. Maybe you should've let that big guy stay in here and watch."

"Mr. Hong?" Rieka chuckled. "I admit he sometimes takes the job a bit too seriously—but then again, that's one of the reasons I hired him."

They continued on in companionable silence, broken only by Lieutenant Verde's one-sided communications with EarthCom Asia. Once the shuttle leveled off in the exosphere, the door opened to reveal Jeniper. "Come on in,

Jen," Rieka said, waving her into the cramped space. "I'd like you to meet your flight crew, Lieutenant Allana Verde and Captain Herald Rieka Degahv."

"No wonder Wang's having a fit back there," Jeniper told her, smiling. "You shouldn't be flying this ship."

"I'm the most experienced person aboard."

"Maybe so, but really . . . it's . . . it's not right. You're the Earth Herald now. You need to consider that."

"I did. For about four seconds." Rieka checked her readouts and nodded to herself. "Verde, I wonder if I could speak to Jeniper alone—if you don't mind. It'll only take a minute or two."

Verde touched a few controls. "Certainly. We're just now coming over the Indian Ocean. I'll be back in about fifteen minutes." She eased out of her chair and, with the help of her magnetic shoes, changed positions with Jeniper.

When the door closed with a soft click, Rieka noted the dusky pink of Jeniper's bibbets, and said gently, "Is everything okay? You seem a little tense."

Jeniper fidgeted and stared at the instruments on her control panel. "A little. The job is new to me. I want everything to be just right."

Rieka nodded and checked their altitude. "I can empathize with that. If you get overwhelmed, say something, Jen. There's no use suffering in silence."

"Yes. Of course."

Sensing that Jeniper had just improvised a generic excuse for her behavior, Rieka decided being subtle might get her closer to the truth. "How'd it go with Robet the other night?"

"Who?"

"Captain DeVark."

"Oh. Well, the captain is quite charming—as I'm sure you know. We chatted about a variety of topics. He is easy to talk to."

"That he is," Rieka agreed. "I noticed you and he left together after dinner," she coaxed, hoping Jeniper would offer an opinion of him.

"Really?" Jeniper asked, sounding more confused than wary. Her bibbets darkened a shade or two. "Oh. Oh, yes."

Now they were getting somewhere. "Look, I don't mean to pry into your private life Jen. That isn't what this conversation is about. But ever since that evening when we all had dinner together . . . you have to admit you've been acting strangely. If Robet said or did anything improper, I'd be glad to speak to him about it."

"Oh." Jeniper's expression shifted from confused to pensive. The bibbets lightened a notch. "Well, I wouldn't go so far as to call it . . . improper."

"He's pushy, I know. And he loves women. I apologize for anything he might have done to offend you." Encouraged by Jeniper's sympathetic expression, Rieka continued. "It was my idea to seat you together, Jen. The whole thing is entirely my fault."

"No, don't blame yourself, Rieka," Jeniper told her, relief obvious in her tone. "It was nothing. Really."

"You sure?"

"Yes. Absolutely." Rieka watched as Jeniper's bibbets faded to a very pale pink.

"Mmm. Well, in that case, I suppose I should relay his message. He apologized for not saying good-bye before he left—he looks forward to seeing you at the Reaffirmation ceremony."

"He told you that?"

Rieka nodded. "Actually, he told Triscoe. I don't have a TC anymore." She paused, trying to gauge Jeniper's mood. "So, it's okay, then?"

Jeniper turned, and Rieka saw the hopeful look in her pale blue eyes. "Yes. Yes, of course. Everything's fine."

Rieka gladly let Verde pilot the *Kimbell* as it made the descent over the Arabian Peninsula. Jeniper had returned to the passenger cabin, and Rieka had no desire to explain the landscape to anyone. She simply wanted to enjoy the view.

"Can we swing out over the Mediterranean before we land?" she asked.

"Sure, Herald," Verde replied.

Smiling softly at the appellation, Rieka leaned closer to the window. The water shone like a thin silver ribbon on the horizon. It widened as they approached, its deep blue mirroring the nearly cloudless sky.

"Crossing the thirtieth parallel now, Herald," Verde told

her. "The ruins of Cairo are about five hundred kilometers due west."

Rieka nodded and rested her chin in her hand, eyes scanning the horizon. Almost eight years had passed since she'd been here, and even in that short time things had changed. The desert seemed dotted with more agro-oases than she'd remembered. And she was almost sure the Char had reached the thirtieth parallel. When they neared the coast, Rieka realized she could see no burned sections amid the various croplands below. Her heart surged with a mixture of pride and relief.

As they shot out over the sea, Rieka noticed that their altitude had dropped considerably. "What's the alt?"

"Six kilometers."

She nodded absently, gazing at the deep blue Mediterranean below them. "I've seen enough water this morning. Swing back east over the mainland at the thirty-third parallel and drop to two kilometers."

"As we speak, Cap—Herald," Verde replied.

Rieka turned away slightly to hide her grin and felt the lieutenant's attention shift from the control panel to her, then back. A silent apology for almost calling her captain, she wondered—or hesitation at traveling over the actual impact site? A lot of people didn't like to look at the scar. For her, it was a reminder of just how long they'd suffered and how far they'd come.

Collision Gulf loomed before them on the horizon. "Slow forward speed to 250 kph." As Verde complied, the panorama before them shifted slightly and grew slowly.

This is how she'd always imagined it, Rieka realized. Riding the meteor's path. Sometimes she could even conjure it in her mind's eye—falling from the sky, plunging into the Mediterranean Sea, and ramming the coastline hard enough to change it forever.

Their speed, though slow, was too fast at this elevation for more than a quick look. Rieka saw waves breaking against the limestone cliffs, a waterfall, then scrub-covered mountains. The *Kimbell* swept over them, and Verde turned the ship south toward the long flat valley once farmed by Humans calling themselves Syrians.

They skirted the blast zone's edge and made their approach to Damascus. Now restored as a tourist base and historical point of interest, Rieka was sure this new, above-ground city would soon become Earth's focal point. She figured anyone visiting the planet, even businessmen and women, would eventually wind up here. Curious about Humanity's past, the Collision, and what had happened in its aftermath, they'd find all their answers, however incomplete, in Damascus's On-Site Museum.

It was the perfect place to hold the Reaffirmation.

After they set down in a shuttle parking facility, Rieka, Jeniper, and Wang walked across a short open space to the Chute that would take them to the terminal and waiting ground transport. Rieka breathed in the heat, the dry tang in the air, and a quality of freshness that invigorated her. "Wonderful, isn't it?"

"Amazing," Wang said before stepping forward and speaking to the person waiting at the Chute door.

"Amazing?" Jeniper asked.

Rieka purposefully said nothing. She waited while Wang finished with the attendant and ushered them into the Chute.

"Amazing how, Wang?" Jeniper repeated when they were under way.

"This place was completely devastated, Jen," he told her, waving his hands to indicate everything outside the Chute. "Gone. A century ago most everything around here was still black. The Char, they called it. Any place within five hundred kilometers of the Site. Burned. Even the ground itself. The restoration is amazing."

Jeniper nodded, apparently comprehending the project's immensity. She turned to Rieka. "And your father and uncle are responsible for the transformation."

Rieka found herself smiling wryly. "Not exactly." The Chute door opened and Wang stepped out. He looked around and signaled someone waiting a few paces away. The two men spoke, and he turned.

"This way, Herald." The ground transport waiting for them looked identical to the one they'd used in Canberra. When they'd settled in their seats, Rieka reached for her datapad and noticed Jeniper doing the same. Wang sat up front with the driver, watchful but relaxed.

The ride into Damascus took only a few minutes. Rieka managed to catch up on her notes and check the calendar before shutting down the datapad to look at the incredible city built to honor the many civilizations of man.

Nowhere else in the Commonwealth would Humans find such a firm foundation of their peoples' past. She saw a building that looked remarkably like the Parthenon, a mosque, a pyramid, and a three-story brick building among modern structures both short and tall. She saw tents of various types, all constructed of something far sturdier than the original woven or hide materials they resembled. There were thatched roofs, totem poles, and great, granite walls wearing parapets like jagged crowns adorning their corner towers.

They passed a huge domed structure, and, even from several blocks away, Rieka could identify it as the On-Site Museum. "We'll need to go there, Jen," Rieka told her, pointing toward its hulking blue form. "Make sure you schedule it sometime before we leave for the Senate meetings on Yadra."

Jeniper nodded and made a note on her small computer. "Did you want to do that before or after the World Zoo?"

"Doesn't matter. But I'm sure Wang'll probably want the entire facility closed to the public when we go—so try to find a time that won't be too invasive to their schedules."

Wang turned at the sound of his name. "It's nice to know I'm appreciated—or at least considered competent."

Rieka smiled. "Oh, you're appreciated, Wang-Chi—even if only for your scintillating conversation."

She watched him absorb her subtle barb, then laugh in that good-natured way she'd come to expect. Since their first meeting, Rieka had sensed that Hong Wang-Chi much preferred criticism to praise. Consequently, they got along quite well when she wrapped one in the other. It was like talking in code.

Watching him turn back toward the driver, Rieka couldn't recall meeting anyone else with hair so black it reflected a blue tint.

"That must be Olympic Stadium," Jeniper said.

Rieka looked left through the trees and glimpsed the immense structure. "The place seats ninety thousand people. How many tickets are left?"

Jeniper shook her head. "Earth NewsNet reported the Reaffirmation's ticket sales at 56 percent this morning."

Rieka sighed. It was almost as if a conspiracy brewed, intent on making the ceremony a circus. Low ticket sales, balky caterers, entertainers backing out. She couldn't imagine her new career starting off on a worse note.

"Shit!" Wang snapped. For a moment, Rieka thought he'd simply been reacting to their conversation. But when he left his seat and reached for something under his jacket, his eyes trained on the stadium, she realized his comment had nothing to do with them.

He pulled the maitu into view, and Jeniper gasped. "Everyone stay here," he ordered. For once, Rieka simply nodded and let him do his job.

Candace Degahv turned at her stateroom door and looked at her personal secretary, Barbara Smith. The Human woman sat at the console studying a News Sheet. Apparently sensing her employer's attention, Smith looked up. "Mrs. D?"

"Schedule my dinner for eight this evening," Candace told her. "I'll be dining with Captain Gimbish. I'll let you know the location later."

Smith nodded, nonplussed. "Of course."

Purposefully, she left the suite and went directly to the captain's quarters. He opened the door with a surprised flip of his ears. "Mrs. Degahv, welcome aboard. I had not realized you would be making this trip." He bowed formally, from the waist.

"An oversight of your registrar, no doubt," Candace said easily.

"Come in please. Make yourself comfortable. Can I offer a refreshment?"

Candace strode into the room and seated herself in a cushioned chair. "No. Thank you, Captain." She studied the Oph's now-familiar coat pattern. Generally cream-colored, Gimbish had darker paws and ears and a mask across his eyes.

Gimbish sat on a nearby chair. "Is there something I can do for you, Mrs. Degahv?" he asked.

Candace smiled for his benefit. "Actually, there is. I'm going to be sending several large shipments to Earth in the next few weeks. And I was wondering if you would be amenable to . . . taking my word as to the contents."

The captain's ears pricked up. "This sounds like an interesting prospect. Can I have some assurances from you that this mysterious cargo is not hazardous?"

"Oh, it's completely benign, Captain. Tools and equipment—things like that. And I plan to compensate you, as usual, for your cooperation." She waited patiently while the Oph considered the proposition.

"The usual fee?" he asked.

"Yes. And I'll throw in a bonus if you can give me any information as to any plans TechLine might have for Earth. You do have access to someone on the executive board, do you not?"

Gimbish seemed to hesitate, apparently unsure of how much she knew and what he could safely tell her. "I have some, limited connection," he admitted. "I am unsure of when I will next have contact."

Candace nodded. "I understand completely, Captain. Of course, compensation will not be forthcoming unless I receive the information. But the cargo business will be handled as usual."

He growled lightly. "Of course."

She glanced around the room and noticed a ceremonial blade mounted to the wall. It was for some part of the Oph Kori-death ritual, but she had no idea of the thing's name or function. Still, it struck a cord Candace had been grasping at since she'd first boarded the *Garner*.

"Was there anything else, Mrs. Degahv?"

"No. Thank you for your time, Captain," Candace said, eyeing him as she stood. "But I would be honored if you dined with me and my staff before this trip is over."

He seemed to consider the invitation, then nodded. "It would be my pleasure," he said, his black lips thinning slightly.

"Good. Tonight at eight in the VIP dining room."

Gimbish hesitated only a moment. "I will look forward to it."

They made their way to the door and Candace turned to study his dark eyes. "You seem to have many more Ophs in your crew than I remember," she remarked lightly.

He glanced away before responding. "Yes. We've had an influx of new personnel during this tour."

"I'm sure I'd love to hear all about it . . . at dinner,"

she said. "Thank you again, Captain." Her face an impenetrable mask, Candace allowed a smile. Sure Gimbish had business with entrepreneurs other than herself, she decided dinner would be the perfect means to find out what was going on, and perhaps find a way to capitalize on it.

ELEVEN

When Triscoe walked through the now-familiar doors at Sati Labs, he was surprised to see Wilmstos waiting for him behind the reception desk.

"Captain Marteen," the man said, a trace of excitement in his voice. He came around the desk and extended his hands, palms up. "I have marvelous news for you, Captain," Wilmstos told him, eyes gleaming excitedly. "Come. Let me show you."

Triscoe followed, but with a good deal less enthusiasm than the doctor. He had convinced himself it would be easy to tell Wilmstos simply to hold the DNA samples until more research could be done or some other way to have a baby could be explored. But the man acted as impatient as a child in an amusement park, and Triscoe sensed telling him to postpone their request would come as a great disappointment.

Instead of going to his office, the doctor led him into the main laboratory building, where they entered a lab observation deck.

"I've brought you here so we can actually see the work in progress," Wilmstos began. "Of course, I could get you clearance to enter the lab proper, but we would have to be sterilized and wear biotech suits. And, frankly, I didn't want to waste the time."

Triscoe nodded as he glanced around the floor below. "I appreciate the forethought, Doctor," he said. "But I'm not sure why you've brought me here."

"I wanted you to witness the people and the place that has created a modern-day miracle," Wilmstos explained. "One which you and your wife instigated."

This was sounding worse than he'd imagined. "It's only been a week since your board accepted our proposal and tissue samples," Triscoe said, a hint of uneasiness in his voice.

"Yes. Yes, I know. And who could have predicted such incredible success?"

Triscoe studied Wilmstos's exuberant face and glanced back over the lab, the technicians busily working and paying them no mind. "I think, Doctor, that we should adjourn to your office."

Wilmstos frowned slightly, then smiled. "Of course, Captain. We need to sit and discuss what will happen next. Timetables. Additional questions you might have. When the Herald will be able to schedule a trip to Indra. And I've taken the liberty of ordering a bottle of *kiova* and some *darvin* to celebrate the occasion."

Triscoe frowned slightly, nodded again, and followed the doctor back to the Chute. Now that the lab both had their DNA and had managed to do something remarkable with it, he needed to find a diplomatic way to explain their new goals without minimizing the achievement, whatever that was. After all, he and Rieka had made the request in good faith. No one should be blamed if plans had changed.

A few moments later, they found their way to Wilmstos's now-familiar office. Seating himself at the doctor's request, Triscoe watched the man collect two small glasses and a short round bottle from a shelf. He pulled the stopper and poured about fifty milliliters of thick white liquid into each glass, enough for a couple of swallows.

Keeping his hands on his thighs, Triscoe waited for Wilmstos to sit, then asked, "What, precisely, has happened?"

"I must tell you first, Captain, that as soon as you approached us, I had a team running virtual simulations and working on techniques that might be useful in our quest. We worked through several dozen possibilities, most of which were unsuccessful, before your samples were even taken. Nine did show promise."

He studied Triscoe for a moment, apparently wondering why his client lacked enthusiasm at the news. Then, with a little shrug, Wilmstos continued his story. "Yesterday afternoon while some preliminary testing was being conducted with sections of the genomes you and the Herald provided—a most astonishing thing occurred. We got natural cohesion. It's unheard of between alien species, Captain. But it happened. The lab notified me immediately as soon as they got a positive turn. I went down and looked at the films, myself. Several pair of chromosomes had correctly aligned themselves. Not all of them, I should add, but enough to show promise. The tech-pro assured me the event happened without our intervention."

Triscoe eased back in the chair and felt light-headed, as if all the CO_2 in the room had been removed. "What are you saying, Wilmstos?" he asked, hoping he didn't sound as alarmed as he felt. "That I could impregnate Rieka myself?" he asked incredulously.

"Of course not. Well, I don't think so, anyway. Not exactly—but this is remarkable. Hundreds of additional processes are still to come. But our job has been made infinitely easier by this affinity between the two species' genetic material. No one's ever tried anything like it before." He stopped and took a breath. "We've gone through that already." He waved his hand, dismissing that old news. "But this is . . ." He shook his head, unable to find the proper words.

"Incredible?" Triscoe offered.

"Beyond that."

Sighing quietly, Triscoe felt the war within him bubble back to the surface. He'd come to tell Wilmstos to delay the attempt, but now nature had accelerated the plans without warning. He did want to have a child. Maybe this remarkable cohesion foretold the possibility of that. But he didn't want Rieka to endanger herself—and that was still a sobering factor.

"Wilmstos, I came here today to make a request on behalf of both Rieka and myself," he began, calling upon all his diplomatic talent.

"Yes?"

"Yes." He looked into the doctor's brown eyes for a moment, then at the glasses of *kiova*. "Yes. The thing of it is, you see, she couldn't possibly have realized the time involved in her duties as Herald until she'd actually become Herald. Which she hadn't when we first approached you.

I . . . other factors have become apparent, recently, forcing us to change our plans."

Wilmstos's smile faded. "I understand. Can you tell me exactly how the plans have changed?"

"We need to . . . postpone the pregnancy," Triscoe told him softly. "I don't know how long—"

"You're halting the process?"

"No," Triscoe said firmly. "We *do* wish to have a child. But Rieka frequently jumps into things without all the facts. The situation now, precludes us having a baby until things have . . . calmed down."

"I'm afraid I don't understand, Captain," Wilmstos said, a wary look on his face. "This interview—indeed—every conversation we have is completely confidential. If there is some unique reason you must postpone the pregnancy, I would like to know."

Triscoe had debated telling him both everything and nothing. Now as he sat here looking the doctor in the eye, he realized Wilmstos had taken a big career risk in supporting their original request. If only for that, he deserved the truth.

"There are two reasons, Doctor. Both quite serious and both, as I assumed you've deduced—have very little to do with Herald's duties."

"I'm listening," Wilmstos said. He picked up his glass and swallowed the *kiova* in one gulp.

Pausing a moment to gather his thoughts, Triscoe finally said, "I have the Gift. When we were married, Rieka was unable to communicate with me mentally without my performing a Singlemind. During the Procyon War, she received a severe blow to the head. When she regained consciousness we found the link had bridged our minds. And it has grown stronger in the last few months."

The doctor's eyes grew round. "You are a Gifted Pair," he whispered reverently.

"I wouldn't go quite that far," Triscoe said. "But there is a significant risk to all three of us if we aren't absolutely sure the fetus will be chemically compatible with Rieka's Human body."

Wilmstos took several deep breaths. "I can see why you are concerned, Captain. This is most serious. It certainly supersedes anything I might say to the contrary. And, since the chromosomes are so compatible, we can shift our attention from whether or not they will attain mitosis to exactly what might grow from that single cell. That, of course, is your biggest risk. And I assure you we planned to investigate thoroughly any possible complications before even suggesting implantation. The extra time—" he made a small gesture with his hands, silently telling Triscoe of his relief, "—will allow a more unhurried approach."

"I am pleased that you're able to accommodate our request without very much difficulty."

Wilmstos smiled, and Triscoe felt thankful the man had understood the situation's complexities without having them explained. "Of course, Captain," he said. "We always intended to move cautiously, of course, but now there will be absolute certainty the cells will be compatible or, I assure you, there will be no mention of implantation."

"Thank you, Doctor."

They sat in companionable silence for a moment, then Wilmstos asked, "And what was the other reason to delay?"

Triscoe shrugged slightly and exhaled through his nose. "There is no delicate way to say this, I'm afraid. It is quite possible someone means to do Rieka harm."

"But who? Who in their right mind . . . would . . . would consider such a thing?" Wilmstos stammered, obviously aghast at the notion. "She's a Fleet hero. Humanity elected her as their united voice. Surely she hasn't made an enemy in the last few days."

"The situation began almost two decades ago, as I understand it," Triscoe began. "Suffice it to say there is at least one individual who—"

The floor suddenly shook. Triscoe's chair shifted. He held on to it and watched Wilmstos lurch forward. An incredible sound assaulted their ears.

"Take cover!" Triscoe yelled, barely able to hear himself over the noise. An explosion? Earthquake? Somewhere in Korval, he decided, though the notion seemed ridiculous.

He dropped to the floor and tipped his chair forward, creating a small but serviceable shelter. Another concussion shook the building. A second tremor or rubble falling from above? He had no idea. Sections of ceiling slammed into the floor around him. Shelves tipped and crashed. Triscoe heard Wilmstos whimper once and hoped the man was unhurt. The air became so thick with dust Triscoe found it difficult to breathe. He pulled his tunic up over his mouth and nose, hoping the cloth would filter enough to keep him breathing until they could escape the building.

Finally, after what seemed like minutes but probably amounted to seconds, the noise abated. He could still hear things occasionally crashing, but the building itself seemed to have stabilized, at least for the moment.

"Wilmstos, are you all right?" Triscoe began what became a complicated process of extracting himself from the chair and the debris that had fallen around him. When he finally looked around, he was astonished at the amount of dust in the air, and the mess. The ceiling had caved in, leaving barely enough room for him to crawl around.

"Wilmstos?" he said again, picking his way through the rubble to the desk's farside. "Doctor, can you hear me?"

A small sigh sounded from somewhere in the vicinity of where he expected the doctor to be. Triscoe carefully picked up chunks of ceiling, books, a smashed picture frame. When he'd cleared enough away to see some of the floor, he heard another sound and saw the doctor's hand protruding from under a fallen shelf.

After checking first to see whether or not moving the shelf would cause an avalanche of debris, Triscoe levered it up as far as he could and braced it against a small table. Wilmstos lay facedown, his right arm twisted at an unnatural angle. He moaned slightly.

Triscoe knew ground assistance was out of the question. Rescue crews would never enter a collapsing building. He clicked on his TC and pulled his tunic back into place. "Marteen to *Providence*."

"Aarkmin here, Captain," his EO replied. "I was about to contact you. There has been an explosion in the vicinity of your signal. Are you all right?"

"An explosion? Not an earthquake?"

"Definitely an explosion. Are you injured?"

"I am fine, Aarkmin," he replied, confusion washing over him. The dust clogged his throat and he coughed. "However, my companion requires medical attention. Have us InterMATted directly to the Medical section."

"As we speak."

In another moment, Triscoe was looking at Vort Twanabok, his medical superintendent. The Vekyan glanced at him and waved at an assistant. A mask attached to a small compressed air cylinder was slipped over his face. Another was placed on Wilmstos.

"I'm fine, Vort," Triscoe assured him through the mask. He pulled it off and took a deep breath. "Swallowed some dust, that's all." He pointed to the unconscious man on the floor.

"See to him, Vort," Triscoe ordered. "His name is Dr. Wilmstos. Helegi Wilmstos, I think. He's employed at Sati Labs."

"I'll report as soon as I know something," Twanabok told him.

Triscoe nodded and left the Medical suite in search of some answers. When he got to the bridge, Aarkmin vacated the command chair. "Captain on the bridge."

"Report," he spit, confusion and anger swirling in his mind like tangible things.

"Sir, there isn't much to say. Shortly after you InterMATted to the surface, Sati Labs was destroyed."

"Only the lab? Nothing else?"

"Nothing else, Captain," she said.

Wang ordered the driver to stop before turning toward Rieka. "Stay here," he said. She nodded, catching a glimpse of the maitu he'd pulled from its holder. She frowned when he began walking across the pavement, holding the small but lethal weapon in full view.

He stopped about ten meters away and gestured the gate attendant to come down from her tower. Once she stood on the ground with him, Rieka smiled at Wang's obvious height advantage. The woman responded to his questions, waving her hands at her tower, the roadway, and the stadium behind her.

"What the hell is going on?" Rieka grumbled.

They watched him speak to the woman for another moment, then turn and stride back to the transport. "Sorry," he said with an apologetic shrug, then instructed the driver where to park. "Security isn't what I wanted. The stadium manager is waiting in the main lobby to show you around.

Before we take his tour, I'll need about fifteen minutes with him. Privately."

Rieka found herself smiling at the determined look on Wang's face. She schooled the expression to a faint curve in her lips, and said, "Whatever you think is necessary, Mr. Hong. This is your specialty. But I'd rather not wait in the transport, if you don't mind."

"That can be arranged." He turned as they parked and the driver opened the door.

"Oh, and Wang—"

"Yes, Herald?"

She smiled. "I don't mind the inconvenience."

They had just finished touring the stadium and were walking toward the third-level VIP lobby when Jeniper looked up from her datapad, confusion and concern clearly written on her face. Rieka felt her heart speed up when Jeniper's bibbets actually darkened.

"What's happened, Jen?"

She watched Jeniper work her jaw for a second, then she managed to say, "Herald RadiMo is . . . missing."

"What do you mean missing?" Rieka snapped, snatching Jeniper's proffered datapad and looking at the missive. His aide, CariMo, clearly stated the Herald had been expected in New SubAtlanta. When he did not arrive at the scheduled time, a search was conducted. Neither he nor his *skiff* could be found anywhere on the Australian or North American continents. Searches on the other five continents were still under way.

"Well, this is just great," Rieka mumbled. She handed back the datapad and tried to think where he might have gone. "Dammit. As if things weren't already a mess. I suppose I should be prepared for stuff like this."

"I don't see how," Jeniper advised. "You aren't responsible for the Bournese Herald. In fact, he has been on Earth at his request."

"True. But that doesn't really make any difference, Jen," Rieka told her. She signaled Wang that she was going back to the transport, then turned and led her people to the ground level, where the vehicle waited.

When they'd all taken their seats and the transport had turned down the long, landscaped driveway, Wang asked,

"Where are we going?" His look told her he took Rad-iMo's disappearance quite seriously.

"Well, they've already scoured New SubAtlanta," she replied. "We'd probably do well to start in New SubDenver."

"I was wondering when we'd get a look at the central office," Jeniper quipped.

"Then you don't have long to wait. We'll be there in a few minutes."

Jeniper frowned. "I don't understand. It'll take at least an hour and a half—if a shuttle is ready to go—which I wouldn't expect since this is an unscheduled trip."

Rieka smiled and glanced at Wang. She activated her own datapad and tapped at the pads. Seconds later, she looked back at Jeniper. "The *Capitol* is now in orbit. And though under normal circumstances we'd shuttle in our destination, I'd say this situation requires my immediate attention. I'm proclaiming a diplomatic emergency. We're InterMATting to SubDenver. In fact, as long as there's a ship within range, we're InterMATting everywhere until RadiMo is found."

Wang's frown had appeared and seemed glued to his face. "But—"

"No 'buts' from you on this, Wang," Rieka told him. "We've got an emergency. I'm responsible for both Earth and its image. The day after I officially become Herald, a visiting Herald disappears without a trace. Does this sound like coincidence? Not to me." She paused for a breath and looked at Jeniper. "Am I sounding paranoid to you?"

"I don't know. This could all be quite innocent," Jeniper told them, glancing at Wang. "On the other hand, it could be very serious. At the moment, there's no way to tell."

Rieka leaned her elbow on her seat's armrest and dropped her chin into her hand. RadiMo's disappearance had obviously been planned carefully. Only someone who knew both why he'd been on Earth and his daily agenda could pull off the Herald's kidnapping. How many people had access to that kind of information? Not many, she figured. But for one of them, abducting a Herald wouldn't be terribly difficult. After all, she'd already done it at least once.

Now, she only had to deduce Candace's intent. To intimidate? Or was there a larger scheme? Thinking back to her conversation with RadiMo, she couldn't tell if he'd been behaving with characteristic shyness—or had been deliberately obtuse. With the Bournese, it was anyone's guess.

"Wang-Chi," she said, and he immediately jerked to attention.

"Yes."

"You're with me from now on. Every minute. Is that understood?"

He nodded, a look of conviction in his eye. "Of course."

"And I expect you to hire someone you trust to do all the itinerary work—what you've been doing yourself, so far. He or she will coordinate between you, Jeniper, and wherever I happen to be planning to go, if possible."

"Right." He gave her a slight nod. "I . . . I think I know someone who can do that."

"Good. Now, I can't predict where I'll be going after New SubDenver, but I can give you a few places that you need to secure."

He pulled his own datapad from his pocket while Rieka consulted hers.

"Is there something I should know?" Jeniper asked warily, her bibbets flushing a delicate pink.

"Not yet, Jen. Let's not all worry about things that may simply be phantoms." Jeniper said nothing, but Rieka noticed her bibbets darken slightly. "Okay, Wang. Odds are I'll be in SubDenver, SubAtlanta, Winnipeg, and possibly Jerusalem—sometime within the next twenty-four hours. I'll be InterMATting whenever possible, so there won't be any forewarning on the receiving end, if you understand my meaning."

"Unfortunately," he grumbled, and began tapping commands into his datapad.

"If we go anywhere else, it'll be equally unpredictable. Only the InterMAT chief on the *Capitol*, or whatever ship we use, will be privy to that knowledge. Does that ease your palpitations even a little?" she asked, smiling wryly.

He didn't return the expression. "Not exactly. Can I ask why we're doing this?"

"You can ask whatever you want. And this time I'll even try to reply. Someone wants to control my Heraldship—wants me to keep Earth isolated rather than opening it up to the Commonwealth for repopulation and trade. If I'm

guessing correctly, she's decided to go a different route.
Now, she intends to tarnish my image, raise questions about
my abilities, stir up old lies about my loyalty. All this she
can do without ever threatening me. A clever plan, I have
to admit. And somehow, I have to figure a way to throw
it back in her face."

"Who would do this to us—I mean to you?" Jeniper
asked, a tremor in her voice evidence of her concern. "I
mean, who could possibly have that kind of power?"

"Plenty of people, Jen," Wang volunteered without looking up from his computer. "Especially those with interplanetary businesses."

"But you have someone specific in mind, don't you,
Rieka?" Jeniper persisted.

Rieka nodded, thankful again for Wang's expertise in
things beyond his ability to protect her physically. "Right
now, I'm betting it's Candace Degahv. But knowing her,
that will be difficult to prove."

"Your mother!" Jeniper gasped.

"A lovely woman," Rieka quipped. "If you're lucky,
you'll never have to be in the same room with her."

"Have the records come in from Atlanta, yet?" Rieka
asked, looking across her desk and Wang's head to catch
Jeniper's glance. They'd been in New SubDenver for three
hours, and reports were coming in slowly. The local community directors in Winnipeg, New SubBrasilia, and Canberra had all sent identical communiqués. RadiMo was not
anywhere to be found.

"No," Jeniper answered. "Mr. Moore's secretary said
there was a problem in one of the school facilities, and he
went to see to it, personally. She assured me he'd send
word as soon as he had any information."

Wang shifted in his chair and looked at her. "You seem
safe enough, here. Do you think you can survive without
me for about an hour?"

"I suppose so."

"Don't you want to know why?"

"I know why, Wang-Chi," Rieka said. "You've been
studying those résumés for, what—two hours, now? You've
made the decision on whom to employ to replace you as
security chief—so you can do what you were hired to do."

He made a face at her. "Do you read minds, too?"

"Only one," she replied trying to keep a straight face. "Thankfully, not yours."

He grumbled, and Jeniper cleared her throat. Rieka waved him off. "Go, Wang. I have the maitu you gave me here, in the desk. I know how to use it. Jeniper and I will be okay for an hour or two."

He stood but didn't leave. When Rieka looked up to see a strange expression on his face, she offered him a one-sided smile. "Yes, Wang," she admitted, glancing once at Jeniper, "I can kill if I have to." When shock did not register on his face, she continued, echoing the same things he'd told her during his interview.

"It was during the war. And given a choice, I would have found another way. But when it's a them-or-me situation, there is no choice."

He watched her for a moment, then apparently made his decision. "I'll be back in an hour. If you need me, my datapad page will be on."

She waved him off, again. "Good luck."

When the door had closed, Jeniper moved to sit in the chair Wang had vacated. "You really . . . killed someone?" she asked gently.

"That comes as a surprise, Jen?" she asked, allowing only a trace of sarcasm. "Aren't we Humans expected to be barbaric—capable of every imaginable atrocity?"

When Jeniper looked at her as if she'd lost her mind, Rieka shook her head. "Sorry, just repeating something my mother once said."

"I still can't understand how she could hate you—her own daughter."

"It's a long story."

Jeniper's datapad beeped, and she moved to the desk console to receive the incoming message. Rieka didn't pay much attention to her until the printer spit a hard copy on the desk.

"What's this?"

"Just came in from EarthCom. It's the report you asked for on your father's shuttle crash."

Rieka nodded and grabbed up the sheets of paper. Glancing through them, she nodded to herself. "Nothing

much new here. The shuttle had been inspected by the pilot
and ground crew prior to liftoff."

"That's routine," Jeniper commented.

"True. But I wonder if this is?" She pulled the last page
from the others and studied a column of names.

"What?"

"The ground crew that serviced the ship was made up of
Ophs." She looked up into Jeniper's confused frown. "That
seems a little odd, don't you think?"

"I have no idea," she confessed. "Is it?"

"Twelve individuals of the same species on the same shift
sounds more than a little strange, to me." She raked her
fingers through her hair and tried to think. "Okay. The
next step is to verify how those Ophs were assigned. Eighteen years ago we were still using Fleet equipment. If there
aren't records here on Earth, Admiral Nason should have
them on Yadra."

Nodding her agreement, Jeniper tapped some notes into
her datapad. "I'll find out about the Earth records, first. If
they're inconclusive, I'll request Fleet records."

The plan sounded reasonable, but Rieka's sense of apprehension resurfaced. "Ask for both, now. We may find
they don't match."

Jeniper's bibbets paled slightly, but she said, "Of
course."

Her console beeped, and Rieka saw that the report from
Atlanta had arrived. "Director Moore looks to be a good
record keeper," she said, sifting down the index of residential, travel, and communication files. "From just looking at
this I can tell our next stop will be Atlanta."

"I've been told you get a breathtaking view of the Atlantic from several above-ground sites," Jeniper said.

"Really?" Rieka said. "I can't remember. Last time I was
there it was at night. And cold, too. Did you know the city
used to be about three hundred kilometers from the coast?"
Jeniper shook her head "no." "At any rate, by the time
we're done in Atlanta, I'll be ready to head back to Damascus." She tapped in an access code to NorthAm Comm to
find out if any Fleet ships were in orbit. Much to Rieka's
displeasure, the *Capitol*'s captain, Durana, hadn't seen RadiMo's disappearance for a few hours as an emergency, but

fortunately, she'd been willing to accept Rieka's need to InterMAT. "Oh, good."

"Good—what?" Jeniper asked.

"The *Currency* is due to attain orbit in about ninety minutes. I'm sure Bilik would love to help."

TWELVE

Captain Gimbish of the C.F.S. *Garner* sat alone in his room and thought about his cargo, his cousin, and what she planned to do.

He had always respected Gundah. She was older than he, held an enviable position in the Oph Herald's entourage, and enjoyed rough intercourse more than any other female he knew. She had wooed him to support her with tales of her unhappy adolescence and he had sympathized. Empathized. Sworn to help her right the wrongs.

But in the last few months, her suggestions had become requests and, finally, orders. Knowing she kept him caveblind for his own good, Gimbish hadn't questioned what she did or why. Lately, though, he'd begun to realize Gundah's behavior was far from predictable. While on the one paw he credited that to her genius, on the other, he couldn't help but wonder if she required mental therapy of some kind.

Thus far, the cargo she'd transported on the *Garner* had been innocuous. Things in mismarked boxes. Shipments of goods they both knew were either damaged or defective. But now, she'd suddenly swayed political. And try as he might, Gimbish could not get past the feeling of blatantly breaking his Command Oath.

With a muffled growl, he slid a communication chip into his console and typed in her Ophiuchus address along with the encoding instructions to prevent the document from being read more than once. When the camera flashed its record prompt, Gimbish took a breath and began.

"Gundah. Greetings. As requested, I am notifying you that I have done as you asked. But I have grave concerns for this strategy. I see no point in risking everything in order to bait your quarry. I realize you have not told me the entire plan, but this does not sit well."

Both knowing and fearing her ire, Gimbish was glad many light-years separated them. He took a breath and continued. "RadiMo has told me this 'excursion' off Earth is unexpected. He seems upset that you have changed the original plan. I have done everything in my power to keep him happy—but who can tell such a thing with a Bourne?" He let his black lips pull tightly against his teeth, then twitched his nose.

"In any case, I will continue to hold him isolated from the crew and, as per the plan, deliver this last shipment before our next meeting. His carton will be addressed to you and will be waiting for your arrival at Mars Colony.

"I anticipate our next *grussha*. Gimbish."

He switched off the recorder and collected the communiqué chip. Staring down at the piece of plastic in his paw, Gimbish recalled how Gundah had helped their extended family financially. How she'd taught him the basics of investing and how he'd come to possess a small fortune from that knowledge. He closed his eyes and remembered how her fur rose when he panted in her ear just so, and how she growled at the back of her throat when he sniffed her.

Of late her eccentricities had diversified, but he still trusted her judgment. She had requested his help, and he looked on it as a repayment for all she had done. Her promise of wealth, power, and a harem on Oph only fueled his dedication to her. She was the cleverest person he'd ever met. How could he doubt her success?

Still, that small warning sounded at the back of his thoughts. Why hadn't she told RadiMo she wanted to see him before the Earth ceremony? And why did she keep her plans so secret? Had she become irrational, or were her tactics so incredibly complex they defied logic?

Gimbish realized he simply had to have faith in his cousin. She'd supported him and expected support in return. Knowing this was his last opportunity to back out of the plan and save his reputation, he took a breath, pushed out of his chair, and headed for the communications room.

*   *   *

The usual soft popping sound accompanied Setana Marteen as she transported from the *Currency* to New Sub-Denver. Rieka stood a short distance away, a huge, dark Human behind her. Their expressions bespoke both concern and curiosity.

"Setana," Rieka said, stepping forward and offering her hand. "Welcome to Earth. I'm glad you're here—but I was expecting to see Captain Bilik."

"He'll be along later," Setana assured her, gripping her daughter-in-law's hand. She let go and offered a firm embrace.

Rieka returned the hug, then stepped back. "Something bad has happened, hasn't it?" she asked softly.

Setana nodded, unsurprised by Rieka's intuition. "We must talk. Privately."

"Of course." Rieka turned and gestured toward the man behind her. "This is Hong Wang-Chi, my personal bodyguard. Circumstances demanded I step up security. Wang is never more than a room away."

Setana felt herself stiffen slightly. Rieka couldn't possibly have known what had happened on Indra. Her increased security had to be the result of something here, on Earth. For Rieka to take such measures, the problem had to be quite serious. "A pleasure to meet you Mr. Hong," she said pleasantly, offering her right hand. "I am Setana Marteen, the Indran Herald."

"I'm honored, Madam Herald," he replied. He shook her hand and stepped back, indicating he would follow them. Setana felt uneasiness in him as well and began to wonder at the scope of their combined problems.

"Let's go, then," Rieka offered. On the way to the guest suite, she explained that Wang had had a team go through it and several others in the Embassy's housing wing. She currently knew of four Heralds and a dozen offworld administrators who would attend the Reaffirmation.

"But I'm hoping a lot more will show up," she finished with a wry grin. "We can quarter them in other cities, but not with the level of security Wang has established here."

Mr. Hong stepped up to the lock and opened the keypad. He tapped in some numbers and eased back. "Now if I could have your left palmprint, Herald Marteen," he said.

"Of course." She placed her palm on the faceplate, and he tapped in another code.

"Thank you. We're set now. This door will only open for the three of us. If you need anyone else to access your quarters, let me know, and I'll add their print."

"Perhaps my husband and my adjutant. But neither of them is with me at this time," she told them.

When the door slid open, Rieka led the way into the suite. Mr. Hong positioned himself just inside the threshold.

"How bad?" Rieka asked, motioning Setana to sit on a sofa.

She settled on a cushion, deciding straightforward answers would be the easiest for her daughter-in-law to digest. "Bad enough. Would you sit, too, dear?"

Watching her carefully, Rieka eased onto a chair. "It isn't Triscoe, or I would know," she said softly.

"That is true," Setana agreed. "Even without the Gift, you would know if his life force had . . . departed. But this does have something to do with him—and you."

She watched Rieka frown, take a small breath, then gently ask, "What, Setana?"

"I was on Perata at the time—still involved with the problem that kept me from your inauguration," she began. "Triscoe had just come from Earth. He had a meeting with Dr. Wilmstos at Sati Labs."

"Yes. I know. He went to tell them there was no rush for a pregnancy. We had decided to . . . let things settle down a bit before attacking that problem."

"Yes," Setana said. "So Triscoe mentioned. But while he was meeting with Dr. Wilmstos, there was an accident."

"Accident? What kind of accident?" Rieka glanced once at her bodyguard. "The News Sheet this morning said something about an explosion in Korval. Is that what you're talking about? Are you sure he's okay?"

"Yes. Everything is fine. He is unharmed," Setana assured her, relieved when the sense of bright red alarm she received from Rieka eased off into a warm, orange concern. "Actually, that isn't quite correct. His message to me on Perata included a brief report not publicized on the News Sheets. I'm sorry to tell you—Sati Labs is . . . destroyed."

She felt Rieka recoil, but plunged ahead, knowing she needed to disclose every bit of information. "It was determined that someone used an antimatter device to consume the top twelve floors of laboratories. The entire building is unusable. Triscoe is fortunate he was on the ground floor when the explosion occurred."

She watched Rieka's reaction to the news. Her eyes widened, and her jaw dropped before she could snap it shut. She looked again at Mr. Hong. The man had gone motionless enough to remind Setana of one of Yadra's Living Statues. The sense of red flared again.

She watched Rieka stumble for something to say. "Sati Labs is destroyed? Did Triscoe say anything about—our samples?"

Setana tried to impress a sense of calmness in her words. "Yes. Triscoe wanted me to tell you Dr. Wilmstos said the samples achieved a partial natural cohesion, and he'd been encouraged by that compatibility."

Rieka nodded uncertainly. "And now all that work is . . . gone."

"Yes."

She took a deep breath. "Good. That's good, I think."

Surprised by that reaction, Setana sat straighter. "You've changed your mind about having a child?"

"No! Just readjusted my priorities. We'll find a way, eventually." She gave Setana a brief smile. "When Triscoe explained—showed me how the Singlemind really works— I realized how presumptuous I'd been. We decided to wait until a better time. Maybe even change the strategy." She shrugged, and Setana decided not to question her further.

"Considering the circumstances, you made a wise decision, dear."

Rieka appeared to be studying her hands, so Setana gave her a moment to reflect on what she'd been told. Glancing at Mr. Hong, she got a sense of uneasiness. His eyes skimmed from Rieka to her, then back to Rieka again.

"What's happened here?" Setana asked hesitantly. "You haven't been threatened since you've been sworn in, have you?"

"No. Nothing like that. RadiMo is missing." Rieka paused, but before Setana could comment, added, "I'm guessing you know about Candace abducting me."

"Triscoe mentioned it," she answered. "I can't say I'm surprised. Your mother has always been able to get what she wants—one way or another. But what do you mean, RadiMo is missing?"

"The day after my inauguration, we went to Damascus to tour Olympic Stadium and visit the Site." Rieka stood and paced behind her chair. "While we were there, we got a report that RadiMo had not shown up in New SubAtlanta as scheduled. We've been looking for him for two days. He's . . . gone."

"Or hiding," Setana suggested. "The Bournese are known to require several days of solitude when they become overtaxed."

"No." Rieka shook her head. "He's not aground. CariMo would know. And she has no idea where RadiMo is."

Setana sat back and wove her fingers together on her lap. "This does warrant serious consideration, Rieka," she said. "You don't even know whether or not he's still on Earth?"

"No. Not for sure, anyway. The *Capitol* was in orbit when he disappeared. And the interplanetary shuttle to the Moon and Mars has come and gone since then, too. He wasn't listed on any manifest."

Silently, Setana wondered how many challenges her daughter-in-law could take on at once. "Tell me how I can help you," she said. "I am expected on Yadra in three days, but my attaché there can take my place. This situation is infinitely more important."

Rieka seemed to deflate. She eased back into the chair, and the expression on her face reflected both relief and astonishment. "You'd do that?"

"Of course, dear. Not only are you Earth Herald, you are my family. I regretted having to miss your inauguration, but had I known you needed me, I would have come sooner."

Setana sensed Rieka's relief, yet could tell she held a great amount of thought and emotion in check. Dreading the addition of another enigma to their conversation, she knew it would be indecorous not to speak. "There is one other thing," she said softly.

Rieka stiffened. "What?"

"One of the reasons I was on Perata last week was to speak to the Oracle." She watched Rieka frown slightly. "During my audience, he asked that I relay a message to you. He said to beware for the children. Success or annihilation rides with them."

When Rieka lifted her brows, Setana understood her unasked question. "I am sorry. He did not explain further."

Rieka then let out a long sigh and sank back into the chair. "Whose children, Setana? Triscoe's and mine? Did he mean the samples destroyed in the lab? That prediction's both premature and late," she said sarcastically.

Setana didn't blame her for being pessimistic. "I don't think so," she replied evenly. "He seemed to mean the term in a broader sense. As in children belonging to more than one person."

"And his message was meant specifically for me?"

"Yes."

She shrugged. "Well, I haven't a clue what he's getting at—but I don't suppose I should be surprised. The man's an enigma."

Setana relaxed a bit at Rieka's light tone. "That he is," she agreed.

"But if he meant that for me, specifically, then we've got to assume he's referring to Earth—since it doesn't look like I'll be having children of my own anytime soon. Earth's children—meaning Humanity? Or children living on Earth?"

"I really couldn't say."

"Well, that isn't the most pressing problem on our agenda." She frowned. "What we really need to do is concentrate on finding RadiMo."

"Page me if anything comes up," Rieka said, looking into Jeniper's blue eyes. "We can be back in a few minutes."

"Of course," the Aurian woman replied, her bibbets remaining faintly pink.

"Captain Bilik on the *Currency* is standing by," Wang told her, touching a finger to the left side of his jaw where his new toy perched, an external TC clipped around his ear and activated by touch. Integrated with the Fleet's frequencies, the little device had enough power to reach a vessel in orbit.

"I'm ready," she said, picking up a small scanner. With the TC, they no longer needed to use an InterMAT chamber to lock the signal. Silently envious of her bodyguard's latest gadget, she stepped to Wang's side, and added, "Request transport for two individuals to RadiMo's apartment in New SubAtlanta."

Wang repeated the request and a heartbeat later they stood in what seemed to be a black void. Nothing appeared out of the blackness and the cool air held a distinctly stale odor. Obviously everything had been shut down for a long time.

She felt Wang tense and heard him draw his weapon. "Lights," she commanded. The apartment's environmental system immediately kicked on, revealing a typical biped habitation. Wang looked around warily but holstered the maitu.

"When Director Moore received my request to search this apartment, he said once it had been checked out by his people everything had been shut down, Wang-Chi," she said jauntily. "Judging by the stale air and coating by dust on everything, it doesn't look like anyone other than the search crew has been in here in some time."

"It stinks."

Rieka grinned. "Put your gloves on, hold your nose, and have a look around. I'll try checking some surfaces with the scanner." She busied herself with the small device, identifying individuals who'd left their cells on the computer console and the kitchen table.

While she worked, Rieka wondered why RadiMo had chosen this apartment rather than a VIP suite or one that more closely resembled a Bourne environment. This one held all the typical Human trappings: individual rooms containing chairs, tables, closets, beds. With his *skiff,* he really didn't need anything else. Maybe the conveniences were for his associates.

Wang caught up with her in RadiMo's sleeping room. "Kitchen is clean. Nothing in the cool units. The pantry's almost empty. None of the other bedrooms has anything either. Closets are clean. Find anything in here?"

"Nothing but this," Rieka replied, gesturing toward what appeared to be a platform bed. "It looks like a portable den of some kind."

"It is," Wang replied, stepping up for a closer look. "I've been reading up on the Bournese. They can use their *skiffs* for days at a time—but long-term visits away from the home den wear on them. These things," he added, squatting down for a better look, "provide all the comforts. Plus they have quadruple the space."

Rieka shook her head at the complexities spacefaring travelers dealt with and perched on the habitat's edge. About two meters across, the thing really did dwarf a *skiff*. A control panel of some kind hung on the wall. "What do you think this is for?"

Wang stood and examined it. "Let's find out." He touched an indicator and half a dozen holes opened on the platform.

"Interesting." Rieka tried looking down a hole, but couldn't see anything. "Does that thing control internal illumination?"

"Coming on now," he said.

The faint light didn't improve her vision. Frustrated, Rieka wished she could climb down a hole, but despite the spongy texture, the outlet wasn't even wide enough for her head.

Wang joined her on the mattress, peered down another hole and stuck his arm in up to the elbow. "Can't feel anything. Until I did some research, I didn't think they ever left their *skiffs*," he admitted, sitting up and bouncing lightly on the rubbery surface.

"Neither did I."

Wang stood and rubbed his hip. "I don't know what the Bournese call comfortable, but this thing's definitely got some hard spots."

Not quite sure why, Rieka studied the slight indentation he'd made. There wasn't any holes near it, so she chose one a short distance away and slid her arm down it as far as it would go. Her fingers felt nothing more than the tunnel's smooth sides, about twenty centimeters across.

Curious, Rieka activated the scanner and aimed it at the place Wang had sat.

"Is there something down there?" he asked.

"Maybe. Have you got a knife?"

He stepped closer, digging into a trouser pocket. "It isn't very big."

"Doesn't need to be. What I want is only fifteen centimeters down." She took the pocketknife and activated the laser. One swipe opened the bed's outer surface. "Remind me to tell Jeniper this comes out of my expense account," she muttered.

The second cut went deeper. Rieka deactivated the knife and handed it back to Wang. She shoved her hand down into the slit she'd made and pushed her fingers through the foam until she touched a solid object. She traced the surface to an edge and pulled it up.

"A datapad," Wang whispered, amazed. "Stowed in his bed. Looks like the Bournese Herald had a few things he didn't want anyone to know about."

"Could be," Rieka agreed, holding the compact machine and silently kicking herself for not personally searching the apartment two days ago. "But they're very private creatures—beyond simple shyness. Even checking the file directories can be construed as invasive."

"If he's in trouble, and we don't check for some kind of clue in this"—Wang pointed at the datapad—"we could be considered negligent."

"Tough decision."

"Not really."

"You'd just switch this thing on and find out whatever you could?"

He nodded. "Damn right I would. Lives are at stake."

"Maybe." Carrying both RadiMo's datapad and her scanner, Rieka went back to the computer console in the other room. She set both devices down, then reached for the datapad and activated it.

The machine turned on but refused her access without the proper user ID. She could still hear Wang moving around in the sleeping room. "How do I hack my way past this datapad's access lock?" she called.

"You don't," he answered, coming toward her. "Let me. If this isn't too customized, I should have you in in a couple of minutes."

Rieka stood up and gestured for him to take the seat. "Then by all means, Wang-Chi, work your magic."

An hour later, Rieka leaned over his shoulder. "You're going to wear the battery down."

"I'm almost in," he said, waving her away.

Returning to the chair she'd been sitting in, Rieka realized she'd heard him say that at least four times already. "Uh-huh. Maybe you should define 'almost.'"

He looked up and took a deep breath. "What do you want to know?"

She bounced up from the chair and slid the datapad from beneath his fingers. "None of your business, Wang. This is RadiMo's private stuff. You don't have authorization to—"

"—hack my way through the access code?"

"I asked you to do that," she snapped. When he glared at her with his face an imperturbable mask, she relented. "Okay. Look through the filenames and see if anything seems significant."

Together, they studied the entries and decided to open three directories. One involved notes he'd made during his stay on Earth, one had to do with Yadra, and the other looked to be a catalog of his offworld communications.

They checked the Yadra notes first, expecting to find some reference to her mother. When there wasn't one, they searched RadiMo's documentation on Earth. Most were dry reports on mineral deposits, geology, and the like. His communications had generally been to Bourne, but there were four messages sent to Ophiuchus 70, the star around which the planet Oph orbited.

"That's a bit odd, don't you think?" Wang asked.

Puzzled, Rieka rolled back to the directories and found a file for Oph. Unfortunately, the file had been recorded in Bournese, a language she didn't understand. A glance at Wang told her he didn't, either. She went back to the communications files and called up the messages sent to Oph. They were addressed to Herald Cimpa's office. Frowning, Rieka looked over other recent communiqués, but those were personal, to RagiMo on Bourne.

She sighed loud enough for Wang to comment. "Whadya think?"

"RadiMo's sent four and received two communications from Herald Cimpa's office in the last month. Most everything else looks personal. He doesn't usually have a lot of contact with other Heralds—as far as this log goes."

"So let's look in the files written to Cimpa. I'll bet he recorded them in the standard language. That would be a start."

Rieka made a face, but touched the proper spots on the datapad's surface. The most recent message switched on.

RadiMo's small face took up most of the screen, making his location impossible to guess.

"Adjutant Gundah," he began. The electronic translation sounded strange, almost contrived, but at least they understood it. "Greetings to Oph. This creature is most confused as to your request, but shall do his best to gain entry to the answers you seek. Business does well, here. It is not an unpleasant place. Not abundantly populated. Most work hard, readying for the Reaffirmation. I will bring the information with me the next time I travel to your planet. The travel is expected for two days after the Earth ceremony. I rejoice that our business will soon be concluded. RadiMo."

Rieka sat back and looked at Wang once the system shut down. "What's he up to with Cimpa?"

"No way to tell. Those little Bournese are too clever for their own good, if you ask me."

"I didn't. But I happen to agree with you." Rieka glanced back to the file and checked the date. "He sent this seven days ago. Could be Cimpa wanted his report earlier than RadiMo intended to give it."

"Could be," Wang conceded. "What could the two of them possibly have in common?"

"I have no idea. But Cimpa could have sent someone here to collect RadiMo. And even though there isn't a transport record for him on any Fleet ship, I'm willing to bet we'll find RadiMo on Oph."

Gundah reclined on her well-appointed bed and snarled at the video screen suspended from the ceiling. Jonik Tarrik's insipid Aurian face stared back at her like a frightened *kreget*.

Nibbling a chunk of raw beef, she said, "I don't care if she thinks you work for her. You work for *me*." She spoke in tones imperious enough to cow an Oph, though she had no idea of the effect on the furless being.

He turned his head, and she saw a bibbet grow dark. "Yes, I know. But—"

"There is nothing to add, Tarrik. You were sent for the item. Did you get it?" She watched as his eyes roved but wouldn't focus on his video pickup.

Finally, he mumbled, "I got it."

"Good. I expect you to bring it to Earth as soon as possible and wait for me to contact you, there. The Courier's ticket you've been issued will only pay for transit to Earth. Don't try to run out on me, Tarrik. I have many . . . acquaintances in the Fleet."

He nodded but refused to look into the camera. "I'll bring it."

She smiled and smacked her black lips as she dangled another bloody tidbit over her tongue. Savoring the flesh, Gundah gave in to the sense of accomplishment. Her plans were coming together nicely. Tarrik's part in them would soon be over, and she found herself anticipating his demise. The demise of everyone who stood in her way, in fact. She found the possibility of actually outliving the Human race uniquely entertaining.

Her amused smile wrinkled her nose and bared her upper teeth. "Perform well, Tarrik, and I may consider your debt paid," she said.

"But that was the deal," he whined. "You said this was the last thing I'd have to do."

"So I did," Gundah agreed, almost impressed that he'd stood up for himself. "Then all you need concern yourself with is getting to Earth. I want you there at least two days before the Reaffirmation—with the item."

"I understand."

"I'm so glad," Gundah drawled. She reached and deactivated the comm unit. She never ceased to amaze herself. She hadn't dared to dream she'd achieve her goal so quickly, so easily. Stumbling upon an Aurian who would do anything to pay off his debts, she'd seized the opportunity fate had handed her.

What Stephen Degahv had started almost thirty years ago, she would finish. They would call her Gundah the Redeemer, she thought, purring with anticipation. Her actions would restore the Ophs to their former economic dominance and bring an end to the puny whelps called Humans.

Gundah reached for her goblet of *sallanni* and held it high. "To me," she announced to the furniture. "Gundah the Redeemer."

THIRTEEN

"I would really feel better if you stayed on Earth," Rieka grumbled at Jeniper when the escort had left them alone in the *New Venture*'s guest suite. Aware of the potential danger involved in retrieving RadiMo, she couldn't shake the fact she considered Jeniper a civilian. Conversely, her own self-image was still that of a Fleet captain. Rieka wondered how long she'd be a Herald before she actually felt like one.

Jeniper sat on the sofa, leaned back, and stretched her legs out in front of her. "I've already told you—the staff will handle all the minor details. The new caterer is coming from Yadra and won't arrive for three days. The touring itineraries for Damascus, the Site, and World Zoo are mapped out, and my assistants can handle any little problems that come up."

"I'm sure they will," Rieka replied absently. She sighed and ambled restlessly around the room. Waiting was her least favorite pastime and the four day round-trip to Oph yawned before her like an eternity. Not discounting the necessity of retrieving RadiMo, she wanted this trip to be over before it began.

Glancing around, Rieka had to admit, this ship did look better than the *Venture* the Fleet had lost to the Procyons. The suite had three sleeping rooms with attached baths, a meeting area, and this socializing area, complete with comm console.

"With everyone doing their respective jobs on Earth, I doubt you'll be missed for a few days," Jeniper went on. "Herald Marteen is quite able to, how did she put it? 'See to things.' And in light of what we've found out so far about the events surrounding your father's death—going to Oph ties in with that, too."

Rieka nodded as she tried to walk off her sense of frustration. Jeniper's preliminary report on the evidence was woefully incomplete. Totally circumstantial. They needed to dig a lot deeper before they could begin to prove the accident had been staged.

She glanced at Jeniper. "I agree with you about the odd coincidence that the 'repairs' the shuttle required were both evaluated and performed by only Oph tech-pros," she said. "But I remind you we're looking for incriminating evidence against my mother, not someone on Oph."

"You've got to start somewhere."

"True. But it doesn't have to be now. I should never have listened to Setana," she grumbled. "Nothing is as it should be."

"Well, that's a comforting thought," quipped a voice from the doorway.

"Midrin!" Rieka hurried forward as the Indran woman entered and hugged her tightly. "Or should I salute and address you as Captain?"

"Midrin will be fine," she said, grinning. "You look as though the role of Herald fits you well."

"Looks are deceiving," she replied cryptically. "But a command of your own seems to suit you."

"Most of the time," Midrin replied with a smile.

"Did many of the crew get reassigned to you—or did they stay on the *Prodigy*?"

"A few," she replied. "Gorah is my Security chief. She's pregnant with her first pup."

"I'll have to make a point of saying hello," Rieka said, smiling. "I can just see the hair on her shoulders stand straight up when you tell her a Herald has asked to see her. Don't tell her it's me."

"Impossible, I'm afraid. Gorah knew the exact moment you came aboard. It was she who suggested this suite. And, you'll find she's changed a bit since her mating. Much more confident."

"Well, good for her." Rieka turned and tugged her old friend farther into the room. "Midrin, I want you to meet Jeniper Tarrik, my adjutant. Jeniper," she began, turning to see the Aurian had risen and come forward, a thoughtful expression on her face as she studied them.

"Captain," Jeniper offered, her hands stretched forward in the Indran custom. "You honor us by this visit."

Midrin returned the greeting. "The honor is mine, Ms. Tarrik."

"Everything looks wonderful," Rieka told her former executive officer. "Is the *New Venture* very different from the old one?"

"Not really. Once we're under way I'll give you a tour. You can decide for yourself."

"I'd like that."

"I know this trip was arranged on short notice," Midrin added, looking Rieka in the eye. "It sounds as if there's a problem."

Rieka recognized the question in her voice. "There is. Actually, several."

A door behind them slid open, and Rieka turned as Wang came out of his bedroom. "Everything is clean," he said, his comment directed toward her as he looked at Midrin.

Rieka nodded and gestured him to come forward. "Hong Wang-Chi, I'd like you to meet the captain of this ship, Midrin Tohab."

"A pleasure, Captain." He offered a hand, and Midrin shook it.

"Captain Tohab was my executive officer aboard the *Venture* and *Prodigy*," Rieka added. "The best EO in the Fleet. That's why Admiral Nason gave her this command."

Midrin sighed. Rieka clapped her on the shoulder. "And she *still* doesn't take compliments well."

"As if *you* ever did," Midrin shot back.

When Rieka laughed, Wang announced, "I'm Rieka's bodyguard," and brought the conversation to a standstill.

After a few silent seconds, Midrin looked up at him, and asked, "Is there a security problem I should be aware of?"

"Not aboard the *New Venture,* Captain," he replied. "But I'm not about to take any chances."

"I should think not, Mr. Chi."

"Actually, it's Mr. Hong," Rieka corrected.

"Mr. Hong," Midrin said with a nod. "Shall we sit?" She

gestured toward the sofas. "I'd like to know exactly what is going on and how the *New Venture* may be affected."

When they'd all taken their places, Rieka explained about RadiMo's disappearance and the problems Candace had created. Jeniper jumped in and added background information involving the curious circumstances of Stephen Degahv's death.

When the room was finally quiet, Midrin sighed and looked at Rieka. "I wish I could do more than provide you with transport to Oph, but my scheduled stop is actually the third planet in the system, Grita, and I won't even be able to stay with you long enough to—"

"Don't worry about us, Midrin. I'm sure we'll be fine. This is a surprise visit, and with just the three of us, we don't pose any kind of threat to whoever has got RadiMo. I'm sure we can see Cimpa, get some answers, and go from there. We'll leave as soon as we can."

"The advantage of unpredictability has been useful in the past," Midrin said, nodding. "But you're a Herald now, Rieka. Is it really wise to do this? I'm sure Captain Marteen would advise against it."

Rieka smiled ruefully. "Well, he'd have to take that up with his mother," she said, suddenly feeling a bit more confident about her travel plans. "Setana suggested this trip."

"Really? Well, then I suppose I shouldn't feel quite so . . . apprehensive about the idea."

Wang nodded and said, "And both the *Providence* and *Prospectus* are scheduled for deliveries at Oph soon after we arrive. The plan is for Captain DeVark to pick us up and get us back to Earth in plenty of time for the Reaffirmation ceremony."

Rieka watched Midrin glance from Wang to Jeniper to her. "Knowing this lady, Mr. Hong, plans tend to go awry. You may well need plenty of what you Humans call luck."

Jeniper watched Rieka come out of Herald Cimpa's office and walk down the corridor to the waiting area. Having known Rieka for several weeks now, Jeniper realized she could read her boss's expression even from a distance. She looked to be both disappointed and angry.

With a glance at Wang, Jeniper said, "Be back in a minute." She stood and hurried toward Rieka. When she got close enough for a private conversation, Jeniper asked, "What did Cimpa say?"

Rieka shook her head. "Nothing," she grumbled softly. "He doesn't know anything. And I mean that, literally. His office reeks of *ciffa*. It's a wonder he knows his name and what day it is."

"It can't be that bad."

"You're probably right, but he's never liked Humans, and I'm sure part of it was an act to make me go away." She sighed. "I'm not leaving here without some answers."

Jeniper recognized the frustration in Rieka's tone. "Maybe his adjutant knows something," she offered. "RadiMo did mention her name. The Herald may actually be as incapacitated as you say. If that's true, she probably runs the office during his rutting time."

"I sure hope somebody does."

"Let me talk to her," Jeniper told her. "Her name is Gundah. She's been the adjutant for nearly two decades. She's bound to know if RadiMo has had any contact with Cimpa."

She waited patiently as Rieka's face went through a variety of expressions while she weighed the decision. Finally, Rieka sighed and nodded. "Give it a try, Jen. It really burns me we came all this way for nothing. I was so sure that entry in RadiMo's diary meant he'd come here."

"He might have, and Cimpa doesn't know it. Almost anything is possible." She glanced at the clock on the receptionist's desk. "Gundah can see me in fifteen minutes—I already checked with her secretary. You and Wang go back to the Earth Embassy, and I'll meet you there when I'm done."

She watched Rieka take a deep breath and then smile with one side of her mouth. "You know, being a Herald is a lot like commanding a ship," she said. "Do it." Then she collected Wang and left Jeniper in the waiting area, still wondering what she'd meant.

The wait to see Gundah went by quickly. Jeniper busied herself with her datapad, trying to find a correlation between the Oph company, OSSI, and Candace Degahv. She figured if Candace had had a hand in Stephen Degahv's death, she would have been in contact with the company that built and maintained the shuttle in which he died. Who else would have the expertise to stage such a crash and make it look like an accident?

"Gundah will see you now, Miss Tarrik," the receptionist announced. "Third door to the left."

Jeniper shut down her datapad and walked toward the indicated door. She knocked once and entered before Gundah could reply. "Good morning, Adjutant Gundah," she offered, "I am Jeniper Tarrik, adjutant to Herald Degahv."

The Oph behind the large desk had a dark gold coat. The jewelry fused to her left ear was quite ornate, though Jeniper immediately noticed she wore no stones indicative of having had pups.

"Welcome," Gundah told her, rising and coming around the desk. She executed the straight-backed Oph bow of greeting and the traditional body sniff. Jeniper returned the bow only. "It is a pleasure to meet you, Adjutant Tarrik," Gundah continued smoothly. "Sit, please. May I offer a refreshment?"

Jeniper sat in the proffered chair and accepted a cup of *colan.* "Thank you."

She watched Gundah sip her drink and smile with black lips. "One is curious, Ms. Tarrik. With Earth so close to its time of Reaffirmation, why are you here, on Oph?"

Having anticipated this question, Jeniper replied cautiously. "It is a matter of some urgency. And discretion," she said, watching to see Gundah's reaction.

The Oph was unreadable. "I see."

"Herald Degahv just met with Herald Cimpa. The conversation left many questions unanswered. I thought you and I might have a more productive talk."

Gundah nodded and put down her cup. "On what topic?"

"Herald RadiMo."

Jeniper watched Gundah go very still for a moment, then flip her ears, apparently confused. "What about him?"

Hoping her strategy would work, Jeniper said, "Having spent the last several months on Earth, he is now missing."

"Really? And what has that to do with anything here on Oph?"

"He left documents on Earth indicating recent business transactions with Oph natives," Jeniper said, keeping her bibbets as pale as she could. "It was natural to assume he may have come here. Would you happen to know if he's made a recent visit?"

Gundah leaned back in her chair, and Jeniper could see something going through her mind. Unfortunately, she had no idea what. "Of course this office isn't privy to every individual itinerary," Gundah began, "but we are aware of all visiting dignitaries. To my knowledge, RadiMo has not been to Oph in the last several months. In fact, I believe he's spent the entire time on Earth."

"Yes," Jeniper replied patiently. "We know that."

"One moment." Gundah activated her console and tapped at the keys for a moment. "Yes. He visited here with his mate, RagiMo, just after the Procyon War, five months ago."

"That was an 'official' visit, I'm sure," Jeniper told her. "I'm wondering if there is a possibility he has come to Oph in another capacity. Perhaps under an assumed name."

"If that is so, this office would not necessarily be aware of it," Gundah replied. She pulled her black lips into a thin, tight smile.

Jeniper nodded. "Yes. But you have access to certain data. And a Bourne—any Bourne—coming to Oph would have specific physical requirements. . . ."

Gundah looked at her screen a moment, then glanced at Jeniper. "Naturally. They require a *skiff* when they travel."

Jeniper waited patiently while Gundah requested more information from her computer. A moment later, the Oph nodded and made a soft groaning sound. "It seems, Ms. Tarrik, that a Bourne may have come into the system several days ago. From Earth. Yona, our smaller moon, records the arrival of a crate having the dimensions of a *skiff*: point seven-five meters by one meter by two meters."

"Is there a colony on Yona?"

Gundah gestured with a paw. "A mining colony. The director there is a Lomii." She smiled. "Named Klikt."

Jeniper sat a bit straighter. Now they were getting somewhere. "Are there travel restrictions to Yona? Would I need any kind of clearance to see Klikt?"

"None," Gundah replied. Jeniper noticed a small light on the desktop begin to flash. Gundah glanced at it and slid her chair back from her desk. "You must excuse me,

Ms. Tarrik, the Herald requires my presence immediately. If I can be of any further assistance, please let me know."

Jeniper stood and, as Gundah left her office, said, "Thank you for your cooperation. I will."

"Well, then, I guess the decision's up to you, Wang," Rieka said. Uncomfortable in Oph's strong gravity, she leaned back into her chair's cushions and looked at him over the massive desk. Despite feeling as if she weighed almost twice what she did, Rieka had been delightfully surprised by the Human contingent here at the Earth Embassy. The office looked good and appeared to be running efficiently.

She glanced at Jeniper, seated in a nearby chair. Her news about the mining outpost had brought an unwelcome feeling of uneasiness, but Rieka decided to let Wang handle all the safety issues.

"You're sure this Lomii won't talk to you? Maybe you could try again," he asked.

"I doubt it would be worth the effort," she told him. "Lomii are very . . . uh . . . visual, Wang. Even with a two-way screen, it's not the same. And it would be very bad manners to use my position as Herald to examine the suspected *skiff* without a short audience. I may need Lomiian support in the future. Offending them isn't a good idea."

Jeniper looked at Wang. "I'll go and talk to him."

Wang shook his head. "We shouldn't split up."

"Then what do we do?" Rieka asked.

"We shuttle out to Yona, talk to Klikt, and check this . . . object, ourselves."

"You're sure?" Rieka asked, surprised he'd give in so easily.

Wang sat forward and looked her in the eye. "You're at risk wherever you are, Boss," he began. "As long as I can secure the shuttle and get a layout of the mine, we should be fine. This little excursion is so completely unpredictable, I don't see how it could be a trap."

"Okay." Rieka nodded at him. Glancing at Jeniper, she said, "You two make the arrangements for this trip. I'll work on my Lomiian sign language and book our passage back to Earth." She'd already called up the Fleet schedules and found that even though the *Providence* would arrive in another three hours, it would be going on to Aurie. The *Prospectus* would arrive at Oph tomorrow but could take them directly back to Earth.

Thanks to Wang's efficiency, they set down at Yona just two hours later. The shuttle's small DGI gave them an exterior image. The mine consisted of a series of seven domes connected by transport tunnels. The domes served as both air locks for the mine shafts and some other purpose, such as housing, administrative offices, storage facilities, and the like. The shuttle pilot docked inside one of them. Rieka looked out a portal and saw only one other shuttle.

After Wang inspected the terminal and found it empty, she disembarked and waited while Jeniper opened a comlink to the mining director.

Once video had been established, Rieka made a series of introductory gestures at the screen. Klikt responded in kind and bowed, which for a Lomii meant floating up a bit, then coming back to camera level. After a flurry of complex hand signals, most of which she didn't understand, Klikt's image disappeared from the screen and a map appeared. Wang stepped closer as a pair of indicators began to blink.

"We're here," he said, pointing. "And this must be where Klikt is. We'll just grab a personal transport and ride on out to him. It'll be a whole lot easier than trying to negotiate walking in this moon's weak gravity."

"It is about half what we're used to," Rieka agreed. "But definitely better than Oph." She noticed Jeniper try to walk toward one of three transports parked in the terminal. She leaned awkwardly before managing to right herself, then tipped again.

When they'd selected a transport and strapped into the seats, Rieka activated the locator system and programmed their destination. "It looks like he's near the mouth of shaft three," she said. "We'll have to go through two pressure domes before we get there."

Wang hit the accelerator. "Then let's get this over with."

During the ride, Rieka sensed Wang's increasing unease. He didn't like this situation any better than she did, but neither of them could find a reasonable excuse to leave. Protocol demanded she see Klikt before they inspected the *skiff*.

Finally, the last air lock appeared and they made their

way through it. Klikt, folded delicately into his own transport, met them near the shaft's sealed entry. Wang stopped
their vehicle a short distance away and Rieka stepped off.
She waited while Klikt extracted himself and balanced
lightly on his six elongated toes. He began a long, formal
sign-greeting accompanied by the high-pitched squeals the
Lomiians called language.

Rieka replied as best she could, knowing Klikt could interpret her five-fingered hand motions. She wondered,
though, if he pitied her for the handicap of having only ten
digits. When she began to ask him if he knew where RadiMo was, Rieka realized she didn't know how to sign individuals names, so she used "Bournese Herald."

Klikt's pale blue, bony hands replied, "No."

Frowning, she asked about the recent shipment that included the *skiff*-sized box.

Klikt's sixteen fingers blurred with their immediate reply.
Rieka raised her hands, palms forward, and he slowed to
a point where she could catch the general intent. When he
finally let his long, elegant digits relax, Rieka was sure she'd
misinterpreted him.

"What'd he say?" Wang asked.

"I . . . I think he said a *skiff* did arrive last week. He
hadn't requested one and sent it on a shuttle to Oph. As
far as he knew, it was empty."

"So we're back to square one?" he asked.

"Possibly. But if someone wanted to hide a Bourne, a
mine would be just the place, don't you think?"

"I've already thought of that," Wang replied. He draped
his wrist over the steering wheel and scanned the dome.
Rieka silently wondered what else he might be thinking.

Jeniper leaned forward from the transport's backseat.
"Could a Fleet ship locate RadiMo if he were here?"

"Not specifically, Jen," Rieka said. "But it can detect the
number of life-forms in a place. And once we know how
many individuals are here on Yona, it's just a matter of
mathematics."

"If RadiMo's alive."

Rieka shot Wang a disapproving look. "We assume that
he is, Wang-Chi. There's a reason he's missing."

Klikt began to sign again, and Rieka snapped her attention back to his fluttering fingers. "Apparently, that wasn't

the first *skiff* to be sent here. Klikt's returned two others in the last four months. Odd, don't you think?"

"I'd call it suspicious," he said. "Not to mention the fact that the Herald's office told us the *skiff* was here. We've come for nothing."

"The object was *skiff*-sized," Jeniper corrected. "They didn't know for sure."

When Klikt signed he knew no more about *skiffs,* Rieka thanked him for his time and wished him high profits. He signaled her a similar response, then folded himself into his transport and exited through the air-lock corridor to shaft number four.

Rieka flopped into the seat next to Wang. He turned the transport around to head back to the shuttle port.

When they stopped to wait for the air lock to open, Jeniper asked, "Are you going to request a ship to check for life signs?"

"Absolutely, Jen. The *Providence* should be here soon. Even the threat of an official protest from an Oph senator wouldn't stop Triscoe. It's always much simpler to apologize for doing something than waiting to get permission to do it."

"I don't think I've ever thought of things quite like that," she admitted.

"You're too caught up with protocol," Wang said. "People who get things done don't bother with—"

He didn't get to finish, Rieka thought perversely, as she slammed into him. The jolt that had pitched her in his direction sent Jeniper off the cart. With Yona's low gravity, the Aurian woman went sailing in an arc over their heads while Wang struggled to control the vehicle.

"What the—?" She gripped the handholds as the little transport skidded for a brief moment, then plowed into the wall. Wang had already slammed on the brakes, but the momentum bucked them back off the wall and they bounced sideways, tipping precariously.

"Get out!" he yelled, shoving at her.

Rieka let go and pushed off the seat. She floated up briefly, then hit the ceiling and fell back to the floor. She lay there, dazed, trying to decide what had happened, what she needed to do. The sound of a lethal crash snapped her attention back to the present and she pushed off the floor.

"Wang!" She saw that the transport had finally come to a stop about twenty meters down the corridor. It lay on its side. Wang was gone. She guessed, hoped, he was somewhere under it, maybe stuck between it and the wall.

A soft moan behind her made Rieka turn. Jeniper had ended up on the floor, a long streak of blood behind her, evidence of how far she'd slid once the minimal gravity had pulled her down from the tube's ceiling.

Struggling to her feet, Rieka stumbled forward. "Jeniper? Can you hear me?"

No reply. Rieka gnawed at her lip and watched for any movement. A labored breath. Good. "Okay. I'm here, Jen. You're going to be fine." Rieka ran her hands along Jeniper's arms and legs, looking for any injuries. She found nothing, then realized a puddle of blood was forming under Jeniper's neck. Following the dark, sticky path upward, she discovered a gash in her scalp.

"You'll be okay, Jen," Rieka whispered, yanking off her overtunic and ripping out the lining. "You're going to have a nasty headache, though."

Once she'd tied the bandage around Jeniper's head, Rieka covered her with the remains of her tunic and turned toward their mangled vehicle. Unused to the low gravity, she stumbled more than walked. The distance seemed to have grown in the last few minutes, but she finally managed to arrive, thankful the transport had slid no farther.

"Wang, where are you? Can you hear me? Are you okay?"

She found him, unconscious, pinned between the steering column and the wall. Rieka wedged herself against the backseat, pushed her feet against the wall, and shoved as hard as she could. The vehicle shifted slightly. "Guess low gravity is good for something," she told herself, then took a deep breath and shoved again. Two more tries gave her enough room to slide Wang from his seat. When she'd got him stretched out on the floor, Rieka reached for his communicator. But it wasn't in his ear. She looked around the floor and couldn't find it. Once she'd made sure he was stable, she'd have to go looking for a comm board.

He had a big knot on his forehead and a few scrapes but didn't seem to be suffering from any other damage. Rieka patted his arm. "You'll be okay, Wang-Chi," she assured him. "I'm going to get help."

She rose slowly, fighting unwelcome dizziness. Her own head ached mightily from having contacted the tube wall, and she had to blink several times before the floor looked level. She thought she remembered seeing a comm board near the shafts. One couldn't be too far beyond the next air lock.

Rieka took a few steps forward, swayed, and steadied herself against the wall. "Can't be far," she told herself. "Get going." She picked up one foot and put it down in front of the other. It slid helplessly out in front of her. Scrambling, she caught herself with her hands and realized she couldn't breathe. Her vision blurred and she rolled onto her side. When she forced her eyes open again, she realized the overhead seam in the tube's skin had breached. Just a crack, but the pressure difference was enough to pump all the oxygen out into space.

"Damn," she murmured, before the blackness enveloped her completely.

FOURTEEN

As the *Providence* approached Oph, Triscoe felt a growing sense of unease. Nothing seemed out of the ordinary, and yet the closer they came to achieving orbit, the stronger his anxiety became. Something was *wrong*. It took him a moment to realize the feeling had nothing to do with his perception of his ship or the crew. It had to do with Rieka, though that seemed absurd, here at Oph.

His heart lurched as the connection solidified. Rieka was here. And in danger. No. More than that, she'd been hurt. Closing his eyes, Triscoe concentrated on their subconscious connection. He reached out. Where was she? What had happened?

Once he identified a general direction, Triscoe glanced at his helmsman before calling up a tactical display of the Oph system. "Lisk," he announced, "we're detouring to Yona. Get us there immediately."

"As we speak, Captain," Lisk replied, no hint of curiosity in his tone. "Our ETA at Yona is three minutes."

"What has happened?" Aarkmin asked.

Triscoe gestured for her to be patient as he thumped a toggle on his console. "Zonne, security," the voice answered.

"Lieutenant, I require a team in InterMAT Station One immediately," he said.

"Yes, Captain. They're on their way."

"Rieka is in trouble," he told Aarkmin softly. "You are in command until I return."

The look she gave him spoke of both astonishment and concern. "Understood."

On the way to the Chute, Triscoe activated his TC. "Marteen to Kyliss."

"Station One. Chief Kyliss here, sir."

"Scan Yona, Chief. I'm sure the Earth Herald is there. If she is, another Human is with her. I'm not sure of anyone else."

"Scanning, sir."

He switched off his TC once he reached the InterMAT suite. Zonne's team had arrived and were awaiting orders. Kyliss looked up from his screen.

"I've got signals for about two dozen sentients on Yona, Captain," he began. "Most of them are cool—probably Lomii. But there are three stationary readings in a corridor near the shuttle dock that are much warmer. And—"

"—and what, Kyliss?" Triscoe demanded, waving the four security people into the chamber.

"There's a hull breach, Captain. That whole section is losing pressure. I don't know if there's time—"

"Out!" Triscoe shouted at the security team. While they scrambled to exit the chamber, he turned back to Kyliss. "Get those three up here. Now."

"As we speak, sir." Kyliss, ever efficient, had already been locking onto the heat signals. Seconds later three bodies appeared in the chamber, followed by a soft popping sound.

"Send for Twanabok immediately," Triscoe said, shoving past a wide Vekyan ensign as he made his way to the chamber. Rieka lay on the floor next to Hong Wang-Chi and Jeniper Tarrik. How had they gotten to an Oph moon? And why? She looked terribly pale but he saw her chest rise and allowed his anxiety to relax a notch.

Rieka?

He knelt and touched her face. Cool. The skin looked as pale as he'd ever seen it. His eyes swept over the others. Jeniper's head had been crudely bandaged, the cloth soaked through with blood. Wang's forehead had a huge swollen area over his right eye.

Twanabok arrived with a medical team and three mobile bodypads. Triscoe lifted Rieka and placed her on one while the doctor issued orders to his assistants. Once the bodypads activated, Twanabok studied the readings and muttered a few unintelligible sounds.

"How are they?" Triscoe asked, managing to keep his voice calm.

Twanabok gestured for his people to take the patients to the medical suite. He followed them, Triscoe at his shoulder. "None is critical," Twanabok said quietly. "The Herald will be fine in an hour. The male is the most serious. Concussion. Dislocation of the right shoulder. Fractured humerus. Possible kidney damage—I'll require additional scans since the bodypads are only designed to determine injuries for triage. The Aurie woman has a scalp wound and possible concussion."

"And Rieka?"

"She needs oxygen therapy. The others do, too." They crowded into a Chute and Twanabok ordered it to the Medical suite.

"And that's all?"

"Yes."

"There is no sign of . . ."

"Of what?"

"Mistreatment."

"If you're asking whether these injuries were the result of an attack—I'd say no." Twanabok glanced at him as the Chute door opened, then addressed one of his assistants. "Take the male to the surgical suite. The women go to the ward for treatment."

Triscoe waited until the Chute was empty before heaving a sigh of relief. He'd feel better once Rieka had regained consciousness, but Vort's lack of concern for her provided an ironic sense of comfort. She'd be fine. He followed the small parade of stretchers and crew through the wide entry doors but remained in the outer office.

He clicked on his TC. "Marteen to Memta."

"Clear as the morn, Captain," his engineering superintendent replied.

"Something odd has happened on Yona. I want to know what caused a breach in the conduit wall. And I need to know why three people were seriously hurt."

"An equation requiring multiple answers. Three engineers will I send to factor the variables," Memta's gurgling voice replied. "Will they require security?"

"Whether required or not, have Zonne send a team with them," Triscoe answered.

"Understood, Captain. I shall report to you as the first light touches Varannah."

"Good. Marteen out." He reactivated his TC and asked for Aarkmin. "Any communication from Yona?"

"None yet, Captain," she replied. "There's a small mining colony on the moon. The director there is a Lomii named Klikt. I've tried to reach him, but the comm system is automated, and apparently Klikt isn't currently accessible."

"Keep trying. I want to speak to this Lomii as soon as possible.

Rieka sensed Triscoe's anxiety before she realized she wasn't cold or struggling for breath. She blinked her eyes open and found herself clamping them shut again against painfully bright lights.

Triscoe, where are you? Where am I?

Here, love. I am here. You are fine.

She felt his hand on her cheek. He kissed her, and she smiled and opened her eyes again. "The lights are bright," she whispered.

He reached to adjust the control. "Better?"

"Yes." When Rieka saw the look on his face, she almost wished she were still temporarily blind. Finding her must have terrified him.

"You're on the *Providence* under Vort Twanabok's care."

"Where are Wang and Jeniper?" she asked. Her throat was painfully dry. She tried to swallow, but her tongue stuck to the roof of her mouth.

"Here, too. Wang is in surgery at the moment. Jeniper is in the bed to your left."

"Water?" she asked. Triscoe filled a cup, and she pushed herself up against the pillow before he handed it to her. She took a few sips, then gulped the rest. She felt him squeeze her hand as she looked at Jeniper. A bandage covered the top part of her head. Her eyes were closed, and her bibbets looked pasty white.

"She'll be fine," Triscoe assured her. "Vort says she's had a slight concussion in addition to the scalp wound."

Rieka took a deep breath and let it out. "And what about Wang-Chi?"

"A bit more serious," he said. Rieka sensed Triscoe's concern but couldn't be sure of its depth. "Vort is setting his arm and repairing an internal organ, I think. I'm sure he'll give us a full report once the procedures are completed."

Rieka nodded and watched Triscoe's brown eyes as he kept his own questions to himself. Finally, she smiled softly and squeezed his fingers. "By the time Setana got to Earth, we were dealing with our own little crisis."

"Tell me."

"You sure you don't want to tell me about Sati Labs, first?"

"I will tell you. Everything," he promised. "After you explain why you were on Yona."

Rieka nodded and sat up higher on her pillow. "By the time Setana got to Earth, we'd been looking for RadiMo for about forty hours. He's gone, Tris. Disappeared."

He frowned at the news. "Could he be aground?"

She shook her head. "No. His attaché, CariMo, wouldn't have reported him missing if he'd just gone into seclusion."

"I suppose."

"Wang and I found RadiMo's personal diary. There were some clues in it pointing to Oph. Your mother offered to look after things on Earth while Jeniper, Wang, and I talked to Cimpa. He didn't know anything, but his adjutant, Gundah, discovered that an object with a *skiff*'s dimensions had recently been delivered to Yona. We took a shuttle there and talked to Klikt, the mining director. Nothing." She shrugged, still confused about the accident. "Then . . . when we were leaving . . . something happened with the ground transport."

"Deliberate?" Triscoe whispered.

"I don't think so." She frowned at his cynical expression. "I don't know. It all happened too fast for it to be a setup, don't you think? There's no way Candace could have planned it. No one except Setana and Midrin knew we were coming."

Triscoe stood straight and crossed his arms over his chest. Rieka recognized the determination on his face. He watched her for a moment, then flicked his eyes toward Jeniper. "Memta has a crew investigating the—accident," he told her. "We'll know more once he reports."

"I suppose." Rieka sat, absorbed in her thoughts, picking up vague sensations of what Triscoe was thinking. She sighed again, loudly. "So tell me about the lab. The news release didn't say much. Was anybody hurt?"

She watched him purse his lips slightly for a moment, a habit she recognized as a stall for time. "Forty-two people were killed instantly when the antimatter shell decayed. Another fifty-seven were injured—Dr. Wilmstos included."

Rieka felt her heart leap. Setana had said nothing about the huge loss of life, probably to keep her from worrying overmuch. The News Sheets had only reported an explosion, claiming an unknown number of dead and injured. "Seriously?"

"Yes."

"No. I mean—was he seriously injured?"

Triscoe shook his head. "No. I was with him at the time. We were in his office. I wasn't hurt at all, but a section of ceiling fell on Wilmstos. Vort patched him up and sent him to the Korval Care Center for continued medical supervision. But the laboratory was destroyed. They had made amazing progress in their study of—combining our gametes. Wilmstos was very encouraged with the testing."

Rieka said nothing for a moment. "Then it's probably best that we . . . decided to wait." She sighed. "I'm sure there's an ongoing investigation by the local authorities as to the cause, but do they have any suspects? Should we be thinking Candace had a hand in that, too? Or am I just getting paranoid?"

"In your case, paranoia is preferred," Triscoe said.

"Very funny." While she watched, he tightened his jaw and glanced at Jeniper. "Is there something wrong?"

He shrugged, shook his head, and refocused his attention on Rieka. "They haven't found any evidence to point at a suspect yet—as far as I know. Since a Fleet captain was present, Admiral Nason has managed to gain access to unpublicized information. He has not mentioned anything to me."

"Yet," Rieka added.

"Yet," he agreed.

"I wish I knew if any of this is related to Candace," she grumbled. Her head ached, though it was probably nothing compared to what Jeniper would suffer when she finally woke. "Or maybe it's all coincidental."

"Be careful," Jeniper whispered.

Rieka turned immediately, causing her head to feel as if it had been split in two, but saw the Aurian woman was still asleep. Triscoe walked around the bed and stood near Jeniper's feet.

"Careful. She's a threat. She means it," Jeniper said softly.

"She's still unconscious," Triscoe whispered.

"Seeyouinbywong."

"What language is that?" Rieka asked.

Triscoe frowned. "I didn't recognize it."

"She means it," Jeniper repeated. Then she took a breath and settled into a deeper sleep.

"I wonder what that was all about," Rieka said softly, still eyeing her unconscious companion. "I wonder who 'she' is. Candace, maybe?"

"I don't know. Your anxiety may have rubbed off on her."

Rieka shot him an accusing look. "Well, thanks a lot."

Twanabok entered the ward and examined the readouts on Rieka's bodypad. "Nothing to keep you here, Herald," he told her. "I'll sign you out. But report back if you experience dizziness, nausea, pain—the usual."

"Thank you, Vort, I will. How is Mr. Hong?"

"Stable," the Vekyan replied, negotiating his wide body past Triscoe so he could examine the console at the end of Jeniper's bodypad. "The fracture is hairline and internal damage was not significant. He should be functional in a few days."

Rieka nodded and swung her legs over the side of her bed. "And Ms. Tarrik?"

"Suffering from a severe blow to the head." Twanabok clicked his claws together and stepped closer to examine his patient's bandage. "Lost some blood. Aurian and Human head wounds tend to bleed quite a bit. She will be fine."

"Thank you, Doctor," Rieka offered, smiling at his big green face. "You always seem to be patching me up. I'm grateful."

"This is my job." He shrugged, heaving his chest out and

in, then shifted his attention from Jeniper to Rieka. "We all serve the Commonwealth to the best of our abilities. Now go . . . and be diplomatic elsewhere. My patient needs rest."

Rieka couldn't resist a little chuckle. "You're a treasure, Twanabok." She pushed herself off the pad and stood on the floor. When the room didn't spin as she'd expected, she nodded at Triscoe, and they left the ward.

In the corridor, Rieka stopped. "Have you recovered our equipment? Jeniper and I had datapads. Wang had a mobile TC, a maitu, and probably some things I didn't know about."

"I'll find out," Triscoe told her as he gestured toward the open Chute door. "Let's get you cleaned up, first."

Some minutes later, as she zipped up her fresh jumpsuit, Rieka heard the distinct gurgle of a Boo voice. She shoved her feet into a pair of soft boots and stepped into the living area of Triscoe's quarters to discover Memta taking up what seemed like half the room.

The engineer swiveled his head toward her and double-blinked. "Captain Herald Degahv. A pleasure to see you on the morn," he said.

Rieka smiled and closed the distance between them. "Your visage is like a glimpse at Varannah, Commander," she said. "How do you function?"

"In balance," Memta replied, though he waved his starfish hand at her. "To a point. This I am equating to your husband captain."

"Then don't let me interrupt you."

She saw Triscoe pick something up from the low table in front of the sofa. "Your datapad," he said, handing it to her. "Memta's crew found Jeniper's and Wang's equipment, too."

"Were you able to determine what caused the accident?" she asked, looking up into the Boo's huge, multifaceted black eyes.

"The transport's tires are an inflatable type. Not magnetic," Memta replied, then inhaled a breath of chlorine from his compensator. "The right rear tire was defective as Schlimb's sails. Scanning shows a weak spot in the wall like Baro in the line at Horrahn. Three on the transport exceeded the pressure parameters. It blew."

Rieka nodded, relieved the explanation seemed innocent. "And what caused the ceiling to open?"

Memta made another gesture with his hand and wriggled a bit of flesh over his left eye. "This tire released pressure as an eruption of stored energy. A section of the material shot up like the waves into Trenno. It was enough to open the ceiling. The internal pressure in the conduit widened the fissure as Toroon displaced the air of Guye."

Rieka glanced at Triscoe. His face was unreadable and he even felt calm through their link. "So you're saying this . . . was an accident?" she asked. "It would have happened . . . eventually?"

Memta blinked at her again. "You perceive this like the dawn at Varannah, Captain Herald," he said.

"Thank you for the report, Commander," Triscoe said. "The information is vital to the equation."

"I am pleased to provide such important factors." Memta saluted them, turned, and left.

Rieka clutched her datapad and sat down. She looked up at Triscoe and sensed a color. A disconcerted reddish brown. Was he unconvinced by Memta's report? "What are you thinking?" she asked.

"I'm thinking I want you three back on Earth as soon as possible. RadiMo will turn up eventually—with or without your assistance."

Rieka felt her jaw drop at his tone, but snapped it up and used her own captain's voice on him. "You're being overprotective again, Triscoe," she warned. "Memta said this was just an accident. RadiMo disappeared while on Earth. I'm responsible for his safety."

She saw him clench his jaw and turn slightly away before he looked directly at her, and said, "I am also thinking that the easiest way to have you murdered—and avoid being suspect—is for someone to make it *look* like an accident."

That brought her up short. He'd just described her theory of her father's death. She took a deep breath and raked her fingers through her hair. "Okay, Tris. We'll transfer to the *Prospectus* as soon as it arrives—and return to Earth. Maybe RadiMo will have turned up by then."

As the *Providence* slid into orbit around Aurie, Triscoe heaved a small sigh of relief. He'd transferred Rieka, Jen-

iper, and Wang to Robert DeVark's protection before he'd
left the Oph system. If the *Prospectus* had not yet arrived
at Earth, it would shortly. He hoped they would stay in one
piece until he arrived there himself, at the end of the week.

His helmsman, Lisk, announced their orbit was stable.
A moment later V'don reported incoming communications.
"Tell them we'll begin standard cargo transfer immediately," Triscoe advised V'don. "Commander Aarkmin, you
may begin."

"Understood, Captain."

Triscoe listened to the interplay between the bridge and
cargo hold while he scanned through their transfer schedule. They had roughly eighteen kilotons in their hold to
send to the surface and were expecting to receive about
half that amount. Glancing through the list of vendors, his
eye settled on one. Tarrik Enterprises.

He accessed that file and found they were receiving nothing and sending out only one point six metric tons of cargo,
all bound for Oph. Having just come from there, Triscoe
wondered why Tarrik didn't wait for a ship that would run
a direct route to his product's destination. Then he realized
once the merchandise had been loaded on a Fleet ship,
Tarrik could claim delivery.

His interest having been piqued when he'd met Jeniper,
Triscoe had found Tarrik Enterprises' stock had been dropping steadily for six months. Unable to fathom why, since
other agro suppliers had not suffered similar losses, he wondered if Tarrik himself had problems. Remembering Jeniper's cryptic words in the medical suite, Triscoe decided a
few moments alone with her brother might be prudent.

While Aarkmin continued to coordinate their cargo
transfer, Triscoe leaned toward his communications officer.
"V'don, see if you can reach an individual named Edrin
Tarrik. He runs Tarrik Enterprises. If you cannot speak to
him directly, tell his secretary I require a meeting in person—as soon as possible."

Robet strode purposefully down the *Prospectus*'s main
corridor and hesitated only a moment before he rang for
admittance. Hoping he wasn't giving Jeniper the wrong impression, he schooled his bibbets to a soft pink and took a

breath. The idea of seeing her privately had excited his libido more than he thought it would.

The door slid open, and Jeniper stood there, her pale eyes visible below the bandage. "Captain DeVark," she said. "This is a pleasant surprise."

"I hope I'm not intruding," he offered, the words sounding contrived, even to him.

"No. Please, come in. I was just doing some research."

She backed away, giving him room to enter. He stepped across the threshold and eased into a chair as she gestured for him to sit. "How are you feeling?"

Jeniper touched the bandage and sat in the chair next to him. "I'm fine. I don't really need this anymore."

Robet nodded and groped for something else to say. "I hope the room is satisfactory. If you don't like it, there are others. Rieka's fear the Reaffirmation won't be well attended seems frighteningly accurate."

"The room is fine . . . Captain." She reached to switch off her datapad. Robet had already glanced at the screen. She'd been "researching" a company called Tarrik Enterprises.

"Robet," he corrected. "All my friends call me Robet."

He watched her fiddle with the datapad before she said, "Well, yes. But we're on your ship now. It wouldn't really be proper—"

"—you're absolutely right," he conceded gallantly, "in certain circumstances."

"And this isn't one of them?"

"No." He heaved a sigh, thankful to be past that hurdle. "I . . . enjoyed having dinner with you after Rieka's inauguration."

"Thank you," she said smiling. "It was too bad I had to run off so early."

Robet found himself smiling simply because she did. "You should have stuck around. When I came back from my walk, Rieka got Alexi on the dance floor."

"That must have been a sight," she replied, her slender fingers reaching to pat the hair around her bandage. "I mean, they're both vivacious, but Rieka is thin compared to her uncle. Still, I think Alexi has lost some weight recently. I understand he's had some health problems." She stopped and smiled strangely.

Through the elastic gauze, Robet saw her bibbets darken slightly before she said, "I'm rambling, aren't I? I don't usually do that." He noticed her hands couldn't seem to find a place to light. "Really. Robet," she persisted, "I can't tell you—"

"—Jeniper, stop." Robet reached and caught her right hand. He held it loosely, allowing her the choice to pull away. She didn't. She did exactly what he asked. She stopped. Talking. Moving. Breathing.

"What's wrong?" he whispered softly, holding her hand a bit tighter. "You can trust me, Jeniper. If there's anything I can do to help you—just name it." He liked this woman, and although comforting her hadn't been on his mind when he'd been in the corridor, Robet realized she needed him as a friend right now more than anything else.

She shook her head. "It's nothing."

"I don't think so," he insisted gently.

Jeniper closed her eyes and seemed to pull into herself, even though she let him hold her hand. "Please," she whispered.

For a brief moment, Robet felt as though his world had tilted. Did she want him to please help her—or please leave her alone? This woman *needed* help, and he wanted to give it, but he had no clue what to do. Never having faced such roiling emotions, he let his bibbets darken and held her hand tighter. "Jen? Are you in pain? Is it your head?"

Her eyes snapped open and she looked at him. "No."

"Well then . . . tell me," he coaxed. "Whatever it is— is tearing you up. Don't do this to yourself." To me, he added silently.

"I'm . . . frightened," she said slowly. She pressed her lips together and looked away as though trying to decide what to tell him.

"Frightened of—what? Of me?"

She shook her head and for a moment, Robet thought she wouldn't answer. Then she sighed. "Everything's such a mess, and it's all my fault." She pulled her hand from his and brushed her fingers against bibbets that had thickened and darkened considerably. "Just look at this. I'm falling apart. I can't even control . . . myself." She dropped her face into her hands and gulped her breath.

"No. No, don't cry. Please," Robet pleaded. Dark bibbets he could handle, but not tears. He pushed out of his chair and moved to sit on the arm of hers. He slid his hand across her back. She was so tense it felt as if he were caressing a statue.

"Talk to me. I can't help if you don't tell me what's wrong. What's happened?"

She gulped great breaths of air, and not knowing what else to do, he rubbed her back. "Why would you want to . . . help me?" she asked finally, wiping her eyes with the backs of her hands.

Robet turned and sat on the table's edge so he could face her. He didn't touch her, but leaned as close as he dared. "I like you, Jen." He shrugged and looked into her pale eyes. "Honestly, I'm attracted to you. Very attracted. But if you're in some kind of trouble, I think you need a friend right now more than you need a—relationship."

She blinked at him, then sniffed. "My brothers are in trouble."

Robet shook his head. "What kind of trouble?"

"I . . . don't know. I don't know anything!" Jeniper stood and walked to the bathroom. A moment later, she came out with a wet cloth and pressed it to her eyes and bibbets. "My younger brother, Jonik . . . He's always in debt. Always trying to get ahead with crazy schemes or by working for people who—who flagrantly disregard the law. He's borrowed thousands and thousands of credits from me. The last time he asked, I told him no. But he was worried. He said someone had threatened him—and maybe they'd come after me."

"Did you believe him?"

"No. Yes." She waved her hands aimlessly. "I don't know." She sighed. "He always says things like that when he needs money. But this time his bibbets got really dark. I wasn't sure if he was truly scared or had learned how to make them do that."

"And when was this?"

"A few weeks ago. On Indra."

Jeniper sat down in her chair again and looked at Robet with such a painful expression he wanted to go find this guy and teach him a few lessons, himself. He brushed aside the sudden anger he felt toward her callous brother, and asked, "Have you spoken to him since then?"

"No. But he's sent messages to Earth. I was supposed to meet him . . . but he couldn't come. He left a video note for me. Another warning." She sighed. "And now, this!" She gestured to the bandage on her head.

Confused, Robet returned to his chair and leaned toward her. "But what happened at Yona wasn't anyone's fault. The transport had a defective tire."

"Yes. Of course it did," she agreed. "And there was no security problem at the stadium in Damascus and RadiMo isn't missing and the lab in Rhonique didn't blow up." She glared at him, daring him to disagree.

"Jeniper, those are all unrelated incidents. Two of them don't even have anything to do with you."

"They do—indirectly," she countered. "I'm the Earth Herald's adjutant. Whoever is trying to hurt me may be—"

"—or maybe not. It's possible this isn't directed at you at all," Robet told her using his best don't-argue-with-me captain's voice. "Rieka's got plenty of her own troubles. You may just be caught up in that. Do you know who is threatening your brother?"

She sighed and shook her head.

"I'm guessing you haven't spoken to Rieka about this."

"No. You said yourself—she has enough to worry about."

His mind churning, Robet nodded. "That's . . . what I said." Concern for both women made him forget his bibbets. He looked away from her long enough to get them back under control. Then, reaching for her hand again, he said, "I don't know what's going on, but I'm going to find out. While you're aboard the *Prospectus,* I promise you'll be safe. Once we get to Earth, we'll figure something out. Everything will be fine."

"I'm not so sure. My other brother, Edrin, is experiencing huge financial problems. It's like some kind of conspiracy. He can't make anything happen the way it used to."

"You can't be sure the two are related."

"I can't be sure they're not."

Robet sighed. Talking to Jeniper was like talking to Rieka, neither woman could be convinced their assumptions might be wrong. "Why don't you send Edrin a communiqué? Ask how he's doing. Tell him about the younger brother and that you've seen the market reports—and offer your support. See what he says."

"Just like that?"

"The direct way is usually best," he said.

He watched her consider the idea and make a decision. "I'll do it. I've got to do something. I need answers. And Edrin may be in danger, too, and not even know it."

FIFTEEN

"Captain Marteen, it's a pleasure to meet you. I'm Edrin Tarrik." The Aurian standing in the middle of the room looked at least a decade older than his sister, but the similarity of their features made it obvious they were siblings.

"Mr. Tarrik," Triscoe replied. They exchanged the formal Aurian greeting, a bow from the waist.

Tarrik gestured for him to sit and took his place behind a large desk. "I beg your pardon . . . Captain . . . but I don't believe my schedule—"

"It was short notice, Mr. Tarrik," Triscoe apologized.

Tarrik nodded, then glanced at the screen on his desk console. "If you will excuse me for one moment, Captain Marteen." He tapped furiously at his keyboard for a moment, studied his screen, then began tapping again. Finally, he took a deep breath and leaned back in his chair. "What is it you wish to discuss?"

Triscoe glimpsed the bibbets on the left side of Tarrik's forehead. They seemed dark, and he wondered if it had to do with the information Tarrik had just received, or perhaps his own unanticipated presence. Treading carefully, Triscoe slowly said, "There . . . is a . . . problem."

"Yes. That seems to be my *hoshan* of late." Tarrik banged the desk with a fist. "It's quite obvious, don't you think? Though I hadn't expected they'd send a Fleet captain to complain to me. The potassium conduits were defective when we got them from Oph," he explained, pointing a finger at Triscoe. "And as far as we've been able to tell, the oxygen and nitrogen mix synthesizers were also not up to standard."

"I see."

"And that doesn't even begin to explain the mismarked shipping cartons or why we're suddenly unable to get our suppliers to fill our orders."

"Suddenly?" Triscoe frowned at that fact but let Tarrik continue.

The Aurie waved absently. "Our parts have been backordered, in some cases for months. It's infuriating."

"I can well imagine."

"In each instance we are obligated to notify the customer. If the problem is defective equipment, we offer to replace the faulty hardware at no cost," Tarrik explained. "I have hired eight additional inspectors to guarantee such problems won't happen again."

"I am pleased to know the situation is under control," Triscoe began, "and that you are taking measures against future occurrences. I am sure this series of incidents has not been profitable."

"Quite frankly, Captain, it has been a nightmare."

Triscoe nodded and watched Tarrik's face. He couldn't sense much from the man, but hoped to pick up whether or not he was lying. "That is more along the topic I wished to discuss with you," he said. "From the published accounts I have studied, you never experienced such problems before."

"Never," Tarrik agreed. "Everything started after the Procyon War. The past six months have been chaos, Captain Marteen. Complaints. Recalls. Our profits are off. Stockholders are furious—as I'm sure you're aware." He braced both elbows on the desktop and leaned over them. "We're doing everything we can, but it will take years to recoup."

"Undoubtedly." Triscoe decided the man would continue to lament his problems if not nudged in another direction. "Do you have any enemies, Mr. Tarrik?"

"Excuse me?"

"Enemies, sir," Triscoe repeated. "I'm looking for a source. Are there people in the Commonwealth who would profit greatly from your ruin?"

Triscoe watched as Tarrik's face went through an array of expressions. "I . . . don't know. Certainly there is tough competition in the hydroponics industry. That is a good thing, of course. It keeps the standards up and prices steady. I sincerely doubt a competitor would want to see us fold."

"Then . . . someone else? Some person or group that would profit if Tarrik Enterprises didn't exist?"

Tarrik looked truly confused. "I don't think I can answer that question, much less believe our current difficulties are a deliberate attack. The idea is completely absurd."

Triscoe nodded. He hadn't picked up anything but surprise. The reports he'd read about Tarrik's integrity must have been true. He could only hope Edrin Tarrik was as conscientious in his personal life as he was in his professional one.

"Actually, Mr. Tarrik, my purpose for this meeting was not to discuss Fleet business, and I apologize for allowing you to think so." He paused briefly and added, "I needed to ask you a few questions about your sister."

"Jeniper?"

"Yes." Triscoe eased himself back against the chair. "Jeniper. She has informed you of her new job, has she not?"

"Yes. Several weeks ago. She's the Earth Herald's adjutant." Tarrik nodded and looked Triscoe in the eye. "Forgive me for being so dense, Captain. I see the connection now. She works for your wife. A big step for her—but I'm sure she can handle it." Tarrik took a deep breath and made a vague gesture with his hand. His bibbets lightened, and the tension seemed to drain out of him. He got up from behind the desk and gestured for Triscoe to follow him through a door.

"I apologize for that frustrated tirade, Captain Marteen," Tarrik said once they'd entered a comfortable-looking room. "I assumed you'd come about our current difficulties at T.E. Quite honestly, I've been expecting the Fleet to renegotiate our cargo contracts." He sighed, and Triscoe watched his bibbets fade to pale pink. "I'm a much better host in a social setting. Can I offer you some refreshment?"

"Fruit-water would be fine," Triscoe replied, and waited while Tarrik ordered beverages at a small console. They sat across from one another on thickly padded chairs. A small servebot rolled up a moment later, carrying two glass tumblers and a tray of snacks.

"Earth chocolate," Tarrik explained, picking up a small hunk of dark brown candy. "I admit I am addicted."

Triscoe smiled. He took a sip of his water and selected a piece of dried fruit. "Are you and Jeniper very close?"

"We are siblings," Tarrik replied after savoring the chocolate. "We keep in touch with one another, but we both have out own lives. I haven't seen her in almost a year, actually. Why do you ask?"

"Jeniper was involved in an . . . accident. Four days ago. On an Oph moon called Yona."

Tarrik leaned closer, his bibbets darkening slightly. "What kind of accident? Was she hurt?"

Triscoe shook his head. "She suffered a minor concussion and a small scalp wound. She was in the company of my wife and her bodyguard. None was seriously injured."

"Well, that's a relief—that none of them were hurt." Tarrik leaned back and Triscoe watched as his bibbets again paled to a neutral tone.

"Yes. But the reason I'm here has to do with the accident. I'm sure you understand my wife's safety is paramount—and that of her staff."

"Absolutely."

"Your sister, while still unconscious, said a most curious thing. And in light of your current business difficulties, I am wondering if there may be a connection."

"What did she say?" Tarrik sat straighter, and Triscoe picked up a distinct sense of anxiety from him.

"She said—while unconscious: 'Be careful. She's a threat. She means it.' Then she said something else in a language I did not understand." He paused for a moment, then said, "Does this . . . have any meaning for you?"

Tarrik set his glass down and tapped his fingers on the arm of his chair. Triscoe could tell he was trying to decide how much to reveal of whatever it was he knew. Softly, he said, "My concern is solely for the safety of my wife and her staff. I have no other agenda."

Nodding, Tarrik replied, "Of course, Captain. I appreciate your bringing this to my attention. And, unfortunately, I have few facts to give you. But I must ask—are you certain this incident involving Herald Degahv was an accident?"

"My engineers found no evidence to prove otherwise."

"But you are skeptical."

"Yes."

Tarrik nodded. "I would be, too. Let me explain, Captain. My sister and I have a younger brother. His name is Jonik. His birth was unanticipated, and though Auries do not give up their children to adoption as other races do, I sometimes think he would have been better reared in another household. My parents had planned and saved only enough for my sister and me to be well educated. Jonik understood at a young age that he would be earning his own way. By the time he finished his primary education, however, I had begun to turn a profit with Tarrik Enterprises. I offered to subsidize his education—but he refused.

"Jonik has worked in a variety of trades, the latest of which has been as a courier. I don't know for whom he works—or even if he's presently employed. He also likes to take risks. He gambles. Speculates occasionally. I have loaned him credit several times. And I know Jeniper has, too."

"How much are we talking about?"

"Tens of thousands of credits. I don't know the exact amount at this moment." Tarrik shrugged. "I have a record of it in my personal papers."

"Has he asked for money recently?"

"About a month ago. He wanted almost sixty thousand. My finances had already been bad for some time. I told him no."

"Do you think he went to Jeniper?"

"Possibly. She's given him money in the past."

"Would she have given him that much?"

"No."

Triscoe sat straighter. "You say that with certainty?"

Tarrik nodded. "I do. That's nearly a year's salary to her. Jeniper doesn't approve of Jonik's lifestyle. She wouldn't have done it."

"So do you think he might have threatened her?"

Tarrik shook his head. "No. Jonik would not threaten anyone." When Triscoe frowned at him, he smiled sadly. "You must understand. Jonik is easily influenced, but harmless. He could be holding a maitu to your head—and you wouldn't feel threatened."

Triscoe tried not to frown. "I'll have to trust you on that. But if not Jonik, then who?"

"I wish I knew, Captain. I'd also like to know where Jonik is."

"Is he missing?"

"Not as far as I know," Tarrik replied. "I simply don't know his whereabouts. He doesn't contact the family very often. Usually only for a loan. But our father's health is failing. I'd like to be able to find Jonik and ask him to spend some time at home."

"Does Jeniper know?"

"I think so. I believe Mam sent the message to Earth last week."

One look at Robet's face made Rieka glad she didn't have bibbets. "Come in, Robet," she told him airily from just inside the doorway of her suite. "Wang, Jeniper . . . would you excuse us?"

Wang hesitated. Rieka chafed at that. "I'm sure Captain DeVark isn't going to harm me, Wang-Chi." She flashed him a false smile. "And he's smart enough to know it would be stupid to try."

Wang gave her a halfhearted shrug and nodded. "I'll wait in my room."

When they were alone, Rieka relaxed. Slightly. "What's gone wrong now?"

"How do you know anything's wrong?"

"Because your bibbets are very pale, Robet," she told him gently. "You always overcompensate when you're trying not to show anxiety. And," she added, gesturing for him to sit on the sofa, "because we're inside Neptune's orbit, which means you've slowed forward speed enough to receive messages."

He frowned at her, his blue eyes cloudy with concern. "You know me too well."

"I know the routine," she corrected, seating herself beside him. "So what's happened?"

"An incoming communiqué, from Nason . . ."

"What about it?"

"He suggested I play it for you once I got to Earth. Of course he couldn't know you'd be on the *Prospectus* when I received it. I don't know whether to wait or—"

"Oh, for heaven's sake, give me the damn thing," Rieka snapped, holding out her hand. Robet fished in his trouser pocket and placed the small plastic square in her palm. He perched on the desk as she inserted it into the slot in her console.

The Fleet logo appeared for several seconds before Nason's face sprang three-dimensionally from the graphics. Rieka noticed the steely expression and the fact that his bibbets, like Robet's, were noticeably pale.

"Captain DeVark, you should be receiving this communiqué as you power down from your slide to Earth. The orders I am about to give you supersede your current tour schedule. I am issuing Contingency Order Three. Upon arrival at Earth, you are to remain there until you receive additional orders from me. Do not, for any reason, leave orbit."

Rieka flipped a toggle to suspend the replay. She looked up into Robet's odd frown. "What's going on? I haven't heard anything about a breach of security."

"Me either, until now," Robet told her. "Switch it back on."

She did. Nason sighed, looked somewhere off camera for a moment, then redirected his attention forward. "Contingency Order Three is being initiated for the following planets: Earth, Oph, and Yadra. And for the Fleet base at Dani. Persons en route to other planets who are *Prospectus* passengers may remain aboard at no charge—or may billet themselves on Earth at Fleet expense.

"The 'official' reason for remaining on Earth is a faulty valve in the exotic matter conduit. Your engineer is receiving a similar communiqué with a more technically complete explanation of the problem."

"Jeez," Rieka complained, "get to the point."

"I also want Rieka Degahv to be privy to the problem as it will quite probably affect her directly. Rieka, as you know, is still on the Fleet roster. It is possible we will have need of her services."

"See," Robet said, nudging her arm with his elbow.

She nudged him back but said nothing. A frisson of energy went through her. Excitement? Anxiety? She wasn't sure. But whatever was happening had to be serious enough for Nason to pull ships off their tours. She wondered if he'd actually recall her.

"Encoded communications between persons in the Fleet and on Earth, Oph, and Yadra have been brought to my attention by Admiral Veridok in Internal Affairs. The missives defy decoding. Once played, the audio and video are rendered unintelligible. This type of programming is virtually foolproof. Copies are equally impossible to comprehend.

"We do not know what is being relayed, nor to whom. I am issuing the contingency order to provide additional security for the planets involved. Other Fleet ships will arrive and depart without having been issued the order. Since this action is covert, your excuse for staying on Earth is the breakdown in your engine system. I may upgrade to Contingency Order Two if and when the parties are identified."

"I can't believe this," Rieka whispered.

"Travelers wishing to transfer to outgoing ships may do so. No one is to be detained. I need you to double-check all manifests for the last four weeks. Look for any inconsistencies—among both cargo and passengers. Even if you find nothing, forward all records to me. Brief only your command-level personnel on this matter. Do not increase ship's security. Do nothing out of the ordinary unless you receive additional orders from me.

"Good luck, Robet. Let's hope this matter will resolve itself as soon as possible."

The screen went blank, but Rieka stared at it for several seconds before switching it off. "Damn, Robet," she said softly. "I don't like this. Do you think it has something to do with the Reaffirmation?" When he said nothing, Rieka felt the hair raise on her forearms. Plans had been crumbling ever since she took office. Her mother's reach was far, but Rieka hadn't anticipated anything like this. It resembled a coup.

She looked up at Robet. His jaw was clenched shut and his eyes were almost closed. He seemed worried. "Do you know something?"

He swiveled his jaw from side to side. "Not about this," he answered. "I'm concerned about Jeniper."

"Jeniper?" Rieka pushed herself up and away from the

console and went back to the sofa to sit. "I don't understand. She's fine now."

He sighed and followed her. She watched him fidget for a moment and swivel his jaw again. "She's so vulnerable right now, that's all," he said finally.

"Jeniper?" she repeated, incredulous. "I'm the one who's being threatened. I'm the one who's lost RadiMo. I'm the one who's plans for Earth's future are in jeopardy. And you think *Jeniper* is vulnerable?"

He had the decency to look contrite. "When you put it that way . . ." He gestured aimlessly with his hands. "It's just that—you're experienced. Gods, Rieka. You've commanded Fleet ships. You took on the Procyons. You're a Herald! Jeniper's just a nice girl from Aurie who works for you."

Rieka took a moment to absorb both what he had and hadn't said. She sighed and raked her fingers through her hair. "I see your point. But in that case, I need to ask—are the two of you . . . seeing each other? Are you worried about her because you care—or because anyone associating herself with me is probably taking a big health risk?"

Robet hesitated before he answered, but looked her in the eye when he did. "Both. Well, no. Actually we aren't physically involved, yet. That will happen . . . eventually. I hope." He sighed and looked at the floor.

"I'm proud of you, Robet," Rieka offered, hoping to ease him out of his apparent discomfort. "After that last horrible relationship you tried to jump into . . . I'm glad to see you getting some confidence back."

"I realized, then, what a fool I'd made of myself. I don't intend to do that again."

"You won't. Jeniper is a wonderful person. I'm sure once she gets to know you she'll see that you're a wonderful person, too."

"Yeah," he said sheepishly. "But now there are more important things to worry about than my social life. Do you have any idea what Nason's found out about those illegal transmissions and why he'd order CO-3?"

"Not exactly," Rieka answered, though her mind had already processed that information, and she'd agreed with the admiral's assumptions. "But I do know that my mother has people working for her who are willing to risk going to prison by programming messages to play only once. I actually received such a message from her. And Candace's base of operations is on Yadra. Since her goal is to stop me, we can assume she's communicating with someone on Earth."

"Then what about Oph? And the Fleet personnel?"

"I'm not sure. It may have something to do with Radi-Mo's disappearance. Or, it may have nothing at all to do with it. We don't have enough information. And though I'm usually willing to speculate on a lot of things, I'd rather not this time."

She looked at Robet and frowned. "As far as I know, my father and I are the only people who have ever successfully crossed Candace. If RadiMo is involved with her, he doesn't stand a chance."

Robet sat straighter. "You don't think she'd . . . murder him?"

Rieka thought back to her own speculation surrounding Stephen's death. They were still digging up evidence, but things were pointing toward something more sinister than a malfunction. Exterior coolant systems had backups and fail-safes. His shuttle should not have incinerated in the atmosphere.

"I suppose you could say with Candace, anything's possible."

SIXTEEN

Rieka couldn't quite suppress a smile for the motley group that followed her out of the InterMAT station at the Embassy in New SubDenver. Jeniper still wore the bandage on her head, Wang's arm would be in the sling for at least another day, and Robet looked as though he hadn't slept in several nights.

"I'm going to my office," she told Wang. "You don't have to come if you've got other things to do. I'm just planning on catching up with—"

"I'm not one hundred percent," he insisted, "but I can still do my job."

Rieka opened her mouth to berate him for his tone, then switched gears before she spoke. "Of course you can, Wang. If I didn't think so, you wouldn't be here." She offered him a wry smile and accepted the small nod she got in return. He still blamed himself for the accident at Yona. She figured she'd wait until his body mended before making any judgments as to his attitude.

Robet, having watched the interplay, took Jeniper gently by the elbow, and said, "We'll come along, too. I know Jeniper has some catching up to do, and I'd like to take a look at Earth security."

"The embassy is a clearinghouse for everything you might need," Rieka said. "Wang can take you through whatever security checkpoints we've got set up—and you can decide what you want to do with the *Prospectus*—security-wise." She watched him nod, and led the way to her office.

When the outer door opened, Rieka recognized Elena, Setana's adjutant, seated behind Jeniper's console. "Welcome back, Herald Degahv," the Indran said, a smile brightening her beautiful, pale face. "Herald Marteen is in your office. We have been rather busy in your absence."

"I can't imagine why," Rieka quipped. With the Reaffirmation now just days away, *busy* was a gross understatement.

Elena frowned, then nodded. "Oh, a joke. Yes. Well, I can certainly understand the value of humor in such a complex situation."

"I'm sure you can." She gestured for Wang to take Robet to the security office, then prodded them with, "Jen and I will be in my office. You can find us there when you're through." She watched Robet nod at Jeniper and follow Wang down the hall.

"I think I'll stay here and have Elena brief me on what she's been doing," Jeniper said.

"That's fine, Jen," Rieka replied. "I'll let you know if I need you." She turned and strode into her office, where she was greeted by Setana.

"I heard about what happened on Yona. How are you feeling?" Setana asked. "How are Jeniper and Mr. Hong?"

"We're all okay. Nothing sinister happened as far as Memta could determine. And there isn't any evidence to suggest otherwise. But that doesn't mean I accept his conclusion. *Something* isn't right." She sighed. "The most disappointing thing is that we still have no idea what's happened to RadiMo."

"It is very disconcerting," Setana agreed. "I do hope he turns up safe before the Reaffirmation."

"I wouldn't hold my breath." Rieka said. When Setana frowned, she realized she'd used another Earth idiom. "It means . . . we'll have to be patient."

Setana relaxed and nodded. "I shall not hold my breath, either."

Rieka covered her smile with her hand. "Right. Why don't you brief me on what you've done in my absence— and then you can go and . . . do what you'd rather be doing."

Setana adjusted her scarf and looked pointedly at Rieka. "I have been perfectly content as your temporary replacement. And I'll remind you I volunteered to help."

"Sorry. I didn't mean—"

"—I know exactly what you meant," Setana scolded. "Do not apologize for someone else's presumed hardship. It places you in a less favorable position." Rieka nodded. "Now then," Setana went on, "Elena has been coordinating the housing problems—there have only been a few—and I have overseen the social events. Everything is ready for the party tomorrow night in Versailles, and nothing untoward has happened in your absence—unless you consider your mother's arrival in that category."

"Candace is here?"

"She arrived yesterday."

Rieka sat back and digested that news. On the one hand, with Candace here to stir up trouble, there might not be a moment's peace. But on the other hand, it would be a lot easier to catch her trying to undermine their plans for Earth.

"Okay," she said, offering Setana a quirky smile. "If she's here, let's put her under the microscope. I'll have Wang order surveillance for her and whatever staff she's got. She might even provide Admiral Nason with some much-needed evidence."

"What is his connection to her?" Setana asked, confusion apparent in her eyes.

"Nothing is confirmed yet. I'll let Robet tell you about that, himself."

"Captain DeVark?"

"The one and only. But let's not digress. Who else is here?"

Setana smiled. "Herald Dets of Aurie arrived yesterday, as did Herald Honutik. We have been notified that six senators will accompany Herald Loome from Yadra. They will arrive the day before the ceremony. Dzan, the Boolian Herald is expected, but we don't know when. Several business leaders are here, as are some Fleet administrators. They're arriving slowly, but Earth is the place to be for the next week."

"Don't you just love the limelight?" Rieka asked, pushing out of the chair to return to her desk.

"Sarcasm? I thought you liked attention."

"In moderation," she explained. "From certain people. Sometimes I'm convinced I must have been insane when I decided to run for Herald."

"But it is your destiny."

Rieka shrugged. Destiny or not, she had the job, for life.

Slightly raised voices coming from the outer office made her frown. "What now?" Rieka went to the door and opened it to find Wang holding a maitu on her mother. Jeniper and Elena stood behind the receptionist's desk, and Robet blocked the outer door. "What the hell is going on out here?"

Everyone began talking at once, though the noise level rapidly elevated to shouting. Rieka rolled her eyes and grimaced at the cacophony, then yelled for quiet. Everyone responded immediately, with the exception of Candace.

"I cannot believe I would be treated with such—"

"Shut up, Mother. Just shut—up. Can you do that?"

The order apparently shocked her into submission. Candace clamped her jaw closed and sighed loudly through her nose.

Rieka glared at her for a moment. "Now . . ." She studied the crowd. "Elena first."

Setana's adjutant offered an odd gesture with her hands. "This woman insisted on seeing you immediately. I explained you were in conference, but she became . . . agitated."

"I have never been—"

"Shut up, Mother. You'll have your chance," Rieka barked. She turned back to the others. "So she started fussing at you, and I'll bet Wang came tearing down the hall with his maitu drawn." He'd already holstered the weapon, but she nodded her thanks.

"Well, yes," Elena said softly. "It all happened very quickly."

"I'm sure it did." She glanced at the faces around her. People looked angry, frustrated, and uncertain. "I think we'd better have a little chat. Mother. Wang." She gestured toward her office. "We're not to be disturbed," she said, addressing Jeniper.

"Of course." After a glance at Robet, Jeniper closed the door behind them.

Silence reigned for a moment, then Rieka shook her head. "Okay, we might as well get this ironed out right now. Conference room." She gestured toward a paneled door.

Wang went to it first, opened it, and switched on the lights. "It's clear," he announced.

Setana caught Rieka's eye as she waved her mother through. "Consider using the DGI, dear," she advised softly. "Perhaps a pastoral mural. Maybe running water. Something soothing."

Rieka nodded and went to the console to program the setting. Before she took her place at the oval table's narrow end, the room's DGI window revealed a forest lit with dappled sunlight. Speakers hidden in the ceiling played sounds to accompany the image of a running brook. The tension in the room dropped several notches.

Now, even though they were eight stories below ground level in the middle of a large city, it both looked and felt as though they could escape everything by simply leaving the room. At the moment, she realized she wished she could do just that.

"Okay. Let's start with introductions. Mother, allow me to introduce you to the Indran Herald, Setana Marteen. And this gentleman"—Rieka gently touched his arm—"is Mr. Hong Wang-Chi, my personal bodyguard." To Setana and Wang, she said, "This is the CEO of PirezCorp of Yadra, my mother, Candace Degahv."

A brief moment of silence passed, then they echoed various words of welcome. Candace, looking pleased with herself, "I didn't realize, Mr. Hong, that a Herald required a bodyguard."

"Under the circumstances, it is a prudent precaution," he replied.

"Under what circumstances?"

"Considering the fact that the last two Earth Heralds have suffered unexpected health problems."

"Such as?" Candace asked.

"Such as . . . let's drop this subject," Rieka interjected, throwing a warning glance at Wang. They'd get nothing out of Candace if they implied her involvement in Stephen's death. And as far as Alexi's liver was concerned, Rieka understood that to be a problem that had developed without Human intervention, though at this point she knew anything was possible.

"Mr. Hong has already saved my life and, fortunately, is on the mend. End of story."

"I don't think I like the sound of that," Candace said.

Rieka ignored the comment. "Your barging in unannounced this afternoon has been rather fortuitous, Candace. I need to ask you some questions. And Herald Marteen can tell us whether you're lying or not."

Candace gasped. "Well, I never—"

"—oh yes, you do. More than you think," Rieka said, recalling how sincere Candace always made herself sound. "But that's beside the point. You didn't want me to be Herald, and now that I am, you're determined to obstruct every effort I make on this planet's behalf, aren't you?"

"I'm sure I have no idea what you are talking about."

"And I'm sure you don't mean that," Setana said.

Candace huffed.

Rieka hid her smile behind her hand, then leaned slightly toward her mother. "You see, you're not going to get away with your scheme—whatever it is. Not everyone is on your payroll. I told you before—my plans for this planet do not include upsetting the Commonwealth's financial balance. Your fortune is safe. Can't you be happy with that? Tell all your people you've changed your mind and leave Earth alone. If you don't, I swear I'll see you prosecuted to the fullest extent of the law."

"I don't have to stand for this!" Candace announced, pushing out of her chair. "You are my daughter. My flesh and blood. I could not be here for your inauguration, but I came for the Reaffirmation—as a Human, as your mother. And look at what I find when I arrive. The Herald does not have time for an audience with me. I waited an entire day!" she hissed. "What kind of treatment is that—for anyone? How dare you sit there and accuse me of—of nothing—when you, yourself are far from blameless, Rieka.

"You carry on about responsibility—that you'll be responsible for Earth and the Commonwealth. But that's laughable. You don't know the meaning of the word. I have never seen or met a worse hostess. And your manners are deplorable. How dare you threaten me. It is unfathomable how you could have been elected, much less make a success of your position as Herald."

She stopped for a moment, her eyes daring Rieka to take the bait. Knowing better, Rieka simply sighed and said nothing.

"And your plans for Earth will fail without my help, certainly," Candace went on. "To expect to house people in these underground cities where everything is contained and accounted for as if you were aboard a spaceship . . . for heaven's sake, it's completely uncivilized. It's like living in a cave. Earth has spent billions with borrowed credit to create these civic abominations—and will never be able to pay it back."

It took incredible effort, but Rieka managed to keep her face relaxed and her mouth shut. She knew better than to try arguing with Candace in front of people. It would only serve to make her look less in control. She suddenly realized all that tongue biting she'd done as a Fleet captain did actually serve a purpose.

Candace continued ranting for several minutes more. Finally, when she paused for a breath, Rieka calmly said, "Thank you for that lovely tirade, Mother. Now, you will please leave us to get some work done. And if you ever barge into my office unannounced again . . . I'll let Mr. Hong shoot you." She looked at the man seated at her left. "Wang-Chi."

He stood and escorted Candace out. At the doorway, she stopped and turned. "You can't be rid of me this easily. And let me assure you, daughter, that even if you don't see how wrong you are, others do."

Ignoring a rumble from her empty stomach, Rieka poured a glass of fruit-water for Setana and joined her on the sofa. The apartment she'd selected was both roomy and well appointed. They sat quietly gazing at the large DGI Rieka had programmed to play a prairie sunset.

"That is quite lovely," Setana said. "Do Earth sunsets actually look like that?"

"In some places," Rieka told her. She heaved a great sigh and leaned her head back against the cushion. "I need more hours in the day."

"Triscoe will be here soon, dear," Setana soothed. "Things will be better."

"I'm sure I don't know what you mean—but I'm also sure I don't want you to explain it to me." She heard a door close and turned her head to see Wang come through the entertainment area. "Why aren't you wearing your sling?"

"Don't need it anymore." He poured himself a drink in the kitchen and joined them. "Nice sunset."

"We were just discussing it," Setana said.

"The DGI in my room is out of alignment," Wang complained. "Everything is blurry. Makes me dizzy to look at it."

"I can probably fix it," Rieka said, sitting up. "Shouldn't take more than a couple of minutes."

"Don't worry about it," Wang said warily.

"Who's worrying? I'm qualified to work on that type of equipment. I was a tech-pro only a few months ago." She pushed off the couch and glanced down at Setana's wry smile. "What?"

"The tech-pro that single-handedly *undid* the *Prodigy's* circuitry, I believe," she said.

Rieka lifted her chin. "I did what I was *ordered* to do, Madam Herald. Wang, I promise if I can't straighten out the problem, I'll admit it."

The big man shrugged and led the way. "Couldn't be much worse, anyway."

"Your confidence is inspiring, Wang-Chi. Be back in a minute, Setana."

They went through the entertainment area and down a short hallway to Wang's suite. His desk and several shelves were cluttered with various computer parts and other sundry hardware. The DGI was off, so Rieka went to his small console and switched it on. Sure enough, the picture looked so blurry she couldn't make it out.

Rieka picked up a pair of dirty socks from the chair and handed them to Wang. "Didn't realize you needed a housekeeper," she said.

"I manage."

Rieka laughed and sat. "Let's see what kind of damage I can do." Thoroughly enjoying herself, she accessed the programming files and called up those pertaining to the DGI. "Here you go, Wang-Chi. Your depth perception is way off. Who set this thing up, a Lomii?" She tapped a few more keys and reset the screen. When the DGI menu came up, she found a North Atlantic shoreline and entered it. "How's that?"

She saw the look of astonishment on his face, then a bit of awe added to it as he turned to her. "You really did it," he said.

She rolled her eyes. "Why are people constantly surprised when I do something completely mundane? It isn't that hard to reprogram a DGI. I'm sure you could have done it, yourself."

He shook his head. "I don't mess with that kind of software. It's Fleet derivative. Now, you want to talk anything else, or hardware—cameras, microphones, private TCs, any security equipment—"

"Rieka!"

Rieka heard Setana's strident calls and was out the door in a heartbeat with Wang on her heels. They ran into the sitting room and stopped short. Setana and Robet were staring at one another. Both looked concerned, almost fearful.

"What? What's happened now?" Rieka barked.

Robet turned to her. "It's Jeniper. I went to her apartment—we were going to a bar upstairs before dinner with you—and she wasn't there."

Rieka told herself to be calm, then looked into Robet's blue eyes and ignored his darkening bibbets. "What do you mean, she wasn't there?"

"I mean she's gone. When she didn't answer the door, I checked your offices and the bar we were going to. Then, I had SubDenver security come and open the apartment. She wasn't inside. Her datapad was on the kitchen table, Rieka. She's gone."

"Okay," she said gesturing for him to stay calm even as a frisson of worry went through her. "Now, Jeniper is pretty methodical. I'm sure she'd tell me if she planned to be late for dinner—which she isn't, yet. Let me just check my incoming messages."

Stepping past Setana, Rieka snatched up her datapad and accessed her comm file. "Here. She sent a message sixty-eight minutes ago. She asks me not to wait dinner. She's got an errand to run and she'll see me later."

Sure Robet wouldn't take her word for it, she handed the datapad to him. "Jeniper's fine." As long as the errand she's running has nothing to do with Candace, she amended silently.

SEVENTEEN

Jeniper took a deep breath and pulled her coat collar up against her neck. She couldn't believe she'd come back to Bywong just because Jonik had asked her to.

The old and new structures looked less frightening in the late-morning sunlight. There were two private vehicles parked near the small office she'd been in before. She stood next to the taxi that had brought her from Canberra and wondered what to do.

"This is so stupid," she told herself. The icy wind licked at her, and a line of strangely dark clouds loomed, blocking out all but the nearest peaks. A small voice in her head urged her to go back to New SubDenver. Now.

An Oph came out of the building. He glanced at her, walked to a vehicle, and got in. She heard a click as the flywheel engaged the electrical systems and watched as it maneuvered around the other car and her taxi. It pulled up alongside her and the window opened.

"He's in there," the Oph said. Then he took off down the narrow winding road that led back to civilization.

The wind picked up and Jeniper shivered. Glancing at the snow line, she realized it wasn't much higher than where she presently stood. The clouds looked closer now. She wondered how long it would be before it snowed.

Taking the Oph's advice, she walked cautiously toward the door. "Stupid, stupid," she muttered, knowing how foolish this gamble was. But she couldn't go on risking Rieka's life because of Jonik's disreputable actions. Somehow, she had to help him out of his current problem. Settle the overdue account. Whatever.

She knocked, but no one answered. Gripping the icy handle, Jeniper pulled the door open and stepped in out of the wind. She blew on her fingers to thaw them while she looked around the room. The blinds were drawn, but even in the gloom she could see there wasn't anyone at the console.

"Jeniper."

She swiveled her head. She had no idea where he'd been hiding, but he stood only a couple of meters away, now. She stared at him, taking in his gaunt features and dark hair that had grown too long since she'd seen him last. Apparently, he'd suffered more than she in that time.

"Gods, Jonik. You scared me. Are you all right?" She stepped closer to him and lifted her arms to offer a hug. He accepted it, and she got a better idea of how much weight he'd lost.

"You're too thin," she chided. "Mam would tell you to eat—that you look like a skeleton."

"I get enough," he said.

"And before we say anything else to each other, I need you to know that Mam sent me a message. Pae isn't well. Mam thinks . . . She thinks we should come home and see him soon. I'll probably go after the Reaffirmation. You should, too."

"He doesn't want to see me."

"He does. I'm sure of it. Mam and Pae always ask if I know how you are, where you are, what you're doing . . ." When he shook his head, Jeniper felt her patience waning. "Jonik, I want you to listen to me. Whatever it is you've gotten yourself into, I can help you. I work for the Earth Herald. I can—"

"—I know who you work for."

Jeniper shook her head. "I'm not the Indran attaché anymore," she said, not knowing how much news he'd heard. "I'm Rieka Degahv's adjutant to Earth."

"I know that!" He shoved her arms away and took a step back, putting the desk chair between them.

Jeniper made herself stay put. If she scared him and he ran, she'd never be able to keep up. She lifted one hand, gesturing for him to stay calm. "I came here because I got your message and want to help you."

"You refused to, before," he spit, the heat of his anger

and frustration darkening his bibbets. "Now things are different. You can't help me the way you think."

She didn't like his ominous tone. "How are things different?"

"She's already tried to kill me. Even after I helped her. I did what she asked, and she didn't care." He hugged himself and turned away.

Jeniper watched him in the room's faint light. She listened to his ragged breath and knew no matter how frustrated and afraid she'd felt, Jonik's terror had to be a hundred times greater. She raked her fingers through her hair, mindful of the healing wound, and tried to think of something meaningful to say.

"You're still my brother," she reminded him softly. "And even if you are a *bimoosh*, I love you anyway." She took a small step toward him. "Jonik, I didn't believe you, before. I do, now. I understand the kind of trouble you're in and—"

"No you don't, Jen. You don't understand anything." He looked at her and she could see the anguish on his face. The skin was so pale, and his bibbets stood out in stark contrast. She started to reply, but he went on. "You think you understand. But this whole stupid mess is my doing. Mine and hers. She'd kill anyone to get what she wants. You can't ask for your Herald's help—or anybody else."

"Rieka Degahv's a good person, Jonik. And she knows what it's like to be wrongfully accused. She's got a lot of power, too—and a lot of powerful friends. She can help you."

"I've already wrecked her life, Jeniper, and she doesn't even know it. I won't consider asking for her help."

"So the accident . . . It did have something to do with you." She had worried over that for days. Speculating whether or not it had been planned had almost driven her crazy.

"It was no accident."

Jonik's sober words doused her uncertainty but fueled her fear. Jeniper sighed and leaned on the desk. "I wondered about that, even after Captain Marteen had his engineer examine the wrecked transport. But of course, that had nothing to do with the hull breach."

He turned to face her, frowning. "What are you talking about?"

"About the accident. On Yona. How I got this." She pointed to the scab on her head. His bewildered expression told her this was news to him. "What are *you* talking about?"

She watched his eyes bulge for a moment, then a mask settled over his features. "I want to give you something, Jen."

"What are you talking about?" she repeated. "Don't change the subject." He shook his head. "Jonik, I'm prepared to help you, but I need some information. Just a fact or two. Anything." He didn't answer and she rapped her knuckles against the desktop. "Damn it, Jonik. You've got to trust me."

"I do. Come with me. I need to give you something."

Not knowing what else to do, Jeniper followed him out the door and toward a gaping hole in the mountainside. "I'm not going in there," she said.

"It's just the old mine," he explained, nodding for her to follow. "The developers have modernized everything. It's a tourist ride now. They finished laying the last of the tracks a couple of days ago. There's nothing to worry about." He walked into the cave's mouth and seemed to be swallowed up in the darkness.

"Jonik!"

"It's okay, Jen," his voice called out. "There's a blackout curtain right at the edge. Just come on through."

The blackout curtain turned out to be three curtains hanging about a meter apart. They'd been stretched and mounted to the cave's roof and floor. She pushed her way through slits in the heavy material, almost choking from the sense of claustrophobia.

"There you are," Jonik said, as she stepped into a well-lit room. "This place'll be open in another few weeks. But we can take a complimentary ride."

She watched him walk confidently to a console behind a large boulder, or more correctly, a console that had been constructed to look like a boulder. A string of dim lights came on down the tunnel, and a trio of connected ore cars with molded seats rolled into the room.

"Get in," he told her. Jeniper nodded and climbed into

the last car. Jonik stood a moment more at the controls, then stepped into the second car. "I turned off the audio," he said. "This'll only take a few minutes."

They rolled down the tunnel and Jeniper could tell it had been reinforced by modern technology and then decorated to appear old. What looked like antique wooden struts framed the underground passage every few meters, both small overhead lights and flickering lamps hung strategically on the uneven walls, lighting the mine shaft. The air smelled dusty, but dry. She imagined that would change once the snow melted in the spring.

He stood as they turned a corner and stretched his hand up high enough to reach the beams as they passed under them. He touched each one, and she realized he was counting them.

"Nine." He put his foot up on the car's seat. "Ten." He stood on the seat. "Eleven." He reached up and pulled something down from a recess behind the beam. Jeniper turned to look where the knapsack had come from, but she could only see shadows.

Jonik reseated himself. She watched him handle the dark cloth bag carefully. He set it on his lap and opened it. A burnished silver-colored cylinder appeared in his hand. It looked to be about the size of a large mug.

"What is that?" she asked.

"Insurance," he answered cryptically.

"For what Jonik? I don't understand. Why won't you tell me anything?"

"The less you know, the better, Jen." He slipped the cylinder back into the bag and leaned across the short space between the still-rolling cars. "Keep this for me. Keep it safe. Don't let anyone know you've got it."

Frowning, Jeniper accepted the proffered sack. "But why?"

"Our lives depend on it."

Robet could never remember being so worried about anyone. He couldn't get Jeniper off his mind. He'd watched her strong independence wilt until she blamed herself for every little mishap. He'd wanted to help her, and she wouldn't let him. Now, she'd mysteriously vanished. Even if the errand she'd supposedly been on had taken more

time than expected, she should have checked in sometime
during the night.

The secretary announced him, and he walked into Rieka's office. Setana Marteen stood before Rieka's desk, tapping notes on a datapad. "Is that all?" the Herald inquired.

"It's everything from her office's appointment book. You
sure you want to do this?" Rieka asked.

"Endless Heavens, dear," Setana quipped. "Who better?" She turned and smiled. "Hello, Captain DeVark.
How are you?"

"Good morning, Herald Marteen, Rieka," he replied,
nodding to them in turn. "I've been better, to tell you
the truth."

Rieka stood and looked him in the eye. "Wang's running
a check on all modes of travel to and from this city. I asked
him to wait until zero-eight-hundred just in case Jeniper
came home late and didn't receive my message." She
glanced at a nearby clock. "It's been almost twenty minutes. There should be something, soon."

Robet nodded. He sensed his bibbets coloring and concentrated on keeping them under control. He tried to think
of something intelligent to say, but nothing sprang to mind.

Herald Marteen smiled at him gently before turning to
Rieka. "I'll just get started on this, dear. If you need me,
buzz my office."

"Thank you, Setana," Rieka said.

Robet nodded as the Herald glided by. When she'd left
the room, Rieka looked at him sternly. "Robet, sit down
before you fall down."

"I'm fine," he said, but he went to her office sofa and sat.

Rieka pounced before he'd even settled against the cushions. "You're not fine, my friend," she chided, sitting next
to him. "You look awful. I've never seen you like this."

"I've never been like this," he admitted. "I mean, I was
worried about you when you'd been arrested for treason—
but it didn't feel like this. It didn't make me empty inside.
All I do is think about Jeniper. I wonder if she ran away or
was taken away. And if she ran—if it was because of me."

"It wasn't you." Rieka said it with such conviction, Robet
took it as fact. "We'll know more once Wang finishes his
search. And we'll get her back. And RadiMo, too."

Robet shook his head. "You don't know that."

"Maybe not, but I think Yillon probably would. And the most recent message he's sent to me is about children. Jeniper is not a child."

"No," he said, trying to remember the last time he'd felt this powerless. "Jeniper definitely isn't a child."

The door slid open and Mr. Hong strode into the office. "You're not going to believe this," the big man said. "Apparently, for some unknown reason, Jeniper went to the spaceport at seventeen-hundred hours yesterday. She purchased passage to Canberra, Australia, on an express shuttle. It arrived there at nineteen-thirty hours, our time. About noon in Canberra." He sighed. "I lost the trail after that. She didn't buy anything or register at any hotels there."

"Was she alone?"

Hong shrugged. "Hard to tell, but I think so. No other tickets were purchased within three minutes of hers. It's usually pretty obvious if people are traveling together. The ticket purchase is recorded almost simultaneously."

"Then why Canberra?" Rieka asked. "I don't get it. What errand could she have had there?"

"I don't know," Hong told her. "There could be a hundred reasons. But I don't think she stayed in Canberra—otherwise, she'd have made a purchase. Food. A hotel reservation. Something."

An idea began to coalesce in Robet's mind. "I think I can find her," he said.

"Australia's a big continent, Captain," Hong said.

"I know. But there's something . . ." He looked at Rieka. "Trust me on this. I think I can find her. It'll be faster if I go alone." He pushed himself to his feet.

Rieka rose and flashed him a skeptical frown. "All right, Robet. You know the rules about InterMATting into potential danger as well as I do."

He stepped closer and put his hand on her shoulder. "I'll be fine."

"Of course you will," she replied, her quirky smile proof of her confidence in his decision. "Just find Jeniper and bring her back safe."

He eased his hand down her arm and gave her fingers a squeeze. When she squeezed back, Robet released her and bowed. "Thank you, Madam Herald."

She chuckled and echoed his tone. "Get going, Captain DeVark."

"See you in a couple of hours." Robet left the office, then switched on his TC to contact the *Prospectus*. A few moments later, he stood on the bridge issuing orders.

"Dimish, I need you to get me some information," he said to the lieutenant at the communications console. "Start with EarthCom Australia and work your way down to someone in Canberra that can identify every taxi service."

"As we speak, Captain," the Indran woman said.

Robet turned to his helmsman. "We're altering orbit, Mr. Viktar. Bring us geosynchronous over Canberra."

"Yes sir." Viktar paused only a moment to check with his computer before adding, "It'll be about twenty-five minutes, Captain."

"Very good. Dimish, if you reach someone before we get back, page me. Strummik," he said softly, gesturing toward his executive officer, "let's have a chat."

"Indeed," the Vekyan said. She eased out of her chair and eyed him curiously before following him off the bridge and to a conference room. "You intend to do something beyond regulations, again, I take it."

"Not exactly," he replied, walking off his anxiety. "The Herald's adjutant is missing. I think I can find her. I'm going to try."

"But sir, I was under the impression that Herald's security office—"

"—I think I can find her, Strummik. That's all you have to know."

"Perhaps," she said.

Robet stopped pacing and looked at her. Strummik stared back, her pink eyes unblinking. He'd been reckless in the past, he knew, and she'd covered for him. He didn't intend a repeat performance, today. Fortunately, his TC clicked on before he had a chance to say anything more. "DeVark."

"Captain," Dimish's voice began, "I've reached the public-transit manager in Canberra. Her name is Emily Vasquez."

"Put her through to the conference-room console," Robet replied, guessing she'd be more responsive if she could see him. Strummik reached across the table and activated the system. He sat down before the console and motioned for her to stay out of camera range.

A dark-haired and dark-skinned Human appeared, her attention focused on something beyond his screen. "Emily Vasquez?" Robet began. "I'm Captain DeVark of the *Prospectus*."

She looked into his screen. "Yes, Captain. I understand you require some information."

"A bit. Is it possible for me to find out where a taxi has taken a fare?"

"Possible . . . yes. You need to tell me which taxi service it was and the approximate date. The patron's name would be helpful, too. Or, an account number."

Robet frowned. "I don't know which service. The vehicle was white with red lettering."

Vasquez shook her head. "They're *all* white with red lettering in Canberra, Captain. It's a standard. How about the account number? That would be the simplest way—though the date would reduce the number of records I'd have to search."

"Commonwealth date 204:279," he answered. "I'm sure of that. I can have the Earth Herald's office forward the account information, if necessary. The name we're looking for is Jeniper Tarrik."

"I'll start with that," she said. "But the number would speed things along. Is there a reason—?"

"Yes, there is. But this is a secure matter, ma'am. I simply require your cooperation and the information from your records."

"I'll do what I can, Captain."

It took only fifteen minutes for Vasquez's computers to receive Rieka's reply to his request for Jeniper's account number and to correlate it with that day's records for the five taxi companies servicing Canberra. He spent the entire time poring over a detailed city map, trying to remember the name she'd given as her destination.

"Captain," Vasquez's image said, finally. "Miss Tarrik took a Green Hills taxi to Bywong. An odd destination. But our records show she made the round-trip."

Robet nodded. That name sounded familiar. "Why is that an odd destination?"

"Bywong is quite a distance northeast of Canberra," she

replied. "And there's nothing much there at the moment. An old gold-mining town is being refurbished as a tourist center. It isn't expected to open for a month or two, last I heard."

Robet nodded, absorbing the woman's skeptical tone. "Can you tell me if another fare has gone there in the last day?"

"One moment." He watched her check the information on her console. "Sorry, Captain. No one has taken any taxi from Canberra to Bywong in that period of time. Although there is a discrepancy . . ."

"What?"

"Corin Cabs is reporting a missing vehicle."

"I'll check that out. Thank you."

"Captain DeVark," she said, stopping him before he could cut the transmission.

"Yes?"

"All our cabs are Bitterlys."

He frowned. Having no idea what a Bitterly was, he asked, "Is this significant?"

"The vehicle uses energy supplied by a flywheel. Depending upon how long ago it was charged, it may not even register on your"—she waved her hand to indicate she had no idea of the correct term—"sensory equipment. And I'm afraid orbital imagery won't be available. It's been snowing in the mountains for several hours."

"Thank you, ma'am. I'll bear that in mind." Not that it mattered much, anyway, he added silently. He intended to do an on-site survey of the place. "*Prospectus,* out."

Jeniper shivered, furious with herself for getting into this situation. She huddled into the mining car's seat and sighed. The last few hours had been unbelievable.

When Jonik left, he'd warned her to wait at least half an hour before heading back to Canberra. He'd thought someone was following him, and he didn't want them following her, too. By the time thirty minutes had expired, snow was falling so hard she couldn't see past the cave's overhang. She saw no point in trying to find the office building, much less the car. The blowing snow would have her disoriented in less than a minute, and she couldn't possibly stand more than a few minutes in the frigid air with the thin coat she'd brought.

Since caves maintained a constant temperature, she went back in and settled into the car. She could only hope Rieka would forgive her once she did return.

"If I ever get out of here," she told the cave, her voice echoed down the winding tunnel, "I'm going to soak in a hot bath until my bones melt."

She looked at her wrist chrono. She'd been stuck here for over two hours. Thirty minutes had passed since the last time she'd checked outside. She flexed her stiff muscles and climbed out of the car.

The snow wasn't quite as bad, now. She thought she could distinguish the building's outside security light in the eerie darkness. Her feet would be frozen by the time she got there, but Jeniper knew she had no other choice. The console had to have EarthCom access. She needed to call for help.

No longer disconcerted by the curtain, Jeniper pushed through the last layer, then stopped. Something had moved. A dark, lumpy shape. The light turned it into a man's silhouette. It lurched toward her.

Not knowing what else to do, Jeniper clutched Jonik's bag and retreated to the cave. Though she'd been struck there for hours, she couldn't decide on a decent hiding place. Finally, she dropped the bag onto the floor of a car and hurried farther down the cave, where she could conceal herself around the first winding turn.

Pressing against the rock, Jeniper heard a noise from above. The cavern distorted everything, but she distinctly made out the sound of footsteps. Whoever it was had come inside.

"Jeniper? It's—" the person's shout had been so loud, the rest of the sentence became drowned out in the echo.

Her breath caught. They knew her name. She looked around frantically and found a shadowy niche. Silently, she eased into it. What else had they said? she wondered. Could it be Jonik, worried that she hadn't made it back to Canberra?

The sound of footsteps came closer. The person came around the corner and she shrank back against the wall, ignoring a rock as it pressed into her back.

The figure held something and turned it directly toward her. It stepped closer. Clad in a parka that covered most of its face, she couldn't even tell the person's gender, but she guessed it to be a man. "Jeniper?"

Whoever it was knew her, and the voice wasn't Jonik's. The object in his hand didn't look like a maitu, but it could be some other type of weapon. She realized Jonik's influence on her when she wondered if her assailant intended to kill her here, or take her someplace else, then do it.

She willed herself to stay calm. What would Rieka do in such a situation? Jeniper had no idea, but she knew she couldn't give up Jonik's treasure without a fight.

Pushing off the wall, Jeniper plowed into the stranger. They spun together for a brief moment, and she jerked away, hoping to run back up toward the entrance. But a hand reached out and caught her arm.

"Jen?"

Thrown off-balance on the uneven surface, Jeniper teetered before she fell. She thought she might still get away until she realized her attacker hadn't let go. They crashed together onto the tunnel's hard floor, the blow knocking the air from her lungs.

"Jeniper? *Shadana,* are you all right?" Robet tugged the parka's hood away from his face and looked down at her. "Why did you run like that?"

Her wide-eyed expression was incredulous. "Robet?" she asked, gasping for breath, "Captain DeVark? Why didn't you say who you were?"

"I did when I came in the cave. And I meant to again just now—but then you hit me." Suddenly conscious of their intimate position, he rolled off her and sat up. Not that he minded the body contact, but this was neither the time nor place. "Are you all right?" he repeated, pushing himself to his feet.

"I think so," she answered warily, scrambling off the ground. "Did you . . . did you just call me your *shadana*?"

Robet helped her steady herself on the uneven terrain. The word had come out unbidden. "Yes. I did," he admitted wincing at how contrite he sounded. "And I beg your pardon, Jeniper. I have no right to lay claim on you. It was . . . disrespectful. And I apologize."

To his amazement, she lifted a hand and caressed his cheek with cool fingers. "Perhaps it was—wishful thinking?"

Even in the tunnel's dim light, he could see her bibbets darken. He had to stop himself from following up on the urge to kiss them. He focused on her eyes, instead. "Perhaps."

Her expression softened, and she leaned closer. Slowly, he brought his lips to hers, brushing them gently, waiting for Jeniper to respond.

When she did, Robet thought he might never again experience such joy. Since he'd played at loving so many women before, this reality overwhelmed him. Somehow, she had become more valuable to him than his life.

"Jen, Jen," he whispered, nuzzling her bibbets, relishing how they thickened under his cheek. "I thought I'd never find you. Don't ever scare me like that again."

"I won't. I promise." Suddenly, she pulled back from his embrace, and he saw fear replace the passion in her eyes. "We've got to get out of here."

Robet nodded. "I told Rieka I'd bring you back to New SubDenver as soon as I found you." He'd almost switched on his TC when she stopped him.

"I have to get something first."

"What?"

"It's not far," she said, catching his hand and pulling him back up the tunnel. "I dropped it in one of the cars."

He followed and watched as she pulled a small knapsack from beneath a seat.

"What's in there?"

"I'm not exactly sure, but it's very important to my brother." Hugging it to her side, she turned to him and nodded. Less than a minute later, they were standing in the embassy's InterMAT station in New SubDenver.

Robet tugged off his thermal parka as they left the chamber. He turned down the hallway to Rieka's office. Jeniper turned the other way.

"I want to stop at my apartment, first," she explained with a shy smile. "I need a cup of *colan*—and I'm a mess."

Robet hesitated only a second before nodding. "Okay. Take this for me?" He handed her his coat. She took it, silently promising they'd be alone later when he went to retrieve it.

EIGHTEEN

Gundah woke to the sound of her comm console beeping. She lifted her head from the pallet and sniffed disapprovingly at both the noise and the darkness. Cimpa had billeted them in the subterranean city called Johannesburg, and despite the light she'd left on, the sense of being underground disturbed her.

Pulling herself to her feet, Gundah stretched before padding to the console. If Cimpa required her services at this hour, she'd never get any sleep. Sometimes she wondered why she didn't kill him and be done with it. She flipped the toggle. "Adjutant Gundah."

Gellath's face appeared on the small screen. "I am uneasy," she began without preamble. "We left Earth orbit three hours ago. The *Prospectus* arrived yesterday and doesn't look as if it's planning to go anywhere."

"Yes, I know," Gundah told her. "I made some inquiries on Cimpa's behalf this afternoon. The ship has a mechanical problem and is awaiting parts."

Gellath snorted. "You do not think this is suspicious?"

Gundah sighed tiredly. "I hardly think a malfunctioning Fleet ship is going to alter our plans. All you need do is rendezvous with the *Barnel* and *Garner* at the appointed place and time. Gimbish will provide you with my instructions, then."

"You are sure we can put an end to Humanity's association with the Commonwealth?"

"Very sure," Gundah replied, curling her black lips into a toothy smile. She sobered quickly, and added, "Do not try to contact me again unless there is an emergency. Gundah, out."

She shut down the console and the room again plunged into darkness. After thumping her pallet until it felt comfortable, Gundah relaxed against the firm support. Gellath's worries were completely unwarranted. The plan had been moving along with great precision and would continue to do so. Very soon, Tarrik would fulfill his part of their bargain, and she'd have the means to destroy the Human race.

When the Reaffirmation failed to be the entertainment spectacular the ads implied, a shadow would cloud Earth's image. Rieka Degahv would founder helplessly for months trying to recover from her naive notions of a productive homeworld. She would be so busy making amends, she would never suspect the ceremony's sabotage might have been a decoy.

Heaving a contented sigh at her foresight, Gundah slid a paw under her cheek. The only thing she hadn't yet decided on was what to do with that vermin, RadiMo.

"What do you mean you left her in the corridor?" Rieka snapped in disbelief. She gripped the arms of her chair and glared across her desk at Robet. Jeniper had been gone for almost twenty hours, and his behavior was completely nonchalant. Exasperated, she said, "I asked you to bring her directly to me, Robet. What were you thinking?"

"That she needed a few minutes to herself," he said, then settled into one of the chairs in front of her desk.

"Well, I suggest you redefine your priorities. Fast."

"There's no point in getting upset," Robet advised. "She's fine. She'll be here in a minute."

"Good." Rieka paused, hoping to control her frustration. "Thank you. And I am not upset. I am . . . disappointed." She heaved a disgruntled sigh. "I expected you to do something and you—"

"Maybe we should clear up that little gray area, Rieka," he said, suddenly on the offensive. "I have orders given to me by Nason to stay here and maintain peace and security until he tells me otherwise."

Surprised by his comeback, Rieka frowned. She pushed out of her chair and came around the desk to sit next to him. "Robet," she began in the calmest tone she could muster, "I appreciate both Nason's orders and you're being here. But what you're forgetting is a Herald's request takes top priority in an emergency situation. And we both considered Jeniper's disappearance an emergency. If this were any other planet, you'd have coordinated with the established authorities. But we're still hiring our peace officers and the resident population is less than a million people. The hierarchy simply isn't set up yet."

"There's no emergency situation," he told her adamantly. "And unless one does occur, I'm not taking orders from you. Possibly not even then."

Rieka bit her tongue to keep from saying things she'd later regret. She wished Triscoe were here, or Setana. Then she might begin to understand what had made her Aurian friend suddenly belligerent.

"Great. Have it your way. And the next time—" The door opened, and Jeniper appeared, effectively cutting her off. "Jeniper. Come in. Are you all right?"

"I'm fine, thank you, Rieka." Jeniper took a few tentative steps into the office. "I need to apologize for my leaving so suddenly. I would have returned sooner . . . but the weather complicated things."

The look on Jeniper's face told Rieka her problems were more than weather-related. "Accepted," she replied easily. "What don't we make ourselves comfortable." She gestured for everyone, including Wang to adjourn to an alcove in her office she called the "sitting room."

Robet and Jeniper sat together on the sofa. "Okay," Rieka began, after settling in the chair next to Wang, "now that we've established that everybody's fine . . ."

"I need to explain," Jeniper blurted. "I haven't been honest with all of you and it's . . . it's gotten to a point where I can't keep it to myself anymore."

A dozen nightmarish ideas swam in Rieka's head, including one that said she'd allowed herself to be manipulated. Again. She watched Jeniper's bibbets fluctuate. They darkened and lightened, then thickened slightly. She looked at Robet, who placed his hand in hers. "Do you know about this?" she asked him.

Robet swiveled his jaw, and he looked both insulted and angry. Rieka felt Wang tense, but Jeniper held up her free hand, and softly said, "No, he doesn't. Nobody knows anything about this. Please. Just let me tell you and . . ."

"And what?"

"And then accept my resignation."

Rieka sat up straighter. That remark had come out of nowhere. "I'll decide that once I've heard your story."

Jeniper took a deep breath. "It started the same day you hired me," she began, glancing once to meet Rieka's gaze, but mostly focusing on the floor. "My brother Jonik is—basically a good person. But he's made a lot of bad decisions in his life. He came to me for money, and I wouldn't give him any. He warned me that someone might come after *me* if he didn't repay the loan."

"Why didn't you say something?" Wang asked.

"I didn't believe him. And Rieka had just offered me the job. I thought the situation would turn out to be nothing."

"But it didn't," Rieka added softly.

"No. It was just the beginning. When we arrived for the inauguration, Jonik had already sent me a message, here, on Earth. He'd asked me to meet him in an old mining town outside of Canberra that's been renovated for tourists."

"Bywong," Robet supplied.

"Yes. When I went there, the place was deserted. But Jonik had sent another message warning me to be extremely careful. He wouldn't supply the name, but he did say that this person was ready to make good on her threats." She sighed. "Two days later, you told us about your mother—how you thought she meant to hurt, maybe kill you." Jeniper glanced at Rieka then away again.

"I remember," Rieka said, strangely enthralled with Jeniper's story. "And so you thought he was mixed up with her." Knowing Candace, the idea wasn't so far-fetched as Jeniper seemed to think.

She nodded. "Then RadiMo disappeared, and we went to Yona. And that accident happened, and I thought it was my fault. We all would have died if it hadn't been for Captain Marteen. I keep thinking—" Jeniper stopped speaking when her voice cracked. Robet slid an arm around her shoulders.

"It's all right, Jeniper," she said gently, handing her a tissue from the container next to her chair. "Can you tell me the rest?"

"When we came back . . ." She sniffed and blew her nose. "When we came back, Jonik was here. I got another message to meet him. I thought it wouldn't take long, so I went. I needed to see him."

"Of course you did," Rieka agreed. "He's your brother."

"Jonik isn't working for Candace Degahv, or any of the companies she owns. He told me he owes a great deal of money, nearly a hundred thousand credits, to an Oph named Gundah."

Wang perked up at the name. "Gundah? The Oph adjutant?"

"I don't know—he didn't know. But *I* think it must be. Gundah was the one who told me about the *skiff* on Yona. Maybe she somehow—"

"—set us up," Rieka finished. "Dammit." She frowned and raked her fingers through her hair. "I can't believe I could have been so blind. I was so focused on Candace, I didn't even consider another angle."

A wave of confusion and guilt washed over her as it had when she'd been arrested for treason. Then as now, she'd done all the appropriate things, made the correct decisions, but it hadn't been enough. The Procyons' machinations had nearly toppled the Commonwealth. She had no idea whether Candace and Gundah were working together, nor could she guess their ultimate goal. But she did know they were shrewd individuals who thought nothing of using treachery to get what they wanted.

"You couldn't have known," Robet told her. "And this might tie in to the reason the *Prospectus* is still in orbit."

She looked at him and noticed his bibbets darken slightly. "Yes, it could."

Wang cleared his throat. "Would somebody like to explain that?"

Rieka waited for Robet to nod before she answered the question. "The Fleet has intercepted illegal transmissions between Oph, Earth, Yadra, and some of its ships. Until they figure out what's going on, one Fleet ship has been assigned to remain at those planets. The *Prospectus* is not awaiting parts from Dani."

She let Wang digest that information and tried to see the situation from a new perspective. She had always known Humans were considered the dregs of Commonwealth society, no matter who claimed otherwise. She had earned respect as a Fleet captain, but even that rank had not exempted her from the undercurrent of xenophobia that prevailed.

She'd been so busy on her crusade for Human equality, she hadn't realized someone might actually take a stand to defend the status quo. And the time to strike was when Earth presented itself as a productive member world. More than once, she'd wondered if the Reaffirmation was being sabotaged and ignored those thoughts as paranoid. Now, she realized her instincts had been right.

While Wang asked Robet a few more questions, she let her military training kick in. They needed to define the enemy and design a suitable counteroffensive.

"Where's Jonik now?" she asked. "We need to get him here so he can be protected."

Jeniper shook her head. "I don't know. He left just before the snow began falling. He wouldn't say where he was going."

"We need to find him. I'll leave that to you, Wang-Chi." He nodded, and Rieka looked at Jeniper. "Do we know when Cimpa is arriving?"

"I think they're already here," she said. "His entourage planned some tours for tomorrow. They'll be in Damascus before the ceremony. They leave for Oph as soon as it's over. He's reserved eight or ten seats. Gundah is probably attending with him."

"I'd bet on it," Rieka agreed, "but as things stand now, our hands are tied. We can't detain her without proof. And we need to know who's working with her."

"I can access her financial record," Wang said. "It might help determine if she's the right individual."

"Is that legal?" Robet asked.

Wang shrugged. "Not . . . necessarily."

"We need some kind of implicating evidence before we can have her arrested," Rieka told him. Wang simply grinned, so she looked at Robet. "You'll look the other way on this?"

He squeezed Jeniper's shoulder and nodded. "I wasn't even here."

"Good." Rieka felt her anxiety level drop a hair. Despite whatever had bothered Robet before, at least he was willing to cooperate. "Who knows, maybe we'll untangle all of this and the Reaffirmation will be a success."

"Yeah." Wang smiled rakishly. "And RadiMo will show up, too. And Candace will recant her wicked ways. And—"

"—and I can see I'm not the only one who can dole out sarcasm."

Rieka sat behind her desk and massaged her forehead with her fingertips. After a long argument, she'd convinced Jeniper to stay on the job, at least temporarily. But her Aurian adjutant's self-confidence had dropped considerably. Even with Robet's emotional support, she wasn't sure Jeniper could defeat the personal demons that still surrounded her. If she couldn't, Rieka knew she would have to let her go.

The console screen activated, and Jeniper's face appeared. "Are you free, Herald? You have a visitor."

Friend or foe? she wanted to ask, but stopped herself just in time. Jeniper offered the information before she had a chance to reword the question.

"It's Admiral Nason."

She frowned. With Nason, one could never predict the objective. "Send him in, Jeniper. And bring some refreshments, please."

"Yes, ma'am."

Rieka had barely enough time to take a deep breath before the admiral marched in the door. He stopped, looked around, then smiled at her. "The job suits you, Herald. You're looking well."

Rising, Rieka shook her head. "I look as though I've pulled a double shift, sir, and you know it." Jeniper entered, pushing a small cart. "Just leave that by the sofa, Jen. Thank you."

Jeniper nodded and left.

"Come in, Admiral. Sit down. Have a cup of *colan* and tell me what brings you here."

Nason nodded and sat. Rieka retrieved a mug from the cart and filled it with the strong-smelling brew. After handing it to him, she poured herself a cup and eased onto a chair so she could face her old boss.

"So, tell me what's gone wrong, now," she said.

Nason chuckled. "I told you I was coming to make a speech at the Reaffirmation. What makes you think anything is wrong?"

"Admiral, I probably shouldn't admit this, but I will. I can read bibbets pretty well. Even yours. As a captain, I picked up a lot of information by reading bibbets. You're controlling yours the best you can, right now," she said, knowing he respected her frankness. "They haven't fluctuated since you came in this room." She leaned forward, her elbows resting on her knees. "That tells me two things. One—you have news. And two—it's bad."

Rieka leaned back against the cushion. "Am I right?" she asked.

Nason pinched at his well-trimmed beard with his thumb and index finger. "First Setana and now you," he murmured.

"What?"

"Individuals—women—who can somehow manage to read me like a book," he admitted. "It's uncanny. And you aren't even Indran."

Rieka chuckled and set her cup down. "I shall be gracious, Admiral, and take that as a compliment."

"So intended. And now that we've shared a few pleasantries, I'm sure you want me to get to the point of my visit."

Rieka smiled tightly and nodded. "I assume this has something to do with those illegal transmissions."

"Unfortunately, yes." Nason took another sip of *colan* and set his mug on the table. "Robet DeVark did show you my communiqué, did he not?" She nodded. "We're still unable to decode them."

"Nothing's been sent recently from here. If it had, Wang would have pinpointed the source, and we'd have someone in custody."

"Wang?" Nason asked.

"Hong Wang-Chi is his full name. My bodyguard and all-around security man. He's in his office now, working on a project. Otherwise, he'd be sitting here making you nervous."

"He's that intimidating?"

"He's that big," she told him. They shared a smile. "Since Wang's people haven't intercepted any illegally coded messages, incoming or outgoing, do you think someone is getting nervous?"

"I wouldn't begin to speculate," Nason said. "All questionable communications stopped abruptly once the Fleet ships in orbit were given CO-3. As much as I would like to think we've put an end to whatever was going on—I sincerely doubt it."

"You're right," Rieka agreed. She considered telling him about Jeniper's brother and Gundah, but decided against it. There wasn't any evidence to connect them to this odd situation, yet, and it would only serve to complicate matters.

The desk console sounded. "Excuse me." He nodded as she got up and went to the desk. She pressed the appropriate spot and Jeniper's concerned face appeared.

"Sorry to interrupt," the Aurian began. "Herald Marteen and Captain DeVark are here. You have a dinner engagement in ten minutes."

"Damn, I forgot. Thanks, Jeniper. Could you access my apartment and see what I've got to wear that's appropriate. And send the Herald and captain in."

"Of course."

Rieka switched off the console and looked at Nason. "Would you care to join me for dinner, Admiral? I'm hosting an intimate dinner for seventy of the Commonwealth's finest business and social leaders."

He chuckled at her facetious tone. "Thank you, Rieka. I'm sure that would be refreshing. Most of my social engagements are with stodgy old Fleet types."

"I beg your pardon, sir?" Robet said as he followed Setana Marteen into the room.

The admiral stood. "Present company excluded, Captain." They exchanged salutes, then Nason turned toward the Indran Herald. "You're looking lovely as ever, Setana," he said, offering her his palms. "Is Ker here, too? I haven't played a decent hand of Cranbonie in months."

"He's coming on the *Providence*," she replied. Rieka detected more than a trace of amusement in her tone. Apparently Ker was an easy mark when it came to Cranbonie.

As long as I've got the three of you here, the admiral said, "I suppose I should present my news."

Rieka came around the desk to stand near Setana. "I was wondering when you'd get around to it."

Nason smiled gallantly and inclined his head. "Officially, I'm here to represent the Fleet at the Reaffirmation ceremony. I'm in your office this afternoon to tell you something you've very nearly heard before." His eyes blazed with a mixture of excitement and anxiety, and his bibbets flushed slightly from pink to rose. "You may take this information and do with it what you will. But I don't want it made public knowledge."

"Of course," Rieka assured him.

Nason took a deep breath. "Just before I left Headquarters at Yadra, an astounding thing happened. I received confirmation that three Fleet ships are off their routes."

"Missing?" Robet asked, his eyes growing large.

"Perhaps. They have been *listed* as missing."

"This sounds far from coincidental," Rieka said. "Whether they're actually 'missing' or not, three ships disappearing at the same time sounds like—"

"A conspiracy," he finished. "Yes, it does. And with the additional fact that I'm about to divulge, I'm sure it will more than *sound* like one."

"What?"

"The missing ships—*Garner, Barnel,* and *Dividend,* are all captained by Ophs."

NINETEEN

The dining area's antechamber overflowed with Commonwealth personalities. They had booked three rooms at the Continental Hotel: a dining hall, a reception area with an open bar, and a quieter visiting room for private conversations. With dinner still thirty minutes away, most all the guests remained here nibbling finger food as they held their beverages in lead crystal.

Above the friendly chatter, Rieka recognized Candace's strident voice. "Of course the Earth was considered a garden spot before the Collision," her mother said. Rieka couldn't see to whom she was speaking. "But that's what I'm saying, don't you see? That it should remain a garden spot. People don't need to be immigrating to this planet simply because they're Human. Why that's the most ridiculous thing I've ever heard."

"Well I certainly don't want *you* here," Rieka grumbled under her breath.

"Do you want me to say something, dear?" Setana asked. "Shall I speak to Candace?"

"No. It'll probably just instigate a tirade on the fact that I'm so weak I can't defend myself."

She watched Setana's gentle face fold into a frown. "I am not a violent person, but I most assuredly would find pleasure in slapping her face."

Rieka laughed lightly at the image of Setana hauling off to smack her mother. "I know that feeling. And compared to you, I *am* a violent person."

Candace's voice rose again. "Unfortunately, my daughter doesn't particularly listen to my advice."

"I've had it," Rieka muttered. To Setana she said, "Be

back in a minute." Jeniper had planned this evening to show off Rieka's plans, not to have them denounced as inappropriate. She wasn't about to let Candace get away with undermining their work.

She eased through the crowd until she found her quarry and Ekatarina Volshoy, one of Earth's senators. Rieka recognized the man standing next to her as her husband, but couldn't remember his name.

"It's good to see you again, Mrs. Volshoy," Rieka said, offering her hand. "Mr. Volshoy."

The senator grasped and shook it firmly, as did her husband. "The pleasure is mine, Mrs. Degahv," she said. "I've been having a remarkable conversation with your mother."

Rieka glanced at Candace. "So I heard. From across the room. I hope you didn't take her seriously."

Her mother grimaced but Volshoy smiled softly and replied, "I . . . try not to discount anyone's opinion until I have some facts."

"As I said," Candace countered, her tone dripping superiority, "my people have amassed a great deal of evidence. I can forward that report to your office, Madam Senator, if you'd like."

"Mother, this isn't the time for your anti-Earth campaign. Please stop it," Rieka hissed at her as quietly as she could.

Whether she'd heard or not, Volshoy nodded noncommittally. "This isn't a business trip, but you may forward the information to my office on Yadra. My door is always open."

"Why thank you, Senator," Candace trilled. Rieka wanted to strangle her.

When the Volshoys moved on, Candace scanned the crowd, apparently for her next victim. "Don't do anything you and I both will regret," Rieka warned.

Her mother's eyes turned cold. "Don't threaten me. You have no idea what could happen to you."

Rieka nodded and set her jaw. "Ditto," she said. "You've been warned."

Candace went still for a moment, then noticed someone else in the crowd. "There's Senator DeWilt. Charming man. I believe I'll say hello."

As she moved off, Rieka doubted that was all she

planned to say. Glancing around, she saw Setana's concerned expression and went to join her.

"It didn't go well," Setana said.

"No."

"Dinner in twenty-four minutes," Jeniper said as she passed them.

Rieka watched Jeniper disappear through the crowd. "It won't be too soon for me," she muttered. Catching a whiff of *ciffa* dust, Rieka turned to look past Setana. "Cimpa is here? I thought his secretary had sent word he wasn't feeling well enough to come this evening."

"That was what I understood," Setana replied, angling in the direction of a small commotion. "Perhaps we'd better investigate."

Rieka saw Wang moving through the crowd from his post near the wall. "Yes. Let's go."

It took only a few seconds for them to squeeze around several guests before they found Cimpa standing in a small knot of fellow Ophs trying to face down Admiral Nason.

"What are you implying, sir? That my people seek to monopolize the hydroponics industry?"

Nason, to his credit, remained unruffled. "I haven't implied anything, Herald," he said, his smile all innocence. "I've simply asked you a question. A *hypothetical* question regarding transport of goods."

Rieka tried to say something, but Setana put a hand on her arm. Instead of speaking, she watched Cimpa's face. He didn't seem himself. He licked away foam from the corners of his mouth.

"And have you brought your *hypothesis* to all the other Heralds as well?" Cimpa demanded, adding a growl.

"I had planned on it," Nason said smiling. "You just happened to be the first Herald I've spoken to this evening."

"Vigaran!" Cimpa growled. "I will not have you defaming my people."

"I've done nothing of the kind, sir."

A female with no gemstones in her ear jewelry put a paw on Cimpa's shoulder. She spoke to him too softly for Rieka to hear, but he calmed almost immediately, so Rieka took the opportunity to jump in.

"Gentlemen, this evening we're celebrating Earth's accomplishments and its entry into the community of productive planets. We're not here to create obstacles or negative feelings. If you have something you'd like to settle, please take it outside and away from my guests."

"Of course, Herald," the female murmured as she edged her way in front of Cimpa. "I am Gundah, adjutant to Oph. The Herald is going through a difficult time. We apologize profusely for any problems we may have caused."

Rieka looked at Gundah's face and could tell the words obviously meant nothing. "Accepted," she said in a tone equally discordant. She then turned to the watery-eyed Cimpa. "Herald, I realize your journey to Earth has been tiring. Perhaps you and some of your staff would care to retire to a more comfortable room. Through those doors is a quiet sitting area. I'll make sure someone notifies you when dinner is ready."

"Very gracious, Herald," Cimpa replied. "Attend me, Grellah . . . Gundah."

Gundah looked pointedly at Rieka before she turned to follow her boss. Rieka inched to trail after them and address the issue of what had happened on Yona. She felt Setana's light touch on her arm and sighed.

"Now isn't the time, dear," the Indran Herald told her softly.

"Now is never the time." She glanced at Wang. "I want them under observation, Wang-Chi," she said quietly. "Subtly."

"I'm on it." He turned and went back to his post.

Rieka welcomed several others as she stood chatting with Nason and Setana. Then, quite suddenly, she heard her name called and turned to see her father-in-law walking toward them.

She waited while he greeted Setana, then said, "Ker, how wonderful that you could come." She purposefully extended her right hand in the characteristic Human greeting. He stared at it for a second, then shook it.

"I wouldn't miss this," he told her. "I rarely get the opportunity to see my family anymore."

"Where is Triscoe?" Setana asked.

"He sends his regards. He'll be a bit late." He studied his wife admiringly. "You are looking lovely this evening, my dear," he offered.

"I thank you for the compliment," she said.

"And you," he returned his attention to Rieka, "look quite elegant, especially wearing a Herald's insignia on your collar."

"I preferred the captain's insignia, myself," Nason interjected.

Rieka felt herself smile. Quite honestly, she thought the same thing. She ignored the admiral, however, and kept her attention on her father-in-law as he watched her carefully. "Ker, you look as if you have a request."

"True," he admitted and a dimple appeared on his cheek that reminded her of Triscoe. "I was wondering, my dear, if you might possibly be able to procure something for me."

"And what is that?" she asked, her curiosity piqued. This was a first for them.

"Well, they're very difficult to find—especially since they're only grown on Earth, you see. And after you sent the first box, I believe I really became addicted."

"The first box?" Rieka searched her memory and frowned. "You mean the macadamia nuts I sent you?"

Ker made a strange face, then sighed. "Do you remember where you got them?"

"The ones I sent were from Australia," Rieka said. "I don't know if they're grown elsewhere, right now. I'll have Jeniper look into it for you. We can probably have some here by tomorrow morning. Or, better yet, I'll see if Jeniper or one of her staff can get you a grove tour. Do you think you'd be interested in that?"

"I would be," Nason interjected. "If you've found something that makes Ker Marteen sit up and ask for more, I'd like to see where it comes from."

"Merik," Ker said, clapping him on the shoulder, "you're welcome to come along. And if you're free later, let's play a few hands of Cranbonie."

"You're on, old man," Nason said.

Candace's voice caught Rieka's attention again. Her mother had attracted a small audience just to their left. Listening to the annoying chatter, Rieka didn't think they could announce dinner one second too soon.

"Candace never gives up," Setana remarked. "I think she's insulted you haven't spent more time with her, Rieka."

"I didn't think it wise," she said.

Ker reached and touched Rieka's jawline. "This obnoxious woman with the white hair is your mother?" Rieka nodded, speechless at this unanticipated sign of affection. "Stay here," he said. "I've heard enough. I'll take care of this right now."

"No, don't—" she began. But he ignored her, and she could do nothing but stare wide-eyed as Ker walked into the fray.

Ker edged his way closer to Candace's voice.

"Of course, she was always a recalcitrant child," she trilled, batting her eyes at a particularly handsome young Aurian male. Ker didn't recognize him, but he instinctively knew the lad would be forgotten the minute he escaped Mrs. Degahv's sight. "She always did whatever she wanted—never did a thing she was told—and of course that trait has continued to this day."

"Why, Mrs. Degahv, how nice to finally meet you," Ker said, shouldering his way forward. "Ker Marteen. Triscoe's father."

For a brief moment, Candace said nothing. Then a smile blossomed on her well-preserved face. "Of course, the resemblance is uncanny." She thrust a hand at him.

Ker shook it, trying not to be offended that she hadn't extended both hands and offered an Indran greeting. His daughter-in-law had earned his respect, but he still held a particular dislike for Humans in general. He wondered if Candace Degahv would soon top the list.

"I have been meaning to speak to you," he told her, purposely keeping his voice light. "Perhaps we can go into the lounge and have a talk before dinner is announced."

He watched her swirl the orange liquid in her glass before nodding. "Certainly, Mr. Marteen. If you'll all excuse us . . ." She gestured to the young man. He stepped closer, and she patted his arm. "I'm sure I'll see you after dinner, Torry."

Watching her performance, Ker began to wonder if he'd have any appetite at all by the time they assembled at the table. Once inside the lounge, Candace walked past several members of Herald Cimpa's party, including the Herald himself, and gestured at a pair of chairs near a small fountain feeding a pool occupied by several large orange-and-white fish.

"Now, Mr. Marteen," she began once they were comfortable, "what did you wish to talk about?"

"Your daughter. Is there any other common subject?"

"I—wouldn't know."

Ker leaned back in his chair. "Perhaps I should begin by explaining that, in general, I cannot tolerate Humans. They are arrogant, selfish, and deceitful. I've known them to lie, cheat, and commit criminal acts to get what they want—with absolutely no regard for anyone who gets in their way."

"I will not sit here and be insulted by you, Mr. Marteen. I don't care whether you consider yourself family, or not." She huffed and began to push out of the chair.

Ker raised both hands innocently. "I meant no offense, madam. But I like to speak plainly. As an astute business-woman, I assumed you'd appreciate that."

When Candace neither replied, nor departed, he took it as a sign to continue. "I am *sure,*" he went on, emphasizing the last word, "you are familiar with the type I'm describing."

"Exactly what is the point of this conversation?" she asked, her voice hard and accusatory.

Ker smiled. Goading her was as much fun as he'd thought it would be. "My point, dear lady, is that nearly all of the Humans with which I've had contact are exactly as I have described, with one rather impressive exception—your daughter, Rieka."

"I don't see—"

"You needn't *see* anything, madam," Ker cut in harshly. "Simply listen and take heed. Your daughter is now the Earth Herald. She represents a planet populated by roughly one million people—hardly an impressive number. She has a great deal to do in order to see this planet gain the respect it deserves."

"But the Earth should not be repopulated to any extent," Candace interjected vehemently. "There are ten subterranean cities completed now and that is enough. Ten million people living here will not have a negative effect on the Commonwealth—or on this planet. But there are plans for over fifty *more* cities to be built. Some of them five times the size of New SubDenver. And who knows what might come after that. The effect on the economy is bound to be dramatic." She tapped her finger on the chair's arm to reinforce her point.

"What you say may be true, Mrs. Degahv. But your attitude toward what Rieka envisions for Earth—your words and actions speak against your daughter. I will not tolerate that."

"How dare you threaten me." This time Candace pushed farther out of her chair, but Ker put a hand on her arm.

"Please," he said in his sternest voice. "Sit. And listen."

Frowning, and obviously furious, Candace slowly sat back. Ker remained on guard, ready to stop her should she decide to make a quick getaway.

"Say what you want then, and have done with it," she told him, her voice steely.

He let go of her arm and nodded. "Thank you, Mrs. Degahv. As I understand it, you've been saying your piece for several days. Now it is my turn."

Ker took a breath and wondered exactly where to begin. "As I have mentioned, I do not like Humans. When I learned of my son's marriage, I was outraged. I thought he must have been insane to consider a Human for a mate. According to the media, she'd also disobeyed a direct order and attacked and destroyed a Procyon ship—thus committing a treasonous act.

"I didn't like her and I didn't trust her. That mistrust nearly cost me my life. I was present at Dani when the Procyons commandeered the *Prodigy*. In the aftermath of the assault, I met your son."

Candace, thus far giving the appearance of boredom, perked up. "Paden? You knew Paden?"

Ker nodded. "I understand you think Rieka killed him. Is that right?"

"She was responsible for his death. Yes."

Candace's steely blue eyes stopped him for a moment. Carefully, he continued the narrative. "Paden didn't trust Rieka, either. Nor did he have any faith in the Fleet's decision to drop the charges against her. I agreed to accompany him aboard the *Prodigy* and stop her before she attempted to do anything that might seem seditious."

He sighed. "I don't know how we were discovered, but

when your daughter arrived and found us held hostage by some Procyons, she traded herself for me." Ker paused, reliving the moment when he realized what Rieka had done. "In the process of negotiating with them, shots were fired and Paden was hit. He died immediately."

He watched as Candace again pursed her lips and made an oddly Human face at him. "And what exactly am I supposed to learn from your little story?" she asked coolly.

"I thought you might learn to trust your daughter, perhaps more than you did your son. She is a very capable Human. I would not say that if I didn't believe it."

"I see." She lifted her chin and looked down her nose at him.

"I don't think you do." Ker sighed and shook his head. Candace's attitude required another tactic. "It is my understanding that you are rather an astute businesswoman."

She shifted in the chair and smoothed her skirt. "That is correct."

"Then you realize that image is very important."

"Rieka's image is not my—"

"I'm not talking about hers, Mrs. Degahv," Ker interjected, leaning forward and looking directly into her eyes. "*Your* image is in jeopardy. One who speaks against a person with high ideals and commendable goals comes off looking the fool. I tell you this from personal experience."

Candace huffed. "Rieka is a child who does not comprehend the complexity of the situation she's in. She thinks that—"

"I beg to differ, madam," Ker said. "She is no child. She has served the Commonwealth nearly all her life—in the Fleet and now as Earth Herald. She knows how to get her job done. All she requires from us is a little faith."

Candace shook her head. "*You* are a fool to believe in her. She thinks that a few million Humans on Earth will cause the Commonwealth to hold *all* Humans in higher esteem."

Ker heard the musical tones signaling the dining room had opened, but Candace continued her lecture. "Trust your instincts, Prefect Marteen. Humans are contemptible creatures. Perhaps my daughter did not murder my son, but she hated him all the same. For that, she will never have my respect." She rose and turned to leave.

Ker stood and hoped he intimidated her with his size. "The same way you hate her, madam?"

Candace had the decency to look shocked before she straightened her shoulders and walked away.

Rieka leaned forward in her chair and tried to listen to everything the Aurian Senator DeWilt said, but a sense of Triscoe kept distracting her. She also felt an unwelcome sense of urgency but couldn't tell if it originated within her or her husband.

"But you do agree," Setana offered, "that the seasonal variety of produce is going to increase consumer interest throughout the Commonwealth."

"Most definitely," DeWilt agreed. "The studies I've seen of Earth's potential grain crops are phenomenal. When the workforce arrives to start achieving that potential—"

"—prices will be driven through the floor," Candace finished.

Rieka itched to kick her mother under the table. But with her target a third of the way around, it would have been too far to reach, anyway. She didn't try to hide her smile, however, when Ker shot Candace a menacing look.

"Not necessarily, Mrs. Degahv," DeWilt said. Rieka couldn't tell whether he'd missed the interchange or simply ignored it. "Our population on Aurie has been growing steadily, and we have several new colonies to support as well. If Earth hadn't been ready to be reinhabited and brought to a productive level, the Senate would now be voting to send several Fleet ships on a mission to search for a similar planet."

"Inhabited or uninhabited?" Robet asked.

"Preferably uninhabited," Senator Ekatarina Volshoy replied. "We terraformed Yadra two hundred years ago— and could terraform another world again, if necessary."

Rieka had only just met Mrs. Volshoy that day and liked her immediately. "Then a productive Earth actually fits into the Commonwealth's future plans," she said, looking pointedly at her mother.

DeWilt nodded. "Very much so. The only things in question are quality and quantity."

"Quality will not be a problem," Rieka said. "Earth, even when all seventy-two self-contained subterranean cities are completed and occupied, won't suffer from the pollution problems associated with several other Commonwealth planets. Water, earth and atmosphere are as pure now as they've ever been. Pests, both animal and vegetable, can be controlled naturally. Processing plants are under construction. As far as agriculture goes, I'd say we're ready to go."

Volshoy nodded, her smile contagious. "And we must credit the Degahv ancestors for their farsighted leadership."

Rieka accepted the compliment with a nod. Everything on Earth today had been built on their shoulders.

"I'm afraid you missed dinner, dear," Setana said.

Rieka turned and found Triscoe standing behind the chair left vacant for him. *Not funny sneaking up on me like that,* she chided.

Thought I'd try behaving like a Human husband, he replied while he smiled at the others, then said, "It's mid-morning to me, anyway."

Rieka introduced him to her distinguished tablemates, and added, "If we're through here, shall we retire to the lounge?"

Senator DeWilt deferred to his redheaded wife. Even before she nodded, Volshoy's husband pushed his chair away from the table. He helped her from her chair.

Rieka let Setana and Ker lead the way in order to have a private moment with Triscoe. They followed as far as the reception area before Robet broke off his conversation with Nason and came toward them.

"What's new?" Robet asked.

"I've learned a few things," Triscoe answered. "I take it the situation here is secure."

Rieka glanced over her shoulder to find Wang positioned near the door. He acknowledged her silent inquiry with a nod. "As secure as it's going to get," she said. "But we still don't know what's become of RadiMo. And Jeniper's got a few problems. Hopefully they'll wait until after tomorrow's Reaffirmation ceremony."

Not everyone can wait that long.

Rieka got an instant sense of Triscoe's desire. She took a breath and tried to push it away. "And . . . uh . . . Robet's got some charming news," she managed.

Totally oblivious to the heat that Rieka felt, Robet launched into the Fleet's current problems. He and Triscoe carried on a short conversation that she could barely follow.

Stop it. Almost immediately the sensation abated.

"And Nason's already had words with Cimpa—even though he didn't imply anything much," Robet concluded.

Rieka frowned as a new thought hit her. "Could be Cimpa doesn't know what's going on."

"You may be right," Triscoe agreed.

"If you are, then our prime suspect is Gundah," Robet said. "Have we got anything on her, yet?"

Rieka looked over her shoulder, again. In the relatively empty room, Wang had come close enough to hear their conversation. "Have we, Wang-Chi?"

"She's clean," Wang admitted, stepping closer. "Very clean," he amended. "Too clean. She's got three personal credit accounts and doesn't spend half of her adjutant's salary. No mate, no kids. A perfect Oph enigma."

"So you're saying this Gundah probably has inaccessible accounts?" Triscoe asked.

"I'm saying her lifestyle and documented spending habits are suspicious. She owns property that wasn't paid for by any traceable funds. She's smart enough to conduct her business in a way normal inquiries won't reach."

"That's suspect in itself," Rieka pointed out.

Triscoe frowned as he watched her, and she could tell he'd thought of something she didn't want to air, yet.

Could you say good night to your guests without appearing impolite? he asked.

Probably.

Then please do.

It didn't take as long as he thought. When Rieka finally returned to the apartment, Triscoe was lounging in a chair, scanning the news channels. He'd found nothing much to hold his interest, save a listing of available SubDenver real estate.

She came in with Hong Wang-Chi and flopped on the sofa. "I hate these shoes," she groused, kicking them off. "See you at zero-six-hundred, Wang."

"Bright and early—if that can be applied to living three hundred meters below ground level."

Triscoe said good night and watched Wang turn the corner to his room. He then picked himself up and settled next to Rieka. "How are you, love?" he whispered after kissing her cheek.

"I feel like I need about four clones of myself to get through tomorrow," she said. "I need to play hostess, tour guide, master of ceremonies—and probably five or six other things I can't even think of."

"Has Mother been of any help?"

"She's been wonderful, Triscoe." He watched her smile wistfully. "I can almost imagine what it would have been like to grow up with a real mother, myself. I couldn't have got this far—and remained sane—without her."

"Good." He reached and put a hand on her shoulder. The thin, shimmery blue material felt like nothing under his fingers. "You're tense."

"Big surprise."

"You don't need to snap, love." He turned her around and put both hands against her neck. "I'm here for at least three days. We'll sort through everything before my next tour starts." He kneaded the bands of stiff shoulder muscles. "We'll have lots of time to relax you."

Her eyes closed and she dropped her head forward as far as the muscles allowed. "Just as long as—ouch, ahh—that hurts."

Triscoe worked the spot, then pressed his lips against it. "Better?"

"Infinitely."

"You were saying?"

"I can't remember."

Her skin, her voice, her scent was intoxicating. He nuzzled her nape and kissed the back of her left ear. She turned slightly and pressed her lips against his.

Doo natti karan, Rieka.

Da nattu, Triscoe, she replied. He could tell she'd become so absorbed in emotion she hadn't even known she'd spoken Indran. Her hands slid up his arms and over his shoulders to lock behind his neck.

"Not on the sofa, I know," he whispered, easing off the cushions and bending to lift her as the door chime sounded.

Rieka stiffened and sighed. She waited until he'd set her

on her feet before grumbling, "What now? Your mother said not to expect them till late."

The chime sounded again, and Wang appeared. Triscoe watched Rieka smooth her dress and nod. Wang hit the switch to open the door.

Jeniper rushed in without preamble. "I just got this from Jonik," she told them, holding a communiqué chip in her hand. "He's been kidnapped."

TWENTY

They huddled around the console screen as Jonik Tarrik's frightened face appeared, his bibbets a dark rose. "Jeniper," he began, his voice wavering, "I need you to bring me the . . . the package I gave you for safekeeping. The person who hired me insists she needs it now."

He looked away from the camera for a moment, licked his lips and sighed. "You need to bring it to me on the Oasis. Nothing will happen if you bring it in an hour. We'll both be free to go once it's here."

His bibbets went darker. "Please don't be late, Jen. And please don't tell anyone. Anyone at all. Gundah says I won't survive any—any more reckless behavior."

The image on the screen faded. Rieka switched off the console and sighed. She knew each of the three other people in the room had his or her own ideas about what should be done. But Jonik Tarrik's plea to his sister had been nonnegotiable. No peace or Fleet officers were to be involved or he would be killed.

She dropped the plastic chip into Wang's outstretched hand. "Do you think you can get anything out of it?"

"Place of origin, probably," he said. "Maybe more. You can never tell." He dropped the chip into his pocket, then gestured to her dining table. "Conference time, Boss?"

Rieka nodded and stood. If anything, Jeniper looked even more tense than she did when she'd come in. "Jen, why don't you fix some *colan*? And maybe make yourself some tea."

"Yes. Yes, I can do that," she replied. Her bibbets fluctuated strangely as she turned and headed to the kitchen.

Rieka gestured toward the table. "Gentlemen."

Patting his pocket, Wang said, "I'll be right back."

Rieka waved him off, then sat and looked at Triscoe. "I need your cooperation on this. I think we ought to let Nason know whatever we decide to do—but the Fleet needs to appear oblivious."

"I'm not sure I understand," Triscoe answered, leaning back in his chair.

Rieka sensed him becoming defensive and knew nothing she said would satisfy him. "I'm saying the Herald's office will handle this, and the Fleet needs to be involved as backup only."

"I disagree."

"And what would you rather do, Triscoe? Make an assault on this place where Jonik says he's being held? Risk a lot of people's lives?"

"No. But certainly there is another way."

"Of course there is. I just haven't thought of it, yet." Frustrated because it would take a direct order for him to do as she asked, Rieka dropped her face into her hands and waited for the others to return.

A few moments later Jeniper set a tray of cups and a decanter on the table. "Servebot's bringing some fruit and cheese," she said softly. "I'll just go and get my tea."

By the time she returned, Wang rejoined them and reported. "The message originated on Earth and was routed through EarthCom to Jeniper's address."

"So, Gundah lied—because there's no city with that name on this planet," Jeniper said.

"Earth origin means everything both terrestrial and in orbit," Wang told her. "I verified the name: Oasis. It's one of three hydroponics labs built to support the restoration crews. It's been orbiting Earth for about 175 years. Dimensions are one kilometer by 100 meters by 100 meters. Energy is provided by a small cold-fusion system. Most of the equipment was salvaged a decade ago. It's pretty much just a shell now. The file says an Indran company bid on it last month. I don't know whether they intend to use the structure or scrap it." He shrugged. "That's all I got."

"It's enough—for now," Rieka told him. She looked at Jeniper. "I need you to tell me what's so important about the package Gundah is ransoming your brother for."

Jeniper shrugged and her bibbets paled. "I don't know.

He gave it to me in the mine just before Robet came. He'd hidden it there. I have no idea what's in it, but he said it was worth our lives."

"Apparently he was right," Triscoe offered. "Unfortunately, Gundah now holds the upper hand. Once she's had the ransom paid, do you think she'll just let your brother go?"

Jeniper paled visibly, bibbets included, and Rieka kicked Triscoe under the table. "Kidnappers like to *think* they have control at all times," she said carefully. "Trust me on this, I've had a lot of experience dealing with them."

As Triscoe bent to rub his skin, he said, "What we need is some information that can be used against Gundah. It seems to me she's one who apparently plans things out in advance. If we can get her to act on impulse, we might have an advantage."

Jeniper shook her head. "If? Might? Those aren't very substantial words, Captain. We're talking about my brother's life."

"The Human term for your attitude is 'wet blanket,' Triscoe," Rieka scolded. "We're searching for possibilities, here. We'll worry about the details later."

Jeniper drummed the table with her fingertips. "I'm supposed to be there in forty minutes. There doesn't seem like a lot of time to work out a detailed plan."

"There's plenty of time, Jen. We're going to use the *Providence* and InterMAT there rather than take a shuttle."

"We?" Triscoe inquired.

"A figure of speech," Rieka said, offering what she could only hope didn't look like a phony smile.

"But Jonik said—" Jeniper began.

"The Fleet is involved," Triscoe told her, "despite Gundah's wishes."

"But—"

"That doesn't matter," Wang cut in, stopping Jeniper's complaint with a stern look. "This Oph craves power. And for some unknown reason, she does it without craving attention, too. She had Jonik record the message in order to remain incognito. She doesn't even know we're onto her. So we'll do what she wants—but not the way she wants it.

That cuts into her power and makes her think on her feet.
Many wrong decisions are made that way."

Hoping they could capitalize on those faulty decisions,
Rieka looked at her wrist chrono. "I've got twenty-three-
twenty. Gundah expects you to show up by zero-hundred.
Let's get ready by changing out of these party clothes and
regrouping on the *Providence*. We'll talk to Nason, there,
and let him decide how visible he wants the Fleet to be."

"Sounds good," Wang agreed. He slid the communiqué
chip across the table to Jeniper and stood. "Give me five
minutes."

Rieka nodded and looked at Jeniper. "Everything will
be fine. Once we're aboard ship we'll have your whatever-
it-is scanned. Maybe that will tell us something, and we can
plan our strategy. Go get changed."

Jeniper nodded nervously. "Should I tell Robet?"

Rieka glanced once at Triscoe. "If you want to—but I'm
sure he'll find out soon enough."

"I appreciate you backing me up on this, Admiral,"
Rieka said as they strode down the corridor toward an
InterMAT station on the *Providence*.

"It seems the most logical course of action," he said.
"We can't make any kind of assault on the station—at this
point, anyway," he added.

Rieka grinned at his phraseology. "I like the way you
think. And you agree we substitute a dummy package for
the real thing? Twanabok supplied us with a metal cylinder
similar to the one Jonik Tarrik gave Jeniper. He said
they're used to transport tissue samples."

"Makes you wonder what's so special in the real one."

"Yes," she agreed, "it does. Especially since Twanabok's
scan was inconclusive."

They entered the station and found Jeniper and Wang
outside the transfer chamber. Jeniper held a small sack containing the stand-in cylinder. Two tech-pros put the finishing touches on Wang's body equipment.

"How's it rigged?" Rieka asked him.

Wang turned toward her. "The TC has been repro-
grammed to pick up both my voice and any other noise in
the room—so you'll be able to hear exactly what's happen-

ing. I've got a regulation maitu here in my pocket and a chemical packet under my shirt."

Rieka nodded and looked at Nason. "We're expecting them to disarm Wang. But they shouldn't be able to detect the smoke bomb. If there's trouble, he can activate it—thus giving us time to InterMAT him out."

"And Miss Tarrik?" Nason asked.

"Jeniper's got a signal tracer injected behind her left ear. The InterMAT is already programmed with her code."

"Then it looks like we've done all we can," Nason commented.

Rieka nodded but remained silent. More and more she felt suffocated by her Heraldship. Not long ago she'd chafed at the idea of being recalled to duty. Now, she realized how badly she wanted to do just that.

Sending two inexperienced individuals into a potentially hazardous situation was not her idea of doing all she could. Her sense of responsibility worked like a double-edged sword. If it weren't for Triscoe's *quantivasta* gift, she'd be preparing to settle the score with Gundah, herself. She could feel her adrenaline pumping at the thought and frowned in frustration.

Nason nudged her, and whispered, "It does get easier in time, Rieka. Right now, though, a smile would help more than a frown."

She forced herself to do as he asked, and said, "When did you learn to read minds?"

"I haven't," he replied. "I've been there—and it was you I sent into the fray."

"But *you* never smiled."

Nason shrugged slightly. "I didn't have the advantage of someone advising me."

Trying not to laugh, Rieka ended up snorting softly. "What's the time, Lieutenant?" she asked.

"Twenty-three-fifty-eight, Herald," he replied.

"Contact the bridge and tell Captain Marteen you're ready to transport."

Rieka left Nason to step closer to Jeniper and Wang. "No fancy heroics, understand? Just trade the bag for Jonik, and we'll get you out of there."

Jeniper nodded. Wang, however, offered a one-sided smile. "Simple plans are the best ones, Boss. See you in a few minutes." He gestured to Jeniper, and they entered the chamber.

Rieka backed away from the door and went to stand with Nason near the console. She listened to Lieutenant Kyliss's conversation with the bridge while he prepared to send his charges to New SubDenver. From there, they'd be rerouted to the Oasis, thus avoiding any suspicion of having involved the Fleet. In a moment, she heard a pop as Wang and Jeniper were sent to the orbiting station via synthetic wormhole.

Jeniper gasped when the two Ophs grabbed her and pulled the bag from her hands. One shoved a maitu against her neck and she closed her eyes, sure he meant to kill her. She realized Wang was receiving similar treatment when she heard him curse. She turned toward him as far as the guards allowed and watched as he was disarmed and pummeled when he fought back.

"Stop fighting," she yelled, her voice echoing eerily in the distance.

Remarkably, all three of them did. Her guard's pushed her forward and they began to walk down a long covered walkway made of strong, metal mesh. Dim overhead lights lit the path and disappeared in the darkness ahead. Hoping they wouldn't be separated, Jeniper listened for Wang behind her. He and his guards stayed a few paces back. She heard them struggling and wished Wang would cooperate.

Finally, they came to a junction with another walkway. When she got close enough to recognize the individual waiting for them, Jeniper took a breath and pushed her shoulders back. Her guards stopped her a short distance away from Gundah.

"Adjutant Tarrik, how nice to see you again. And who have you brought with you?"

"His name is Hong Wang-Chi," Jeniper said. "A Human on the Earth Herald's staff."

Gundah took her time as she looked him over. "Your mate?"

Jeniper decided not to dignify the question with more than a simple answer. "No." She watched as Gundah ambled toward Wang and growled at him in her throat. He looked her in the eye, but didn't move.

"He had this," one of Wang's guards said. He handed Gundah the maitu.

"That's all?" she asked.

The creature nodded and Gundah leaned close to Wang. Jeniper watched him clench his jaw when she sniffed his neck, then jerk violently when she licked him. "Take care, Human," Gundah told him. "Your life is in my paws." She punched him in the chest, sending both Wang and the guards a few steps back. "Mind yourself."

A hiss emanated from the vicinity of the blow and the three men were immediately surrounded with smoke. Jeniper watched as Gundah stepped forward and all but disappeared in the cloud. She heard clothing rip and the sound of the tape being pulled from Wang's chest. When the smoke cleared, Jeniper felt her chin quiver. Wang's shirt was in tatters and his chest raw from the chemical and tape.

Gundah waved off the guards and they stepped back a pace. "He will behave," she said.

Jeniper felt a shiver run down her spine as Gundah casually turned to scrutinize her. "And now Adjutant Tarrik, I believe you and I have some business to attend to." She reached out a paw and a guard handed her the sack.

"Where's Jonik?" she asked, hoping her voice wouldn't betray her terror.

"He is here," Gundah replied casually. Jeniper watched as she hefted the bag.

"On this station?" she persisted.

"Perhaps." Gundah's paws fumbled with the canvas material.

While Jeniper waited nervously for her to open the knapsack, she heard an odd humming sound. Odd, but familiar, she realized. She glanced away from Gundah and felt one of her *ribah* flip. Jonik stood in front of an ornately carved *skiff*.

"I told you she'd come," Jonik said, moving toward her.

"Jonik, are you all right? Is that a *skiff*?" Jeniper asked, knowing that back on the *Providence* they could hear everything being said. She wanted to touch him, but the guards held her arms immobile. Ophs, she knew, were much stronger than any other bipeds. She glanced at the two who stood beside Wang. One had a dark streak near his mouth. Blood? Had Wang actually injured an Oph?

"I'm healthy enough," Jonik said. He looked pointedly at Gundah. "For now."

"Your debt will be paid once I verify the contents of this," Gundah replied, slipping the silvery cylinder from the sack.

Wishing she knew what she hadn't truly delivered, Jeniper thought hard for something to say. "How can such a tiny thing be so important?" she asked.

"That is not your concern, Aurian," Gundah said. "My business with your family is almost complete."

Before Jeniper could respond, the *skiff* slid out into the small area formed by the intersecting walkways. RadiMo popped up from a hole and his digits began to dance over the keys.

"When the Aurians return to Earth, this creature would accompany them," the voice said.

"That wasn't exactly our deal," Gundah replied. A low growl came from her throat. "I told you to wait in the lab."

"This creature no longer trusts Adjutant Gundah of Oph, and will cease to comply with her requests."

As Gundah walked toward RadiMo, Jeniper could tell she had some difficulty with the reduced gravity. "You'll do what I tell you, you little bug, or that bitch of yours won't see her next litter."

"This would be blackmail," RadiMo's *skiff* announced.

"Yes. It would." Gundah turned the cylinder over in her paws and frowned, if that could be said of Ophs. Jeniper felt her breath catch when Gundah walked under a light to examine it more closely.

"We've given you what you wanted," Wang said quickly. "At least let RadiMo and Jeniper go."

"I do not take orders from Humans," Gundah replied, making the term sound vile. She scrutinized the metal and ran her paws over it.

Jeniper looked at Wang and saw him nod at her. He figured Gundah had realized she'd been given a phony whatever-it-was. She wondered if the *Providence* could InterMAT just the four of them back, leaving the Ophs behind, but doubted it. The guards still held her and could probably kill her in an instant.

"You all thought you were very clever, didn't you?"

Gundah said finally, turning to glare at them with yellow-ringed eyes.

Jeniper said nothing. She felt her knees weaken as the Oph approached, but thanks to the guards, remained standing. "I . . . I have no idea what you mean," she managed.

"I am insulted at both your attempt at duplicity and your underestimation of my intelligence," Gundah said easily. "Someone will die for that."

"This is an outrage," RadiMo's *skiff*-voice announced. "You assured this creature no one would be harmed by the plan."

She turned slightly and bared her teeth at him. "I hate to disillusion you, vermin, but I lied." In a movement too smooth for Jeniper to believe it could have been anything other than calculated, Gundah grabbed a maitu from the nearest guard's holster and blasted a hole through the far end of RadiMo's *skiff*.

He shrieked as the device dropped to the floor, then disappeared down a hole. Gundah's barking laugh filled the walkway, but Jeniper distinctly heard Wang say, "Boss? I think we need help."

Rieka couldn't imagine how she'd let the situation slip from bad to worse. Now, as she stood in Triscoe's conference room, staring into his worried face, the beginnings of a plan came to her. She could only hope he'd cooperate. Not daring to form the thoughts into words he'd perceive through their link, she realized she needed to get aboard the Oasis, herself.

She glanced at her companions. Nason and Setana occupied two chairs at the table, and Robet's concerned face lit the console's screen.

Gundah's voice clearly said, "You'll do what I tell you, you little bug, or that bitch of yours won't see her next litter."

"We've got to do something," Rieka insisted. "She doesn't care what's in that cylinder. She'll kill them all."

"InterMAT them here?" Setana suggested softly over Wang's voice asking Gundah to let RadiMo and Jeniper go.

"No," Triscoe said. "The guards are too close to Jeniper and Wang to separate the signals. Plus, there's a brief moment before and after transport in which the guards could discharge their weapons."

"And we need to get RadiMo out of there, too. We just have to find something to distract the guards," Rieka said, raking her fingers through her hair. Unfortunately, she had no idea what that might be.

They eavesdropped on the conversation until Gundah said, "Someone will die for that."

Rieka gasped as they heard the maitu's blast and RadiMo's terrified squeal. Then, Wang's quiet plea did something to her. She felt as if he'd drilled through a facade she'd worn and reached her true self. The urge to act overcame the conventions of her office. Lives were at stake, now, because she'd made the decision to send the fake canister.

Striding past the admiral, she sat in the chair at the console and switched on two-way communications. "Tell her I'm listening, Wang-Chi."

"No," Triscoe barked, but it was too late. They heard Wang relay the message.

"All right then," Gundah's disembodied voice replied. "I will accept that the Earth Herald is privy to this conversation. How does she wish to contribute to it?"

"Ask her what she wants," Rieka said.

Wang relayed the message. They heard Gundah's barking laugh, then she said, "I want Earth under my control, again."

"Again?" Rieka frowned and looked at Nason. He shrugged.

Setana offered, "Perhaps she's deluded herself into believing that—and your Heraldship has altered her warped perception."

Rieka shook her head and looked at Triscoe. "Somehow I doubt that. There's some kind of connection here—but I can't see it."

"However," Gundah's disembodied voice continued, "provided you bring along the genuine canister, I am willing to trade one Herald for another."

"Tell her I'll be there in ten minutes, Wang-Chi," she told him over Triscoe's loud objection. "And if she hurts anyone in the meantime, I'll destroy her merchandise."

"What do you think you're doing? You simply can't—"

It took both Nason and Setana's efforts to quiet Triscoe, but he managed to control himself long enough for them to hear Gundah's reply. "That is acceptable."

"You are Earth Herald," Triscoe insisted, pointing a long finger at her. "You cannot simply trade your life for another. The welfare of your planet rests on your shoulders."

Rieka glared at him, and she sensed the flare of his emotions, but it didn't alter her decision. "Don't tell me my responsibilities, Triscoe," she warned, slapping his finger away. "Those aren't your people being held at gunpoint."

"That would make no difference."

"The hell it wouldn't!" She pushed away from the table to put some distance between them. "You haven't lost—anything. Ever. In your whole life." She turned and glared into fierce brown eyes. "You only *think* you know the burden of responsibility."

"And you do?"

"You're damn right I do." She paused and brought herself under control. "How many people have died under your command?"

Triscoe frowned and shook his head. "That isn't fair."

"Really?" Rieka glanced at Nason. "I'm guessing fewer than twenty. on the other hand, I've lost dozens, including my brother. I'm well aware of the consequences my decisions bring, and I don't intend for anyone else to die on my account."

"That isn't fair, Rieka," Triscoe persisted.

"Maybe not. But we don't have time for discussion. Gundah expects me in nine minutes, and I've got a lot of preparing to do." Rieka glanced at Nason for support, but he simply frowned down at the table, presumably in deep thought.

She realized Triscoe and Setana were communicating silently and turned to leave them alone when Robet's voice stopped her. "I'll go instead," he announced.

Embarrassed she'd forgotten him, Rieka moved to the console. "A generous offer, my friend," she said. "But you aren't the Earth Herald."

"Is that so important?" he asked.

"Apparently. I intend to find out exactly why."

"Good luck, then. *Prospectus* out."

Rieka looked at the grim faces of her companions. Nason's bibbets fluctuated wildly. She nodded at him and hurried out the door. Triscoe's mind-voice hit her in the corridor.

Rieka stop.

No. He continued to try to talk to her, but Rieka discovered that humming to herself did a good job of drowning him out. She went to their rooms and collected the canister from the desktop. She'd almost made it back to the corridor when Triscoe arrived.

"You can't ignore me," he insisted.

"And you can't order me."

He grabbed hold of her arm when she attempted to pass him. "Have you forgotten that we are bound? That if something happens to you, I suffer as well?"

"I haven't forgotten, Triscoe. I simply don't intend to die." She pulled free of his grasp and left the room. He caught up quickly, and they took a Chute to Station Four.

"Your arrogance is astounding, Rieka. You cannot control the future," he argued. "You don't know what will happen."

"You don't trust me, do you?" she snapped.

He stood mutely for a moment as if shocked by her question. "That was uncalled for."

"I disagree," Rieka told him, hands on her hips. "I think I just hit ground zero."

The door opened, and she strode the last few meters to Station Four with him in her wake. "Lieutenant Kyliss, I need two InterMat transponders," she told the chief.

"Right away, Herald," he said, then went through a doorway opposite the chamber.

Rieka went to the console and tapped in the command to receive Wang's TC signal. She boosted the sound until she could hear Gundah speaking clearly. "Dorah, keep that rat quiet."

"Yes, Adjutant."

Triscoe stepped close and doused the volume. "We need to talk."

Kyliss returned with two small disks the size of communiqué chips. "Here you are, Herald. I've programmed your ID into this one just like I did for Jeniper's."

"Thank you," Rieka said pleasantly. She took it from

him, thinking of the best place to wear it. "And the second?"

"It's not coded."

"Okay." She clutched the second one in her palm.

"Clear the Station," Triscoe ordered. "I need to speak to Herald Degahv alone."

"Yes, sir." Kyliss nodded and left.

Rieka turned to face her Indran husband. She knew what had to be done and didn't like it any more than he did. But the emergency facing them had to take precedent over their personal needs.

"Rieka," he said, grasping her by the shoulders, "don't do this."

"Because if I die—you die?"

"I did not say that. But Gundah is like a nuclear reactor with an exposed core. We don't know when she'll blow."

Rieka shook her head. "That's a fine argument, Tris, but RadiMo doesn't stand a chance. We've still got what Gundah wants. That has to be enough reason to believe in my decision." She tugged the jumpsuit's zipper and shoved the transponder into her bra.

"Not for me."

"Because your life is at stake, too?" He said nothing, but the look in his face told Rieka all she needed to know. "All right. Then let's fix that. I've got a couple of minutes left before I'm late. Disconnect me."

He reeled back but didn't let go. "Do what?"

"You heard me, Triscoe," she said, her heart pounding. "Get out of my head. Now."

His normally pale face looked ashen. "I . . . I can't do that. I don't want to. The Singlemind is complete. Without that connection—"

"—what, precisely, will happen?" Rieka interjected. "You don't know, do you? That's because you're convinced this is the same type of Singlemind as that of a 'Gifted Pair.' Well, it isn't, Triscoe. I'm Human. I'm not a Gifted Indran. I didn't begin to understand the difference until you made me . . . get into your mind."

She paused and took a shaky breath. "If you refuse to get out of my head, then I want you to *stay* out. Can you do that?"

Staring at her as if she'd grown a third eye, he nodded. "However, that would not . . . be wise."

"I don't give a damn about what you think right now," she said, her heart aching. She'd gone this far and wasn't about to turn back. If Triscoe could actually separate himself, then maybe he'd be safe if anything did happen to her. It might not be the best idea she ever had, but they didn't have time to explore any other options.

She saw the recognition of her strategy in his eyes. "But I must protect you," he protested.

She aimed a finger at him. "That's another Indran thing we need to work on." Glancing at her wrist chrono, she added, "Another time. Take this"—she thrust the silver cylinder into his hands—"scan it again, and don't send it to the Oasis."

"But you told Gundah you'd—"

"I know what I told her. Now please, Triscoe, trust me. As soon as my signal and this one separate, InterMAT this one." She held out her hand, still holding the chip.

Looking completely dumbfounded, he nodded.

Her throat burned, but at least her eyes hadn't teared up. "Thank you," she whispered, then turned and walked smartly to the InterMAT chamber.

TWENTY-ONE

Arriving at the orbiting station with a soft pop, Rieka realized how alone she suddenly felt. With her mind as her only weapon, she thanked whatever gods might be watching that Triscoe had not called her bluff and disconnected them. Even so, she knew it had to be torture for him not to speak to her.

She moved cautiously along an enclosed catwalk structure, glancing out occasionally into the darkness and imagining the station as it once was, growing every sort of edible plant for the planet below. This place was only one of many gifts the Commonwealth had given Humanity. Rieka wondered why Gundah had chosen it.

The dimness grew brighter and the sound of distant voices became stronger. She crept quietly along the mesh flooring, wondering if the Ophs could either hear her approach or feel the vibrations as she moved.

RadiMo's *skiff*-voice sounded, a loud complaint. She heard the unmistakable sound of metal rending. Someone had discharged a maitu.

Knowing she'd run out of time, Rieka hurried on toward what she could now make out to be the junction of at least two catwalks. The gravity created by the station's spin had decreased a bit as she neared the pivot point, but she still managed to maintain contact with the grillwork under her feet.

Ignoring everything but RadiMo and his *skiff,* she took a deep breath, straightened her shoulders, and strode regally past the guards standing beside Jeniper and Wang. Gundah made some kind of growling noise, and Jonik gaped, but Rieka didn't stop until she reached the Bournese Herald.

"Herald Degahv would greet Herald RadiMo and inquire as to his health," she said.

RadiMo pulled himself up from his hole and typed on his console. "This creature is well. But the Oph, Gundah, has lied, and this creature is displeased."

"All will be well, RadiMo," Rieka said, squeezing the TC transponder in her palm.

Gundah bared her teeth. "You are *my* prisoner, Degahv," she snarled. "You will do as I say, or die."

Ignoring her, Rieka bent to examine the *skiff*'s damage. She could see sparks down one of the holes and caught a whiff of something pungent. "You will require major repairs to this unit, Herald," she said, slipping the transponder onto his console. "I am glad that this area remains undamaged."

Gundah growled again and RadiMo blinked strangely when he saw what she'd done. He typed. "It is just a machine."

"Replaceable, yes. Unlike the rest of us."

"Shoot her!" Gundah snapped angrily.

Still kneeling, Rieka looked directly at the Oph guards. All four held their weapons ready, but none of them appeared very anxious to kill a Herald. "Not a good idea, Gundah," Rieka said pleasantly, "even your men know that. If you kill me, then there's absolutely no reason why anyone would consider bargaining with you. With that hurdle crossed, there's also no reason not to move up the schedule and scrap this station early. Say, in the next few minutes. My guess is a couple of spheres ought to do it."

"You could not do this," Gundah hissed.

Rieka smiled. "Try me." She stood and took a step away from the *skiff*.

"I still have RadiMo," the Oph argued. "The Fleet ships would not attack with him aboard."

A second later, the Bournese Herald and his *skiff* were gone.

Rieka released the breath she'd held and crossed her arms over her chest. "You were saying, Gundah?"

Her nemesis growled strangely. "I accepted the trade, Human," Gundah replied, switching tactics. "You are infi-

nitely more valuable to Earth than the Bournese Herald."
Her nostrils flared and hatred was evident in her yellow-
ringed eyes. Rieka took her emotional state as a good sign
and shifted her attention to assess Jeniper, Jonik, and
Wang.

Even in the minimal light, she could see Jeniper's bibbets
had gone dark under her disheveled hair. Her powder blue
eyes were wide and uncertain, but she nodded slightly that
she hadn't been hurt. Jonik's bibbets were pale, as if in
shock. Rieka wondered if he'd been drugged.

Wang, on the other hand, had a conspicuous bruise over
one cheekbone and a swollen lip. His chest, exposed by the
shredded shirt, looked burned. Rieka couldn't tell if he'd
received any other injuries, but he seemed to be leaning
heavily on the mesh wall. Unable to tell if that was a ruse
or not, she looked him in the eye. "Wang-Chi?"

"I'm okay," he whispered hoarsely.

"Good," she replied brightly, then turned her attention
back to Gundah. "Now, Adjutant, I would like an explanation."

"I do not explain myself to Humans."

"Oh really?" Rieka uncrossed her arms. "My curiosity is
piqued. Do you happen to have a reason?"

"An Oph does not answer to a subspecies."

"I see," Rieka replied, still keeping her tone light, though
she wanted to get her hands around the Oph's throat. Gundah's reasoning might be the evidence she needed to convince others the Commonwealth harbored a double
standard. "Now, would that be subspecies as in subordinate
or—"

"As in—inferior," Gundah spat. "Deficient. Insignificant."

"Second-class?" Rieka prompted, knowing Triscoe could
hear this conversation via Wang's altered TC.

"Precisely. Humans are worthless creatures. They were
unworthy of Commonwealth aid two hundred years ago—
and they are unworthy of possessing their own planet
today."

"What an interesting statement, especially coming from
an Oph," Rieka replied. "And how, precisely, did you intend to rectify the situation? You're holding two Humans

and two Aurians hostage and everything we say is being transmitted to the *Providence*."

"I am not obligated to explain myself to you," Gundah stated, twitching her nose. "I want the container Jonik gave to his sister. The *real* container. Now." She growled again.

Refusing to be intimidated, Rieka waited until the eerie echoes died away. "Sorry. I didn't bring it with me—but I do have it," she assured Gundah quickly. "So let's say I get the canister to you. What then?"

Gundah let a moment of silence pass before she said, "Then, I will consider letting you go."

Rieka shook her head. "I'm afraid that isn't good enough."

Gundah snorted then, and Jonik stepped back. Rieka glanced at him and recognized fear in his face, his stance. She was scared, too, but didn't dare show it. Individuals like Gundah thrived on intimidation.

Gundah's black lips drew taut around her teeth, "Do nothing, Aurian," she warned. To Rieka she said, "You are your mother's daughter."

Thrown by the odd turn in the conversation, Rieka frowned. "You know Candace?"

Gundah raised her chin and grinned. "Intimately."

Triscoe had assembled his mother, Admiral Nason, and Commander Aarkmin in the InterMAT lab. They all heard the conversation unfold, each registering shock every time Rieka goaded Gundah to divulge something.

Cursing himself for honoring his wife's request, Triscoe looked at Aarkmin. "Find Candace Degahv. I want her brought here as soon as possible."

"Yes, sir." Aarkmin nodded and strode from the room.

"Do you think that's wise, dear?" Setana asked.

"Candace has been threatening Rieka since before the election. If she has some connection with Adjutant Gundah, then I want her to explain it to me—before I have her arrested."

"Do you have any evidence?" Nason asked.

"Not yet. But a high-ranking Oph with an admittedly xenophobic streak has just implicated Candace. I mean to find out exactly what is going on."

The admiral nodded, and Triscoe felt his anxiety drop a

notch. Rieka had convinced Gundah not to kill her, and Nason agreed to an inquiry. The situation didn't seem quite so out of control. Unfortunately, he wasn't sure how long that would last. Nor was he certain he could last much longer, himself. *Not* communicating with Rieka had to be the most difficult thing he'd ever done.

"And what shall we do with the cylinder?" his mother asked, gesturing beyond the lab to the innocent looking object sitting on the station's InterMAT console.

"I'm not sure. Our scans have only identified an interior chamber containing discordant strands of molecules."

"What kind of molecules?" Nason asked.

"Simple sugars . . . bases . . . Nothing, apparently."

"Gundah thinks it's something," Setana reminded them.

Nason frowned. "Do you think it *could* have been something once—and has since broken down?"

"If that is the case, then we don't lose anything by letting Gundah have it," Setana said, looking first at Triscoe, then at the admiral.

He felt his mother's scrutiny and knew some strategy was in the works as Nason asked, "Do you think that is wise?"

"I'm not sure," she admitted. "But it does present itself as a possibility."

Triscoe's TC clicked on in his ear and he held up a hand. "Marteen."

Aarkmin's voice sounded in his head. "Candace Degahv is in her quarters on Earth, Captain. In New SubDenver."

"If you've found her, then why isn't she here, Commander?"

"It is zero-two-hundred hours local time, sir. Apparently my rank was only sufficient to warrant waking her. She refuses to comply with my request."

Aware now of where Rieka got her stubborn streak, Triscoe asked, "Do you have the InterMAT coordinates to her quarters?"

"Affirmative."

"I'll access them from here. Thank you, Aarkmin. That's all for now." He terminated the link and looked pointedly at his mother. "Would you mind collecting Candace Degahv for me, Mother?" he asked. "She requires . . . motivation."

*   *   *

From his captain's chair, Robet activated communications with the *Providence,* hoping for news.

"Aarkmin here, Captain DeVark," Triscoe's EO replied.

"Any news?" he asked.

"Captain Marteen and Admiral Nason have been in conference in an InterMAT station and have asked not to be disturbed," Aarkmin offered. "Otherwise, I would put you through to them."

"I see." Robet nodded as a *ribah* flipped, silent evidence of his concern for both Rieka and Jeniper. He had infinite confidence that should either Triscoe or the admiral require his services, they would ask. He set down his cup and tried to smile at his DGI. "Thank you, Commander. If the opportunity arises, please inform the admiral that I've put my ship on standby alert."

"I will sir," she said. "*Providence,* out."

"*Prospectus,* out." Robet flipped the toggle and cut the communication. The Reaffirmation ceremony was only hours away. It would take a miracle to work through this crisis and still go forward with the celebration. Rieka, he knew, had managed a few miracles in the past. He decided to help her however he could.

Working along that idea, Robet let his thoughts slip back to the admiral. Nason had ordered him to stay here to protect Earth. Wondering just exactly what that might entail, he leaned toward his navigator.

"I want you to do a sweep of the inner planets, Pita," he said to the Aurian lieutenant. "Everything inside Mars's orbit. Go above and below the solar plane, too."

"What am I looking for, Captain?" Pita asked.

"I'm not exactly sure, Lieutenant," he answered, frowning. "Anything unusual, unexpected, out of the ordinary."

Rieka blew into her cupped hands. "Just for the sake of curiosity," she began, "is there a warmer place on this hunk of junk? I mean, your fine illumination leads me to believe the power is still on," she added, a touch of sarcasm in her tone when she referred to the dim bulbs along the ceiling.

"The manager's office is warm," Jonik volunteered. "It's one level up."

"Silence," Gundah barked. She grabbed a *maitu* from

the guard near Wang and turned it on Rieka. "I want that cylinder, now."

Rieka saw Wang stiffen as the weapon was leveled. She looked at the maitu in Gundah's paw, then at her eyes. The yellow rings had disappeared. Gundah knew exactly what she was doing.

She shrugged. "I'm not the one with the TC, Gundah," she said. "If you want to talk to the *Providence,* you'll have to use Wang to do it. And, of course, it only works if he's alive."

Gundah glared at her, but turned slightly to address Wang. "*Providence,* I am aiming a maitu at Herald Degahv. Transport the cylinder to me immediately, or I will kill one of my hostages." She waited a moment, then barked, "Well?"

Wang nodded, frowning as if trying to concentrate on what only he could hear. "Okay." He looked at Gundah. "The EO on the ship," he began slowly, "Commander Aarkmin—says that Captain Marteen has given permission to send the cylinder. But he wants to trade it for the hostages."

Rieka gritted her teeth as Gundah growled and turned the weapon on him. He pointed to his ear. "I'm only repeating what she's telling me."

"No hostages," Gundah barked.

A moment passed and Wang shook his head.

"How about two?" Rieka offered. "Send back the Tarriks. They're just excess baggage now, anyway."

Gundah took a moment to consider that option. She looked Rieka in the eye and nodded once. "All right. Tell your captain I will let them go."

"Unharmed," Rieka prodded.

"Unharmed."

Rieka watched Wang as the messages were relayed. "It's in the chamber now," he said.

"Have the guards step away from Jeniper and Jonik," Rieka told Gundah.

The Oph nodded, and they did. Fear and concern in her eyes, Jeniper looked at Rieka while she moved closer to her brother. Rieka nodded once, and Wang said, "Okay, they're ready."

A moment later, the Tarriks disappeared and, to Rieka's

amazement, Candace appeared holding Gundah's ransom. She couldn't imagine Triscoe's reasoning in sending her mother. Did he think, as she'd been wondering herself, that they were working together toward a common goal?

Gundah immediately reached forward and Candace recoiled. "Give me the canister," the Oph barked.

"I will not!" Candace countered, clutching the prize closer to her chest. "I demand an explanation."

"Why do you Humans keep insisting upon explanations when you do not control the situation?" Gundah growled ferociously and lunged.

Rieka watched, amazed, as Candace actually struggled to keep hold on the object. Gundah, of course, had little trouble wrestling it from her, but it seemed almost comical the way her mother wouldn't let go.

As Gundah held up the canister, Rieka watched its polished surface reflect the station's dim lights. "Do you have no curiosity about this, Herald?" the Oph asked.

"Not particularly."

"It contains something of yours."

That caught her attention. "Mine? Is that so?"

"Oh, yes. Your adjutant's brother owed Candace a great sum of money. We struck a deal that when he delivered this to me, I would pay the debt."

Rieka nodded. She glanced at Candace who looked as though she had no idea what Gundah was talking about. "I'm listening," she said. "And I haven't heard anything that remotely involves anything belonging to me."

Gundah grinned, if that could be said of an Oph. "I hold your children." While Rieka frowned trying to figure that out, Gundah went on. "And many more."

Her words registered, and Rieka felt her blood pressure rise. They hadn't scanned the canister to ID anything on the molecular level. "Are you telling me that's what left of—of Sati Labs? That Jonik stole my DNA and then blew up the lab to cover his tracks?"

"Actually," Gundah began, suddenly modest, "it was my plan. And it worked marvelously. No one had any idea your sample survived."

For a brief moment, Rieka found her temper difficult to control. "And what do you intend to do with it?" she managed stiffly.

"Control you. Control Earth. Until you are of no further use, that is."

For some reason, Rieka didn't believe her, but she said, "Blackmail."

"Precisely."

Thankful that Jeniper was safe, but still worried for Rieka, Robet scanned the file he'd retrieved on the Oph Adjutant. He hoped to find some clue as to why she hated Earth so much.

Lieutenant Pita shifted in his chair. "Captain?"

Robet leaned toward him. "What is it, Lieutenant?"

"You said to watch for anything out of the ordinary."

Sensing his bibbets thicken, Robet concentrated on keeping their color light. "That's right, Pita. What's the panoply picking up?"

"Well sir, it isn't exactly out of the ordinary—considering Earth's had a lot of traffic recently. But three Fleet ships have just entered the solar system, about one-point-five AUs from the sun."

Robet sat straighter. "Three ships. Are you sure?"

"Absolutely, Captain."

"Give me a tactical on the DGI. I want them identified." Pita carried out his orders and Robet watched the three-dimensional image form before him. The four inner planets appeared around the sun, their orbits traced by a blue line. Two red spots well above the solar plane blinked, indicating a pair of Fleet ships. A lone red blip appeared below.

"No response on the IDs, Captain. Maybe they're too far to pick up."

He doubted it. "Three . . . ships." He felt his jaw swivel and turned to the ensign manning the communications console. "Contact the *Providence*. I need to speak to Captain Marteen or Admiral Nason immediately."

"As we speak, sir," the woman said.

It took several seconds longer than he hoped, but finally Triscoe's face appeared, slicing the DGI's image into two sections. "Yes, Robet?"

"Tris, I think we have a situation."

"Of what sort, Captain?" Nason's unmistakable voice asked. A moment later, he stepped into the video pickup.

The camera automatically zoomed out, and Robet realized they were in an InterMAT station.

"My navigator has informed me three ships have just entered an area of less than one-point-five AUs from Sol. Their autorecognition beacons have apparently been deactivated. Could these be our missing Ophs?"

He watched Triscoe work the console adjacent to the InterMAT. Nason turned to look at the screen which displayed a two-dimensional image similar to Robet's own DGI. "It is possible, Robet," Nason admitted. "Ready your crew for combat. I'll issue further orders shortly."

"Yes, Admiral."

When the signal had been cut, Robet leaned back in his chair and took a deep breath. After the Procyon War, he never thought he'd need to fire another antimatter sphere. Now, with Earth poised to enter the Commonwealth as an equal partner, he realized Rieka had been right. Humanity and all it represented had not been universally accepted. And he would have to defend this planet and all the individuals on her against once-friendly ships.

The *Barnel*. The *Garner*. The *Dividend*. Pita would ID them soon enough, but Robet instinctively knew it had to be them.

And he knew those captains and respected them. It would not be easy to engage onetime comrades, but he would. He had sworn to protect every Commonwealth planet nearly two decades ago and had lived his life by those words.

Reminding himself to concentrate on what, rather than whom, Robet flipped a toggle on his console. The intercom lit and he spoke into the microphone. "All hands, this is the captain. We are now at red-alert status. Please man your stations and prepare for battle. This is not a drill. Repeat. This is not a drill."

Rieka wasn't precisely sure when Candace's maternal instinct switched on, but once it did, Gundah's earlier reference about their mother-daughter similarities made a whole lot of sense.

"And just who do you think you are, speaking to my daughter like that?" Candace demanded.

The Oph remained unruffled. "I have absolutely no motivation for entering into a debate with you, but since you've served me well in the past, Candace Degahv, I may let you live if you behave yourself."

"Served you well?" Candace echoed. "I have never met you—or done business with you. You must be—"

"Surely you have heard of TechLine Enterprises," Gundah said smoothly.

Rieka watched a number of expressions cross her mother's face. Confusion. Recognition. Disbelief. "Yes," she said, a dubious tone surrounding the word.

"I am TechLine," Gundah announced.

"But there are at least a dozen companies under that umbrella," Candace replied, glancing at Rieka. "No one individual could . . . Why, the combined fortune . . ."

"Is in the quadrillions of credits, yes," Gundah answered easily. "The only entities larger than myself are Extensa Communications and the Commonwealth Fleet."

"Then why risk it all for a few strands of DNA?" Rieka asked.

"Earth has been a growing ulcer for some time. I have managed, in my way, until now. And then the Procyons came along and ruined everything. You," she said, aiming her maitu again at Rieka, "must be controlled. If that is impossible, there are other less-cost-efficient ways to rectify the situation."

Rieka searched Gundah's face and saw more than a hint of evil. She glanced at Candace. Somehow, the Oph had managed to manipulate her mother who, in turn, had control of Paden. Without him as Earth Herald, Gundah had lost her bid for control of Earth. The idea was at once astonishing and absurd. The connection Rieka and Jeniper had been looking for in recent weeks seemed suddenly clear.

"You," she announced, pointing an accusing finger at Gundah. "You murdered him, not Candace."

"You're very clever," Gundah conceded, dipping her head in a small salute.

"Murdered who?" Candace inquired.

Gundah flipped an ear and her jewelry tinkled softly. "Stephen, of course. Your dear, estranged, most uncooperative husband. It was very simple, really."

"Oph ground crew," Rieka supplied. "Accident on entering the atmosphere."

"Could happen to anyone," Gundah said with a faint smile. "I'd be careful if I were you, Herald."

"You had him *killed*?" Candace demanded. "Whatever for?"

Gundah made a small gesture with the paw holding the maitu. "Because unlike you—my small, furless Human chattel—he refused to cooperate. A lesson you should learn soon, Herald."

Rieka refused to dignify that threat with a comment. But Candace huffed and glared at their captor. "I've never cooperated with you," she insisted. "I've never met you until now."

"But you've dealt with TechLine for over two decades. I fed you numbers and you reacted accordingly. Surely you recall your good fortune after the Garacci deal. I believe your investment in Aurian produce netted you enough to buy Paden's administrator's seat."

"I didn't buy his seat," Candace protested.

Gundah gestured with her paw. "For want of a better term."

"I—dear God—can that be true?" Rieka heard the distinctive sound of hysteria in her mother's voice and readied herself to spring. "I can't believe—you have manipulated me. You . . . you killed my husband. You! You . . . animal!"

In her peripheral vision, Rieka saw the maitu come up, but her attention remained on her mother, watching the signs of fear and rage gone out of control. She caught Wang's eye and before her mother could move more than a step toward Gundah, they both lunged.

Rieka saw a guard intercept Wang as she shoved Candace down, but Gundah had already fired. The blast hit Rieka in the shoulder and she heard someone shout her name before everything became shrouded in black.

TWENTY-TWO

"She's unconscious!" Triscoe gasped, raking a hand through his hair. He glanced at Nason long enough to see a concerned frown appear as his bibbets darkened, then began to pace. He tried to list every option in this scenario and their possible results, when his mother entered the InterMAT station.

"What happened?" she asked.

"It isn't good," Nason replied before Triscoe could speak. "How are things on Earth?"

"Organized chaos," she replied. "Damascus and the stadium are awaiting the influx of people—but EarthCom has complied with your request. No shuttles will be launched until you give the word. Jeniper and Ker are personally speaking to as many individuals as they can—asking for their cooperation." She sighed. "What more can we do?"

"Hopefully something," Triscoe grumbled. "Rieka's been stunned."

"Bring her back then, Triscoe. She's wearing a TC signal."

"I can't, Mother. In the moment before the signal takes its full effect, they could kill her."

"I'm not sure leaving her there is a better option," she complained.

Nason pinched at his goatee. "We'll think of something, Setana."

Triscoe's TC clicked on. "Captain to the bridge, please."

"On my way." To his companions, he said, "I'm needed on the bridge." Without waiting for the admiral's permission to leave, Triscoe hurried into the corridor.

As he eased into his chair a few moments later, Aarkmin

gestured at the DGI. "Long-range visual ID shows it's the *Garner,*" she said, indicating a ship maneuvering into orbit. "She doesn't respond to our request for communication."

"Of course not." Triscoe swiveled toward the lieutenant at the comm console. It was still the late shift and it took a moment for him to remember her name. "Stolik, ask EarthCom if the *Garner* has made contact."

"As we speak, sir," she replied and a moment later added, "negative, Captain."

"Link to the *Prospectus.*"

"On-line now, sir."

The incoming signal reorganized the DGI, splitting it in two. Robet's face looked determined but his bibbets remained pale. "Good morning, Captain DeVark," Triscoe began brightly. "From your expression, I take it the *Garner* refuses to acknowledge you, too."

"Can't believe Gimbish would turn traitor," Robet replied, shaking his head.

Triscoe frowned as a new thought hit him. He'd heard Gundah's blatant prejudice as she'd spoken to both Rieka and RadiMo. While her use of words simply disturbed him, the motivation behind them was shocking. Now, he sensed Gundah had a following larger than any of them had imagined. "Perhaps he doesn't see it that way."

"What do you mean?"

"We've been monitoring the standoff closely. Gundah's reach is far and her financial base is greater than we'd guessed. Though we don't know her reasons, she doesn't want Earth to become an equal partner. It's possible she's convinced these Oph captains they're doing the right thing."

"Against Nason's orders?"

Triscoe shrugged. "Without contact, all we can do is speculate."

Robet looked away for a moment. "My position is about thirty thousand kilometers aft of you. I'm picking up the other two ships. Looks like it's the *Dividend* and the *Barnel.* They're not talking, either."

"Are they close enough for you to tell if they've powered up their weapons systems?"

Robet nodded. "They haven't. Yet."

Triscoe turned toward Aarkmin. "Put us on full alert, Commander. I want Becker to man the weapons station."

While she made the announcement, Triscoe contacted InterMAT Station Four. "Kyliss, I need to speak to the admiral."

"Here, Captain," Nason's voice replied immediately.

"Sir, the *Garner* is now in Earth orbit. The *Barnel* and *Dividend* will arrive shortly. None respond to our hails. Perhaps you should come to the bridge."

"I appreciate the offer, Captain," Nason replied. "But the situation is better served if you remain in command. I'll commandeer a conference room on level one and coordinate things from there."

"Understood. Thank you, Admiral." Triscoe closed the channel and leaned back in his chair. Nason's decision to remain off the bridge was at once a relief and an onus. By choosing to "coordinate things," Nason had implied they would soon engage the renegade ships.

A brief moment passed and Nason reopened the intercom. "Yes, Admiral?"

"Gundah has established contact with the *Garner*," Nason said. "I think it's time to risk transporting our people out of there."

"About time, Gimbish," Gundah said, adding a small snarl as she hauled Candace out of the *Garner*'s InterMAT station.

Her cousin looked both frightened and excited, his eyes open wide enough for her to see a narrow yellow ring around his dark iris. He gestured for her to move closer.

Gundah shot Candace a lethal look. "Do not move, Human," she warned.

"I wouldn't think of it," the woman replied.

Gimbish snorted in confusion as Gundah moved toward him. "As per your order, Oasis is destroyed," he reported.

"Were the two Humans rescued?"

He nodded once. "Your request was to wait until there were no life signs aboard. They left almost the moment you did."

Gundah bared her teeth and offered him an approving growl. When he did not relax, she flipped an ear. "Something is amiss?"

"The *Barnel* and *Dividend* are approaching Earth. I cannot possibly launch an attack on the planet and defend myself against so many ships."

"Fool," Gundah whispered. "The *Barnel* and *Dividend* will fight with us, not against us."

"You neglected to mention that," Gimbish snapped, pulling himself to his full height. "It now occurs to me that you neglected to mention quite a bit."

"Whatever I choose to mention to you is everything you need to know, Gimbish," she said. "Now enough of your whining. I have much to do in the next several hours."

His lips thinned, but he nodded smartly.

"I shall need a guard for this Human," she said, gesturing toward Candace Degahv. The original plan had not included her, but when she appeared with the canister, Gundah had had to rethink her strategy. Keeping Degahv hostage made more sense than letting her go. "She and her guard will accompany me wherever I am on this ship—unless she becomes uncooperative," she added loud enough for Degahv to hear. "In that case, you may put her in one of your holding cells unless I decide to kill her."

"Understood."

She waited and watched while the captain used his TC to request a guard for Degahv. "Has my control center been outfitted as I requested?"

"Of course," Gimbish replied, looking insulted. "My people have constructed the room to your exact specifications. As soon as the guard arrives, I will take you there, if that is what you desire."

"It is," she said, glancing back at the Human who seemed to be studying both her and the captain intently.

By the time they reached her control room, Gundah realized that her stomachs were demanding food. She followed Gimbish as he toured the small facility, explaining the console functions and the DGI's abilities. The room also contained a table large enough for eight individuals and a comfortable-looking lounge area. Across the hall, Gimbish explained, were sleeping quarters for both herself and Mrs. Degahv.

"Good," Gundah said, glancing again at the console. "And this directly connects me with your station on the bridge?"

"Correct. You can communicate over the audio channel, here," he replied, gesturing to a toggle, "or via screen, here." He indicated another spot on a light-panel board. "This unit uses verbal-initiate software. No keyboard is required."

"The VI is articulate in Commonwealth Standard or Oph?"

"Both," he replied. "But you need to key in what language you're speaking before you start."

"That should be simple enough." Gundah looked around the room once more, her gaze sweeping past Degahv and the guard standing just inside the door. "This will do nicely, Captain. I expect you would like to return to your duties."

"Yes." He nodded and left.

Gundah turned her attention to the console. She sat before the computerized atoll and began familiarizing herself with each function. "Degahv," she said after listening to her stomachs rumble again, "fetch something to eat."

"I am not your lackey," the woman replied. She'd seated herself at the table without permission and looked as indignant as Gundah had ever seen a Human look. "And I imagine there are plenty in the crew just waiting to serve you." She crossed her arms over her chest. "If I have inadvertently helped you in the past, you can be sure I intend to redeem myself at the earliest opportunity."

Amused, Gundah swiveled in her chair and squinted at the creature who might still be of use in her quest for revenge. Candace Degahv appeared disheveled, but her eyes were sharp and her jaw set. "Ah. Human spirit." Gundah smiled. "That intangible thing that has kept your species going for two very long centuries. And what has it got you?" She paused for a brief moment, then said, "Can't answer for your entire race? Then how about yourself, Candace Pirez Degahv? What has your Human spirit done for you?"

The Human didn't answer, but Gundah sensed the silence was belligerent. "I'll tell you, then," Gundah went on. "Your husband died because of his 'spirit.' And your daughter will live out her life as my thrall. As for you—money, even small amounts of it such as you have, will not buy you respect. You're still an inferior species. And I have made it my personal goal to see that you either accept that—or are exterminated."

Rieka heard moaning and wondered who'd been hurt before she realized the noise was coming from her. She lifted a hand to protect her closed eyes from the invading brightness and thought she heard Setana's voice.

"I think she's coming around, Doctor. Mr. Hong, you stay right there. You've been told several times not to move."

Eyes still closed and covered, Rieka recognized Twanabok's approving hiss somewhere close to her right side. She gritted her teeth through the pins-and-needles sensation where the stun had hit her. From experience, she knew it would be gone in an hour or so.

"You're conscious," Twanabok stated as he shifted his position, moving toward her head. She felt his claws contact her still-unusable shoulder before recalibrating the light. When it dimmed, she uncovered her eyes and looked up at him.

"Everyone okay?"

"Mr. Hong has several contusions and a chemical burn on his chest. He is lucky he did not further damage his arm," Twanabok answered.

"And the others?" She watched the doctor's leathery green face meander through several subtle expressions. His pink eyes skimmed over her, then looked away. She'd been a Fleet captain long enough to interpret this indecision as bad news.

Setana stepped to her other shoulder. "Jeniper and Jonik are fine, dear," she said, straightening the blanket across Rieka's shoulders. "They're both back on Earth. Jeniper felt she needed to make arrangements for postponing the ceremony. RadiMo, of course, has been with us for some time."

"Where's Candace?"

Setana gently ran a finger along Rieka's jaw. "I'm so sorry, dear, Gundah took her."

Rieka sighed. "To keep me in line."

Twanabok took her numb hand and wrapped it around his lower arm. "Squeeze, Herald." She did as best she could, and he grumbled something unintelligible. Then he manipulated her shoulder and jabbed it in two places with a claw coated in something.

"Ow!"

"Neural transmitter," he said, attaching a small device to her upper arm. With the heat light off and his pads now registering on her skin, Rieka realized they'd removed her clothes.

Willing her expression to appear as alert as possible, she looked up into Twanabok's pink Vekyan eyes. "Does that mean I'm ambulatory? I can't stay here much longer. Where are my clothes?"

Twanabok flicked his tongue at her. "I'll authorize your release as soon as I return to my office. Your clothes are stowed in the locker. Herald Marteen has offered to help you into them."

"Why are you being so cooperative, Vort?" she asked warily.

He made a strange sound in his chest. "Nason's orders," he replied before turning away.

"Wang-Chi," Rieka called, and waited until he stood beside the bed before she spoke. "I need a TC like yours."

He looked at her skeptically. "Okay, Boss. Can I ask why?"

"Sure you can"—she glanced at Setana as she opened the clothes locker—"but you'll have to wait for your answer."

He, too, glanced at Setana. "I understand. I'll get one ready." Wang nodded once and left.

Setana turned and studied her with a strange look. "Are you planning something with Mr. Hong?"

Rieka sat up, felt the room spin for a minute, then heaved a grateful sigh as it steadied itself. Having no intention of answering Setana's question, since she would go directly to Triscoe with it, Rieka evaded the issue. Twanabok's resistance to her earlier query propelled her to ask, "You going to tell me the bad news?"

"No," Setana answered brightly. "I'll leave that to Merik."

"Then it must really be bad," she said, taking the bra Setana handed her.

"I watched the nurse remove that," her mother-in-law

remarked, deftly changing the subject. "But I'm interested to see how it goes on."

"Nothing to it," she said, slipping it around her. "Even Triscoe—well it never mind," she added diplomatically. "The jumpsuit may give me some problems, though."

Working together, they got her into the outfit. Rieka slid her feet into her boots and nodded. "Guess I'm ready. Is the admiral still aboard?"

"Yes," Setana answered. "But before you see him, RadiMo would like an audience."

"Okay," she said, nodding. Taking it slow, they left the ward and found Twanabok waiting at the doctors' med station.

"You have been placed on the board," Twanabok told her without preamble. "If you require pain relief, request it."

"Thank you, Vort." Rieka offered him a smart salute. He returned it, then shook his head and shuffled off toward his office. She turned to Setana. "Where's RadiMo?"

Setana led the way, and a few moments later CariMo greeted them at the guest room's door. "Enter, please," CariMo's *skiff*-voice said. She gestured for them to sit and carefully guided her mobile device to a position near RadiMo's.

The Bournese Herald popped up from a hole and frantically began tapping his board. "This creature would thank Herald Rieka Degahv and wishes her to know he owes her a great debt."

Just seeing his little black eyes blink at her gave Rieka a sense of relief. She sighed and nodded. Wondering if she was about to break some kind of taboo, Rieka left the couch and squatted before RadiMo's floating *skiff*. "You gave us all quite a scare, Herald RadiMo," she told him softly. "I am glad to know you are well."

"You may not be," the *skiff*-voice replied. Before she could ask what he meant, his digits danced over the console and the voice continued. "An explanation is in order."

"Yes."

"Adjutant Gundah has plans for Earth. She communicated with this creature many months ago, seeking cooperation and mutual satisfaction. In return for information about Earth subcities, Bourne received a contractual agreement to mine precious metals and gemstones."

Trying to make sense of what he'd said, she asked, "From Earth?"

"From Earth."

"But Gundah has no authority to offer such a contract." Rieka settled herself into a more comfortable position on the floor and glanced first at Setana, then CariMo. "You must have realized an Oph can't negotiate a contract from Earth."

"Gundah owns controlling shares in TechLine. TechLine owns Kaypak Corp. Kaypak holds mineral rights on three Earth continents," CariMo explained.

"Kaypak is a . . . Human-owned company," Rieka said.

"This is true," CariMo agreed.

"But Gundah owns Kaypak," RadiMo said.

Rieka felt her jaw go slack for a moment, then clamped it shut. Too stunned by Gundah's seemingly endless reach, she switched gears. "What did she want to know about the cities?"

"Their precise positions," RadiMo answered.

"And their proximity to geologic faults or other subterranean structures," added CariMo.

"Such as?"

"Caverns. Aquifers. Deposits of oil and gas. New intrusions of magma."

Rieka immediately saw the impact of such information. If Gundah was out to destroy Earth's ability to be productive, the easiest way to do it would be reducing the workforce. Destroying the underground cities by "accident" would accomplish that without suspicion.

Working hard to keep anger from her voice, she asked, "And you agreed to this in exchange for mineral access?"

"Correct," RadiMo replied.

"Did you confer with the Earth Herald before striking the deal?"

"Affirmative," CariMo said.

RadiMo made an elaborate gesture with his upper body, then attacked his console again. "Herald Alexi Degahv would offer similar access but required monetary compensation."

"I see." Rieka frowned.

"And we . . . that is . . . the Bournese tribal council voted negative to deal with Humans," added CariMo.

"For Earth rights," Rieka said, empathizing with his frustration and trying to understand their thought process. This duplicity had to be a Bournese characteristic. Alexi would have altered the deal if he'd known a second party was involved. He had warned her the Bourne were shrewd, but he hadn't anticipated them selling out Earth in order to get their paws on precious gems.

"Yes."

"So you took the easy way out. You didn't have to pay anything and you didn't have to deal with Humans."

"Precisely," CariMo's *skiff* said.

"This creature now understands that our reasoning may have been in error," RadiMo added. "The bargain did not take into account ill effects toward Humans—who are now perceived as valuable citizens. Though we chose not to do business with you, we would not wish to see you harmed."

"Thank you," Rieka said, unsure whether she believed his excuse. She glanced at Setana, then back to RadiMo. "And the agreement you did make with Alexi? What was that for?"

"This was simply a way for our presence to be uncontested. A Herald sanction is indisputable," RadiMo replied.

"I thank you for your honesty, Herald RadiMo," Rieka told him. "If you should wish to continue your business with Earth, I would request you do it only through my office."

"This would be acceptable."

"Good." She got to her feet and offered both Bournese a crooked smile. "For your protection, please remain aboard the *Providence* until Captain Marteen deems it safe to return to the planet."

"We will do this," CariMo's *skiff* said.

"Thank you. Until I return—be well."

"And you," the synthetic voices echoed.

Back in the hallway, Rieka shook her head. "Who would have guessed that 'funny little guy' would have fooled us like that."

Setana made a strange gesture with her hands. "The Bournese are very straightforward—when one asks precise questions. Apparently Alexi did not ask the right questions."

"And made some incorrect assumptions," Rieka added.

They continued walking for a few more moments, then Setana gestured toward a door. "In here," she said.

Wang stepped from a nearby Chute and joined them. "Your TC is waiting for you in the medical suite, Boss," he said.

"Thank you, Wang." Rieka turned and entered the room to find Nason ensconced at one end of a conference table. Judging by the number of discarded cups, datapads, and the like, he'd been there for some time. "Admiral, you're still here," she said lightly as she moved toward him.

"For the duration," he replied. "Sit down. Everyone." He gestured for Setana and Wang to join them. Not bothering to wait for them to comply, Nason looked at Rieka and asked. "You're better?"

"The arm's a little tingly, still. But Twanabok released me."

"Good."

Rieka read something in that singular word. She stared at him for a long moment, steeling herself to the realization. Dread and anticipation warred within her. When she managed to say the words, they didn't sound quite as unpalatable as she thought they would.

"You're going to recall me."

Nason glanced at his screen before focusing his attention on her again. "That's very possible, yes," he admitted.

"Why?"

"Several significant things have happened since you were stunned, Rieka," he began. When he glanced at Setana, Rieka saw her mother-in-law shake her head.

"What haven't you told me?"

"The abandoned station is now destroyed," Nason answered. "We transported you and Mr. Hong here only moments before it happened."

Frowning with confusion, Rieka asked, "How?"

"Gundah's escape was apparently well-planned. She and your mother are now aboard the *Garner*, captained by an Oph named Gimbish. The *Garner* destroyed the Oasis with a sphere—as I said—just seconds after we InterMATted you here."

Rieka digested that information and decided it wasn't anything she couldn't have guessed for herself. But none of that, as far as she could tell, warranted her returning to active duty. Not wanting to seem too eager, she crossed her arms over her chest and leaned back in her chair. "And?"

Nason nodded once. "And . . . the *Barnel* and *Dividend* have entered Earth orbit. They remain unresponsive to our hails and are considered hostile."

"How many loyal ships are in orbit?"

"Two right now, the *Prospectus* and *Providence*. The *New Venture* should arrive shortly. Captain Tohab has two senators aboard who are scheduled to speak at the Reaffirmation."

"So Midrin doesn't know the situation," Rieka said.

"I've just sent her an update," Nason told her. "Fortunately, we've got battle-experienced people manning all three ships."

"You're expecting shots to be fired?" Setana asked.

"I have to anticipate anything. Adjutant Gundah apparently has a plan. We don't know what it is, but with—"

"Wait." Rieka lifted her hand, indicating he should backtrack. "She only wanted the genetic material in the canister, right? And we gave her what she wanted. So what's keeping her here? The Reaffirmation? Jeniper's announced its postponement. What if I tell her to reschedule it for next year? That ought to throw off Gundah's plans."

"It may not be that simple," Nason countered. "She has a hostage and our attention. I think she wants a great deal more."

Setana sighed tiredly. "If only Cimpa was not so . . . disoriented. We might be able to get some information out of him."

"Or one of the other Heralds," Rieka added. "If Gundah struck a deal with RadiMo, she could have easily done it with anyone." Nason nodded and swiveled slightly to study his console.

"True," Setana agreed. "Perhaps I could—" She stopped and looked wide-eyed at Nason. "Merik?"

Rieka glanced back to him to discover his bibbets had darkened considerably in the moment her attention had been directed at Setana. "Admiral?" she asked, echoing her mother-in-law's concern.

Nason ignored them for a moment. He'd already switched on audio communications with the bridge. "I'm monitoring your tactical screen, Captain," he advised. "What do you make of that maneuver?"

Rieka heard Triscoe's voice reply, "They've dropped to a closer orbit and have gone geosyncranous over the Earth city, Winnipeg. It's an above-ground. Many structures pre-date the Collision."

Nason looked at Rieka. "What's in Winnipeg?"

Rieka shook her head, frantically trying to think. "Uh, it's above ground, like Triscoe said. Probably about ten thousand residents. Lots of historical landmarks." She continued to rattle off increasingly insignificant details until she couldn't recall anything else. "I . . . I don't know what she wants there."

"The kids," Wang blurted.

"The kids?" It took her a moment to realize what he meant. "The Blue Planet Future?" In a heartbeat, the faces of the children she'd met flashed across her mind. "That's right. Their Camp Future in Winnipeg."

"Are you sure?" Nason asked.

"Yes."

"Intercept that ship, Captain," Nason ordered. "Do whatever you can to get it away from the city."

"As we speak, sir," Triscoe replied. "Two minutes to intercept."

Rieka glanced at Setana. "Yillon said to beware for the children. I thought he meant the genetic material but do you think he could have—"

"Damnation!" Nason shouted, pounding his fist against the table. "We're too late. They've begun transport."

TWENTY-THREE

Triscoe watched, horrified. The *Garner* had InterMATted a number of individuals from the surface. And Gimbish had used a technique Triscoe had adopted when attacked by the *Venture* during the Procyon War. He'd called up a screen fragment during transport, a simple but effective way of moving objects while still protecting your ship. Did that mean he anticipated friendly fire?

His horror at the abduction was augmented by Rieka's frustration and rage. He'd purposely kept out of her mind, but the involuntary connection still bridged their feelings. He let her snap and squabble with Nason. If the admiral really wanted her back in uniform as he's suggested, he'd have to accept both Rieka's talents and her temperament.

"Update positions on the *Barnel* and *Dividend*," he said.

"They're closing on the *Garner,* sir," the lieutenant replied. "Still ignoring our requests for communication."

"If we knew what she wanted, we'd know how to prepare," he mumbled.

"What was that, Captain?" Nason's voice asked at his elbow.

"I was lamenting that we still do not know what Gundah wants. We thought it was the DNA. Now, it's the Human children. There isn't a pattern to follow, sir."

"You may be looking at the problem too closely," Nason advised. "This Oph has something against Earth. What, exactly, we don't know. She's managed to acquire the allegiance of three Fleet captains—and convinced them to accept her commands."

"You're saying she wants to destroy the Earth?" Triscoe

asked, bewildered. Now that he thought about it, three ships could do that job rather efficiently.

"Or something close to it," Nason replied.

"Captain," Stolik interrupted, "they've opened communications with each other."

"Can you tap into it?"

"I have," she replied, turning toward him with a strange expression on her green, Vekyan face. "It's encoded in such a way the translator won't process it. It throws the garbled transmission back at me."

"Keep trying," Triscoe told her, though he knew it probably would do them no good. Judging from the section of his DGI that maintained a muted image of the *Prospectus*'s bridge, he figured Robet's crew had drawn the same conclusion.

"Sir, they're powering up the weapons systems," Aarkmin informed him.

For a split second Triscoe wondered how to respond. "Power up, Becker," he ordered. "Repulsion screens to maximum."

"As we speak, Captain," the Human at the weapons console replied.

Robet looked into his camera, and the audio suddenly came on. "*Dividend*'s closer to me," he said. "I'll keep them busy. You take the *Barnel*."

Triscoe nodded. "Target the *Barnel*, Becker. Minimally charged spheres to start with."

"Aye, Captain." Becker bent to carry out the order, and Triscoe acknowledged the feeling of dread he'd thus far kept at bay. Having to use weapons rankled, and firing on a sister ship went against the fealthy oath he'd taken when he'd become a captain.

"Admiral," he began, "is there anything—"

"They're InterMATting again!" Aarkmin's strident voice interrupted.

Triscoe snapped his attention to his console screen and felt his heart flip. The *Garner* had transferred cargo to her companions. They were now forced to assume the children had been dispersed to all three Oph vessels. An effective shield, Triscoe realized.

"Hold your fire," Nason said. "No Fleet ship is to fire on them without my express order."

Robet's voice echoed Triscoe's as they replied in unison, "Yes, sir."

"Gods, no!" Becker's voice rang out across the bridge.

Triscoe glanced up from his small screen to the image on the DGI. All three rogue ships had just released spheres headed for the Earth's surface.

Rieka watched Nason's DGI as six spheres converged on a single spot in central North America. They disappeared in the atmosphere, but the imager compensated and she felt her heart cringe as Winnipeg ceased to exist.

Wang dropped his face in his hands, and she gripped the table, her body shuddering at the unspeakable act. "Thousands of people," she managed, her voice rough with emotion. "She's just murdered thousands of people."

Setana's face contorted, but she didn't immediately speak. "What can we do, Merik?" she finally asked, turning toward the admiral. "We can't let this continue."

From the look on his face, Rieka realized Nason was in shock. Who could prepare themselves to face such destruction? While he grappled for a reply, her mind clicked into gear. Maria and little Po's face flashed across her mind. They had to get those children back. All of them.

"Earth doesn't have a squad to handle this sort of thing." Rieka glanced at Wang. "And while the Fleet has security personnel on every ship—this situation is probably beyond anything they've ever handled."

Nason couldn't seem to pull his eyes from the screen. "Unfortunately, that's true," he said.

"So what can be done?" Setana asked.

"We can start by recalling me to active duty," Rieka told them, relieved now that the choice had been so easy.

The admiral's head snapped around. He stared at her for a brief moment before nodding decisively. "I'll process your recall immediately."

"Good."

"Is that wise, dear?" Setana asked, both concern and confusion in her voice.

"No. It's not," Wang interjected.

She shrugged. "It's necessary. That's all that matters. The way things are now, Gundah can destroy Earth piece by piece while I stand by and watch her. A Herald can do almost nothing in this situation. But a Fleet officer can, and I'm going to get those kids back, too."

She paused for a moment to think. "As my adjutant, Jeniper will have to take over my Herald's duties." Rieka glanced at her mother-in-law. "She may need some help."

"Don't worry about a thing," Setana replied.

Knowing they would not disappoint her, Rieka smiled wryly, then looked at Nason. "How long before the *New Venture* gets here?"

"Less than twenty minutes," he said. "What are you thinking?"

"I'm thinking . . . somebody needs to get aboard the *Garner* and stop Gundah before she does any more damage."

The admiral nodded. "And what role does the *New Venture* play in that objective?"

"I think there's someone aboard her who can help me do that."

Wang pulled himself straighter. "Us," he said.

"Us?"

Wang's look told her not to argue. "Herald or captain, it makes no difference. You're not going anywhere without me."

From her position at the table, Candace studied her captor. Gundah opened communications with someone via the Digital Graphics Imager. An Oph in a captain's uniform appeared three-dimensionally near the wall.

The captain curled her lip before she spoke. "What now, Gundah? A third Fleet ship is approaching the planet. I do not have time for—"

"You have as much time as I tell you, Gellath," Gundah snapped. Candace heard the ring of irritation in her voice. "We are three ships. They are three ships. But we have Human children aboard and a planet to destroy below. They will not fire on us."

"Don't be so sure."

"Humans have mush for hearts. They will not sacrifice the children," Gundah assured her.

Gellath shook her head. "The other Fleet ships are battle-experienced, too. This concerns me. My people are following orders—but I sense they are wondering about the objective."

"You have few aliens aboard and none on the bridge. Correct?" Gundah asked.

"Of course."

"Then don't worry. I will contact you when we reach the next target. Gundah out."

The screen went dark and Candace watched Gundah frown. Perhaps things weren't running as smoothly as she had led everyone to believe. Fleet captains pledged an oath to serve and protect all Commonwealth citizens. It seemed reasonable that the Oph officers might be having second thoughts. If she handled this situation correctly, Candace realized, she might do far better than simply coming out of it alive.

"That captain knows what she's talking about," Candace said from her seat at the table. "You're running a big risk taking on the likes of Captains Marteen and DeVark."

"I fail to see any point in discussing this with you," Gundah said. She gave a little snort to punctuate her annoyance.

"Have it your way."

"It is always my way," Gundah reminded her.

Sure the Oph would eventually decide to kill her, Candace taxed her mind for some strategy to delay the inevitable. If she could manage to make herself seem useful, Gundah might choose to keep her on retainer. A good plan, she decided—if the Fleet didn't elect to destroy this ship, first.

That thought inspired a roundabout strategy. "I'm sure you have everything . . . under control." She made her voice sound soothing. "I just hope you haven't left out any of the variables."

Gundah's ears pricked up ever so slightly. "Explain," she said.

Candace gestured with her long-fingered hands. "As you've already noted, we Humans know all about survival. We understand that sometimes a few people have to die in order to save many, many more."

"And you expect me to believe that?" Gundah sneered. "All you creatures do is cry about how everything must be protected from harm. Nothing is to be sacrificed." She growled deep in her throat. "It's uncivilized."

"You underestimate us. My daughter—"

"—your daughter and her father are the only Humans I have ever met with a backbone," Gundah finished. She left the console and went to the table. "Every last one of you worships money more than integrity."

Candace held herself straight, moving only her eyes to look at the Oph. "You're mistaken."

Gundah laughed and peered down at her captive. "This from you, Candace? From the Human so predictable that you have never once done something without my telling you?"

"You said that before," she replied. "And I still don't understand. I've never met you and have done very limited business with TechLine. The Garacci deal you mentioned before had nothing to do with you."

"Didn't it?" The Oph settled into the chair nearest the tray of food and began to move its contents about with an extended, lethal-looking nail.

While Gundah waited, Candace tried to find the connection. "I dealt exclusively with Auries," she replied, shrugging slightly.

"How do you make your business decisions?"

Candace considered that for a moment. She fingered her bracelet while Gundah played with her food. "The way everyone else does," she said, finally. "I watch the trends, consult the market reports, consider sales projections. . . ."

"And if the decisions prove to be wrong?"

"I either change the marketing strategy, downsize the project, or cut production entirely."

Gundah pounded the table with her paw. "Typical Human philosophy," she hissed, jaw clenched.

Surprised, Candace forced herself to sit straighter. She schooled her face into an indifferent mask. "I don't see what is wrong with that. I've built quite a large reputation based upon that philosophy."

"*Everything* is wrong with it," Gundah told her. "You are looking at the Commonwealth through a microscope. One does not get ahead by altering oneself to meet the needs of others. That is passive. That produces nothing."

She pounded the table again, but this time Candace didn't budge. "A philosophy of fools."

"I see." Candace lifted her chin. "And your philosophy?"

"I have changed the Commonwealth to meet *my* requirements," Gundah replied proudly. "You should be honored that I have decided to share this information with you."

"Oh, I am," she said. Her tone betrayed the words, and she wondered if Gundah would catch the sarcasm. "Please, go on."

Gundah studied her a moment and Candace wondered what she might be thinking. Finally the Oph tapped the table and said, "Power, not money, is the key. The two often go together, I will admit," she went on, "but *power* is the key."

Candace nodded. "And that's what you've got."

"Ahh . . . yes." Gundah squinted and sighed, giving Candace the idea this conversation went beyond the words being spoken. It was as if Gundah, despite her hatred for Humans, had chosen to take Candace under wing. "You see me commanding three starships and holding a planet for ransom and think this is the extent of my power." She threw her head back and laughed, the yellow rings visible in her eyes. "This is the beginning!"

Candace shook her head. "From my perspective, it looks rather like the end."

Gundah aimed a paw at her. "That is because your thinking is flawed, Candace Degahv. It always has been. Did I not risk my life for that canister?"

"I wouldn't say that, exactly," Candace replied.

"Fortunately, what you think is immaterial. I have the canister now. And with it I will control Humanity's destiny."

Candace leaned back in her chair. "You'll forgive me for not making that leap."

"That is because you do not know what it contains."

"I heard Rieka say it was a sample of something—from a lab that was destroyed."

"The canister contains your daughter's DNA."

Candace frowned and shook her head again. "Where do you get power from that?" she asked.

Leaning forward, Gundah snatched a bloody tidbit from

the tray and ate it. Candace tried not to watch. "Think of this, Human. The Earth Herald is the advocate of equality for her species. In the past, she has been the one to complain loudest about Human mistreatment. How ironic it would be, don't you think, for her own DNA to destroy her race?"

Realizing the canister was the angle she'd been looking for, Candace knew instinctively how to handle her captor. "Destroy it? How?" she asked, hoping she sounded both curious and interested.

Gundah wrinkled her nose and took another morsel off the tray. "Sati Labs was not the only genetic-research facility in the Commonwealth. I own another—a company I removed from the TechLine umbrella and set out on its own. My people there have assured me they can both alter and replicate a strand of Human DNA. It does not even need to be complete." Gundah smiled to herself at her cleverness.

"Go on," Candace coaxed.

"The Degahv sample will be altered and duplicated and turned over to another little company I own called Pulsar Pharmaceuticals." She stopped when she noticed Candace's confused reaction. "Surely you see where this is leading. Pulsar's main business is providing serum inoculations. It produces almost eighty percent of the vaccinations given to Human infants."

Candace fought to maintain her stoic expression. "What are you doing to do?"

"I won't hurt them," Gundah assured her. "It will take a number of years, though, using this—civilized approach. And the expense will be more than simply controlling your daughter. But I alone will eradicate the Human species and no one will ever know."

"I don't understand how you can do this," Candace persisted. "If you don't plan to harm them—?"

"The vaccine will mutate them slightly," Gundah explained. "Every Human inoculated with serum from Pulsar will be sterile."

Candace forced herself to remain aloof as she absorbed the impact of Gundah's monstrous plan. "I don't understand why you've gone to all this trouble. You could use *any* Human DNA to do that."

Gundah gobbled another morsel of flesh before she answered. "Theoretically, you are correct. But I have my reasons for proceeding with Degahv DNA."

"I'm fascinated," Candace said, leaving forward. "Why?"

"Stephen ruined my life," Gundah replied simply. "When I was still a pup, my father invited him to our home. For some reason that escapes me, he impressed my mother."

Candace nodded, remembering her tall, handsome husband. "In his youth, he was quite—impressive."

Gundah tilted her head back. "I recall he seemed large, for a Human." Her eyes wandered the room and Candace waited patiently for her to continue. "He visited frequently after that first time. Until the day my father caught my mother sniffing him."

"And that was bad?"

Gundah stared straight into her eyes. "A criminal act."

"But . . . Ophs mate for life," Candace said softly, sure Stephen hadn't provoked such an intimacy.

"Precisely." Gundah's voice grew hard. "She was banished from our clan. My father fell into a *vesch*. You would call it—depression. He took up games of chance and lost huge sums of money. Eventually, in my seventeenth season, he took his life."

"And it was Stephen's fault," Candace forced herself to say with conviction.

"Oh, yes."

Cautiously, Candace leaned over the table, and softly said, "I hated him, too. That's why Rieka thought I was behind the shuttle accident. And I can accept why you've taken this stand against Earth. I, too, believe that Humans are base, reprehensible creatures. And while your plan for the inoculations is—nothing short of genius, it will take time."

She waited for Gundah to react, but the Oph simply watched her. "And I'm sure you realize I abhor Rieka's designs for Earth. Perhaps . . ."

"Perhaps what?"

"Well, it just occurred to me . . . it might be amusing if we worked as a team."

At that, Gundah bared her teeth. "I like your choice of words, Human."

* * *

Rieka glanced at Lieutenant Kyliss and offered him a reluctant smile. Pacing across the InterMAT station did little to calm her nervousness, but it was better than talking to Triscoe. True to his promise, he'd kept out of her head, but it didn't stop him from arguing mightily that she should not go through with the plan. While she empathized with his sense of frustration, Rieka could not sympathize with his inherent fear for her safety. They both knew she would do everything possible, including laying down her life for the Humans of Earth. And now that the *Providence* had been placed in battle-ready status, Triscoe faced a similar predicament.

"*New Venture*'s within range, Captain," Kyliss told her.

"Notify the bridge, Lieutenant. We're standing by for transport." Nodding at Wang, who had stood like a statue near the console, she positioned herself in the chamber.

Wang stepped up to her shoulder. He looked good in the Fleet's colors. A black ensign stripe ran up his sleeve. "You love this, don't you?" he asked quietly.

Rieka noticed how comfortable it felt to be in uniform. She wore her captain's rank bar on the blue-and-rust tunic, but had a lieutenant's bar in her pocket that matched the bronze stripe on her sleeve. "Is it that obvious?"

She watched while he tried not to smile. "Only to someone who knows you."

She nodded. "Think of it this way, Wang-Chi, I'm much better at doing something rather than nothing. And while it might seem to you like my DNA is just a strand of molecules, to me—she's got my child. I can't turn my back on that."

Wang sighed. "Gundah's got your mother, too. She seemed genuinely surprised back there—when she found out about Stephen."

Rieka shrugged. "Candace can put on a pretty good act."

"Here we go, Captain," Kyliss said.

Rieka stood straighter. The InterMAT effect began, and in a moment she found herself standing in an identical chamber on the *New Venture*. Midrin Tohab waited for her out in the lab. Rieka smiled and saluted. "Permission to come aboard, Captain."

"Granted, Captain Herald—and Mr. Hong," Midrin replied, returning both the smile and the salute. "We're assembled in the conference room on this level." She shook her head as they moved into the corridor. "Do you really think you can do this?"

"Truthfully I have no idea," Rieka admitted. "But no one can come up with anything better."

Midrin nodded. "You'll do fine I'm sure. They won't know what hit them."

"I hope so."

The door opened to reveal four Ophs seated at the conference table. They stood and saluted her. Rieka returned the greeting and nodded to them in turn. "Good morning, Lieutenant Giffah, Lieutenant Gebrah, Lieutenant Gennath, Lieutenant Gorah."

"Captain Degahv," they replied.

She didn't correct them. Rieka then gestured to Wang. "And this is Mr. Hong."

They eyed him carefully, but said nothing.

"Let's sit down," Midrin said, gesturing toward the table. She took the end seat and Rieka sat opposite her, Wang on her right. "Now, all four of you have volunteered for this duty and the plan has been outlined to each of you. Before we brief Captain Degahv, have you any questions?"

The lieutenants shook their heads, their collective jewelry clinking pleasantly for a short moment. Rieka studied them all and wondered if any had been approached by Gundah in the past. It was possible, she decided, but unlikely. The three ships threatening to redesign the Earth's surface were captained by Ophs and had primarily Oph crews. She knew Nason was kicking himself for not noticing how the transfers and promotions had slowly trickled past him. Gundah, they'd realized belatedly, was both devious and patient.

"Before we start," Rieka said, looking each lieutenant in the eye, "I'd like to know why you volunteered for this mission. It's dangerous, and some of us might not survive."

Lieutenant Gennath, the one with the cream-colored coat, spoke first. "We are mothers," she began, gesturing toward the ornate metal symbol fused to her left ear. In it, two of the four jewel spaces contained stones. "My two sons will respect my decision to save other children. They will be taken care of by my family if I do not return."

Rieka nodded. "I appreciate the help, Lieutenant."

Lieutenant Gorah leaned closer. "You conducted my Advancement, Captain," she said. "I will always assist you whenever possible."

Honored, Rieka simply nodded. "Thank you, Gorah."

"My child grows within my body," she continued, "but our research has found that Gundah went past her prime without seeking a mate or having pups. This phenomenon can make an Oph . . ."

"Insane," Lieutenant Giffah finished. "We believe Adjutant Gundah is suffering from a disorder called Encephalostemic Syndrome. Most Oph females seek chemical therapies if they have no pups. Apparently, Gundah has not. While we are not doctors, it is plain to us that she requires medical help."

Rieka shook her head. "I'm afraid I don't understand. Gundah's behavior doesn't strike me as—insane."

Giffah's fur ruffled slightly across her shoulders. "This is a chemical imbalance," she explained. "It is difficult to explain fully. But a female with ESS appears normal in most respects. Their aberrant behavior is difficult to pinpoint. They become obsessive, deceptive, secretive . . . their desire for intercourse is heightened."

Nodding her understanding, Rieka said, "I can only vouch for the secretive aspect as of right now, but I'm guessing she's probably deceived a lot of people, too."

Lieutenant Gebrah nodded. Her spotted ears reminded Rieka of a stuffed animal she'd once had. "She must not be allowed to achieve her objective, Captain Herald. We intend to help you secure the children and the planet and take Gundah into custody so that she can be examined and treated. She is, after all, a sister Oph."

Rieka accepted their reasons and sighed. She looked down the table at Midrin. "And you're willing to let them do this."

"You're going to need all the help you can get," Midrin replied.

Rieka shot her a cantankerous look. "Thanks a lot, I think." She pulled her attention back to the four Ophs in front of her and looked them all in the eye. "Okay Lieutenants," she began, "this is a covert operation. Admiral Nason wants the hostages off those ships as soon as possible. We've got three targets and six of us. Who is taking the InterMAT detail?"

"I am," Giffah replied.

"And me," added Gebrah.

"Then we'll put you on the *Barnel* and the *Dividend.*" They nodded. "You'll just man the InterMAT stations and transport the kids off the ships. Giffah, you'll be on the *Barnel.* Send the children to the *Prospectus.* Lieutenant Gebrah, you've got the *Dividend.* Transport to the *New Venture.*"

"Gennath and Gorah—you'll be with us." She gestured at Wang and herself. "We'll start with the *Barnel.* You're going to locate the children and bring them to the InterMAT station."

"And what will you do, Captain?" Gorah asked.

"In addition to helping you, Admiral Nason has empowered me to incapacitate the ships. First, Wang and I will disable their weapons systems, then we're going to confer with their engineers."

"How will we keep in contact?" Midrin asked.

"We both have TCs," Rieka answered. "Twanabok glued one into my ear canal because we didn't have time to install it properly. Just ask for Lieutenant Dee and I should receive you."

Midrin nodded. "The admiral hasn't briefed me on what to do if something goes wrong, but I'm sure he'll—"

"Nason doesn't expect me to fail, Midrin. He'll be monitoring our progress as we go, but Gundah may have a few surprises for us. In the event that something untoward happens, I'm sure he'll issue new orders."

"You don't think he'll choose to destroy the ships, do you?" Midrin asked, visibly concerned.

Rieka blinked, surprised she'd ask such a question. Knowing the possibility existed for Nason to do just that, she diffused the suddenly tense atmosphere. "He'd better not—if he wants to stay on my good side."

TWENTY-FOUR

Rieka removed her insignia and pinned the lieutenant's bar on her tunic. She turned toward Wang. "Is it on straight?"

"I guess so."

Annoyed with his answer, she glanced at Gorah. "Is it?"

"Yes, Captain."

"Lieutenant," she corrected, lifting her arm and pointing to the bronze lieutenant's stripe running down the sleeve.

Gorah nodded once. "It's on straight, Lieutenant Dee."

The others joined them in the InterMAT station. Midrin looked anxious but determined, and the three Ophs' ears were perked up a bit more than before. "Let's get started then," she said.

Midrin turned to her InterMAT chief. "Have you coordinated with Damascus?"

"Yes, Captain," the Aurie said. "They're waiting for our signal."

"We'll be all right, Midrin," Rieka assured her, hoping her bravado wasn't transparent. "The *Barnel* won't have any idea we're from the *New Venture*. They'll think we're from Damascus. The odds are with us that Gundah's got some of her people there, waiting to wreck the ceremony. If we need you, we'll call."

Midrin's eyes met Rieka's for a moment, then she said, "Everyone have their stasis cuffs?" Rieka and the others nodded. "Good. Remember—all of you—no TC transmissions over ten seconds."

The Ophs nodded again. Wang clipped his maitu to his waistband and stepped close enough to Rieka for her to feel his warmth. She smiled. "See you in a couple of hours."

Rieka's anxiety moved up another notch as they stepped from the chamber in Damascus. The Boo ensign stationed at the InterMAT controls, who had already been briefed by Nason, saluted and stepped back out of the DGI range. Gorah signaled the ship while the other two Ophs aimed their maitus at Rieka.

"*Barnel*," an Oph lieutenant answered.

"Lieutenant Gorah, here, *Barnel*. We've got a Human in custody and thought it best to secure her aboard one of our ships. Is that acceptable?"

"I do not have the authority for such a transfer. I'll put you through to the captain," the lieutenant said.

"Stay calm," Rieka whispered.

Gorah's nod was slight as a second Oph's face appeared. "Captain Goverah," she began before he had a chance to speak, "we have taken this Human into custody. She apparently knows something of the plan and we are unsure what to do with her. Is it acceptable that we quarter her in your brig until Adjutant Gundah has a moment to decide her fate?"

"This is an unusual request, Lieutenant," Goverah said.

"True, Captain," Gorah replied. Then she began to speak in what sounded to Rieka like growls and yips. The captain nodded slowly. The name Gundah was used several times before the communication terminated.

"Well?" Rieka asked.

Gorah licked her black lips and shrugged. "An Oph that can be bought responds predictably to threats."

"You threatened him?"

"I wouldn't exactly say that, Cap—Lieutenant," Gorah replied. "I simply implied that Gundah would be displeased if anything went wrong." She turned to the Boo that had shuffled back toward the InterMAT control. "The *Barnel* will accept our transport signal."

"Good," it said. "Go now to the cliffs of Rothiwa and search for Varannah."

Rieka couldn't help but smile at Gorah's confused look. To the Boo, she said, "Let us hope Karina remains on the Rock." To Gorah she added, "Let's go," then led the way back into the chamber.

They arrived on the *Barnel* a moment later. Gorah led the way toward the station's attendant, who barked something incomprehensible. Rieka watched as Gorah nodded and gestured toward Rieka with her maitu. Then, she leisurely aimed her weapon toward the attendant and discharged it. He slumped to the floor.

"So far, so good," Rieka smiled. Gorah and Giffah bound the unconscious attendant in stasis cuffs and hauled him into the station's office.

Giffah took her place behind the controls. "I'll hold the children here until I receive confirmation from you, Dee," she said.

"We shouldn't be too long," Rieka told her while she tapped in commands on the InterMAT's auxiliary console, calling up an infrared inventory for the main hull.

"Okay. There's nothing here that points to where they've got the kids. The cargo holds read dark and cold—so my guess is they're holding them in a relatively public place. A conference room, crew's quarters—something like that. We don't even know how many there are. A dozen, at least, I'd guess. Obviously we need information, and we're not going to get it here." She opened a cabinet attached to the wall and searched through the equipment inside. She found a datapad with the power pack missing and picked it up. "Let's go."

"Where?" Gennath asked when they reached the corridor.

"Security office."

The *Barnel* had been refitted after the Procyon War, but that didn't alter its internal structure. Laid out like every other Fleet ship except the *Prodigy*, Rieka led Wang and the Ophs directly to the security office. "We all go in," she told them quietly, "but I'll do the talking. Gennath, you're with me and remember—we do this fast and loose."

A moment later, the door opened and she strode to the counter. Gesturing at the inoperative datapad, Rieka addressed the lieutenant on duty. "Engineering sends me to install an energy grid where they're holding the kids—but I didn't understand the commander. I heard the captain doesn't want to be bothered—so I figured we'd come in and ask you. Where am I supposed to set up? I can't even order up the right equipment if I don't know where to set up."

"Quad B second level dining hall," the Oph replied.

Rieka smiled. "Thanks, Lieutenant." She pretended to consult the datapad then glanced at Gennath. "Oh, sorry, Gennath. Your turn."

The lieutenant lifted her maitu and fired. While Rieka watched Gorah and Gennath secure the unconscious Oph with stasis cuffs, she asked, "You sure you haven't done this before?"

"This is too easy," Wang whispered as they approached the dining area. One Oph stood outside the door. Rieka figured there were at least two more inside.

"They're not expecting us," she replied softly. "Relax, Wang-Chi. Gorah, this time you do the honors."

Gorah moved forward. "This is the holding room, correct?" she asked.

The ensign guarding the door nodded. "We've got two more Humans to put in with them." Gorah gestured at Rieka and Wang.

The ensign stepped aside. They went through the door and stood near the menu counter. Three Ophs had positioned themselves around the room. The children had been seated at the tables and given food, probably to keep them occupied. Glancing around quickly, Rieka estimated twenty-five children were there, all wearing pajamas. She could imagine them being kidnapped from their beds and wondered what they must have thought when they found themselves aboard a Fleet ship. Judging by the noise level, Rieka wondered if they even knew they'd been kidnapped.

Two Oph guards approached, but Rieka let Gorah and Gennath handle them. Smiling, she wound her way around the table toward the third guard and recognized Maria seated nearby. The teenager seemed nervous and looked up as Rieka and Wang slowly came forward.

Sensing the girl wanted to call out to her, Rieka shook her head slightly. Maria, apparently understanding, deliberately looked down.

A glance in Gorah's direction told her they weren't yet ready to take down the guards. Quietly, she said, "Sit down, Wang."

"What?"

She pulled out a chair. "I said sit. We need to wait until there aren't any children in the cross fire."

Parking himself in the proffered chair, he grumbled, "That could take days."

She smiled at him. "You're such a comedian." Turning to a nearby child who reminded her of Po but looked a bit older, she said, "I'm Dee."

"I'm Joe."

"Guard's watching us," Wang whispered.

"It's nice to meet you, Joe," she replied, ignoring Wang. "I was wondering if you could do me a favor."

Joe looked skeptical. "I guess."

"It's nothing hard," she assured him. "Can you pass a message to the others?"

Joe shrugged. Wang tapped his fingers on the tabletop.

"Okay. Here's what you tell them: when Dee yells 'Down,' hit the deck. Do you think they'll know what that means?"

"I guess," Joe told her. He tapped a child at the next table and whispered to her, then got up and spoke to an older boy at another table.

Rieka watched the message cross the room and saw that Gorah and Gennath had positioned themselves near the other guards.

"No one's said anything to this guy, and he looks suspicious," Wang informed her.

She glanced at the guard. "I'll take care of it, right now." She stood and he reached to stop her, but Rieka was faster. "Just be ready," she told him and moved in the third guard's direction.

When she'd got close enough for a clear shot, a boy at Maria's table called out, "It's Herald Degahv!"

"No, Garret," Maria warned.

Before the Oph guard could make the connection, Rieka shouted, "Get down!"

Having received the message, most of the children complied. She aimed her maitu and fired, but the guard was moving she only hit an arm. Rieka heard the other maitus discharge while the guard scooped up the boy next to Maria.

Wang had already taken a position a few meters away, his maitu aimed steadily at the Oph.

"All clear here, Dee," she heard Gennath call.

"Understood," she replied. Keeping eye contact with the

Oph, she said, "Okay now, kids, I need you to move behind us toward the door. Can you do that?" They began to crawl away from the tables. "Your turn, Wang-Chi," Rieka said conversationally. Then, while he got himself into position, she addressed the guard and his hostage. She needed to keep him occupied so that he didn't have time to use his TC and call for help.

"Let him go."

"Not possible."

"Oh, it's entirely possible, my friend," she replied. "And it would make things so much easier."

"I have sworn not to make anything easy for you."

"You really are Herald Degahv, aren't you?" the boy persisted, apparently thrilled to be the center of attention.

Rieka sighed. She hadn't anticipated this. The Oph shifted his aim between her and Wang. Slowly, she lowered her maitu. "Yes, I am," she admitted. "And you need to do what I tell you—Garret, is it?"

"Uh-huh."

Held as he was by the guard, Garret would suffer from Wang's forthcoming stun. She needed the Oph to remain against the wall and the boy out of his grasp. Fortunately, she realized, the restraining arm was the one she'd stunned. "Good. Now, do you know the tickle game?"

"Sure."

Rieka smiled. "Then let's play and he's it." She nudged her chin forward to indicate the guard.

Instantly, Garret began to wiggle until his pinned arms reached the Oph's sides. Rieka didn't have any idea whether Ophs were ticklish, but she hoped the unexpected attack would be enough.

A second later, the Oph jerked. Then he jerked again, his arm coming up for a better grip on Garret's waist.

"Keep going, Garret," she coached. Hands free now, the boy went at his task enthusiastically. The Oph groaned and lurched, his hold on Garret gradually loosening, his maitu all but forgotten.

Rieka decided to speed up the process and unclipped the dummy datapad from her belt. Knowing Wang would fire at the first opportunity, Rieka lunged, smacking the data-pad's edge against the Oph's elbow. At the same time, she grabbed Garret and pulled as hard as she could.

She heard Wang fire and the sound of a body hitting the floor. Taking a deep breath, she set Garret down. "Are you okay?"

"Sure," he chimed. "That was a-mazing."

"Yes," she agreed, looking over his head at Wang. "It sure was."

Maria appeared at her shoulder. "The Ophs told us we were supposed to stay here until the ceremony. But that's not what Mrs. Giovanni told us. What's going on?"

While Wang dealt with the stunned guard, Rieka turned to see that Gorah and Gennath had secured their guards and gathered the other children near the door.

Rieka knew they'd never make it to the InterMAT station unless each one cooperated. She slid a comforting arm around Maria's shoulder. "I'll tell you, but I need you to promise that you'll do exactly what I ask. It's very important."

Maria and the others nodded. "Something has happened involving Earth and the ceremony today . . . and the Blue Planet Future."

"We were all together at Camp Future and then they transported us here," Maria explained. "Then they brought us to this room. Where are the others?"

"You're on the *Barnel*," Rieka said. "And you can't stay here. It isn't safe. I've come to make sure you're transported to the *New Venture*."

"Why?" another child asked.

"Because . . . some confused people don't like Humans. It would take me too long to explain more—and we haven't got a lot of time. I need you all to go with Lieutenants Gorah and Gennath. Go as quietly as possible. They'll take you to the InterMAT and make sure you get to the *New Venture*. Can you do that for me?"

Most of the children nodded that they could. Maria asked, "Aren't you coming, too?"

"I've . . . got something else to do. I'll see you all again soon."

It took a few minutes, but they finally got the youngsters queued up in two lines at the door. Rieka went out first and stunned the ensign. Wang helped her lug the body inside while Gorah and Gennath led their charges to the nearest Chute door.

"We'll send the children on and wait for you at the station," Gorah said, then hurried to catch up with Gennath.

Rieka led Wang in the opposite direction and took the nearest Chute to the weapons lab. She didn't expect it to be manned or guarded but checked the entire lab before stationing Wang as lookout while she went to work. Although the easiest way to incapacitate the ship would be via the panoply systems, Rieka avoided those panels. The bridge would be alerted the moment she touched them.

"How long is this going to take?" Wang whispered.

"Not long."

Rieka opened the access panels to the IRB and sphere-production circuitry. Setting her maitu on its lowest energy level, she discharged it against the IRB board. The panel matrix went from clear to opaque, and she knew she'd charred the circuitry. She did the same to the sphere-production unit and clipped the panels shut.

"We've been aboard fourteen minutes," Wang told her as she headed for the hardware storage area where the backup panels were kept.

"I'm going as fast as I can."

Suddenly, Rieka felt a wave of anxiety wash over her. Triscoe. She sensed his mind concentrating on the bridge but a worried shade of ocher came through the link. His concern was genuine and, apparently, for more than her. Was he preparing for battle? Without speaking to him directly, she couldn't tell.

Rieka sighed. She couldn't risk finishing the job in the hardware storage area. If the *Barnel* tried to fire its weapons and found them disabled, repair crews would be dispatched immediately. There was no way she could find the backups, corrupt them, and get off the ship without being discovered.

"Dammit." Frustrated, she turned and hurried back toward Wang.

"What's wrong?"

"Nothing." Together, they headed for the InterMAT station.

Wondering how he could break the news to Rieka that New SubBrasilia had been destroyed, Triscoe looked up from his console when the DGI switched on the *Prospectus*'s audio. "What do you make of that?" Robet asked.

He studied the tactical display for a moment. "Looks like they're planning to regroup over the northern section of the Pacific Ocean," Triscoe said. "What's there? Nothing that I can see."

"Only two population sites nearby, Captain," Aarkmin reported, studying her own console screen. "There's a city about 150 kilometers inland on the Asian continent, New SubBeijing. And about fifteen hundred kilometers east of it, there's another one still under construction. It's called New SubKyoto."

"Both are underground," Robet said. "It's going to take them several rounds like it did with New SubBrasilia."

Watching the three ships slowly regroup to form a triangle, Triscoe frowned. "A piece of this puzzle is missing," he murmured. He'd eavesdropped for a moment or two when his mother and Rieka had spoken to RadiMo, but hadn't heard the entire story. He'd realized enough, though, to understand that the Bournese Herald knew something of Gundah's plans.

Mother.

Triscoe?

What did RadiMo tell Rieka about the Earth cities?

She paused for a moment, then replied, *Their deal was to scout the local geology in exchange for mining rights.*

For what purpose?

I'm not sure. He said they were looking for faults, aquifers, oil deposits. That sort of thing.

Thank you. He brought his attention back to the bridge as Midrin Tohab's face split the DGI into a third section.

"Captains," she began, "one-third of the missing property has been recovered. My people are still working on the problem."

Triscoe saw Robet's face brighten at the news. Honoring his promise not to contact Rieka, he'd been following her progress silently. She and the others were already aboard the *Dividend* and had located the second group of children.

"Thank you, Captain Tohab," Triscoe said. "Right now, we're wondering what our . . . friends are planning in the North Pacific."

"I've been monitoring them," Tohab said. "My guess is they're going to target New SubKyoto."

"Why?"

"Earth history records the detonation of two atomic bombs over this island chain, Japan. It's relatively small and located on a line of geologic instability called the Pacific Rim. The bombs may or may not have caused additional stress fractures in the strata. Your other possible target, New SubBeijing, the nearest populated city, is hundreds of kilometers from either an active or dormant volcano."

"That's true," Triscoe agreed.

"The other possible strategy, though I doubt she's going to use it, would be to simply target stress points in the crust to stimulate undersea earthquakes. This is potentially more devastating than destroying a single city—since the resulting tsunamis have a tremendous impact on the coastline."

Triscoe saw Robet frown. "How do you know so much about this?"

"I served as Rieka's EO for several years, Captain DeVark," she said. "It is difficult to be in her company and not learn . . . Earth trivia."

"Why wouldn't Gundah opt for this, do you think?"

"It would take too long. Hours, in fact. She made a decisive move when she annihilated Winnipeg and New SubBrasilia. It seems to me she wants to make an immediate statement."

Triscoe smiled. "And we appreciate the fact that you were paying attention. The question now is: What do we do?"

"Do you think we could stop their spheres with ours?" Tohab asked.

"In space, I would try just about anything," Robet offered. "But we're dealing with a planetary atmosphere. That's risky."

Triscoe nodded. "I agree. Even though we don't know their target for sure, I suggest we begin evacuating New SubKyoto. Until we can engage the ships themselves, I suppose we can't do much more than that."

"Captain," Aarkmin began, "two of the ships are firing."

Triscoe watched the DGI as four dots indicating spheres

descended on Earth. The *Barnel* had not fired, he noted. Rieka had managed to disarm it. He waited helplessly along with his companions, to see what damage the Ophs would do.

When the DGI registered the explosion, Becker turned. "They didn't hit the city, Captain," he said.

"What?"

"They didn't hit it. Of course it's underground, anyway. But the detonation point is northeast of Kyoto, midway between it and Lake Biwako."

It took a moment for the information to register, but Triscoe understood the implication immediately. He flipped a toggle and Nason's face replaced the map of Japan on the DGI. "Did you hear that, Admiral?" he asked.

"Yes. And I want the *Providence* and *New Venture* to begin immediate evacuation of all life signs in New Sub-Kyoto. Activate every station aboard until that city is empty. The *Prospectus* will stand by for the scheduled transport initiated by Lieutenant Gebrah."

"Understood, Admiral," Tohab said. Her image left the DGI as she ordered her crew to comply with his orders.

Robet nodded, though he looked somewhat disappointed. "Yes, sir."

Triscoe disconnected the admiral's channel and relayed the orders to his InterMAT chief. Before Kyliss had the three other stations working, Triscoe had Lisk move them closer to the island.

The lieutenant complied, bringing them in from the north. "Why the hurry, Captain?" he asked.

"It seems that Gundah likes to watch a progression of disaster," he replied. "If the admiral is correct in his assumption, New SubKyoto will be flooded by that lake in a matter of moments."

Rieka ground her teeth when she felt Triscoe's shock and frustration. Some new horror had befallen Earth. She was sure of it. Staring at the computer decks in the *Dividend*'s weapons lab, she couldn't quite suppress a fountain of rage, herself. Not bothering to think, she reset her maitu and destroyed the banks controlling the IRB and sphere production.

Knowing both repair and security crews were being dispatched, she clicked on her TC and hurried toward Wang, stationed at the door. "Dee to Gebrah. Got those kids off yet, Lieutenant?"

"Last five are leaving now."

"Good. You're going to need to transport us directly from here. We're about to be pinned down."

"What did you do?" Wang whispered as they heard the muffled sounds of voices and footsteps approach.

"Lost my temper," she mumbled. Studying the lock's programming panel, she tapped in her command-code override and hoped no one over the rank of lieutenant would be dispatched to investigate the lab. If a commander accompanied them, the override wouldn't buy much time. "As soon as you're ready, Lieutenant."

"Understood," Gebrah replied.

Rieka felt the InterMAT effect begin and a moment later found herself crouched beside Wang in the *New Venture*'s chamber.

She stood and walked out the door and into what seemed like a sea of children. She looked over the smaller ones' heads to Lieutenant Giffah. "Why aren't they in the Medical suite?"

"They wanted to wait for you," Giffah replied.

Rieka turned as a small popping sound behind her announced the arrival of Lieutenants Gebrah and Gorah. "Everything go okay?"

Gorah shrugged as she stepped around a young boy. She leaned forward and said softly, "I had to fuse the lock to the station's door—but we got out without incident."

She nodded, knowing Gorah tended to underplay problems. "That's fine. I told you it would get progressively harder. They'll be waiting for us on the *Garner*."

"I expect so."

Rieka took a breath and looked out over the ragtag group of young performers. The *Dividend*'s party had responded to the teenagers' leadership and followed their orders to the letter. "Okay, everybody. You've seen me, and I've seen you. And we all made it to the *Prospectus* in one piece. If you could please go with Lieutenant Giffah to the Medical suite, we'll get the rest of your group off the *Garner*."

She watched the kids leave the InterMAT station, then

glanced at Wang, Gorah, and Gebrah. "Ready for round three? It's going to be a little different."

When they nodded, she clicked on her TC again. "Link to main computer."

"Linked," the animated voice said.

"Request name of engineering superintendent on the *Garner.*"

"Commander Bashid," the voice replied.

"End main computer link. Link with *Garner.* Lieutenant Dee to Commander Bashid."

"I know no Dee," the Boo's voice gurgled after a moment.

"That is my TC registry, Commander," Rieka said. "In truth you speak to Captain Herald Degahv, newly recalled."

"You have been resting at the parallax too long, Captain," the Boo told her.

Rieka wholeheartedly agreed with that, but answered, "I suppose so. My question, Bashid, is—do you follow Gimbish and Gundah—or Nason?"

A moment of silence passed before Bashid replied, "The Ophs are on a nonlinear path of destruction. They slide far from the quanta. It is the zone Milari took before she fell from the White Cliffs."

Rieka nodded. The reference to Milari made sense. But the commander hadn't answered her question. "But do you follow them?"

"If Nason issues order to me, I will act upon them."

Chastising herself for bringing the admiral's name into this, she asked, "Then would you assist me in following his orders?"

"The Karina of the Rock? You are as a high pass of Morado. Even Herald Dzan would follow Karina."

"He would, eh?" Rieka smiled at both the thought and Wang as he frowned, listening to the one-sided conversation. "Bashid, I need you to cut power to your weapons system. And I need to come aboard."

"These requests show symmetry."

Gorah looked up from the console. "The *Garner*'s repulsion screens have been activated."

Rieka frowned, though she'd expected Captain Gimbish

to have set the screens before now. "Bashid, we cannot transport safely through your screen."

"Then it shall fluctuate for the next twenty-four seconds."

"Clever, Commander. I'm heading for the chamber now."

"I will await your arrival."

"Dee out." She turned toward the InterMAT operator. "Good morning, Lieutenant," she said.

"Morning, Herald . . . Captain . . . ma'am." He replied, saluting.

She responded with a less-than-enthusiastic salute, and said, "For the moment I'm just Lieutenant Dee. I need you to pick up Commander Bashid's TC signal on the *Garner* and transport the four of us to him." She gestured behind her as Wang, Gorah, and Gebrah made their way into the InterMAT chamber.

"Yes, Lieutenant . . . ma'am." With a task to perform, he attended to his console.

By the time Rieka stood next to Gorah, the lieutenant was nodding at his board. "Commander Bashid's signal is coming in clear and the ship's repulsion screen is pulsing regularly. I'm in sync with it, so you're clear to transport."

Rieka nodded. She nudged the maitu strapped to her hip. "We're ready," she said, and hoped that they were.

TWENTY-FIVE

"It may have been unwise to bring only three," Bashid said as he towered over her.

Rieka looked up at the huge blue being. She heard the slow click of his kroi and watched his eyes double-blink. "Possibly, Commander Bashid," she said. "But nature shows us how easily a small stream becomes a raging river. Like the Driel over Kolini Falls."

The flesh above his eye wrinkled. "This is true," he said.

"Will you assist our cause again?"

"Should the factors follow your tangent." He double-blinked at her.

Rieka nodded. She turned to her Oph companions. "This is Lieutenant Gennath and Lieutenant Gorah from the *New Venture*. They will coordinate with you when they require alterations in the power grid."

Bashid's starfish hand made a sweeping gesture toward the rest of the engineering suite. "My control of this ship is extensive," he said. "I will follow the equation and induce it toward a satisfactory outcome."

She nodded. "And this is Hong Wang-Chi," Rieka said. "He is my Watcher—as Karina before the Light."

"Understood," Bashid gurgled. He double-blinked at Wang. "See that your eyes bring Karina to the Light."

Obviously perplexed by the request, Wang nodded once. "That's my job."

Rieka looked at Gorah and Gennath. "Okay. This time we need to split up right away. Don't use any InterMAT stations. Coordinate transport through Commander Bashid."

"What about you?" Gorah asked.

"Don't concern yourself with us, Lieutenant. The two of you go find those kids and get them off this ship."

"The Earthlings have been moved like a flock from a cargo hold to the weapons lab on level three," Bashid rumbled.

Gorah nodded. "Thank you, sir." She and Gennath saluted him and left the suite.

Rieka craned her neck to look up at Bashid, again. "My function here is to neutralize Gundah and secure the ship. May I count on engineering as a factor?"

His kroi clicked again, this time the cadence lighter. "I can float this over the equation, Dee," he said ominously. "Roda!"

"Chief," a paler Boo replied as it came toward them, clicking its kroi with a rhythm Rieka identified as curiosity. Roda wore a lieutenant's bar pinned to the drape that fell across broad, sloping shoulders.

"This Human has need of your datapad. It is hers until she departs the *Garner*. Further, like factors in a double-star system, you will now follow her orders."

Roda handed over the datapad. Rieka took it. "I don't need another companion."

Bashid leaned closer. "Perhaps you will," he rumbled, then waddled off on his three stumpy legs.

"Okay then Roda," she began dismissing the engineer from her mind, "we need to neutralize Adjutant Gundah's control. I've used an attack-and-retreat strategy so far. But now I think it's time for a direct frontal assault."

Gundah cursed and cut communications with Gimbish. "Buffoon," she muttered. She'd seen the readouts on the repulsion screens when they'd fluctuated. It had only happened for a few seconds. But InterMAT transport was nearly instantaneous. Whoever had gotten aboard the *Barnel* and *Dividend* had quite probably made their way onto the *Garner*. At least Gimbish had not argued about stepping up security and ordering a search.

She glanced over her shoulder at Candace Degahv. The woman looked up from her Human food and gestured with a hand. "Is something wrong?"

"Nothing significant. Captain Gimbish is sometimes difficult. He forgets who is in charge."

Degahv nodded. "I have several employees like that."

Gundah squinted and studied her further. The Human's attitude had changed once she assumed she'd become something of a partner in this endeavor. "I see we are more alike than I originally thought," Gundah said smoothly. "Now," she added in a businesslike tone, "I require some information. I want to know where the Heralds and senators are."

Candace shrugged. "There's no way we could possibly get that information. The ceremony has been canceled by now. They could be anywhere."

"Well, I suppose that's true—to a degree," Gundah conceded. She'd seen the short announcement Jeniper Tarrik had made about postponing the event. "I am guessing the Indran, Human, and Bournese Heralds are on the *Providence*. Cimpa is probably still in SubDenver. That leaves Herald Honutik. I know I saw Senators Volshoy and De-Wilt at the banquet," Gundah went on. "Did you happen to notice any others?"

"I'm afraid I didn't," Candace said.

Gingerly reaching for proof of the Human's loyalty, Gundah pressed her. "Had they briefed you on any contingency plans? Where to go in case of an emergency?"

Candace shrugged and shook her head. "All there was—was a brief notice on the back of the guest room's door. To evacuate New SubDenver, you take the stairs to the surface."

Dissatisfied by the Human's generic reply, Gundah inhaled and let the air escape her lungs accompanied by a low growl. "That's hardly helpful."

Candace rubbed her temples. "Maybe we should do a little research."

"Maybe I'll destroy Damascus." Gundah thrilled at the flash of horror that crossed the woman's face. "It won't take a minute," she assured her. "I've already practiced on Winnipeg, SubBrasilia and SubKyoto. And . . . of course, they're only Humans."

Candace leaned toward her, her lips drawn in a tight line. "You're doing this the wrong way, Gundah. I thought the plan wasn't to hurt anyone else. I thought you wanted to control Rieka and sterilize the next generation of Humans.

If you continue to openly attack Earth, the Commonwealth
will return fire."

"I'm just having some fun while motivating your daughter to do as I say." To herself, she thought: or I could kill
you and anyone else who disagrees with my thinking.

"The Fleet might decide to destroy this ship," Candace
countered. She left the table and began pacing the length of
the room. "You have everything to gain if we leave, now."

"But I still have unfinished business," Gundah said, hoping to draw the Human out. Surely a mother would know
her child well enough to predict her actions. And Humans
were such homebound creatures. "Your daughter strikes
me as a doer—rather than a spectator. One of my ships
has had their weapons circuitry damaged and the other is
completely incapacitated. I find that rather odd, don't you?"

Candace frowned. "I'm not following you."

"The Procyon War's venerated hero. Earth Herald.
RadiMo's savior. It just doesn't follow that she'd sit back
and let others do the work."

Candace made a strange face and puckered her lips.
"Captain Marteen is very protective of her."

Gundah glanced back at her console. "So I've heard. But
I've also heard he doesn't always get his way."

Candace said nothing.

Abruptly, Gundah snatched up her maitu. She flipped
a switch on her console and Gimbish's face appeared on
her screen.

"Yes?" he asked.

"We're leaving Earth orbit, Captain. Have your people
set a course for Oph. Begin acceleration as soon as the
course is set."

He nodded. "Understood."

"Well, it's about time," Candace Degahv said. She
heaved a sigh and sat down.

"We're leaving because I have the information I needed,
thanks to you."

"But I didn't say anything."

"Of course you did. You told me that Rieka Degahv is
aboard the *Garner*. And now we are taking her away from
those who could protect her. I could not have planned this
better, myself."

*   *   *

Triscoe suppressed a shudder as he watched the *Garner* suddenly depart Earth orbit. The other two ships took off on divergent paths but remained close to the planet. He flipped a toggle. "Admiral . . ."

"I see what's happening, Captain," Nason replied. "Do not pursue the *Garner*."

"But sir—"

"Trust me, Captain. I had a surprise scheduled for Herald Degahv later today. The surprise will work equally well for Adjutant Gundah."

"I don't understand, sir," Triscoe replied, frustrated and confused by Nason's reply.

"That's because I didn't explain it to you. Let's just say I have a reunion of sorts planned. Right now I have other orders." Triscoe watched him open communications with the other two ships. "Captain DeVark, Captain Tohab, once again we have Fleet ships prepared to do battle with Fleet ships. Since there are no longer children aboard either the *Barnel* or *Dividend,* your orders are to attack and disable them."

Triscoe glanced first at Aarkmin then at Becker. They nodded, indicating their readiness.

"Is there any specific strategy you wish to employ?" Tohab asked.

"Negative," Nason replied. "Use whatever method you see fit. But I want the ships disabled—not destroyed."

"Understood, Admiral," she said.

"Do we coordinate through you, sir, or among ourselves?" Robet asked.

Triscoe didn't know whether to feel worried or relieved when Nason replied, "I'll stay out of it—unless you require my input. Nason out."

"Yes, sir." Triscoe watched Robet cut his channel to the admiral, then address his DGI pickup. "Well, how do you want to do this?"

Triscoe replied automatically though he wasn't sure he liked the ease with which he solved the problem. "The three of us should target each ship in turn. We'll use our spheres and try for simultaneous impact on their screens."

Tohab nodded. "That will remove their only defense."

"And then do what to disable them?" Robet asked.

"A single, low-charged sphere to the panoply ought to do it," he said.

"Take out their ability to see, aim, and navigate," Tohab said with a sigh. "But they will retain the ability to fire on us."

Triscoe agreed with Tohab's reluctance. "If Gellath and Goverah don't surrender once we've incapacitated them, then we'll take the admiral up on his offer—and request his input." A physical assault was the logical next step in such a scenario, but he resisted giving such an order without Nason's counsel.

Tohab's face took on a determined look. "Which one first?" she asked.

He glanced at the tactical display on his console. "The *Dividend* hasn't fired any weapons since Rieka was aboard. Let's start with the *Barnel*."

"Gorah to Dee," the TC said softly in her ear.

Rieka allowed Lieutenant Roda to exit the Chute first as she said, "Dee. What's your status?"

"Unable to extract the cargo," Gorah's gravelly Oph voice said. "Still examining alternative methods."

"Understood. Dee out." She sighed. Gundah knew they'd get aboard and attempt a rescue. She'd probably planned a strategy for that and implemented it as soon as the children turned up missing on one of the other ships. But Rieka hadn't figured on Gundah attacking a second target so soon.

The *Barnel*'s inability to fire would have alerted the Oph long before any of the guards turned up missing. By now both the *Barnel* and *Dividend* must have reported their hostages gone. The *Dividend* wouldn't be using her weapons anytime soon, but the *Barnel*'s tech-pros might have repaired the minimal damage Rieka had done. She would've liked to confirm her assumptions with Triscoe via TC, but didn't want to risk going past the ten-second limit.

Gundah had also correctly guessed a rescue team would board the *Garner*. She needed to buy herself some time, which was why she'd kept her hostages heavily guarded.

Rieka empathized with Gorah's frustration. They both needed to find a way through the obstacles as quickly as possible. At the same time, she knew Lieutenant Gorah wouldn't do anything to risk either herself or the children. Fortunately, the lieutenant was both patient and methodical. Her own team had already taken two Chutes to avoid security personnel in the corridors.

Roda stopped and leaned his great head toward her. "Commander Bashid communicates. We slide from Earth orbit."

Rieka frowned, then realized Bashid had sent the message via Roda so that he wouldn't have to speak to her directly. Even he didn't want to chance the communication being traced. And she credited Gundah with enough paranoia to be tracing every signal.

"All three ships?"

"Negative. Just the *Garner*," Roda replied.

"Not good," Wang whispered.

Rieka nodded. "Tell Bashid my thanks for this information are exponential."

Roda wiggled the fleshy patch over his eyes and double-blinked. His kroi clicked, stopped, and clicked again. "He is pleased to assist like the dew of the morn."

They continued slowly down the empty corridor. Rieka felt like kicking herself for making Triscoe promise to stay out of her head. She needed information now, and the only one she could access was Bashid. On the other hand, avoiding contact made things safer for them. The paradox confounded her, and she began to wonder if they'd ever sort it out.

Roda stopped, and she realized they'd arrived. "Mautu on stun?" she asked softly.

"Ready and waiting, Boss," Wang said.

"The door is a short *vondine* down that intersecting corridor," Roda's translator box said. His starfish-shaped hand indicated a cut in the main hallway about two meters to the right.

She nodded. "Wang and I will deal with the guards. You need to disconnect whatever equipment she's got in there." With an unwelcome sense of foreboding, Rieka realized that if Gundah had decided to make a run for it, she might be pursued. If that happened, shots would be fired. "Ask Commander Bashid to power down the weapons from engineering. I don't think the captain will do anything stupid once Gundah's in custody, but I don't want to chance it."

"Captain Gimbish is predictable as *pi* in most situations," Roda agreed.

"Good. Let's go then." To Wang, she whispered, "If there is more than one guard at the door, take the right."

They crept toward the intersection, turned the corner, aimed and fired. Rieka doubted the Ophs even knew they'd been attacked. Leaving the stunned bodies on the deck, she studied the door. Remarkably, it wasn't locked. Roda entered first and Rieka hid behind his immense bulk until they were inside. Then she stepped out from behind him, aiming her maitu at the first Oph she saw.

Candace stood in front of it, effectively blocking off a clear shot. As a bolt of energy barely missed her head, Rieka realized Gundah, on her far right, had a weapon, too. A gut-wrenching sound emanated from Roda. He'd been hit. But Boos was incredibly sturdy beings. He remained on his three stubby feet and fired off a return blast at Gundah.

While Rieka ducked and rolled behind a chair, Wang scuttled away, obviously trying to find a better angle at the guard. For some unknown reason, Candace stayed in front of the Oph, acting as a shield.

"Mother, for heaven's sake, get down," she ordered.

"You have no idea what you're doing," Candace told her.

Rieka watched as Wang squeezed off another ineffectual shot at the guard. The deck below her feet shuddered. Turning, she saw Roda had fallen. His kroi clicked strangely, and he didn't try to speak.

Peeking out from behind the chair, Rieka once again saw Gundah's yellow-ringed eyes as she ducked behind her console. The Oph was breathing hard, her maitu clenched unsteadily in a paw. Roda had hit her at least once.

Rieka didn't allow herself the luxury of satisfaction. She knew Gundah understood the situation was a standoff and anything might happen. A quick glance at Wang showed him behind a table, still trying for a shot at the guard.

Figuring she'd been right about Candace all long, Rieka toyed with the idea of shooting her, too. But Gundah was the main threat here, and Candace was unarmed, so she focused her attention on the Oph.

"I want the canister, Gundah."

"You'll never find it."

"I'll have it even if I have to kill you to get it."

Gundah snorted. "Your fragile Human sensibilities wouldn't allow you to murder me, Herald."

"I wouldn't assume anything if I were you, Adjutant," Rieka told her.

"You see?" Candace spoke from somewhere across the room. "I tried to warn you about her."

"Stay out of this, Mother. This is between me and Gundah."

She heard the Oph respond with a barking laugh. "So you would like to think. The stakes are much higher than you can conceive, Human. And I alone will save Oph and the Commonwealth from the scourge your planet has inflicted upon us."

Rieka consciously ignored that remark, not wanting to give her opponent the satisfaction of knowing she'd hit a tender spot. Right now, she needed to tip the Oph off-balance, either physically, mentally, or both. "I'm afraid you've got it all wrong, Adjutant. You've already lost," she said in her best captain's voice.

"I? What have I lost?" Gundah demanded.

Rieka could tell that Gundah had moved, her voice had come from a different direction. She wondered how much of Roda's stun had managed to hit her after all. "The Fleet knows your identity. And that you're running back to Ophiuchus."

"And once I get there . . ." Gundah paused and took a deep breath. "Once I get there, I'll be safe. You'll never find me."

Rieka found her patience flagging. The guard and Wang exchanged shots again, but Rieka paid them no mind. She could hear Gundah crawling around behind the console, planning to do—what?

Suddenly, Gundah moved. Rieka raised her weapon to take aim, but the guard fired at her, effectively stopping her shot. She ducked and fired anyway, but Gundah had already slipped out the door.

"Dammit!" Rieka banged the floor with a fist.

"Boss, you okay?" Wang asked.

"Yes," she hissed.

"The guard's down. What do I do with Candace?"

Frowning because she hadn't heard Wang fire, Rieka stood to find him holding his weapon on her mother. "Cuff the guard," she told him. "I'll take care of her."

Wang nodded and pulled the last set of cuffs off his belt. While he tended to the unconscious guard, Rieka glared at Candace.

"Where'd she go?"

"I have no idea."

Glancing at Roda, she saw his chest move in and out and saw him suck from his atmosphere compensator. He'd be fine in a few hours.

Two steps brought her within arm's distance of Candace. "Don't give me that, Mother. You're protecting her. What's the payoff, this time? Controlling shares in one of Tech-Line's companies?"

To her credit, Candace pulled herself straighter and lifted her chin. "Don't be ridiculous. I have nothing to do with her. I never have."

Rieka shook her head. "You are quite a piece of work. I'm actually supposed to believe that?"

"I'm not lying to you."

"Right." Silently, Rieka wished Setana were here to verify that. Unfortunately, the only evidence she had was to the contrary. She nodded solemnly. "So, what am I supposed to believe, instead? That you protected him because you had feelings for him?" She indicated the guard.

"Don't be impertinent," Candace argued. "I almost had her trust. She would have told me what she'd done with your DNA."

Rieka wanted to believe her, but couldn't. Holding her maitu in Candace's general direction, she watched Wang finish dealing with the Oph. "Shut down those consoles Wang-Chi," she said. She clicked on her TC. "Lieutenant Dee to Captain Gimbish."

"This is the captain," his barking voice replied. "I have no officer aboard named Dee."

"How astute," Rieka commented. She looked down at Roda again. He double-blinked at her, but spoke with only slow clicks of his kroi.

She heard Gimbish tap at his console, then he addressed her directly again. "Who is this?"

Rieka debated divulging her identity. She'd met Gimbish once or twice before at Fleet functions and couldn't remember much about him. She glanced at her mother and figured Gundah had probably already contacted Gimbish, herself.

"You're speaking to Captain Herald Rieka Degahv."

"Impossible."

"Nothing is impossible, Gimbish. We learned that in the Procyon War."

"Captain Degahv no longer exists," Gimbish persisted. "She is now the Earth Herald and would be a fool to risk her life to rescue my hostages."

"I've been called lots of names before, Captain, fool included," she said. "But that's not the issue here. Surrender command to me, and we'll see if we can't work something out with the admiralty."

"Never. Humans *are* inferior beings," Gimbish insisted. "You can't win, Captain."

"*We* most certainly can."

The link cut off abruptly and Rieka's anxiety level jumped. The last voice had been Gundah's. She looked into Wang and Candace's expectant faces and knew something awful was about to happen. "We've got to get out of here, right now."

"I don't understand," Candace said.

"We've got to move!" Rieka shoved her mother toward the door. "Out of here, now." She turned as Roda tried to push himself upright. "Can you make it, Lieutenant?" she asked.

His kroi clicked positively, and she nodded. "Wang, help me." She realized that, for the time being, she'd have to trust Candace. "Mother, watch the corridor." Together, they steadied Roda on his three stubby feet. He wobbled a little, but remained upright.

"Someone's coming," Candace reported, excitement threading through her voice. "But I can't see them, yet."

Roda followed them toward the door and Wang sniffed the air. "Do you smell something?"

Rieka nodded. "They're gassing the room." Knowing the effort would be all but futile, she willed Roda to hurry out the door. Seconds later, it closed behind them.

"They're here!" Candace gasped.

Rieka looked down the corridor to see a squad of six

Ophs running around the corner, their weapons drawn. Pinned in the short hallway, she stepped forward beside Wang.

"Shoot. Shoot!" Rieka ordered. She lifted her maitu and discharged it just as they received return fire.

TWENTY-SIX

She looked at the guards where they'd fallen, then at her own unorthodox crew. "Roda, can you make it to the Chute?" she asked. His kroi clicked again, and he blinked at her. She took that as a yes. "Okay. Let's go. Wang, you take the rear and keep an ear out."

"Right."

Rieka took the point and felt oddly secure when her mother stepped in behind her. She still didn't know how much she could trust her, if at all. But feelings, she knew, had little to do with facts. "Chute's just down here," she said. "Won't take a few seconds to reach it."

They moved along as quickly as Roda could manage and Rieka clicked on her TC again. "Dee to Bashid."

"Bashid," the Boo engineer's voice replied.

"Gundah is still in the equation and the captain's plans are reciprocal to ours, Commander. He does not wish to slide to Varannah—and seeks another place—like the vortex of Drazid."

"His is a calculable endeavor, Dee. I shall be vigilant with the factors."

"Then add this to the equation—he gassed the conference room."

"Understood."

The connection switched off as they reached a Chute door. Rieka triggered the motion sensor and stood ready with her maitu when the door opened. Fortunately, the car was empty.

"Roda, inside," she said, looking up into his dark multi-faceted eyes. "You have done well, my friend. Karina hopes you find Varannah."

His kroi clicked in response, and she ordered the Chute to the main engineering deck. "Bashid will see to you," she told him, then saluted quickly as the door closed.

"What about us?" Wang whispered.

The light above the door pulsed as a second car arrived to take the other's place. She replayed the same precautions with the new car, but it, too, was empty. "Everybody in." While she waited for Wang to take a final look around the corridor before he joined them, Rieka contacted Gorah.

"We found a way to get to the kids, Dee," she said softly. "We're in the enviro lab. It's secure."

"We'll meet you there." She clicked off the connection and ordered the Chute's destination. "Environmental lab, level two."

"Why are we going there?" Candace asked, irritation obvious in her voice. "Why don't we just get off this ship?"

Rieka couldn't bring herself to make eye contact. "Because I said so."

Triscoe felt a wave of relief when Rieka's emotional state eased from an alarmed, fiery red to a more controlled gold-orange. But he still hated the thought of her aboard the *Garner* as it increased its speed away from Earth.

He'd managed to move the *Providence* into the path of every sphere the *Barnel* sent their way. Using his own repulsion screens to neutralize the attack, Triscoe's strategy to keep the Earth from suffering any more damage had thus far worked. But he knew Lisk couldn't keep at it indefinitely.

His weapons specialist, Becker, had unfortunately endured nothing but bad luck. Trying to coordinate the counterattack with his counterparts on the *Prospectus* and *New Venture* proved to be nearly impossible. With the ships dodging every which way to intercept spheres, their positions were constantly changing with regard to the target.

They'd already tried half a dozen volleys against the *Barnel* to no avail. Repulsion screens cold be worn down eventually by many contacts in close succession, but that would take minutes they didn't have. What they needed was a simultaneous hit that would disrupt the *Barnel*'s defense screen.

He watched the Human lieutenant pound a fist on the

console and mutter an oath when their latest attempts failed. "What was the margin this time?" Triscoe asked.

"Three-tenths."

"We'll do it, Lieutenant," Triscoe said with assurance. "The *Barnel*'s crew will eventually tire. Be patient."

"Yes sir." Becker shook his head, then bent toward his board once again. Three-tenths of a second seemed like nothing to them, but to the computer in charge of the repulsion screen, it was more than enough time to recover from a strike.

The *Dividend* had apparently been rendered defenseless. It had moved south, far away from the battle, and had fired no spheres at all since Rieka had been in their weapons lab. The only viable strategy was to keep after the *Barnel* until Captain Goverah either surrendered on his own, or was forced to.

"V'don," Triscoe said, switching his attention to the lieutenant in charge of communications, "can you link to the *Barnel*?"

V'don's fingers attacked his console. He nodded. "Go ahead and activate your position, Captain," he said.

Triscoe flipped a toggle. "*Providence* to *Barnel*. This is Captain Marteen," he began briskly. "I wish to speak to Captain Goverah."

He let five seconds of silence pass before he said, "As you may or may not have guessed, Admiral Nason has issued a warrant for Adjutant Gundah's arrest. She is wanted for treason. Any efforts on your part to support her will be considered additional acts of treason committed of your own volition. Please feel free to both verify this fact with EarthCom and pass on my message to Captains Gellath and Gimbish."

Not expecting a response, Triscoe nodded at the DGI pickup. "*Providence,* out."

A few seconds later, Lisk sat straighter in his chair. "They're firing again, Captain."

Rieka cautiously peered out of the Chute into the empty corridor. No Fleet personnel lurked in either direction. She found that odd for a ship with known intruders on the loose. Then, considering Gundah was in charge, Rieka accepted their good fortune. It seemed as though Gennath's assumption had been accurate. Gundah appeared to be lucid, but several of her decisions had been far from logical. Why had she murdered Stephen? Why did she need to control Earth? None of it made any sense.

"Okay, let's go," she said. "The environmental lab is just on the right."

While they headed for the lab, she clicked on her TC. "Dee to Gorah. We're here. Is the door locked?"

"I'll have Gennath open it," Gorah's voice said before the connection went dead.

Wang reached the door first and turned to look at her. Rieka nodded for him to go in, but he hesitated, glaring suspiciously at Candace. "Watch yourself, Candace," he warned. "I'm not above using this on you." He pointed the maitu at her.

"Watch yourself," Candace replied, stepping past the threshold.

Shoving him into the lab, Rieka whispered harshly into his ear, "You just watch my back, Wang-Chi. I said I'd take care of her." As Gennath secured the door, she added, "Stay here, you two. Guard the exit. No one else is expected."

"Yes, Captain," Gennath said.

Rieka turned and found Gorah surrounded by a sea of equipment and young people. The Oph lieutenant had somehow managed to keep them seated and quiet, no simple feat when dealing with Humans.

"Status, Lieutenant?" she asked, stepping forward.

"Everyone's out of the weapons lab, Dee," Gorah told her. "We cut our way through from this side and neutralized the guards. Then we brought the children in here and resealed the opening. What happened with Gundah?"

"She . . . got away," Rieka replied, trying not to sound fatalistic. As far as she could see, it would take a miracle to bring Gundah in alive.

Gorah sighed and licked her black lips. "I understand, Captain," she said softly. Her eyes seemed sad. "She may be beyond help. But I am glad you are unhurt. And most importantly, the children are safe."

She nodded for Gorah to follow her and moved away from their young audience. "Just between us, that . . . that may be premature," Rieka replied softly. She shrugged apologetically at Gorah's questioning look. "We're not in Earth orbit anymore. There's nowhere to InterMAT them to. Gimbish is preparing for a slide to Oph. Commander Bashid is still powering down nonessential systems, but it might take a while."

"Understood," Gorah said, her ears pinning back slightly.

Rieka was still smiling her keep-the-faith captain's smile when the ship shuddered hard enough to knock anyone standing to the deck. Her natural instinct when she went down was to fall to absorb the impact. Unfortunately, a chair slid into her path and caught her in the midsection. She rode it for a moment before it slammed into a console.

Gorah clambered to her side and pulled her around to sit in the chair. "Are you injured, Captain," she asked.

Rieka nodded both no and yes. Her diaphragm had momentarily ceased to function, and she couldn't get her lungs to move. Finally she managed to reply, "Fine. Go. See to them." Gorah nodded and went to calm the terrified children.

It was then that she realized two of the group had come to stand by her. She looked up and into Samantha's frightened blue eyes.

"Are you okay, Herald?" she asked. "What happened?"

Someone touched her shoulder, and she turned to find Po. "Can't you talk?"

Rieka nodded. She tried to inhale and managed a short breath. Po rubbed her back, and she took in a little more air. "Thanks, Po," she said, finally. "Is everyone all right?"

"We're okay," he told her. "The Ophs gave us ice cream."

Rieka found enough breath to laugh, but it came out sounding like a cough. "They did?"

"Yes, but we didn't like the way they dragged us around," complained Samantha. "I mean one second we were all sleeping in our beds and suddenly we were here."

"I know." Rieka drew another painful breath. "The Ophs on this ship are—confused. We're doing our best to get you all back to Earth safe." She couldn't tell them the painful news of what had happened to Winnipeg and the other cities. That would have to wait for later.

While she squeezed Samantha's hand, her mother appeared out of the crowd of children. "What happened just then?" she demanded.

Rieka shook her head, and whispered, "I'm not sure." She pushed out of the chair. "Samantha, Po, I need you to do something for me."

"What?" Po asked, excitement crossing his cherubic face.

"You need to keep the others calm. Things might get worse before they get better." She looked at Samantha. "Can you all stay together and out of the way?"

"Sure," Samantha assured her. "Come on, Po."

Rieka smiled encouragingly. "It might help if you told them I want everyone to sit down against the back wall."

"Okay," he said.

While Samantha dragged Po away by his arm, Rieka touched the nearest console's comm board. "Environmental to Engineering."

"Engineering." Watching the small screen, Rieka was glad the gravelly voice belonged to a Vekyan rather than an Oph. The lieutenant flicked out his tongue and looked off screen as if distracted.

"We don't have a DGI here," she explained. "What's happening?"

"Could be bad, Lieutenant," the Vekyan replied. "Captain Gimbish is not standing down."

"Standing down? To what?"

"The *Prodigy*." Abruptly, he terminated the link.

Rieka's mind reeled. The *Prodigy* was here? An image of the huge ship designed for both defense and deep-space research flashed across her thoughts. She'd captained that ship and knew the damage it could do. What in the world was Gimbish thinking?

She considered cutting back through to the weapons lab to disable the equipment, then figured that would both take too long and expose the children to greater danger. It seemed they'd run out of alternatives. No longer caring whether or not the signal was traced, Rieka clicked on her TC.

"Degahv to Gimbish." She heard the link connect but Gimbish didn't reply. "Are you insane? Captain Saxen has more than double your firepower. Stand down, Gimbish."

"Never," the Oph growled in her ear. "Never will I surrender to a Human or a Human-lover!"

The connection went dead before she could say anything more. She decided another strategy was in order. "Link to the *Prodigy*."

A tinny automated voice replied, "Intership links are unavailable at this time."

"Dammit. Dee to Bashid."

"Commander Bashid."

"What's our power situation, Commander?"

"Sixteen minutes left—if the captain continues sphere production."

That wasn't a question, in her mind. "Can we get through to the *Prodigy* somehow?"

"Negative, Dee," he replied. "Another equality remains beyond the horizon."

"Okay. I'll try to think of something. Dee out." She clicked off the TC and looked around. Beyond her mother's disapproving scowl, the seated children had gone amazingly quiet. It was then that she heard the singing. Peering over the console, she saw Samantha and Po leading several of the younger ones is a soft, slow, repetitive children's song. As she watched, Gorah nodded approvingly, adding her voice. Rieka smiled at them.

"Well, what are you going to do?" Candace rasped instantly in her ear.

She turned and glared. "I'm thinking, Mother." She eased back in the chair and set her elbows on the console before her. If the *Prodigy* hadn't arrived, she'd have had a whole lot more than sixteen minutes to figure a solution.

There wasn't much she could do from the environmental lab. Other than a comm board, the console controlled nothing of great import. In front of her, she recognized pressure gauges, a set of indicators for mixing elemental gasses, filtration and temperature controls. The board behind her controlled oxygen and nitrogen production, and the air scrubbers. Nothing useful, there. She hadn't felt this helpless since she'd been arrested.

A thought hit her. "Gorah," she called.

The lieutenant came immediately. "Yes, Captain?"

"Have a look at this console." She leaned back so the Oph had an unobstructed view while she moved around Candace who stood steadfastly in the way. "Can we mix the right elements in the right proportions to generate a knockout gas? And can we pump it directly to the bridge—like Gimbish did to Gundah's conference room?"

Gorah studied the indicators for a moment. "I don't know this equipment very well, Captain. But ammonium nitrate is available. If we heat it, we'll get nitrous oxide. That should do it."

Rieka looked up at her skeptically. "Laughing gas?"

Gorah shrugged and sniffed. "Maybe it makes Humans laugh."

"What does it do to Ophs?"

"In high concentrations, it's deadly. Otherwise, it will do just what you asked."

Rieka nodded. "And how can we route it to the bridge?"

Gorah pointed to a light board on her far right. "That panel down there controls individual vent sections."

"Okay." Rieka nodded approvingly. "You heat the ammonium nitrate. I'll figure a way to pump it."

Rieka found the computer easier to use than she'd imagined. She'd very nearly worked out the route, closing some vents and opening others, when Wang's strident voice filled the room.

"They're cutting their way in!"

Rieka glanced up to see sparks in the vicinity of the doorway. "Damn." Not bothering to look up from her task, she knew Candace was still nearby. "Can you handle a maitu, Mother?"

"I think so. Yes."

"Do I have your word you won't use it on me?" After a moment of silence, Rieka looked up at her mother's indignant expression. "Answer the question, please."

"Of course I won't shoot you."

"Then take mine and find something to hide behind—but don't let anyone in that door." Rieka reached and pulled her maitu from her waistband.

Candace took it. "They'll regret if it they try," she muttered, striding away.

"I've got positive ID for nitrous oxide, Captain," Gorah said.

"What's the pressure?"

"Minimal now. Less than point-five pascals. We're going to need to triple that to one-point-five if we want any speed built up."

Rieka nodded and worked another calculation on her board. "It's going to have to travel thirty-eight meters through the vents to reach the bridge. Can you tell the ratio of the mix in that volume of air?"

"It should be enough to knock them out—but not be fatal."

"Good." A squeal from beyond the console pulled at Rieka's attention. Samantha and her companions stared wide-eyed at the door. More sparks were flying as the Ophs cut through the metal. Rieka clicked on her TC. "Dee to Bashid. We're in the environmental lab on level two. The door is locked and an unknown number of security personnel are cutting their way in. Can you assist?"

"Hold steady, Karina. Help comes."

"Point-seven," Gorah said.

"Not enough." Rieka's finger hovered over the release switch. "I'm not so sure we can wait, Lieutenant."

Gorah looked up at the door, now nearly breached. Her eyes had gone wide and yellow-ringed, but her voice remained steady. "I think you might be right, Captain." She glanced down at her board. "One-point-one."

Rieka counted to three and punched the button. The board began to flash with indicators announcing the gas's progress. Together, they watched it flow toward the bridge.

Addressing the twenty or so children Samantha and Po had moved to the back wall, Rieka said, "Some Boos are going to help us. When I know you're safe, Lieutenant Gorah, Mr. Hong, and I are going to go to the bridge. Everyone is to stay here and do exactly what Lieutenant Gennath says. Is that understood?"

The young people nodded. "Good." She smiled, hoping to boost their confidence, then turned and went back to the console.

"They should be feeling some effect by now, Captain," Gorah told her. "I'm reading ten percent N_2O on the bridge, and I've terminated production."

"Good. Grab your maitu. We'll be heading there once we handle this mess."

Gorah tapped at the console and followed her toward the door. Almost immediately it was kicked from the outside. Wang instinctively stepped back and braced for the onslaught, his maitu aimed at the door. Rieka grabbed her weapon from her mother's hand as she joined her behind some equipment. "Everybody get ready."

The door shuddered twice before it fell in. More Ophs than she thought possible stormed through the opening. Fortunately, it was narrow enough for them to be cut down by maitu fire before they could get very far.

Unfortunately, the Ophs returned fire.

Some of the smaller children began to scream. Rieka doubled her firing speed, hoping to draw the Ophs' attention away from her young charges. The noise grew to an unbearable level before the room grew eerily quiet. She heard thumping sounds from outside and a large blue head peered over the pile of bodies in the doorway. A single little girl shrieked again, and was silenced by Samantha. The Boo's dark eyes double-blinked for a moment, and she heard the distinctly solemn click of kroi. "Karina of the Rock?"

"Here," she said, stepping away from the scorched console.

"You are steady," it told her. "The equation seeks its conclusion."

She nodded and looked back at the terrified faces of the Blue Planet Future. "You did great," she told them. "Now, remember to do what Lieutenant Gennath tells you. Samantha, Po, thanks for your help."

For once, Po had nothing to say.

Rieka winked at him, then gestured for Gorah to follow. They climbed over the stunned Ophs on their way to the corridor. "How long until we're out of power?" she asked the lieutenant. Before he could answer, she saw Wang and her mother come out the lab door.

"Another nine is the estimate," the Boo reported. "We have attained the Symmetry of Six. Sphere production is discontinued."

She nodded to him and looked at Candace. "I want you to stay here, Mother."

"You're not going anywhere without me," Candace said, her tone defiant.

Deciding it would be worse to stand there arguing, Rieka shrugged. "Fine. It's your funeral."

Wang sighed. "I wish you wouldn't say things like that."

*   *   *

"Finally!" Becker shouted. In his excitement, he jumped up from his chair.

Triscoe smiled. "Congratulations, Lieutenant." He turned toward the DGI. "Robet, you and Midrin can see to things now that the *Barnel* is disabled. I'm going after the *Garner*."

Robet nodded. He flashed a triumphant smile as his bibbets returned to their normal pale pink tint. "We won't start the party until you get back."

Triscoe didn't bother to give that comment more than a nod. "Lisk. Let's go. Maximum speed."

"Course has been plotted and updated, Captain," Lisk replied. "We're looking at an ETA of about twenty minutes."

Triscoe groaned inwardly at the time, but said nothing. He could tell Rieka wasn't in immediate physical danger, but that situation could change. Knowing her, he predicted it would. Frustrated and fearful, he silently wished the InterMAT could traverse great distances.

Nason's face appeared on his screen. "Status, Captain?" he asked.

"You've been monitoring, sir, I'm sure," Triscoe replied, snapping back to attention. "Earth is secure, and we're on an intercept course with the *Garner*."

Nason nodded. "Do you confirm there have been shots fired between the *Garner* and *Prodigy*?"

Triscoe consulted his tactical board. "Yes, Admiral."

He watched as Nason sighed, then tapped at his own console. Triscoe realized he'd set up a comm link with the big ship. "Admiral Nason to Captain Saxen on the *Prodigy*," he began. "Cease fire. Repeat. Cease firing on the *Garner*."

Maitu at the ready, Rieka held her tongue as Wang eased his way onto the bridge ahead of her. The six Ophs within were either slumped in their chairs or on the floor. Gorah held back, and she couldn't blame her. The sweet taste of nitrous oxide remained in the tainted air.

"We'll handle this, Lieutenant. Mother, stay with Gorah." While Wang checked the bodies, she stepped to the weapons board and shut it down before hurrying on to the comm console. Shoving the unconscious Oph onto the floor, Rieka tapped out an order for an intership link.

"*Garner* to *Prodigy*," she said. The DGI melted quickly from a view of the stars to an austere-looking Indran face. "Saxen, cease fire. I've shut everything down."

"Who is speaking?" the Indran captain inquired.

"It's Rieka Degahv. Nason put me here to get control of the ship."

She saw him study his own DGI before saying, "The admiral has just informed me of the situation. I see that you've managed to get the job done, Herald. Or is it Captain?"

"Either will do," she commented dryly. "Can you possibly lend me a hand, though? I need a safe haven for the children. They're in the environmental lab."

"We'll bring them aboard right away."

"Thank you, sir," she said with an approving nod. "With regard to the crew, the bridge and engineering are secure—but I don't know what else. Don't know how many I can trust."

"I believe we can manage that," Saxen began, "in one of two ways. We can either contain them on the *Garner*, or sequester them aboard the *Prodigy*."

"I hadn't thought of that," Rieka admitted. "They'd be easier to manage in a couple of your cargo holds—if you have any available."

"Several," Saxen said. "How many squads do you think it will take?"

Rieka shrugged. "As many as you've got, Captain, so long as none of them are Ophs. I know that's a strange request—you'll just have to trust me. I'll explain it as soon as I've got a minute."

Saxen inclined his blond head. "I'll be waiting."

She watched while he began issuing orders to his crew and noticed Gorah slip into the room.

Wang had assembled a small pile of bodies. "Looks like Gundah's still on the loose, Boss," he announced.

"Put your maitu on the lowest setting and stun them, Mr. Hong," Gorah said. "I doubt the nitrous oxide effect will last much longer."

"Be glad to." Rieka watched as he set the weapon and, with Gorah's assistance, stunned the prone bodies.

Rieka tapped in another request on the communications board. "*Garner* to *Providence*."

"*Providence,*" V'don's voice answered. A split second later, the DGI image reconfigured to show their bridge. All positions were manned, the officers tending to their specific jobs. At the center back sat a worried looking Triscoe.

"Your status, Rieka?" he asked.

"Fairly secure," she replied, glancing over her shoulder to watch Gorah and Wang lift Gimbish out of his chair. Candace had edged into the room and stood watching them. "We've been in contact with the *Prodigy,* and Captain Saxen is collecting the last group of hostages and sending a few squads to secure the entire ship."

"Will that be enough?"

"Don't know. He's going to transfer the prisoners to a cargo hold."

Triscoe nodded, agreeing with that strategy. "Our ETA is about ten minutes. How is everyone?"

"We're okay," she said, studying the navigation console to verify his statement. "Gundah's still at large, and we need to find the canister."

"Don't go after her on your own," he warned.

Rieka shook her head. "She's getting desperate, Triscoe. And we've pushed her hard. She might do anything. We can't wait."

TWENTY-SEVEN

As Rieka finished telling Bashid he could put the reactor back on line, Gorah called her name. "What?"

The lieutenant sat at a console, a schematic on her screen. "I'm reading activity in the quad B perimeter hold. Section Three."

"A team from the *Prodigy*?"

Gorah shook her head. "One individual."

"What's in the hold?" She caught Wang's inquiring glance and shrugged a shoulder.

Gorah consulted the computer. "Manifest lists for the section include two ground transport vehicles, four cases of industrial recyclers, a shipment of textiles, and an interplanetary shuttle."

"Gundah's going to try to make a run for it. Reset the hatch overrides. Command level only."

"As we speak," Gorah replied, her paws flitting over her board.

"And secure that door." Rieka saw her mother move toward the exit. "Where are you going?"

Candace turned, a determined look on her face. "The same place you are. That cargo area."

Rieka sighed. Another lie? Impossible to say. Her better judgment told her to wait. With Gundah effectively locked in the hold, they could afford to proceed slowly. On the other hand, Gundah probably had the canister with her. When she found out she'd been trapped, she might decide to destroy it. The shuttle had an onboard cold-fusion reactor. If she get desperate enough, Gundah could even blow the reactor and scuttle the *Garner*.

She'd rescued the other children. Now it was time to tend to her own.

Something on her face must have given away her decision. Wang smiled and gestured toward the door. "After you, Boss—until we get to that cargo hold."

Triscoe paced the floor in the conference room as Nason and his mother watched. "She's anxious," he growled. "She's gone to apprehend Gundah. I just know it. What's wrong with that bodyguard of hers? Why doesn't he stop her?"

"Do you actually think he'd accomplish that any better than you?" Nason asked quietly.

"Merik, please," Setana chided. She caught Triscoe's eyes. "Why don't you just speak to her?"

"I promised I wouldn't," he said, trying to keep from sounding ridiculous.

His mother frowned. "Why?"

"It's Rieka's attempt to keep me from harm in the event she's . . . she doesn't survive."

Setana put a hand to her throat. "This is unprecedented."

"*Rieka* is unprecedented," he said, swiping a hand through his hair. "Sometimes I think Father was right. Marrying her was insane."

"Don't be ridiculous, Triscoe," Setana chided. "Now, we'll be there in a few minutes. Surely she can keep out of danger until then."

He sighed at her and looked at Nason. "Admiral, with your permission, I intend to leave Aarkmin in command of the *Providence* and board the *Garner* as soon as we reach InterMAT range."

Almost smiling, Nason said, "Granted, Captain."

"Thank you, sir." Leaving his elders to think whatever they wished of him, he saluted, then turned smartly and strode out the door. On the way to Station Two, Triscoe promised himself he and Rieka would settle this risk-taking business before the day was out.

Rieka checked that her maitu still had a reasonable charge, then glanced at Wang, Candace, and Gorah. "Unlock it, Lieutenant," she said.

While Gorah tapped in her code, Wang sidled in front of her. "No heroics, Boss," he whispered.

She made a face at him. "You wound me, Wang-Chi. There's only one Oph in there—and three of us."

"Four," corrected Candace.

"It's impolite to eavesdrop, Mother," Rieka said. "And I want you to stay out here."

"It's unlocked, Captain," Gorah said.

"Open it."

The door slid aside and they peered into the hold. The interior lights were on, enabling them to see everything clearly. Boxes were stacked in neat rows, vehicles parked end to end. Gorah stepped inside and moved quickly to crouch behind some crates.

Wang nudged Rieka. "Go. I'll cover you."

With a warning glance at Candace to do as she'd been told, Rieka moved to join Gorah. By the time Wang slipped next to her, Rieka was frowning. "We need to check the vehicles," she whispered, silently kicking herself for not collecting some sensory equipment first. A general infrared sweep would have been able to pinpoint Gundah's position. "My best guess is she's hiding in one of them."

"Okay."

Rieka led the way to the first vehicle, a ground transport. Looking through the clear windows, they found no evidence of either Gundah or the canister.

The shuttle was next. Designed to travel relatively short distances through space, it stood just over four meters high. Rieka estimated its length at about fifteen meters. It had been floated in through the cargo doors and sat on an immense platform. The air lock wasn't open, but the gangplank had been extended to the floor.

"Check the perimeter, first," Rieka told them. Cautiously, they moved down the ship's port side. Wang stayed a short distance in front of her. She saw him tense when he turned a corner, but he continued around and headed back toward the entry port. She'd almost caught up to him when they heard a small sound.

Rieka pivoted instantly. She retraced her steps around the little ship's aft area. Gorah was gone. Cursing herself for underestimating Gundah, she hurried back to Wang.

"Gundah's out here, somewhere," she whispered. "She surprised Gorah."

Wang's jaw tightened as he looked down at her. "This is your show, Boss."

She nodded, and called out, "Lieutenant?"

"Your misguided friend can't answer you, Herald," Gundah's unmistakable voice replied.

Wang pointed to the right. Rieka nodded. The sound had come from that direction. "Keep her talking," he whispered, then crept off behind a stack of crates.

Trying for a conversational tone, Rieka said, "Actually, I'm not particularly surprised. Is she dead?"

"Not yet," Gundah's disembodied voice replied. "I'm waiting for just the right time."

"I see," Rieka answered. "Why kill Gorah now—when you might use her to control me?"

"Precisely, Herald. I do like the way you think."

Knowing she needed to keep speaking in order to cover whatever noise Wang might make, Rieka grasped for something else to say. "So . . . what kind of a deal did you make with Candace?"

"I'm not about to discuss that with you."

The direction of her voice had moved. Rieka was sure of it. "But surely you came to some . . . mutual understanding." They hadn't come too far into the hold. She wondered if Candace could hear this, too. "I mean, you've used her in the past."

"Without her knowledge," Gundah added.

The voice had moved again. Rieka took a few tentative steps around the shuttle. Three rows of crates were stacked on the right. Both Wang and Gundah were back there. "Oh, of course not. But she knows what you're doing, now. Your objectives. Your strategy," Rieka coaxed.

"Possibly," Gundah hedged. "I never tell anyone all my secrets. On the other side of the coin, I still require the assistance of certain Humans. And your mother is . . . well beyond the reproductive years. Her price is worth the cooperation."

Rieka frowned. Beyond the reproductive years? What in the world did that mean? "I'm sure it is. So . . . is that what we're doing now, Gundah. Working out a deal to secure *my* cooperation, too?" Rieka left the shuttle and crept toward the first row of crates.

"Possibly."

Gundah's voice had come from behind the third row. If she would just stay in one place for another few seconds, Wang could grab the opportunity to stun her.

"What's the deal, then?" she asked.

"I've been thinking about that," Gundah replied conversationally. "I've decided to help you with your greatest desire—in exchange for your cooperation."

"My greatest desire?" Rieka couldn't imagine what that might be.

"You want a child," Gundah's voice answered. "I can give you one. I own a research lab similar to the one I destroyed on Indra."

"A child in exchange for . . ."

"Your life."

Gundah leapt around the far side of the shuttle's gangplank, surprising Rieka. She crouched instinctively, bringing her weapon to bear on Gundah's chest. She'd been sure the Oph had been behind the crates.

"What good is a baby if I'm not alive?" she asked. Her maitu was aimed, but then so was Gundah's.

Gundah bared her teeth and issued a barking laugh. "Even with you dead, I can produce your children. As many as I want. Hundreds of them."

Gundah lifted her maitu higher. Rieka had waited for some small distraction, and realized something must have happened to Wang. She watched the Oph's eyes, gauging the moment when she would fire.

A second later, Rieka dropped to the floor and rolled to the left, hoping to squeeze off a shot since Gundah now had to come past the gangplank to correct her aim. Wang appeared then, hurtling himself toward Gundah as he came around the shuttle's far corner.

"No!" Rieka shouted, but it was too late to stop him.

Wang leapt on the Oph, fouling her aim and knocking them both to the floor. The blast hit a crate above her. Rieka scurried away and got to her feet as it tumbled to the floor.

"Wang, get loose of her," she shouted. She didn't dare

shoot and hit Wang by mistake, though she did consider the possibility of stunning them both.

She watched helplessly while he tried, but Gundah wouldn't let go. They rolled, crashing into the shuttle's platform. Wang grunted, and she knew he couldn't last much longer. Taking a chance she'd rather not, Rieka ran up the gangplank to get a better angle. She aimed her weapon and fired.

Gundah's howl echoed across the hold, but Rieka realized instantly she'd only been hit in the leg. Then, in a maneuver that looked almost unreal, the Oph lifted Wang like a shield in front of her and got to her knees. He struggled mightily, clouting her with vicious kicks, but she ignored his blows.

"Humans," Gundah managed, "are so tedious."

Rieka barely saw Gundah move. But she heard a loud snap and saw Wang's body go limp. In the second it took for her to realize his neck had been broken, the Oph flung his body at her. His foot knocked the weapon from Rieka's hand. Before she could recover it, Gundah had snatched up her own maitu from the floor, aiming it with unwavering precision.

"You said you'd let me handle her," Candace's voice rang out, breaking the eerie silence. "We had a deal."

She kept her eyes locked on Gundah, but in her peripheral vision, Rieka saw her mother come forward. Her heart breaking over Wang's senseless death, she realized it had been foolhardy to trust Candace even a little bit. Not knowing how much time had passed since they'd been on the bridge, Rieka held her breath.

Triscoe?

Silence.

Gundah glanced momentarily at Candace when she came a step closer. "I gave you your chance. Apparently you have no more control over her now than you did when she was a child."

Triscoe, answer me! Silently berating herself for ever suggesting they disconnect, Rieka realized the irony of that demand. In a few seconds she would probably die. Without their intimate mental connection, at least she knew he'd survive.

"I have my own way of doing things," Candace snapped. "She would have done exactly as you asked."

Gundah shrugged. "Too bad we won't have the opportunity to test your theory."

The look appeared in her eye, again. Rieka recognized it for what it was. Gundah experienced a strange type of ecstasy when she held someone's life in her hands. The Oph savored it for a moment, then smiled.

Rieka dropped to the floor as the maitu went off. Her hand slid under Wang, and she groped for her weapon.

"You can get up now," her mother said.

Looking past Wang's body, Rieka saw that Candace was still standing and Gundah had collapsed onto the floor. While she took a second to figure out what had happened, Candace stepped up to the ramp and extended her arm. In her open palm, she held what had to be Gorah's maitu.

Gingerly, Rieka lifted the weapon and saw it had been calibrated for the highest stun setting. Hoping her voice still worked, she asked, "Do you know where the canister is?"

"Inside the shuttle."

Triscoe looked around as soon as the InterMAT deposited him in the *Garner*'s cargo hold and saw a strange tableau. Two women stood over a pair of bodies. Not knowing what had happened, he gestured for the security team to wait while he walked toward Rieka and her mother.

"Rieka?" he asked cautiously. Closer now, he recognized Wang and knew from the stillness of his body that he was dead. "Rieka?"

Her attention shifted from Candace to him. He saw her nostrils flare and could sense she was on the verge of an emotional collapse. He knew that feeling well, himself. The last few minutes as the *Providence* approached the *Garner* had been torture.

She held two maitus in her hand and offered them to him as he approached. "Just let me . . ." She stopped, pressed her lips together, and took a deep breath. "Candace is under arrest. Have your men look for Lieutenant Gorah. I'll be right back."

She strode up the ramp and went through the shuttle's air lock before he had time to formulate a question. Trusting her word, Triscoe turned to his people, and said, "Place

Mrs. Degahv in custody and secure the area. Report if you find Lieutenant Gorah."

Triscoe desperately wanted to be with her, but knew Rieka would not accept his comfort until she'd done what she'd set out to do. He didn't know what had happened here, but was glad when one of his people led Candace away.

Rieka returned holding the silvery cylinder. She stopped and knelt near Wang's body. He watched as her trembling fingers gently touched him. "His hair is the most interesting color," she whispered, smoothing a wayward lock. "It's so black it looks blue."

A moment of silence passed, and she stood. Triscoe saw the tears pooling in her eyes and felt the chaotic swirl of her anguish. Carefully stepping around Wang, he took her in his arms.

She shuddered, and he squeezed her tighter. He wanted to tell her it would be all right. That she was safe, and that's all that mattered. But he couldn't lie to her. Rieka had known the stakes. And she'd paid the price.

She took a deep breath and leaned back to look at him. "I'm sorry, Triscoe," she said, her voice gravelly. With her free hand, she wiped her cheeks. "I should never have suggested we . . . disconnect."

"Don't apologize, love. I should have trusted you."

Oddly, she frowned and gave a little shake of her head. "Sometimes . . . sometimes doubt is a good thing."

Triscoe nodded. He wiped another tear as it slid down her cheek. "Wang didn't doubt you. He was a good man." He watched her clutch the cylinder tighter. "The best."

Rieka sat on the sofa with a pillow in her arms, finding it odd to see both Nason and Setana here, in the rooms she shared with Triscoe aboard the *Providence*.

"Perhaps you should rest now, dear," Setana suggested.

"I'm fine," she said, her voice steady again. She'd cry for Wang later. There were still too many unanswered questions. "I simply want to interrogate Candace. Is there something odd about that request?"

"No," Nason said as Triscoe came in the door. "I just want to make sure you're up to it."

She glared at him for a long moment. Not even a Fleet

admiral could dent her determination in this. Finally, Nason looked at Triscoe and nodded. He went back to the door and led Candace in.

Eyeing her mother carefully, Rieka said, "If you don't mind, I'd like to speak to my mother privately."

"Of course," Triscoe said. He gestured for Nason and his mother to leave. Before he followed them out, he added, "We'll be outside."

"You murdered her," Rieka began without preamble, watching Candace. She stood regally near the console as if nothing could touch her. "I want to know why."

"She was going to kill you," Candace countered.

Rieka shook her head. "I chose my words carefully. I said you *murdered* her. You could have stopped Gundah without seeing her dead." She looked sharply into Candace's eyes. "You reset the maitu."

"I—may have."

Rieka set the pillow aside and stood. "You know something, Mother. I can see it in your face. You felt justified, didn't you? She'd already been shot twice. There wasn't a chance she could have survived three hits in a row like that."

"I'm not a weapons expert. I had no idea—"

"—and you waited until after she'd killed Wang to act."

Candace faltered briefly. Rieka saw her frown. "I . . . I wasn't able to help him. I would have—but it took time to find Gorah's maitu."

Frustrated by the answers she got, Rieka balled a fist. "Too much time," she said, the words infused with accusation.

Candace lifted her chin. "Do you intend to have me charged with murder?"

Rieka recognized that defiant look. She'd seen it in the mirror. Shaking her head, she muttered, "No. I doubt any court would even hear the case." Feeling oddly detached, she walked the room's length. "But I still don't have the answer I'm looking for. There is more to this than some kind of retribution for her having Dad killed. What else did she tell you?"

Candace looked at her a long moment before heaving a tired sigh. "Two things."

"And they are?"

Candace sank down in one of the chairs. Rieka realized the day had been grueling for her, too. "Gundah's business acumen was incredible. Her holdings were easily a hundred times greater than mine. She owned TechLine, for heaven's sake. I do business with them on a daily basis. Almost everyone does." She stopped speaking and shot Rieka a defiant look.

"Go on, Mother," she prodded.

"You uncovered part of it." Candace glanced at her once, then studied the floor as she spoke. "Gundah admitted to manipulating me. For years. She thought she owned me and did these things to protect her investment. She studied me well enough to be able to predict my reactions to certain situations—and then she made them happen."

Gundah's strategy came as less a surprise than her mother's admission of it. Rieka nodded sympathetically. "Do you believe me now?"

"About what?"

"That we've been deliberately degraded. That individuals like Gundah have worked hard to keep us in the Commonwealth's debt."

"At this moment," Candace admitted, "I'd believe just about anything."

Rieka nodded and returned to her chair. "So. She manipulated you and had Stephen killed. You said there was another thing."

Her mother frowned and pressed her lips together. "I'd rather not say."

Rieka huffed. Did Candace really expect to be excused with that lame answer? She aimed an accusatory finger. "I don't care what you'd rather do, Candace," she said, her jaw tight. "Adjutant Gundah is dead now by your hand. And Wang by hers. I want my questions answered."

Another moment passed before Candace said, "She intended to destroy Humanity."

"What?"

"She could have used any Human's DNA to do what she planned. But it was very important to use yours."

Frowning, Rieka shook her head. "That's sheer fantasy. How could she possibly pull something like that off?"

"She intended to sterilize an entire generation."

For a moment, Rieka could think of nothing intelligent

to say. The statement was unbelievable. Perhaps the Oph lieutenants had been right after all. Finally, she stammered, "That—that's insane."

Candace shook her head. "Her influence was incredible, Rieka," she said quietly. "I believe she could have done exactly what she planned to do."

Pushing past acceptance of the plan, Rieka wondered, "Why my DNA, then?"

Candace looked away to study her lap. "I don't think you want to hear this." She paused, but went on before Rieka had a chance to prompt her. "There was some sort of connection between Stephen and her parents. She blamed him for her father's death. Her family's fortune was all but wiped out. Everything she did—she did for revenge."

Rieka nodded. "So she hated him and decided to take it out on all Humanity. Earth's restoration must have felt like a personal insult," Rieka went on. "When Stephen's plans actually started to come about, she created the accident to stop him. Uncle Alexi continued the plan, but at a much slower pace. I wonder if it's coincidental that he's been suffering from a variety of illnesses since he took the office."

Rieka paused and studied her mother. "She influenced you, and probably planned for Paden to become Herald." She shook her head. "This is . . . I'm at a loss for words. If the Procyons hadn't killed Paden, he'd be Earth Herald now and Gundah . . ."

"Gundah would be using *his* DNA to commit genocide."

Rieka took several deep breaths, trying to overcome her shock, indignation, and rage. Purposefully, she tried to think of what to do next. How to proceed. How to behave. Unfortunately, nothing seemed clear. Finally, she said, "And how about you? When you found out what she had planned—"

"—I wanted my own revenge," Candace told her. "I convinced her the two of us could keep on as we were. That all I wanted was the money."

Rieka nodded. Candace's revenge had had nothing to do with insanity. As usual, it had been cold and calculated. And now Gundah was dead. She sighed. "This remains between the two of us, Mother, I don't want anyone else to know." Of course Triscoe had access to her thoughts, but he'd honor her request, and her mother didn't need to know about that part of her relationship with him.

"And," she added, "since you're obviously going to profit from your bargain with her, you're going to stop your petty verbal attacks of me and my office—or I will prosecute you. Is that clear?"

Candace nodded. "I know how to keep a secret."

Rieka studied her for a moment. "I'm sure you do."

Triscoe held Rieka firmly in his lap even after Jeniper and Robet entered the apartment. He'd considered staying aboard the *Providence* for a day or two, but realized Rieka needed to be on Earth. Or in it, he thought wryly, considering they were several hundred meters below the surface.

"How are you feeling this morning?" Jeniper asked.

"I'm fine. I wish people would quit treating me as though I were made of porcelain." She squirmed again, and Triscoe released her to sit beside him.

"Good. Then you're ready to hear my news."

"You've not going to believe this," Robet added, beaming.

Rieka raised both her hands. "Okay. The two of you sit down and tell us your news."

Jeniper and Robet sat. "We're betrothed," he announced.

Triscoe leaned forward and smiled. "Congratulations."

Rieka poked him with her elbow. "I'm glad I didn't listen to you," she murmured, snapping a glance at him.

Jeniper cocked her head. "What is that supposed to mean?"

Before he could respond, Rieka said, "He didn't think you were right for each other. I did." She smiled, her first for the day, and Triscoe breathed a relieved sigh. "I'm really happy for you."

"I am, too," he said.

"But there's more," Jeniper said, moving to the edge of her seat. "I know how disappointed you were, Rieka, when we had to announce the Reaffirmation Ceremony needed to be postponed indefinitely."

Triscoe felt her stiffen. "We decided it was for the best," she said softly.

"Yes. Well, apparently no one else did." Jeniper gestured

with her fingers splayed. "Our office has been inundated with calls. Heralds, business people, the general public— everyone thinks Earth needs to be rededicated as soon as possible." Her voice had the ring of excitement. "They want us to announce the new date today."

Rieka shook her head. "We can't possibly put it back together anytime soon. There are hundreds of details . . ."

Triscoe watched Robet's bibbets darken slightly before he spoke. "You don't seem to understand. These folks want to cooperate."

Jeniper nodded. "They want to help. Participate. They've been telling me they want to welcome Earth—not the other way around."

The room stayed quiet for a moment. Rieka seemed to be studying the floor, but Triscoe knew better. She was overwhelmed by the impact of what Jeniper had said. Finally, she nodded. "When, then?"

Jeniper's eyes glowed excitedly. "Next week?"

"Do you think so?"

"You're the miracle worker."

Rieka chuckled softly. "Okay. Set up a broadcast time for this afternoon, Jen. If we're going to give them what they want, we might as well get started."

"I'm on it." Jeniper stood, and Robet followed as she fairly danced toward the door. "This is the most wonderful thing that's ever happened in the Commonwealth, Rieka," she said, turning and flashing them a huge smile. "And it's all because of you."

When they were alone again, Triscoe squeezed her shoulder. "I should have trusted you from the start," he said softly. "Things might have ended differently if I had."

Rieka turned toward him and he saw confusion in her blue eyes. "Are you saying Wang's death is your fault? You're no more to blame than I am for not stunning both of them when I had the chance."

Triscoe felt as if someone had reached into his chest and squeezed his heart. He had failed her on a most basic level and still she forgave him. He glanced across the room to the dining table where the canister set. "We cannot undo what has been done—no matter how hard we wish it. But I want you to understand you are more precious to me than anything else I could possibly imagine."

She put her hand over his. "I know. I feel the same way about you."

"No matter what the future brings, I never want to lose contact again."

"No matter what?" Rieka asked skeptically.

Triscoe rolled his eyes and squeezed his Human wife's shoulder. "Yes, love. I trust you."

At that, Rieka smiled her quirky, one-sided smile.

Five hours later, Rieka sat amazed at what Jeniper had managed to pull together. Not only had she organized a Herald's News Conference, she'd coordinated entertainment to go along with Rieka's speech.

Seated beside Triscoe in New SubDenver's media room, she went over the hastily prepared speech one more time. A variety of entertainers had already performed, including the Blue Planet Future.

Senator Volshoy began Rieka's introduction. She took a deep breath to quell a sudden wave of anxiety.

"Are you all right?" Triscoe whispered, squeezing her hand.

"I think so." She tried to smile. Rieka felt him close in her mind and knew he meant her mental state rather than her physical one. She looked beyond him and saw her mother, seated next to Setana and Ker. They nodded their support.

Volshoy said her name and she went to the podium. In addition to the now-recognizable faces of the Blue Planet Future, she noticed Admiral Nason, Midrin Tohab, and the *Prodigy*'s Captain Saxen. Rieka smiled at them, then grinned when she noticed Jeniper seated next to Robet.

Glancing once more at her speech, she began. "Welcome, Commonwealth citizens, to my planet. As Earth Herald, I am privileged to invite you to experience the wonders my home has to offer. From Damascus, to the restored equatorial rain forests, to undersea laboratories, to the incredible World Zoo—I know you will find yourselves fascinated, educated, accommodated, and entertained."

Glancing away from the camera, she saw Jeniper give her an encouraging nod. Perhaps this speech wasn't as sappy as she thought. She took a breath and went on.

"Additionally, I am proud to announce that the Reaffirmation will take place one week from today. On that day, the Earth will begin to repay the Commonwealth for the investment it made two centuries ago. Our ancestors understood value and potential—and saw both in the Earth and its peoples." There was a smattering of applause from the audience. Smiling, she waited until it died down, then continued.

"Our civilization works on the principle of business, and it has been brought to my attention that some individuals are concerned with the idea of a productive Earth. To them, I say simply—wait and see. There are winners and losers in every business transaction, but I assure you we will work very hard to see that everyone profits. And we will work just as hard to ensure the Earth both achieves its potential and maintains the high standard of ethics so important to the Commonwealth today."

Rieka raised her left hand in a cautious gesture. "But success is never without obstacles," she added. "I can promise the future holds many hurdles for all of us. And I can likewise predict we will gain an amazing return for that effort.

"It is my wish that all of you within the sound of my voice remember this moment and pass on to your children and to their children the sense of excitement and challenge you feel right now. For this is what it is like to be Human and to have your feet on the soil of your homeworld. To remember where you've come from, to hold a vision of the future, and to be proud of who you are."

She paused and looked out onto the sea of faces before her, then returned her attention to the camera. "Welcome to Earth, my friends. I hope you have brought with you an appetite for adventure. I guarantee you won't be disappointed."